PENGUIN TWENTIETH-CENTURY CLASSICS

THE GORSE TRILOGY

Patrick Hamilton was one of the most gifted and admired writers of his generation. Born in Hassocks, Sussex, in 1904, he and his parents moved a short while later to Hove, where he spent his early years. He published his first novel, *Craven House*, in 1926 and within a few years had established a wide readership for himself. Despite personal setbacks and an increasing problem with drink, he was able to write some of his best work. His plays include the thrillers *Rope* (1929), on which Alfred Hitchcock's film *Rope* was based, and *Gas Light* (1939), also successfully adapted for the screen (1939), and a historical drama, *The Duke in Darkness* (1943). Among his novels are *The Midnight Bell* (1929), *The Siege of Pleasure* (1932), *The Plains of Cement* (1934), a trilogy entitled *Twenty Thousand Streets Under the Sky* (1935), *Hangover Square* (1941) and *The Slaves of Solitude* (1947). *The Gorse Trilogy* is made up of *The West Pier*, *Mr Stimpson and Mr Gorse* and *Unknown Assailant*, which were first published during the 1950s. J. B. Priestley described Patrick Hamilton as 'uniquely individual ... He is the novelist of innocence, appallingly vulnerable, and of malevolence, coming out of som[illegible] mysterious darkness of evil.' Patrick Hamilton died in 196[illegible]

PENGUIN TWENTIETH-CENTURY CLASSICS

THE GORSE TRILOGY

Patrick Hamilton was one of the most gifted and admired writers of his generation. Born in Hassocks, Sussex, in 1904, he and his parents moved [illegible] early years. He published his first novel, Craven House, in 1926 [illegible] published [illegible] readership [illegible] himself. [illegible] personal [illegible] with drink, he was able to [illegible] some of his best work. His plays include the thriller Rope (1929), on which Alfred Hitchcock's film Rope was based, and Gas Light (1939), also successfully adapted for the screen (1939), and a historical drama, The Duke in Darkness (1943). Among his novels are The Midnight Bell (1929), The Siege of Pleasure (1932), The Plains of Cement (1934), a trilogy entitled Twenty Thousand Streets Under the Sky (1935), Hangover Square (1941) and The Slaves of Solitude (1947). The Gorse Trilogy is made up of The West Pier, Mr Stimpson and Mr Gorse and Unknown Assailant, which were first published during the 1950s. J. B. Priestley described Patrick Hamilton as [illegible] individual [illegible] He [illegible] the [illegible] innocence [illegible] specifically [illegible] and [illegible] mysterious darkness of [illegible] Patrick Hamilton died in 1962.

PATRICK HAMILTON

THE GORSE TRILOGY

The West Pier

Mr Stimpson and Mr Gorse

Unknown Assailant

PENGUIN BOOKS

PENGUIN BOOKS

Published by the Penguin Group
Penguin Books Ltd, 27 Wrights Lane, London W8 5TZ, England
Penguin Books USA Inc., 375 Hudson Street, New York, New York 10014, USA
Penguin Books Australia Ltd, Ringwood, Victoria, Australia
Penguin Books Canada Ltd, 10 Alcorn Avenue, Toronto, Ontario, Canada M4V 3B2
Penguin Books (NZ) Ltd, 182–190 Wairau Road, Auckland 10, New Zealand

Penguin Books Ltd, Registered Offices: Harmondsworth, Middlesex, England

The West Pier first published by Constable 1951
Published by Viking 1985
Published in Penguin Books 1986

Mr Stimpson and Mr Gorse first published by Constable 1953
Published in Penguin Books 1987

Unknown Assailant first published by Constable 1955
Published in Penguin Books, as part of *The Gorse Trilogy*, 1992

The Gorse Trilogy first published 1992
1 3 5 7 9 10 8 6 4 2

Made and printed in Great Britain by
Richard Clay Ltd, Bungay, Suffolk
Filmset in Monophoto Sabon

CONTENTS

THE WEST PIER

Author's Note

Although a complete story in itself, *The West Pier* is the first of a series of novels dealing with the character of Ernest Ralph Gorse.

There may be some readers who, on learning this, will feel that *The West Pier* is *not* actually a complete story in itself. The author is anxious to assure any such reader that it really is.

Author's Note

Although a complete story in itself, *The West Pier* is the start of a series of novels dealing with the character of Ernest Ralph Gorse.

There may be some readers who, on learning this, will feel that *The West Pier* is not actually a complete story in itself. The author is anxious to assure any such reader that it really is.

Contents

PART ONE

THE BOY GORSE

Chapter One

I

There is a sort of man – usually a lance-corporal or corporal and coming from the submerged classes – who, returning to England from military service in distant parts of the earth, does not announce his arrival to his relations. Instead of this he will tramp, or hitchhike, his way to his home, and in the early hours of the morning will be heard gently throwing pebbles up at his wife's bedroom window.

It is impossible to say whether he does this because he hopes to surprise his wife in some sinful attachment, or whether it has never occurred to him to use the telephone, the telegraph service, or the post. If the latter were the case one might suppose him to be merely unimaginative: but this type of person is actually far from being unimaginative.

What concerns us here is that such a person certainly belongs to a type, rare but identifiable. There may exist only one in a hundred thousand, or more, people: but, by a shrewd observer, they can be discerned and classified without mistake.

The main feature which characterizes these people is, of course, their silence – their almost complete dumbness and numbness amidst a busy and loquacious humanity. They are not, in fact, inarticulate: at certain times they will talk at great length. They are able, also, to laugh, though this is usually at a joke of a commonplace, cruel, or dirty nature. But although they are able to talk and laugh, they seem to do this only spasmodically and on the surface: beneath this surface they are dreaming, dully brooding, seeming incessantly and as it were somnambulistically to contemplate themselves and the prospects of their own advantage.

They are almost exclusively a male species. Seventy-five per cent of them belong to the submerged classes: the remaining (and perhaps most interesting) twenty-five per cent are scattered amongst all kinds of higher strata. They all tend to drift into the Army. During wars, or in periods of social upheaval, they appear, as if vengefully, to come into their own, to gain ephemeral power and standing.

As boys at school they are generally bullies, but quiet ones – twisters of wrists in distant corners. As adults, naturally, they can no longer behave in such a way, and some of them wear on their faces what may be a slow, pensive resentment at being thwarted in this matter.

They use few gestures, and, like most great inner thinkers, they are great walkers, plodders of the streets in raincoats.

They are conspicuously silent and odd in their behaviour with their wives or their women. In public houses, or in tea-shops, they are to be seen sitting with women without uttering a word to them, sometimes for as much as an hour on end.

It is extremely difficult to guess what goes on beneath the surface of their minds. It is only from their surface behaviour, and surface utterances, that the depths can be dimly understood or estimated.

It would be wrong to suppose that they are all of the same character, that there are not innumerable variations within this species. They are not all bullies at school, and they are by no means all bad and harmful. Indeed, it is likely that many of them serve a purpose as calm, honest, useful, though extremely dull citizens. On the other hand it is beyond dispute that it is from this type that the most atrocious criminals emerge.

We feel that the poisoner Neil Creame, the bath-murderer George Smith, and many others of a similar way of thinking belonged to this type.

Of this type Ernest Ralph Gorse, who was born in 1903, was clearly one or the other sort of member. He showed as much as a boy.

2

During a Thursday afternoon of the winter before the First World War, at Rodney House Road, Hove, there occurred, in a changing-room, an episode which was originated by Ernest Ralph Gorse.

Rodney House was a preparatory school for about forty boys, accepting pupils from many different classes of parents in the town. What may be roughly called an aristocracy of five or six boys came from the squares and avenues – Brunswick Square, Grand Avenue, First Avenue, and the like: what may be roughly called a *bourgeoisie* (the sons of merchants, dentists, estate agents, doctors, clergymen, retired officers, and well-to-do local tradesmen) came from the roads – Wilbury Road, Holland Road, Tisbury Road, Norton Road: while the rest came from the villas – Hova Villas, Ventnor Villas, Denmark Villas – or from obscure crescents and streets at the back of Hove or of Brighton, or from humble western regions verging upon Portslade. A few of this third class approximated to the *sansculottes*: at any rate, their clothes were laughed at, and they were known to be 'common'.

Of these three classes the quietest, for the most part, were the aristocrats and the *sansculottes* – the former, perhaps, because of their smooth home atmosphere; the latter because of their rudely published inferiority and consequent timidity. It was the middle class which made all the noise, the middle class which, in the pursuit of its many varied and violent pleasures, caused the establishment, out of working hours, to resound to the skies.

These pleasures, like all pleasures, were subject to fashion, and fashion of an even more fickle kind than that which operates in the adult world. For a short period, for instance, the eager, clamorous delight of almost all the pupils would centre around the persecution of a single boy, who would be accused of being a thief, or a cheat, or a 'sneak', or unclean in his personal habits, or all these things together. Such a boy, however, would all at once be rescued from the utmost spiritual and physical torment, would be permitted to sink into a blissful state of nonentity, by the chance appearance at the school of a mere water pistol of a new design. Not the human boy, but water pistols of this design would now be the rage, though not for long. Water pistols would be soon submerged in a suddenly recurring wave of, say, model battleships, and so it went on throughout the year, a single one of which would embrace vogues moving from boy-persecution to water pistols, from water pistols to model battleships, and from model battleships to electric torches; to catapults; to regimental buttons; to pocket knives; to miniature trains; to fretsaws; to pistols exploding pink caps; to miniature soldiers, guns, and forts; to whistles; to balloons; to instruments into which one could hum tunes with a greatly enlarged volume of sound; to small mirrors which sent mischievous reflections of the sun into the eye of a distant enemy or friend; to highly coloured tin beetles which raced along the floor; to tops; to cameras; to 'transfers'; to white mice; to chewing gum; to miniature aeroplanes; to solid imitations of spilt ink, and so on and so forth. All these popular passions, ephemeral but returning in cycles, were accompanied by the perennial and perpetual creation and throwing of paper darts and gliders, and the collection and exchange of cigarette cards.

On that remote Thursday afternoon of that remote winter, an interest in small electric torches was approaching its peak; and Ernest Ralph Gorse originated the episode in question by removing one of these from the pocket of one boy and putting it into the pocket of another. He was able to do this unseen, because he was the first to return to the changing-room after military operations on the County Ground, which was within six minutes' walk of Rodney House.

Thursday was the day on which Rodney House School, forsaking games, applied itself diligently to military exercises. In the morning there appeared a 'sergeant', who, establishing himself in a shed in the back garden, taught a number of privileged boys (those whose parents desired to pay for it) to shoot at a target pinned on a wooden box. Such boys, in an expectant and excited condition, were called in twos by rota from their classrooms. They left the room with silent, valiant, and dramatic air (which gave the impression rather that they were going to be shot than going to shoot) and returned about ten minutes later with their targets, riddled and showing their scores, in their hands. These targets, despite the vigilance of the masters, usually succeeded in being passed from desk to desk around the room and coming back to their owners.

All this, in the morning, was pleasant and intelligible to the boys: the afternoon was unpleasant and almost completely unintelligible. In the afternoon they were dressed in the boots, puttees, tunics, and caps of private soldiers, and, carrying wooden imitations of rifles, were marched down to the County Ground and drilled – made, with their coarse puttees tickling their immature legs, to shoulder arms, present arms, port arms, form fours, right dress, stand at ease, etc., never, never satisfactorily, and again and again and again until they were stupefied.

It was, oddly enough, not difficult to stupefy the boys of Rodney

House. They were, in fact, during the greater part of their day at school, either making a noise which rang to heaven, or in a state of stupefaction at their tasks. In the latter condition they wore a bewildered, staring, idiotic, Bedlam, Bridewell look – many of them, during class, biting their nails, blinking their eyes, or showing other nervous twitching gestures.

This habit of staring, brought on by bewilderment and boredom, was almost certainly the original cause of the myopia which would make so many of them in later life wear spectacles.

Ernest Ralph Gorse was, however, not in any way bored by Thursday afternoons: the unintelligible was to him in some way intelligible. His boots were always clean; his puttees were rolled neatly and expertly; his buttons were the brightest of all; his execution of the requisite movements was so good that he was often called from the ranks to make a model demonstration and shame his fellows. Thursday afternoons stimulated rather than stupefied Ernest Ralph Gorse.

Even his expression and demeanour changed. A slim boy, with ginger silken hair which came in a large bang over his forehead, and an aquiline nose which seemed to be smelling something nasty – a boy with thin lips, a slouching gait, a nasal voice, and a certain amount of freckles, Ernest Ralph Gorse's normal expression was the dull, thoughtful one of a person proposing to remember an evil done to him. But on Thursday afternoons there was something different: his look was less obtuse and hoarding: he became, even, in his own way, lively.

It was, perhaps, an excess of this lively spirit which put into his mind, and inspired him to perpetrate, the mischief with the torch.

3

The changing-room was a dark, bare-boarded room in the basement – in the day overrun by boys, in the night by beetles. It was lined with lockers which did not lock, with hooks, and with benches. About twelve boys changed in here – those who occupied, roughly, an upper middle station in the school. A select band of seniors and a mob of juniors changed in their respective rooms elsewhere.

After Ernest Ralph Gorse (who, having removed the torch from the one pocket to the other, was by this time unrolling his puttees) there entered two boys.

One of these was named Ryan and the other Bell. Ryan was a carefree, impulsive, good-looking boy who did not pretend to be clever and did not specialize at anything; while Bell was a spectacled, old-looking boy who was extremely clever at his lessons and who specialized in the use of long words. He was using long words as he entered with Ryan.

'The relation of your proboscis appertaining to your external physiognomy,' he was saying to Ryan as he entered, 'occurs to me to be somewhat superfluous.'

This remark of Bell's came completely out of the blue: nearly all such remarks of his did. Bell would go into a sort of trance, would remain absolutely quiet for a moment or so while preparing such sentences, which, though painfully obscure, were nearly always to be recognized as being of a bald, rude, gratuitous, and challenging nature.

Ryan now had to do some quick thinking. He had not understood what had been said: but he was certain that whatever had been said was unfavourable to himself. 'Proboscis', he at any rate knew, was long-language for nose: so presumably something nasty had been said about his nose. But what? Had it been called red, long, dirty, ugly? He floundered about in doubt (as Bell had indeed intended he should) for a matter of ten seconds, and then, unable to make a retort in kind, rather shamefacedly took the easiest way out.

'So's yours,' he said, and a moment later added, 'only worse . . .'

'That *happens* to be a *tu quoque*,' said Bell without hesitation, and Ryan, having been recently taught in class what a *tu quoque* was, this time did not hesitate.

'You're a *tu* silly ass,' he said. 'And I should say you've got a bit *tu* above yourself.'

This was definitely witty and clever, and it was Bell's turn to be momentarily dumbfounded. He paused for as long as he had previously made Ryan pause, and at last was only able to manage:

'Really . . . Your *brain* . . .'

'Really,' said Ryan, '*yours* . . .'

Honours might now well have been considered even, and so the argument might well have been allowed to drop. But the Ryans and Bells of life never on any account allow such arguments to drop. Only when a school bell rings, a master enters, or their attention is fortuitously distracted elsewhere, do such arguments end. There was now a pause during which the adversaries, while rapidly changing their clothes, and while other boys entered to change, were clearly mobilizing their forces behind the lines. Then Ryan went into the attack.

'Bell . . .' he said in an innocent voice, as if he intended to ask the other a detached or even amiable question.

'Yes?' said Bell.

'*Nothing*,' said Ryan, with the firm and gleeful air of having most cunningly enticed and then snapped a trap upon Bell.

This device, commonplace and, in fact, beneath contempt, yet had the power to hurt: for to the Ryans and Bells of life, in argument, there is hardly any ruse considered too conventional or too low.

'Very clever,' said Bell. 'Very clever indeed. You ought to have your bumps examined – by a phrenologist – just to see how clever you are.'

'I've got quite enough bumps, thank you,' said Ryan, 'playing football. And barges, too.'

Now Bell saw an opportunity of employing a counter-device. This device was, perhaps, not quite so base as the one just used by his opponent – but was, all the same, cheap and facile beyond measure. It consisted of repeating, word for word, and merely for the sake of annoyance, what the other person had last uttered.

'*"I've got quite enough bumps, thank you,"*' Bell quoted, '*"playing football, And barges, too."*'

Ryan thought for a moment.

'Are you trying to imitate me?' he then said.

'*"Are you trying to imitate me?"*' said Bell.

'Don't be a fool,' said Ryan. 'Anybody can do that.'

'*"Don't be a fool,"*' said Bell. '*"Anybody can do that."*'

'It's not funny, you know,' said Ryan.

'*"It's not funny, you know,"*' said Bell.

There was a pause.

'Well – I just won't say anything, that's all,' said Ryan.

'*"Well – I just won't say anything, that's all,"*' said Bell.

There was now a silence of nearly a minute's duration, in which it seemed that Ryan intended to adhere to his resolution. This silence was embarrassing and hateful to both, for to the Ryans and Bells of life there is nothing more unnatural and detestable than not talking. Much as he desired it, it was impossible for Bell to break the spell, for, had he done so, Ryan, he knew, would have at once started repeating his own words, and the whole position would have been fatally reversed. It was Ryan who at last relieved the situation. This he did by adopting a new tactic – or rather a familiar variation in this barren and frustrating form of conflict.

'Bell,' he said, 'is the silliest fool at Rodney House.'

Now what? Without proclaiming himself the silliest fool at Rodney House, Bell was unable to maintain the ascendancy by continuing in the same course as before. Should he, then, remain silent? No – for that would be an admission of defeat. Also, being a Bell of life, Bell, as has been said, was temperamentally incapable of remaining silent. He saw that he had to compromise, and did so.

'Bell,' he said, 'is *not* the silliest fool at Rodney House.'

'There you are. Got you!' said Ryan. 'You couldn't repeat me.'

'"*There you are. Got you!*"' said Bell. '"*You couldn't repeat me.*"'

'You didn't repeat me, and it's no use pretending you did,' said Ryan.

'"*You didn't repeat me, and it's no use pretending you did,*"' said Bell.

Now it seemed to Ryan that, owing to his own folly, he was back exactly where he was before. Ryan, however, was an indomitable boy, and he used indomitability.

'Bell,' he said again, firmly, 'is the silliest fool at Rodney House.'

'Bell,' Bell replied with equal firmness, 'is *not* the silliest fool at Rodney House.'

'Bell,' said Ryan, 'is the silliest fool at Rodney House and is not able to repeat Ryan's words.'

'Bell,' said Bell, 'is *not* the silliest fool at Rodney House and *is* able to repeat Ryan's words.'

'Bell,' said Ryan, 'is so Abso-Blooming-Lutely silly that Ryan doesn't intend to speak to him any more.'

'Bell,' said Bell, 'is *not* so Abso-Blooming-Lutely silly that Ryan doesn't intend to speak to him any more.'

Who, now, was the winner? Who could ever be the winner? Ryan, undoubtedly, was morally and logically in the right, but appearances, which are all-important to the Ryans and Bells of life, were against him. He could not, by any means, establish his moral and logical superiority, and he could never get the last word.

How long this would have gone on, and what the outcome

would have been, cannot be said. In a sense fortunately, the insoluble was at this moment solved by misfortune.

Misfortune, striking Ryan like a thunderbolt, caused him to go white in the face, and to dismiss from his mind all other things.

'Hullo,' he said frantically and whitely, going through the pockets of his coat. *'Where's my torch?'*

4

At first Bell, who was fundamentally of a humane nature, did not at all take in the seriousness of what had been said.

'"*Hullo,*"' he repeated automatically. '"*Where's my torch?*"'

'No, shut up, man,' said Ryan. 'I've lost it.'

And still Bell did not understand, and repeated Ryan's words again.

'No. Do shut up, really,' said Ryan. 'It's gone from my *pocket*!'

At this a hoarseness, even a hint of tears, in Ryan's voice caused Bell to look at Ryan and see that his face was pale and his manner agitated beyond measure. Seeing this, Bell abandoned frivolity, though reluctantly.

'What do you mean – it's gone from your pocket?' he said. 'Don't be an *ass*.'

'It's gone,' said Ryan, still searching feebly, 'that's all.'

And now something of the real and peculiar horror of the situation was communicated to Bell. The horror was of a peculiar nature because of the character and reputation of Ryan's torch. Ryan's torch, in fact, dwelt in a heavenly realm above and beyond all other torches – was famous, one might say fabulous, in the school just at this time. To be permitted to look at it was a privilege, to hold it was an honour; to use it, even with its owner's sanction, was almost a blasphemy, frightening. This was to a certain extent because it was so wonderfully thin and small and covered with imitation crocodile leather; but principally because it had, at the top, a sliding apparatus which enabled its user to change the white light to red, and then to white again, and then again to green! What specific purpose, if any, this was intended to serve, nobody had as yet asked: everyone simply and instinctively knew that no one could ask for more. During the whole week it had been the making of Ryan: Ryan's being was the torch and the torch was Ryan's being. Ryan was a torch. If, then, the torch was lost, was not Ryan utterly lost, suddenly a nothing? Bell, looking at him, was genuinely appalled, and attempted kindness.

'Go on, man,' he said. 'Have another look. It must be there somewhere.'

'But it *isn't*.'

'But it *must* be.'

Bell was not entirely disinterested, and his voice also betrayed terror. For when he was not quarrelling with Ryan he had more than once been allowed to use the torch and had looked forward to much pleasure of this kind in the future.

Here Ernest Ralph Gorse, who, while methodically changing, had been listening to every word which had passed between these two, spoke.

'Are you sure it was in your pocket?' he asked Ryan.

'Yes. I know it was.'

'Absolutely sure?' asked Ernest Ralph Gorse.

'Yes,' said Bell. 'You might have left it somewhere else.'

'No, I didn't,' said Ryan. 'It was in my *pocket*.'

'Then someone must have pinched it,' said Ernest Ralph Gorse.

Ryan considered this for a moment. 'But *who* could have pinched it?' he said, and then, returning to life, he burst forth angrily and addressed the entire room. 'Look here,' he said. 'Is someone trying to be funny? Has someone pinched my torch?'

'Look here,' said a boy named Kerr. 'Are you accusing me?'

'No. I'm not accusing anyone. I'm just asking who's jolly well pinched my torch.'

'You'd better not accuse me, you know,' said Kerr, now anxious to be accused, and endeavouring to create the illusion that this had already happened. 'Because I'll jolly well punch your nose.'

'And you'd better not accuse me either,' said another boy named Roberts, perceiving and rushing and with all his belongings towards the glorious Yukon of quarrelling which Kerr had discovered. 'Or I'll jolly well punch your nose, too.'

'I'll jolly well punch anyone's nose who's pinched my torch,' said Ryan. 'Come on. Who is it? Come on!'

Ryan himself was now, it can be seen, affected by the wild spirit of the gold rush, and assumed without further question that his torch had been stolen.

'Why not institute a search?' said Ernest Ralph Gorse.

This brought in Bell's support because he liked the long word 'institute' (of which he took a mental note).

'Yes,' he said. 'Let's institute a summary investigation.' (He was glad to have beaten 'search' with 'investigation' and was very pleased indeed with 'summary'.)

'Nobody's jolly well going to summary investigate *me*,' said Kerr. 'I'll jolly well summer and investigate their noses, if they do. And winter, too, if it comes to that.'

At this delightful play upon words, many of the boys could not resist openly giggling, while others reluctantly half smiled, and it looked for a moment as though a painful and strenuous situation might break up in humour and lightheartedness. But now another boy named Wills, changing in a far corner, poisonously re-introduced seriousness.

'I'll bet it's Rosen . . .' he said.

Rosen was a dark, Jewish, short, quiet, passionate, long-haired boy, destined in later life to become a successful municipal and BBC musical conductor. His quietness and aloofness, his gift for the violin (which enabled him most enviably to escape, during the week, quite a few hours in the ordinary classroom), together with his hopeless inability to keep a shred of his temper when falsely accused of the foulest crimes, all served to make him unpopular, a victim. He, above all, was one of those characters whom only vogues for water pistols, torches, model battleships, etc., could save from persecution. Now it seemed that the prevailing torch-mania, instead of mercifully hiding him, was by a wicked paradox fated to bring him into the limelight yet again.

'Yes, *I'll* bet it is, too,' said another poisonous boy.

For a few moments nothing was said, and in the silence it was generally felt that it was Ryan's business to make a formal accusation against Rosen. This Ryan did not at once do. Being, like his friend Bell, a humane boy, and not believing for a second that Rosen had stolen his torch, he was loath to begin. The continued silence, however, at last began to fill him with a sense of having to shoulder a public obligation, and, in a gingerly manner, he plunged in, or rather began to paddle.

'Have *you* taken it, Rosen?' he said, with an imitation of some hostility, but actually almost apologetically.

Rosen, who was already getting dangerously angry, made the

pretence of considering it beneath his dignity to reply, and went on changing his clothes rapidly.

'Well. Go on,' said Kerr. 'Answer – can't you?'

But still Rosen, in his anger changing his clothes even more rapidly, affected mute and sublime dignity.

'Oh – so you can't answer,' said Kerr. 'Well – that's a proof of guilt, anyway. That's jolly well a proof of guilt.'

'Yes – that's a proof of guilt,' said Roberts, who was Kerr's shadow. 'Come on, hand it over, you dirty little thief.'

This caused the pent-up Rosen to explode. He stood as if at bay, his body quivered, and his eyes dilated.

'How *dare* you say that!' he said. 'How *dare* you! You *pig*!'

Alas, Rosen had succumbed yet again to his inveterate weakness – his inability to keep a shred of his temper when falsely accused. His mother had constantly spoken to him about this – so had his father: he himself completely accepted and eagerly agreed with what both his mother and father said; but it was all of no avail. He was totally unable to control himself when unjustly treated at school. A success in later life, certainly, he was going to be, with a fame to which his present tormentors (themselves having drifted into money-seeking, undistinguished, or even sordid obscurity) would allude with pride and pleasure, basely preening themselves with a morsel of his glamour: but here and now he created nothing but ignominy and suffering for himself. This was aggravated by the fact that when he lost his temper he always did so with the utmost *gaucherie*, bringing forth, in his lonely, alien, Jewish way, absurd, alien, outmoded expressions. At Rodney House, or at any preparatory school of its kind at that time, you simply did not say 'How *dare* you!' Nor, though in certain contexts you might abusively use the word 'pig', did you ever permit yourself the ridiculous, declamatory 'You *pig*!'

'Did you call me a pig?' said Roberts, fixing Rosen with a steady, detached, questioning look. 'Did I hear anyone calling me a pig?'

Rosen's answer was simple enough.

'You're a *pig*, a *cad*, a *swine*, a *hog*, and a *liar*!' he said.

'Oh – so I'm –' began Roberts, when Ryan cut in.

'Never mind about that,' said Ryan. 'All I want is my torch, and all I want to know is if you've got it, Rosen.'

'How *dare* you say I've got it!' said Rosen. 'How dare you *suggest* I've got it! Do you want to search me? Go on. Search my clothes! Search my locker! Search my desk upstairs! Search everything!'

'All right. We will,' said Roberts, and moved over towards Rosen's locker.

'If you *dare* to so much as *touch* my clothes I'll kill you!' said Rosen, contradicting himself.

'Oh – so you're afraid, are you?' said Roberts.

'No. I'm not afraid. Ryan may search. It's his torch. Go on, Ryan. Search!'

'No, *I* don't want to . . .' said Ryan, but Rosen would have none of this.

'Go on. Search!' he said. 'I *insist* that you search! I *demand* a search!'

Ryan still hesitated, but the other boys egged him on, only one of them recommending him to refrain from searching, and this not for Rosen's sake, but because of the inconvenience which Ryan might have to endure from 'the smell'.

Ryan began to search, and the others crowded round to watch him.

All at once a gasp of incredulity and ineffable exultation arose from the boys. Ryan had found the torch in Rosen's pocket.

'My *Aunt* – my Sainted *Aunt*!' said one boy, and 'Phe-e-e-w!' said another, and others said, 'My Giddy *Forefathers*!' and 'By George' and 'Great Scott' and 'Great Jehoshaphat' and 'My *Hat* – my Giddy *Hat*!' and Bell said solemnly, 'By *Nebuchadnezzar's Toe-Nails* . . .' (Nebuchadnezzar's name was very frequently upon Bell's lips, because Nebuchadnezzar's name was so long.)

Then they turned upon Rosen. 'Well – what about it now, my young friend?' said Kerr. 'What about it now?'

'It's a trick! It's a trick! It was never there! It's a *conjuring* trick!' said Rosen in his old-fashioned way. 'Someone must have put it there! Someone put it there by *sleight of hand*!'

'Oh,' said Kerr. 'So you're accusing other people now. You're not content with stealing – you start accusing people of playing tricks.'

'Legerdemain . . .' said Bell.

'I tell you it's a trick!' said Rosen. 'And you all know it! If I'd taken it I wouldn't let you *search*. I *demanded* the search. Didn't I?'

'Yes,' said Bell fairly. 'He certainly requested an examination of his external apparel.' And the other boys were struck by the curiousness of this. They might, indeed, have remained in some sort of benevolent doubt had not Ernest Ralph Gorse, still standing apart and quietly changing, now cut in again.

'That was just a try-on,' he said. 'He knew he was caught, so he tried it on. He thought we wouldn't look. It was his last fling.'

'Yes,' said Kerr, highly grateful to Gorse for having so astutely readjusted the case against Rosen. 'It was your last fling, you filthy little thief, and now you're trying to use it as an excuse.'

'Filthy low thief yourself!' shouted Rosen, and 'What did you say!' shouted Kerr, advancing upon Rosen to make a physical attack, when there was an interruption from outside. Mr Oakes, a junior master, put his head round the door.

'There's a lot of noise going on in here,' he said, and then suavely suggested: 'Shall we have complete silence until you're all changed and upstairs?'

5

Mr Oakes's suggestion was not really a suggestion at all: it was a command: and Mr Oakes was capable, even with this violent, hardened, and for the most part brutish mob, of inspiring the greatest fear.

This was strange, because Mr Oakes was not in fact formidable, either in himself or to himself. Only twenty-two years of age, with a chubby face, curly fair hair, and spectacles, Mr Oakes was in his private life lonely, miserable, and afraid. He had a tendency to spots on his face; he suffered a good deal from earache; he caught colds easily; and he was treated, it seemed to him, contemptuously and basely by the headmaster. He had a mother who lived in Clapham, and to his mother he wrote letters which were on the surface hopeful and courageous, but in reality filled with great pathos. Over and above his unhappiness at the school he was 'in love', and the one he loved, also living in Clapham, he could not 'understand'. Also, it was clear that she did not 'understand' him. She had originally 'understood' him, had, he believed, 'loved' him, and that was what made it all so much worse. In addition there was a nagging mystery as to whether or not there was somebody *else*. He wrote to her almost daily (receiving much less frequent replies) and harped upon this mystery. She stated that there was nobody else: but this she did in an indifferent, and therefore cruel, way, and even if he had believed it he would only have been unhappier still: because in that case there would be no explanation for her erratic and extraordinary attitudes. Then, again, she might simply have *changed*. He only wanted, he told himself, to *know*. And so on and so on and so on, and so forth and so forth and so forth.

Yet the youthful Mr Oakes, weak and tottering as a private individual, had witch-doctor-like power in the school and was able to cause dread amongst savages. He had a mystical alliance and direct means of communication with the study-god, the headmaster Mr Codrington, whose hideous vengeance, with a 'report', he could at any moment summon into action. The boys were quite silent for fully a minute.

Then, one of the boys having crept to the door and ascertained that Mr Oakes was not within hearing distance, they began to whisper, and then, softly, to talk.

'Well – what are we going to do with him, Ryan?' said Kerr. 'It's up to you.'

'He jolly well ought to have his nose punched,' said Ryan.

'He jolly well ought to be stewed in boiling *oil*,' said Roberts.

'Except for the smell,' said the boy who had already pointed out the danger of any sort of physical approach to Rosen, and who did not desire this contribution of his own to the matter in hand to be overlooked.

'Yes. There is *that*,' another boy agreed, and then said 'Pooh!' as though he could already smell something.

'Stewed in boiling oil, turned upside down, have his guts taken out, and sent to Coventry for a week,' suggested Wills, Rosen's original accuser.

'*Cave!*' said the boy nearest the door, thinking he had heard Mr Oakes returning.

There was now a long, cautious silence, which gave Bell the time and peace necessary for creative thought.

'The advisability of dismissing the delinquent to the City of Cycles,' said the gifted Bell, 'is not to be dismissed. But to submerge his physiology in the oleaginous substance does not appertain to civilized behaviour.' There was a pause. 'I therefore suggest,' Bell went on, 'that the venerable and much-respected Order of the Boot be applied by means of pedal extremities to his nether proportions, and that the culprit be summarily dismissed.'

Bell had surpassed himself.

'*Cave!*' said the boy nearest the door, and this time it was not a false alarm. Mr Oakes again put his head round the door.

'Did I hear someone talking?' he asked, and most of the boys cried '*No*, sir!' indignantly; and Bell, who had, in addition to a command of length in language, nerve, said sweetly, 'By no manner of means, sir' – and there was thenceforth actually no word uttered in the changing-room until the school bell rang.

6

Rosen was sensible enough to prolong his changing until the exact moment at which the school bell was rung, and was the last to enter the third-form classroom.

This was a dreary and uncomfortable room, now rendered, owing to the time of year and day, even more dispiriting by the electric light which shone down upon it from two bright bulbs, with white porcelain shades, suspended from the ceiling.

Three rows of three age-worn desks (each of which seated, and harboured the school belongings of, two boys) confronted the smaller and higher master's desk, which contained, for the most part, objects which had been confiscated owing to their illicit circulation in class.

The boys, when brooding, looked either at this desk and the master seated behind it, or at a blackboard on a stand to the left, or at an enormous coloured map of England, showing each county in a particular colour, which hung in the middle of the wall facing them. They usually stared at the map, gloomily realizing, for the thousandth time, that Rutland (in pink) was indeed, as they had been told, the smallest county in England, and very small.

This afternoon, under the supervision of Mr Oakes, history was being examined, and history had recently arrived at the French Revolution. But this brought about no response, caused nothing but electric-lit, map-staring torpor in the spirits of the pupils. Nor was Mr Oakes responsive, his complications at Clapham and a threat of recurring earache almost wholly occupying his mind. While the boys read given pages, he himself pretended to read.

The boys' reading, too, was little more than a pretence. They relied on their wits somehow to see them through when Mr Oakes questioned them, and engaged themselves in many fervent underground communications.

Ryan, seeking in his mind for any sort of means of relieving his tedium, suddenly realized that Rosen had, certainly, to all appearances, behaved atrociously towards him in stealing his torch, and used this as an excuse for sending a note to a plump, spectacled boy named Appleby, who shared a desk with Rosen.

This note, which merely said, '*Kick Rosen for me and tell him just wait*,' was made remarkable by the elaborate manner in which it was addressed:

Appleby,
    Desk nearest door,
        Front Room,
            Rodney House,
                Hove.

– and was passed along to Appleby, who in three minutes' time had sent back a reply.

'*Can't kick him properly because he's too near, but told him to wait,*' wrote Appleby, using the address:

Ryan,
    Desk nearest window,
        Front Room,
            Rodney House,
                Hove,
                    Sussex,
                        England.

Ryan, who had in the meanwhile been reading a little, and had come across in his book the curious name St Just, now inadvertently let Rosen escape from his mind, and sent another note asking, 'Do you think *St Just* was *Just*?' with the address:

Appleby,
    Desk nearest door,
        Front Room,
            Rodney House,
                Hove,
                    Sussex,
                        England,
                            Europe,
                                The World.

To which Appleby replied, 'No, because he *Robed* himself with

Spears,' which was a subtle allusion to St Just's colleague, Maximilien Robespierre, and was addressed to Ryan as follows:

Ryan,
Desk nearest window,
Front Room,
Rodney House,
Hove,
Sussex,
England,
Europe,
The World,
The Universe.

This set Ryan a by no means easy problem, which he at last solved, he believed satisfactorily, by writing, 'Tell Rosen I'll *guillotine* him,' and using the address:

Appleby,
Desk nearest door,
Front Room,
Rodney House,
Hove,
Sussex,
England,
Europe,
The World,
The Universe,
Not Mars.

This, in its turn, was tasking Appleby to the utmost. How, now, could the point occupied by Ryan in eternal space conceivably be presented with more agonized clarity or accuracy?

However, after much thought, Appleby, like Ryan, solved the practically insoluble. He wrote:

Ryan,
RIGHT HAND SIDE of desk nearest window,
Front Room,
Rodney House,
Hove,
Sussex,
England,
Europe,
The World,
The Universe,
Not Mars.

and was just about to add, as a *coup de grâce*, 'AND NOT VENUS EITHER' (which, in fact, opened illimitable possibilities) when Mr Oakes, who had had his eye on both of these boys for some time, asked Appleby what he was doing.

'*Nothing*, sir,' replied Appleby in an injured tone. Yet, though injured, he blushed.

Mr Oakes then replied that Appleby certainly ought to be doing something – he ought to be reading – and Appleby began to stare hard at his book.

And so the afternoon, and the Rosen episode (originated by Ernest Ralph Gorse), bleakly wore on.

7

Between the ringing of the bell which broke up the class and the ringing of the bell which summoned the pupils to tea, there was no time to resume the assault upon Rosen in a systematic way. At the long tea-table itself Rosen occupied a seat next to another junior master, and immediately after tea came 'prep'. Most of the boys did this under supervision in the front room, but others were allowed to go home, where it was presumed that they did their homework, though they certainly did not unless there was something on paper to be shown next morning. Amongst the latter were Rosen, Ryan, Wills, Appleby, and Ernest Ralph Gorse.

Because these boys had recently slipped into the habit of making a great noise in the changing-room before departure, it had become the business of a junior master to see them quickly off the premises. Rosen was thus again temporarily protected.

Nevertheless, during tea, a plot had been hatched, between Appleby and Ryan, who sat next to each other, to attack Rosen as soon as he was outside the school and in the dark. Appleby, in fact, had been inspired by a plan which served the double purpose of vengeance upon Rosen and use of the torch which he was supposed to have stolen.

This plan was curiously complicated and carefully rehearsed in theory beforehand. Ryan and Appleby, it was agreed, would get into their outdoor clothes with the utmost speed and leave the school by the back door, from which Rosen would presently emerge. When they were outside they would prepare to 'ambush' Rosen, but not together. While Ryan was to take his station at the door, Appleby was to stand at twenty yards' distance in the darkness.

Then, as the other boys came out, Ryan was to 'signal' to Appleby with his torch. If the boy who came out was not Rosen, but another, a green light would be flashed to Appleby, whose nervous vigilance and strain would thus be momentarily relieved. If Ryan believed that Rosen was 'just coming' the white light would be flashed on three times (and this three times in succession) and Appleby would brace himself for the coming ordeal. When Rosen himself did come out, the red light, of course, would be used. Action, however, was not to follow instantly. It was now Appleby's business to 'track' Rosen, while Ryan followed Appleby – Appleby himself having an ordinary torch with a plain white light with which, behind his back, he would himself 'signal' to Ryan – and this in 'Morse', which he professed to have mastered. What was to happen after this had not been discussed, and the main point, really, was that light had been most cleverly thrown upon an obscure matter – sense and a positive utility had at last been found in what might have been thought a totally senseless and useless sliding apparatus at the top of Ryan's torch.

But all these plans came to nothing because the passionate but clever Rosen, on coming out of the back door, at once sensed that something was afoot, ran in an unexpected direction, and made his escape. It was impossible even to make an attempt at a chase. Ryan shouted and 'signalled' to Appleby, and they joined each other at the back door.

'It's no good. He's gone,' said Ryan, and at this moment Ernest Ralph Gorse, coming out into the night, heard what had been said.

'Who's gone?' he asked.

'Rosen,' said Ryan. 'He did a bunk and got away.'

'Well, that doesn't matter,' said Ernest Ralph Gorse. 'You can get him tomorrow.'

'Yes,' said Ryan. 'I suppose we can . . .'

Ryan spoke without enthusiasm, for he did not in his heart believe in Rosen's guilt, and, unlike most of his fellows, was not the sort of boy who was even more anxious to persecute the guiltless rather than the guilty. He was only anxious to make use of his torch. This he now did, turning on the white, the green, the red, the white, the green.

The other two boys stood observing these flashes, and a rather funny silence fell upon all three. This silence may have been due to their absorption in the unspeakably beautiful, the absolutely divine colours piercing the blackness: but it may, in addition, have been due to something else. It may, to a certain degree, have been caused by the fact that Ryan and Appleby, without knowing it, did not wholly like Ernest Ralph Gorse, and felt his presence to be an interruption of their pleasure.

'You'll wear out the battery,' said Appleby at last.

'Got three more in reserve,' said Ryan, and there was another silence . . .

'What are you going to do to him,' said Ernest Ralph Gorse in his level, nasal voice, 'when you catch him tomorrow?'

Such a return to the question of Rosen, in the midst of the divine flashes, was instinctively felt by Ryan and Appleby to be a little coarse, boring, unnecessary, and odd.

'I don't know,' said Ryan half-heartedly. 'What would you?'

'I'd tie him up,' said Ernest Ralph Gorse, 'if I were you.'

And this extraordinary remark succeeded in surprising Ryan and Appleby on a conscious level.

'What do you mean?' said Ryan with a casual air which concealed his bewilderment.

'Yes. That's what I'd do, if I were you,' said Ernest Ralph Gorse. 'I'd tie him up.'

But he had not thrown any further light upon his meaning, and Ryan, flashing his torch off and on, made a brief mental endeavour fully to comprehend what had been said. Tie Rosen up? Why? And what when he was tied up? Or was 'tying up' some sort of new invention by Gorse, something to be regarded as a punishment in itself?

Ryan was unable to find a satisfactory answer, and was not the sort of boy to seek one for long. Asking a patient Appleby whether he now wanted to 'have a go' with the torch, he dismissed the matter from his mind, and here the Rosen episode came to an end, for no one brought the matter up again next day.

Something more than a quarter of a century later, however, those words of Gorse, uttered while the torch flashed in the darkness of that night, were to return to Ryan, and were to have meaning.

Chapter Two

I

Those flashes of the little torch in the night – the red, the white, the green! Were these, to Ernest Ralph Gorse, in any sort of way what they were to Appleby and Ryan?

Did he, as they did, standing there in excitement and rapture, see little holes being pierced into the blackness, holes through which one might gaze into paradise – now a cool green paradise, now a blazing red paradise, now a blinding white paradise in which the visible and glorious filaments of the bulb might have been the crystalline flower of paradise itself?

Seemingly he did not. He did not even wait to ask Ryan to allow him to use the torch. Without saying goodnight, he left the other two in the darkness and entered the lamplight of Rodney Road.

If not inspired by paradise, in what, then, could this boy be interested? Was he interested in anything at all? Yes – for he took pleasure, as has been seen, in military exercises, and he was, apparently, sufficiently interested in human nature to desire to see the results of surreptitiously slipping a torch belonging to one boy into the pocket of another.

Again, were these pure, artistic interests? Did he enjoy military exercises and the observation of human nature for their own sakes? Or was there something more to it than this? Did he, perhaps, dimly perceive and relish the huge potentialities for the infliction of universal pain behind the seemingly innocent and childish military drill? And was his little experiment with human nature in fact conducted mostly for the sake of watching the misery of the victim?

No certain answer can be given. The type to which Ernest Ralph Gorse belonged cannot ever be fully understood at depth: only shrewd or inspired guesses can be made.

Now that the boy was out under the lamps on his half-mile walk back to the house in which he lived in Denmark Villas, he had further business of an uncommon sort to do.

This consisted of sticking a large pin, which he carried for the purpose in the lapel of his overcoat, into the tyres of as many bicycles as he might find, on his way home, propped up against the kerb in dark places.

Although, in those faraway nights, there were many such bicycles, Gorse's task was by no means easy. To avoid detection, a good deal of preliminary observation and lurking was necessary, and the deed required histrionic ability – the simulation of an air of nonchalance as he approached the bicycle, of a detached interest in its make or style. Often, in the pursuit of this hobby of his, Gorse would arrive home twenty minutes or more later than he would have in the ordinary way.

Tonight he met with nothing satisfactory to work upon until he was within fifty yards of his own home: but here his watchfulness was rewarded with a machine in a situation of the most delightful vulnerability. Here he had, also, the pleasure both of knowing that it belonged to a neighbour and of knowing who the neighbour was. He stuck his pin twice into the front tyre and twice into the back one, and half a minute later he was indoors.

Ernest Ralph Gorse never knew – because he felt that it was too dangerous to wait and see – whether these pricks with his pin brought about an almost immediate deflation of the tyre. He confidently believed, though, that a slow puncture was begun in nearly every case, and he was certain that eventual damage of some sort had at any rate been achieved.

2

Ernest Ralph Gorse's mother and father were dead: he lived with his stepmother: and he had a home background which caused him intuitively not to ask friends back to tea.

He had taken, indeed, even at this early age, a dislike to his social beginnings, and this in spite of having been often told that he had much to be proud of in his father, George Gorse, who had been, in his day, a successful, and in certain circles even well-known, commercial artist – the creator of a famous cartoon advertising a toothpaste. But the precocious Ernest Ralph was not interested in art of any sort, and he did not fancy a connection with advertising and toothpaste.

Also, his father's second wife had at one time served behind a West End bar, and although Ernest Ralph was not aware of this, all his instincts informed him that there was something out of order in this second marriage.

He could remember nothing of his mother, and little of his father. A solicitor uncle, Sydney Gorse, was his guardian, and frequently paid visits to the house in Denmark Villas.

His stepmother was one of those remarkable, fat, excessively genial women who are, for some reason, despite their somewhat advanced age and fleshiness, never without quite serious admirers. Known as good 'sorts', or great or grand 'sports', they seem to have the power of enslaving men physically purely by the warmth of their spiritual nature. (Service behind a bar undoubtedly has some occult connection with the creation of this type of woman.) Mrs Gorse was now fifty-seven, but little as her stepson could conceive such a thing, it was not totally impossible that she had notions of marrying again, and that she was actually in a position to put such notions into practice.

The relationship between Mrs Gorse, who made little active endeavour to conceal the fact that she had sprung from the people, and Ernest Ralph Gorse, who already knew that it was inadvisable to ask his friends round to tea, was of the weirdest kind, and marked by suspicion and caution on both sides.

The fault, needless to say, did not lie with the genial second Mrs Gorse. She had made every attempt to make the boy happy and reasonable, and, conscious without being ashamed of her social origins, had been scrupulously careful not to 'stand in his way', as she put it.

Although she believed that she might be capable of 'passing', she never attended, as most parents did, any of the cricket matches, sports, fireworks, parties, prize-givings, and plays given by the school: she never, in fact, made any appearance at the school, or had any interview or direct communication with the headmaster: all that was necessary in this way was left to the uncle.

All the same, she did not like the boy, and was unable to force herself to do so. And, although an extremely fine judge of character, as such a type of ex-barmaid always is, she was unable quite to name to herself what it was which she found so distasteful, if not almost detestable, in her stepson. She contented herself with telling herself (and her intimate friends) that he was a 'funny' one, an 'odd' one, a 'rum' one, and she predicted that his future would be curious. She said that she never knew 'what he was thinking'.

To dislike and distrust anyone – let alone a child, and a child so closely connected to her – ran so much against the grain of Mrs Gorse's character that it caused her whole personality and manner, when in contact or conversation with him, to change. Normally a carefree, laughing, nearly boisterously uninhibited woman – one who was the life and soul of parties in the private rooms of the public houses which she still discreetly visited – with Ernest Ralph Gorse she was actually timid, shy. When she spoke to him she spoke quietly, and looked at him. Often, when not speaking to him, she would look at him. And this for as much as a minute on end, as if she still sought to discover his secret.

Mrs Gorse's manner to himself seemed to be, and almost certainly was, a matter of indifference to Ernest Ralph Gorse. With such a character any kind of behaviour – kindness, cheerfulness, sourness, spitefulness, or even physical brutality – would have produced the same outward response. These would have been, in any event, the same slouching, inimical demeanour: the same slightly nasty smell under the nose.

3

Tonight, when her stepson returned, Mrs Gorse was not at home.

She had, in fact, been out most of the day, and was at this moment drinking stout with familiars in a remote private residence at Preston Park. But Ernest Ralph knew nothing of her whereabouts.

Nearly every week she was twice or three times away from home when he returned from school, but he was not neglected. A maid-of-all-work, Mabel, who was nineteen years of age and who slept in, was there to look after his needs.

The sentiments of Mabel in regard to Ernest Ralph Gorse were, unlike those of Mrs Gorse, uncomplicated: they were those of sheer hatred. This was not because she was, like Mrs Gorse, a fine judge of character. An inexperienced, lumpy girl, she was anything but this. She simply hated boys of this age on pure, academic principles. She had had to live with young brothers and her mind was warped in this direction, perhaps for life. She was, therefore, being unfair to the young Gorse, particularly because in point of fact he gave her very much less trouble (or 'sauce') than nearly any other boy of his age might have given her. He was not the sort of boy to give trouble of the conventional kind to which she was habituated.

Ernest Ralph Gorse did not make a noise, and was orderly in his habits. Also, curiously enough, he had hobbies which kept him quiet. It was curious that a boy who was not interested in paradise could be interested in hobbies. This contradiction was, however, possibly explicable on the grounds that his interest in hobbies was not essentially disinterested. He pursued hobbies for the sake of vainglory and prestige at his school. He had the largest and finest collection of cigarette cards at the school, and the largest and most intricately made fleet of model battleships. But he was a hoarder rather than a genuine collector. He would slowly assemble his fleet of battleships in secret, and then one day appear at school with a huge cardboard box containing them under his arm. Having caused general curiosity, he would open this box at an appropriate and if possible dramatic moment, and become the centre of attraction. All rivals would be snubbed, and he would glow with quiet, ginger-haired, level-eyed power.

He was clever with his hands, and was at present engaged upon an elaborate piece of fretwork. Fretwork was in the air at the school just at this time, was due to succeed torches, and by the employment of foresight he proposed to outshine his fellows with a masterpiece.

He had a hobby room on the first floor at the back, and to this he retired at once on returning. Here he remained until his supper at seven-thirty.

Mabel would cook Ernest Ralph's supper and lay it on the dining-room table, with an air of being meticulously just. However much she might abominate him, his supper was his due, and she was not going to let him gain any moral advantage by not getting his supper properly and punctually.

'Your supper, Master Gorse!' she would cry up from below, but the words, which in print would seem cordial enough, were shouted in a way which filled them with vindictiveness and the resentful intimation that she was keeping *her* side of the bargain.

'All right!' he would shout down, and these, on most evenings when they were alone together, would be all the words which passed between them.

Then Master Ralph would wash his hands (he was clean in his personal habits) and go into the dining-room to eat.

After eating, this evening, he returned to his fretwork for an hour, and then, taking his cage of white mice with him, wen the bathroom and had a bath.

Then he took his five white mice from the cage and made them swim in the bath. This he did almost every night, whether he himself was bathing or not, and the ceremony seldom took less than half an hour.

His furry pets, their heads held painfully high, would scramble and scamper through the water from one end of the bath to the other and back again. It would be impossible to say for certain whether they enjoyed this on the whole or not: but probably they did not. Master Gorse would endeavour to engineer 'races' between different mice, but this was always a failure, as it was impossible to arrive at a decision with creatures who did not know what they were being set to do and every now and again gave signs of extreme panic.

Neither Mrs Gorse nor Mabel knew anything about this nightly immersion of his white mice. Had they done so, they would have put an end to it.

Having roughly dried off his white mice in the dark and merciful recesses of a bath towel, Ernest Ralph put them back into their cage, took the cage into his bedroom, undressed, put out the light, and went to bed. Before sleeping he lay on his back, and thought.

4

It may be assumed that the material for thought for boys of his age in those days was very different from what it is in these; but such was not, really, the case. There was remarkably little difference. The games were the same – cricket in summer and football in winter – there was the motorcar, the aeroplane, the battleship (from 'dreadnought' to submarine), the steam train, the bomb, the revolver, the air gun, the electric torch, and electrical equipment of all kinds, even including 'wireless' in its early state – almost precisely all those things, in fact, over which the juvenile mind today might brood blissfully before sleeping.

What went on in the social adult world of that day, on the other hand – a world not as yet emancipated from its watch chains, and still subservient to the walking stick – a world in which the horse-cab continued to plough its way through streets filled with a squat, bowler-hatted, vindictively moustached middle class and proletariat: a world whose 'politics' manifested itself in the wearing of Conservative or Liberal favours: a world menaced by the militant suffragette yet enlivened by the 'hobble-skirt', the 'tango', the 'knut', and 'ragtime' – what went on in this world certainly differed considerably from what goes on at the present day, but entered only in a blurred, practically meaningless way into the consciousness of the juvenile – was, in fact, as remote and freakish to him as it would be to a man of the present era attempting mentally to reconstruct that past. He would give it no thought in bed.

As Ernest Ralph Gorse lay awake tonight he could hear, even from this distance in Denmark Villas, the English Channel crashing against the beach in the dark – crashing in the dark against the watch chains, the walking sticks, the horse-cabs, the hobble-skirt, the knut, the tango.

The voice of any sort of water beating against any sort of shore at night may be construed in a multitude of ways – as soothing, as menacing, as cynical, as reminiscent, or as prophetic. If the English Channel had been prophesying that night there was certainly no one listening in the town who could have effectually interpreted its obscure though pounded and reiterated utterances – least of all any allusions it might be making to those expeditionary forces of soldiers which in the very near as well as more distant future were destined to float upon its own bosom.

Chapter Three

I

To all those boys at Rodney House, that summer was the longest and most golden of their lives, and this was not because it was (as it was in fact) an exceptionally long, fine summer; it was because it was the one immediately preceding the world war of that era. It was to stand out in their minds in rich, warm contrast with the four black winters to follow. Wars, on the whole, are remembered by their winters. Also, when the war was over, the boys were older, and so the summers were naturally shorter.

Under the arrangement that the boys of Rodney House should play and drill on the County Ground, it was in addition permissible for them to enter the ground free of charge when county matches were in progress. In term-time, under the supervision of a master, they were taken down to watch such matches in the late afternoons, and in the holidays very many of them would separately or in couples take advantage of this privilege. It thus came about that the commencement of the war was to many of these boys ever afterwards to be sunnily and rather weirdly connected with the County Ground and cricket.

One sunny evening, shortly after the gentle tea interval of a county match, something almost resembling a scene, or even a disturbance or riot, took place inside the County Ground. About a dozen men, wearing uniforms and blowing through brass instruments, began to march around the outer path encircling the seats and the stands. The noise they made could not possibly be ignored, and they were almost at once followed by a crowd of small boys as well as many inquisitive adults. Others, watching the cricket and desiring to continue to do so, did not quite know what to do, or what exactly this noise was intended to convey.

Before long, however, the intention became more and more clear. This blowing through military brass was being directed against the flannelled fool still at the wicket while his country was in peril; and soon enough the attention of the entire crowd was divided equally and rather uglily between the game and the band.

This entirely unnecessary, gratuitous, and largely bestial assault upon the players (curiously akin in atmosphere to the smashing up of a small store by the henchmen of a gangster) beyond doubt ended in the victory of the aggressor – though at the time of its happening very few people present were able vividly or exactly to understand what was taking place.

Ernest Ralph Gorse was amongst the crowd of small boys following the band – so also were Ryan and Bell. Ryan and Bell were delighted simply by the music. Gorse was not the sort of boy to whom music in itself appealed; nevertheless, he was much more pleased than they were.

He could not have said why. He inhaled unconsciously the distant aroma of universal evil and was made happy, that was all.

Astute and precocious as he was, he was unable to tell himself in so many words that his day had come.

2

Ryan and Bell were innocently delighted by the music; and, paradoxically, they were at first almost equally delighted by its sequel; for there was a good deal of paradise for the Ryans and Bells of life in the early days of the First World War.

There was colour: an air of a festival: flags. To the charms of the Union Jack they were almost dulled by familiarity: but the French Flag, the Belgian Flag! And even the Union Jack was tricked out in new ways, with likenesses of the King and Queen set in its middle, or displayed in conjunction with the French and Belgian flags. Then there was the royalty – the King and Queen, of course, but, better still, the Tsar, and, again, even better still, the King of the Belgians! Then the leaders – the plumed General Joffre, the medalled Sir John French, the more simply attired but by no means less inspiring Sir John Jellicoe! – their bright images littering every kind of place – even, indeed particularly, the lesser sweet-shops, where it was possible to buy, instead of sweets, small, glazed, coloured discs of any of these national figures – these discs being attached to pins which one might stick into the lapel of one's coat. The war was, to the Ryans and Bells, very much a small-sweet-shop war.

The 'Red Cross' itself, contributing its own flag, added further vivid colour: not least when assisting the return of wounded 'Tommies', who were depicted with bandages set heroically aslant one eye of their weary faces, and as carrying captured German helmets in their limp hands.

And against the 'Tommy' the 'Uhlan', and against the 'Uhlan', at a distance, the 'Cossack!' – and Kaiser and Kitchener, and new figures and flags and events each day to stir irresistibly the happy imaginations of Ryan and Bell.

Slowly, however, the hues of heaven began to fade from all this: the photograph of the scene, as the winter set in, was no longer tinted; it became, like any ordinary photograph, the colour of mud, possibly even muddier. By Christmas Ryan and Bell were looking forward to the end of the war, and were conscious of doing so. They said as much.

With Ernest Ralph Gorse, naturally, there was throughout an entirely different reaction to contemporary events. These never at any time bore the hues of heaven: nevertheless, he was stimulated and satisfied beyond measure in his own way. As on the drill-ground in peacetime he was brighter and more alert, a different boy. After all, was not what was happening the realization, on a vast and unforeseen scale, of all the latent suggestions and aspirations existing in the drill? Gorse did not talk much about the war (he never talked much about anything), but he studied the maps and the illustrated papers with a thoroughness phenomenal in one of his years, and with a peculiar look of complacency on his face – a look which never varied. Victories or defeats in arms for the Allies or for their enemies seemed to make exactly the same impression upon him. It was as if all were equally satisfying.

Many of his school companions at this period spoke of their anxiety to be in the forces, and of their regret that their age did not permit this. Such talk was, needless to say, pure nonsense and boyish pretence on their parts. Gorse, on the other hand, never made any such protestation, but it was likely that he in fact genuinely desired to be in the middle of the conflict. At any rate, he envied the wearing of an adult uniform – an officer's uniform, of course – with so profound a feeling that he was blinded to any perils that it might entail. He had now, as later, a sort of mania for uniforms – a fixation.

As the Christmas Term of 1914 at Rodney House wore on, and was followed by the Easter Term of 1915, life grew blacker and bleaker for the Ryans and Bells. Games were still played in sweaters and shorts, but moral precedence, as well as an enormous amount of free time previously allotted to games, was now given over to drill in uniforms with puttees which made the legs itch incessantly. The boys were made to march during what would normally have been happy breaks and half holidays: they were even made to march to and from their games – the whole day throbbing hideously to the tune of Left-left,-left-right-left. As a crowning horror, on the night of November 5, 1915, there were no organized fireworks as before; instead there was a torchlight parade in the back garden of Rodney House. Parents were invited and the boys drilled and sang patriotic songs in front of them.

Three days before the Christmas Term began, that is to say three days before the end of the holidays of that long, uncanny summer before the First World War, a long and slightly uncanny interview took place between Mr Codrington, the headmaster of Rodney House, and a policeman dressed in plain clothes.

3

Throughout this interview, which took place on yet another sunny evening, Mr Codrington, a thin, spectacled man, was evasive, and at first he did not fully understand, or at any rate he pretended that he did not fully understand, what the precise point of the interview was.

The policeman, also, was politely evasive, though he fully knew what he was about. He had on his person a long statement, which he did not actually show to Mr Codrington, but which told a story which he roughly outlined to the headmaster.

The story seemed to be a peculiarly odd and unpleasant one to Mr Codrington; though to the experienced officer it was nothing very much out of the way.

A few evenings previously, it seemed, a young girl of eleven had been found in a shed underneath the grandstand of the County Ground. She had been found tied to a roller, and screaming in panic for help.

A junior groundsman, working late, had heard cries from a distance, and had finally located her and released her. He had then taken her home crying to her parents – humble people who kept a small tobacco-and-newspaper shop in George Street, Hove. The father had then taken the child, now mollified and perhaps not altogether displeased by the limelight which the adventure as a whole had cast upon her, to the police station, where she had been talkative and made a detailed statement.

This statement, though doubtless entirely truthful, had all the weirdness and unreality of nearly every statement made to the police under such circumstances. When read in court and afterwards published in the newspapers, they almost always puzzle, baffle, and even irritate the reader, who feels that there is something indirect, forced, and false about them. This, almost certainly, is owing to the fact that although they have all the appearance of being a series of direct utterances poured forth spontaneously, they are in reality the result of wearisome and plodding questions put to the witness during a long period of time.

Fragments of the statement made by Ethel Joyce, the little girl from George Street, will serve to illustrate this point as well as to give some impression of what took place on that summer's evening at the County Ground, Hove.

Having given her name and address and age, and after other preliminaries having thoroughly established her identity, the little girl went on thus:

'I was on my way home to George Street. I stopped at the sweet-shop in Alwyn Road, which is near the back entrance of the County Ground. The name of the sweet-shop is Gregson's. I am familiar [*sic*] with it. I go in there often. I went in to buy lemonade powder.

'When inside I spoke to a little man. He seemed to be a little man. He may have been a boy. I think he was a boy. He wore no hat, but carried a green cap in his pocket. I think it was a school cap. I am not certain but think so – it was definitely [*sic*] green. He had very fair hair. I would know him if I saw him again. He spoke to me and offered me a drink of lemonade . . .'

Ethel Joyce then described how she drank two glasses of lemonade with the boy and then continued in the same irritating, because slightly mysterious and not fully comprehensible, way:

'After we left the shop he suggested that we enter the County Ground by the back entrance. I agreed. He said this was for fun. The back entrance was locked, but he said we could climb over. He assisted me to do so. There were spikes on the gate, but he showed me a way of avoiding them. We climbed up and jumped down from a pillar at one side.

'Having entered the ground, he took me to a shed underneath the big wooden stand. Here he found a rope. He did not have this rope when I met him, but I think he knew it was in the shed. I had a skipping-rope with me, but this was not a skipping-rope.

'He then suggested that I should tie him up for fun. I did as he said, and when I had untied him he suggested that he should tie me up as well. I agreed to this, and he tied me to the roller so that I could not free myself.

'He then left me, and as he did not return I became frightened and called out. He then returned and put his hand over my mouth and told me to be quiet.

'He had been gone about two minutes. Perhaps it was not as long as that – I cannot be certain. It was long enough for me to be frightened.

'I then asked him to untie me, but he was rude and said he had no intention of doing so. He seemed excited.

'He then said, "What have you got on you – eh?" and he took my purse from my pocket. The purse contained sevenpence-halfpenny – a sixpence and two coppers. He then put his hand over my mouth again and told me I had better keep quiet after he had gone. He said, "It will be the worse for you if you don't." He hurt me and bruised my face in putting his hand over my mouth.

'He then ran away and I was quiet as he had told me. He took my purse with him. After five minutes alone in the shed again I became frightened and began to cry out . . .'

The child then went on to describe how she was found by the groundsman, released, and taken home to her parents. Towards the end of her statement she repeated her description of her assailant – the 'little man' who on reflection she believed was a boy.

'I am sure,' she said, 'that the cap he had in his pocket was green. His hair was very fair. I was struck by his fair hair. I would know him again by it.'

Mr Codrington, listening gravely, not to this statement but to a précis of the story generally given by the policeman, only just succeeded in disguising a slight change of countenance – a sudden sharpening of interest in his eyes – when the green cap was mentioned. Here, he realized, was the matter with which he might conceivably be concerned. For the Rodney House school cap was of a startling green colour; and it was by virtue of wearing this cap that the boys were permitted by the turnstile attendants to enter the County Ground free of charge when county matches were in progress. The green caps were, in fact, a minor but familiar feature of the ground.

Mr Codrington also found himself disguising a thoughtful look behind his spectacles when mention was made of the unusual fairness of the boy's hair. He endeavoured rapidly in his mind to summon up any of his pupils who might be described as having fair, or outstandingly fair, hair, and for some reason which he could not understand he found his mind almost instantly fixed and concentrating upon Ernest Ralph Gorse.

He was the less able to understand his own lightning mental processes because Gorse's hair was not what one would, strictly speaking, call 'fair'. It was 'red' – or 'ginger'. With so many boys with genuinely fair hair in the school, why should his mind have been attracted with that astonishing magnetic speed to a boy whose hair was ginger?

As the policeman talked he attempted inwardly to find an answer to this problem and met with a certain amount of success. His mind had rushed headlong to Gorse, he believed, simply because his hair was of a remarkable colour, and the child who had been tied up and robbed in the shed had made it clear that she thought the hair of her assailant remarkable. Many boys at Rodney House had fair hair, but by no means in any remarkable way.

The small girl, Mr Codrington noticed, had made no mention of ginger or red hair, and if Ernest Ralph Gorse had been the delinquent, this was odd. But then the small girl was a small girl, and as such likely to be bewildered and unreliable: she had shown complete confusion of mind by first of all making that queer allusion to a 'little man' to whom she had spoken, and then afterwards saying that he was a boy.

Then something else occurred to Mr Codrington. He knew the shed underneath the stand to which the policeman was referring, and he knew also that this was used as a base for hide-and-seek, as a 'den', and for other childish, mischievous purposes by certain of his pupils: he had more than once had to clear the shed of these boys. And he knew, over and above this, that Gorse had always been present when such clearances had been made. He had always felt, in fact, that Gorse had been the ringleader of any boys playing in this shed. It had been, as it were, Gorse's shed.

Having reflected on these lines – and such reflections occupied less than a minute in time – Mr Codrington had a fairly good idea why his mind had in the first place flashed at once to Ernest Ralph Gorse.

His having succeeded in understanding his own mental processes did not, however, make Mr Codrington in any way disbelieve in his intuition about Gorse. On the contrary, it supported it. As a consequence his eyes, behind his spectacles, grew more and more watchful, and his manner became subtly more guarded. For Mr Codrington was not anxious for it to become known in public that one of his pupils had tied up a small girl in a shed, seriously frightened her, and robbed her of her purse.

Towards the end of the interview the policeman came candidly to the point. He explained that the green school cap, taken in conjunction firstly with the fact that the assault and robbery had taken place in the County Ground, and secondly with the fact that the juvenile assailant and robber was evidently acquainted with the County Ground (so far acquainted as to know of the existence of a rope in one of its back sheds), made it seem likely that a boy from Rodney House was concerned in the matter. Could Mr Codrington be of any assistance? Was there at Rodney House any boy with exceptionally fair hair whom Mr Codrington might feel justified in suspecting – any boy who had, perhaps, to Mr Codrington's knowledge, at an earlier date, misbehaved himself in some such manner?

At this Mr Codrington made an elaborate pretence of thinking disinterestedly yet earnestly, and then answered in a negative manner which simulated entire bewilderment. He said that there were certainly several boys with fair hair in the school, but that did not take one anywhere. There were boys with fair hair in every school. There was certainly no boy at Rodney House who had ever, to his knowledge, committed anything resembling any such offence.

Then, although the interview was conducted throughout on the most friendly terms and in the spirit of co-operation, Mr Codrington went, as it were, over to the attack. He suggested that what had been assumed to be a boy might, after all, have been a 'little man', or at any rate an older and more mature boy than any at his own preparatory school. He said that there were many other schools in Brighton and Hove whose pupils wore caps incorporating the colour green, and he mentioned one or two of these schools. He admitted the singular and undivided greenness of the Rodney House cap, but he did not think that this amounted to anything. How much of the cap did the plainly rather unreliable little girl see sticking out of the boy's pocket? Finally he made what he thought was a strong point. Why, he asked, should any boy from his school find it necessary to effect a difficult entrance into the County Ground by a spiked back entrance when, by virtue of being a pupil at Rodney House, he was entirely at liberty to enter in the proper way at the front? Were not the front gates open at the time of the incident, and was it not in fact a matter of the utmost ease to enter at these gates at such a time and such a season of the year, unseen by anyone? Was there not, therefore, every indication that the boy had no connection with the school and probably belonged to a rough, hooligan type?

The policeman, throughout the interview as shy and guarded in his manner as Mr Codrington, seemed to agree with most of this, and made it clear that he had visited Mr Codrington merely on the off-chance of gaining information or assistance. Soon afterwards he left, shaking hands with Mr Codrington, and talking about the weather and the war.

When he had gone Mr Codrington was only dimly aware that he had failed to tell the truth, the whole truth, and nothing but the truth. He had all the same failed to do this. He had not seen fit to tell the policeman that he was for certain reasons well acquainted with the shed underneath the stand, and it had therefore been impossible for him to say that this shed was associated in his mind with Ernest Ralph Gorse. He had also been disingenuous in his remarks about the spiked back gate to the County Ground, for if he had searched his mind thoroughly at the time he would have remembered that he in fact knew that there were boys from his school who liked to climb over this gate when it was locked. These boys had a passion for defeating the spikes for the sake of adventure, and only two summers ago he had, in the course of an admonitory lecture about various matters to the school as a whole, threatened to punish such dangerous folly. Finally, he had failed to tell the policeman that as the story had been unfolded the figure of Ernest Ralph Gorse, the boy with the remarkable hair, had flashed at once into his mind.

Though normally an honest man, Mr Codrington had on this occasion been dishonest, both to himself and to the policeman. For this reason, after the policeman had gone, he was faintly disquieted in his conscience.

As he had a lot of letters to write and work to do that evening in preparation for the coming term, this feeling of disquietude soon left him, and when he thought about the matter next morning he was confident that his attitude had been entirely correct. Any suspicions he might have had about Ernest Ralph Gorse were, of course, fantastic. The whole thing, as connected with any boy at Rodney House, was fantastic.

The small girl had undoubtedly imagined or invented a good deal in what could have been nothing worse than some sort of prank, and, moreover, had come to no harm beyond the loss of sevenpence-halfpenny and a purse.

The policeman did not call again; nothing further ever came to light; and Mr Codrington almost entirely banished the story from his mind.

Nevertheless, when Ernest Ralph Gorse appeared at the school on the first day of the new term Mr Codrington found himself looking at him. And, as the term progressed, he for some reason still found himself looking at him. He would look at him in class for as long as thirty seconds, very much in the same way as Mrs Gorse would look at her stepson. It became a sort of habit. He would look particularly at his hair, and try to get an impression of its exact colour.

This habit became less easy to break because in the Easter Term which followed Gorse was promoted to the senior form, which was the one which Mr Codrington most frequently took. In fact, at last Mr Codrington reached a stage at which he had definitely to resolve to himself not to look at Gorse. But he was unable to achieve this.

Towards the end of the Easter Term the boy's guardian, Sydney Gorse, called upon Mr Codrington. He explained that the stepmother was moving to London – to Chiswick – and that the boy was to be sent to school not far away – to Colet Court in Hammersmith. Later he would go on to St Paul's.

At the end of the term Mr Codrington invited Gorse to his study in order to give him the conventional headmaster's valedictory discourse. During this discourse he looked at him, behind his spectacles, more closely than ever. What was going on in Mr Codrington's head, during these last few moments of his acquaintanceship with Gorse, it would not be easy to say. Probably Mr Codrington had no idea himself.

It may be guessed, though, that Mr Codrington, in addition to being the first individual to protect Ernest Ralph Gorse from the results of a serious misdemeanour, was also (apart from Mrs Gorse) the first faintly to suspect that the boy had a remarkable future.

PART TWO

GETTING OFF

Chapter One

I

Towards dusk on a summer's evening three years after the First World War, two girls of about eighteen years of age walked arm in arm along the Brighton front.

One of these girls was exceptionally pretty; the other seemed to be exceptionally plain. The latter, who wore spectacles, was certainly not as plain as she seemed to be; her plainness was much exaggerated by the observer because she was seen beside her friend, who was indeed spectacularly pretty.

The fact of their walking arm in arm, as well as the way in which they did this, revealed the sort of class to which these two girls belonged. Though remarkably well dressed, they quite evidently came from a poor quarter of the town and were of working-class origin and occupation. The way in which they walked made manifest, too, the real object of their walking; so also did the time and place at which they walked – the hour of dusk on a sea-front. They were looking forward, or at any rate laying themselves open to, encounters with men, or with boys of their own age.

It may be thought curious that, their object being what it was, one of them should have been so pretty while the other was so plain. It might be supposed that normally a pretty girl would pair with a pretty girl, and a plain one with a plain one. But such is not the case. Owing to some mystifying law of psychology or expediency, couples of this sort are more often than not composed of such opposites, and this law has always been as dismaying as it is mystifying to those young men who are also walking in pairs and desiring to talk to girls. Who is to take, to put up with, to be palmed off with, the 'other one'?

The causes of this law must be numerous and complicated. Perhaps the pretty girl adopts the ugly one quite selfishly in order to enhance her own beauty by means of contrast. On the contrary, she may be moved by pity, an anxiety to help her friend. She might, indeed, have both these ideas in her mind at the same time. Then again she may choose to walk abroad with an ugly girl so that there is no question of a rival. Or she may do so for the sake of base vanity, of showing off her powers of attraction in front of one who, incapable of attracting men herself, will be duly impressed and will offer up incense. On the other hand, the relationship may often practically be forced upon the pretty girl by the ugly one. The latter, in order to bathe in something of the glamour of the former, may make herself so useful to her in a variety of ways, may show herself so wonderfully willing to listen to confidences, to advise and sympathize, or even to play the part of a go-between, that she makes herself at last almost indispensable to the other. Plain girls may have solid useful qualities which pretty girls may not be so foolish as to disregard. Whatever the answer to the riddle is, in any given case, there is probably some hidden bargain behind such partnerships.

These two girls were walking from the direction of the Palace Pier towards the West Pier, which they had nearly reached.

At about a hundred yards' distance from the West Pier some sort of suggestive nudging took place between their interlocked arms, and they turned away to the left to the railing overlooking the sea. They leaned over these railings and gave an imitation of observing the beauties of what remained of the sunset.

'Go on,' said the pretty girl to her companion. 'Have a look *now*.'

'No,' said the ugly girl. '*You look*.'

'No – *you* look,' said the pretty girl, and she was in due course obeyed. The pretty girl is usually ultimately obeyed on such occasions, for, in addition to her ascendancy for other reasons, she is the initiator, the senior officer, the skilled and experienced campaigner in operations of this nature.

'Yes,' said the ugly girl. 'Here they come.'

She was alluding to three young men whom they had believed to have been following them.

'All right. Just pretend to be looking out at the sea,' said the mature strategist, in a quiet, steady tone which in fact betrayed some nervousness by virtue of its quietness and steadiness.

'It's a lovely evening,' she added. 'Ain't it?'

2

The pretty girl bore a pretty name – Esther Downes – and the ugly girl bore an ugly one – Gertrude Perks. Fortune, in the case of these two girls, had made up its mind to use no half measures of any kind.

After they had been gazing out over the sea in silence for a minute or so – and after they had intimated to each other, by further imperceptible (indeed practically immaterial) nudgings, that each knew that the three young men who had been following them had caught them up and passed them from behind – Gertrude Perks spoke.

'I think,' said Gertrude, 'they're going on the Pier.'

'Oh – are they?' said Esther, and there was in her voice something which suggested that she felt that she was about to receive a challenge of some sort.

'Yes – they're going on now,' said the vigilant Gertrude.

'Oh well,' said Esther, 'maybe *we'll* be going on too.'

Now Esther's voice showed quite clearly that she thought a challenge had been thrown at her – if not a positive affront. During the last few evenings these three young men had been passing and re-passing her and her friend in a manner which vividly conveyed only one thing – that they desired, and intended soon, to come up and speak to them, to 'get off'. Indeed Esther had been almost certain that they would do so tonight. And here they were coolly going on the Pier by themselves!

The Pier was intimately and intricately connected with the entire ritual of 'getting off'. Indeed, without the Pier, 'getting off' would have been to some minds inconceivable, or at any rate a totally different thing. The Pier was at once the object and arena of 'getting off', and usually the first subtle excuse made by the male for having been so bold as to 'get off' was his saying that he thought it might be 'nice' to go on the Pier. An invitation to go on the Pier was like an invitation to dance; it almost conferred upon 'getting off' an air of respectability. And so now these three young men, by going on the Pier by themselves, had, as it were, established their independence doubly – firstly by the act itself, and secondly by proving that they were in no way anxious to avail themselves of any excuse.

'All right. Let's go on, then,' said the eager and inexperienced Gertrude Perks.

But the wiser Esther replied that there was 'no hurry', and she continued to gaze out at the sea.

3

Esther had much to consider and weigh in her mind. Had she been affronted, and, if so, was the offence too gross for her to stomach? Was she making a mountain out of a molehill, or was she in danger of losing face by making a molehill out of a mountain? If she went on the Pier now, might it not be a clear case of the unthinkable – of 'following' them? And, apart from any injury to her own pride, would not such a thing amount to an appalling mistake from a purely tactical point of view? On the other hand, was it not absolutely the truth that she had, when she had come out this evening, intended to go on the Pier in any case? Why, therefore, should these three impudent young men (if indeed they were intending to be impudent) be allowed to interfere with her original plan? Then there were her purely aesthetic desires to be considered. She genuinely liked walking on the Pier for its own sake: she liked its lights, its band, its slot machines, its smell of tar, its rusty foundations, its noise of people's footsteps clacking incessantly on wood just above the satin-surfaced sea, its curious iron-grille quadrangle at the end, and its vast views of twinkling Brighton and Hove. Why should she be deprived of these pleasures for the sake of childish pride or laboured devices? Who did these young men think they were? Did she not disdain to think of such things as devices in connection with them?

Convincing herself that she did, she at last made up her mind.

'All right,' she said. 'Let's go on.'

But that she still had devices, or pride, or the three young men somewhere at the back of her mind, she proved by her next utterance, which she made as they were walking on again, arm in arm, towards the turnstile of the Pier.

'After all,' she said, 'it's free for anyone to go on, ain't it?'

4

As the girls passed through the turnstile the three young men were outside the West Pier Theatre playing with a slot machine behind whose glass were miniature images of German soldiers on a field of battle. These Germans were waiting, in various positions and postures, to be shot down by a sort of pistol operated from outside the glass. It was necessary to aim between their eyes, and if a reasonable percentage of them were shot down the marksman was rewarded not only with the glamour of achievement but with the pecuniary profit of not losing his penny.

The young man peering through the sights of the pistol at the moment had a great deal of dark hair, a fine profile, and a generally graceful air in spite of his immaturity. This was Ryan, whose torch, several years ago, had mysteriously disappeared in the changing-room of Rodney House School. His two companions also had been educated at Rodney House. One was Bell (who had at that period specialized in the use of long words) and the other was Ernest Ralph Gorse.

All of these three wore grey flannel trousers – what they would have called 'bags'.

With these trousers Ryan wore a well-cut coat originally belonging to a dark blue lounge suit; Gorse wore a pepper-and-salt tweed jacket; and Bell wore a jacket of brown tweed.

None of them wore hats. Ryan probably had the smartest appearance, but he was followed closely by Gorse. The spectacled Bell was far behind: his jacket was shoddy and rumpled, his trousers were not creased, and his collar and tie were out of place. Love of long words had in the course of years led to a love of Learning, and the learned disdain too great an attention to their clothes. He bit, learnedly, a curved pipe.

Ryan and Bell were clean-shaven, but Gorse wore what he could manage in the way of a toothbrush moustache. Ryan and Bell had been to Brighton College. Gorse had been to St Paul's School in London.

Ryan was simple, eager, and shy in his demeanour and thoughts. Bell, in spite of affectations, such as curved-pipe-biting, was really very much the same as Ryan. Gorse was very different from both, in his demeanour and in his thoughts.

Gorse was reasonably tall and had a good figure. His reddish moustache improved him. It largely succeeded in removing what had been so noticeable in his face as a boy – that expression of smelling something nasty immediately underneath his nose. The expression was still there, but could only be seen every now and again, and then fleetingly, by someone who knew him well. A casual acquaintance might never observe it.

He was clean, and neatly dressed, and many might have thought him good-looking. He had even acquired a sort of dashing charm – a charm which, when he took the trouble to exercise it, not only made him seem more good-looking than when he was behaving otherwise, but drew attention away from that other defect he had had as a boy, and still had, a most unpleasantly nasal voice.

5

Gorse was not making any attempt to be particularly charming with his two companions at the present moment, and when, following Ryan in putting his penny into the slot machine and peering through the sights at the German soldiers, he spoke, his looks and voice were on the whole displeasing.

'Well,' he said. 'Do you think the "Birds" are on yet?'

Young women – and particularly young women of working-class origin walking along sea-fronts with a view to encounters – were in these days usually alluded to as 'Birds' by this class of young man. Gorse was asking his companions whether they thought Esther Downes and Gertrude Perks were already on the Pier; and they understood him without difficulty.

'What makes you think they're *coming* on?' said Ryan. He spoke a little nervously.

'Oh,' said Gorse, shooting down a German with a lazy, level accuracy all his own, 'they'll be on all right.'

'How do you know?' said Ryan. 'You seem to be jolly certain about everything.'

And now there was something closely resembling a gulp in Ryan's voice, a gulp of disappointment or grief. It was as if he believed that some fearful mistake had been made.

The truth of the matter was that Ryan loved the sight of Esther Downes – and this passionately. He had done so ever since he had been passing and re-passing her during these soft summer evenings: and passionately to love the sight of anyone, for a male of Ryan's temperament and Ryan's age (which was eighteen), is the equivalent of passionately (though almost sexlessly) loving them themselves – without any reserve. Alluding contemptuously to Esther Downes as a 'Bird' was pure defence and pretence on Ryan's part. If it could be done Ryan would have married Esther Downes tomorrow – married her and have sat in the dusk on the Pier with her (perhaps 'kissing' her) and have taken her to the pictures and caressed her hand, and have taken her into the country on the back of his motorcycle, and so on and so forth for ever and ever with the blessing of the law. No wonder, then, that there was a gulp in Ryan's voice, and that he resented the calmness of Gorse, who, he believed, had lost an opportunity which might never return.

It was all Gorse's fault. For Gorse was to Ryan and Bell, in matters of this sort, as Esther Downes was to Gertrude Perks – the initiator, the experienced campaigner, the acknowledged leader.

That this was so was, really, surprising, and for two reasons. Firstly, Ryan was actually and quite transparently a very much more attractive creature than Gorse. He was indeed one for whom 'all the girls', in the expression of that day as well as this, 'fell', and he might, therefore, be expected to be playing the dominant part in this trio of cavaliers. Secondly, he was by no means fond of Gorse, whom he inwardly and instinctively disliked and distrusted – as much now as when they were both children at Rodney House – and shy as he might be in his thought and demeanour, he had not the sort of character which would accept much domination of any kind.

The explanation was, almost certainly, that Ryan, despite his opportunities, had an attitude towards 'girls' singularly lacking in vulgarity and totally different from that of Gorse, and that he was, in the ordinary way, too easy-going generally not to submit to the mood and manners of anyone with whom he happened to be. So, with Bell as a nonentity hard at work at his pipe, Gorse was allowed to take the lead.

There was remarkably little in common between these three boys, who were now walking together in Brighton through the instrumentality of a letter-writing Gorse. Gorse was an assiduous writer of extremely lengthy letters. It was a sort of passion with him and, in order to appease this passion, he kept in touch with innumerable school companions, even those from his earliest days at school. His letters were largely facetious, and he fancied his own style immeasurably. This was of a fearful Wardour Street, Jeffery Farnol kind – packed with 'Thou'st', 'I would fain', 'Stap me', 'Beshrew me', 'A vast deal', 'Methinks', 'Albeit', 'Where-anent', 'Varlet', 'Knave', etc. – a style commonly used, for reasons hard to ascertain, by people either with very naïve or very unwholesome minds. But the mind of Ernest Ralph Gorse was by no means naïve.

Through all his days at Colet Court, and later at St Paul's, he had written regularly to Ryan and Bell, and now, as all three happened to be in Brighton at the same time, they had at Gorse's instigation met, and had taken to walking with each other.

All three had left school for good and were on holiday before embarking upon adult life. Ryan was to enter a firm owned by his uncle, an estate agent, in London; Bell was hoping before long to Matriculate and afterwards gain a footing in the scholastic world; Gorse had nothing particular to go to, but had expressed (to his stepmother and uncle guardian) a desire to be connected with the motorcar business. With the makes, intricacies, and secondhand prices of the motorcar, Gorse was, for his age, phenomenally well acquainted.

Although she still disliked him, perhaps because she did so, Gorse's ex-barmaid stepmother was singularly indulgent with him, and had urged him, barmaid-fashion, to 'have a good time' while he was 'young enough to enjoy it'. It was also possible that she was a little more indulgent with him than she might otherwise have been because her conscience was a trifle uneasy. Still, notwithstanding her decidedly mature age and figure, she was loved, and permitted herself to be loved by, elderly men – was 'having a good time' herself, in fact. Discreet as she was in these affairs she felt that, from the point of view of conventional respectability, she was here not playing quite fair with her stepson, who, she suspected – quite rightly – was not unaware of what went on. Gorse's uncle, now getting old and becoming increasingly less interested in Gorse, took a good view of the motorcar business, which he believed belonged to the future. At the age of twenty-one Gorse was due to inherit enough money at least to keep him from destitution.

All these three boys were, of course, in what is deceptively called the 'morning' of life – deceptively because the vigorous word 'morning' does not at all suggest the clouded, oppressive, mysterious, disquieted, inhibited condition through which the vast majority have to pass at this age. Ryan and Bell – in spite of their social cheerfulness – in spite of the one's motorcycle and the other's pipe – certainly belonged to this majority, but perhaps Gorse did not. No ordinary human rules applied to the baffling Ernest Ralph Gorse. He was certainly neither clouded in his ideas nor inhibited in his behaviour. To such a character this period may indeed have been a strange sort of 'morning'.

6

Gorse, having shot down his Germans and retrieved his penny, put in the same penny and shot the Germans down again, and then again put in the penny and retrieved it – all this with the air of an adroit executioner rather than a juvenile pier-gambler.

The others watched and waited in silence as he did this. Gorse never showed any dislike either of waiting or of keeping people waiting.

'Well – let's go and see,' he said at last. He was alluding, as his companions knew, to the 'Birds', concerning whose presence on the Pier he was so certain.

'Where?' asked Ryan.

'Follow thou in my footsteps, rogues, rapscallions, and rascally roisterers,' said Gorse, who enjoyed the art of alliteration along with the style of Jeffery Farnol. 'Thou shalt not be led astray.'

He now, in a large manner befitting his style of speech, put his hands patronizingly on the shoulders of the other two, and steered them down the Pier again in the direction of the shore, choosing the right-hand side of the seated and sheltered partition which ran from the Theatre towards the Concert Hall – the east side of the Pier, that is to say. He had a reason, as the anxious Ryan quickly and gladly perceived, in choosing this side. What there was of a breeze that night was westerly and, apart from a few eccentrics, all who were walking or sitting on the Pier had naturally chosen the east side because it was protected from the breeze by the partition.

Also, quite unaccountably, this side of the West Pier has, from far-distant times until the present day, been strongly favoured by the whim of the public.

They had walked scarcely thirty yards before Esther Downes and Gertrude Perks were observed.

The two girls had found a place, as near to the Concert Hall as possible and therefore amongst many other people, on the free seating accommodation which edged the Pier. With their backs to the sea they were looking at the passers-by and enjoying the music wafted from the Concert Hall.

No sooner had they been seen than Gorse began to hum in a gentle, meaning way; and, when he had finished humming, a deadly silence fell upon all three young men.

Absorbed, perhaps, by the music, and the passing people, and the faint, soothing sound of the sea beneath them, Esther and Gertrude were caught unawares.

It was, indeed, not until the three young men were within ten yards of them that Esther and Gertrude saw them, and Esther, for once, lost her head.

Catching Ryan's eye, she turned with absurd haste and looked down at the sea, while the spectacled Gertrude, thus abandoned and in a hideous state of fear and embarrassment, could only glance glassily at the three young men, at the other people passing, and at nothingness – all at the same time, as it were, and with the self-conscious stiffness of a chained, alert macaw being too closely stared at on a perch at the Zoo. This, needless to say, made the ill-starred Gertrude look even uglier than usual – one might fairly say repulsive.

When this gruesome little episode was over, Gorse was the first to speak.

'The saucy wench showeth disdain,' he said. 'Doth she not?'

'Yes, she certainly does,' said Ryan, and from his voice it would have been difficult to tell whether he was disappointed or pleased by what had just happened.

On the one hand he was inclined to interpret Esther's gesture at its face value and as a firm rebuff: on the other hand it had been his own eye that she had caught, and he was not so completely lacking in self-assurance and sophistication not to suspect that extreme coyness had been her motive, and that such coyness was a good omen.

'And what about the other one?' said Gorse. 'I hadn't realized it was as bad as all that.'

'No,' said Ryan. 'She's certainly no beauty.'

And here both Gorse and Ryan gave a little look at Bell, who was silently biting and nagging at his pipe.

Why did Ryan and Gorse thus look at Bell?

Almost certainly this was due to the all too familiar but none the less horrid problem of the 'other one'.

It is not always realized that there are male as well as female 'other ones'. And poor Bell, because of his spectacles, his learnedness, and his general contempt for glamour or even ordinary tidiness in his clothes, had, it seems, either in the conscious or subconscious minds of his two companions, come to be regarded as 'the other one' in this situation.

Now the 'other one' has worse to suffer than the mere humiliation of being what he is. He has duties to perform. It is, in fact, his business to take, to put up with, be palmed off with the 'other one' on the other side. 'Other ones' are supposed not to mind this; indeed in the thoughtless baseness of human nature, they are supposed rather to like it. They are even assumed to have (most conveniently) a *penchant*, if not some sort of inexplicable longing, for their counterparts: like is said, after all, to attract like. But nothing could be further from the case. 'Other ones' worship at the shrine of pure beauty as much as – perhaps, because of their disadvantages, more than – the fortunate ones.

So Gorse and Ryan glanced at Bell – Ryan, possibly not without a distant twinge of conscience. What Bell was thinking was well concealed by his pipe-biting. The matter, though, was of grave importance. Was Bell willing to undertake his responsibilities? Indeed, in view of the recent disaster – the finally established absolutely awful hideousness of Gertrude Perks – would anybody in their right senses be willing to undertake such responsibilities?

Nor was this the only difficult matter. Even if Bell could be taken to be out of his mind and prepared to withdraw Gertrude Perks from the arena, who, then, was to be the 'other one' in regard to the lovely Esther Downes? Ryan or Gorse?

In addition to having very little in common, these three boys knew very little about what each other was thinking. Bell, as we have seen, was an enigma to Gorse and Ryan, both of whom he found enigmatic, and Gorse was an enigma to Ryan. It was only the shrewd Gorse who knew at least one thing, and that was that Ryan, without having met her, was infatuated by Esther Downes, was unable even properly to keep an outward composure about her.

Ryan, then, would have been indisputably anxious to defeat Gorse, though, his nature being as amiable and easy-going as it was, he probably did not think of things in this way.

But what were Gorse's feelings about all this?

Again, because no ordinary human rules could be applied to this boy, the question is not an easy one to answer. Of one thing we may be sure – Esther Downes by no means infatuated him. His was a character incapable of infatuation – it was so for women at any rate. (Military uniforms and slow schemes for secret power are another matter.) He probably admired Esther Downes considerably, however, and had already fitted her into some roughly formulated plan for the future. In the meanwhile he was clearly enjoying his tacitly acknowledged leadership in the chase as well as the exercise and exhibition of his ingenuity as a leader.

7

'Well, what do we do now?' asked Ryan, and Gorse, having said, Drake-like, that there was 'plenty of time', walked on and on, almost off the Pier. He did at last turn, however, and then persuaded his companions to lean over the railings near the shore, and to look down, not at the sea, for that did not rise as high as this, but at the beach, which was now almost in the darkness of the night.

Talking of detached matters, he kept them at these railings for about six minutes – which seemed to a frantic Ryan to be little less than sixty – but he at last relented and permitted a return journey in the direction of the spot at which it was presumed that Esther Downes and Gertrude Perks would still be sitting.

Wrongly presumed, though, as the unimportant Bell, oddly enough, was the first to perceive.

'Ah-ha,' said Bell, 'I see our "Birds" are flown.'

This was a pun, and as such might have been thought beneath such an austere thinker as Bell, it was, though, a Learned pun, and therefore perhaps permissible. Bell was imitating the famous remark of Charles the First on his entry into the House of Commons to arrest the five members who had departed, and whose names, as a knowledge-thrusting Bell would have been only too glad to remind Ryan and Gorse, were Pym, Hampden, Hazelrigg, Holles, and Strode.

But he was given no chance to do this, and his companions, in fact, did not know that he had made a pun at all and simply took his remark at its face value.

Ryan and Gorse had little Learning, and were, if anything, eager to expunge from their minds rather than retain what they had been forced to digest during the last twelve years or so.

'Yes, they've gone,' said Ryan, and added, in the phrase popular at that period, 'They've Done the Giddy Bunk, all right.'

Gorse was masterfully silent.

'And now they're *all* coming off,' said Ryan in despair.

The band had evidently played 'God Save the King', and the greater part of the populace had risen and was making its way to the turnstiles.

'Never mind,' said Gorse. 'When dirty work's afoot, the fewer the better.'

He now led the other two as far as the Theatre again, and then, inclining to the left, took them along the side of the Theatre to the extreme edge of the Pier proper.

Only the grilled quadrangle now lay between themselves and the French coast, but on the farthest edge of the quadrangle, gazing towards the French coast, were Esther Downes and Gertrude Perks. Dark as it now was, their figures were easily recognizable.

'Ah – here we are,' said Gorse, and leaned over the railings, staring through the heavy twilight at the two girls. Ryan and Bell submissively did the same as their triumphant leader.

'I fancy', said Gorse, 'that our Birds are trapped, should we be desirous of courting their favours.'

This was true. There were only two ways, on the east or the west side, of their leaving the quadrangle, and, when they did so, the young men could easily see which side they were choosing and without any haste be in time to intercept and accost them.

'But *are* we desirous? That's the point,' said Bell.

'Ah – that's a different matter,' said Gorse, still gazing at the sea-gazing figures. 'What think'st thou, Ryan?'

'Oh – I don't know,' said Ryan, 'I'll leave it to you.'

He spoke thus indecisively, not because he did not really know his own mind, but because now that a real opportunity had arisen, and a decision had to be made, he was desperately afraid. Also, he wanted to re-establish in front of Gorse an attitude of indifference which he knew he had failed to maintain during the last twenty minutes.

'Very well, then, leave it to me,' said Gorse.

Ryan had to make the best he could of this. Did Gorse, with his 'Very well, then, leave it to me', mean that he definitely proposed to undertake and lead the way in an almost immediate operation? Or had he not as yet made up his mind, and did he merely mean that the decision as to whether or not they were to accost the girls at all was to be left to him?

Ryan, dreading either answer, glanced at Gorse, seeking to discover his intentions.

But Gorse wore that composed and utterly noncommittal expression such as Satan, one imagines, unintermittently wears.

Soon the girls moved to the eastern side of the quadrangle, and then again stopped to look at the view – at the pretty lights of the Palace Pier, it seemed. They had an air, though, of being in conference and of trying to come to a decision themselves.

Then, after a minute or two, they walked in a determined way shorewards (as if anxious to go home), and up the stairs near to which Gorse, Ryan, and Bell were leaning. They could, of course, have chosen the stairs on the other side, and the fact that they did not do so possibly assisted Gorse in making up his mind.

As soon as Esther and Gertrude had reached the top of the stairs Gorse turned and spoke in a loud, cheerful voice.

'Hullo, girls,' he said. '*Quo Vadis* – eh?'

Now had come the agonizing moment – agonizing for Ryan in particular, but almost equally for all the others – except Gorse. Gorse was as immune from this sort of agony as he was from infatuation.

Was Gorse to be answered or totally ignored – given, as they would have said, 'the bird'?

(In the language of Getting Off, 'bird' was in those days used in two senses.)

There was a pause.

Then 'Quo *Whattis*?' said Esther, and she and Gertrude stopped.

The sharpest agony had passed, and the climax had been at last reached.

The West Pier, resembling in the sea a sort of amiable, crouching, weird battleship – a sex-battleship – had, at its prow, yet again revealed its peculiar, traditional uses.

The Getters-off were Off.

PART THREE

OFF

Chapter One

Second sight and telepathy, along with other immaterial means of communication, are probably used by those engaged in these unearthly preliminaries to Getting Off.

Something he could not name had led Gorse to lead the other two to the prow of the Pier, and as soon as they had arrived there Esther Downes, though still gazing towards the French coast, had suspected that she was being watched from behind and who was doing the watching.

In taking Gertrude to the east side of the quadrangle to look at the Palace Pier lights she confirmed her suspicions beyond all doubt. She glanced upwards and sideways and unmistakably saw the young men – saw them, although in the darkness they were not in fact properly visible.

In looking at the lights of the Palace Pier, she had not actually been in conference with Gertrude but making up her own mind as to whether, on returning to the Pier, she should or should not choose the steps nearest to the young men.

She had chosen, as we have seen, those nearest, knowing what must be the almost certain result of doing so.

That she had been followed to the limits of the Pier in this way had completely assuaged her pride: and she was, now, weary of immaterial skirmishing, and eager for battle.

She had never intended, if honestly accosted, to avoid battle completely. This was because (just as Ryan loved the sight of Esther) Esther loved the sight of Ryan. But this did not mean that she felt anything at all of what Ryan felt. She belonged to a different and, at the age of eighteen, a much more mature, cold, and enlightened sex.

She would not have married Ryan tomorrow; indeed, unless he behaved as she required she would not even meet him again tomorrow evening. She was extremely suspicious of Ryan, though she loved the sight of his unusually good looks.

She was extremely suspicious of all three, with the exception, possibly, of Bell, whom she had at an early stage of the proceedings identified as a typical 'other one', and who did not, therefore, really 'count'.

She was, in fact, abnormally suspicious, and, for one of her experience, abnormally inclined to caution.

This was largely because there were three of them – three against two (or rather two against one, since neither Bell nor Gertrude 'counted') – and largely because she was aware that they did not come from her own class. They had, it seemed to her, clearly been educated at what she would have called 'College', and for this reason were what she would have called 'gentlemen'.

Now the much-got-off-with Miss Downes was by no means absolutely unacquainted with 'gentlemen', but she was certainly not so much at ease with them as she was with young men of her own class. Though she had not as yet come to any sort of harm from 'gentlemen' she could still not quite rid herself of a picture of them as cads and traducers.

Also, they had either a flippancy which differed altogether from the crude flippancy of young men in her own sphere of life, or, however shy they might be, an ease which robbed her of her own ease and, therefore, of something of that complete ascendancy which she was accustomed to her beauty bringing her.

Nevertheless, she had made up her mind to take any risks of this sort, and, with her 'Quo *Whattis*?' had shown as much, and could not retreat.

Chapter Two

I

It has been said that the sharpest agony had passed: but there was still much agony, of a different kind, to be endured. This was the agony of that laboured punning and fatuity in conversation which those who have just Got Off are absolutely forced to employ in order to conceal their embarrassment.

'*Quo Vadis,*' repeated Gorse. 'Meaning "Whither Goest Thou?" Latin. Ancient. In common parlance, where are you toddling off to, girls?'

'We're toddling off home,' said Esther, 'if that's all you want to know.'

'But it isn't all. By no means,' said Gorse, and added: 'Oh, excuse me, girls, I don't think you know my friends. Mr Ryan, Mr Bell.'

Gorse had now adopted his dashing and most amiable manner, and was completely in charge of things. The others smiled and murmured 'How-do-you-do' in a shamed way.

Ryan and Bell (and Ryan in particular) were ashamed of Gorse's vulgarity. To hear Gorse calling the girls 'girls' like that caused Ryan the acutest torture, and he trusted that Esther was not going to think of him as another Gorse. At the same time he was grateful to Gorse for what he had achieved and was achieving – which, really, could not be brought off without a certain amount of vulgarity.

'And may we escort you homewards?' Gorse went on. 'For that is whither we wendeth our own ways.'

'Certainly,' said Esther awkwardly, and as they all began to walk together shorewards there was a long, long, long pause – one which even the resourceful Gorse seemed unable to break.

Ryan now thought that he must, for the sake of his manhood, say something, and he did so, trying at the same time to dispel the atmosphere of vulgarity created by Gorse.

'Do you come a lot on the Pier?' he asked Esther, who was on his right. (She was on Gorse's left.)

'Yes,' said Esther, 'quite a lot. It's nice to hear the band and have a look at the people.'

'To *Peer* at the people on the *Pier* – what?' said Gorse.

'That's right,' said Esther, smiling politely at this, his first shot in the inevitable play upon words.

'And did you see us three *Peering* at you?' asked Gorse.

'Oh yes. We saw that all right,' said Esther, looking ahead of her with a demure complacency which fascinated Ryan beyond measure.

'And a very nice *Pair* we thought you,' said Gorse.

'Did you?' said Esther, and there was a pause.

'Yes,' said Ryan, himself plunging into fatuity in his determination not to be left out of things. 'Without *Peer*, in fact.'

'Yes. Beyond com*Pare*, certainly,' said the quick-minded Gorse, and he looked at his hands. 'By the way, I'd've *Pared* my nails properly tonight if I'd known we were going to meet – just to be Pre*Pared*.'

This absurd, irrelevant, untrue, and unfunny remark caused laughter.

'Well,' said Gertrude Perks, now feeling that she must somehow establish herself as a fellow wit, and speaking for the first time, 'we can't give you a *Pear*, as a reward, because they're out of season. Ain't they?'

But nobody laughed at this. 'Other ones' seldom cause laughter. They are not, really, supposed to speak at all. Instead of laughter there was some dim sniggering.

'Are they?' said the polite Ryan, and there was silence.

Now Bell, emboldened by hearing his opposite 'other one' speaking, broke into the conversation for the first time.

'"A drunk delight of battle with my *peers*,"' said Bell.

Learned again, needless to say. Bell was quoting from the poem *Ulysses* by Alfred, Lord Tennyson. Bell's quotation was even less relevant than the previous remarks of Gorse and Gertrude Perks, and, in his eagerness to disseminate the seeds of learning, he had neglected to notice that the word 'peer' had already been used by Ryan.

'Drunk *what?*' said Esther.

'"Far",' continued Bell imperturbably, sonorously, and not without grandeur, '"on the ringing plains of windy Troy."'

'I don't follow,' said Esther, and appealed to Ryan. 'Is your friend always like this?'

'Oh yes. Don't mind him,' said Ryan. 'He's probably quoting poetry. Aren't you, Bell?'

'Tennyson,' said Bell. 'To be precise.'

'Well,' said Miss Perks, 'the only kind of Tennyson *I* know is Tennis on the Lawn. Do you chaps play? You look as if you do.'

'Chaps', Ryan felt, was even worse than Gorse's 'girls'.

'No,' said Esther, who was anxious to educate herself, and had therefore a certain respect, an exaggerated one possibly, for learning. 'Was that Tennyson? I used to be taught him. I used to know *The Brook* right off by heart.'

'Oh – you did – did you?' said Bell eagerly. '"I chatter over stony ways . . ."'

'"In little sharps and trebles,"' said Esther with equal enthusiasm.

'"I bubble into eddying bays,"' said Bell.

'"I babble on the pebbles!"' said Esther triumphantly.

What was this? Was the 'other one', the uncouth and dishevelled Bell, to be the one to capture the beauty after all?

'"Till last by Philip's farm I flow,"' Bell went on, but this sort of thing had to be put a stop to, and Gorse firmly did so.

'Well,' he said, 'as we're all so poetical tonight, what about sitting down and drinking in the poetry of the scenery? What say you?'

They had now reached the long sheltered partition dividing the middle of the Pier, and Gorse indicated, with a sweep of his hand, where they might sit.

'All right,' said Esther. 'Though we haven't got long – have we, Gertie?'

'No – it's getting a bit late,' said Gertrude.

And so now they all sat down – Gorse by methods which were mysterious but did not permit of disobedience, arranging who should sit where. Esther sat between Ryan and Gorse, and on Gorse's right was Gertrude, and next to her was Bell. Bell was thus thrust into outer darkness, having the hideous Gertrude on his left and nobody at all on his right. This was probably a punishment given him by Gorse for getting above himself and gaining favour with Esther by quoting poetry.

Why he had made them all sit down no one exactly knew – not even Gorse. There was no question, for instance, of any of those things which precede, or go with, Kissing. The lights were quite bright here, and there were too many people still about, and they themselves were too ill-assorted, and unacquainted, and large in number.

Nevertheless, sitting down was the thing to do. Perhaps it paved the way, established a precedent for conceivable future sittings-down – these in darker places and when some sort of assortment and separation had been worked out and agreed upon by the individuals concerned.

'That's better,' said Gorse. 'Now – what were we talking about?'

'Poetry, wasn't it?' said Ryan.

Ryan, whose arm was touching Esther's, and who was gazing out to sea at the fairy lights of the Palace Pier, was in what may be called a 'poetical' mood. He had also been much impressed by Esther's interest in poetry, which he took as a sign of remarkable culture, sweetness, and intelligence in one of her class.

It may be said, however, that even if Esther had in the immediate past been totally foul-mouthed and low, Ryan would have found an excuse for her, and, more, somehow twisted things so as to see her in a favourable light for being so.

'Ah, yes. Poetry,' said Gorse, speaking to Esther. 'And Tennyson's your favourite poet, is he – Miss – I'm so sorry I didn't quite catch your name.'

'I don't remember giving it,' said Esther, with an air rather closer to that of flirtation than to that of snubbing.

'Ah, no. So you didn't. But you can now. Come along, then. What is it?'

'Why do you want to know?'

Esther felt a curious reluctance in disclosing her name. Girls do, on occasions like this. They are like new boys at school, afraid of having their names laughed at, or despised.

'Oh – we must be sociable, you know. Come along now.'

'Downes . . .' said Esther after a pause, shyly. 'Spelt with an *e* . . .' She was aware that the *e* gave it all its prettiness, and that without it one thought of things like the Sussex Downs to the north of Brighton.

'And very nice, too. And what's your name, Gertie?' said Gorse.

'How did you know it was Gertie?' asked Miss Perks.

'Because I heard Miss Downes calling you it just a moment ago. Come along now.'

'Perks,' said Gertrude, 'if you want to know.'

'Ah, very suitable for both of you. So when your friend's in one of her *Downes*, you *Perk* her up? What?'

'Yes. That's right,' said Gertrude. 'That's my job.'

It is intensely difficult to believe that sane young people ever talked like this. They did, however. Furthermore, they undoubtedly still do. Let the unbeliever sit on piers in the evening, and eavesdrop.

'Well – now that's all over, let's go back to Poetry,' said Esther, talking to Gorse. 'Who's *your* favourite poet then, Mr – you haven't told us *your* name, by the way.'

'Mine? Gorse. Ernest Ralph Gorse. Known as Ralph – pronounced Ralph or Rafe, whichever you prefer. Which are you going to use?'

'I don't know that I'm going to use either . . . Well – go on – who's your favourite poet, anyway?'

'Mine? I don't think I know. Or at least I know, but I don't know his name. He wrote a wonderful poem. Now – how did it begin? "There was a young lady of –" No, perhaps I'd better not go on with that.'

'No – I don't think you'd better,' said Esther.

There was a pause.

'And who's *your* favourite poet, as you know all about Poetry?' said Gertrude, speaking challengingly to Bell. She knew that Esther expected her to handle and to pair with Bell eventually, and she thought that the time had come to make a start.

'Mine?' said Bell. 'Well, there's a pretty extensive field – isn't there?' said Bell. 'I should say that my taste was eclectic, and that –'

'*Electric*?' said Gertrude sharply, and with all the bitterness with some people have against a word which is curious and unfamiliar to them.

'No, eclectic,' said Bell, rather cowed.

'Well, I'm glad to hear *that*,' said Gertrude, but there was still acerbity in her tone.

'I flit from flower to flower, you see,' Bell went on, 'and still can't settle anywhere. One day it's Chaucer, then Milton, then Shelley, then Keats, then Byron (the noble lord), then Coleridge (the opium-eater). Then I'll suddenly tire of the Romantics and return to the clipped austerities of Pope.' (Bell, though cured of the grosser manifestations of his schoolboy malady, had not completely lost his love of long words.) 'I should say, though, that for lasting satisfaction, and real greatness and depth, the real master is Wordsworth, and if I had to vote for anyone I'd vote for him.'

'Oh no,' said Ryan. '*Not* Wordsworth, surely.'

'Why not Wordsworth?'

'What – *We Are Seven*, and *The Idiot Boy*, and *Goody Blake and Harry Gill*, and all that?' said Ryan, revealing a knowledge which neither Bell nor Gorse had suspected he possessed.

'Well,' said Bell, 'I'll admit that our Lakeland friend was capable of carrying simplicity to an exaggerated degree – even at times to the point of ridiculousness.'

'He certainly was,' said Ryan.

'Yes,' said Bell, 'but we've got to take him all in all. I mean to say, for instance, a man who can write such things as "Earth has not anything to show more fair, Dull would he be of soul who could pass by, A sight so touching in its majesty: The City now doth like a garment wear, The beauty of the morning, silent, bare, Ships, towers, domes, theatres, and temples, lie . . ."'

Bell was reeling off his favourite poet's sonnet at a good speed, with no expression, and apparently without any intention of stopping until the end had been reached.

'Yes – I know,' tried Ryan, but Bell went inexorably on.

'"Open unto the fields and to the sky; All bright and glittering in the smokeless air . . ."'

This was not quite so terrifying to Ryan as it was to the others, for Ryan knew that there were only fourteen lines altogether, and that eight of them had been used. The others had no such advantage. For all they knew, Bell might be intending to go on until midnight, or dawn, or beyond.

'"Never",' continued Bell, '"did sun more beautifully steep, In his first splendour valley, rock, or hill; Ne'er saw I, never felt, a calm so deep! The river glideth at his own sweet will . . ."'

At this point Ryan became fascinated beyond measure in conjecturing as to how Bell proposed to finish the construction of the prodigious sentence upon which he had embarked. It had begun with 'I mean to say, for instance, a man who can write such things as "Earth has not anything," etc., etc., etc.,' and it was still going. How would Bell wind it up? Grammatically, with 'is worthy of consideration' or something like that? Or would Bell draw breath and start again, with something like – 'Well – I mean to say, a man who can write like *that* is worthy of consideration'?

The precise Bell now solved the problem in a way which Ryan had rather fancied it would have been solved.

'"Dear God,"' said Bell, '"the very houses seem asleep; And all that mighty heart is lying still" – is not to be lightly dismissed. Don't you agree?'

'Oh yes,' said Ryan. 'He's fine when he's in form.'

'Nor,' said Bell, 'would I like to say –'

'But he's not always –' said Ryan.

'*NOR*,' went on Bell, now completely inebriated by the exuberance of borrowed words, and practically shouting Ryan down. 'Nor can we allow such inspiring passages from the Lucy poems as "She dwelt among the untrodden ways, Beside the springs of Dove, A maid whom there were none to praise, And very few to love. A violet by a mossy stone, Half hidden from the eye! Fair as a star, when only one Is shining in the sky. She lived unknown and few could know When Lucy ceased to be; But she is in her grave, and, oh –"'

Here Ryan, who knew that the last line was just coming, again waited in a sort of anguish for the accurate completion of the sentence. 'Nor can we allow such inspiring passages from the Lucy poems as' had been the beginning, and then the poem had followed. Would Bell repeat his idiotic adherence to the strictest rules of grammar – which was really an idiotic pretence that he was not really declaiming poetry, as if invited to do so on a platform?

Bell did.

'"The difference to me," be regarded,' said Bell, 'as anything other than in the front rank of English verse.'

'My word,' said Gertrude. 'You can't half spout.'

'And then even the familiar "Daffodils",' said Bell. '"I wandered lonely –"'

But here Ryan was completely at home and able to take the ground from under Bell's feet.

'"As a cloud,"' said Ryan, raising his voice,

> '"That floats on high o'er vales and hills,
> When all at once I saw a crowd,
> A host, of golden daffodils . . .
> Ten thousand saw I at a glance,
> Tossing their heads in sprightly dance"'

Ryan was doubtful if this was enough, and so, as a *coup de grâce*, gave a little more.

'"Continuous as the stars that shine
And twinkle on the milky way
They stretched in never-ending line
Along the margin –"

but we can't go on pouring out poetry like this all night – can we?'

'Well, I sincerely *hope* not,' said Gertrude, but Esther was very much impressed.

'So *you* know all about Poetry too?' she said to Ryan, looking gravely at him.

'No,' said Ryan. 'Only a bit. Nothing like Bell.'

Gorse, who did not care for Poetry and so knew nothing about it, had been perforce silent all this time. Gorse did not like being silent or left out of things. When such a thing happened his expression was thoughtful and displeasing; that faint smell under his nose came back.

Now Ryan had silenced Bell, Gorse saw a chance of entering the conversation.

'And what about the Immortal Bard?' he said. 'What about the Swan of Avon?'

'Oh, he goes without saying,' said Bell.

There was a pause.

'I have, as a matter of fact,' said Bell, 'a copy of Wordsworth on me.' He produced a selection from the poet's work – a cheap paper edition – from his pocket.

'Handy for the pocket,' he said, 'and, as you can see, extremely well Thumbed.'

It was indeed well Thumbed. It was a good deal more. Bell being in the habit of reading at meals – particularly breakfast and tea – the book, in addition to being well Thumbed, was well Fingered, well Porridged, well Marmaladed, well Jammed, well Baconed, well Coffeed, well Tea-ed, well Cocoa-ed, well Crumbed, well Biscuited, and well Buttered. Nor would a keen examiner with a microscope have found the book totally unsausaged, unspinached, unpotatoed, uncauliflowered, unstewed-plummed, unapple-charlotted, unriced or uncurried.

'Yes,' said Gertrude. 'It certainly looks well read. And so that's all Electric, is it? Or Effectic, or whatever you call it.'

'Eclectic,' said Bell.

'And may I ask what that means?' asked Gertrude. 'It sounds funny to me.'

'Oh – gathered from all sources – taken from all schools.'

'You've been to a lot of schools, I should say – by the look of you,' said Gertrude, gazing at him. 'Haven't you? One or two too many, I should say.'

'No – no more than my friends here.'

'We were all at school together,' said Ryan, breaking into the conversation because he felt that the too determinedly philistine Gertrude was being over-harsh with the too determinedly cultured Bell.

'Well, anyway,' said Gertrude, looking at the book, 'if that's Wordsworth, you seem to've got your Words *Worth* out of it all right.'

'Yes,' said Bell, finding nothing else to say.

Gertrude had now as it were come into the lead in the fatuity race, which we are not compelled to follow any further. It may, however, be mentioned that these five, having exhausted the subject of their Favourite Poet, went on to discuss the matters as to Who was their Favourite Musician, Who was their Favourite Painter, Who was their Favourite Sculptor (this originated by Bell), Who was their Favourite Actor, Who was their Favourite Architect (Bell again), and, finally, Who was their Favourite Character in History.

Then Ryan, who was getting very tired of all this, put in a remark about the pretty lights of the Palace Pier. Other lights on the front were then discussed – including those of the Hotel Metropole.

Then the Hotel Metropole itself was discussed – this with results very much more momentous than any one of these young people would have been able to conceive.

'Would you like me to take you there one evening?' said Gorse to Esther.

All heard this, but no one knew exactly what to say. Esther at last replied.

'I'd like to see you doing it,' she said, showing clearly that in her mind the supreme heights of fatuity had been reached.

'Very well, then, you shall,' said Ernest Ralph Gorse.

Esther now used these absurd heights as an excuse for saying what she had wanted to say for a long time.

'Well,' she said, 'we've got to be buzzing off home. I don't know about you.'

She half rose, the others half rose, and then all rose completely and walked towards the shore.

2

By the same semi-mystic yet adamant measures which Gorse had employed while seating the company, he now arranged how it should go off the Pier. Gertrude Perks, Ryan, and Bell went ahead. Gorse and Esther walked behind – so far behind, finally, that they were out of earshot of the other three.

But the anxious Ryan saw to it that all of them met at the turnstiles. They went through these, and it was clearly time to say, 'Well . . .'

'Well, when do we all meet again?' said Ryan, and Gorse said 'Yes, when?' and there was a general atmosphere of 'Well . . .'

Then Gorse suggested that they should all meet at the entrance to the Palace Pier (to make a change) tomorrow evening at seven-thirty.

All agreed to this, and all looked at each other with great shyness and suspicion.

But there was more than the usual shyness and suspicion which takes place on occasions like these. There was a funny, shifting glitter in everybody's eye.

This was probably because Gorse, while walking alone with Esther, had made a private arrangement with her, and the others, quite subconsciously, suspected it.

PART FOUR

GORSE AND ESTHER

Chapter One

1

Getters-off do not usually disclose their home addresses at the first encounter: indeed, more often than not these are never disclosed at all.

Even Gorse, in spite of his private arrangement with Esther, had made no inquiry as to any such thing, and the thought of actually doing so would never have even entered Ryan's mind.

This does not mean that Ryan had not longed to do so – in order to dispel that peculiar dread necessarily attendant upon the hours intervening between a first meeting of this sort and the second – the dread that the other party may vacillate, change its mind (or perhaps it never even *had* any mind to keep its promise), 'think better of it', and so not 'turn up' and, having left absolutely no clue as to where it might be sought, disappear for ever.

Ryan that night, on his bed in the darkness of his bed-sitting-room in Tisbury Road, Hove, lay awake a long while wondering where and how Esther lived.

2

The where, actually, would have furnished a fairly vivid picture of the how. The lovely Esther lived in conditions of grave squalor in Over Street, near Brighton Station, and no one who lived in this street at that time lived otherwise.

Esther shared a bed with a small brother and sister. Her father was a porter at Brighton Station, her mother an ex-seamstress who still made a little money by sewing and mending.

Another family, of three, lived in the same house, whose passages were densely perambulatored.

Over Street, then, was a slum, and Mr and Mrs Downes were not happy people. That they were less acutely wretched than they might have been was because of a sort of apathy, even towards the wretchedness, had overtaken them. Overwhelmed and overworked boxers are sometimes called 'punch-drunk': Mr and Mrs Downes might have been called 'slum-drunk'.

Of the two, Mr Downes, the porter, perhaps suffered the most.

Some people in this world totally fail even to know, while others fail fully to appreciate, the fact that being a porter involves what nearly all people on this earth detest more violently than nearly anything else on earth – namely, *Carrying*. Indeed, they detest this so much that they will part with money in order to get other people to carry the lightest articles over the smallest distances. Being a porter also entails what many people detest even more than Carrying – that is, *Waiting About* – waiting about, sometimes, in the coldest, wettest, or vilest weather – waiting about, worst of all, hopefully, and, as often as not, with hopes dashed to the earth and so without any monetary gain.

Again, a porter is compelled to endure what many people dislike even more than carrying or waiting about – that is, being snubbed, or even insulted, continuously. People who have just alighted from, or who are about to get upon, trains are usually of an anxious, foreboding temper; and this usually manifests itself either in an air of disdain, in irritability, in furious excitability, or, lastly, in sheer savagery. The porter is made the butt of all these types of behaviour.

In those distant days, of course, it was permissible (for the rich at any rate) to indulge in disdain, irritability, excitability, and savagery to a degree in which the youthful gentle reader will not be able to believe. And the amount of money Mr Downes earned, and the amount of hours of the day and night which Mr Downes spent in carrying, waiting about, and being virtually spat upon, would, if revealed and believed, make such a reader's hair stand on end.

Over and above all this, Mr Downes was asked questions by people all day and night. This may be thought of as some sort of compensation, for people, on the whole, like answering questions. But the novelty soon wears off, and Mr Downes was questioned by passers-by in an incredibly rude way. Indeed, more often than not he was hardly what could be called questioned: he was brutally cross-examined.

It may be added that sometimes – something more than a dozen times a year – Mr Downes, on account of some imaginary piece of inefficiency or insolence, would receive no payment at all for an arduous service. And for this Mr Downes had no redress.

There would, however, be a rare saint, lunatic, or drunkard, returning from a successful day at the races, who would give Mr Downes as much as five shillings. (Or even half a sovereign!) Such characters Mr Downes and his fellow sufferers would, in those days call 'toffs'.

It may be fairly said that without these occasional 'toffs', and the hope of serving one, Mr Downes's miserable existence could hardly have continued.

From all this it may be assumed that Mr Downes looked upon himself as a being who had indeed sunk low in the world. But not at all. Mr Downes was confident that he had risen in the world, and believed that he was a success. This was because Mr Downes had vivid memories of his father, with whom he often compared himself.

3

Mr Downes's father had also been connected with Brighton Station – but not in any official capacity. Mr Downes's father had worn no uniform – he had worn rags, and he had not worn shoes. He was not allowed on to the platforms: instead of this he hung about the horse-cabs outside the Station.

When a train of any importance came into the Station, Mr Downes's father would eagerly watch these cabs as they were loaded with luggage by the uniformed porters, and, with a discrimination learned from long experience, would choose a cab, which he would follow, running, to its destination. He did this because he hoped that when it reached its destination, wherever that might be, he might be permitted to help with the unloading of the luggage, and be given a copper for doing so.

Mr Downes senior – who was, by the way, a consumptive – was not obliged to move at a great speed while his cab was moving along thoroughfares in which the traffic was thick, but when the emptier streets or roads were reached he had to run like mad. And, if he was unlucky, he had to run like this for a matter of three or four miles.

Was the hopeful Mr Downes senior, at the end of the pursuit, rewarded with the copper he had sought?

The answer is that nine times out of ten he was not. On the contrary, he was ordinarily threatened and shooed away with the greatest violence. Policemen were mentioned menacingly, and, if one happened to be present, used.

In extenuation of this cruelty on the part of the users of the cabs it should be mentioned that the consumptive Mr Downes senior, small as he was, at the end of his run presented an appalling sight – a frightening sight. The users of the cabs were frightened, and did what they did largely in panic. It must also be remembered that the man was looked upon as a beggar, and a beggar in those days was roughly identical with a criminal of the worst sort.

But the same extenuation cannot be extended to the servants of the households at which Mr Downes pantingly arrived. These were by no means afraid of the runner, and, in their treatment of him, were much more cruel than their employers. It is a mysterious and hideous truism that the oppressed are often much more harsh with the oppressed than the oppressors.

Again the youthful gentle reader will be finding it practically impossible to believe that people of the type of Mr Downes senior existed in the Edwardian era. But they did, and many men alive today, men no older than forty-five, will testify that they did. Moreover, such men have been, and for the rest of their lives will be, haunted painfully by the memory of what they saw as children – by the picture of one of these agonized, humble creatures as they asked gently to help carry in the luggage (which they were hardly capable of doing), and then, after vindictive expulsion, the way in which they hesitated for a moment, like dogs, and at last turned, and slunk wearily back to the Station from which they had come.

It is astonishing that characters like Mr Downes senior are capable of reproducing their kind, but, weirdly enough, in this direction such persons seem to be as, or more, prolific than the healthy and well-to-do. Mr Downes senior succeeded in having two children, a daughter who died at the age of three, and our Mr Downes – though neither was born in wedlock.

No wonder, then, that Mr Downes, with memories of his father and his mode of living, looked upon himself as one who had risen in the world. He wore a uniform; he lived in part of a house; he had married (above himself); he had three children who were decently fed, clothed, and shod. Despite his general misery and slavery to the Station, he knew he had much for which to be thankful.

4

Mr Downes saw remarkably little of his daughter Esther: working as he did, he hardly had any time in which to do so. But sometimes, on a Sunday, he would see her for an hour or so, and even eat at the same table with her.

He was aware that she dressed extremely well, and that she was beautiful. This made him proud. But it also frightened him, for, not altogether unreasonably, he associated beauty, in one of her origin and class, with the danger of sin.

Esther, on the other hand, was not proud of her father. She was ashamed of him, or at any rate of his profession and manners – this without disliking him. Nor did Esther take the view that the Downes family had risen in the world. She imagined that it had sunk low, because her mother had married beneath her.

Esther's mother was in fact of higher social origin, and had been more kindly educated than Esther's father. She had at one time been a housemaid, and afterwards a nurse, with a well-to-do middle-class family in First Avenue, Hove. She was still acquainted with this family – the mother of which still gave her a good deal of sewing, as well as recommending her, for the same task, to other women of the First Avenue type. In this way Mrs Downes – an ailing, tired, but fanatically industrious woman – made quite a good deal of money, and she was rich in comparison with the average Over Street wife. This money was hoarded, or spent upon her children – upon Esther in particular.

Thus Esther was, in a variety of ways, singularly blessed in her mother. For such a mother, having lived in households and nursed children of a much higher class than her own, had taught Esther graces of habit, speech, and manner which would otherwise have been denied her. Also, Mrs Downes, being an expert sewing-woman, not only made for Esther remarkably good and remarkably cheap dresses, but taught her the art of dressing well. She gave money to Esther, too. Most of this Esther herself had to hoard – but she was permitted to spend some of it frivolously upon herself.

Over and above this, Esther made a little money for herself. She worked and served at the counter in a sweet-shop – a rather large and rather low pink-and-white sweet-shop – particularly pink-and-white because it specialized in Brighton Rock – and popular in the season because it was situated in the Queen's Road. Swarming day-trippers, arriving at Brighton Station, and desiring to reach the sea as soon as possible, were then, as they are now, compelled to use the Queen's Road.

Esther, herself looking slightly pink-and-white in this thronged pink-and-white atmosphere (and fully conscious of each minor sensation caused throughout the day by her extreme prettiness), was a good deal happier than her fellow worker here, Gertrude Perks.

All the same, she would not concede that she was happy. Miss Downes was, probably, 'spoiled' and, if not already 'above herself', likely to become so. With all her advantages and good fortune for a girl in Over Street, she pictured herself as one in a miserable, penurious, and frustrated situation, from which she was anxious to escape as soon as she possibly could. She was acutely ambitious.

To return to Over Street, after an evening on the West Pier in the company of young men, and to sleep in the same bed with her small brother and sister, made her very seriously despondent. And as she lay awake long into the night – as she nearly always did, listening to the movement of trains and other station sounds – her depression and anxiety became deeper and deeper.

This slowly increased nocturnal melancholy was almost certainly partially attributable merely to her nearness to Brighton Station.

Large stations (termini especially) are at night evil things. To the listener in bed they seem to be making semi-hellish suggestions: they cast forth an aura of wickedness which extends as far as a quarter of a mile away from themselves, if not further.

It is difficult to discern in what this wickedness of large stations consists. Conceivably it is because they convey, to the sleepless mind, all the pain, futility, and folly of travel, of coming and going – the horrible inevitability, like that of birth and death, of arrival and departure.

They are boisterous and disquieting things during the day as well, and they can never be quite at ease in their souls who dwell near one.

Brighton Station was, as usual, the distressing audible background to Esther's thought: and she had much to think about.

She had to review in her mind the evening she had just spent on the West Pier. She had to appraise the characters and intentions of

Ryan and Gorse. She did not have to worry about Bell. He was too spectacled and silly.

5

Ryan and Gorse (and even Bell) were what Esther thought of as a 'gentlemen'. Esther flattered herself that she could 'tell' a gentleman 'the moment' she saw one.

Esther, the lovely walker on the front so often accosted, had some experience of gentlemen: and on the whole, as has been said, she distrusted their intentions and disliked their bearing. They were either too flippant ('la-di-dah'), or too sure of themselves, or too indifferent, or too much inclined to use obscure idiom far removed from her own.

At the same time Esther had a great hankering after gentlemen. She wanted to marry one of the right sort.

Ryan and Gorse, to her way of thinking, were good types of gentlemen – Ryan in particular. Indeed she entertained strong suspicions that Ryan was a 'perfect' gentleman. She also thought him almost divinely good-looking and attractive. She would have liked to marry Ryan, but she would not have entered into such a bond with the same precipitancy as Ryan would have entered into it with her. Though junior in age to Ryan by several months, she was, by virtue of her sex, at least three years his senior mentally in some ways. Before marrying Ryan she would have wanted much time in which to discover and ascertain many things.

Gorse presented a totally different problem. He was probably not a 'perfect' gentleman. Esther even doubted whether he was fully a gentleman. This was because of his swaggering manner, and of his rather distasteful nasal voice and look, which made themselves apparent every now and again.

All the same, Gorse had an air – an effrontery which did not displease, which rather engaged, Esther. And, what far exceeded these advantages, he had made a most astonishing and exciting proposal to her. He had invited her to drink a cocktail with him at the Metropole Hotel.

This had happened during the brief period in which Esther and Gorse had somehow fallen behind while the five were leaving the West Pier.

'And what about you and I having a cocktail at the Hotel

Metropole one evening?' Gorse had said. It will be remembered that this hotel had only just recently been discussed by all of them.

Esther had thought he had been joking, and had replied, 'Don't be so silly. I'd like to see you and I sitting in the Metropole.'

'No,' said Gorse. 'I mean it all right. What about tomorrow night? Do you think I don't mean it?'

At this Esther looked at him, and met his eyes, and had a sudden mad feeling, a sort of uncanny inspiration, that he did in fact mean what he said. She obeyed this inspiration.

'All right,' she said. '*I* don't mind, if you don't.'

'All right,' said Gorse. 'That's settled. But we've got to do it cleverly, if we want to be alone.'

'And how do we do that?'

'Listen,' said Gorse. 'When we all meet up again in a minute, and decide where to meet again, I'll see that it's outside one of the piers. Well, if they choose the Palace Pier, you and I meet outside the West – and *vice versa*. And at the same *time* that's chosen. Got the idea?'

'Yes.'

'And you'll do it? You'll fill the bill all right?'

'Yes,' said Esther. 'I'll fill the bill.'

And less than a minute afterwards they had perforce joined Ryan and Bell and Gertrude at the turnstiles.

6

At the time of agreeing to this proposition Esther, completely staggered, had hardly known what she was doing. Now, lying in bed listening to the trains, she was only a little less staggered, and knew practically nothing about what she actually intended to do.

A cocktail at the Metropole! With a 'gentleman' – secretly and deceptively! The decision she had now to make involved such vast and hideous intricacies as this old campaigner in Getting Off had never encountered, had never dreamed of encountering.

First of all, did he mean it? Would he 'turn up'? Was he not making (or trying to make) a fool of her?

Somehow she instinctively still believed that he was serious. But, even if he was, how could such a young man, a stripling certainly not much more than a year older than herself, take her into the *Metropole* and give her a *cocktail*? 'Gentleman' he possibly was, but how could he have the nerve?

She could have swallowed the idea of a cocktail, though this frightened and rather thrillingly scandalized her, but the *Metropole*! – that palace of mad, Oriental opulence, that haunt of the fantastically rich, the gorgeously successful theatrical, the aristocratic – that vast cathedral to Mammon outside which she had so often lingeringly passed, and through whose revolving doors she had caught glimpses of fur coats and cigars – the Metropole was too much for her. How could he *afford* it, in any case? (She had a subconscious idea that you had to pay something like five pounds even to pass through those doors, and even then have to produce credentials of some sort.) Even if he was a 'gentleman', she was certain he was not a rich one. He had worn grey flannel trousers and no hat – a thing which the rich Metropole-haunter would, she knew, not do. But did he perhaps have a hat, and a proper suit, which he would wear tomorrow?

And what about her own dress? Could she possibly dress up for the Metropole? She believed that, owing to her skill in dress inherited from her mother, by the skin of her teeth she might possibly 'pass'.

But he was so young, young, *young*! And she was younger still. Would they not (if not actually refused admission) be laughed at cruelly? Would they be served with a cocktail? Once more she suspected that it was a joke, and that he would not turn up.

But even if he did turn up, there were countless other difficulties with which she had to contend. She would, if she met him outside the West Pier, be guilty of a deception of the most crude and brutal sort. Her close friend Gertrude, and Ryan, and the other one (as ill-assorted a trio as you could find in the world) would meet in the open outside the Palace Pier and find themselves betrayed – betrayed while she sat inside the palace sipping a cocktail. What excuse could she make afterwards to Gertrude for not turning up? And what (and this could so easily happen) if she was found out?

Or could she let Gertrude into the secret beforehand? This seemed not impossible, indeed quite easy, for Gertrude was her admiring subordinate and might eagerly encourage her in such a scheme – but still this meant the betrayal of Ryan.

And this brought her to the question of Ryan. Was not Ryan far and away her favourite – the possibly 'perfect' gentleman, the one whose looks and manners she loved, the one who, she believed, strongly admired her, the one whom, after proper investigations, she would be willing to marry?

What if Ryan 'found out' – discovered her hideous treachery? Nothing could be more likely. Would he forgive her and continue to know her? Almost certainly not.

Was she, then, to forsake Ryan for Gorse, for whom she had no particular feeling? Was she to lose Ryan for the sake of one absurd, flashy, material vanity – a cocktail at the Metropole?

Or was there some way round? Need Ryan find out – and even if he did, could not some excuse – a lie, of course, and one made in collaboration with Gorse – be found, and might not Ryan accept this? Might she not without undue exertion eat her cake and have it too?

Esther rebuked herself for contemplating succumbing to treachery on behalf of a material pleasure. But here she wronged herself. What she had in mind was, really, a romantic pleasure. Cinderella's motives could hardly have been called material. What the Ball was to Cinderella, the Metropole was to Miss Downes of Over Street. The romance of Ryan conflicted with the romance of the great seaside hotel – that was all.

Finally – and, in view of her ignorance of Gorse's real character, pitifully – she decided in favour of the Metropole.

She came to this conclusion at about a quarter past one in the morning. She knew that this was the time because she had just heard her father come in – the porter returning after his day and night of waiting, carrying, and being insulted.

Chapter Two

I

Ryan, Gorse, and Bell, after leaving Esther and Gertrude that night, had soon parted, and had made no arrangement to meet each other until all three met the 'birds' again outside the Palace Pier the next evening at seven-thirty.

Purely by accident, however, at about eleven on the morning of the next day, Ryan ran into Bell in a small tea-coffee-cake restaurant in Preston Street. Bell was seated at a table eating a large ice-cream.

Ice-cream, really, does not consort with Learning: ice-cream lacks austerity; it is not food befitting a sage. Milton, letting his

> lamp at midnight hour,
> Be seen in some high lonely tower

would certainly not, even if such a thing had been obtainable, sustained himself with ice-cream.

Bell, therefore, looked a trifle ashamed of himself – and perhaps the more so because Ryan, the comparative philistine, ordered a sophisticated coffee.

They talked about various matters, and then came to the proposed meeting with the two girls in the evening. Bell suggested that he himself should not appear at this. He was, he said, 'odd man out'. Ryan at first warmly persuaded him to come. Ryan was anxious to be polite: and also he secretly felt that Bell was not actually odd man out: it was Bell's function to draw off the hideous Gertrude.

But Bell persisted. Bell also was privately conscious of his real function, and he had no desire whatever to fulfil it.

Ryan at last gave in. It was really a matter of indifference to him. Only Esther was his object and only Gorse was his possible rival.

He was not, really, at all certain that Gorse was his rival. He was quite sure that Gorse had no feeling towards Esther to be remotely compared with his own. Ryan even doubted whether Gorse was capable of natural, commonplace reactions towards girls. Gorse was an unpredictable and curious as well as slightly distasteful character. Gorse, though, by mere virtue of his indifference and calmness, might be all the more powerful a rival.

Ryan left Bell and spent the greater part of the day on his motorcycle. He had a late high tea in his bed-sitting-room in Tisbury Road, and then dressed with great care.

In his anxiety to be early for the appointment he somehow managed (as people in the same situation so often do) to be late for it – by two minutes. People get it into their heads that they have an enormous amount of time to spare, and consequently walk about the streets in the vicinity of the meeting place, almost disregarding time altogether.

Outside the Palace Pier, Gertrude was waiting. Neither Esther nor Gorse was present.

2

'Oh – hullo,' said Gertrude, and Ryan said the same, and apologized for being late, and they clumsily shook hands.

'Where've your friends got to, then?' asked Gertrude.

This was Gertrude's initial indirect lie. She had more to tell. She knew perfectly well at least where one of Ryan's friends was. He was, unless he had proved a deceiver, drinking, or about to drink, a cocktail at the Hotel Metropole.

'I don't know,' replied Ryan. 'At least I know about Bell. He's not coming along. But I don't know about Gorse.'

Now he came to the matter horribly nearest to his heart.

'Where's yours, by the way?' he asked with fairly well-assumed indifference.

Here Gertrude braced herself for the great and indirect lie. Esther, at the sweet-shop that morning, had confided almost all the truth to her, and had instructed her in regard to the falsehood she was to tell.

'Oh – I'm ever so sorry,' she said rather breathlessly. 'Esther sent a message she can't come. She's got a little brother who isn't at all well. He's got a temperature. And Esther's got to stay in and look after him. She told me to say she's ever so sorry, and she hopes she'll meet you again.'

Esther, having invented this lie for Gertrude to tell, had been visited by pangs not only of conscience, but of fear. She was a victim of that curious superstition, and consequent inhibition, under the spell of what human beings feel that if they say that one who is near and dear to them is ill, then Fate, or an angered God, will make that person ill in fact.

Because Gertrude was not a good liar, and spoke breathlessly, Ryan was at once suspicious.

'Oh,' he said. 'I'm sorry. What's the matter with him?'

'He's got a bad sore throat and a cough,' said Gertrude. 'And with a temperature, too, you don't want to neglect that sort of thing – do you?'

The bad sore throat and cough had also been Esther's invention, and she had thus secretly scared herself dreadfully. For, according to this strange superstition, God, provoked, gives the imaginary invalid precisely the illness he or she is imagined to have, and in a much more severe and dangerous degree than is originally pictured. Esther, therefore, had a vision of her little brother dying, within a few days, of influenza, bronchitis, or pneumonia.

'No,' said Ryan, still suspicious. 'I know one mustn't neglect that sort of thing. Is he seeing a doctor?'

'Yes,' said Gertrude. 'I think he's coming tonight.'

This was Gertrude's own invention. Esther had not thought about the necessity for a doctor.

'Well – I'm very sorry,' said Ryan and, though still not quite credulous, realized that he could not press the matter further. Instead he said: 'Well, I wonder where our friend Gorse has got to.'

Ryan, of course, was very seriously disappointed about the absence of Esther, but not in despair: for Gertrude had at any rate turned up with a message from Esther, and through Gertrude he could send messages to her and arrange another meeting later – tomorrow, perhaps. He meant, also, to get Esther's address from Gertrude.

But what on earth was he going to do about Gertrude this evening? How was he to get rid of her? The prospect of spending a whole evening with this plain, spectacled, common girl was too awful to contemplate. And yet he could not see how, in common politeness, and if she desired it – and she clearly looked as if she did – he could do otherwise.

This being so, he longed for Gorse to appear. Gorse would at least help him out. Indeed, Gorse was such a deep and resourceful character that he might well invent some remarkable excuse for both of them to get away quickly.

'He's very late, ain't he?' said Gertrude. 'You were late yourself, but he's later.'

'Yes. He certainly is,' said Ryan. 'Well, we'll give him five minutes – shall we?'

It had occurred to Ryan that Gorse quite probably would not appear. Gorse, he knew, was an extremely punctual person: he was also an extremely unpredictable one. Gorse, Ryan felt, would either be at an appointment on time, or not turn up at all. That is why he gave Gorse only five minutes – anyone else he would have given ten minutes, or a quarter of an hour.

'Yes,' said Gertrude. 'Let's just give him five minutes.'

Something frightened Ryan in this utterance of Gertrude. Perhaps it was the word 'just'. That word betrayed an eagerness to give Gorse as little time as possible. And that, in its turn, indicated a wish to spend the evening alone with Ryan – conceivably a strong desire. And such a thought was decidedly intimidating.

Ryan and Gertrude stood talking about the weather and the passing people for five minutes, and then Gertrude said:

'Well, his five minutes is up. Let's go on by ourselves, shall we?'

By 'go on', she meant go on the Palace Pier. Ryan had been right about her attitude. Bold and extraordinary thoughts had entered the unfortunate Gertrude's head.

3

Gertrude had been given, by her friend Esther, many lessons and lectures on the subject of young men and the manner in which they were to be captured and, when captured, treated.

At the end of these lessons Gertrude had frequently pointed out to Esther that they were of little use. They did not, she would say, properly apply to herself. For, whereas Esther was beautiful and attractive, she, Gertrude, was plain and lacking in magnetism.

To which Esther would reply – half out of politeness but half because she believed it to be true – that it was not Beauty that mattered, it was *Personality*. *Personality* and *Boldness* – cheek, sauce, courage, wit, the art of repartee, a way with one.

Esther would also never concede (but here she was lying in order to be kind to the other) that Gertrude was plain. Now Esther was an extremely kind girl and a fine liar. As a consequence she had made Gertrude believe quite often that she was not anything like as plain as she thought she was, that she was, perhaps absurdly, underestimating herself.

Being in her best dress, and 'got up to the nines', she was tonight in one of these optimistic moods, and there had come into her mind the staggering notion that she should take advantage of the present favourable circumstances and employ Personality and Boldness upon Ryan, and conceivably capture him by such measures!

It must not be thought that Gertrude had any idea of behaving treacherously to Esther in thus trying to win Ryan's admiration or love. She had never suspected for a moment what was in fact true, that Esther was emphatically interested in the good-looking young man. This was because Esther had in another way been untruthful. In her pride she had always pretended, in front of Gertrude, that young men as a whole are contemptible, to be treated disdainfully, merely used. Gertrude certainly did not think in this way about young men, but she believed absolutely that Esther did. Therefore, it was quite clear to Gertrude that Ryan was not a person of the smallest consequence to Esther, and there was no question of her 'stealing' him.

And so she had said to Ryan, 'Well, his five minutes is up. Let's go on by ourselves, shall we?'

4

Ryan, staggered and terrified, tried to do some rapid thinking. But no amount of thought, quick or slow, could extract so kindhearted a being as Ryan was from the situation in which he found himself.

And so he said, 'All right, then. Let's.' And they moved towards the turnstile.

Here Ryan, who was by no means rich, realized that he had to pay for this torture, and he did so gracefully.

As soon as they had got through and were walking on the planks seawards, Gertrude was the one who was trying hardest to think quickly. *Boldness* and *Personality*, she kept repeating to herself. But Boldness of the kind she contemplated was, she realized, of no use until it was Dark. At the moment the sun had barely set in a cloudless sky.

How then, until night had fallen, could she at least exercise Personality?

Thinking of these things, she said nothing, and, Ryan having nothing to say, there was a long, very embarrassing silence as they walked along.

At last Ryan was compelled to descend to banality.

'It's a lovely evening, isn't it?' he said.

'Yes, it is,' said Gertrude. But she could not go on, and there was another silence.

'In fact, we've really had a lovely summer,' said Ryan. 'Taking things all round.'

'We have,' said Gertrude. 'Really.'

And again there was silence.

At last, as they approached some slot machines, Gertrude saw a chance of bringing Personality into play.

'Are you a kid, like I am?' she said. 'And like to play with slot machines?'

'Oh yes,' said Ryan. 'I love slot machines.'

'Ah – then you are a kid,' said Gertrude. 'I thought you were.'

'I suppose I am,' said Ryan.

'You look like one, anyway,' said Gertrude. (Personality, sauce, cheek, an air!)

'Do I?'

'Yes, you look as though you want taking in hand and looking after – to *me*.'

'Do I?' said Ryan.

'You certainly do,' said Gertrude. 'Come along. Let's be kids and play at one of these.'

Ryan assented, and they went up to a machine behind whose glass were small and crude images of moustached footballers. These footballers, on one side, wore green jerseys, and, on the other side, red. The stitches which had gone to make these jerseys were greatly out of proportion. They would, if they had been worn by real footballers, each have been as large as, or larger than, footballs.

To play at this game it was necessary to put in two pennies – the winner receiving one back. Gertrude offered to put in her own penny, but the chivalrous and generous Ryan would not permit this. '*More* money!' was Ryan's thought. But he meant, before he had parted from Getrude that night, to get Esther's address from her. And that would be worth his entire fortune. Ryan put in the pennies, and they began to play.

The reader will possibly blush in his soul almost as much as Ryan did on learning that, as they played this game, Gertrude, while peering through the glass to decide what sort of shot to make with her side of footballers, put her head and hair so close to Ryan that they almost touched his own. She did this more than once, too. But at last Ryan managed to shoot a goal and was temporarily relieved.

They next went to a machine again requiring two pennies and behind whose glass were imitations of race horses.

At this game it was impossible for Gertrude to assault Ryan in the same way – it was too quick.

Ryan, therefore, made them play the game as much as five times. He won the first two races, and then suggested giving her a 'start'. Gertrude won the last game, and they moved on again.

Now some clouds had appeared in the sky and it was darker, but not dark enough for Gertrude's intentions.

She therefore took Ryan to the end of the Pier, and then made him walk four times around the Palace Pier Theatre. This she supplemented by making him stop at other slot machines.

At last it was dark enough. She led him towards a deserted covered bench which she had in mind and which faced the West Pier.

'Come on,' she said. 'Let's come and sit down here.'

And (she hoped fascinatingly) she took his arm in order to compel him to do so. He complied. For about ten minutes she talked, and he answered as well as he could.

Now it was really dark enough. She had not yet released his arm. 'Yes,' said Gertrude reflectively, 'it isn't half a lovely night – isn't it?'

'Yes, it certainly is,' said Ryan.

'Or a night for love,' said Gertrude. 'Which?'

'I don't know,' said Ryan.

'Don't you?'

'No . . . I don't . . .'

'Sure?'

'Yes.'

'Well – *I* think it's a night for love.'

And here Gertrude put ('nestled' is the word vulgarly used) her head on Ryan's shoulder.

He had anticipated abominable enough things, but nothing so eerily ghastly as this. He felt he must say something.

'Do you?' he said.

'Yes. Don't you?' said Gertrude.

'I don't know,' said Ryan.

There was a pause.

'You're Cold,' said Gertrude. 'Ain't you?'

Here Ryan made the perfectly honest mistake of believing that she was alluding to the temperature of the Pier.

'No,' he said, 'I'm quite all right, thank you.'

'No,' said Gertrude. 'I don't mean Cold in that way.'

'Oh,' said Ryan. 'Don't you?'

'No,' said Gertrude. 'Don't you know the way I mean it?'

'No. I don't,' said Ryan yet again.

'Oh yes, you do.'

'No. I don't. Really,' said Ryan.

Now, of course, he was not telling the truth.

'Well – shall I tell you?'

'Yes. Do.'

'Well. Not Warm. Warm in the Heart.'

'Oh. Aren't I?'

'No.'

'Oh. I'm sorry.'

'Not warm in the heart,' said Gertrude. 'Not warm in the heart towards poor little Gertrude.'

And, to cap this horror, she put out her hand and began, with her fingers, to play flirtatiously with the middle button of Ryan's coat.

'*Are* you?' said Gertrude.

'I don't know,' said Ryan (it now seemed for the eightieth time).

'Don't you?'

'No. I don't . . .'

'I'm warm in the heart about you, anyway. I was, ever since I set eyes on you, and I am still.'

'Are you?'

'Don't you think you could ever get warm in the heart about your little Gertie-Wertie?'

(*Gertie-Wertie!*)

'I don't know.'

'Well, I wish you'd make up your mind –' Here Gertrude paused. 'What's your Christian name, anyway? I've told you mine.'

'Peter,' said Ryan.

'Peter,' repeated Gertrude. 'That suits you. I like it. Don't *you*?

'I don't know,' said Ryan.

5

It is not necessary further to embarrass, or tire, the reader with a narration of Gertrude's further Boldness during the next twenty minutes.

It need only be said that she continued to be Bold, thinking that she might wear him down (Esther, in addition to Boldness and Personality, had unfortunately recommended Persistence to her) and that Ryan went on saying 'I don't know' and 'Are you?' and 'Do you?' and 'Don't you?' until he was nearly out of his mind.

Then, quite suddenly, Gertrude gave in. She withdrew her head from his shoulder, and her hand from the middle button of his coat, and she looked at him, pityingly and pitifully.

'No – it ain't any good, is it?' she said.

'I don't really know. What do you mean?' said Ryan.

'Oh yes, you do,' said Gertrude. 'And I know *why* it ain't any good.'

'Why?'

'It's because I'm not pretty – ain't it?' said this now very genuine girl. 'It's because I'm so darned ugly.'

'Don't be silly,' said Ryan. 'You're not ugly. You're very pretty.'

He had not meant to say this last. It had slipped out in his sorrow for her pathos.

'No. You don't mean that.'

'Yes, I do. Of course I do.' What else could he say? And how could he say it without pretending as cleverly as he could that he meant it? And yet how cruel he was being, and what unutterable confusion he was causing in the wretched Gertrude's mind!

For, so convincing was his manner, that Gertrude half believed he was speaking the truth. And if this was so, why did he not accept her advances?

Gertrude, hoping for the best, but feeling in the bottom of her unhappy heart that she was probably deceiving herself, alighted upon an explanation.

'It's *She* you're after,' she said. 'Isn't it?'

'Who?'

'Esther.'

There was a pause.

'Is that her name?' asked Ryan.

'Ah – so you're ever so keen to know her Christian name – ain't you? It *is* her you're after – ain't it?'

'I don't know . . .' said Ryan.

'But I do,' said Gertrude. 'And I can't say I blame you. She's very beautiful – ain't she?'

'Yes. She's certainly very pretty.'

'Not ugly. Like I am.'

'You're not ugly. Don't be silly.'

'Oh yes, I am. And you and she'd make a proper pair. She doesn't think much of boys as a rule, but I think she might like *you* – if you tried.'

'Do you think so?'

'Yes.'

'Really?'

'Yes. I think so. And you're ever so keen to know – ain't you? Come on. Own up. You're crazy about her – aren't you? There's plenty that are – I can tell you.'

'Well – I do think she's very lovely . . .'

Gertrude persisted.

'And you're crazy about her – ain't you?'

'Well – perhaps I am. A bit.'

'Yes. I thought so.' Gertrude was in a way pleased because his confession confirmed her hope that it was only because he loved Esther that he had rejected her advances. Being pleased, she was very generous.

'Well,' she said, 'can I help you in any way? I know her very well – and what I said might count.'

'Do you think you could?' said Ryan. 'It's very nice of you.'

'Yes. I think I could. What do you want me to do?'

'Well – I'd like to know her address, really. Just in case we didn't meet on the front again and I couldn't find her.'

'All right,' said Gertrude. 'It's Over Street. Two hundred and six Over Street. Can you remember it?'

'Yes. I can remember. Two hundred and six. Over Street. Thank you. It's very good of you.'

'And do you know where Over Street is? It ain't a very swell district.'

'No.'

'It's just by Brighton Station. I don't know I ought to be telling you all this.'

'Oh, it's all right. Really. I wouldn't take advantage. It's only just in *case*, you see. To write to her.'

'Yes, I see,' said Gertrude. 'And anything else, Mr Peter Ryan?'

'No – I don't think so. No – I'm sorry, there *is* just one other thing.'

'And what's that?'

'I don't know if it's all right for you to tell me – but tell me if you can. It's just that I want to know whether it was true that her little brother was ill tonight. Or was it just a sham, because she didn't want to turn up?'

'What makes you think it wasn't true?'

Gertrude said this in order to gain time in which to think. She had temporarily forgotten the problem of Esther having lied, and of probably being with Gorse at the Metropole at the present moment.

What was she to do? She was maternally eager to help Ryan, but how could she do so without betraying Esther? She would like Ryan to know, too, that his alleged friend Gorse was betraying him. And had not Esther betrayed him as well? Gertrude fully understood Esther's motives, and had already forgiven her, had even warmly supported her in what she had done. And Esther was to be further forgiven, too, for she had had no knowledge of Ryan's feelings towards her. Had she had, she would probably have acted differently.

As these thoughts rushed through Gertrude's head, Ryan answered her.

'Oh – I just thought it might not be true,' he said. 'There was something in the way you said it, I think. Not that I can complain. There's no reason why she shouldn't make an excuse and not turn up. I know I probably don't mean anything to her. Not at present, at any rate.'

He spoke with such *naïveté*, charm, and simplicity that Gertrude was tremendously tempted to be of assistance to him by telling him the truth. But no – she must resist this. Esther came first. And tomorrow morning she had to get instructions from Esther about this new state of affairs.

'Oh no. It was quite true,' she said. 'Her little brother's ill all right – and that's the only reason she couldn't come.'

'Oh well – I'm very glad to hear it,' said Ryan.

What on earth would happen, Gertrude wondered, if she and

Esther and Gorse were found out? Esther had, she realized, caused a complication dangerous from innumerable aspects.

'I mean,' Ryan went on, 'that as long as she wasn't making an excuse, she might even be a bit interested in me, or come to be later.'

'Yes,' said Gertrude. 'I'm sure she might. And there's plenty of other opportunities – ain't there? I'll be seeing her tomorrow, and so do you want me to give any message to her?'

'Oh,' said Ryan. 'Would you? It's terribly good of you, and you're terribly nice.'

'No, I ain't. What do you want me to tell her?'

'Well. Would you ask her if she could meet me?'

'Where?'

'Well – what about the same time and place that you and I met – outside the Palace Pier – seven-thirty?'

'And when? Tomorrow evening?'

'Well, yes. If her little brother's better and she can manage it.'

'Oh – I expect he'll be better, and that she'll manage it. Anyway – that's the message I'll give her.'

'Well – thank you so much. You're terribly nice.'

'Don't be silly . . . And now I think it's time we was toddling off home – don't you? Me, at any rate.'

'Oh no. Do let's stay, if you'd like it,' said the kindhearted and grateful Ryan. He was so grateful that he would have stayed with Gertrude till midnight, or beyond, if she desired it. But this was not what he wanted to do. He wanted to go home at once and dream and scheme about Esther, and brood upon his probable meeting with her tomorrow evening.

'No. It's quite late, and I'll only get into trouble with Mother,' said Gertrude. 'Come on. Let's wend our way.'

And she rose.

Ryan rose too, and they began to walk towards the shore.

They began to speak about Brighton – its climate and amenities.

When they had passed through the turnstile and were on the front, they stopped and looked at each other shyly.

'Well,' said Gertrude, 'I suppose its goodbye. I'll give Esther that message all right, and I'm sure she'll be here. You've got her address, anyway, now, haven't you?'

'Yes. I have. Thanks to you. I really can't thank you enough. Just tell her seven-thirty – just here – where we're standing – will you?'

'Yes. I'll tell her that.'

At this, chivalry and gratitude again attacked Ryan.

'And will you be coming along too?' he asked. 'I hope you will.'

'No. I don't think I'll be along.' Gertrude smiled at him. 'I don't think *that'd* be very wise, would it?'

'Oh yes, it would. Surely it would. Do come along.'

'No. I won't come. But thanks for asking me all the same.'

'Well – we'll be meeting again – won't we? Of course we'll be meeting again.'

'Yes. I daresay we'll be meeting. Especially if you get friendly with Esther.'

'Oh yes, we *must* meet,' said Ryan. 'All *three* of us must go out together.'

His earnestness, sweetness, and *gaucherie* completely overcame Gertrude.

'You ain't half a baby – ain't you?' she said. And she kissed him on the cheek, and ran away before he could reply.

Soon after they had parted, the minds of each began to work roughly on the same subject – that of Esther and Gorse. Ryan wondered what Esther was doing now, and he wondered why Gorse had not turned up.

Gertrude, who knew all, wondered what Gorse and Esther were doing now, and what they had been doing all evening.

What, indeed?

Chapter Three

Gorse had arrived at the West Pier three minutes before the time appointed. Esther, on principle, had seen to it that she was half a minute late.

Esther was dressed as well as she knew how to dress – which meant that she was dressed very well; and Gorse, for one who remembered him in his jacket and 'bags' of the previous evening, was a transformed being. He was in a well-made dark blue lounge suit; he wore a fawn-coloured trilby hat, a stiff white collar, and a striped but modest tie.

Our dear old friends The Nines, in fact, had been paid due respect by both. But this discreetly – not too officiously or subserviently.

Esther was enormously reassured on seeing Gorse dressed so well. Now it did not seem so incredible that they would be allowed into the Metropole. Her main concern was as to whether she herself would 'pass': but on the whole she believed she would.

Having shaken hands, Gorse said, 'Well. Off to the good old Met. That's where we said we were going – wasn't it?'

'Yes,' said Esther. 'That's what you said.'

'Bon,' said Gorse, and nothing further was said as they crossed the road: nor was anything said as they walked along in the direction of the Metropole. At last Esther found the silence embarrassing, and she decided to break it.

'Do you go to the Metropole a lot?' she asked.

'Oh yes,' said Gorse. 'Quite a good bit.'

But this was a complete lie. Gorse had never been inside the Metropole in his life. Moreover, he was almost as frightened by the idea of doing so as Esther was herself. Indeed, in a manner, he was more so. For whereas Esther had him to lean upon, to believe in, he had no such prop. He had to lead the way, find a table, deal with the waiter. Even the cold, inscrutable Gorse on certain occasions knew the meaning of the word 'cowardice'.

This was why he said nothing as they walked along. This struck Esther as being curious, for he had been so loquacious, too much so, yesterday evening.

Without having uttered another word they reached the entrance and walked up the steps to the revolving doors.

These were swung round for them by a porter from within. The porter did this rather too quickly, and there was something of a rush and panic as Gorse made the trembling Esther go through first.

Then they were inside, and Gorse was face to face with his difficulties.

He now regretted deeply having told Esther that he had been in here before, for he was, in fact, entirely bewildered, and felt that she would detect his falsehood.

'Well. There're a lot of places we can sit,' he said. 'Where would you like to go?'

'I don't know,' said Esther. 'I'd rather leave it to you.'

As they had as yet not been turned out she was regaining confidence.

'Well, let's try down there – shall we?' said Gorse, and he led her straight forwards. About twenty-five yards ahead he had spotted an adult couple seated at a table drinking. He had also seen a vacant table not far away from them.

Nothing was said as they walked towards this table.

Esther, in spite of her more confident feeling, was too overwhelmed by the grandeur of the place and the people and the carpets to speak; Gorse did not speak because he was too frightened, and too much on the watch in order to behave properly.

This state of mind in Gorse caused him, as such a thing does with many more ordinary people, to lift his chin high and to put on an air of the greatest *hauteur*.

Then suddenly he realized that he had not taken off his hat, and he believed this was highly incorrect. He therefore snatched it off clumsily, and so lost the impression of *hauteur*. Then, having lost it, he resumed it with even greater and more painful intensity.

At last the table was reached, and he motioned to Esther to sit down, and sat down himself. Now he did not know what to do with his hat. He thought of putting it on the table, but he was visited by the hideous idea that he ought not to have a hat with him at all: that he should have put it in the cloakroom or something.

And so, hoping that no one had seen him do it, he put it under his chair. But Esther had seen him do it, and had noticed his furtive look.

Now what was he to do? How was he to find a waiter? Esther still had not uttered a word, and he was conscious that she was looking at him. The couple opposite were taking no notice of them, and Gorse was at least grateful for this. (Esther was glad of this too. It helped to make her feel that she had 'passed'.)

By the grace of God a waiter came hurrying by. Gorse put up his hand and snapped his fingers. He had an impression that it was vulgar to snap one's fingers (particularly so loudly), but he could not risk losing the waiter.

The waiter turned and came up to them.

Now Esther was wondering whether Gorse looked old enough to be served with drinks, and Gorse himself had doubts.

'Yes, sir,' said the waiter, and bent over them politely. This was better. Gorse suddenly regained confidence.

'Well,' he said, looking and smiling at Esther. 'What's your choice?'

'I don't know,' said Esther, who had suddenly and completely lost confidence again. 'Really . . .'

'Well, you must make up your mind, you know,' said Gorse, and now he smiled almost confidentially, or even winkingly, at the waiter.

'I don't really know,' said Esther.

'Now. Come along,' said Gorse. 'You've got to make up your mind, you know.'

'I don't know.'

Esther was in a panic.

'But you must know,' said Gorse. 'Surely it's easy enough to think of a cocktail – isn't it?'

Esther absolutely lost her head.

'Oh – very well, then,' she said, 'I think I'll have a Benedictine.'

The unfortunate girl had heard of Benedictine, and had always somehow imagined that it was a cocktail.

'A *what*?' said Gorse in a shocked way. He had no particular desire to humiliate Esther, but he wanted to keep up his dignity in front of the waiter.

'A *Benedictine*,' repeated Esther in a wretched attempted at defiance. But she knew she had made some shocking error, and she blushed.

'Well,' said Gorse, 'you can have a Benedictine if you like – but it's not a cocktail – is it? And I think you'd find it a little sickly if you have it before dinner.'

Young as he was, Gorse – along with his many other rapidly developing snobberies – was an incipient wine-snob (perhaps the most unattractive form of snobbery on this earth), and he already knew something about these matters.

'Don't you agree, waiter?' he said, once more very nearly winking.

'Yes, sir. It might be.' The waiter smiled.

Humiliated almost unbearably, Esther at last saw a way out.

'Well – what are *you* going to have?' she asked.

(Why on earth, she wondered, hadn't she asked this before?)

'Well, I'm going to have a Gin and It,' said Gorse. 'Will you try one?'

'Yes. I think I'll have that,' said Esther. She put in the word 'think' in order to make it seem that she was making a choice. But in fact she did not know the name of any cocktail.

'Good,' said Gorse. 'Two Gin and Its, then, waiter.'

'Yes, sir. Thank you, sir,' said the waiter, and he went away.

There was a silence.

'Sorry if I made a fool of myself,' said Esther. 'But I'm not used to cocktails and places like this, you see.'

'You didn't make a fool of yourself at all,' said Gorse. 'And it's very easy to make mistakes about these things. I used to myself, anyway. Actually Benedictine's a liqueur – not a cocktail.'

'Is it? And what's a liqueur? I don't even know what *that* is.'

Gorse began to explain, and soon the waiter returned.

Gorse paid, tipped the waiter handsomely, and was thanked with the utmost deference. Gorse was now beginning to feel splendidly at home in the Hotel Metropole.

But he, as well as Esther, looked at the drinks (which had a cherry stuck into them at the end of a stick) with some diffidence.

Esther was certainly not going to tackle her drink until Gorse had tackled his and she had been given some intimation of the proper way to approach a cocktail with a cherry in it.

Gorse hesitated for a moment. Then he put the cherry into his mouth, and the stick on to an ash tray, and he raised the glass to his mouth and said, 'Well – cheerio,' to Esther.

Esther did exactly the same.

'Like it?' said Gorse.

'Yes,' said Esther. 'It's ever so nice.'

But although she had not objected to the cherry, because of its sweetness, she had really hated her first sip at the cocktail.

After they had been talking and sipping for about five minutes, however, Esther found that she disliked the taste of the drink much less. Also, she experienced a warm feeling in her heart, a not unpleasant giddiness in her head, and a curious temptation to behave much more audaciously than she had so far. She succumbed to this temptation.

'That's a nice tie you're wearing,' she said. 'Where did you get that?'

'This? Oh – it's just an old school tie, as a matter of fact.'

'Really?' said Esther, secretly awed. 'What school?'

'Westminster,' said Gorse.

The tie Gorse was wearing was in fact an old Westminster tie. But Gorse had been to St Paul's, and he was, therefore, masquerading in such a tie.

Gorse had not thought St Paul's quite good enough, and had chosen Westminster. He had contemplated adopting Eton or Harrow, but had then thought that this might be going a little bit too far. Westminster was his compromise. He only seldom wore this tie, for he was afraid of being exposed as an impostor.

But on special occasions – and bluffing his way into the Metropole tonight was certainly such – he would put it on with his best blue suit.

Westminster conveyed practically nothing to Esther. She thought only of Westminster Abbey. Only Eton and Harrow – or, because she had been brought up in Sussex, Brighton College or Lancing – would have impressed her very much.

The drink by this time had just affected Gorse's head.

'Yes,' he said in a languid way. 'All my people went there, from time immemorial, so I had to go there too.'

This again awed Esther, and she was once again bolder than she would have been if she had not taken drink.

'And what sort of people are yours?' She spoke in a saucy way, which failed to conceal her deep curiosity.

'Oh – Army People,' said Gorse. 'Nearly all of them. They're a dull lot, really.'

Gorse, when he said this, believed he was lying. But, if what he had said were to be taken literally, he was not. His ancestors, on the whole, *had* been 'Army People'. They had been, very many of them, low and lewd privates in slightly second-rate wars.

'Well,' said Esther, who was more impressed than ever. 'I wish I had some Army people in *my* family. *My* people are pretty humble, as I expect you've guessed.'

'What do you mean?' said Gorse. 'We're all the same – aren't we – under the skin? The Colonel's Lady and Judy O'Grady are sisters under the skin – what?'

He was quoting Rudyard Kipling. Gorse, though he disliked poetry intensely in a general way, was not completely lacking in appreciation of the baser sort.

Esther did not know that he had quoted Kipling, but understood his general meaning.

'Yes,' she said. 'I suppose we are. All the same, I wish I'd been born to better things. I work in a sweet-shop all day, and it's pretty nearly a slum, where I live.'

'Well, if you work in a sweet-shop – that's bringing coals to Newcastle – isn't it?'

Esther did not understand this compliment – Gorse's first.

'What do you mean?' she said.

'Well – a perfect sweet amongst the sweets – what?'

She understood this.

'Don't be so silly,' she said, not displeased.

They continued to talk in this way, and then Gorse insisted that they should have another cocktail, and Esther, after a few protests, succumbed.

Half-way through the second cocktail Esther was hilariously happy (she did not know why, for she did not connect drinking with hilarity). Then she suddenly felt 'swimmy' and knew that she must stop drinking. She therefore made Gorse finish off the remaining half of her drink.

Gorse did this quickly, and was, by now, himself quite inebriated. Gorse, throughout his life, was never able to take drink very well.

He suggested that they should go and walk on the West Pier, and Esther gladly assented.

On the way to the West Pier, and while walking on it, Gorse did something which, throughout his life, he always did when he had taken too much to drink. This was his 'Silly Ass' act.

The 'Silly Ass' act had a patter which he had half invented himself and half borrowed from 'Silly Ass' actors on the stage or the music-halls. There was a great deal of 'I say!' 'Bai Jove!'

'Weally!' in it, and before he started his performance he took a monocle from his pocket and stuck it into his eye.

Needless to say, the cultured, watching this, did not, in their shame, know where to look; but the uncultured were often genuinely amused, or fascinated simply to see someone genuinely making a fool of himself.

Esther, though clever, was not very cultured, and tonight the drink had gone to her head. She was therefore highly pleased by Gorse's performance. She laughed at it, and encouraged him to go on with it.

At last, however, he put away his monocle and behaved normally and quietly again. By this time it was dark, and Gorse suggested that they should sit down. He chose the same spot as the five had used last night.

Looking at the lights of the Palace Pier (had she had a telescope and had it been light), Esther could have seen the bold Gertrude and the agonized Ryan sitting beside each other. Esther became pensive and serious. Gorse sensed her mood and imitated it.

After a while Esther said: 'My word – I haven't half got a conscience about those other three.'

'Which other three?' asked Gorse.

'Why – your two friends – and Gertrude.'

Of course she really had no conscience about Gertrude (who was in the secret) or about Bell (who didn't count). But she did feel conscience-stricken about her own deceitfulness, and about Ryan, who, she was certain, must have been disappointed not to see her.

'Oh,' said Gorse. 'I wouldn't bother about them. They'll be getting on all right.'

'Yes. But they must've been waiting for us to turn up.'

Another lie – for Gertrude had been there to tell that she, Esther, at any rate, was not coming because of the illness of her little brother. The Over Street girl was beginning to have some glimmering of what a tangled web we weave when first we practise to deceive.

'Oh, I don't expect they'll wait long,' said Gorse. 'If I know my Ryan, he's not the sort to wait long.'

'Is that his name?' asked Esther. 'I know you introduced us last night, but I didn't take it in. But I can remember yours. It's Gorse – isn't it? Like what you see on the Downs.'

'That's right.'

'And what's your friend's Christian name? I mean the better-looking one – Ryan.'

'Well, of all the cheek,' said Gorse facetiously. 'Here am I taking you out, and you ask Ryan's Christian name, but not mine. And on top of it you call him good-looking.'

'Oh – I'm sorry. Well – what is it? I mean yours.'

'I told you last night.'

'Well – I didn't take it in. I wasn't taking a thing in, somehow, last night. Go on. What is it?'

'Ralph,' said Gorse. 'Pronounced Ralph or Rafe – whichever you prefer. Which do you?'

Esther thought about this.

'I think I prefer Ralph,' she said. 'Rafe's a bit too La-di-dah.'

'Very well, then. And will you call me Ralph, Esther? I remember your name all right, you see.'

And here Gorse moved closer to Esther, and put his arm around her waist.

'Oh – I don't know about that,' said Esther.

She was fighting for time. She had had many previous experiences of this kind, and believed she knew how to deal with them expertly. But Gorse, somehow – was a new type of problem. She now believed that he was a 'gentleman'. His blue suit, his hat, his manner and success at the Metropole, his old school tie – all these had practically convinced her. Also, she thought she 'liked' him. He had dash, and she had laughed a good deal at his 'Silly Ass' act. But still there was just something wrong which made her suspect and *not* altogether like him. This was to a certain extent instinctive in her, but there was also the concrete fact that he had shown duplicity in making a private arrangement with her to go to the Metropole. If he could deceive others, could he not deceive herself? (In thinking thus, Esther completely overlooked her own deception.)

'Come along, Esther, now,' said Gorse. 'Won't you call me Ralph?'

'All right, then. If you like,' said Esther after a pause.

'Well, go on. Say it. Say Ralph.'

'All right, then. Ralph.'

'Good. And will Esther gave Ralph a kiss?' said Gorse.

'Oh – that's *quite* a different proposition,' said Esther.

But she had hardly got the words out of her mouth before Gorse was kissing her on the mouth.

This, although she submitted, Esther greatly disliked. She always did with any young man.

Then Gorse kissed her again, and Esther discovered that there was something unusual in the way in which he was kissing her. There was about it an intensity, even a viciousness, to which she was not accustomed. No 'gentleman', or proletarian of her own class, had ever kissed her in this way. They had been too timid.

And this lack of shyness, restraint, and inhibition, Esther, averse as she was to kissing, did not exactly dislike.

'Now then,' she said at last. 'That's quite enough of that.'

Gorse obeyed her, but, leaning back in the seat, still kept his arm around her. He did not speak, and she thought she must break the silence.

'Well – what *is* his Christian name, anyway?' she said. 'You still haven't told me.'

'Who?'

'Your friend's.'

'Ryan, you mean?'

'Yes.'

'Peter, if you must know. But I still think it's damn sauce for you to ask me, you know.'

'Don't swear.'

'Do you call "damn" swearing?'

'Yes.'

'Well, in that case you're going to hear a lot of swearing before your life's finished.'

'I think it's Unnecessary,' said the demure beauty.

'And I think it's unnecessary for you to ask me someone else's Christian name while you're out with me. And by the way, if you're so interested in Christian names, why didn't you ask me Bell's?'

'Is that the name of your other friend?'

'Yes . . . Well, why didn't you want to know *his* Christian name?'

'I don't know,' said Esther.

'Don't you?' said Gorse. '*I* do.'

Thus Gorse had shrewdly discovered something of Esther's feelings towards Ryan.

'You know a lot, don't you?' said Esther.

'Yes. Quite a lot. I'm not such a fool as I look. And I hope I don't even *look* too much of a fool. Do you think I do?'

'No, you don't look a fool. Anything but. Except when you're playing the silly ass,' said Esther, alluding to his act.

'Ah – but that's put on.'

In this semi-flirtatious way they continued to talk for about half an hour. Then Gorse began kissing her again, and Esther was again slightly fascinated by his lack of restraint.

Having asked the time, Esther found it was unexpectedly late, and she said that she must 'fly' home. Gorse made no attempt to make her stay and they walked towards the turnstiles.

When they had passed through these Esther stopped, as if to say goodbye.

'Don't you want me to see you home?' asked Gorse.

'No, thanks. I'd rather rush off by myself, really. I wouldn't like you to see where *I* live, anyway.'

'Oh – what does it matter? Won't you let me?'

'No. Honest. I'd rather go by myself.'

'Very well. Have it your own way. But let me know when we're going to meet again, at any rate.'

Well – that's up to you.'

'All right. Let's make it seven o'clock tomorrow evening – just here. Then we'll go and have another cocktail. That suit you?'

'Yes. That sounds all right to me.'

'All right. Seven o'clock tomorrow – at the hour of the setting sun. Just here. *Eau voir*, madame,' said Gorse, and offered his hand.

Esther shook hands with him, said 'Goodbye' shyly, and went away, almost running because of her shyness.

As soon as her walk had returned to a normal pace she realized that she had not offered him a word of thanks for the evening, and she reproached herself bitterly for such a breach of good taste – particularly with a 'gentleman'.

This failure was made all the worse by the fact that he had spent a lot of money on her and given her an entirely delightful evening. She could not remember ever having spent a more delightful one. He had taken her to the Metropole and she had 'passed'! And he had been responsible for all this.

She was grateful to him and liked him enormously. She was sure of that.

But was she sure? She did not quite know. Still there was something about him which intuitively made her suspicious.

In spite of his generosity, did she like him as much as Ryan? No – of course not. He was not so good-looking, anyway, and he was not so 'perfectly' a 'gentleman'.

She would like, if he was all he seemed, to marry Ryan. She did not somehow take to the idea of marrying Gorse.

Nice as he undoubtedly was.

PART FIVE

ESTHER AND RYAN

Chapter One

I

Though very busy, Esther and Gertrude had plenty of time for conversation, though some of it had to be furtive, at the sweet-shop at which they both worked.

Gertrude, therefore, next morning, had no difficulty in describing to Esther her evening with Ryan, and in letting Esther know that Ryan was 'crazy' about her.

She also told Esther that she had made an appointment for her to meet Ryan outside the Palace Pier at seven-thirty that evening.

All this disturbed Esther very much. She had had no idea that Ryan's feelings were so strong; she liked Ryan much the better of the two; and yet she had made an appointment to meet Gorse at seven o'clock outside the West Pier.

She could not, in honour, abandon Gorse. (And, because of his Metropole and his cocktails, she didn't really want to!) But she desired intensely to meet, not to lose, Ryan. Could there not be some compromise? Could she not somehow again contrive to eat her cake and have it too? Could not cleverness find a compromise?

Cleverness could. Cleverness combined with wickedness. She had arranged to meet Gorse outside the West Pier at seven o'clock. The appointment which Gertrude had made for her with Ryan was at seven-thirty outside the Palace Pier. Was it not possible to meet both? Might she not meet Gorse, lie to him, and then rush off to meet Ryan? Then, having met Ryan, spent a little time with him, at least kept him in tow, she might even return to Gorse.

She wondered what lie, if she did this, she would tell Gorse. What, but her little brother? She felt herself sinking deeper and deeper into crime. She would, she felt, in fact kill her little brother if this sort of thing went on.

Then it occurred to her that those two – Ryan and Gorse – might easily meet and compare notes. Thus she would be disclosed as an adventuress, and probably lose both.

But she felt that there was some way of forcing Ryan (her slave, after all) to hold his tongue. She could do this either by telling him some lie, or, even, by telling him the truth.

Truth has always been the liar's most able and trustworthy lieutenant.

And what if she did fail in these schemes and was put to shame? Did it matter? Did she not despise young men? Had she not always avowed her scorn of them to Gertrude – and must she not stand by her words? Was not the whole matter of the smallest account to her? Were there not 'plenty of other fish in the sea'?

Esther thought of these things all day as she worked, and at last came to a decision.

She had decided again to take the risk of killing her little brother.

2

Because she had a conscience and wanted to get her lying over quickly, and because she wanted to be in good time to meet Ryan afterwards, Esther abandoned feminine principle and was actually outside the West Pier three minutes before the appointed time. Gorse arrived two minutes later.

They shook hands, and she dashed into it at once.

'Look,' she said, 'I'm ever so sorry, but I can't spend tonight with you – at least not all of it. I've got my little brother ill at home. He's got a temperature and I've got to go back and mind him while Mother's out. I'm ever so sorry.'

'Oh dear,' said Gorse. 'What's the matter with him?'

'I don't really know. But he's got a nasty cough, and a temperature, and he's in bed. I'm ever so sorry.'

'Oh – that's all right. But can't you stay a little while?'

'No. I think I ought to be off, really. But I'll tell you what. I could meet you later, if you liked. But I don't expect that'd suit you.'

'Well – what time, about, were you thinking about?'

'Oh. Nine – or something like that.'

'Well, do you think you could make it eight-thirty? Then it'd be worth while. Otherwise I might as well go to a cinema.'

Esther pretended to hesitate. Then 'Yes,' she said. 'I think I could make it eight-thirty – if that's all right by you. I might be a bit late.'

'Yes. That's all right. And where shall we meet?'

'Oh, here. That's the best place, isn't it? And now I'd really better be popping off.'

'All right. Eight-thirty. I'll be here.'

'What are you going to do in the meanwhile?' asked Esther. 'Going to have a cocktail in the Metropole by yourself?'

She asked him this in order to find out where he was going to be during her interview with Ryan, so that she could see to it that there was no possibility of their running into each other. She wanted Gorse absolutely safely at the Metropole. Esther wanted practically everything. Esther, the beauty in danger of becoming 'spoiled', had recently developed the bad habit of wanting practically everything.

'Yes. I think I probably will,' said Gorse.

'Good. Then you'll be nice and comfy,' said Esther in a voice which was warm because this had made her feel nice and comfy herself. 'Well. So long.'

'So long,' said Gorse.

'Oh, and I'm ever so sorry,' said Esther as an afterthought, 'but I never thanked you for last night. It was a lovely evening, and thanks ever so much.'

'*Pas du tout*, madame,' said Gorse. 'The pleasure was all mine.'

'Well. Ta-ta!'

'Cheerio,' said Gorse, and Esther, having waved, raced off.

Esther now had some time on hand, and she made for the small streets behind the front which she knew intimately and in which she could, as it were, hide, and waste time, until she met Ryan outside the Palace Pier at seven-thirty.

She had believed Gorse when he had said he was going to the Metropole. But it is hardly necessary to say that Gorse had no such intention.

Gorse was not so credulous as Ryan, and although Esther was a better liar than Gertrude, he was not to be taken in by ill little brothers.

And so he followed Esther.

To do this, undetected, amongst the small streets behind the front was no easy matter. Nevertheless, Gorse did so.

And at the end he observed, from a distance, Esther meeting Ryan outside the Palace Pier.

Esther's mother had incessantly told Esther never to Tell a Lie. To do so, she had explained, would only be to attract very evil consequences.

Chapter Two

I

Esther, returning to her principle, made herself two minutes late for Ryan.

She saw him looking in a sort of despair in many directions, and was reassured in her belief that he was her slave.

'Hullo – how are you?' she said, softly stealing up from a direction in which he had not thought to look, and taking him by surprise.

'Oh, hullo!' he said, and they shook hands.

'Hullo. I hope I'm not late.'

'No. You're just on time, I think,' said Ryan nervously. 'I'm so glad to see you. I thought you mightn't be able to manage it.'

'No. I managed to make it, all right.'

'And how's your little brother? Is he any better?'

Her little brother was beginning to get slightly on Esther's nerves. She never knew what exactly had to be said about his state of health. It had to vary.

'Well – he's better. But he's not all right. And that's why I'm terribly sorry I can't stay very long with you tonight. I'm afraid I'll have to be home about eight-thirty.'

'Oh dear. What a pity. But when somebody's ill, it's got to come first – hasn't it?'

He led her automatically towards the turnstile of the Palace Pier; they went through, and walked seawards.

Ryan was so happy merely because Esther had appeared that he could not be downcast because she had to leave him so soon.

'Yes. It must come first,' said Esther. 'But I'm sure he'll be better very soon now.'

This was said to placate God, and so possibly secure her little brother's endangered life.

'And what did the doctor say?' asked Ryan.

This took Esther completely aback. She had no idea there was a doctor. Gertrude had failed to tell her that she had last night been compelled to invent one.

'Oh,' she said after a slight pause. 'He says he'll be all right. So long as he stays in bed. And he *is* better today, too. A *lot* better.'

(Esther was again speaking to God.)

'Oh well. That's good,' said Ryan.

2

As they walked along Esther looked at him. He had no hat; he still wore grey flannel trousers, and had made few concessions, if any, to The Nines. All the same he seemed to her to be even more divinely attractive than when she had first met him. His shy manner, too, confirmed her in her suspicion that he was a 'perfect' gentleman – more 'perfect' than Gorse.

But Gorse had the Metropole behind him! He was drinking cocktails in there now. Ryan, hatless and in grey flannel trousers, would never, she imagined, be allowed into the Metropole.

They played at a few slot machines, and walked to the prow of the pier, and then played at a few more slot machines. Although it was getting dark Ryan made no suggestion that they should sit down, and this made the experienced Esther admire him the more. It was a sign either of his shyness, which she so much liked, or conceivably of indifference, which she did not exactly like, but which made him all the more desirable.

When they were somewhere near the middle of the pier Esther asked him the time, and was told it was five past eight. She said that she must be hurrying off, and they walked towards the turnstiles.

'Well,' said Ryan. 'May I meet you again soon? It's been very short this time, and it'd be nice if we could have a bit longer together.'

'Yes,' said Esther. 'Of course you can. Certainly. I'd like it very much.'

'Well, I'll tell you what,' said Ryan. 'I've got an idea. I've just got a new motor bike, and I thought that if you didn't mind sitting on the back – it's very comfortable – we might spend an afternoon in the country together. Would you mind? It's quite easy to sit on the back.'

'No,' said Esther, who had actually sat on the back of more than one motor cycle already. 'I wouldn't mind it at all. I'd like it. But I don't know about an afternoon. I'm a working girl, you know.'

'Yes. But don't you ever get an afternoon off? A Saturday, for instance? Or what about a Sunday?'

'Yes,' said Esther. 'I get each other Saturday.'

'And what about this one?'

'Yes. I'm off this one.'

'Well,' said Ryan. 'Could we meet – do you think? Then I could take you out to the country, and we could have some tea somewhere.'

The day was Thursday.

'Yes. I'd like to. Very much. That's the day after tomorrow, then.'

'Yes. That's right. I'm so glad you can manage it . . . Well, where shall we meet?'

'I don't know. I'd better leave that to you.'

'Well – what about outside the West Pier? About two-thirty. I'll be waiting for you there. And then, if it isn't fine, we might go to a cinema.'

'Yes. That suits me. Two-thirty – outside the West Pier – Saturday afternoon.'

'Yes. That's fine.'

Now Esther realized that the time had come to practise a further deception, one which she had worked out in her mind carefully beforehand.

'Tell me,' she said. 'Will you do me a little favour?'

'Why, yes. Of course I will. I'd do anything. You must know that. You've only got to tell me.'

This was Ryan's first open intimation of his adoration of her.

'Well,' said Esther. 'You know that friend of yours – the sort of ginger-haired one – I think his name's Gorse or something, isn't it?'

'Yes. That's right.'

'Yes. Well – do you meet him a lot? Do you go about a lot together?'

'Yes. We meet quite a lot. Why?'

'Well,' said Esther. 'I know you'll think it's funny – but will you *not tell* him that you've met me tonight and that I'm going out with you on Saturday?'

'Why, yes. Certainly. But why on earth?'

'Well, now, I know it seems ever so funny and silly, but just at present it's a little secret. I've a reason. There's nothing of any importance in it, but it's a little secret. I'll tell you later. But will you do what I say – just for the time being?'

'Yes. Of course. As long as you promise it's not important. And as long as you'll tell me afterwards. Will you?'

'Yes. It's not the tiniest bit important. And I'll tell you afterwards.'

'Promise?'

'Yes. I promise.'

A conscience-stricken Esther was on one hand sorry to have had this promise extracted from her. On the other hand, if Ryan turned out to be all he seemed to be, she certainly meant to tell him everything afterwards. For if Ryan was the Ryan she hoped and believed he was, all this might easily become a matter of Love. And in Love, Esther had always believed, there were no secrets.

'Well – that's all right, then. I promise, too,' said Ryan.

When they were on the front again Ryan asked her whether he might see her home.

'I know your address, you know,' he added.

'Oh – and how do you know that?' asked Esther flirtatiously, because, through Gertrude, she in fact knew how he knew it.

'Well, I asked your friend – Gertrude – last night. Well – may I see you home?'

'No. I'd really rather you didn't – though thanks ever so much. I wouldn't like you to see where *I* live. It's only a slum, you know. Or pretty near it.'

'Well – does that matter? It certainly doesn't to me.'

'Well. It does to me. No – thanks ever so – but I'd really rather go off alone. Well – thanks for the meeting – and I'll see you on Saturday – two-thirty outside the West Pier?'

'Yes. That's right.'

They looked at each other shyly. They did not shake hands. They were already on too exciting and intimate a footing.

'Ta-ta,' said Esther, and 'Goodbye,' said Ryan, and she hastened away.

In order to reach the West Pier again she used the same streets she had used in coming thence, and on the way she reflected deeply upon Ryan and his motorcycle. Quite apart from Ryan's other charms, Ryan's new machine almost cancelled out Gorse's hotel.

Because of her flurried state of mind she was three minutes early for Gorse, who was waiting for her.

They went at once on to the West Pier, and much the same happened as last night. Gorse did a little more 'Silly Ass', and, when they were seated, kissed her again in the same uninhibited way, and Esther found this even more pleasing, or rather less displeasing, than she had the night before.

After this Esther practised the same deception on Gorse as she had practised on Ryan an hour or so earlier. She asked Gorse not to tell Ryan that she and Gorse had met. She said that she had a 'reason' and that it was a 'secret' which she would finally tell him. But whereas with Ryan she did hope finally to confess, she had no such intention with Gorse. She did not at present totally like or trust him: she was merely irresistibly bewitched by his hotel.

Gorse at once promised secrecy. He said he would not have told Ryan in any case.

As they were parting outside the West Pier, Gorse asked her when they might meet again, and then suggested tomorrow evening, Friday. He said he would like to give her cocktails at the Metropole again.

This, of course, suited Esther down to the ground. Ryan had not asked to meet her until Saturday. She agreed; she thanked him for the evening; and, having arranged to meet once more at seven outside the West Pier, they left each other.

At this moment Ryan was already in bed at Tisbury Road, dreaming about Esther. Ryan, blinded by love, absolutely believed in her story about the 'funny' little 'secret' in regard to Gorse. He had given the matter little further thought.

But Gorse, now returning to his room in Norton Road, of course had not believed her story. He had seen Esther meeting Ryan, and he would not have believed it in any case. And, unlike Ryan, he gave the matter a great deal of thought. Gorse was a great thinker.

PART SIX

WELL-WISHER

Chapter One

I

On returning home from work to Over Street, the next evening, Esther's mother told her that there was a letter for her. Her mother said, with an air of discretion, that she had left it in Esther's bedroom.

Miss Downes of Over Street received letters very seldom. And this letter was addressed in a hand unfamiliar to her mother. That was why her mother had had an air of discretion.

Esther, on hearing about this letter in her bedroom, at once thought that it had come from Ryan. He had told her that he knew her address. The idea filled her with both pleasure and fear. She would be delighted to have a letter from him, but it might be one putting off the motorcycling appointment tomorrow afternoon.

What she found inside, when she opened the envelope, completely surprised her.

She found, pasted upon a plain postcard, some letters, mixed with whole words, which had obviously been cut out from a newspaper. These, all askew, went to form the following disgusting (because anonymous) message:

look out for R y an I KNOW
him Do Not go out with HIM ON cycle
d an G er OUS Take WARN in g
A WELL WISHER

Esther did not for a moment suspect that this had come from Gorse.

But, naturally, it had.

Gorse had not, of course, actually known that Ryan would invite Esther to go on his motorcycle. But he had been almost certain that Ryan would do this.

2

Esther's reactions to this communication were those, first of surprise, then of bewilderment, then of fear, and then of panic – a panic which very nearly sent her rushing downstairs to her mother.

But she restrained herself. Her relationship with her mother, as regards the matter of young men, was, although loving and sincere, rather strange, shy, and furtive.

Esther's mother was fully aware of Esther's beauty, and she had on more than one occasion given Esther advice upon the serious dangers which attended this. Esther had always promised her mother that she completely understood these dangers. Her mother had then said that she completely trusted Esther in every way.

For this reason Mrs Downes, although she knew that a great deal took place on the Brighton Front, and the West Pier, made a point of questioning Esther as little as possible. As a consequence a kind of convention had at last arisen between them that nothing should be said at all about these things. And so Esther did not at once rush downstairs to her mother.

Instead she began to dress for her meeting with Gorse at seven-thirty. Doing this soothed her, and to a certain extent assuaged her feeling of fear. It also prevented her temporarily from giving the matter too much thought.

As soon as she had left the house, however, and was on her way to the West Pier she began to think violently.

Now her fear had left her, but this was replaced by that sort of nausea, that overhanging pall of filth and evil which an anonymous letter always creates – even if it is not (and this one was not) of a threatening nature.

The main question was, of course, who on *earth* could have *sent* it?

Who on earth knew about her meeting with Ryan yesterday? Who had *watched* them? Could it be, possibly, some boy of her own class whom she had in the past rejected or been cruel to? She had a few such boys on her conscience. Moreover, she felt certain that message was of low-class origin. It had a slum air about it.

She had looked at the envelope and had seen that it had been posted in Portslade. But she knew no one in Portslade. And, of course, the poster might have been careful to post it far away from where he lived.

Then, who on *earth* could know that Ryan had a motorcycle?

Who, but Gorse?

Or the other spectacled one? She could not bring herself to believe that the latter had done this. He was not the sort of boy who 'counted' enough to get up to such a thing.

But what about Gorse? He would know about the motorcycle, and she still faintly distrusted him.

Could he possibly be capable of such infamy?

She thought it just possible – only just.

But, on the other hand, what could his motive be? He knew nothing about her meeting last night with Ryan (Esther, of course, was wrong here) and so he could not in any way be jealous.

Or did Gorse in fact know that Ryan was 'dangerous'? And had he, for some obscure reason, chosen this way of warning her?

And *was* Ryan dangerous? She simply could not bring herself to believe this.

And yet had not her mother often told her, and had she not often read, that the greatest villains are usually infinitely more plausible and charming than others?

And dangerous in what way? If she went out into the country with him, would he attempt to assault her? Or kill her? Or both? Esther was a reader of *The News of the World*.

Or dangerous merely in the sense of being a seducer and trifler? She was quite sure she could deal with *that* sort of thing.

But she did not believe that the message intended to convey this lighter meaning. She was certain that dangerous in the fullest sense of the term was being conveyed to her.

It was all hideously disturbing, and she was so upset that she was outside the West Pier six minutes before the time, and Gorse was not there.

He arrived three minutes later, saying politely that he hoped he was not late, and she had to concede that he was not. This normally would have annoyed Esther, as she would not normally have liked to be found 'hanging about', three minutes too early, for any young man. Tonight, however, she was too upset even to think about it.

Gorse, after his success the night before last, had now completely lost his fear of the Metropole, and he was loquacious and cheerful as they walked along towards it. But Esther was distracted, and could only answer him briefly. Gorse noticed this in Esther, and, as the sender of the anonymous message, suspected its cause.

As they went through the revolving doors and entered the Oriental palace Esther was still so worried that she was not in the smallest way impressed by its splendour. She walked and behaved like one who went into the Metropole every evening of her life.

The table they had found the night before last was again vacant, and they sat down at it. The same waiter served them with the same drinks.

Esther had not taken many sips at her own before she began to experience that warm, confident feeling which had come upon her that other time. She was still very worried indeed, but inclined to look upon her trouble more lightly.

By the time the second drink had appeared Esther was not only feeling confident: she was feeling confiding.

Why not, she thought, confide in Gorse?

It was all but inconceivable that he could have sent so foul a message. And, even if he had (but he *couldn't* have!), there would be no harm in confiding in him.

She would, she was sure, be able to detect any deception on his part. Esther thought that she was very clever at this sort of thing.

And then, if he was innocent, which she was certain he was, he might be able to give her some advice – which she seriously needed. She decided to confide in him.

This involved some humiliation and confession.

'Listen,' she said. 'I'm afraid I've got something to confess to you.'

'Oh. What's that?'

'I hope it won't make you angry.'

'I'm sure it won't. Go on.'

'Well – you know when we made that secret appointment to go to the Metropole together . . .?'

'Yes. Go on.'

'Well – the next day I told Gertrude to make an excuse to your friend Peter Ryan. I don't know why I did it. I suppose I just thought I was being rather mean – not turning up – and I don't know for the life of me why I didn't tell you – really.'

'Yes. Go on. Anything worse?'

'Yes. Quite a lot . . . Well, Gertrude met him and he asked her if he could meet me outside the Palace Pier the next evening. And I don't know why – I suppose I felt sorry for him or something – but I thought I *would* meet him – just for a little while. And so I came and told a fib to you.'

'About your little brother?'

'Yes. Are you angry?'

'No. Not a bit. Anything more?'

'Yes . . . There's still a lot. Well, I *did* meet him, and he asked me if I'd go out on his motor bike into the country on Saturday. That's tomorrow.'

'Yes? . . .'

'Well – and then I came back to you at the West Pier. I don't know why I didn't tell you, and I'm sorry. I was afraid you'd be angry, I suppose. I was just being silly.'

'Yes. It was a little silly – I'll admit that. You see what trouble one gets into if one doesn't tell the truth? I didn't believe in that little brother story for a moment.'

'Didn't you? Why not?'

Esther was not altogether pleased to learn of her failure as a liar.

'Oh – I don't really know,' said Gorse. 'I just didn't. But go on. If there's any more.'

'Yes, there is. I'm just coming to the real point – now I've confessed.'

'Well? . . .'

'Well – I made this appointment to meet your friend, you see – and then, this evening, I got a most horrible letter – if you can call it a letter.'

'Really? What was it about?'

'Well, I've got it on me, if you'd like to see it. Would you?'

'Yes. I would. Certainly.'

Esther produced it from her bag, and handed it to him.

Gorse took the card from her, and looked at it. Then, feigning bewilderment and short sight, he took out his 'Silly Ass' monocle from his waistcoat pocket and looked at it again. The glass of his monocle was quite plain. Later in life he was clever enough to have a lens made.

'Ah,' said Gorse after scrutinizing the document from several angles for more than a minute. 'Most interesting, very interesting indeed.'

There was a pause.

'Well – what do you think about it?' said Esther impatiently.

'I don't really know. Just at the moment,' said Gorse. 'But on first thoughts I'd say that there are just two things you ought to do with something of this sort.'

'What? Which two?'

'Well – one is to put it straight into the wastepaper basket and forget about it. And the other is to take it straight to the police. They're nasty things – anonymous communications – like this.'

With his mention of the police, and by his general attitude, Gorse completely duped Esther. She had, now, not the slightest doubt that Gorse was not the originator of the situation.

'Oh – I don't want to go to the police,' said Esther, rapidly and with determination. The very idea of the police scared the humble Miss Downes out of her wits. And, when she had been naughty as a child, her mother and father had often frightened her with the police.

'Well, then, put it into the wastepaper basket.'

'Yes. But what if it's *true*? What if there *is* something dangerous about him? Should I go out in the country on his bike?'

'Ah, yes,' said Gorse. 'I was coming to that aspect of the matter. Now that, I must admit, is a different thing.'

'What do *you* know about him? You were all three at school together, weren't you? Do you *know* anything about him?'

'Well, we were only at school at Hove together. I've written to him since then, but I haven't seen him all the time I was at –' (Here Gorse inadvertently very nearly said St Paul's but saved himself in time.) 'Westminster,' said Gorse.

Along with Gorse's astuteness there was, occasionally, a curious folly and lack of caution. He had worn an old Westminster tie for Esther's benefit. Now it was quite possible that he and Ryan and Bell and Esther might meet again, and that Esther might mention that he had been to Westminster. In which case Ryan and Bell, who knew for a fact that he had been to St Paul's, might easily expose him.

All impostors, of course, must take risks: but this particular risk had never even entered Gorse's head.

'Yes,' said Esther. 'But you did know him at your first school, and you know him now. Do you *know* anything about him?'

'Well, now, that's not quite a fair question, is it? If I did know anything against him it wouldn't be right for me to tell tales about a friend – would it?'

'Yes. I think it would. You're my friend, too, aren't you? And I'm really very worried. I think it'd only be fair to *me*.'

'Ah – I don't know about that,' said Gorse, putting his fingers together, leaning back in his chair, and looking at her in a manner which hinted that he had a good deal to tell if he could.

Esther rose to this suggestion in his eye.

'I believe you *do* know something, you know. Come on. You must tell me. If you do. Do you?'

'Well, now,' said Gorse, still looking at her meaningly. 'That's rather difficult to say, you know.'

'No, it isn't. Not if it's going to help me it isn't – is it? Go on. Say it.'

'Well, I'll say this much, at any rate,' said Gorse. 'I don't personally really trust Ryan. And I don't really think he's the sort of person *you* should trust.'

'But *why*?'

'Oh – it's only a feeling – probably. Perhaps I'm doing him an injustice.'

'No. There's something else. You know something more. Go on. Tell me.'

'Well . . .'

'Yes?'

'Well. There *were* some rather funny things which took place at school – I'll admit that.'

'What sort of funny things?'

'Oh. Just funny things.'

'But what? Did he steal or something?'

'No. He didn't *steal*.'

'Well, *what*, then?'

Gorse paused.

'You know, really it's not the sort of thing I'd like to discuss.'

'But you *must*!'

'No – it's not the sort of thing.'

Esther braced herself to speak more boldly.

'But you must. Tell me. Go on. Was it something to do with –' said Esther, here hesitating before she took the plunge. '*Sex?*'

'What made you think that?'

'I don't know. It just came into my mind. Was it?'

Gorse did not answer.

'Go on,' said Esther. 'Was it? Because if you don't answer you make me think it was. Go on.'

'Well . . .'

'Go on.'

'Well . . . Yes.'

There was a pause.

'What *sort* of thing to do with sex? Come on, now. Tell me. We're both grown up, after all.'

'No. Now you're going too far. That's not the sort of thing a gentleman discusses with a girl.'

'But what was it? How could it make him "dangerous", as that beastly card says? Could it?'

'Well . . . it *could*. But I really don't want to go on talking about this.'

'You mustn't go on mystifying me like this. Tell me. Something about sex?'

'Well,' said Gorse. 'I'll tell you this much. I think Ryan thinks a little too much about sex. We all do, of course. I do myself. But Ryan carries it a little bit too far, and he's not at all scrupulous in the methods he uses of getting what he wants. There, now, that's enough for you, surely.'

'No. It's not. I want to know if *you* think he's dangerous, and if I ought to go out with him tomorrow?'

Gorse was again silent.

'Well. *Do* you?' said Esther.

'Do you want me to tell the truth?'

'Yes.'

'Well. I don't think you should. It *might* be all right, but I wouldn't advise it. Not after you've received this card. It's signed Well-Wisher, and he may really know something. I have a feeling that things have got worse since Ryan's school days. Now – let's leave the subject, shall we?'

'But I can't leave it. I've got to make up my mind about tomorrow!'

'Well – you've been given my strong advice. You must just take it or leave it. And so now let's drop the subject, shall we? Will you?'

'Well, I suppose I must. If you say so. But it's very worrying. Who on earth could have *sent* the letter?'

'Well – that's the mystery. It couldn't be Ryan, of course . . .'

'No. Of course it couldn't.'

'But it might, of course,' said Gorse humorously, 'be me.'

'Don't be silly.'

'But it *might*, you know. Didn't that ever strike you?'

'Yes, it did. Just for a moment – if you want the truth. But of course I know it's absurd, now.'

'Well, it is actually, you know. If I'd wanted to warn you I could have done it by word of mouth – very easily – couldn't I? I wouldn't have sat up all night pasting bits of a newspaper on to a postcard. It must be hard work – finding the words and letters – apart from the pasting.'

'Yes. It must. That's what makes it so beastly. Do you think it could be that other friend of yours – the one in spectacles?'

'Bell? . . . No,' said Gorse benignly. 'I don't think poor Bell would do a thing like that.'

'Did *he* know about this – Sex thing?'

'I don't really know. Possibly.'

'Then he *might* have done it. He seems to have got a pretty funny mind – with all his jabber, jabber, jabber about Poetry and all that.'

'No. I think we can exclude Bell. I like and trust Bell, in spite of his eccentricities,' said Gorse. 'He's not the type – although one can never be absolutely sure with human nature – can one?'

'No. And it must be a pretty low type. It couldn't be a gentleman. The whole thing *looks* sort of uneducated – doesn't it?'

'It certainly does.'

'That's what makes me think it might be someone in *my* class. But how could they know about the *motorbike* and all that?'

'Yes. It's all very baffling, I must say. But I'm very sorry you began to suspect me.'

'Don't be so silly. But you see that's what a thing like this does to one. It makes you suspect *everyone*, and it sort of hits at you every way – if you see what I mean.'

'Yes. I certainly do.'

'And so your advice is for me not to go tomorrow?'

'Yes. That's my advice. My *very* strong advice.'

'Well. I'll have to think about it.'

'Yes. It's for you to make up your mind. But if you *should* decide to go, by the way, I hope you won't tell him what I've said about him. I still feel in a way I shouldn't have told you.'

'No. Of course I won't. I wouldn't dream of it.'

'And if I were you, I wouldn't dream of going. But that's your business. Now let's change the subject – shall we?'

'Yes. Let's.'

But Esther could not change the subject – at least not with any pleasure. She kept on coming back to it.

Tonight she was so distraught that she finished her own second cocktail, and, though she felt a little dizzy, the drink did not go to her head as it had last night.

Then Gorse suggested that they should go, and they rose and went out into the air.

'Where are we going?' said Esther, and it was clear to Gorse that in her present state of mind she had no desire to go on the West Pier and repeat the performance of the two previous evenings. He was wise enough not to invite her to do such a thing. He stopped.

'You know, I don't think you feel like the Pier tonight – do you?' he said. 'I think you'd rather go home – wouldn't you?'

'You know, I honestly think I would. I don't want to disappoint you, but I'd really rather. It's very nice of you to think of it. Would you mind if I did?'

'No. But may I see you home?'

'Well. Part of the way.' She smiled. 'You know I don't want you to see where I live. Come with me as far as the Clock Tower – will you? That's quite near where I am.'

'Very well. Always your humble obedient servant. To the Clock Tower.'

When they reached the Clock Tower Esther said, 'Well – here we are,' and Gorse asked her when he might meet her again.

'Well – I don't think tomorrow – do you? I still *might* decide to go out with him. What about the day after?'

'Very well. That'll be Sunday. What about seven-thirty again, outside the West Pier? And then we'll go to the Metropole.'

'Yes. That'd be lovely. You're ever so good to me. And thank you ever so for the evening, although it was a little bit spoilt. Goodbye, then, and thank you again.'

And feeling suddenly grateful for his kindness, his generosity with his cocktails at the Metropole, and the fact that she had him at least to turn to in her trouble, she impulsively kissed him on the cheek. Then she ran away.

This was the first time that Esther had ever been the first to kiss a young man. She had made a strange choice in the one she had singled out for such an honour.

Gorse returned to Norton Road very deeply satisfied with the evening, the success of his schemes, and his knowledge that he had entirely deluded Esther.

What, it may be wondered, were Gorse's motives in all this? They were, roughly, threefold.

He had no particular feeling for Esther. His vicious kisses were feigned. Lovely as she was, there was no question of his being in love with her. Gorse was never, in all his life, capable of sentimental emotion. But he knew that she was lovely, that she dressed beautifully, and that in a right setting, such as that of the Metropole, she definitely 'passed'. Hence he liked to be seen with her: everybody looked at her with admiration, and then, of course, looked at him and envied him. In this way she was an asset: and he had no intention of losing her. He was only just trying his wings in places like the Metropole, and she was of the greatest assistance to him. Such was his first motive.

Not being in love with her, he was not particularly jealous of Ryan. He saw, however, that Ryan was a danger, and he had taken steps to meet this danger. This was his second motive.

His third motive, however, was really much more powerful and irresistible than the other two. It was the sheer pleasure of scheming and deceiving, of knowing that he alone possessed a secret – and one with which he could wield secret power.

He had almost intoxicated himself with pleasure while pasting those letters on to the card. He had found it much more deliciously easy than he had expected. He had done it from only one evening paper. He had easily found the 'Ryan' (which he had thought might be considerably difficult) by using an 'R' and 'Y' (in headline letters) – followed by the first two letters of the word 'and'. And the rest had been child's play.

He was even more exhilarated by the restraint and brilliance of his performance with Esther at the Metropole this evening.

He did not think that Esther would meet Ryan tomorrow. His schemes had succeeded. He had, as he put it to himself in his own dirty way, 'done the trick all right'.

Chapter Two

I

Gorse, for once, was wrong.

Esther, for some reason – possibly some obscure physical cause – woke up in a peculiarly calm frame of mind the next morning.

The anonymous card, she found as she dressed, was not anything like the horribly disturbing thing she had found it last night. She even thought that she had made a mountain out of a molehill.

This balanced mood continued as she worked at the sweet-shop. She was very busy because it was Saturday morning and the trippers were in full force. And hard, bustling work soothes the mind in much the same way as cocktails do.

A picture of Ryan was in her mind almost incessantly as she worked, and she simply could not bring herself to believe that he was what the author of the anonymous message had said he was. And, if he was not, what right had she to break the appointment? Would he not be infinitely pathetic – desolate – if she forsook him? And did he not know her address and be bound to continue his pursuit in any case?

And did she not, very nearly at any rate, Love him – like him a hundred times more than any other boy she had met?

And if he *was* 'dangerous' – could he be so in public? Clearly not. What was his present idea of what they should do this afternoon? He had suggested that they should go out on his motor cycle and 'have tea somewhere'. Well – he certainly couldn't do anything 'dangerous' while she was on the back of the motor cycle. Nor could he do anything in a tea-shop.

But what about Quiet Lanes? What about Shady Nooks? What about Woods? Suppose he invited her into one of these? Well, she could always refuse to accompany him. She could make some excuse to keep him in the open. And if he insisted she could become angry and leave him.

Finally, was she not in duty bound to defy an anonymous letter writer? Was not such a one so low a creature that he (or it might be a she) must be treated only with the supremest contempt?

Esther at last made up her mind to meet Ryan.

2

Ryan was outside the West Pier twelve minutes before the time. He filled in the time he had to wait for Esther with polishing and playing with his delightful new machine.

So absorbed was he in this that he did not notice the arrival of Esther, who was herself early.

Men are at their best when quietly absorbed in the workings of a machine. There is something charming, disinterested, and childlike about it. Her heart grew even warmer towards him than ever before as she approached him. Oh – if only that *filthy* thing had never been sent to her!

'Hullo,' she said, completely surprising him. 'Is that the bike?'

'Oh. Hullo!' he said. 'I didn't see you. Yes. This is it. What do you think of it?'

'It looks lovely to me. I'll bet you aren't half proud of it – aren't you?'

'Yes. I must say I am, a bit.'

They gazed at it.

'Yes. It's lovely,' said Esther.

'Well,' said Ryan at last. 'Where would you like me to take you with it?'

'Anywhere you like. I'll leave it to you.'

'Well, I'll tell you what. I have an idea. Do you know Hassocks? It's a little village about seven miles from here.'

'Yes. I've heard of it. I've never been there.'

'Well, I thought we might go there. And then go on to Hurst – do you know Hurst? – for tea. Do you know Hurst? It's about three miles away from Hassocks, and I know a tea-shop there.'

'Yes. That sounds fine.'

'You see, I was born at Hassocks, and I know all the walks round there. There're some lovely walks all about there.'

Esther did not this time reply that this sounded fine. She was far too frightened. Some Lovely Walks. Did not Lovely Walks possibly imply Quiet Lanes, Shady Nooks, Woods?

'Oh – are there?' she said.

'Yes. I thought we might go for one, if you liked.'

'Yes,' said Esther, and added awkwardly, 'well – we'll see when we get there – shall we?'

This rather mysterious remark made Ryan glance at her. And, of course, the glance, innocent as it was, again frightened Esther. She read it as a glance with some meaning behind it – she did not know what exactly.

'Well – let's start, shall we? Now – I'll get on, and then you get on. I think you'll find it quite comfortable. Have you ever done this before?'

'Yes. I have. Once or twice.'

'Oh . . . Good.'

Soon they had adjusted themselves and started. Ryan made for the London Road.

'It's a glorious day – isn't it?' Ryan shouted back to her against the noise of the machine.

'Yes. It is!' she yelled.

After this they said practically nothing until they were past Preston Park and approaching the country. Then Esther spoke.

'Where's the walk you're thinking of taking me?' she asked. 'Have you got a special one in mind?'

'Yes. I have, as a matter of fact. It's where I used to walk as a child. It's along by the railway line. I love walking by railways – don't you?' Both were yelling, of course.

'Yes. I do.'

'It's what we used to call the Cinder Path when I lived there. It may be still, for all I know.'

'The Cinder Path?' said Esther, and added, 'you mean a sort of *public* Path.'

'Yes. That's right.'

Again Ryan thought there was something curious in what she said, but he was, of course, unable to glance at her. Esther was slightly reassured by his assurance that the Path was public. All the same she still wondered about Quiet Lanes, Shady Nooks, and Woods leading from this Path.

Now the Gorse-created evil of Ryan's situation resided in this. He was a young man in love – desperately and sentimentally so. And what, pray, is a young man in such a condition likely to think of most when taking the loved out into the country? What, but Quiet Lanes, Shady Nooks, and Woods?

He had, in fact, a Wood in mind. It adjoined the Cinder Path. Here he had picked primroses as a child, and here he proposed to take Esther. He meant, furthermore, to take her into the middle of this wood, and tell her that he loved her. Then, if she would permit such a thing, he would kiss her. And then, if his wildest hopeful dreams came true, she might consent to be his own. She might become *Engaged* to him! Or, failing that, Promise to Think about it.

He knew that a romantic setting was necessary for this, and so he had chosen his Wood carefully.

Because he loved Esther so much he was desperately afraid of the immediate future, but he was swearing to himself, as he drove along, that he would show courage and determination.

Ryan had never before taken a girl into a Wood, Nook, or Lane. But girls had more than once made him go, reluctantly, into such places; and because this had happened he did, at moments, have a feeling of confidence.

3

At the entrance to the Cinder Path Ryan stopped, and both dismounted.

He left his motor cycle at the side of the road.

The Cinder Path at Hassocks runs southwards, parallel to the Southern Railway, and very near it. It is little frequented on weekdays, but on Saturday afternoons Hassocks villagers and others use it a good deal.

This was Saturday afternoon, and, to Esther's unspeakable relief, a dozen or more people had passed them before they had been walking a quarter of a mile along it.

Ryan's Wood, however, was about three quarters of a mile away, and, as they approached it, people became scarce.

They stopped, every now and again, to watch a passing train, and talked about trains. Ryan was an expert on trains (his father and himself shared a model railway), and he interested Esther with his talk and explanations.

But, at last (and alas!) the Wood was reached. It was on their left and could be entered without difficulty at any point. Ryan began to talk less and less. Esther talked less, too. She had noticed that Ryan was talking less, and she had noticed that, on their left, was a Wood which could be entered without difficulty at any point.

At last Ryan found his courage.

'Let's go in here, shall we?' he said. 'It's awfully pretty. This is where I used to pick primroses when I was a child.'

And he led the way into an easy path through the wood. Esther, trying so hard to think quickly that she was unable to think, followed him.

She had, though, seen a man walking at a distance along the Cinder Path in their direction. Otherwise she probably would not have followed Ryan.

When they had walked about fifteen yards into the wood, Esther suddenly stopped and looked around at the trees.

'Yes. It's ever so pretty,' said Esther, and she tried to make every motion of her eyes and body imply that it was very nice to have gone fifteen yards into a wood in which he had once picked primroses, but that it was now obviously time that they returned to the public path by the railway.

Ryan immediately sensed that she did not want to go any further. But they were fifteen yards inside, and not visible to a passer-by. Therefore, summoning up all the courage he had promised himself all the afternoon that he would, he said: 'Well, shall we sit down for a bit? I'm a bit tired, I don't know about you. It looks quite dry and cosy here. Shall we?'

He indicated a dry place on the ground, filled with last year's leaves.

Esther said 'Yes,' and, with Ryan's assistance, sat down.

Ryan sat beside her.

The man in the distance, Esther reflected, must be much nearer by now. And they were, after all, very near the path by the railway, and other people must soon be passing.

Ryan began to talk – again about trains. He had never thought that his knowledge of trains would be of such service to him.

But trains were not enough. Something else had to be said or done. He forced himself to do it. He put his hands upon hers as he talked.

Esther did not at once withdraw her hand. One of the reasons for this was that her attention was at the moment elsewhere. She was listening to the sound of footsteps. They were obviously those of the man whom she had seen in the distance.

She heard him (but there was no way of seeing him) as he came striding by.

Then his footsteps died away, and there was complete silence.

There was not even the sound of a distant train. Also, Ryan had stopped talking. He was looking at her.

She drew her hand away, and uttered meaninglessly the word 'Yes . . .'

Ryan pretended not to notice this, and went on talking. Then he took her hand again.

Once more, because she heard people approaching, she let him retain her hand. Then the people passed, and she took it away.

But he persisted, and a few minutes later once more tried to take her hand. But this time she drew it away at once.

'You mustn't do that,' she said.

'Why not?' asked Ryan.

'I don't know you well enough,' said Esther feebly.

Now the Gorse-created evil of Esther's situation was this. She was enormously attracted to Ryan. She wanted him to hold her hand. She even wanted him to kiss her – a thing she had never really desired from any young man in her life before. But what is a young girl, confronted with her Prince Charming, to do, when she suspects that the latter may be a dangerous lunatic, a sex-maniac, some kind of *News of the World* slaughterer? She remembered Gorse's warning, as well as the anonymous letter.

If she let him hold her hand, it would be definitely encouraging him. It would lead to further things, and the hypothetical maniac might be seized by his mania.

'I know you don't know me well,' said Ryan, making no further attempt to take her hand. 'But a lot can happen in a little time, can't it?'

There was a pause.

'*What* can happen?' asked Esther.

'Well – one can get attracted – can't one? May I call you by your Christian name?'

'Yes. If you like.'

'Well – Esther – well, you see, it's hard to explain. But there *is* such a thing as love at first sight, isn't there?'

'Is there?'

'Yes. You know there is. Do you know the words of the old song:

"I did but see her passing by
And yet I love her till I *die*?"

Well – that's what's happened to me, that's all.'

Esther did not like his use or stressing of the word 'die'. To begin with, it reminded her unpleasantly of death! And it was too passionate a thing to say at this stage of their acquaintanceship. It confirmed her fears.

'Well,' she said. 'I don't know what to say.'

'Don't you like me at all?'

'But I don't know you. I don't know anything *about* you.'

'But that's not the point. The point is do you like me?'

'I don't know.'

'Well – do you think you could *come* to like me? Do you think if we went on meeting you could *come* to like me?'

'I don't know. I'd have to know more *about* you.'

'Why do you keep on saying that? I mean about knowing *about* me. There's nothing particular to know about me. I'm just an ordinary person, and I'm terribly in love with you.'

'Well, then I want to know you better, let's say.'

'Well, I hope you will. Tell me. Is there anybody else? There must have been dozens of people in love with you – but is there anybody *you're* in love with?'

Esther hesitated before replying. Suppose, she thought, it was later somehow proved that Ryan was incapable of wickedness, that the anonymous sender of the letter was the foul slanderer which such a person must almost certainly be, and that Gorse was mistaken? Surely she must give Ryan some sort of chance. And if, now, she said there was somebody else, she would lose him. He was (if innocent) not the type to persevere after being told such a thing, Esther imagined.

'No,' she said. 'I don't know that there's anybody.'

'Oh – then there *is* some hope, then. Say there is.'

'I don't know . . .'

Here Ryan made a fatal error.

'Oh – *do* say there is,' he said, and seized her hand – this time more violently. Worse still, when she tried to release it, he did not immediately permit her to do so.

There was, indeed, something not far removed from a struggle, and Esther, when her hand was released, at once rose.

Ryan rose too.

'I'm sorry,' he said. 'I'm really sorry.'

'It's all right,' said Esther. 'But I think we'd better be getting on – don't you?'

'Yes. Perhaps we'd better. I'm sorry. Let's go back to the bike, and then we'll have tea.'

Thus Gorse, after all, had 'done the trick' – temporarily, at any rate. If it had not been for this young man's crafty intervention Esther would have allowed Ryan to hold her hand, and afterwards to have kissed her. And after that, almost certainly, it would not have been long before Ryan would have realized his ultimate ambition. They would have become 'engaged'.

But instead of this they walked back to the path by the railway, and then returned in the direction of his motor cycle.

Ryan changed the subject. He was not utterly crestfallen. He thought that Esther's attitude might easily derive from maidenly coyness, and that he still might have a chance. There was, though, in her attitude, something which he could not define and which slightly puzzled him.

He told her some things about his childhood, and she told him something about her own.

When they were not far away from the motor cycle, he pointed out that it was Sunday tomorrow. Because of this she would be free, and perhaps able to meet him. He asked her if he might take her to the Palladium Cinema in the evening. There was a film he particularly wanted to see, and would like her to see.

Esther remembered that she was meeting Gorse tomorrow evening. She would have liked nothing better than to go to the Palladium with Ryan. There could be no 'danger' in that. But she could not do so, and had, she supposed, to tell another lie.

She was seized suddenly with a violent revulsion against these incessant falsehoods. Why not, for once, tell the truth – and afterwards tell Gorse that she had done so? She saw nothing against it, and attempted it.

'Well, that's going to be difficult,' she said. 'You know that friend of yours. His name's Gorse, isn't it?'

'Yes.'

'Well, I ran into him last night – quite by accident.'

Esther saw that, in her magnificent attempt at truth-telling, she had told yet another lie. Oh – what *was* she to do!

'Yes?' said Ryan.

'And he took me to have a drink at the Metropole.'

'The Metropole!' said Ryan. 'I say – *he's* going it a bit – isn't he?'

'Yes. I suppose he is. And he asked me if I'd meet him tomorrow for another drink. And I don't see how I can let him down, really. You don't mind, do you?'

'No, not a bit,' said Ryan. 'But why didn't you tell me before?'

'It just didn't come into my head.'

Another lie, thought Esther.

'Where did you run into him?' asked Ryan, slightly suspicious and disturbed.

'Oh – on the front. Between the two piers.'

And another!

'And what did you have to drink?'

'Oh – Gin and It, I think it was.'

'How many did you have? Didn't it go to your head?'

'No. I was all right. We only had one.'

And another.

'And what did you do afterwards?'

'Oh – we just said goodbye outside the Metropole.'

And another still.

Truth, it seemed, was out of the question, beyond her powers. She had told him that she had had only one drink, because she did not want him to be shocked. And she had told him that Gorse had left her outside the Metropole, because she did not want to hurt him by letting him know that Gorse had escorted her most of the way home – a privilege she had not granted Ryan on Thursday. She did not want Ryan to think that she was in any way interested in Gorse.

Now they had reached the motor cycle. They mounted it and drove off towards Hurst.

This was a great relief to Esther.

The noise of the machine excused her from talking, and so, briefly, from telling further lies.

4

It was only after they were seated at the tea-shop in Hurst, and after the tea and bread-and-butter and cakes had been put before them, and Esther (being 'Mother') had poured out the tea, that something occurred to her which, for some extraordinary reason, had never occurred to her before.

Why should she not tell Ryan about the anonymous postcard and give him a chance to defend himself? And why had it never crossed her mind to do so?

This was precisely what these hideous communications did to one. In addition to all else, they threw you off your balance – robbed you of your normal reasoning powers.

What could be wrong with this proposition? She looked at Ryan. He was eating his bread-and-butter, and sipping at his tea, and looking out of the window at the pretty garden with a sort of dejection and quietness which touched her heart immeasurably. Why should she not put him out of his pain – and, perhaps, by candour – and fearlessness and truthfulness – escape from her own pain?

Something held her back. There were, after all, reasons why she should not do this. In the first place, if he was in fact guilty and 'dangerous', he would certainly not confess that he was. He would lie with all the charming plausibility which he so obviously possessed.

Then (supposing he *were* 'dangerous') Esther perceived that above all things she must be cautious. She must think about it carefully; and this she could not possibly do while sitting with him over a tea-table.

Then, supposing he was innocent, she was afraid of offending or disgusting him. Her real belief still was that the postcard came from someone in her own class – her own low class. Would not a gentleman, and particularly a 'perfect' gentleman, be so horrified by such a thing that he would decide to abandon her, utterly disconnect himself from such slum-filth?

This was all getting too much for Esther. To whom could she go for help?

At this point it occurred to her that she might tell her mother. Then she decided that she would do this. She loved and trusted her mother, who had always told her never to tell lies, and who, as a wise woman, might extract her from those upon which she had embarked.

5

After tea, a subdued Ryan peacefully drove her back to Brighton.

There was a discussion as to where he should leave her. Ryan knew that Over Street was near Brighton Station, and suggested the Station itself. To this Esther agreed.

Ryan had a minor motive in naming Brighton Station. Here, he knew, he could get the latest edition of the evening paper. He was anxious to read the Cricket Results. At Ryan's age such things as Cricket Results can enter the head of even the most dejected or frenzied lover.

When they had got off the machine Ryan told her that he wanted to buy a paper and asked her if she would accompany him to the stall in the Station. She consented.

But she had no sooner done so than she regretted it. She had remembered that she might easily encounter her father inside the Station, and she did not want to be seen by him with a young man. Esther's father, unlike her mother, had no tacit mutual arrangement about her young men. Esther's father, really, was not supposed to know that young men happened at all. (And, in fact, he was too busy a man to know fully that they did.)

When he had bought his paper Ryan made the foolish and unnecessary mistake of trying to say goodbye inside the Station.

'Well,' he said. 'I suppose this is goodbye, isn't it? Just for the present. When can I see you again? Tomorrow evening seems to be out – *so what about the evening after that*?'

Because of a great noise of engines, and because of the flood of returning Saturday trippers, almost bumping into them, Ryan raised his voice.

Esther, already alarmed by the thought of her father seeing her, was further disconcerted by Ryan's raised voice, and the noise of the engines, and the danger of trippers bumping into them – so much so that she could hardly think. She had promised to go out alone with Gertrude one night early in the week, but she could not remember which night this was.

'I don't know,' she shouted back. 'I've got to go out with Gertrude one night. I just can't think at the moment.'

And now a sort of panic seized both of them. Standing where they were, in the midst of the noise and bustle, they both got the impression that one or the other of them had to catch a train. Moreover, they quite madly thought that the train was going out at once, and that they had only a few seconds in which to speak.

It was this insane unconscious impression which had originally panicked Ryan into saying goodbye here instead of peacefully outside.

Esther, too, imagined that she had seen her father at a distance – her father coming in their direction.

What if her father came up and spoke to them? Such a thing was extremely likely, and then she would be shamed doubly. There would be the shame of being discovered by her father with a young man, and the shame which would be caused by Ryan seeing that her father was a member of a low profession – that of a porter. In addition to this, Esther knew that her father, apart from his being a porter, had the appearance of a low person. He was bowed, and he wore a moustache which he frequently neglected to wipe.

And so her panic increased. All she wanted to do was get away. And when Ryan said, 'Well – couldn't you *think* of a day?' all she could reply was, 'No. I don't know. I can't think.'

Esther's panic had increased Ryan's.

'But you *must* think!' he shouted against a violently hissing engine. It was as if he were speaking harshly, and shouting – not against the engine – but at Esther. This further frightened, and slightly offended her.

'But I can't. Just at the moment. And I *must* go, you know,' said Esther, again thinking that her father might be upon them at any moment. 'I'm ever so late.'

'But when are we going to *meet*?' cried Ryan in despair.

It still did not occur to either of them that they might walk out of the Station to his motor cycle, and there say goodbye and make their arrangements peacefully.

'I don't know,' said Esther, looking at him miserably.

The atmosphere of trains and journey-taking gave Ryan an inspiration.

'Well, can I *write* to you?' he said. 'I know your address.'

'Yes. That's right. You can write to me. You know my address.'

'All right. I'll write. And you'll answer, won't you?'

'Yes. I'll answer all right.'

'Promise?'

'Yes. I promise.'

'All right, then. Well, I suppose it's goodbye for the present.'

'Yes. I suppose it is. Well – goodbye, then.'

She shook hands with him and fled from the Station.

As soon as she was back at Over Street and had calmed down, Esther perceived that she had yet again failed to thank a young man for taking her out. Esther, whose ambition it was to behave like a 'lady' in whatever circumstances, bitterly reproached herself for this omission.

Ryan, deeply disturbed, went into the Station Buffet and had yet another cup of tea.

Upset as Ryan was, however, he did not fail to open his paper and look at the Cricket Results.

PART SEVEN

SAVINGS

Chapter One

Gorse was in excellent form when Esther met him on the following Sunday evening, and he took her with great dash to the same table at the Metropole.

'Well, what news on the Rialto?' he said, when their drinks had come. 'Eh?'

And he stuck his monocle into his eye and looked at her ruminatively.

He was really seeking to confirm his conviction that his ruse had succeeded, and that Esther had not gone into the country with Ryan.

'I don't think there's any, really,' said Esther. 'At least none of any importance.'

Something evasive in the way Esther said this gave Gorse an idea that his ruse had failed after all. He came straight to the point.

'Did you go out with our friend Ryan?' he asked. 'Against your Uncle Ralph's advice?'

'Oh yes. I'd forgotten about all that.' (But Esther had not forgotten about all that.) 'I *did* go, as a matter of fact, after all. I thought I was making a mountain out of a molehill, and that I knew how to look after myself, and so I decided to go after all.'

'Oh – you did – did you?'

'Yes. And – oh – by the way, there's something I ought to tell you.'

'Oh – what's that?'

'It's not of any importance. It's just that I suddenly got tired of telling lies, and so I told him I'd met you, and had a drink in here, on the Friday evening. I told him I met you by accident, and you took me in here.'

'But that's still telling lies, isn't it?' said the quick-witted Gorse. 'Because you didn't meet me by accident – did you?'

'No. But you've got to *try* and tell the truth. You've got to get as near it as you can – haven't you? And it didn't do any harm – telling him – did it? *You* don't mind, do you?'

'No. Not in the least. And I'm all for telling the truth, whenever it's possible, certainly.'

'Yes, I knew you would be. So that's why I told him. And I told him I was meeting you tonight. That's all right, too, isn't it?'

'Perfectly,' said Gorse, still looking at her. 'And tell me. Did anything happen?'

'Happen? When?'

'When he took you out.'

'What do you mean by "happen"?'

'Come along now. You know perfectly well what I mean.'

Esther hesitated.

'Well. No . . .' she said, and added, 'If you mean he tried to hold my hand, he did. But that's all.'

'And did you let him?'

'No. I didn't . . .'

'Sure?'

'Yes.'

'And where did all this take place? I hope you won't think I'm cross-examining you. But I'd just like to know.'

'Oh, just in a place by the railway. It was at Hassocks.'

'What sort of place?'

'It was a wood.'

'Ah. A wood. Really,' said Gorse, with much meaning.

'What's wrong with a wood? It was only just inside, and there were quite a few people about.'

'And did anything happen after he'd held your hand?'

'What sort of thing?'

'You know what I mean.'

'Do you mean did he try to' – Esther dragged the word out – '*kiss* me?'

'Yes.'

'No. Not a thing like that. I didn't even let him hold my hand properly. And then he gave up, and we walked back to where his bike was.'

'And did you make any arrangements to meet again?'

'No. No appointment. He said he'd write to me.'

'Oh – he did – did he?' said Gorse, again with much meaning.

'You know,' said Esther, 'I've thought it out and I'd swear there's nothing really wrong in that quarter. I don't really believe that awful letter, and even if he *did* do something wrong as a boy I'm sure he's all right now. I'd swear to it. I would – really.'

'Well,' said Gorse. 'You certainly seem to have got over your fright about the letter.'

'Yes. I am getting over it. I don't think I ought ever to have got in such a state about it. It ought to have been treated with contempt. He behaved so *well*, you see.'

'Yes. But that's just what they do – isn't it?'

'What do you mean?'

'Well – they behave well three or four times, and then, when they've got your confidence – something happens.'

'What?'

'Oh – something.'

'Tell me. Won't you still tell me what happened – what he did – at school?'

'No. I won't,' said Gorse. 'But don't look so frightened. And don't think I'm trying to damage Ryan in any way. He may be a perfectly decent chap. Uncle Ralph's just giving you his worldly advice, that's all.'

'I know. And it's very good of you. But all I can say is that he behaved like a perfect gentleman – that's all.'

'And what do you mean by a perfect gentleman? What do you mean by a plain gentleman, if it comes to that?'

'Oh. You know.'

'No, I don't. What?'

'Oh – don't be so silly.'

'No, I don't. You've said Ryan's a gentleman. Would you call me one?'

'Yes. Of course you are.'

'Why?'

'Why – it's written all over you.'

'What's written?'

'Oh – you know well enough. You've been to College and all that. You were born better. You're not like me. I'm not a gentleman – I mean a lady. Although I try to be.'

'Why aren't you? *I* should say you are.'

'Oh, don't be so silly. It's a question of *birth*,' said the tormented Esther. 'Birth, and where you're brought *up*.'

'Is it? Well, how were you born? Who were *your* people, if you *must* go on about it? Who's your father, for instance?'

Esther paused.

'My father's a porter at Brighton Station, if you want to know. And I live in something pretty near a slum. I've told you about the slum before. But I haven't told you about the porter.'

'Well, what's wrong with being a porter?' said Gorse. 'I've no doubt he's a very worthy man.'

This last remark was typical of Gorse. He had spoken fairly gracefully to Esther so far, but now he had slipped up. Even the struggling, bewildered Esther somehow knew that it was very seriously caddish to allude to a person's father as one who is 'no doubt a very worthy man'.

Gorse was to do this sort of thing all his life, and it did not help him.

Esther, having much finer taste than his, took offence a little.

'He's a very nice man, anyway,' she said.

'I'm sure he is,' said Gorse. 'And what about your mother?'

'Oh – she's a bit different. She's in a much better sort of class, really. She worked as a nurse to some children in a very good family. They lived in First Avenue, in Hove. They were related to a General – General Sir Arthur Atherton-Broadleigh. I don't know if you've ever heard of him . . . So you might call my mother a much better class.'

Esther, if the truth must be known, had brought in this General as a kind of counter-blast to Gorse's Army People.

There was, really, remarkably little social snobbery about Esther. But she did, as we have seen, desire to 'better herself'. And she thought it politic, on certain occasions, to 'hold one's own'. And so she had dragged in this obscure connection with an obscure General obscurely related to a family in First Avenue, Hove.

'And who were your grandparents?' asked Gorse. 'Do you know about them?'

'No. Not much. Mother's mother was a sewing woman, I know that. But I hardly know anything about my father's father.'

Esther's grandmother had, actually, been a hideously sweated seamstress of the type in which Beatrice Webb had interested herself. About Esther's grandfather, the consumptive runner, we know.

'So you found Ryan a perfect gentleman, did you?' said Gorse, returning to their previous conversation.

'Yes. I did. I must say I did.'

'More perfect than yours truly, for instance?'

'Don't be so silly. Of course not. You're both the same.'

Gorse had been profoundly chagrined to learn that Esther had after all been out with Ryan. This, still, was not because he was really jealous of Ryan. It was because his plotting had unexpectedly failed. (While discussing Esther's parentage he had been wondering what his next move was to be.)

The time came for their second cocktail, and Esther made a proposition.

'Won't you let *me* pay for a change?' she asked. 'I know it's not done, but I don't see why *you* should always go on forking out.'

'What!' said Gorse. '*You* be seen paying in a place like this! No – I don't think that'd quite do.'

The flash of the cad again – shaming her. She flushed faintly.

'No,' she said. 'I didn't mean that. I meant doing it all secretly. Or waiting till we got outside.'

'Well – that's very good of you,' said Gorse. 'But I really can't accept it.'

'Well, I wish you would – just once. It seems unfair on you all the time.'

'And are you as rich as all that?' said Gorse. 'I thought you said you were so poor.'

'Well, I *am* poor. But I've got a little put by. In fact, I've got quite a lot, for a girl like me. It'd surprise you. My mother always made me save, you see.'

Esther had, indeed, what she looked upon as a great fortune. And of this she was proud. She liked to tell her intimates about it.

'What do you mean by quite a lot?' asked Gorse.

'Oh – lots.'

'Pounds, shillings, or pence?'

'Oh – pounds. A lot of them.'

'Five?'

'No.'

'Less?'

'No.'

'More, then? Ten?'

'No.'

'More?'

'Yes.'

Esther was enjoying this game, and had no objection to disclosing the great amount of her savings. Not only was she proud, in a general way, of these. In this particular context, in the Metropole with Gorse, they might give her a further sense of satisfaction. If she disclosed the great amount she might seem of much more consequence, both to Gorse and herself. The General, taken together with her savings, were, she fancied, impressive, if only in a small way.

'Fifteen?' asked Gorse.

'No. More,' said Esther. 'You see, my mother makes quite a lot on the side by her sewing, and she's given me money to save ever since I was a kid.'

'Twenty?'

'No.'

'Twenty-five?'

'No.'

'*Thirty?*'

'No.'

'More?'

'Yes.'

'*Forty*, then?'

'No.'

'Am I getting warm?'

'Warmer.'

'Fifty!' exclaimed Gorse.

'No,' said Esther primly. 'More.'

'All right. We'll try sixty.'

'Ah, now you *are* getting warm.'

'Then what about seventy?'

'No. You've gone just too far. It's sixty-eight pounds, fifteen shillings, if you want to know.'

'Well – I'd call that a pretty tidy little sum – if you ask me,' said Gorse. 'And where do you keep it all?'

'In the Post Office. Of course, I hardly ever draw on it. But it gives you a sort of feeling of security.'

'Yes. It must,' said Gorse.

'And I do draw on it a little, every now and again. That's why I wanted to pay for a drink tonight . . . And now I've got to tell you I've gone and told you another lie . . .'

Esther could not resist having yet another of her wretched little shots at the truth.

'What is it this time?' asked Gorse.

'Well – my money isn't really in the Post Office. My mother tells me to say it is, that's all. It's at home.'

'At home!' said Gorse.

'Yes. My mother feels that way about money.'

'What way?'

'Well – she doesn't like *putting* her money into anything. She's had friends who've lost all they've got that way. She likes to keep it at home.'

Esther was again speaking the truth. Esther's mother was, in fact, a victim of this eccentricity – an eccentricity to be found more amongst the very poor than any other class. Mrs Downes, sane as she was, did not fully trust even the Post Offices or Banks. She had painfully forced herself to put a small proportion of her money into the Post Office, but most of it was at home. This was kept in her own bedroom, in an extremely inaccessible place. Esther's money was kept in an extremely old tin safe, which was hidden amongst old clothes in an old tin trunk in Esther's bedroom.

There is probably more ready cash available in little streets like Over Street than in the largest and most opulent Avenues, Crescents, or Squares of this world.

'Well – it doesn't sound very wise to me,' said Gorse. 'You're losing a tidy bit of interest to begin with . . . And how much have you got on you tonight, pray?'

'Three pounds. It's got to last a while, though. And it's really money for a new bag that I've got to buy sometime this week. This one's worn out.'

'Is it? It looks all right to me.'

'Oh no, it isn't. You're only a man so you wouldn't know. And the lining's all gone inside, anyway.'

'Can I have a look? Or is there anything private?'

'No. There's nothing private,' said Esther, handing it to him. 'And you just look at that lining.'

Gorse took the bag and looked inside it.

'Yes. It certainly is a bit torn,' he said, and handed it back to her.

'Thank you,' said Esther, herself examining the lining. 'And that beastly letter's still in here, I see. I suppose I ought to put it on the fire.

'Oh, is it? I didn't see it.'

'Yes. Here it is all right.'

Gorse had, really, seen it, but he had to pretend not to have done so, because the card had now been put into its envelope, and he had not been shown this before.

Gorse, a few nights ago pasting the letters from the newspaper on to the card, had suddenly grown tired of his amusement. He had therefore decided to address the envelope in a disguised hand. He knew that there were certain risks attached to this: but he fancied himself as a forger.

He had not sent the postcard without an envelope, for he feared that a postman might report the matter either to Esther's father or mother, or even the police, and in this case it might never reach her.

'Perhaps,' said Esther, 'you didn't see it because of the envelope. I didn't show you that before.'

'Envelope? Oh – so there was an envelope, was there? No – you didn't show it to me before. But of course there must have been. The other side was blank. And I *did* see an envelope in there. Could I have a look? It's in somebody's hand, and it might throw some lights on things.'

'Yes. Here you are.'

Gorse looked through his monocle carefully and at some length at the envelope.

'Portslade postmark, I see . . .' he said.

'Yes. But you don't know the handwriting – do you? It isn't any friend of yours, is it? Not your friend what's-his-name? Bell?'

'No. At least it's very cleverly forged if it is. And as you suspected me for a moment, I may as well tell you it's certainly not mine. I use a fountain pen with light blue ink. This looks like an ordinary pen, and the ink's pretty well black. If you still suspect me, would you like to see my fountain pen? I've got it on me. And would you like to see a specimen of my handwriting? You could take it to a handwriting expert, and he might prove it was me.'

'Oh – stop ragging me about that,' said Esther. 'I've said I'm sorry.'

When Esther was half-way through her second drink she began to feel dizzy, and she made Gorse finish it for her.

When he had done this they went out and on to the West Pier

once more. Gorse repeated his 'Silly Ass' act, took Esther to the same seat as usual, and kissed her as before.

She again allowed him to escort her as far as the Clock Tower. But here, as they said goodbye, something unexpected happened.

'I say,' said Gorse. 'Something's just struck me. Do you think you could do me a favour?'

'Yes. I hope so. What is it?'

'Well, the truth is,' said Gorse, going through his pockets, 'I'm pretty well completely out of ready cash. That doesn't matter, because I don't want any tonight. But tomorrow morning I've got to be up with the lark to go and see an old uncle of mine over at Preston Park. He's a bit of a tyrant and a martinet, but as he's absolutely rolling in money, and I'm hoping a lot of it's coming to me, one's got to toe the line, if you see what I mean.'

'Yes? Well?'

'Well, although I've got enough of the ready to get home tonight, it's going to be the devil tomorrow morning waiting for the bank to open and then get to Preston in time. And I hate being without money on me. And so I was wondering if you could loan me something.'

'Yes. Of course I can. How much?'

'Well – could you manage a quid? Or even two – if you can manage it. I hate not having enough on me. And then I can go to the bank when I've left the old boy, and pay you back tomorrow evening. You can meet me tomorrow evening – can't you?'

'Well, I'm not quite sure,' said Esther.

She was, though she tried not to show it, decidedly taken aback by what Gorse had asked her.

Apart from the smallest sums to intimate girlfriends, she had never lent money before. And the sum he had mentioned – two pounds – quite staggered her.

And over and above this, he was not an intimate friend. She had only met him three or four times. And he was a man, not a girl – a very different thing in money matters. And, further still, he was a man she still did not instinctively fully trust or like.

She knew exactly what her mother would say about this. She would say that it was very wrong of Gorse to have asked such a thing from a working girl: that it was a thing she didn't 'like the look of', and that it would be highly rash, asking for trouble, to let him have the money.

Then he had said that he would pay her back tomorrow evening at the Metropole. But tomorrow evening she had promised to go out with Gertrude alone.

She could, of course, put Gertrude off until another evening. But, if she decided to do this, she certainly would not mention her appointment with Gertrude to Gorse. Firstly, her putting it off would give him too great a sense of his own importance; secondly, it would look as if she were too anxious to get her money back quickly.

Gorse was speaking to her.

'Why? What's the matter?' he was saying. 'You've got the money on you – haven't you? But I don't want to press it, of course. I can manage easily enough.

'No. It's not that,' said Esther. 'It's just that I've got to buy things with it. There's that bag, for instance.'

'Oh. Can't you put the bag off, just for a day? One never wants to rush at buying, you know. It's a good policy to wait.'

Esther made her decision.

She desired to 'better' herself: it was for this reason that she liked mixing with 'gentlemen': and Gorse was one. But if one mixed with 'gentlemen' one had to behave in a gentlemanly way. And ladies and gentlemen, she had always imagined, did not fuss about small money matters. A matter of two pounds would be a small one to them.

Furthermore, a gentleman would certainly not like to find a lady not trusting him. Gorse might easily take offence, and that would be the end of the Metropole.

'Oh – I suppose you're right,' she said. 'And it was only the bag I was thinking about. How much do you want?'

'Well, I'd like two. But one would see me through.'

'No. You have two.' She gave them to him. 'There you are.'

'That's very nice of you,' said Gorse, pocketing the notes. 'And thank you very much indeed.'

'Not at all. And now I must be buzzing off.'

'You know I thought for a moment you didn't trust me,' said Gorse, smiling at her. 'Did you think I was going to run off with your hard-earned savings?'

'No, it was only the bag. I've told you. I promise you it was only the bag.'

'Well, I *might* be a crook, you know,' said Gorse. 'Anyway, now you'll *have* to turn up tomorrow – won't you? If only to get your money back.'

Esther suddenly thought of telling him frankly about her appointment with Gertrude. But she decided against it. If she did she would have to meet Gorse on another, later evening, and she did not want this. She wanted, she knew in her heart, to see the colour of her money as soon as possible!

And so that she could do this, poor Gertrude had to be sacrificed.

'Yes,' she said. 'I'll be there. Seven o'clock, West Pier?'

'That's right. And then we'll go to the good old Met. again.'

'Fine. Well – ta-ta!'

'Cheerio,' said Gorse, and they parted.

Gorse indulged in more deep thought on his walk back to Norton Road.

He now had two schemes on hand. One concerned Ryan. The other concerned Esther. Esther's sixty-eight pounds, fifteen shillings had interested the precocious and enterprising young man very much.

Chapter Two

I

On Monday morning Esther received another letter. Before she had opened it she was sure it was from Ryan, and it was. It read:

Dear Esther,

Please forgive me for writing to you so soon, but I know how you must be booked up, and I thought it best to be in good time.

When we left each other yesterday evening we were in such a fluster (I don't quite know why) that it must have been difficult for you to have thought of a free day.

Would Thursday do? Say seven-thirty, outside the West Pier? Could you let me know? I know you are busy, but you need only just write a line, and I am enclosing a stamped addressed envelope. I never told you *my* address!

I am so much looking forward to seeing you again, and I do hope that you can manage Thursday. I thought we might go on to the Pier, if it is fine, but if it is wet we could go to the Palladium. I still very much want to see the film I told you about, and I would like you to see it too.

I hope you are keeping very well.

Yours,

Peter (Ryan)

Esther found this letter charming, and she spent a good deal of time in trying to find out whether he had signed himself 'Your', which was passionate, or 'Yours', which was less so. He had purposely put a little squiggle after the *r*. He had wanted to write 'Your', but thought it might be too bold, and 'put her off', and so he had hit upon this clever ambiguity with his pen.

Esther also admired his modesty in the way he had signed his name – the 'Ryan' in brackets. She would not have liked a plain Peter nearly as much. The perfect gentleman had hit (as he had tried to do) upon the perfect compromise.

2

From Ryan's point of view this letter (although he had feared he had sent it too early) had arrived a little too late. For by this time Esther, as she had promised herself she would, had confided in her mother, and her mother's advice about Ryan detracted from the charm of the letter.

Esther had confided in her mother on the Sunday night – shortly after she had left Gorse.

The opportunity had arisen quite accidentally, and Esther had taken advantage of it. She did not have to 'go' to her mother. Her mother, on hearing her come in, had invited her into the sitting-room to join her in a cup of cocoa, which she was just about to make for herself.

Mrs Downes had had no motive save that of having the companionship of her daughter for a quarter of an hour or so.

Cocoa is not, like alcohol, a great stimulant: but, if taken in front of a warm fire at the end of the day, it induces confidences.

Esther plucked up her courage and told her mother very nearly the truth, the whole truth, and nothing but the truth.

3

She began with the first meeting of all five on the West Pier. Then she told her mother about Gorse, and about her having gone to the Metropole with him.

The nature of the hotel surprised and slightly alarmed Mrs Downes. But some pleasure was mixed with her alarm – for she had always felt certain that her lovely daughter was destined to enjoy astonishing delights. And she believed, as have all mothers since civilization began, that young people nowadays get up to extraordinary things for which allowances simply have to be made.

But then Esther came to the anonymous postcard, and her mother was horrified. On Esther's showing it to her, she became more horrified still. Indeed, after a lot of staring at it and thinking about it, she said she would keep it and show it to Mr Stringer. Mr Stringer was an elderly ex-policeman who lodged in a small room three or four doors away in Over Street, and he was a personal friend of Mrs Downes, whom he awed with what he believed was an intimate and intricate knowledge of the law.

So, Esther reflected, it was going to the police after all! She almost regretted having confided in her mother. She only trusted that poor Ryan was not, through her instrumentation, going to have the police set upon him!

Then Mrs Downes began to advise Esther. She said, first of all, that she must never see Ryan again. The message on the postcard might well be purely malicious, and untrue, but no risks could possibly be taken. In cases of this sort, she said, there was only one thing to do – and that was completely to remove oneself from the sphere of evil. When mud of this sort was being thrown near one, however pure Esther might be, some of it might strike and stick to her. And this was no ordinary mud: it was dangerous, and endangered Esther perhaps physically as well as socially.

Then Esther pleadingly told her mother how she had been out into the country with Ryan, and how he had behaved, throughout the entire afternoon, like a perfect gentleman.

But this made no impression at all on Mrs Downes. He might easily, she said, behave like a perfect gentleman at the beginning.

This, Esther noted secretly, was an almost exact repetition of Gorse's advice. Could both be wrong?

'But what if he *writes* to me?' asked Esther. 'He knows my address and said he would that evening.'

'Well,' said her mother, after reflection. 'You mustn't answer it, that's all.'

'But suppose there's nothing really wrong about him? Wouldn't it be rude and unkind to not answer?'

'No,' said Mrs Downes firmly. 'You mustn't answer. You've got to risk being rude and unkind. You've got to be kind to yourself, and keep out of trouble at all costs.' A thought struck Mrs Downes. 'You're not at all – keen – on this young man, are you, by the way?'

Esther could not quite bring herself to admit that she was.

'No,' she said. 'I like him very much, though – what I've seen of him. And I've told you he behaves like a perfect gentleman.'

'Well – I'm glad to hear you're not,' said Mrs Downes. 'You must keep out of this.'

'But what if I *meet* him again, on the front? I can't very well refuse to speak to him.'

'No. But there're ways and means – and I'm sure you know how to use them. I expect you've had to do things like that before. You can be cool and cut the meeting short – can't you? You'll know how to choke him off.'

'Yes. But if he's really all right I don't *want* to choke him off,' said Esther, and then asked about Gorse. Should she go on meeting Gorse?

Esther's mother gave this matter some reflection, and then said that this might be permissible. But Esther must take the utmost care. It would really be preferable, she said, if Esther never saw any of these boys again.

Then Esther asked whether she should not show the postcard to Ryan and give him a chance to exonerate himself. But Mrs Downes said that such a thing would be useless: he would certainly not admit any guilt, and have some extremely plausible lie ready to hand.

And, said Mrs Downes, repeating her exhortations, Esther must certainly not voluntarily see Ryan again. In addition to this, Mrs Downes said that she herself wanted to keep the letter and show it to Mr Stringer.

Finally Esther said that she would take her mother's advice, and her mother, adopting her usual method, said that she completely trusted her daughter, and she kissed her as she went to bed.

Hard as she had tried, Esther still had failed to tell the whole truth, or even the truth, to her mother.

Her mother, for instance, had asked her what she had had to drink at the Metropole with Gorse, and Esther had said that she had had lemonade. This had been done in order not to shock her mother, but it was another plain lie.

She had failed to tell the whole truth in two ways. She had not told her mother about Gorse's hints concerning Ryan's strange crimes at school. She had been, somehow, too eager to defend Ryan to do this. And she had not told her mother that she had lent Gorse the sum of two pounds that very evening. She knew that this would scandalize her mother, who would probably make her promise not even to see Gorse again.

Esther was up early the next morning, and found Ryan's letter in the hall before her mother was down.

She knew that it was her duty to show this letter to her mother. But what harm could there be in reading it first? She did this in her bedroom.

When she had read it, and had been charmed by it, she thought that she would like to think about it before she showed it to her mother. What harm was there in this? Anyway, her mother was at the moment, she could hear, very busy, and she could show it to her in the evening. Her mother had made her swear no oath.

During her day at the sweet-shop, because her mother had not made her swear any oath, she decided that she would not show the letter to her mother at all, at present. And she decided that she would write to Ryan and agree to meeting him on Thursday evening.

Esther Downes was not a dishonest or untrue girl – rather the contrary. But she was not yet eighteen: she was weak, and found herself in unique circumstances. Any circumstances created by Ernest Ralph Gorse were almost always of a unique character.

4

On Monday night, Ryan, returning to his bed-sitting-room yet again to think and dream, himself received a letter.

This at once puzzled him: for his name and address on the envelope, instead of being written in the conventional manner, had been cleverly formed by letters from a newspaper being pasted on to it. And, on opening the envelope, he found a postcard upon which other letters had been pasted.

These letters went to make the following message:

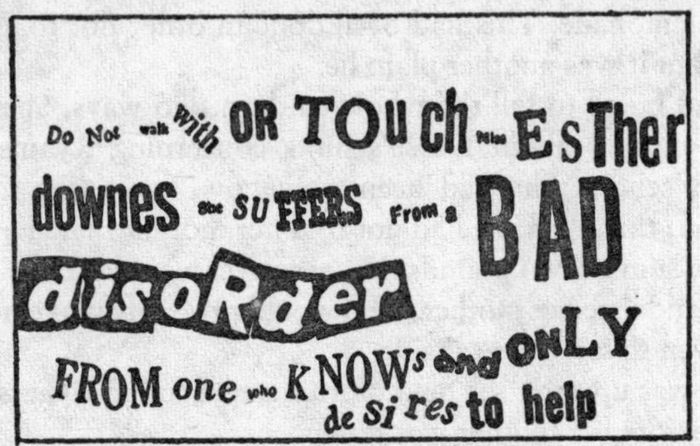

Do Not walk with OR TOUch him EsTher downes She SUFFERS From a BAD disoRder FROM one who KNOWs and ONLY deSires to help

Ryan was not as frightened by this postcard as Esther had been by hers. But now it was his turn to think as laboriously as she had.

Chapter Three

Gorse was again in splendid form when he met Esther outside the West Pier on the Monday evening.

Perhaps the writing of anonymous letters removes from the blood of the sender that amount of evil which it casts upon others. The evils of this life, after all, should be shared.

They found, at the Metropole, the same table and the same waiter; and Gorse ordered the same drinks. The moment these had been paid for and the waiter had gone away, Gorse, feeling in his hip pocket, said:

'Well – to begin with first things first – here's the money you lent me last night. Here we are. There you are.'

He put two pound notes down on to the table.

Esther did not quite know in what manner to take these. It was an entirely new situation for her. In her anxiety to be a 'lady' against his 'gentleman' (and in her flurry of happiness at seeing the colour of her money!) she even thought of trying to refuse the notes – to give them to him. But her common sense saved her from doing this.

'Oh well,' she said, picking up the notes and putting them into her bag. 'That's very kind of you.'

Before she had finished saying this Esther realized that it was absurd and not ladylike. A lady would never had said that it was 'kind' to repay a loan.

'How do you mean – "kind"?' said Gorse. 'It was just a debt which I've paid back – that's all.'

The cad once more. It seemed that Gorse could never resist letting Esther know when she made a fool of herself. But there was possibly some motive behind this: it kept her in her place and increased his power over her.

'No. It was silly of me,' said Esther, and changed the subject. 'Well, how did you find your uncle?'

Gorse had almost forgotten about his invented uncle at Preston Park; but had no difficulty in extemporizing.

'Oh – he's not a bad old boy, really,' he said. 'Bit of a martinet, you know, as I said. You know – retired Colonel type.'

Gorse made him a Colonel as a means of utterly squashing Esther's faint, faint, faint, pathetic connection with a General.

'In fact,' he went on, 'you might say he had a heart of gold – beneath a rather frightening exterior. He's got a purse of gold, too – and a very large purse. And although I don't want to be mercenary – one does have to take that into account. Because I think he's taken a bit of a fancy to yours truly – I can't imagine why – and when he dies I have an idea most of his money's coming to me.'

'How old is he?'

'Oh – well into his seventies, and I have a feeling he's not going to last very long. Not that I want the old boy to go. I'm very fond of the old thing in an odd way.'

'What's his name?' asked Esther quite innocently – that is to say with no intention of trying to cross-examine Gorse to catch him out. She entirely believed in this Colonel uncle.

Gorse had neglected to invent a name. He hesitated.

'Why do you ask?' he said, to gain time to think of a name.

'Oh, only curiosity,' said Esther. 'I don't really know why I asked.'

'He's a Gorse too,' said Gorse. 'My father's eldest brother. He's a Ralph Gorse, too, like me. Colonel Ralph Gorse. Perhaps that's why he's taken such a fancy to me.'

'Well,' said Esther, 'I wish *I* had expectations from a rich uncle.'

'Yes, I suppose I *am* pretty lucky, one way and another.'

'You certainly are.'

There was a pause.

'Oh – by the way,' said Gorse. 'I've got something for you.'

Esther had noticed, the moment she had met Gorse, that he was carrying a neat parcel, and she had somehow felt as though it contained something which he was going to give to her.

'Really?' she said. 'What's that?'

'Here you are,' said Gorse, handing her the parcel. 'You open it yourself and find out.'

Esther undid the string, and removed the paper, and found a flat cardboard box. On opening this she found tissue paper, and on removing this she found a woman's handbag.

'Good heavens!' she said, and took it out and gazed at it, shocked with delight. It was a handbag such as she would never have dreamed of possessing. She guessed that it must have cost two pounds at least. She was right. It had cost Gorse two guineas.

'There you are,' said Gorse. 'You said you wanted a bag, so I thought I'd save time for you and get you one.'

Accidentally Gorse had said this in such a way as to fill Esther with the dreadful suspicion that it was not a present – that he had merely bought this fearfully expensive article on her behalf. She had to be reassured at once.

'But I can't afford a thing like this,' she said disingenuously. 'It's good of you to have thought of buying it for me, but it's too expensive!'

'What do you mean – "afford"?' said Gorse. 'It's a present.'

'But you can't! You can't!' said Esther.

'I can, I will, and I do,' said Gorse. 'If you'll accept it.'

'But what can I say? I mean how am I ever going to thank you?'

'Don't thank me,' said Gorse. 'Thank God. He gave me the wherewithal to buy it – so I should thank God.'

'But it's lovely! It's lovely. I simply don't know how to thank you.'

'I've told you. You're not to try. I'm only too grateful that you like it.'

Esther, dizzy with pleasure at the gift, looked at the giver.

He was looking at his best, and behaving at his best. Was there, she thought, perhaps much more 'to' this young man than she had ever thought there might be before? The gift had truly captivated her. Was it possible that he himself might come truly to captivate her? At that moment she thought such a thing far from impossible.

'Well,' said Esther. 'I can only say thank you – from my heart. In fact, I'd like to kiss you for it, if I could, in a place like this.'

'Well – I can only say I wish we weren't in a place like this.'

'No. You're sweet. You are really. What shall I do? Put it back in the box?'

'No. Put the old one back in the box and wear the new one.'

'All right.'

She gleefully emptied the contents of the old bag, and put them into the new one, and then put the old bag into the box. Then she held up the new one to the light and gazed at it.

'Look at it!' she said. 'What on earth'll people think? They'll think I'm getting above my station.' An unpleasant thought struck her. 'Oh lord,' she said, changing her tone. 'What'll my mother think?'

'What's your mother got to do with it?'

'Well – I don't think she likes me taking presents. And I'm afraid an expensive one like this is going to shock her a bit. She's very old-fashioned, and she'll want to know all about you.'

'Well, you can tell her – can't you? There isn't anything to conceal, is there?'

'No. I suppose there isn't.'

'Or you could hide the bag.'

'Yes. I suppose I could.'

'That is, if you think your mother wouldn't approve of me. Do you think she wouldn't?'

'I can't see why on earth she wouldn't.'

'Well, I hope she would. Because I have an idea she's got to do a lot more approving before she's done.'

Esther did not at all get anything of his meaning.

'How do you mean?' she said.

'Well,' said Gorse, 'things might go further, mightn't they?'

'In what way?' said Esther, now roughly following his drift.

'Well – they might get a lot further – mightn't they? Then we *would* have to ask her approval. Your father's too.'

Though unable to believe her ears, Esther had an impression that Gorse was alluding to marriage – or an engagement to marry.

'How do you mean?' she said. 'How much further? And why should my father and mother come into it?'

'You know what I mean.'

'I don't really.'

'Well – must I explain?'

'I wish you would.'

'Well – just suppose – it's only a supposition – suppose I asked you to marry me. And suppose – and I expect that's even more unlikely still – that you – accepted me. We'd have to tell your father and mother then – wouldn't we?'

Here even the experienced Esther blushed, half with pleasure and half with embarrassment.

'Well,' she said. 'It's only supposing, isn't it?'

'No,' said Gorse. 'It *isn't*. I'm extremely serious.'

'Look here,' said Esther. 'What are you doing? Are you trying to pull my leg? Are you trying to say you're proposing marriage or something?'

'I don't quite know. I'm looking into the future. We don't know each other very well just at present, do we?'

'No. We don't . . .'

'But things do happen – don't they? In fact, things are happening. To me, at any rate. And if things go on happening, and we get to know each other better, I can see myself asking you to marry me – that's all . . . Tell me – if I did – do you think there'd be any chance of your saying yes?'

'Look here,' said Esther. 'Are you being serious?'

'Extremely serious,' said Gorse, looking seriously into her eyes as he leant back in his chair. 'I'm a very serious person. Though I may not seem to be on the surface. But tell me. Do you think there'd be any chance?'

'I don't know,' said Esther, looking away as he looked at her.

'Well,' said Gorse. 'I just thought I'd tell you that's the way my mind's working. I'm ready to wait – because you don't know me properly yet, and I know it's wise to wait. But I'm pretty sure that that's what's going to happen on my side.'

'But how *could* you marry me! It's all so absurd.'

'What's absurd?'

'You and me. We're not in the same *class*. It'd never work.'

'What's the difference in class?'

'Well – you're a gentleman and I'm just a shopgirl. It's absurd.'

'Well – even if you're right – *I* don't see that it matters. If there's one thing I'm not, it's a snob. I think you can see that.'

'No. You're certainly not a snob.'

'And I know that I'd be proud to have you for my wife. Anybody would. And, after all, that sort of thing happens every day nowadays. Peers marry chorus girls almost every other day. Not that I'm a peer, or that you're a chorus girl. So that side of it doesn't matter. You've only got to read the newspapers.'

'All the same, I still say it's absurd.'

'And I still say it isn't. Now will you tell me something else?'

'Yes.'

'Is there anybody else?'

'No.'

'Sure?'

'Yes.'

'You're not enamoured of our mutual friend Ryan, for instance?'

'No.'

'Sure?'

'Yes.'

'Not that I'm against him. Let the best man win's my motto. Have you heard from him, by the way?'

'Yes. He wrote to me.'

'What did he say?'

'He asked me to meet him on Thursday evening.'

'And are you going to?'

'I don't know. I suppose I might as well.'

'Where are you meeting him, and where are you going?'

'He asked me to meet him outside the West Pier. And he said we might either go on the Pier, or to a cinema. I can't see any harm in that – can you? It's a public place.'

'No. So long as it's in a public place it's all right. But see that it's in a public place – won't you?'

'Yes. I will.'

Gorse changed the subject.

'And now the time's come for me to finish your cocktail – hasn't it?' said Gorse about ten minutes later. 'That is, if you don't want it yourself.'

'No, I don't want it.'

When Gorse had finished drinking they went out of the hotel. On the way out Esther again spoke fervently about the beauty of the bag he had given her.

When they were in the street Gorse asked her what she would like to do.

'I don't know,' she said. 'I'll leave it to you.'

She presumed that he was going to ask her to go on the Pier, where he would again kiss her. But Gorse was too clever for this.

He knew that going on the Pier must entail kissing. And he knew that Esther would think, when he kissed her, that he was seeking a return, exacting a reward, for his generosity about the bag. She would be, as it were, under an obligation – and Gorse saw that this was inadvisable.

Gorse was not capable of sentimentality, or even sentiment, towards women. He had at times strong and unusual sexual desires, but he was otherwise cold.

In spite of this, or perhaps because of it, he had, throughout his life, a remarkable tact, skill, and understanding of the mentality of girls and women he met. He showed this quality tonight.

'Well, I'll tell you what,' he said. 'I've had rather a hard day, and I'm a bit tired, and I've got three letters I ought to write tonight – so shall we say goodbye early tonight? It's just as you like.'

Esther was inwardly delighted. Charmed as she was by Gorse, she certainly had no desire to go on the Pier and be kissed by him. Now she would get off scot-free with her bag! Gorse had read her mind correctly.

'No. I'm a bit tired too,' she said. 'I'd like an early night.'

'Well, then, may I just see you back as far as the Clock Tower again?'

'Oh no. Don't bother. I can easily go by myself. And you're tired, too, and it's right out of your way.'

'No. Please let me. I'd like to, really.'

He took her back to the Clock Tower, and on the way made an appointment for the following evening.

At the Clock Tower she thanked him for the evening, and again for the bag. Then, as on the previous night, she kissed him lightly on the cheek and quickly left him.

As each went homewards tonight it was Esther who was thinking the hardest. She had to grind over in her mind Gorse's amazing suggestion, his near proposal of marriage.

Could she marry Gorse? She believed almost that she could.

Since meeting him tonight she had completely lost her distrust of him. She did not quite know why this was. Perhaps it was the way he had instantaneously returned the money she had lent him. Perhaps it was the bag. Perhaps it was his talk of marriage, and what she thought was his complete lack of social snobbery. Perhaps it was his manner tonight – his generosity, chivalry, and reticence. She now believed that he was, along with Ryan, a 'perfect' gentleman.

Would he ask her to marry him as he had prophesied that he would? She believed so. And was the idea of marrying him as absurd socially as she had proclaimed it to be at the Metropole?

Did not peers, indeed, marry chorus girls? And was she not remarkably beautiful, and had she not always felt in her heart that she was destined for remarkable things? Even her mother had hinted as much.

She told herself that she must not make the fatal mistake of underestimating herself.

PART EIGHT

ADVICE

Chapter One

I

Ryan, as has been said, had not been as frightened as Esther on receiving his anonymous postcard.

His first impulse had been to tear it up and forget about it.

But he did not do this because he wanted to study it, to discover the sender, to have it, perhaps, as evidence.

This is another evil of the anonymous letter: their recipients hoard them. They simply cannot part with them.

And then, slowly, though he was still not really frightened, the muddy filth and nagging puzzlement attendant upon these things crept over Ryan, and at last completely gripped him.

'Do not walk with or touch Miss Esther Downes she suffers from a bad disorder from one who knows and only desires to help.'

Ryan began to reflect. 'A bad disorder'. What did this lewd expression mean?

Did Esther suffer from some plague – so serious that it was dangerous even to 'walk' with her?

Or did she have some dreadful rash or something, which was concealed by her clothes and infectious to one who 'touched' her?

Or was venereal disease being suggested? Ryan knew little about the latter, but his lack of knowledge made him dread it the more.

Ryan thought that, on the whole, this was being hinted, but surely you could 'walk' with such a victim. Surely you could 'touch' such a one.

'Touch'. Could this conceivably be the reason why Esther, at Hassocks that day, had been so reluctant to allow him to 'touch' her, to hold her hand?

Ryan, for whom 'all the girls fell', had not before encountered such reluctance. He had thought it strange at the time, and had put it down to her extreme beauty, which enabled her to behave in a high-handed way with young men.

But there had been other strange little things about her behaviour. Could Esther have been trying to protect him from some malady from which she suffered? Such a thing seemed not at all unlikely.

Then Esther had confessed to living in a slum. There were many slum diseases, he imagined.

Did Esther have lice on her body? Or in her hair? Such a thing might account for the words 'walk' and 'touch'.

Or was she consumptive?

Then, of course, there was the problem of who on *earth* could have sent the message. Ryan, as had Esther with her pasted post-card, felt that it must come from the slums – from some incredibly low quarter.

But how would such a person know his address?

Who, in Brighton (the letter had been posted in Brighton), knew both his address and the fact that he had met Esther? Only, so far as he knew, Gertrude Perks, and Bell, and Gorse.

He could not possibly believe such a thing of the ugly but amiable Gertrude. She had tried to help him – had made an appointment with Esther for him.

True, as an intimate girlfriend of Esther's, she would be in a position to know more about any malady than any man. And, of course, Gertrude might be a villainess – angry because he had rejected her advances, and jealous of Esther. This might be her way of taking her revenge. All the same, he could not believe it of her.

Bell? No – that was utterly out of the question.

Gorse? That, too, was surely out of the question. Ryan somehow disliked and distrusted Gorse, but it would be absurd to think him capable of baseness of such an order.

Ryan went over and over the thing, and backwards and forwards, late into the Monday night.

He hoped, on Tuesday morning, to have a reply from Esther to his letter, and that she would have consented to meet him on the Thursday as he had suggested. Now, more than ever, he could hardly wait to see her.

He decided that, on the Tuesday morning, he would ask advice from a friend. He had only two of these in town – Gorse and Bell.

Now Gorse was far and away the most sophisticated of the two, and likely to give the best advice. Nevertheless, Ryan decided to go to Bell.

There was still just enough of that little suspicion of Gorse to make him choose the naïve Bell.

2

The naïve Bell was lodging with an aunt in a little house in Bigwood Avenue, which was not far away from their old school, Rodney House.

In the morning no letter had come from Esther, and Ryan, in a state of impatience, took out his motorcycle very early and arrived at the house in Bigwood Avenue before Bell had quite finished his breakfast.

The naïve Bell was at his naïvest. He was smoking his curved pipe with the remains of his coffee, and was studying a chess problem on a small folding chess set which lay open upon the tablecloth.

Bell was by no means displeased to be accidentally discovered in this learned posture.

Indeed, instead of going to the door and letting Ryan in (he had seen him arrive on his motorcycle), he had let the maid do this, and had carefully held the chess picture of himself until Ryan had entered – and for some time after Ryan had entered.

'One moment,' he said, staring at the board. 'I'm delighted to see you, but I suspect I have just found the key move, and I don't want it to elude me. Sit down. I'll be with you in a moment.'

Ryan did what he was told, and waited patiently while Bell went on making an idiot of himself. This Bell did, in silence, for something like a minute.

Then 'No,' said Bell, still gazing at the board. 'No. It won't do. It has eluded me again. A question of discovered check which I had missed. We'll have to abandon it for the time being. It's only a two-mover, but the ingenious problemist has defeated me for more than three quarters of an hour.'

Bell rose.

'Well, my dear Ryan,' he said, very nearly saying 'Watson', for at the moment he had a strong impression that he was Sherlock Holmes being called upon at an early hour by an anxious client.

'I'm delighted to see you. You come at an early hour – and the earlier the better.'

He had nearly added, 'And what can I do for you, sir, pray?' but realized just in time that he was not really Sherlock Holmes.

But he puffed mightily at his pipe, and took a rapid, nervous sip at his coffee – thus giving a clever impression both of smoking 'poisonous shag' and of being a drug addict.

'Yes. I know I'm early,' said Ryan, who saw through all these affectations and now rather regretted having called. 'But I thought it'd be nice to see you again. I'm sorry if I'm too early.'

Ryan did not want to confide in Bell until the latter had stopped making a damned fool of himself – had calmed down.

In about ten minutes' time Bell had done this. He was once more natural, and showing that somewhat sweet and pathetic nature which was really his.

At last, 'As a matter of fact, there's something I want to talk to you about,' said Ryan. 'I want to ask your advice.'

'Oh. Do you? Go ahead. I'm only too pleased to help in any way.'

'Well – it's rather a long story,' said Ryan.

'Go ahead. The longer the better.'

Ryan then reminded Bell of the first meeting of the five on the West Pier, and he told Bell that he had taken Esther into the country, and he confessed that he was 'rather keen' on her.

'Ah yes,' said Bell. 'I rather fancied that Cupid's dart had struck home in that quarter.

'"Cupid and my Campaspe played
At cards for kisses – Cupid –"'

Bell perceived, in fairly good time, that he was reciting poetry which was utterly irrelevant to Ryan's problem, and stopped himself and went on to say, 'However. Proceed.'

'Well, I've had the most funny letter,' said Ryan. 'And I want to know what you think about it.'

'Really? Have you got it on you?'

'Yes. Here it is,' said Ryan, producing it. 'I think it's absolutely filthy, and I ought to tear it up and forget about it. But I'd like you to look at it and give me your advice.'

Bell read the pasted postcard carefully.

'Yes,' he said at last. 'I agree with you. I'd put it on the fire.'

'But who *sent* it?' said Ryan passionately. 'And could there be any *truth* in it?'

Now, at Bell's age (unless one has received one oneself, and one is personally concerned), anonymous letters are regarded as low, but not as being of tremendous importance. Therefore, Bell did not understand Ryan's passion and was of little assistance to him.

'Who cares who sent it?' he said. 'One simply doesn't consider such things. The only thing is the fire or the wastepaper basket. May I put it in this one – here and now?'

'No. I'd rather keep it, I think,' said Ryan. 'I don't know why, but I rather would.'

'Well, I think you're wrong – but here you are,' said Bell, handing it back to Ryan. 'My advice to you is to throw it away and forget all about it.'

But, as Ryan subconsciously perceived, Bell had not *received* the letter and was not *concerned*!

'Yes, that's all very well,' said Ryan. 'But supposing what it says is *true*. What about that?'

'Oh – I don't know about that,' said Bell lightly.

'Do *you* think it might be true? Go on. Tell me.'

'No, I shouldn't think so. It probably comes from some filthy rascal in a low district, and he may be jealous or something.'

'But do you think it *might* be true?'

'Well. Yes. It *might*, of course,' said Bell unconcernedly.

For Bell, having not received the letter, was not concerned.

'But then who *could* have sent it? How did they know my *address*?'

'What does it matter? I've given you my advice. Just forget all about it.'

'But it *does* matter, you know. Tell me. Do you think it might be that friend of hers – the ugly one – Gertrude Whateveritis?'

'It might be.'

'But do you *think* it is?'

'*I* don't know. And I don't care. Neither should you.'

But Bell did not care because he had not received the letter and was not concerned.

'It might be her,' said Ryan. 'I think she's got a bit of a crush on me, and she might be jealous.'

'Yes . . . She might . . .'

'You think it's possible?'

'Yes. It's possible.'

'But then I don't think she knows my address. And that brings me to something else I want to ask you. There is a person who knows my address – and you'll probably think me mad for even thinking of such a thing – but do you think it *could* somehow – be Gorse?'

'Well, I know your address, too – don't I?' said Bell.

'Don't be silly,' said Ryan. 'I'm just asking you if you thought it might be dimly on the cards that it was Gorse. Tell me. Do you think so?'

Bell puffed at his pipe for about ten seconds.

'No,' he said. 'I think that's entirely out of the question. I think you're letting your imagination run away with you. I've told you. Forget it all. It's certainly not Gorse.'

'Well, then. We have to fall back on Gertrude Whateverhernameis. But I still don't really believe it's her. So who could it be?'

'I don't know. What does it matter?'

But it did not matter to Bell because he had not received the letter and he was not *concerned*!

Ryan was becoming slowly infuriated by Bell's complacent and inconsequent attitude – so much so that he had a strong feeling that he would like to get up and knock Bell's pipe out of his mouth. At the same time he knew that Bell was giving him the correct advice. It was exactly the advice he himself would have given to another.

Anyway, there was no sense in nagging at Bell, who clearly was not going to be of any assistance to him. He gave in.

'Well,' he said. 'It's no use going on about it, I suppose. Would you like to come out and have a ride on the bike?'

'Why, yes,' said Bell. 'That's very kind of you – I would. And it certainly might be as well to rid ourselves of the nauseous fumes of tobacco, and inhale the pure oxygen of the open air.'

In three minutes' time they were outside the house and driving away on Ryan's machine.

Ryan took Bell as far as Worthing, where they had a cup of coffee, and then they returned to Brighton. Doing this soothed Ryan considerably. Next to Esther he loved his motor cycle. And, after his motor cycle, Cricket Results.

Chapter Two

1

On Wednesday morning Ryan was further soothed by a letter from Esther. She wrote:

Dear 'Mr Ryan',

I was very pleased to receive your letter, and will much look forward to meeting you outside the West Pier on Thursday – 7.30. Hoping you are keeping well.

Yours

Esther Downes.

Ryan was very glad that she had put 'Mr Ryan' in inverted commas. He had never for a moment hoped for a plain 'Peter'. He noticed that she had spelt 'receive' incorrectly. Apparently she had not been taught the '*i* before *e* except after *c*' rule. He was touched by her mistake, and loved her the more for it.

That night he put the letter under his pillow, and, defying a fear that he might be contracting some obscure contagious disease, kissed it several times.

2

On Thursday evening, Esther, not being particularly flustered, maintained her usual principle and arrived a minute and a half late for Ryan.

Esther had shown her mother the bag which Gorse had given her, and her mother had not disapproved very greatly. Esther had also told her mother that Gorse had a rich uncle who was a retired Colonel. Perhaps this had made Mrs Downes disapprove of the present of the bag less than she would ordinarily. The truth was that Gorse had succeeded in deceiving Mrs Downes almost as much as he had deceived her daughter.

Indeed, Mrs Downes at moments had even gone so far as to entertain high hopes about this mysterious young man.

But Esther had not told her mother that she had written to Ryan and agreed to meet him.

The squalid spiritual tumult caused by the two anonymous letters had, by Thursday evening, with both Esther and Ryan, somewhat subsided. They were both worried, but there was no panic.

They said 'Hullo', and shook hands shyly, and talked about the weather, and went through the turnstile, momentarily forgetting the cloud which overhung them both. But, having no conversation as they walked seawards along the west (the least populated) side of the West Pier, the cloud returned.

In sending an anonymous letter to Ryan as well as Esther, Gorse had, really, made yet another of those curious and gross blunders which he was to make throughout all his life.

Ryan had only to show his own letter to Esther, and all would have been well between them. Esther would have at once shown hers to him, and they would have both realized that there was a conspiracy against them. And they would, because of this, almost have been thrown into each other's arms.

But Gorse was, on this occasion, lucky. Or perhaps Gorse, in the extreme depths of his extremely deep mind, had been wise. Perhaps, in these depths, he knew that these two would not disclose such a secret to each other. He had, possibly, a sort of genius in regard to anonymous letters – knowing the curious effect, the passion for secrecy, which they have upon the minds of their recipients.

Just as Esther had never (until she had been at tea with Ryan at Hurst) for a moment thought of showing her own letter to Ryan, so it had not, as yet, occurred to Ryan that he might show his to her.

Esther and Ryan went to the extreme end of the Pier and looked, in a romantic atmosphere, towards the French coast. As it grew darker they returned, and played the slot machines outside the West Pier Theatre.

It was while they were doing this that there came to Ryan the same inspiration which had come to Esther at Hurst. Why not show her the letter, and free his mind from the beastly thing for good and all? Would it not, also, only be fair to her? What was against it?

Well, on second thoughts, there were reasons why it might be better to keep the thing secret.

In the first place, because the letter and the suggestions contained in it were so low, he would find telling her about it a hideously embarrassing thing to do. And it would not only be embarrassing to him: it would be even more so for Esther. It would shock her dreadfully if the letter had no truth in it; and if there were any truth in it the situation would be more awful still.

Then, quite apart from truth and falsehood, merely to show her such a filthy missive would be to disgust and frighten her. It was not a thing a proper person – a man with sensitive and decent feelings – could really do. It was, really, his duty, as Bell had advised, absolutely to ignore the thing. And if he did otherwise she might easily be 'put off' him – quite rightly put off.

But Ryan's father had always taught him to charge at difficulties – and to do so, really, belonged to his own temperament. Therefore, he did not quite put from his mind the notion of showing her the card.

It was now dark, and Ryan, leaving the matter in abeyance, manoeuvred Esther towards the part of the covered bench, facing the lights of the Palace Pier, upon which all five had sat upon that first meeting and to which Gorse had always taken Esther when he meant to kiss her. Such is the force of habit.

Esther was not much afraid of sitting with Ryan here. The place was dark, but a few people passed, and she was certainly within screaming distance of help.

After about ten minutes of talking Ryan tried to take Esther's hand, but she withdrew it.

'I told you you mustn't do that,' she said.

'But why?' said Ryan. 'What's the matter with it?'

'There's a lot the matter with it,' she said, being unable to think of anything else to say.

But there was, accidentally, something in the words she used and the way in which she used them which struck Ryan forcibly. Was Esther, conceivably, trying to intimate to him that there was something the matter with herself – that she suffered from some malady which made it dangerous to 'touch' her, as the missive had put it?

In which case had not his opportunity come? Should he not show her the letter, or somehow lead her on to talk about herself, or tactfully ask her about herself?

The impulsive Ryan believed that his opportunity had come and that he would be a fool to let it go by.

'But what *is* the matter?' he asked, looking at her earnestly.

'Well . . .' was all Esther could manage, and this encouraged Ryan further.

'Go on. Tell me,' he said. 'There *is* something the matter, isn't there?'

At this Esther was tempted to tell him about her own anonymous letter, but remembered her mother's advice not to do so.

She was merely silent, and Ryan was encouraged further still.

'Go on, tell me. What *is* the matter?' Ryan took the plunge. 'Tell me, is there anything the matter with you?'

'With me? How do you mean?'

'Well. The matter. With you. Personally. Tell me.'

'Personally? How do you mean?'

'Well. Personally. Is there anything wrong with you?'

'How?'

'Well – do you *suffer* from anything?'

'From any what?'

'From any illness. It's hard to put, but you must tell me. I have a reason. Now. Go on. Tell me. Do you, or do you not, suffer from any personal illness?'

Ryan was so eager and emphatic, and his question was so mysterious, that it struck Esther that he might be out of his mind. In that case, the warning on the postcard was a genuine one.

'What on earth do you mean?' she said. 'Do I suffer from a personal illness?'

'Just what I say.'

'Of course I don't,' said Esther. 'What on earth should make you think I do? I've never had any illness in my life so far – apart from the measles and whooping cough as a child, and an occasional cold.'

Because she was speaking the truth Esther's statement was utterly convincing, and Ryan was utterly convinced.

He bathed in delicious relief. At the same time he reproached himself for ever having even entertained such a suspicion. He should have taken Bell's advice and completely expunged the thing from his mind. He had behaved in a low way.

Esther, on the other hand, was now more than ever inclining to the opinion that Ryan might be mad. She therefore pursued a subject which Ryan was now only too anxious to drop.

'What on earth made you ask me such a question?' she asked.

'Oh – I don't know . . .'

Ryan, as well as feeling, was looking ashamed of himself.

'But there must have been a reason. Go on. What is it?'

'No. There wasn't.'

'But there must. Go on. Tell me.'

'No. There wasn't.'

'There was. I can see there was. Come on. Tell me.'

Ryan hesitated.

'Well,' he said. 'There was a little reason – but it was an absolutely absurd one, and I don't want to talk about it.'

'But please do.'

'No,' said Ryan. 'It's a little secret. I'll tell you one day, perhaps, when I know you better.' Ryan had an inspiration. 'By the way – talking of little secrets, what about *your* little secret? The one about Gorse. You said you'd tell me later.'

'No,' said Esther. 'That's still a little secret. Like yours.'

Esther now had a shot at some more truth.

'By the way, I've been out with him twice since I last saw you,' she said.

'Oh. Have you? I knew you were meeting him on Sunday evening, of course. Did he take you to the Metropole again?'

'Yes. He did.'

Gorse, if he had been listening to the dialogue which had just passed, would have been disquieted. Esther and Ryan had very nearly disclosed to each other their separate secrets. But now the danger had passed, and Gorse would have been relieved.

'And did he give you another cocktail?'

'Yes.'

A cocktail and a *half*, thought Esther, would have been the real truth.

'Well, he certainly *does* seem to be going it,' said Ryan. 'What did you do afterwards?'

'Oh – he just saw me home – part of the way.'

'How far?'

'Oh – just as far as the Clock Tower.'

'Oh – he did – did he?' said Ryan, and added, after a pause, 'Do you think he's keen on you? Like me?'

'Oh no, there's nothing of that sort.'

Remembering the kisses which had taken place on the very spot upon which they were now sitting, together with Gorse's near proposal of marriage, Esther knew that she had told another flagrant lie. On the other hand, it might be thought of as a legitimate lie. It was not Ryan's business, and his question had been, really, impudent – 'sauce'.

Ryan, as we know, was not really afraid of Gorse as a rival.

'No,' he said, 'I didn't really think there would be. I somehow don't believe Gorse really likes girls. At least not in the way other people do.'

That's what *you* think, was what Esther wanted to say. She was, of course – remembering the kisses and marriage offer – quite certain that Ryan was wrong.

But, actually, it was Esther who was wrong.

'What makes you think he doesn't?' asked Esther.

'Oh. I don't know . . . It's just an instinct.'

'What sort of instinct?'

'I can't really say. He's rather a funny one, our friend Gorse . . .'

'Funny? In what way? I don't see how he's funny.'

'Don't you? Well – I can't put my finger on it – but there it is. It's only an instinct. No doubt he's really very nice.'

'Well. I don't see anything funny about him. I think he's very nice.'

Esther, who now completely trusted (and, almost with her mother's approval, was contemplating marrying Gorse), was annoyed by Ryan's attitude. Also, she felt that it might derive from spite and jealousy. Also, she knew that 'funny' people were the first to call other people 'funny'. And all this not only lowered her opinion of Ryan as a completely sane person, but refreshed her grave suspicion that he was mad.

Ryan sensed her annoyance at once.

'Yes,' he said. 'I just *said* I thought he's probably very nice. Don't be angry.'

'I'm not angry.'

The subject was changed, but Esther continued to be slightly annoyed, and said that it was time for her to go home a good deal earlier than she might have otherwise.

As they walked towards the shore Ryan asked her if he might meet her tomorrow evening. She told him that she had arranged to meet Gorse – which was the truth.

'Oh,' said Ryan with a rather irritating lack of concern. 'Then what about Saturday?'

'No, I'm afraid that's no good. I've got to work this Saturday.'

'Oh yes. I'd forgotten. But couldn't we meet after your work – in the evening?'

'Well, no. I'm afraid that's no good. I get very tired, and I always spend the evenings with Mother on the Saturdays I work.'

Esther (the nearly 'spoiled') had now worked herself into a temper.

They had passed through the turnstile.

'Well,' said Ryan. 'Now may I see you home? Just as far as the Clock Tower?'

'No. I'd really rather go alone,' said the bad-tempered girl. 'I'd really rather – if you don't mind.'

'No. Of course I don't mind,' said Ryan, his calm infuriating Esther more than ever. 'But when am I going to see you again?'

'I don't know.'

'Well – what about Sunday? Perhaps we might go out on the bike again.'

Esther, in her anger, and the perturbation caused by her anger, thought that she must certainly not at present risk going into the country with Ryan again.

'No,' she said. 'I'm afraid I can't manage Sunday afternoon. My father's home on Sunday afternoons, and I don't see much of him, and so I have to stay in. I'm sorry.'

'Well, then – what about Sunday *evening*?'

Ryan was now getting a little angry himself.

'Yes,' said Esther. 'That seems all right.'

'Good. Then shall we meet just here? Seven-thirty. Sunday evening? All right?'

'Yes. Right you are. Seven-thirty – Sunday evening.'

She thought of thanking him for the evening. But she was in a temper, and he had only taken her on the Pier (not to the Metropole), so she did not.

'Very well, then,' said Ryan. 'Goodbye.'

And he offered his hand in rather a cool way. She shook his hand with equal coolness, and left him quickly.

Ryan, as he walked home, was fully aware that something very nearly approaching a quarrel had just taken place. But this did not bother him. It might, even, be taken as a good sign. Other girls had quarrelled in this way with Ryan, and such quarrels had certainly not shown disinterest on their part.

A little later, on his walk home, it struck Ryan that Esther was, perhaps, just a silly little ass, or a coquette whom he ought to leave stone cold – who should be allowed to stew in her own ridiculous juice.

Many things she had said and done pointed to this conclusion: and Ryan was for a few minutes exhilarated by the notion of quickly and dramatically abandoning Esther.

But this mood and theory did not last long. Our poor, infatuated Ryan, after a few minutes, was unable to sustain and fortify himself with this new idea.

PART NINE

THE CAR

Chapter One

I

When Esther met Gorse outside the West Pier on the Friday evening she found him in a state of subdued excitement.

This was feigned by Gorse, but Esther was completely taken in by it.

'Well – where are we going?' he said. 'The good old Met. again?'

'That suits me, if it does you.'

'Yes. That's what I'd like.' He took her arm as they crossed the road. 'And let's get there quickly, as I've got some news.'

'Yes. I thought you had. Good or bad?'

'Oh – good. Decidedly good, if only everything goes all right.'

'What is it? Tell me.'

'No. Let's wait till we're sitting down over our drinks. It needs a lot of talking over quietly.'

'Why – do you want my advice about something? Or does it concern me?'

'Yes, as a matter of fact, it *does* concern you. I hope, of course, that everything that concerns me concerns you – but this, as a matter of fact, concerns you in any case.'

'It all sounds very mysterious. Won't you tell me?'

'No – not until we're sitting down and drinking.'

'Very well.'

As soon as their drinks had come, at their usual table inside the Metropole, Esther said: 'Now then. The time's come. Go ahead.'

Gorse took a sip at his drink, sat back in his chair, and put his fingers together.

'Well,' he said. 'What would you think of yours truly as the owner of a car?'

'A car!'

'Yes, and not only a car – but one of the sweetest little semi-racing things you've ever seen in your life.'

'It sounds lovely to me. But where do I come in?'

'I'm coming to that in a moment. As I said, it's the loveliest little thing I've ever seen in my life. It's secondhand, actually – but as good as new, and going for a song. I know a lot about cars – I've been brought up with them as a child.'

'Yes. I'm sure it's wonderful, but I still don't see where I come in.'

'Well – would you like to be part owner of a car?'

'How'd I do that?'

'Oh – just put in a little money for it, and then you'd be part owner. And then, when I've sold it again, you'd get your percentage – double your money back, probably. If I can only get it, it'll be one of the finest investments in the world.'

'But why is it going so cheap?'

'The man's hard up for ready cash. I know that for a fact. He's having to make a rush sale. I've known him since I was a kid.'

'Who is he? What's his name?'

'Gosling,' said Gorse, who had prepared himself for this question. 'He's got a garage out on the London Road . . . Well – are you coming in on it? It's the chance of a lifetime, I can assure you.'

'But how much would I have to put in?' asked Esther. 'About?'

'It's not a question of "about". I know the exact sum. It's fifteen pounds.'

'Fifteen pounds!' exclaimed Esther. 'But I couldn't manage all that!'

'Don't be silly. Of course you could, if you've got all that money saved. And you're going to make double – or only a little under.'

Esther did not like this at all. The two pounds she had handed over to Gorse (and had back) was one matter. Fifteen pounds was another.

'And what's the full price of the car?'

'Ah – that I'm not quite sure. It's going to be pretty stiff, and I'm going to haggle.'

'Then how do you know it's so cheap?'

With this Esther nearly tripped Gorse up.

'Oh – I know roughly,' he said. 'He's mentioned eighty, and it'll only be a matter of five or ten pounds either way. Well – are you in?'

Esther was deeply reluctant. Fifteen pounds! She thought of what her mother would say about all this.

She decided to make a stand.

'You know, I'd really rather not,' she said. 'I don't like "speculation", or whatever you call it, and I know my mother wouldn't approve.'

'But you needn't tell your mother.'

'No. But I don't like it myself. Honestly I don't. I'd really rather you left me out. It'll be your car – so why don't you buy it on your own? I'd really rather not. Do you mind?'

There was a pause. Gorse took a sip at his drink, and leaned back again, and looked at her.

'Well,' he said. 'To tell you the truth, I'm afraid it's a bit too late, and you've *got* to come in.'

'*Got* to? How?'

'Well – you've got to unless I'm going to lose it – and it's the chance of a lifetime.'

'How? I don't see.'

'Well – it's all rather a long story.'

'Tell me.'

'Oh dear – I'm afraid you'll think I'm trying to borrow money from you again, but I'll tell you all the same. You see, it's a question of a deposit.'

'Deposit?'

'Yes. You see, there are a lot of other people after it, and if I'm going to get it I've got to give this man Gosling a deposit – and he's asked for fifteen pounds. He's so hard up that he wants even that. And I said I'd give it to him.'

'Then why don't you? If you've got the money to buy the car!'

'Because I haven't got fifteen pounds.'

'Not fifteen pounds if you're going to buy the car for eighty?'

'No. Now I'm coming to the story. I haven't got all that money just at the moment, and if I don't give him the fifteen pounds tomorrow, Saturday, it'll go to somebody else. I *know* it.'

'But when will you get the money – I mean the fifteen pounds?'

'On Monday – absolutely for certain. That's when my stepmother pays my allowance into my account. She does it monthly. So I can pay it back to you on Monday. And then, on Wednesday, unless there's any hitch, there's a hundred and fifty pounds coming to me, and all's well.'

'A hundred and fifty! Where's that coming from?'

'It's coming from my aunt. She died two or three months ago, and left it to me.'

Esther reflected that Gorse went in for rather a lot of aunts and uncles. There had been, so far, only one uncle and one aunt, but still this somehow seemed to her too many.

'And why haven't you got the money – if she died three months ago?'

'Oh – you know all these maddening legal delays. Or perhaps you don't. I do – I've had to suffer from them enough. It's a question of probate, and all that. I don't expect you know what probate means. However – it's all over now. I had a letter from my lawyer only this morning and he said I should get the cheque by Wednesday – or Thursday at the latest. I think I've got the letter on me.'

Gorse began to fish in his breast pocket. 'Would you like to see it, or do you still not trust me?'

'No,' said Esther. 'Of course I trust you.'

Gorse had expected her to say this, but was relieved that she had. Otherwise he would have had to pretend that he had left the letter at home.

'Well,' he said. 'I'm very glad you do. If you don't trust me, that means you really don't like me, and that's the end of all my hopes, isn't it?'

'What hopes?'

'You know exactly what I mean. But as I can't make love to you in the lounge of an hotel, perhaps we'd better drop the subject and return to where we are. Tell me now – will you help me in the chance of a lifetime? I've put all my cards on the table. Don't if you don't want to – of course.'

'No. It's not that. It's just that I hate speculation, as I said. And I know my mother wouldn't approve. And it was she who *gave* me all that money – wasn't it?'

'Yes. I know,' said Gorse. 'But do be a sport. I always thought you were one, and I believe you are still. Won't you?'

'I can't make up my mind,' said Esther, clearly weakening.

'I know your mother must be very nice,' said Gorse. 'But all mothers are old-fashioned – aren't they? And one's got to be modern and a sport – hasn't one? One's got to take risks – that's doing things the right way. And if one doesn't do things the right way, one never gets anywhere. One just gets stuck where one is.'

Thus Gorse, with that peculiar insight into women's minds which characterized him, was playing cleverly upon Esther's strongest inner passion – the passion to 'better' herself, and, in order to do this, to behave exactly as those 'better' than herself did. His use of the words 'the right way' won the day for Gorse.

'Well,' said Esther. 'Perhaps you're right.'

2

Gorse saw that he had won the day.

'Of course I'm right,' said Gorse. 'And just think of it. You and I, going wherever we like, and driving up to the Metropole in one of the smartest little cars on the road. Of course, it's not a Rolls, or anything like that, but I'll bet you there'll be plenty of Rolls owners who'll envy us. You just wait till you see it.'

Esther, already a little intoxicated by her cocktail, was additionally intoxicated by this picture.

Esther, although she had been on the back of motorcycles, had never actually stepped inside a car in her life. And the idea of doing so, and driving up to the Metropole, completely went to her head. All her fears left her.

'All right,' she said. 'Then it's a go.'

'Good,' said Gorse. 'I knew it would be. I knew you were a sport.'

A thought struck Esther.

'But how am I going to get the money to you? It's got to be by tomorrow, you say, and I have to work all Saturday.'

'Yes. It's got to be tomorrow – and tomorrow afternoon, too – or I'll lose it. Can't you take it to your work – and then meet me somehow?'

'Yes,' said Esther. 'I suppose I can.'

'I'll look in at your shop and buy some sweets early in the afternoon, shall I?' said Gorse. 'And then you can slip it to me. The money's got to be with Gosling by four o'clock.'

'All right. If you don't mind seeing me at my worst.'

'How worst?'

'Well – serving behind a counter.'

'I don't think you'll be at your worst. There's no worst with you,' said Gorse. 'At least not to me, at any rate. Everything's always the best.'

After this compliment there was a pause.

Then another thought struck Esther.

'Are you old enough to drive a car?' she asked.

'Ah,' said Gorse. 'There are ways and means.'

And for Gorse there certainly were. The precocious Gorse was more precocious in the matter of cars than in any other department of life. When it came to car-buying, car-selling, or car-trickery, Gorse probably knew more than any other young man of his age in England, Europe, or the world.

'Then, when I meet you after that,' said Gorse, 'I'll take you for your first spin in it. I know he'll let me take a run or two in it before I've actually got it. If he will – what about going out in it on Sunday afternoon?'

'Oh – I'm sorry. Sunday afternoon's bad for me. It's about the only time I ever see my father, and Mother likes me to stay in.'

'Well, then – Sunday evening?'

'Oh lord – that's no good either. I've gone and promised to meet your friend Ryan.'

'Oh – I'd forgotten about Ryan,' said Gorse truthfully, for, in the somewhat strenuous extraction of the fifteen pounds from Esther, he actually had. 'How did you get on with him?'

'Oh – all right . . .'

'Where did you go?'

'On the Pier.'

'And what did you do there, pray?'

'Oh – we walked, and played with a few slot machines, and sat down for a bit, and then came home.'

'Is that all?'

'Yes.'

'Did he hold your hand again?'

'He tried to.'

'But you didn't let him?'

'No.'

'Why not? There's not much harm in holding hands, if there're people about.'

'Oh – I don't know. I suppose I'm a bit afraid of him.'

'Naturally. And what did he do when you refused him?'

'Oh – he behaved all right. But you know, I *do* think there's something funny about that boy.'

'Ah-ha. So you're beginning to see that your Uncle Ralph knows a thing or two, after all. But what did he do funny?'

'It wasn't what he did. It was more what he said.'

'What did he say?'

'I don't know. It was just *funny*, somehow.'

'But he must have said something. Go on. What was it?'

'I can't quite remember now. But he asked me if there was anything the matter with me – whether I suffered from any illness.'

At this moment, for the first time, Gorse saw that he had made a serious blunder – that the two might compare notes. He looked thoughtful, and there was a pause.

'How very strange,' said Gorse. 'And what did you reply?'

'I said of course there wasn't, and I asked him if he'd gone mad.'

'And what did he reply?'

'I've forgotten how it went now.'

'Did you ask him why he asked?' asked Gorse.

'Oh yes. So I did.'

'And what did he say?' Gorse, although Esther did not perceive this, was looking gravely yet anxiously at her.

'He said it was a secret – a little secret. He wouldn't tell me. And that's funny in itself.'

'It certainly is,' said Gorse, breathing again.

'I mean *why* should he ask such a question?' said Esther. 'Can *you* think why?'

Gorse thought before replying, and was inspired.

'Well. I *could* make a guess,' he said.

'What?'

'No. I'd rather not say.'

'Now. Come on. You're my friend – aren't you? And you're advising me. You can't keep me in the dark if you're doing that. It's not fair. Go on.'

'Well – it's very difficult to put.'

'Go on. Out with it.'

'Well, if he wanted, later on, to go further than – just holding your hand. And if he wanted to go further even than kissing you – well –'

'Go on. What do you mean by further than kissing me?'

'Really. This is a bit indelicate, you know.'

'Go on.'

'Well, if he wanted to – to –' said Gorse, hesitating. 'Well – to *go the whole hog* – if I've *got* to say it. You know what I mean . . .'

'Yes. I know. Go on.'

'Well, if he wanted that, he might want to make certain beforehand that you were quite well, in a certain way. I don't know if you know it, but there *are* certain diseases, you know.'

'Yes. I know. But what a filthy idea.'

'Yes, very filthy. But people with twisted minds develop filthy ideas – don't they? Of course I may be wrong – I may be completely maligning him on this particular point.'

'I hope you are,' said Esther. 'But it was a funny thing to ask me. And then the funny thing about it all is that he called *you* funny.'

As soon as she had made this indiscretion – one forgivable because characteristic of girls of her age – Esther regretted it. She had, she realized, started 'making mischief'.

'Oh, he did – did he?' said Gorse. 'Did he say in what way I was funny?'

'No. He just said he thought you were – a bit.'

'And did you ask him why he thought me funny?'

'Yes.'

'And he said?'

'He said he didn't know.'

'A very curious character,' said Gorse. 'Do *you* think me funny?'

'Me? No. Anything but. *You've* got your head screwed on all right. Anybody can see that.'

'Well, I believe I have, fairly well,' said Gorse, and added, 'Of course it's typical of funny people to go about calling other people funny.'

This, it will be remembered, was exactly the thought which had visited Esther at the time.

'Yes,' she said. 'I know it is.'

'But you're still going about with him?'

'Well, I don't see really how I can get out of it. He's very polite and he hasn't done anything wrong so far. And I'll see that it's always in public places.'

'Very well,' said Gorse indulgently. 'Go your own way. But if you get into trouble don't say your Uncle Ralph didn't warn you. And now let's change the subject – shall we?'

The subject was changed, the second drinks were finished, and they went outside and on to the West Pier.

When it was dark enough Gorse took her to the familiar spot, and kissed her in the familiar way. While doing this he said: 'You know, I'm going to ask you a very important question very soon now.'

'Are you?' said Esther.

'Yes,' said Gorse. 'Have you any idea what sort of answer you're going to give?'

'I don't know,' said Esther.

'Very well,' said Gorse. 'Uncle Ralph'll have to wait. He's a patient fellow – is Uncle Ralph.'

'Is he?'

'Yes. But he knows what he wants, and quite often he gets what he wants,' said Gorse.

Esther allowed him to escort her as far as the Clock Tower. He arranged to call at the sweet-shop at two-thirty tomorrow (Saturday) afternoon in order to collect the fifteen pounds. Then they were to meet at seven-thirty outside the West Pier on Monday. He would then, he said, have the money to pay her back.

Esther was lighthearted as she left Gorse, but Gorse had a lot of thinking to do.

3

Ryan had had the effrontery to call him 'funny' to Esther.

Also, Esther and Ryan, despite all Gorse's efforts, were still meeting each other. And, this being so, they might easily still disclose to each other their anonymous letters from himself.

Previously Gorse had had little jealousy or hatred of Ryan. The anonymous letters had been sent mostly for the pure pleasure of the thing. But now Gorse, in working against Ryan, had two definite motives.

Ryan, if he went on meeting Esther, might at last show his letter, and, by doing so, perhaps win her. In this case Gorse's plot in regard to the car might fall through: for Ryan (who also knew a lot about cars) might advise and sway Esther.

Gorse's other motive was that of revenge. He did not propose to be called 'funny' without returning the blow – and this with double force.

Gorse, on his way home, decided that what he called to himself 'stronger measures' would have to be taken with the person he called to himself 'Master Ryan'.

Chapter Two

I

On Saturday morning Ryan again arrived early, and on his motor cycle, at the house belonging to Bell's aunt in Bigwood Avenue.

Because Bell's lighthearted advice about the anonymous letter had shown itself to be so entirely and beautifully correct, Ryan's heart was warm towards Bell, and, as a reward, he proposed to take Bell for a long trip into the country. The Sage, Ryan knew, enjoyed riding on the back of a motor cycle as much as he enjoyed ice-cream.

Bell saw and heard Ryan arriving, but, as chance would have it, he had neither folding chess set, nor book, nor even pipe, to hand: and so there were no means of making an ass of himself. He went unaffectedly to the door, and invited Ryan to come into his front room.

They talked for a little while, and then Ryan said:

'Oh, by the way – about that anonymous letter – you were quite right. It was simply drivel. I've found out for a fact. I ought to have taken your advice in the first place, and thrown it into the waste-paper basket. I'm sorry I didn't, and I want to thank you for it.'

'Not at all,' said Bell. 'Only too glad if I've been of any help.'

'And as that cloud's passed,' said Ryan, 'and it's another cloudless day, what about you and I having a nice long trip on the bike into the country?'

Bell readily agreed to this, and in five minutes' time they were both on the motorcycle.

They travelled that day over a great deal of Sussex, having lunch at Haywards Heath, and tea at Hurst. At about six they returned to Bigwood Avenue, and washed, and then strolled down to the Brighton Front.

Between the two Piers they saw Gertrude Perks, who was walking alone.

They did their utmost to cut her, but she came up to them, saying, 'Hullo – how are you two boys getting on?'

2

Ryan and Bell were walking in the direction of the Palace Pier.

After Ryan and Bell had greeted her politely, Gertrude walked with them in the same direction.

Ryan and Bell now tried very hard to do two things – to remain polite, and to think of an excuse for getting away from Gertrude. They were fairly successful with the former, but not adroit with the latter.

As all three drew near the Palace Pier, the situation was extremely, almost unutterably, painful.

Because of its painfulness, the naïve and *gauche* Bell could not resist giving Ryan a Nudge with his elbow.

Because Bell was so naïve and *gauche* this Nudge was an enormous one – ridiculously so. So much so that Gertrude herself observed it.

Ryan, agonized both by the Nudge and by his almost certain knowledge that Gertrude had observed it, was thrust into two minds – several minds.

Did the Nudge mean merely 'Isn't this awful?' Or did it mean 'What are we going to do? For heaven's sake get us out of this. You're more experienced than I am and you ought to find a way'?

Or did it mean, perhaps, that Bell wanted to be alone with Gertrude?

Ryan inclined very strongly to this last point of view. Wishes are, unfortunately, and, as we all know, the parents of points of view, even with such sincere and delicate-minded people as Ryan. All Ryan wanted to do was to escape at the earliest possible moment – to run for his life, in fact – and here was his chance.

His reason, in due course, childlike, began to obey his wishes. Was not Bell an 'other one'? Was not Gertrude an 'other one'? Did not 'other ones' naturally desire to pair with each other? Would it not be simple tact on the part of Ryan, would it not, perhaps, be his *duty*, to leave these two alone?

When they were within about fifteen yards' distance from the entrance to the Palace Pier, Ryan made his decision.

'Well – this is where I have to buzz off,' he said, stopping and looking at his watch as if he had suddenly realized he was in a dreadful hurry. 'I've got to put the bike away, and the garage closes at eight. So will you two forgive me?'

'Yes,' said Gertrude with alacrity. 'Of course. If you're in a hurry. Nice to have met you. I only hope we'll meet again soon.'

'Yes. I hope we will. Well – I *must* go. So long – both.'

'So long!' said Gertrude cheerfully.

'So long,' said Bell.

Thus Ryan had done his duty by Bell, and should have been pleased with himself. But, unluckily, as he had left the couple together, he had looked at Bell's face, and had caught an unspeakably forlorn and deserted expression upon it.

And so, as he walked home, Ryan had an uneasy feeling that he had not, really, done his strict duty.

3

Gertrude had, as Ryan feared, observed Bell's enormous and ridiculous Nudge.

Now the real meaning of Bell's Nudge had been merely 'Isn't this awful?' – nothing more at all. But Gertrude had interpreted it quite differently.

Gertrude had, in fact, put exactly the same construction upon it that Ryan had. With Gertrude, as with Ryan before her, a wish had given birth to a thought. Not that Gertrude was in any way attracted by Bell. She thought him plain, affected, eccentric, and what she would call 'soppy'. But Gertrude was susceptible to flattery, and if the Nudge meant what she thought it did – 'I want to be alone with this girl' – it was a compliment of a serious kind.

And this made her see Bell in a new light. His 'soppiness' and other defects practically all vanished and she believed she could even discern in him some charm.

The unfortunate thing was that Ryan had absolutely confirmed her interpretation of the Nudge by his hasty departure with an obviously false excuse.

4

'Well,' said Bell weakly. 'What are we going to do now?'

'Well – as we're outside the Palace Pier – what about going on it?'

Bell tried to think of an excuse, but the feat was beyond him. Also, in common politeness, he could not make an excuse so immediately after Ryan had made his. The wretched girl would know that she was being left stone cold – stranded.

'Very well,' he said, and they went through the turnstile, Gertrude offering to pay, but Bell not permitting this.

As they walked seawards remarkable thoughts entered Gertrude's head – thoughts very similar to those she had entertained some nights previously when she was with Ryan.

What if 'other ones' (she thought) were, after all, destined to pair with 'other ones'? What if they had no other choice? What if they must simply make do with them?

And here was Bell, who had nudged his friend in order to be alone with her. Would she not be foolish to reject him? Was it not her business to encourage him?

Though he was now much more attractive in her eyes than before, Gertrude still could not say that she had any feeling for Bell. But, apart from anything else, after her rebuff, kindly as it was from Ryan, she was in desperate need of reassuring herself – of proving that she could at least magnetize someone. And here was her chance.

Bell was very untalkative as they walked along, and Gertrude put this down to sudden shyness or fear.

Was it not, therefore, her business to dispel this shyness and fear? Must she not, in fact (as with Ryan before), employ Personality and Boldness? She decided to do this.

'Do you like playing with slot machines?' she asked.

'I don't really know,' said Bell. 'Do you?'

'You seem doubtful,' said Gertrude. 'Do you think it too childish?'

'Well – quite apart from the expense involved – I'd certainly say I should regard it as a somewhat puerile – indeed, I might say sterile – form of activity. Don't you?'

'I don't know. You see, I don't know what "puerile" or "sterile" means. What do they? What's "puerile"?'

'Oh – just boyish – as of a boy. Derivation from the Latin.'

'And "sterile"?'

'Well – arid – leading to nothing. Unproductive.'

'And what does "arid" mean?'

'Dry,' said Bell. 'Dried up.'

'You know, you're a bit dry yourself, you know,' said Gertrude, 'with all your long words. Have you *got* to use them?'

'No. I haven't got to. I just like the right expression, that's all. I like to hit upon the *mot juste*.'

'The Mow *What*?' said Gertrude rather violently.

'The *mot juste*,' repeated Bell. 'That's French and means exactly the correct word.'

'*Joost* the right word, in fact?' said Gertrude jocularly.

'Yes,' said Bell. 'If you like to put it that way.'

'You with your French and Latin,' said Gertrude. 'You know, a lot of people might think you're a bit conceited.'

'Might they?'

'But I don't,' said Gertrude. 'I can see through you all right.'

And it had just occurred to Gertrude that she could, indeed, see beyond Bell's affectations. Furthermore, it now seemed to her that these were so childish that they might come to be slightly enchanting rather than a flaw in his character.

'Well, I certainly hope I'm not conceited,' said Bell.

'No. I don't believe you are. You're just a baby, really, in spite of all your long words,' said Gertrude, and she took his arm and led him towards the footballing slot machine with which she had played with Ryan. 'Now come and forget all about your French and Latin and have a bit of fun with me.'

Reluctantly Bell obeyed her. He tried to put in both pennies, but she would not allow this, and put one in for herself.

There is little skill required in this game, but there is just enough to make a person with enthusiasm and his wits about him beat a person who is devoid of either. Needless to say, Bell lost. Gertrude made him play again, and he again lost. Then, at the third game, she instructed Bell and absolutely forced him to win.

As with Ryan previously, while playing, Gertrude managed to get her head extremely near to Bell's. This did not terrify him as much as it had Ryan. In his inexperience he thought it must be an accident, or even as something necessarily belonging to such a game.

He was rather pleased at winning the third game, and when Gertrude (taking his arm again, which he did not like) led him on to the next machine (the race-horse one) he was more willing to play.

Of course he lost again. But Gertrude cleverly deluded him into the thought that he had won the third race by his own merits, and she could see that he was again not displeased.

'Third time lucky seems to be your motto,' said Gertrude. 'You can beat me easy when you learn. Only you're such a slow starter, that's all.'

In this last remark there was a double meaning which Bell completely missed.

She took his arm again, and they walked on.

They did not have to walk long before it was dark enough for Gertrude's purposes. She took him to the same seat to which she had taken Ryan. The force of habit again.

After a while Gertrude repeated, exactly, her tactics with Ryan.

'It's a lovely night – ain't it?' she said. 'Ain't it?'

'Yes. It certainly is.'

'Or a night for love?' said Gertrude. 'Which?'

The foolish Bell still had no inkling of her meaning or intentions.

'Yes,' he said. 'Gazing at the stars in their firmament is certainly an ennobling experience – small as it makes one feel.'

'Yes,' said Gertrude. 'It makes one feel lonely. Doesn't it you?'

'Yes. It certainly does,' said Bell gravely.

Bell had said this in all innocence, but Gertrude, remembering that he had nudged Ryan in order to be alone with her, was certain that he meant it as an invitation. And, remembering his shyness, she decided to take the initiative. She put her arm round Bell and endeavoured impulsively to 'nestle' her head against his shoulder.

But she was too impulsive and something went wrong. Instead of arriving on Bell's shoulder, her head somehow bumped into Bell's face, and her spectacles hit his own, with a clattering noise and very nearly knocking them off.

Only spectacle-wearers who have been embraced awkwardly by other spectacle-wearers will be able to comprehend fully the ineffable gruesomeness of the noise made by the clatter of lens against lens, and rims against rims.

Bell nearly jumped up, but managed to remain seated, and a moment later Gertrude had properly 'nestled' her head upon his shoulder.

'Aren't *you* lonely?' said Gertrude. 'Aren't *you* lonely – like poor little me?'

'Yes . . .' said Bell. 'Indeed . . . Yes. I am . . .' Then he managed to throw in 'I suppose . . .'

'I thought you were,' said Gertrude. 'You're like me. You're all solitary. There you are. There's one of your long words for you – "solitary".'

Bell, fantastically unsophisticated as he was, now knew roughly the sort of thing Gertrude was after, and tried to think of some means of defence.

All Bell had learned in life had been Learning – and so his mind at once flew to this. He had never thought that Learning would be of assistance to him in a predicament such as this.

He loved, in his own way, Learning for its own sake, and he also hoped to advance in life by using it. But now it was to be used on a Pier in the darkness against an importunate girl!

'Ah, yes,' said Bell. 'Solitude. A serious problem indeed. In the words of Keats, "O solitude! if I must with thee dwell, Let it not be among the jumbled heap. Of murky buildings; climb with me the steep – Nature's observatory – whence the dell, Its flowery slopes, its rivers' crystal swell, May seem a span; let me thy vigils keep, 'Mongst boughs pavilioned, where the deer's swift leap, Startles the wild bee from the fox-glove bell. But though I'll gladly trace these scenes with thee, Yet the sweet converse of an innocent mind, Whose words are images of thoughts refined, Is my soul's pleasure; and it sure must be, Almost the highest bliss of humankind, When to thy haunts two kindred spirits flee." Very finely put – don't you think?'

'Yes,' said Gertrude, who had not understood a word of the sonnet, and who, of course, did not want this sort of thing at all. However, she decided to go on trying.

'I like to hear you reciting Poetry,' she said. 'Go on. Recite some more.'

'Some more about what?'

'About solitude. It's romantic. Go on.'

Bell was silent.

'I can't think of one about solitude,' he said – weakly, because exhausted by thought.

'Well – about anything romantic. Go on.'

Bell went on thinking.

'Well,' he said. 'As it's dark – what about darkness? Complete darkness. What about Milton on his own darkness? You know your Milton? You know that he was blind?'

'Yes,' said Gertrude, who did know this.

'Very well,' said Bell. 'Let's try this – "When I consider how my light is spent, Ere half my days in this dark world and wide, And that one talent which is death to hide, Lodged with me useless . . ."' And Bell completed a second sonnet.

Gertrude, who was still hardly able to understand a word, was, however, quite clever enough to see that Bell had been clever enough to dodge Romance.

'Yes. That's nice, too,' she said. 'Now go on. Let's have some more.'

'But what?'

'Oh – anything. Just about the night and the stars, *I* don't mind.'

Keats's *Bright star, would I were as steadfast as thou art* came into Bell's head, but he was quick enough to see that the end of this would be most appallingly and pertinently romantic.

'Are you interested in the stars?' he said, with a new clever idea in his mind. 'In Astronomy?'

'Yes,' said Gertrude. 'I like hearing about Astrology.'

'No. I said Astronomy – not Astrology,' said Bell.

'What's the difference?'

'Well – one is the art of divining the future by the stars – that's Astrology. The other's the science of the stars – of the constellations.'

Bell felt that he was getting nearer the shore, and that, if only he went on swimming hard, he might reach it.

'All right, then,' said Gertrude. 'Tell me about your old Astronomy.'

'Very well,' said Bell. 'You see that star, there? The large one just above the extreme tip of the West Pier?'

'Yes.'

Luckily, amongst the branches of Learning which Bell had climbed, a little knowledge of Astronomy was included. He now proceeded, for a matter of ten minutes, to explain constellations to Gertrude.

He had reached the shore. Gertrude gave in. She was deeply hurt. So she could not even touch the heart of another 'other one'!

But she was not a resentful girl.

'All right,' she said at last, forgivingly interrupting Bell's flow of talk, and removing her head from his shoulder. 'We can't go on talking about the stars all night – can we? They're cold – and I'm cold, too. Shall we go off home? It's getting late.'

'Yes. It is a bit late, and I'm rather cold, too,' said Bell, and they rose and walked towards the turnstiles.

Bell offered to see her home, but she would not allow him to do so.

Deflated and wearied by her experience, Gertrude walked home.

Exhilarated and stimulated by his escape, Bell did the same. These two made a very tragic couple.

For, when Bell was in bed, he remembered the warmth of Gertrude's body against his own, and half regretted what he had done. He even hoped he might meet her again. Gertrude, in bed, also remembered the warmth of Bell's body, and that night she cried before going to sleep.

They were not fated to meet again.

Bell was a bachelor all his life. Gertrude, on the other hand, by a mixture of divine luck and intense labour, married the son of a fishmonger in George Street, Hove. The fishmonger died, and his son inherited his father's business. Gertrude had three children by this son. These were hideous, noisy, and ugly, but consoled her. Bell consoled himself with the thought that Learning was to him both wife and mistress.

But Gertrude and Bell were not effectually consoled.

Chapter Three

1

Esther and Ryan met outside the West Pier on Sunday at the time appointed and spent an evening which was not particularly eventful.

Esther was amiable and in an unusually carefree mood.

She had completely thrown off that fear she had momentarily had that she was 'speculating' and might not recover her fifteen pounds.

Gorse had called at the sweet-shop on the Saturday afternoon, and, serving him with sweets for which he had jokingly asked, she had secretly passed the notes over to him. He arranged to meet her on the Monday evening, and he said that, if Gosling would allow it (and he was almost certain he would), he might have the car with him when he met her.

She had liked the joke with the sweets (he had asked for pear drops and had been very amusingly particular about their size and colour), and when he had gone she knew she was beginning to like and trust Gorse more and more.

Also, she was excited about the car itself, in which Gorse had said she might still have a share, if she liked. She almost contemplated doing this.

Esther, as we know, had never stepped inside a car in her life, and the thought of doing so exhilarated her to a degree which cannot easily be understood by those who have entered or driven cars. Esther, in fact, was looking forward tremendously to tomorrow evening – could hardly wait for it.

2

Ryan, of course, benefited by her good spirits, which he at once sensed, and which made him happier and more hopeful. If he had known to whom and what he was indebted for this renewed hope and happiness, his spirits would have fallen low.

When it was dark, and they had played gaily at several slot machines, Ryan tried to take Esther to the usual spot on the covered bench. But this, for once, was occupied. They therefore went to the other side of the Pier, and sat down on a bench facing Worthing.

The very distant lights of Worthing Pier were just discernible, and Ryan told her that when it was so clear that Worthing Pier was visible from Brighton it was usually a sign of bad weather to come. Esther told him that she knew this. It is, in fact, an old Brighton legend.

They began to talk about Brighton. Ryan knew it well, but Esther knew it better and chattered to him cheerfully.

Then Ryan took her hand, and Esther did not withdraw it.

Ryan had by now, of course, almost completely forgotten about his own anonymous letter. And with Esther the passage of time, together with her excitement about the car, had very nearly removed the cloud. As these two sat facing Worthing at this moment neither of the two letters was in the minds of either of them.

Having held her hand in a variety of increasingly affectionate ways, Ryan was emboldened to kiss Esther. She allowed this, and he put his arm round her, and kissed her again from time to time.

Esther in some ways enjoyed Ryan's kisses more than Gorse's, but in some ways she did not. After Gorse, Ryan seemed a little timid, tame, even lukewarm.

Then, all at once, Esther recalled the hypothesis that Ryan was a dangerous lunatic, and she said, 'We mustn't go on doing this, you know.'

Ryan at once assented. His highest hopes had been exceeded; he was a good deal more than content; and he knew that this was the moment to leave well alone.

It was he himself who, after looking at his watch, suggested that it was time to go home.

When they were on the front again he asked if he might see her home, and she said, 'Oh no – don't bother.'

Determined not to press anything, Ryan at once agreed to leave her, but asked her when he might see her again.

'Now, let's think,' she said. 'Tomorrow's no good. Nor the day after. What about Wednesday?'

She had thus easily dodged telling him what she was doing tomorrow evening. She did not quite know why she implied that she was engaged on the day after. Perhaps it was because, if Gorse had the car on Monday, he might also have it on Tuesday, and then she would get two drives in it on successive evenings. The car had gone to Esther's head.

'Very well,' said Ryan. 'It's a long while to wait, but I'll put up with it somehow. Seven-thirty – here – Wednesday?'

'Right you are.'

They shook hands, and Ryan thought he would throw in a final compliment.

'You know I'd wait for you – don't you? For however long,' he said. 'You know I'd do anything for you. I'd die for you.'

'Would you?'

'Yes – die or do *murder* for you,' said Ryan solemnly, and he looked at her with burning eyes. 'Goodbye.'

Coming from one who was possibly a raving maniac, this remark was not a happy one.

Nor were the burning eyes exactly of any help to Ryan.

Chapter Four

I

On the Monday evening Gorse was waiting for Esther at the usual place, and as they walked towards the Metropole Esther noticed that Gorse was talking in a rather strained, self-conscious way.

Outside the Metropole, Esther observed, among a few other cars, a slim, exquisite, beautiful, open car, painted bright red – a dream-car.

She looked at this, and then at Gorse, who, it seemed to her, was purposely, and with an effort, not looking at it.

2

Her heart leapt with joy and hope. Could it be possible?

Once, when Esther was a child, she had been taken to a Christmas party for children. At this party there had been a Christmas tree, and, on this Christmas tree, presents for the children had been hung. Amongst these was a small doll's house, with miniature furniture, and on this doll's house, the moment she had seen it, Esther had set her heart passionately. She wanted absolutely nothing else on earth. Could it conceivably be for her? She had been compelled to wait in anguish until the Christmas presents were given to the children, and then, to her indescribable joy, she was given the doll's house.

Her emotions now were almost exactly the same as then. Could this dream-car be the one Gorse had acquired – or rather was in the process of acquiring? She wanted absolutely nothing else on earth.

3

They found their usual table at the Metropole, and as soon as their drinks had come, and they had sipped at them, Gorse said, 'Well – a little business transaction first, I think,' and began to fish in his back trouser pocket.

'Oh – must we be so businesslike?' said Esther, very pleased that he was being so, for all that.

'Yes, we must,' said Gorse. 'At any rate, in the present stage of our relations. Perhaps a time'll come when all my money's yours and all yours is mine. My money arrived all right.'

Another near-proposal of marriage, Esther observed.

'Well, here you are,' Gorse went on, counting the notes and putting them on to the table. 'Unless you want a share in the car, and you want me to keep it for you. But I don't think you want that – do you?'

The curious thing, now that she had seen the money, was that Esther was not absolutely certain that she did not want precisely this. Indeed, if the car was the red dream-car outside, she really believed that she would like to have a share in it. She did not pick up the notes from the table, and she played for time.

'Oh – I don't know,' she said. 'I've been wondering about that. Tell me. Did he let you have the car this evening?'

'Yes. He did. And if you're agreeable we'll go out for our first little spin in it together this evening.'

'Where is it? Where have you left it?'

'Ah – never you mind. It's not a long walk, though.'

'Tell me. What *sort* of car is it? What does it look like?'

'You're very curious, aren't you? Well – curiosity killed the cat. You must hold yourself in patience for a little. You'll be seeing it soon enough.'

Esther was now quite sure that the red dream-car was the one.

'Well,' she said. 'It's difficult to make up one's mind – I mean about taking a share.'

'Ah – so you're seriously contemplating it?'

'Well, I am *thinking* about it. It *would* be an investment, wouldn't it?'

'Oh yes – it'd be that all right. As I've told you, I'm going to sell that thing, after I've had some fun with it for a bit, for pretty nearly double the price – if not quite. I know about cars, as I've told you too, and I know when I'm on to a good thing. And it's not the first time I've done it, by any means – though my previous deals have only been more or less with little tin Lizzies.'

'Well – if it *is* an investment, I don't see why I shouldn't.'

'In which case I retain the fifteen pounds?'

'Yes.'

'And give you a receipt for it?'

'Yes. I suppose so.'

Gorse looked at Esther. He had not anticipated that Esther would trust him to this extent. He had to make up his mind quickly as to what he was to do in this new situation – to see if he could exploit it in any way.

After a pause in the conversation, he hit upon what he thought would be the best thing.

'No,' he said. 'I'm not going to let you.'

'Why not?'

'Well – you said you were afraid of speculation – didn't you? And I don't want to be the one to introduce you to bad ways – if you call them bad.'

'I don't. And I'm not really afraid any more. Honestly.'

'No. I know you think you're not. But I believe you still are at the bottom of your heart. And I'm sure your mother is.'

'Oh. That's a different matter. I needn't tell her.'

'No. I think it'd be wrong not to tell her. She gave you all your money, after all. And if you tell her, she'd be shocked. I know these old-fashioned mothers. And I want to keep the right side of your mother, above all things.'

'Why?'

'You know why.'

She did, but had to pretend that she did not, and said, 'No, I don't. Why?'

'Well, if you should look favourably upon a certain proposition which I've told you I may make very soon, your mother'd be a very important person, then, wouldn't she? And so would your father.'

'Oh – I don't think he'd count very much. Although he's very nice.'

'No,' said Gorse firmly. 'I'm not going to let you. I've got an instinct it's wiser not to. Although there *is* another idea.'

'What's that?'

'You keep the fifteen pounds, and let me *give* you a share in the car – fifteen pounds' worth.'

'No,' said Esther. 'That's certainly out of the question.'

'Why?'

'It'd be the same as giving me a present of fifteen pounds.'

'It'd be giving you thirty pounds, actually, when the car's sold. But I still don't see what's wrong.'

'Well, I do,' said Esther. 'It's out of the question, and that's *that.*'

'Very well, have it your own way,' said Gorse, and he picked up the notes and handed them to her. 'There you are. Put them away safely and don't lose them.'

'All right, then, and thank you very much,' said Esther, taking the notes.

Here, although he had no notion that he had done so, Gorse had made yet another of those strange, sudden, appalling blunders which he was always to make in spite of his astuteness generally.

He had returned to Esther the identical notes which she had given him, and if she had taken note of the numbers she might have noticed it, and this would have proved that no deposit had been paid to the man Gosling.

The man Gosling did not actually exist. But a man named Randall did. He dealt in cars, and Gorse had gained his confidence. He had let Gorse, a prospective buyer, use the car tonight. He had previously let Gorse use the other cheaper cars. He had asked for no deposit.

In returning to Esther the fifteen pounds, which he had in the interval kept in his pocket, Gorse was using a very old-fashioned, one might say hackneyed, method of gaining confidence.

Fortunately for Gorse, Esther, reader of *The News of the World* as she was, knew nothing about this stale trick. Even more fortunately for Gorse, Esther had not looked at the numbers of the notes, and so did not realize that she was being given back just those which she had given Gorse.

Had she done so, Gorse's game might well have been up. Expert and resourceful liar that he was, he would have had great difficulty, on the spur of the moment, in explaining the matter away. Certainly he would have lost a little of her trust. And, if he was to achieve his ultimate object, he wanted all of Esther's trust, all the time and until the very end.

'And all in my new bag, too,' said Esther. 'You aren't half generous to me. Oh lord – I shouldn't say "aren't half".'

'Why not?'

'It's common. I know that. I ought to've said you're *very* generous to me.'

'I don't see that it matters. I like the way you say and do everything. And it's easy to be generous when you feel like that.'

'All the same, you *are* generous. I've never known anyone so generous. And if I say "aren't half" again – will you tell me off?'

'If you like.'

'And if I make any other mistakes, will you tell me? I try hard enough, but I don't always know, and I'm always tripping up.'

'All right, I will. All the same, I like you as you are.'

'Yes, but I don't like myself, and I'd like your help. I'd like you to teach me.'

This, perhaps, was the greatest verbal concession Esther had so far made to Gorse.

'That's very flattering,' said Gorse. 'And it makes me feel very hopeful.'

'Does it?' said Esther, and blushed.

Gorse changed the subject.

'And did you meet our friend Ryan last night?' he asked.

'Yes.'

'And how did he behave?'

'Oh – he was very harmless.'

'Did he hold your hand?'

'Yes.'

'Did he try to kiss you?'

'Oh,' said Esther, eluding the question. 'You know how boys go on. I know how to deal with them all right.'

'Are you sure?'

'Yes. Of course I do.'

'Yes. I believe you do – with the normal boy. But I'm afraid I don't think Ryan *is* a normal boy. Aren't you ever going to take Uncle Ralph's advice? When are you meeting him again?'

'Wednesday evening, I said.'

There was a silence, for Gorse was again thinking. He was wondering how this would fit into the plan he had in mind.

'Wednesday – the day after tomorrow – eh?' he said. 'Very well, do as you like. And now I think we'd better finish these drinks and go for a little spin. I'd suggest having another, but I don't want to be had up for driving under the influence.'

They went outside, and he led her to the red dream-car.

'There you are,' he said. 'What do you think of it?'

Esther was enraptured. It was, indeed, a sensational car – of the type at which connoisseurs, passing by, stop to look. There was a man looking at it as they approached it, and another man stopped to look. There was, Esther realized, practically a crowd! – and one of which she, in a way, was the centre of attraction. At that moment Esther was a deeply, deeply happy girl.

'It's *glorious*!' she said.

'Very well,' said Gorse. 'Step in.'

He opened the door for her, seated himself at the wheel, and drove away.

4

Gorse was an even more expert driver than he was a liar. He made no blunders.

He took Esther to the back of Hove, and then into the country, towards Devil's Dyke.

As they sped along the country road, Esther, exhilarated by the air as well as all else besides, said:

'You know, I wish you *would* let me have a share in this.'

'No,' said Gorse. 'This is where your Uncle Ralph puts his foot down sternly. You can have a share if you like, but I won't take the money.'

'Well,' said Esther. 'I think it's mean of you.'

'No. It's not mean,' said Gorse. 'Just wise. And, anyway, you might come to have a share in it in quite a different way. But I admire your attitude.'

'What attitude?'

'Oh – taking a risk. Not that it *is* a risk in this case. But that's the only way to do things in life. Do things in the proper style. That's what makes the difference between, well – *proper* people, and those who aren't.'

'You really mean common people and gentle-people – don't you?' said Esther.

'Yes,' said Gorse, after deliberating. 'If you like to put it that way. And you've proved to me to which type you belong.'

These words were to have a great effect upon Esther's future conduct with Gorse. They had been intended to do so.

Gorse was clever enough to stop the car on a lonely road and kiss her. He drove as far as the Devil's Dyke, and then said that they must get home quickly or Gosling's garage would be shut.

He drove home with all his skill at a thrilling speed. He left her at the Clock Tower, arranging to meet her again tomorrow evening – Tuesday.

As Esther walked back to Over Street that night she did more than tell herself that she would like to marry Ernest Ralph Gorse: she hoped that he would quickly and firmly make the proposal.

PART TEN

WARNING

Chapter One

1

Returning from her work on Tuesday evening, and entering the house in Over Street with the object of dressing before meeting Gorse, the smashing blow fell upon Esther.

Her mother was out; so were both the children, who were with their mother.

The house was quiet, and seemed to be empty. On the floor of the perambulatored passage on the ground floor lay a letter.

It was addressed in letters from a newspaper pasted on to the envelope.

Because the house was quiet, and seemingly quite empty, Esther went whiter in the face than she might have done otherwise.

2

Esther took the letter up to her bedroom. Now her face was red. She opened the letter.

She found, inside, a card upon which letters from a newspaper had been pasted. This read:

You WERF WARNED but DIS obey
ed you AR- WatcheD ALWAYS If
you MEET RYAN JUST onCe
More you WILL sufFer FROM
WELL – wisher not Only Mind BUT your
pretty Body very seriously ADVISE
OBEY ANGRY but still WELL WISHER

Esther read this three or four times in order to discern its full meaning behind its lack of punctuation.

Her impulse, then, was to rush down to her mother. But her mother was out, and the house, she believed (and actually it was), was entirely empty. She looked at the letter in the dusk (it was a cloudy night) and listened to the emptiness of the house.

She began to dress herself for Gorse.

When she was almost completely dressed, and ready for Gorse, she heard her mother come in with the two children. All three went into the sitting-room on the ground floor.

She thought of calling her mother up to the bedroom. But she had not told her mother that she had met Ryan again, and so would have to reveal that she had betrayed her mother's trust in her.

Also, if she were going to meet him at the appointed time, she would be late for Gorse. She would have to talk to her mother for at least a quarter of an hour.

She decided that she would tell her mother later – or not tell her at all – and she slipped out of the house quietly without even greeting her mother or the children.

3

Gorse was again in very good spirits when he met Esther outside the West Pier, and he was loquacious as he took her to the Metropole. Esther noticed that the red dream-car was not tonight outside the hotel. But she was not now really interested in the red car.

'I'm sorry,' said Gorse. 'But we haven't got the car tonight. Old Gosling's a bit sticky about it.'

'Is he?' was all Esther could say.

'Yes. Very sticky, as a matter of fact,' said Gorse. 'Tell me, though – you seem a bit worried. Is there anything on your mind?'

'Yes. There is.'

'What?'

'I'll tell you when we're inside,' said Esther.

'Serious?'

'Yes. Very,' said Esther. 'I want your advice.'

'You shall have it,' said Gorse.

Their usual table was occupied, but they found one opposite

it. When the drinks were ordered Gorse said, 'well. Go ahead.'

'No. I'd rather wait till I've had a drink.'

The drinks came, and Gorse said, 'Well – go ahead,' again.

Esther sipped at her drink, and said, 'Well, I've had another – that's all.'

'Another what?'

'Another of those letters,' said Esther.

'Yes. I rather thought so,' said Gorse. 'If you've got it on you, will you let me see it?'

'Yes,' said Esther, producing it from her new bag. 'Here it is.'

Because of the seriousness of the occasion, or because Gorse desired to make the situation seem as serious as he possibly could, he did not put on his monocle to read the card.

He scrutinized it carefully for something like two minutes. Then he spoke, still looking at the card.

'Now this is serious – you know. Really serious,' he said. 'In fact, it's very dangerous.'

'Yes. It's pretty awful – isn't it?'

'Yes,' said Gorse. 'In fact, I should say that this is now definitely a matter for the police.'

'Oh no. Not the police. Surely.'

'But it is. In fact, if you'll let me have this card I'll take it to them myself,' said Gorse. 'Will you?'

'Oh lord. I don't want the police dragged in.'

'But I don't think you understand how serious all this is. The other letter was just a warning. This is a threat. And a very nasty threat. Did you read that bit about the body?'

'Yes. Of course I did. It's terrible, though I don't quite know what it means.'

'Well – it might mean anything – you know. You don't want to be set upon in a dark place – you don't want to be disfigured for life – do you?'

Esther went whiter than she was already.

'What do you mean?' she said.

'I mean what I say. This obviously comes from a very low quarter, and the type of person that doesn't stop at anything – *anything* – do you understand? I don't think you know the shadier side of life. How should you? I happen to have come across them – on racecourses, and other places. And the bad part of Brighton's as bad as any place on earth. This is a matter for the police.'

'Oh dear. I still don't want to go to them.'

'Well – even if you don't, your other course of action is absolutely clear now.'

'What other course?'

'I mean about Ryan. It's quite clear that you can never meet him again.'

'Oh lord . . . But I've *promised* to meet him, tomorrow night.'

'Well – you just don't turn up – that's all.'

'But supposing he's *innocent*? Supposing there's nothing behind these filthy letters?'

'You just can't afford to take the risk, and that's that. Anyone can see this man – the man who wrote the letter – means business. He must be a low type himself. He *may* be warning you for your own good, but he's probably got a grudge against Ryan. Ryan mixes with some very low people. I can tell you that, because I've seen him with them – unknown to himself.'

'Have you?'

'Yes,' said Gorse, moving away from the subject. 'And then has another thing struck you? You've been watched – incessantly watched. You've probably been watched coming here, and you'll be watched going home. And that brings us to another interesting thing. You and I must have been watched as well. But he's got no grudge against me, and you've been out with me more than Ryan. So it looks like a grudge against Ryan – I should personally say a justified one, but that's not the point. The point is that you're not going to meet Ryan again. That's absolutely certain, if ever anything was.'

'Oh dear,' said Esther. 'It does seem –'

'You see,' said Gorse, interrupting her, 'these sorts of people stop at nothing, and they usually strike through the girl. They've got twisted minds, and it's one of their pleasant little habits. It's the girl they go for. The girl's weaker.'

'But what could he do to me?' said Esther. 'I mean – "disfigure" me.'

'Oh, please don't let's go into that. I'd really rather not. The point is that it happens. It's happening incessantly. You've only got to read the newspapers. Isn't it?'

'I suppose it is.'

'Now. Will you promise me you'll do what I say?'

'I suppose I'll have to.'

'But *do* you? Solemnly?'

'I'd like to think about it. You see, if he's innocent, it does seem awful not to turn up – just leave him waiting there . . . He's never done me any harm. He's always behaved like a gentleman.'

'Believe me, gentlemen – or so-called gentlemen – can be more dangerous than any others in the world. You must know that.'

'Yes – but if he *is* all right. It does seem mean.'

'By the way,' said Gorse, 'you're not in love with him by any chance, are you?'

'Good heavens, no,' said Esther. And, in her present state of perturbation, she certainly was not. 'It only just seems mean – with him waiting there.'

'Well – there's a way round that.'

'What?'

'You can write to him and tell him you're not coming.'

'But it wouldn't reach him in time. Not even if I wrote it and posted it tonight.'

'No. But you could write it tonight and post it in the morning. Then it'd probably reach him before he left in the evening.'

'Yes. I suppose it would.'

'Then write it tonight and post it in the morning.'

'But what am I to *say*? What excuse am I going to make?'

'Oh, you can make any excuse. That's easy enough. But what you ought to do is to tell him that you don't want to meet him again at all. And an excuse for that might be just a little more difficult.'

'It certainly would.'

'But not impossible. In fact, on second thoughts, it's perfectly easy. Can't you just tell him there's somebody else?'

'I suppose so. But it's difficult.'

'Say there's been somebody else all the time – someone you're in love with. And then you can say that this someone's put his foot down at last, and said that you mustn't go out with anyone else. You can say you're very sorry, and all that.'

'But I told him – that day in the country – that there wasn't anyone particular.'

'Well – tell him that you weren't telling the truth. That's easy enough, isn't it?'

'Yes. I suppose so. But, if he's really all right, I still think it's mean. Especially if he doesn't get the letter in time. I *still* don't quite believe there's anything wrong with him, and I hate to think of him standing – waiting there.'

Esther, it will be seen, was putting up a brave, indeed a noble, fight for her romance – for her ideal of Beauty. For she thought Ryan beautiful, and he was the one she really loved. But Gorse was too much for this ignorant, frightened girl.

'I don't care if he stands and waits for hours. You've got to get *out* of this. When there's evil going around you've just got to run away from it. You've got to get out of its orbit.'

Esther did not know what the word 'orbit' meant, but she realized that Gorse was giving her almost exactly the same advice which her mother had given her.

'Yes,' she said. 'I know all that.'

'Have you told your mother about all this?' asked Gorse, by pure luck hitting upon Esther's thought.

'Yes,' she said. 'Some of it. Not all. And she said just what you said.'

'Of course she did. And you ought to have told her all. And now I can tell you this. If you don't do what I say, *I'll* do something. You've had enough threats already, and heaven knows I don't want to start threatening you. But I'll tell you this. If you don't do as I advise, I could go to your mother myself – couldn't I? In fact, I could go to your mother and father. And you know what'd happen then – don't you? *They'd* soon put a stop to it – wouldn't they?'

'Yes. They would . . . But I don't want you to go.'

'Neither do I. But it might be my duty – just my plain, simple duty. Now – will you promise to write that letter tonight?'

Esther paused.

Then she said:

'All right, then. I'll write the letter.'

(I've promised, but if I change my mind I needn't post it, was her thought.)

'Very well. That's a good girl. I know I can trust you, and you've taken a weight off my mind.'

'Oh – lord,' said Esther. 'I don't half feel bad – I mean I feel bad. Not not half. I'd like another drink. Can I?'

'Of course you can. And you shall drink all of it tonight.'

'It looks as though I'm going to the bad, doesn't it? – taking to drink.'

Esther spoke jokingly, but she had come very near to the truth.

In later life Esther was to drink a great deal too much, and this brought upon her many evils. It is disasters (of the proportions of the one from which Esther was suffering now) which, taken in conjunction with early youth and the use of alcohol, bring about the habit of heavy drinking.

'Don't be silly,' said Gorse, and ordered more drinks.

They talked about other matters, but Esther could not properly bring her mind to them. When she was half-way through her second drink (which went to her head) Esther suddenly burst out with:

'You know I *still* don't believe there's anything wrong with that boy.'

'Now then,' said Gorse. 'Don't let's go back to that. You've made your promise, and that's that. You won't weaken at the last moment, will you?'

'I hope not.'

'Well, I'll jolly well see that you don't. Listen. What time are you supposed to be meeting Ryan tomorrow evening?'

'Seven-thirty.'

'Good. Now I'll tell you what. You meet me in here at seven o'clock. I'll be sitting here waiting for you. Then I can hold your hand – well, in a metaphorical sense, anyway. Will you do that?'

'Yes. All right.'

'Promise?'

'Yes.'

'Good.'

They again went on to discuss other matters, but Esther was still unable to concentrate.

At last, 'It's no good, is it?' said Gorse. 'You can't think of anything else.'

'No – I'm afraid I can't.'

'Very well, then, drink up that and we'll go off home. And I'm going to see you the whole way home tonight.'

'Oh no. Only as far as the Clock Tower. Please. It's so awful where I live.'

'Well, then, as far as the street. I want to see you going safely into your house tonight.'

'Why? Safely? I haven't done anything wrong tonight – have I? I mean wrong by this awful person, whoever he is?'

'No. You haven't. But I like to take every precaution. And I have a little idea. I want you and I to leave each other outside the

Metropole. Then, at a distance, I'm going to follow you. You're probably being watched tonight, and I might find something out about the gentleman – what he looks like. I'll probably fail – but it's on the cards. So I'll just see you to the end of your street, and see you go into your house. Agree?'

Gorse, of course, was only trying to terrify Esther further with all this nonsense. He succeeded.

'Oh lord,' said Esther. 'It's pretty awful – this feeling you're being watched.'

'Yes. But remember you're being watched *over*, too. You've got me there to look after you – haven't you?'

'You're very good to me,' said Esther.

'It's very easy to be good to you,' said Gorse. 'And now let's get going – shall we? We'll just say goodbye in a normal way outside.'

'Very well,' said Esther, and they rose.

As they walked towards the revolving doors Gorse said:

'And you'll promise you'll write that letter tonight?'

'Yes. I promise.'

When they were outside Gorse said goodbye to her in a rather exaggeratedly normal and loud-voiced way.

Esther walked home.

Although it was not strictly necessary for his purposes, Gorse did in fact follow Esther to the end of her street and watch her go indoors.

He had a feeling that Esther would look back occasionally on her walk home, and that it would be polite to be seen following.

He was right. She did look back, once or twice. And, when she reached the door of the house in which she lived, she saw Gorse standing at the end of the street.

Chapter Two

I

That night Esther wrote a letter to Ryan, using much labour in its composition. Its final version read as follows:

Dear Mr Ryan,

I am very sorry I cannot meet you tomorrow night.

I have also to say that it is impossible for me to meet you at all in the future.

I am afraid I have not played quite fairly with you. You asked me in the country whether there was anyone else and I said there was not. But there is someone else, who I love, and he says that I must not go on meeting you.

Please do not make any attempt to get into touch with me, either at the above address or by letter. It will be of no use.

I feel sure you will understand. I apologize for my bad behaviour, but I feel sure you will understand. I will always have very pleasant memeries of our friendship.

Yours gratefully and sorrowfully,

Esther Downes.

Esther put this extremely pathetic letter into an envelope and addressed it. But she left the envelope open, and she did not stamp it because she had no stamp.

She left the envelope open because she wanted to read the letter again in the morning.

She slept well, and in the morning was a good deal less frightened.

On her way to her work she bought a stamp and stuck it on to the envelope. But she still did not post the letter, or close the envelope.

All day she brooded upon her trouble, and still, still she had a feeling that Ryan was guiltless, and that she should defy the author of the low, menacing letter. For this reason she still refrained from posting the letter to Ryan, and had it in her bag when she met Gorse at the Metropole at seven that evening.

2

Gorse rose directly he saw her, and shook hands. She noticed that there were two drinks ready on the table.

'Never been so glad to see you,' he said. 'Now sit down and have a drink.'

Esther did so.

'I saw you following me last night,' she said, after she had had her first sip.

'Yes,' said Gorse. 'And I saw you looking back. You shouldn't have done that, really. A watcher doesn't like to know that the one who's being watched is trying to watch him. But it doesn't matter.'

'Well – *was* there a watcher? Did you find anything out?'

'Not a thing. He was probably behind – watching me. Or he may not have been there at all. He's as clever as paint, whoever he is. Well – did you write the letter?'

'Yes . . .'

'And post it?'

'No . . . I didn't.'

'Why not?'

'I don't quite know. I've got it here in my bag. I suppose among other things I wanted you to see it first.'

'Well – that's foolish in a way, you know. Now Ryan'll have to wait outside the Pier. However, may I see the letter?'

'Yes. Here it is.'

Gorse put his monocle into his eye and studied the letter.

'Yes,' he said. 'That seems all right. Very good, in fact. And now we'd better post this – hadn't we?'

'Oh lord. *Must* we?'

'Yes. And at once.' Gorse licked the envelope and closed it. 'I can do it here. In the hotel.'

Gorse rose.

'I won't be half a sec,' he said.

'But *must* we? Can't we wait a bit? I've got an idea.'

'Yes. I'm afraid we must,' said Gorse, and walked away and put the letter into the hotel box, and returned to Esther.

'Well,' he said, sitting down again, 'what's the idea? Or rather what *was* it?'

'You shouldn't have posted it, you know,' said Esther, ignoring his question. 'I started with "I'm sorry I can't meet you tomorrow night", and it ought to be *last* night, now.'

'Well, that doesn't matter – does it? That's your fault for not posting it. Now he's got to stand waiting, that's all. But what was your idea?'

'Well – *has* he got to stand waiting? Why shouldn't I be brave and meet him, after all? Why not show him those two filthy letters and give him a chance to defend himself?'

'Out of the question,' said Gorse. 'Don't be silly.'

'But I don't see why it's silly. The letters might just have come from a harmless lunatic. I've thought about it.'

'*Might* is the word you used,' said Gorse.

'And couldn't we *both* go along to meet him? Then we could all talk it over. I'd have a man with me.'

'Now listen,' said Gorse. 'You're talking complete nonsense and you know you are. He'd never admit anything. He'd just lie – I happen to know he's one of the best liars existing – and you don't get anywhere. And you'll have disobeyed the instruction in the letter. And that means dangers. I don't want to talk about Disfigurement again –'

'Oh – don't do that, for heaven's sake.'

'No. I don't want to. But I'm telling you this. If you go out and meet Ryan tonight, I know exactly where I'm going tonight. I'm going straight to your father and mother in Over Street, and tell them everything. And you know what'll happen then. I'm sorry to be so stern, but there we are. And you know in your heart I'm right. Don't you?'

'Yes,' said Esther, after staring miserably at nothing for a few moments. 'I suppose I do.'

'Very well, then – the subject's closed, and the letter's posted anyway. You know, you ought to think yourself very lucky to have someone like myself to advise you.'

'Yes. I know,' said Esther. 'I'm very grateful, really.'

'Well, let's say no more about it – shall we? Let's talk about other things.'

'All right,' said Esther. 'Let's.'

And it was with these words that Esther, after her very fine struggle, finally lost Ryan – though she was destined to meet him once more in Brighton.

3

Gorse entertained Esther with his conversation and succeeded fairly well in holding her attention until twenty minutes to eight. Then she broke away.

'Oh, it is *awful* to think of him waiting there!' she exclaimed.

'Now then,' said Gorse. 'Don't be foolish. He's probably gone by now. He's not the type that waits.'

'I should have thought that's just what he is.'

'No. You don't know him as well as I do – believe me. However, I'll tell you what I'll do. I'd like to do it in any case. I'll just hop out now and see if he *is* waiting. I might see someone else too. He must be watching, and I might still find something out. Do you mind if I leave you?'

'What? All alone here? I can't sit in a place like this all by myself. I'd look silly – and it's wrong – isn't it? – for a girl to sit in a place like this all by herself.'

'It depends on the girl,' said Gorse. 'And if you're embarrassed, I'll go and get you a newspaper to hide behind. They've got some papers at the porter's desk. Excuse me, I'll go and get one at once. I want to hurry.'

He went to the porter's desk, bought a newspaper, and returned to Esther.

'There you are,' he said. 'You read the news and tell me all about it when I come back. I'll only be about ten minutes. Cheerio.'

He left Esther, who saw him pass hurriedly through the revolving doors.

All this nonsense was, again, only perpetrated by Gorse in order to frighten Esther, and he was again extremely successful.

She sat, longing for his return, in anguish – anguish about the waiting Ryan, anguish about the whole situation, and anguish about sitting alone in the great hotel.

Esther, temporarily, had lost her taste for Oriental splendour.

Gorse, who (largely because it was still light outside) had never had any intention of going anywhere near the West Pier to look at Ryan, walked about in the small streets behind the front. He did this for nearly twenty minutes. He knew exactly what sort of anguish Esther was suffering from, and he thought it desirable to prolong it, and thus increase it.

Then he returned, apologizing for being so late. Curiosity, he said, had got the better of him.

'And was Ryan there?' said Esther.'And did you see anybody else?'

'Yes,' said Gorse. 'Ryan was there. And, to do him justice, I must say he stayed longer than I thought. In fact, he only left a little before I did. And I drew a complete blank about anybody else. There was no one loitering or looking suspicious at all.'

'Didn't Ryan see you loitering? It's still quite light outside, isn't it?'

'No. I'm sure he didn't. I'm pretty good at that sort of thing. Now let's have another drink.'

They did so, and the subject was changed. Esther again finished the whole of her drink.

When it was time to go Gorse said:

'I don't imagine you want to go on the Pier tonight. I expect you'd rather go straight home.'

'Yes, I would rather.'

'Very well,' said Gorse. 'And tonight, if I may, I shall escort you as far as the Clock Tower. There's no sense in following you, like last night. You've done what you were told, and the danger's over now.'

'You think it is?'

'Yes. Of course it is. Well, let's go, shall we?'

On their way home Esther asked Gorse, quite accidentally, an amazingly shrewd question.

'Tell me,' she said. 'Suppose whoever wrote those letters had told me I wasn't to meet *you* – not Ryan. What would *you* have done?'

Gorse was very nearly knocked out by this: he was certainly on the floor while the referee started counting. But somehow he managed to survive.

'Ah,' he said. 'That's a very difficult question.' He was silent, and then went on. 'That's a very difficult question indeed . . . Very difficult . . . But I think I know the answer.'

'What?'

'Well – it sounds an awful thing to say, but I think there'd only be one thing I *could* do. I'd have to stop meeting you.'

'What – completely leave me?'

'Yes. It sounds awful, I know – but I don't see any other way.

There'd be two reasons. One would concern me, and the other yourself.'

'What are they?'

'Well, in the first place, I personally don't like to get mixed up with that sort of thing. As I told you, you've just got to run – get out of its orbit. And I think anyone with any pretensions to being a gentleman would do the same. But that's only me. What's more important is you. I couldn't possibly expose you to such a risk. And so for your sake I'd have to leave you. There'd be nothing else to do. I need hardly tell you it'd break my heart. *And* ruin all my hopes for the future into the bargain. And I hope it would hurt you a little. Would it?'

'Yes,' said Esther, simply and candidly. 'It would.'

'But the question's an absurd one, really,' Gorse continued. 'Ryan's Ryan and I'm myself. Ryan has obviously done something very wrong somewhere, and he obviously mixes with very low people. Well – I *don't* mix with low people, and I've never done anything very wrong – so far as I know, at any rate. And so of course I'm not the sort of person to *get* a letter like that – or even to be mentioned in one. Do you follow me?'

'Yes,' said Esther meekly. 'I do.'

The referee had counted six and Gorse was up.

As they said goodbye at the Clock Tower, Gorse asked her if he could meet her tomorrow. She said, truthfully, that it was really time that she gave Gertrude an evening.

Gorse allowed her to do this, and arranged to meet her, not outside the West Pier, but inside the Metropole, at seven-thirty, on the day after tomorrow.

He was secretly glad to have missed a day. Doing so fitted in with the schemes he had in mind.

Chapter Three

I

Ryan's first emotions, on receiving Esther's letter next morning, were those of one suffering from great grief and irretrievable disaster.

But, as the day wore on, his mood changed.

Having read the letter about twenty-five times, he decided that there was something 'funny' about it.

To begin with, it had been posted (as he saw from the postmark) in the evening, but she had begun her letter with 'I am very sorry I cannot meet you *tomorrow* [Ryan's italics] night.'

Did this not point to the fact that she had hesitated a long while, perhaps a whole day, before posting it, and had only at last done so reluctantly? And was not this a hopeful sign?

But there were other 'funny' things. He could not quite make himself believe in this 'someone else'. He did not appear to be a nice character, anyway – forbidding her to meet anyone else – threatening her, it seemed.

There was something strange, too, in her 'Please do not make any attempt to get into touch with me, either at the above address or by letter.' Why should he not at least write to her – even if it was only a letter of farewell? This seemed to confirm the idea that she was being threatened.

Then she had signed the letter, 'Yours gratefully and sorrowfully.' The 'sorrowfully' struck him as being written in all sincerity. And this was further reason for hope.

Then Ryan was touched by the immaturity of her handwriting and her misspelling of the word 'memories' as 'memeries'. He felt that she was in trouble, ignorant, and needing help.

But what was he to do? Clearly he must not visit her or write to her. But might he not contrive somehow to meet her, apparently by accident?

And, even if there was a genuine 'someone else', had he not been brought up to believe that faint heart never won fair lady, and that all was fair in love and war?

He was anxious to consult someone, and thought of Bell. But he remembered Bell's abilities and enthusiasm as a consultant on a previous occasion.

Gorse came into Ryan's head, and he saw that there were advantages here. Gorse was in the habit of meeting Esther: he took her to the Metropole.

Might he not get Gorse to plead for him – plead for another meeting, at any rate?

Gorse, also, was much more sophisticated than Bell – indeed more sophisticated than himself. He might have good advice to give.

The idea of going to Gorse was distasteful; for Ryan, as we know, disliked and somehow distrusted Gorse. The advantages, however, seemed to outweigh these sentiments, which after all were only faint and instinctive.

By the end of the day Ryan had decided to seek advice from Gorse.

2

Ryan, the early riser and motorcyclist, called at an early hour upon Gorse on the next day, Friday.

Gorse was still in bed with his breakfast.

When Gorse's landlady announced Ryan, Gorse was for a moment a little alarmed. He feared that objects in his room might disclose some of his occupations – such objects as paste, scissors, postcards, and clipped newspapers. But a glance satisfied him that all of these were effectually concealed.

'Ah-ha,' said Gorse from his bed. 'Our worthy Ryan. Thou callest at an early hour – dost thou not?'

'Yes. I'm sorry,' said Ryan. 'Do you mind?'

'No. I'm delighted,' said Gorse. 'But what bring'st thou here? Any matter of urgent moment? Thou wearest an anxious look. Come and sit on the bed.'

Gorse had also been struck for a moment by the fear that all had been discovered, and that Ryan had come round to fight with him.

'No, nothing frightfully urgent,' said Ryan, sitting on the bed. 'I've really only come round to ask your advice about something.'

'Go ahead. Only too glad to help in any way.'

'Well,' said Ryan. 'You know that girl – Esther Downes?'

'Yes. I do indeed. I've taken her out.'

'Yes. I know. She told me. Well – it's difficult to put – but I've got pretty keen on her.'

'Yes. I rather thought so. You showed it that first night.'

'Did I?'

'Yes. It seemed obvious to me. But go ahead.'

'Well – before I do that,' said Ryan, 'will you tell me something?'

'Certainly. If I can.'

'*You're* not keen on her by any chance – are you? Tell me if you are.'

'Not in the slightest,' said Gorse, more than ever convincing because he was telling the truth. 'I can give you a straight answer there, I promise you.'

'Then why do you take her out? Don't think I don't believe you, but why do you go out with her?'

'Well – it's rather hard to explain. I suppose it's vanity, really. I like to be seen with a pretty girl. She's not my type, but she's tremendously pretty and she dresses beautifully. I've even taken her to the Metropole. Though I don't share in your feelings – I completely understand them. Well – go on.'

'Well,' said Ryan, producing Esther's letter from his pocket. 'I thought I was getting ahead pretty well with her, but yesterday I got this letter. There seems to be something funny about it, and I want your advice.'

'Funny?' said Gorse. 'Let me look.'

Gorse read the letter carefully.

'Well,' said Ryan. 'What do you think?'

'Well – I don't want to hurt your feelings – but at the moment I don't see anything funny about it at all.'

'You mean it means what it says – that there *is* someone else?'

'I'm sorry to have to say it, but I do, frankly – yes.'

'Tell me,' said Ryan. 'Has she ever spoken to *you* about anybody else?'

Gorse deliberated.

'Now, that's interesting,' he said. 'As a matter of fact, she has. She's given very strong hints that there is. And the funny thing is that it crossed my mind that it might be you.'

'Then your advice is to take the letter at its face value?'

'You know, I'm very sorry to have to say that it is. I wouldn't worry too much. There're plenty of other fish in the sea, you know.'

'Now there's something else,' said Ryan. 'Thank you for your advice. I'm not sure it's right, but thank you for it. But I was wondering if you could help me. Are you meeting her again?'

'I am indeed,' said Gorse. 'In fact, I'm meeting her again this very evening. At the Hotel Metropole.'

'Now, *that's* funny, too,' said Ryan. 'If this "somebody else" objects to her meeting me – why shouldn't he object to her meeting *you*?'

'Oh – that's very easy to explain,' said Gorse. 'She's probably told him that you're "keen", as you put it, on her. And she's probably told him that I'm not – that I'm quite harmless. Do you see?'

'Yes. I suppose I do,' said Ryan.

'But how can I help?'

'Well – if you're meeting her again – tonight – I was wondering if you could put a word in for me. I still think there's something mysterious about it all, and why I'm not allowed even to write to her *or* see her, I can't see.'

'Yes?'

'So would it be possible for you to ask her why? To ask her if we couldn't have just *one* more meeting, at any rate? You're detached, and so she'd respect your advice. And you might find out about this "somebody else". Could you help me?'

'Yes. Of course I could,' said Gorse. 'And I will. I'll speak to her tonight. Honestly, I don't think there's much hope, because I believe there *is* somebody else. But I'll try and pump her, and do everything I can for you.'

'You know, this is awfully good of you,' said Ryan, genuinely grateful to Gorse, whom he decided to flatter. 'And I know you're awfully good at that sort of thing.'

'I don't know that I am. But I'll certainly do my best.'

'And I nearly thought of going to Bell for advice!' said Ryan.

'No,' said Gorse. 'I don't think that'd have been wise, exactly. Bell's an admirable character, but not of much use in cases like this, I fancy.'

'By the way,' said Ryan, who at the moment liked and completely trusted Gorse. 'I suppose I couldn't come *along* to the Metropole tonight and join you, could I?'

'No. I think that'd be fatal. You can, if you like, of course, but I don't advise it. She's said you're not to meet her, and young ladies

– particularly pretty ones – don't like to be disobeyed. It'd be butting in and might ruin everything. You take my advice, and leave it all to your Uncle Gorse. I can't promise anything. In fact, I don't hope for much, as I told you. But I'll do my best. You know in your heart I'm right – don't you?'

'Yes,' said Ryan miserably. 'I suppose I do. And thank you very much.'

'*Pas du tout*,' said Gorse. 'And now I suppose it's time for the Emperor – Gorse the First – to arise from his bed.'

'No – Gorse the Good,' said Ryan, and then asked Gorse, because he wanted to reward him, whether he would like to ride on the back of his motorcycle.

But Gorse, the motorist, was above motorcyles – very much above riding on the back of them.

He politely rejected the offer, and Ryan, who was anxious to soothe himself with riding, asked him when they were to meet again so that he could hear the news.

'Now, that's difficult,' said Gorse. 'I've got to spend all tomorrow with an ancient and venerable uncle of mine at Preston. Suppose you call on me, at the same time, on Sunday morning. I don't mind how early you are.'

Ryan again thanked his benefactor, who was left to his thoughts.

PART ELEVEN

RELIEF

Chapter One

I

On returning home from work on that Friday evening, Esther, going upstairs to dress before meeting Gorse, was called down by her mother, who asked her to come into the sitting-room.

There was an air of mystery about her mother, who was alone in the sitting-room, and who asked Esther to shut the door.

Esther, already frightened, was made more frightened by what her mother said.

'Another of those letters has come,' said her mother. 'But it's all right.'

'Oh lord,' said Esther. 'Where is it?'

'It came in the afternoon,' said Mrs Downes. 'It was addressed to you, but I couldn't keep from opening it. You don't mind – do you?'

'No. Of course not. But where is it? What did it *say*?'

'It's all right,' said Mrs Downes, producing it from a drawer in a sideboard. 'In fact, it's good.'

'Good. How *could* it be good?'

'It *is* though,' said Mrs Downes. 'You read it.'

Esther took the postcard, and rapidly ran her eyes over it. It read:

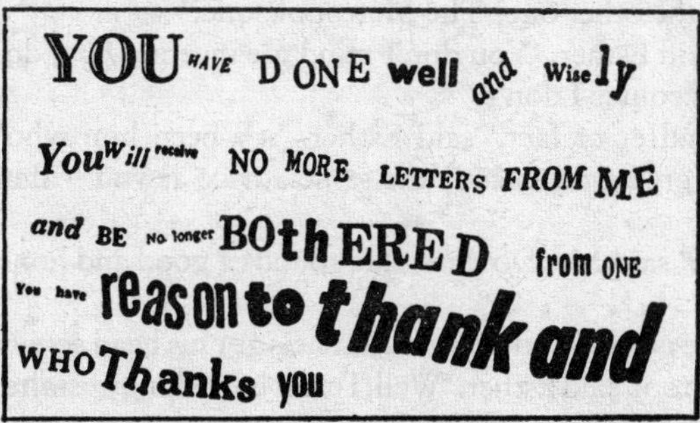

YOU HAVE DONE well and Wisely
You Will receive NO MORE LETTERS FROM ME
and BE No longer BOthERED from ONE
You have reason to thank and
WHO Thanks you

'Well, that's better, isn't it?' said Esther's mother. 'In fact, you're out of the wood now – aren't you?'

'Yes. I suppose I am,' said Esther, still dazed.

'Aren't you glad now that you did what I advised you?'

'Yes. I am,' said Esther.

There was no sense in telling her mother that she had not done what her mother had advised – that she had done exactly the opposite, and met Ryan.

'Well – now you're *right* out of the wood,' said Mrs Downes, and kissed her daughter congratulatorily. 'Mother always knows best about everything, you know.'

Here Mrs Downes was inaccurate. Mother usually knows best about everything, but not always. In this instance, as Esther perceived, she knew a great deal less than Esther.

After she had been kissed, Esther said: 'Yes. I know. And just think of it. I *am* out of the wood, aren't I?'

'Of course you are.'

And now Esther, who had come out of her daze, began to feel surges of inexpressible relief and joy.

'Well, what shall we do with the letter? Tear it up or keep it?' said Esther's mother.

'Oh no. I think I'd like to keep it,' said Esther impulsively. She was so joyous she wanted to hug it and look at it again and again.

There is only one type of anonymous letter capable of bringing joy – that which, after previous anonymous menaces, promises there shall be no more. But it seems that all anonymous letters have to be hoarded.

'Very well,' said her mother. 'It doesn't matter either way, now.'

'Yes. I'd like to keep it,' said Esther. 'And as a matter of fact I'd like to show it to someone I'm meeting tonight.'

'Is that the other one? The Metropole one?'

'Yes,' said Esther. 'You don't mind me meeting *him*, do you?'

'No. Of course I don't.'

'As a matter of fact,' said Esther, 'it's been him who's all the time been giving me exactly the same advice as you – almost word for word.'

'Did he?' said Mrs Downes. 'He sounds a good and honest boy to me.'

'Yes. He *is* good and honest. And he's got his head screwed on the right way, too,' said Esther. 'Well, I must be rushing upstairs to dress.'

She kissed her mother again and ran upstairs.

As Esther dressed her joy and relief grew greater, and, as she was walking on her way to meet Gorse at the Metropole, they grew greater and greater still.

It was the wording of the letter in her bag which particularly pleased her. She already knew them by heart. '*You will receive no more letters from me and be no longer bothered.*' The words carried complete conviction. Then '*From one you have reason to thank and who thanks you.*'

She liked the way he thanked her. And perhaps she *did* have reason to thank this unknown. Perhaps he was a good character who had been absolutely forced, for some reason, to use underhand methods.

She inclined strongly to this view. After all, why should the man, whoever he was, go to the trouble, unless he was good, of writing her a third letter to reassure her and thank her?

It may be said that all this time the thought of Ryan had hardly entered Esther's head.

Anger atrophies fear: a really angry man will strike another man much larger than himself. So does great relief atrophy other emotions. Esther was impervious to regretful or romantic thoughts.

2

When Esther arrived at the Metropole (noticing the red dream-car outside) Gorse had risen from their usual table to greet her. Esther was radiant, and radiantly beautiful, with joy. Only a satanic creature, such as Gorse was, could, surely, pursue, as he did, his dark plans with so lovely a being.

'Hullo,' she said, sitting down. 'I've got something to tell you. I've got some good news.'

Gorse had seen her mood as soon as she had entered. It gave him pleasure and satisfaction. It was exactly the mood he had intended to induce in her when he had sent her the final letter.

Tonight was an important night for Gorse: the success of his plans hung upon what happened between Esther and himself in the next hour or two: and so he wanted Esther to be in a good mood.

'Have you?' he said. 'Well, I've got a bit of news too. But what's yours?'

'No,' said Esther rapturously. 'Let's wait till our drinks come. That's what you make *me* do.'

'Well, that won't be long,' said Gorse. 'I've taken the liberty of ordering them.'

'And what's *your* news? Good or bad?'

'Well, it could have been bad. But I think it'll be all right. In fact, I know it will. Though actually I want a bit of *your* help this time.'

'Well, you shall certainly have it,' said Esther, in her own happiness not taking Gorse's trouble in any way seriously. 'You help me, and I help you. That's only fair – isn't it?'

The drinks came.

'These glasses are larger,' said Esther.

'They're larger drinks,' said Gorse. 'I wanted a bit of bucking up, and I thought we might make a change. Well, go on. What's your news?'

'Here you are,' said Esther, producing the anonymous letter. 'Read that. I'm out of the wood now all right. And it's all due to you, really. I'm pretty grateful, you know.'

Gorse pretended to read the letter. Then he said:

'Oh yes. This is wonderful. You're out of the wood all right – there's no mistaking that. Well, let's drink to it. Congratulations. Well done.'

They drank.

'Shall I tear this up?' Gorse said.

'No,' said Esther. 'Give it back, will you? I want to keep it. I want to go on looking at it.' She took it back from him. 'And now. Tell me. What's *your* trouble? And how can I help *you* or advise *you*, this time?'

'Well – it's not really so much advice I want as help.'

'Go on, then. Tell me.'

Gorse paused, and took another sip at his drink.

'Well,' he said. 'It's this. That money – the money from my aunt – hasn't come through.'

'What about it? It hasn't *fallen* through, has it?'

'Oh – good heavens no. Nothing like that. It's just been delayed again. It'll be here on Monday for certain.'

'But what does it matter, then?'

'It wouldn't, normally, but just at this moment it matters more than anything else on earth. It means that I lose that car outside.'

'Lose the car?'

'Yes. Unless I get some help.'

Esther saw roughly what was coming, and her soul was emptied of joy.

'What sort of help?'

'Well – what do you think? Monetary help.'

'A lot?'

'Yes. A great lot.'

Esther's soul was now not only emptied of joy. Grave anxiety was pouring into it.

'But *why* do you lose the car?'

'Because the deposit of fifteen pounds I gave Gosling only lasts till twelve noon tomorrow. And if I don't fork up by then I not only lose the fifteen pounds, but the car as well. But don't look so worried. You can help me, and it's going to be all right.'

'Help you how much?'

'Well – in a pretty big way. I'm sorry, but there's nothing else to do. Thank heavens I've got you to come to.'

'But *how* big a way?'

'Well, I'll give you the details. The car's going – for a song – at eighty-five pounds. I've paid fifteen as deposit. That means seventy more to come.'

'Well?'

'Well, I went to Bell this morning, and he lent me five. He hadn't got it himself, but his aunt had. She happens to like me, fortunately. So that leaves sixty-five pounds to be found.'

'Well?'

'Well – don't you see? It all fits in. With your sixty-eight you can just do it for me. You get it back on Monday, and now I'm determined to give you a real share, and every sort of security as well. You and I are going to make a lot of money – between us.'

'But I *can't*!' said Esther. 'I *can't*! Not all that money.'

'Oh, don't be silly,' said Gorse, utterly coolly and casually. 'It's as simple as pie – simpler. All you've got to do is to dig out the money tomorrow morning – early – and it'll have to be early, and then –'

'But I *can't*! said Esther. 'It's all the money my mother gave me.'

'What's that got to do with it? You're going to get it back on Monday. And a lot more, too. I don't see where the trouble is.'

Gorse was still beautifully casual.

'But it's all I've *got*!' said Esther, and spoke incorrectly in her excitement. 'I ain't rich like you.'

'Not "ain't". I'm *not*,' said Gorse. 'You told me to tell you these little things.'

'Well, then, *not*. I'm not rich like you – and I just can't do such things.'

'I don't know what you're getting so excited about,' said Gorse. 'It's just a plain business transaction. If you go on like this I'll think you're mean or something. Or that you don't trust me. And that'd be worse. You *do* trust me – don't you?'

'Of course I do. You know that. But there must be some other way round.'

'I wish you could tell me what,' said Gorse.

'Well – this man who's selling the car – what's his name?'

'Gosling.'

'Well – if you give him a little more money – say another fifteen pounds – won't he wait?'

'Don't you think I've tried that? I've been haggling with him all this afternoon. The man's as hard as nails. And he's got everything in writing. I'm going to show you all the documents later. I don't like the man, but I don't blame him for being a bit hard. He knows I'm getting a bargain of a lifetime, and he knows, now it's too late, that there're dozens of people after the car – people who'd be only too glad to pay double the price, if not more. He's only praying in his soul that I don't stump up.'

'But your money from your aunt might come through tomorrow morning.'

'Not a hope. I've got a letter from my solicitor – I'm going to show it to you in a moment – and beyond any suspicion of doubt it'll definitely be here on Monday morning – but not a moment before.'

'But *still* there must be a way round. What about Bell's aunt? Wouldn't she help?'

'No. I tried that one. That's no good. Not a penny more than five pounds from *her*. Though she's got the money. It's funny how the richer people in life are so mean, and the poorer ones so generous.'

'Then what about your uncle – the one in Preston?'

'If you can get water out of a stone you might get threepence out of my Uncle Ralph. But I don't think you can get water out of a stone – can you?'

'Then what about your people – your stepmother?'

'Yes. She'd probably give it to me in the long run. In fact, I'm sure she would. And my solicitors would advance the money on Aunt Lucy's legacy. But it's a question of *time* – don't you see? There's no way of getting the money by *twelve o'clock tomorrow morning*.'

'Then what about a money-lender?'

'Well – first of all, I don't know a money-lender in Brighton. And then I don't like dealing with money-lenders. I never have and never will. They're dangerous people. And, then, even if I found a money-lender in Brighton, I'd never get the money in time. They put you through thousands of formalities, because they want security – quite naturally. Now you're *not* a money-lender, but I *am* going to give you security.'

'What does security mean – exactly?'

'Well – something which makes it absolutely sure that you get the money back.'

'What security are you going to give me, then?'

'You sound very stern and businesslike.'

'I'm sorry. But tell me. I can't help being anxious.'

'Well – I'm coming to that in a moment. But first of all I want to show you all the documents. You're quite right, really. In business one's got to be businesslike.'

'I don't really want to see them. I probably wouldn't understand them, anyway.'

'Oh yes. They're quite simple,' said Gorse, feeling for papers in his pocket. 'Now. Here we are. Exhibit one.'

Gorse now produced three documents – all typed.

The first purported to be a copy of an agreement with Gosling. In this agreement Gorse had promised to forfeit his deposit of fifteen pounds if he had not produced the remainder of the money for the car by twelve noon, Saturday.

The second purported to be an agreement, signed over a stamp, by Gosling, in which the latter acknowledged the receipt of the fifteen pounds' deposit, and declared that he would sell the car to Gorse for £85, provided the remainder of the money was given to him by Gorse by twelve noon, Saturday.

The third document seemed to be a letter from a firm of solicitors. It had imposing-headed notepaper from a perfectly genuine firm of first-class solicitors. Gorse had acquired the useful habit of stealing notepaper from any hotel, club, firm of solicitors, or other owners of imposing-headed notepaper.

The letter from this firm of solicitors was half formal, half informal. It was apparently signed by one of the directors of the firm, whose name appeared upon the headed notepaper. The letter apologized for the unexpected and annoying delay in the sending of the cheque, and assured Gorse that it would reach him by Monday without fail. The name of this firm of solicitors was 'Rose and Loughborough'.

'That's Sir Charles Loughborough, Bart.,' said Gorse. 'It's pronounced Luffborough. I used to pronounce it wrong when I used to meet the old boy as a kid. I expected you've heard of him. He was pretty well known in his day.'

Esther had not heard of Sir Charles Loughborough, but she was awed by the name, and believed in the letter.

'No. I haven't,' she said. 'Are you related to him, then?'

'No,' said Gorse. 'No connection at all. Nothing so grand. You'll see the letter's signed Rose – Ronald Rose. That's the connection. The Roses are sort of distant cousins of mine. Ronnie's a jolly good sport – and a friend of mine, as you can see by the letter – but the rest of the firm's all very pompous and stuffy.'

Although Esther entirely believed in these documents, and in Gorse, she still did not want to part with sixty-five pounds.

'You know, I *still* don't want to do it,' she said.

'Well – you haven't got to,' said Gorse. 'It's your choice. I've just got to lose fifteen pounds, and let's see – what's the exact double of eighty-five pounds? Yes – that's a hundred and seventy pounds to be precise. Well – I've got to lose that, if you won't help me.'

Esther did not perceive the flaw in his mathematics.

'But you haven't got to,' Gorse went on. 'In a way it's just fifteen pounds down the drain, that's all. But I lose the *car*! That's what's so important to me! However, there we are, if you feel that way. I'd have thought those letters would have been sufficient security for you. Actually –'

'Yes. I know *they're* all right. It's just I don't like the whole idea – that's all.'

'Now that's not speaking like the Esther I know – the Esther who does things in the right way. You know you've got to take risks if you're going to get anywhere. You've got to do things in style. Not that there's the tiniest risk on earth in this case. The whole thing's as safe as houses.'

'Yes. But I'm so *poor*. My *family's* so poor. Don't you see that –'

'No. Let me go on. You interrupted me just now. I was going to say that actually I've got much more security than I've shown you.'

'Have you?' said Esther miserably. 'What?'

'Well – first of all, I can give you an IOU for the money. You know what an IOU is – I take it?'

'Yes. I've heard of them, anyway.'

'Well – if it's signed over a stamp it's absolutely valid in law, and I could write it here and now. Then, if anything went wrong, you could sue me. Unless you think I'm going to vanish into thin air? Do you?'

'Don't be silly. Go on.'

'Well – even if I did vanish – I mean if I was run down by a bus – you could claim on the estate – the Gorse estate.'

'Could I?'

'Yes. But that's not all. You can ring up my solicitors – Rose and Loughborough – and simply get them to tell you that the money's there, and reaching me by Monday. You can't do it tonight – but you can early tomorrow morning. Of course, it's Saturday morning, and they may not all be there. But there's bound to be somebody in charge to tell you. Ronnie Rose himself'll almost certainly be there – though, as a matter of fact, I know that he likes, when he's given the chance, to sneak off and get a game of golf on a Saturday morning. He's a crack golfer, and he likes to play the whole of Saturday when he possibly can.'

All this wealth of inventive detail was convincing Esther more and more. Nobody, she thought, could possibly *invent* detail like this.

And, in fact, Gorse, had he not been what he was, might have been a highly successful novelist.

'But even *that's* not all,' said Gorse. 'There's more.'

'Is there?' said Esther, slightly less miserably. 'What more?'

'Well – it's half sentimental and half businesslike.'

'Sentimental?'

'Yes. It concerns a ring.'

'What sort of ring?'

'Well – not an engagement ring, or a wedding ring, actually. But this ring – the one I'm wearing. It's a signet ring. Would you like to have a look at it?'

'Yes. I've noticed your ring,' said Esther. 'And I've wondered what it was. I like it. It suits you, somehow.'

'Well, I should imagine it'd suit anybody,' said Gorse, taking it off and handing it to Esther. 'I'm very proud of it. Just take a look at it.'

Just as Gorse had adopted an old school tie which he had no right to wear, so he had adopted, falsely, a family relationship – a relationship with the peerage.

The ring he wore was of gold, with a cornelian stone, upon which was engraved the image of a horse's head – a head like that of a chess knight. A person related to Lord Belhaven and Stenton might have worn such a ring.

Gorse, whose real social snobbery was deep and bitter, had also thought it might be useful to exploit social snobbery for commercial purposes.

About a year ago, while he was lazily yet greedily turning the pages of *Debrett* in a Public Library, this crest had caught his attention, and appealed to his imagination as being a suitable one to adopt. The family to whom it belonged, it seemed to him, was of the correct type. It would be flying neither too high nor too low. It will be remembered that Gorse had been clever enough, when choosing a tie, not to have gone to Eton or Harrow.

He had had the ring made at Spinks's, and it had cost him as much as ten pounds.

'Well – what do you think of it?' he said.

'It's lovely. What is it – exactly?'

'Well – it's been handed down in my family – that very thing you're holding now – from generation to generation. The crest's Belhaven and Stenton – Lord Belhaven and Stenton.'

'Good lord,' said Esther. 'Are you connected with a lord?'

'You got rather a lot of lords into that sentence,' said Gorse jocularly. 'Yes. I am. But it's all extremely distant and only on my mother's side. She had another name – the Belhaven family name. You can look it up in *Debrett's* if you like.'

'What's *Debrett's*?'

'Oh – just a reference book about all these things. You'll find one in any Public Library. There's probably one in this hotel, if we ask. However, it's a lovely ring – isn't it?'

'It certainly is.'

'And do you know how much it's worth?'

'No. Not the faintest idea.'

'You don't know about antiques at all?'

'Not a thing.'

'Well – it's worth about fifty pounds. It might be a little more or a little less. You see, it's got historical value. I couldn't tell you the exact date – but it's well over a hundred years old. And that sort of thing fetches money.'

'Yes. I suppose it does,' said Esther, quite believing all this piffle, and she tried to hand the ring back to him.

'No,' said Gorse, waving it away and looking at her earnestly as he leaned forward. 'I don't want it back. That's just the point. I want to give it to you – or at any rate lend it to you. That's half as security for you, and half sentimental.'

'How sentimental?'

'Well – don't you see what I mean? Quite apart from any question of security, I'm giving you something of great sentimental value, for great sentimental reasons. You must know what I mean.'

'No . . . I don't . . .'

'Listen, Esther. You know I've told you I'm going to ask you something soon – to ask you if you'll marry me. Well – I am. And I'd ask you tonight if I could, but your mind's on other things. So's mine, if it comes to that. But I want you to take that ring as something more than security. I'd like you to say that it means that there's a bond between us. Heaven knows I wouldn't give it into the keeping of anyone else – apart from its money value, its sentimental value's too great. And so I want you to say that it means there's a sentimental bond between us. Will you?'

'Well – there's certainly a bond between us, after what I've been through, and the way you've taken me out and helped me. I can certainly say that, though we've only known each other such a short time.'

'You know, it seems to me that I've known you for about five years. Funny, but there it is.'

'Yes. I feel I've known you a long time too.'

'And will you take the ring? Please say that you will.'

'All right. I'll take it. If you want me to.'

'And, although it's not an engagement ring – couldn't we look upon it as a sort of *half* engagement ring? Couldn't you say that we're sort of *half* engaged? It doesn't commit you to anything.'

'All right. I'll say it.'

'Thank you. I don't think you know how happy you've made

me. Now don't let's say another word about it at the moment. You might say something to spoil everything. Now, you put that ring in your bag – it's too big for any of your little fingers – and let's get back to business.'

Esther, dazed and by no means unhappy at this firm proposal of marriage – her first from what she called a 'gentleman' – had almost forgotten about the horrible business on hand. But, somehow, it was much less horrible now. The large drink, too, was going to her head.

'Yes,' she said. 'I'd forgotten business.'

'Well. Just let me run through the details, and I'm sure you'll agree there's nothing in it – one's only making a mountain out of an absurd little molehill. Now, remember what your securities are. One, there's those letters I've shown you. Two, there's my IOU, absolutely valid in law. Ask a lawyer. Three, you can ring up my solicitors. Their telephone number's on their notepaper and I can give it to you now. Fourthly and lastly, but by no means least, there's that ring, which I wouldn't part with for anyone else on earth. Now, say you'll just help me out for ever such a little while. Will you?'

Esther hesitated. Then suddenly, and believing in Gorse's valuation of the ring, and not without the aid of the larger drink which Gorse had purposely bought for her, Esther was utterly convinced by Gorse's story, and was sure that she was secure.

'All right,' she said. 'I will. I suppose I'll have to.'

'Thank you for saying that. I can promise you you won't lose by it. In fact, you're going to gain a great deal. Because I'm now going to *insist* that you have a share in the car, and that means a share in the profit when it's sold. And now let's change the subject and be gay. It's worth celebrating. We're going to have good times ahead in that little bus. Come on. Drink up.'

They drank, and the subject was changed.

But soon Gorse saw that Esther's mind was unable to fix itself upon other subjects.

He had won a technical victory, probably a real one – but Esther still had a night and morning in which to change her mind.

Gorse had anticipated this situation and had up his sleeve what he believed was an unbeatable card.

The reader may be interested to learn, at this point, that Gorse was, in fact, the owner of the car.

The youthful but highly experienced speculator in cars had paid for it in cash only that morning.

It may also interest the reader to learn that all of Gorse's recent persuasion of Esther was merely an exercise in his own powers of persuasion. He had an unbeatable card, but he wanted to prove to himself that he could win the game without it. He was deliciously satisfied with his success.

But now, as he saw that Esther's mind was wandering back to the car and to her promise, he decided to play his unbeatable card.

He interrupted the conversation suddenly, and said:

'Oh, good heavens! What a fool I am!'

'What? How?' said Esther.

'About the car. It's just come to me this moment.'

'What?'

'Well – I needn't have gone into all that palaver at all. I've got a *much* better security for you than *all* those I've mentioned.'

'What?'

'One that'll cut out all the IOUs and the telephoning, and all that. Although you can still have all that. It's so simple! And I didn't see it!'

'But what *is* it?'

'Why – the car *itself*.'

'How?'

'Listen. Tomorrow morning I can go to Gosling early, and I know he'll let me have it for the morning. If he didn't trust me he wouldn't let me have it now, and anyway, he's charging me three bob an hour for the loan of it – the old Shylock . . .'

'Well?'

'Well – all I've got to do is to call for you in the car early tomorrow morning. At the end of Over Street if you don't want the house. Then you give me the money. Then we pay Gosling – you can come with me while I do it. And then you need never let the car out of your sight. You can put it into any garage, of your *own* choosing, and tell the garage people it's *yours*, and that no one else – including me – can take it out. Either that, or leave it outside your house all day and night. In fact, you can *sleep* in it, if you want to. And it'll jolly well be *yours* until you get your money back on Monday. You see how simple it all is?'

'Why, yes. That does sound simpler than IOUs, and all that. But you mustn't think I don't trust you.'

'I know you trust me. But this way's so much simpler. It's *I* who've been so "simple", as they say. In fact, I'm afraid, if you *should* accept an offer I'm going to make so very soon, you'll be engaged to a complete idiot.'

He saw a glow of relief on Esther's face. Another of his reasons for telling her the long circumstantial story had been to put this glow of relief into Esther's soul. Gorse, all his life, was an expert exploiter of the emotion of relief in women.

'Well, it does seem simpler – though I'd hate you to think I don't trust you,' said Esther joyfully. 'In fact, the only trouble I can see is I'll be late for work tomorrow.'

'Well – you can get round *that*, can't you, for an occasion like this? Can't you pretend you're ill?'

'Yes. I could. Or I could get my little brother to go round and say I'll be late. They're very good to me round there.'

'There we are, then. By the way, there's only one other little thing. You might think the car might not be worth the money. But you can get the garage people, the people *you* choose, to assess that, and, believe me, they'll agree with me. There. Now let's have another drink and go for a little spin again. But only a small one this time. No driving under the influence.'

Gorse and Esther had another drink, Esther taking all of her own. Then, in a state of great exhilaration, Esther went for a ride in the car with Gorse.

He finally left her at the end of Over Street, arranging to be there, with the car, at nine o'clock tomorrow morning.

As Esther walked to her humble home she believed that she had fully decided to accept Gorse's offer of marriage or an engagement, when he made it.

Though she had pointed out that it was now unnecessary, Gorse had insisted upon her keeping the signet ring. Among other things, Esther did not totally dislike the notion of marrying one who was related, however distantly, to a 'lord'.

She looked many times at the ring in the dim gaslight of her bedroom, and she put it on to several of her fingers.

She was a good sleeper, and she slept beautifully.

Chapter Two

I

The car and Gorse were at the end of Over Street next morning, five minutes before the appointed time, as Esther saw from her bedroom window.

Of course Esther had not told her mother about the car and the temporary surrender of her savings. Her mother would not approve: she would argue. This would cause delay and Gorse had only until twelve. Also, her mother might want to meet Gorse, and this would embarrass him. It would embarrass herself, too, for Esther was ashamed of the mother she loved. She was not so much ashamed of her as she was of her father, but all the same she was ashamed – afraid.

She therefore bribed her little brother with twopence and asked him to take a note to the sweet-shop. The note said that she would be late, and that she would explain why when she arrived. She would think of an excuse later: it would depend on how late she was. She made her little brother swear to keep the matter secret from her mother. He readily agreed.

Having met Gorse, Esther got into the red dream-car, and gave him (apart from three pounds fifteen shillings) her entire savings. She had taken these from the old tin safe, hidden amongst clothes in her old tin trunk, the night before.

'And now to our friend Gosling in his royal residence in Portslade,' said Gorse when the car was moving.

'But I thought you said he was in the London Road,' said Esther.

'Yes. That's where his garage is. But it's Saturday morning, and he's over at his private house.'

'Oh lord,' said Esther. 'That's going to take some time, isn't it?'

'Oh no – not long,' said Gorse. 'With any luck we'll get the whole thing signed and sealed under an hour.'

They had not been driving long before Esther, who was very worried about being late for her work, and who utterly trusted Gorse, said that she would rather not accompany him to Portslade. She asked him if he would drop her near the sweet-shop at which she worked.

Gorse had rather fancied that she would do this. The matter had not bothered him, however, for he had many tricks to play had she not done so.

2

Gorse, on leaving Esther near the sweet-shop, said that, after he had paid Gosling and was the owner of the car, he would call in the car at the sweet-shop and buy some sweets.

He did this at eleven-thirty. She saw the car outside. He bought some sweets and spoke to Esther. He said that the car was now his – and hers. He asked her when they were to go to whatever garage she had chosen.

His future plans were such that he did not even care in the least if she insisted on a garage, or watching or sleeping in the car.

She said that she had chosen no garage: she trusted him. And she had his ring, she said jokingly.

He said that he could not meet her that evening because he had to go again to his uncle in Preston. What, then, he asked, was to be done with the car?

Esther said that she thought it advisable to take the car and drive over in it to his uncle in Preston.

'The old boy'll be a bit taken aback,' said Gorse. 'But the point is, when do I meet you again? What about Sunday afternoon and a real spin in the country?'

'Well,' said Esther. 'I'm supposed to give that up to seeing Father.'

'Oh – can't you make an exception?' said Gorse. 'This is a pretty big occasion, after all, isn't it?'

'All right, then. I'll manage it somehow,' said Esther. 'Where and when on Sunday?'

'Well – what about two-thirty – outside the Metropole? I'll be waiting there in the car.'

'All right,' said Esther. 'That sounds fine.'

'All right. Two-thirty – outside the Metropole – tomorrow. And in the meanwhile will you work out what sort of answer you're going to give to that question I'm going to ask *you*? I'm going to ask you it tomorrow afternoon.'

'Yes. I'll try and work it out.'

At this Esther had to serve a customer, and Gorse left her.

Gorse, having no uncle there, was, of course, not going to Preston. He had made the excuse simply because he preferred to spend the evening alone.

The girl and her company bored him.

It would have been possible, now, for Gorse to have fulfilled his plans at once – in which case Esther would not have seen him again.

But Gorse intended to meet Esther tomorrow. He wanted to recover his ring.

Chapter Three

I

Esther, finding herself unexpectedly without a friend on a Saturday evening, became lonely as the evening wore on, and was even assailed by remote doubts and fears in regard to Gorse. These she shook off easily, but her loneliness remained.

For this reason she took the unusual step of calling upon Gertrude, who lived in another little street near Over Street, with the object of asking her to take a walk with her.

Gertrude was at home, but she was not free. She had arranged to go to the cinema with another girlfriend, who was paying for the seats.

Esther knew perfectly well that she had no reason to be offended by Gertrude's having made an arrangement to go elsewhere with another patroness: all the same, she was slightly displeased. The slightly 'spoiled' girl had come to look upon her slave-companion, the ugly Gertrude, as one who would be ready to come out with her whenever called upon to do so.

But this is characteristic of slave-companions. They are finally compelled to lead some sort of life of their own, and, nearly always, at the very moment when they are most wanted by their owner-companions, are engaged elsewhere.

The matter was made worse because Gertrude (as she had to explain to Esther) could not very well invite Esther to join herself and her friend at the cinema. Her friend (who was unknown to Esther) was most generously paying for the seats, and it would look rude.

Also, Esther did not relish the idea of Gertrude having another patroness at all. However, she showed nothing of these somewhat base feelings, left Gertrude with a pretence of cheerfulness, and decided to go for a walk by herself along the front.

2

Ever since the receipt of the final anonymous letter, and the excitement caused by the car, a thought of Ryan had hardly entered Esther's head.

But Ryan, needless to say, had been thinking of practically nothing else besides Esther.

He had been forbidden to write to her or see her. But could he not possibly manage to meet her accidentally?

After his early-morning meeting with Gorse, he haunted the front and the West Pier – morning and night. He also tried the Palace Pier.

Then he thought that, although he had been forbidden to call at her house, he had not been forbidden to look at it, or at any rate haunt its vicinity. He made inquiries about the whereabouts of Over Street, and found it. He did not dare walk down it, but he loitered at one end of it, in the same place that Gorse had loitered and met Esther in the car.

He did this more than once, had cups of tea at Brighton Station, and was in the neighbourhood a great deal.

It was because of this that he ran into Esther on that Saturday evening after Esther had left Gertrude and was making for the Brighton Front.

He met her at the bottom of Queen's Road, very near the Clock Tower. There were many people passing on the pavement. The encounter was brief and most unpleasant.

3

'Hullo!' said Ryan, completely surprising her, for he had come up from behind her. 'Well – fancy running into you.'

'Oh – hullo,' said Esther, who did not smile and went white in the face.

Esther's emotions were of a mixed and peculiar nature. Ryan had not been in her mind for two days, and he belonged to, was the central figure of, a horrible episode in the past. In this past she had been tortured, and then she had been relieved of this torture.

Now a feature of torture, physical or otherwise, is this. The victim will endure much: some victims, indeed, will endure an incredible amount of it, without flinching. But, once having been relieved of torture, there are few, if any, victims who can tolerate the thought of having to submit to it once more. In the case of physical torture to extract a secret, it is usually at this point that the victim gives in.

Ryan symbolized Esther's recent torture, and the sight of him filled her with horror. She could not go back to it again.

In fact, her affection for Ryan had turned into a complete revulsion.

'How are you?' said Ryan.

'I'm all right . . .' said Esther, still white.

'It's very nice to see you again,' said Ryan. 'And funny meeting you here, of all places.'

'Yes, it is,' said Esther. 'And I told you I didn't want to meet you again. You know that.'

'I'm sorry. It was quite an accident. I was just in this part of the world.'

'Yes. And why were you in this part of the world – so near to where I live?'

'Oh – I don't know . . .' said Ryan, his whole manner and tone suggesting that he had been hanging about in the neighbourhood.

'Have you been hanging about and following me?'

'No – of course I haven't been following you,' said Ryan, and added foolishly, 'I'll admit I've been hanging about a bit.'

'Yes. I thought so,' said Esther. 'And I don't like it. You got my letter – didn't you? So will you leave me now?'

'But why?' said Ryan. 'I don't understand. Why can't we *meet*, even if there *is* someone else?'

'We can't. That's all,' said Esther.

'But *why*?' said Ryan. 'Anyway, couldn't I just have one more little talk with you? Couldn't we go into a coffee-shop or something *now*, and just have a little talk?'

'No. I'm afraid we couldn't.'

'But just tell me *why*,' said Ryan, unwisely raising his voice. 'It all seems so utterly *absurd*!'

Esther saw that his raised voice had attracted the attention of a passer-by. She anticipated some dreadful scene in public. This threw her into a panic. At the same time she realized that the unknown writer might still be watching her – might be watching them both at this moment. Her panic increased.

'I've told you why in my letter,' she said, also raising her voice. 'Now will you please go and leave me *alone*!'

Her anger was real. It was also, in a way, simulated and made to look greater than it was. This was for the benefit of the possible watcher.

'I can't see why you're so angry!' said Ryan, almost shouting. 'At any rate, there's nothing to be *angry* about!'

Now it seemed to Esther that people were definitely standing and watching them. She was in a public brawl. She was filled with even greater fear and rage.

'Look here, will you leave me this *moment*?' she said. 'Or am I to call a *policeman* and make *him* make you leave me?'

This, quite naturally, put Ryan himself into a violent temper.

'All right, I'll leave you,' he said. 'But I think you're a silly little fool – that's all – a damned silly little fool. Goodbye!'

He left her, walking in the direction of Brighton Station. Esther walked on towards the front.

4

As arranged, Ryan called upon Gorse early on Sunday morning. The ginger-haired young man was again found in bed with his breakfast.

After greeting Gorse, Ryan came straight to the point.

'Well,' he said. 'I ran into that girl again last night.'

'Really?' said Gorse, who was disturbed by this news. Those two, then, might still have compared notes about their anonymous letters. What Ryan said next, however, relieved Gorse.

'And it looks as if it's all over, as you said.'

'Why? What happened exactly?'

'Oh, we met in the street, and she wouldn't even speak to me. She ended up by threatening to call a policeman.'

'A policeman!' exclaimed Gorse.

'Yes. A policeman,' said Ryan. '*Me! A policeman!*'

'Yes. That does sound a bit stiff, I must say.'

'However,' said Ryan, 'I thought I might just call and ask if you found anything out. Did you?'

'Yes. I did my best for you. I sang your praises, and I pumped her as much as I could.'

'And what was the result?'

'It was just what I thought. There *is* somebody else, beyond any doubt, and that's just that. She was absolutely firm about it. I'm afraid you'll have to call it a day. I'm sorry, but there it is.'

'What sort of person is it? Did you find that out?'

'Not exactly. She was a bit reticent. But I gathered, pretty well for certain, that it was someone in her own class. They make strange choices, these girls.'

'Yes, I suppose they do. However, as you say, that's that, and there's nothing more to do about it. I'm pretty well fed up, anyway. Particularly after that threat about a policeman.'

'Yes,' said Gorse. 'That was rather low. But then, you see, they *are* low, these people, and that's why you're so well out of it. It's an awful thing to say, I know, but breeding does tell in the end. If they come from that class it always comes out somehow, though sometimes you have to wait for it.'

'Yes. I suppose you're right. But I thought her different, somehow.'

'Yes, She was a little unusual.'

'Yes. She was. She got under *my* skin, I must say. But now the whole thing's made me feel so fed up that I've decided to cut my holiday short and get away from Brighton. I'm packing up and going home this afternoon.'

'Well – funnily enough – I'm feeling just the same. I'll probably be going myself, tomorrow or the day after.'

They talked about other things for a little, and then Ryan prepared to go.

'Well,' he said. 'It's been a funny holiday. Nice in some ways – nasty in others – for me, at any rate. Anyway, it's been nice seeing you and Bell again. I hope we'll all be meeting again sometime.'

'Yes. I certainly hope so. By the way, have you got my address – my home address?'

Gorse had a minor reason in asking this.

'No. I did know it – I think – but I'm afraid I've lost your letters, and it's gone from me.'

'Well, it doesn't matter,' said Gorse. 'Because we're moving in about two weeks. And I'm going to be on the move for a bit. However, I've got yours and I'll write.'

'Good. Do. And now I think I'd better be buzzing off. Well. Goodbye and good luck.'

'Same to you.'

They shook hands.

'Oh, I'm sorry,' said Ryan, at the door. 'I completely forgot to thank you for trying to help me. It was really good of you, and thank you very much. Well. Goodbye.'

'Not at all. I was only too happy, and you're more than welcome. Goodbye,' said the nasal-voiced, imperturbable doer of good deeds.

PART TWELVE

JOURNEY

Chapter One

I

Esther found Gorse waiting for her in the car outside the Metropole at two-thirty on Sunday afternoon. He wore a motoring cap, and she was pleased by his appearance.

He drove her out into the country.

After about half an hour Esther, as they drove along, said:

'Oh – by the way, hadn't I better give you back that ring?'

Thus Esther had volunteered to give it back to him. If she had not, he had plenty of tricks with which to extract it from her: but he was glad that she had brought the subject up herself, and glad, too, that she had it with her. Otherwise he would have had to go to the trouble of using further tricks to make her go back to her house and get it.

'No,' he said. 'That's just what I don't want you to do. I love you keeping it – apart from all that security nonsense. And talking of rings, I've got another ring. I bought it yesterday.'

'What ring?'

'It's very cheap. It cost me exactly two bob, in fact. But it's an engagement ring. It's only a temporary one. Tomorrow, when my money comes through, I'll get another one – a proper one. That is, if you're going to give a favourable reply to a question I'm going to ask you this evening.'

Here Esther very nearly said, 'Why not ask it now?' For she had decided to become engaged to Gorse. She was not absolutely certain that she would marry him (though she thought she would), but what harm could there be in an engagement? What, after all, were engagements for? To enter, surely, into an arrangement which was not entirely binding.

'Oh – it's to be this evening, is it?' she said.

'Yes. Over our drinks, at the Met. I want you to be in a good mood, you see,' said Gorse. 'But I'll tell you what.'

'What?'

'If you've got it on you, I might as well wear it just while I'm with you. I feel sort of naked without it.'

She produced the ring from her bag and gave it to him. He stopped the car and put the ring on his finger.

'I was terrified of losing it, anyway,' said Esther.

At about a quarter to five they were in the vicinity of Shoreham.

'Now we're near Shoreham,' said Gorse. 'And I've got a bit of a bore to go through. I've got to go to my uncle.'

'What? *Another* uncle? Here?'

'Oh no. Not that sort of uncle,' said Gorse, giving a little giggle. 'Haven't you heard the expression "my uncle" – meaning a pawnbroker? I'm short of cash, and I've got to pay for tea soon, and drinks at the Metropole tonight. You see, Monday morning's an important day for all of us.'

'But isn't a pawnbroker a money-lender? And I thought you disapproved of money-lenders. And anyway, will he be open on a Sunday?'

'No – pawnbrokers aren't anything like money-lenders. And my friend Mr Fenton is a very high-class pawnbroker. And I'm calling at his private house. I arranged it yesterday over the phone.'

'You don't half arrange things – don't you?'

'Not "don't half". You told me to tell you.'

'Sorry. You *do*. And thank you for telling me.'

'Not at all. Well – I've got my typewriter in the back there, and Mr Fenton has promised to lend me a fiver on it.'

Gorse spoke the truth when he said that he had his typewriter at the back of the car. All his belongings were there too.

'But it's got to be delivered in an hour's time, or he might be out,' said Gorse. 'And that means we've got to go miles beyond Shoreham. And I want my tea – don't you?'

'Yes. I must say I do.'

'But needs must when the devil drives. You haven't got any money to see me through, have you?'

Gorse had seen pound notes in Esther's bag when she had given him back the ring.

'Yes. I've got a bit.'

'How much?'

'I've got three pounds and a few coppers. It's what's left over from what I took out.'

'Oh well. That's fine. If you'll just loan it to me we can have tea at once.'

'What? The whole three?'

'No. Two'll be enough. More than enough, really. I can give you any change at the end of the evening. Well – shall it be that, or shall we wend our weary way to Mr Fenton?'

'No,' said Esther. 'Let me lend it to you.'

'Well – that's very good of you.'

'And have the whole three,' said the generous girl, taking the notes from her bag.

'All right,' said Gorse. 'It's all the same. I can give you the change in the evening. I certainly hope we're not going to spend three pounds. But there *may* be an occasion to celebrate in a big way – mayn't there?'

'There might,' said Esther. And she gave him, as he drove, three pounds. These, removing one hand from the steering wheel, Gorse put into a pocket of his coat.

Much as we may dislike the character of Gorse, it must be conceded that he did things thoroughly.

2

Gorse knew a large inn, a mile or so to the north of Shoreham, at which teas were provided, in the summer, in the garden at the back.

It was called 'Ye Olde Wheatsheafe', and it was of partially genuine, partially vilely restored Elizabethan architecture.

Gorse drove towards this. Then, at a walking distance of about two minutes away from it, he stopped the car in a quiet lane.

'We're just there,' he said. 'But we'd better leave the car here. It's one of those swanky places, and if you drive up in a car like this they stick up the price. I'm sorry to be so mean, but I know the place.'

They walked to Ye Olde Wheatsheafe, outside which there were one or two cars. Esther was deeply delighted by the foolish architecture. She was deeply happy in every way.

3

Gorse took Esther through Ye Olde Wheatsheafe (whose name enchanted her) to the garden at the back.

Here there were a few people having tea – few because it was late for tea.

Tea was brought to them by a pleasant waitress.

They had bread-and-butter, strawberry jam, and cakes.

After tea Gorse smoked a cigarette (Esther, although invited, would not do so in public) and then said that he would like to wash his hands before they returned to the Metropole. He asked her if she would like to do this. She said that she would.

'Well – who'll go first?' Gorse asked.

'I don't mind.'

'You go first, then,' said Gorse.

Esther left him, and returned to him in about four minutes' time. Gorse was smoking another cigarette.

He rose politely.

'Well,' he said. 'Now I'll just go and do the same. Will you excuse me? My hands are absolutely filthy after all that driving. Not at all the way to appear at the Metropole. I won't be a sec. And talking of the Metropole, I may tell you I'm pretty worried about what's going to happen there tonight.'

'You needn't be,' said Esther. 'At least not *too* much.'

It seemed that Gorse had the power to extract the last ounce of everything from this girl, who, really, was by no means more credulous or stupid than other girls of her age. He had not only taken her savings: he had recovered his ring; and had deprived her even of the three pounds left over from her savings. Now, in having made her tell him that he need not worry too much about what would happen at the Metropole, he had most ironically extracted from her what was as good as an admission that she would engage herself to him, or marry him. It is difficult not to believe that, had he desired them, he could have taken from her the clothes in which she stood.

In much later years it was rumoured that Gorse had Hypnotic Eyes with women. Indeed, pictures of these alleged Hypnotic Eyes, isolated from his face, were published in the newspapers. But all this was mere press folly and sensationalism. Gorse had no hypnotic quality: all he did was to use common sense and take the greatest pains in a particular field of activity in which he was naturally gifted.

4

Left alone, Esther looked around at the pretty garden. There were now only two other couples left, and their tea was finished.

Esther watched one of these couples paying the bill and leaving the garden. Then she listened to the song of the birds, and watched the waitress clearing away the table which the couple had just left.

Amidst the song of the birds it would have been just possible for her to distinguish another noise – that of the engine of a car moving away at a high speed. This was the red dream-car, and Gorse was driving it. But Esther did not consciously hear this noise.

Gorse had had not the slightest difficulty in reaching the red car. He had walked straight and boldly through the hotel, and out to the front. Then, in the same calm way, he had turned to the right and reached the quiet lane in which he had left the car.

Then, because he believed (correctly) that he was unobserved by anyone, he had begun to run towards it.

In less than a minute after this Gorse had started the car and was on his way to London. He wanted to reach London before it was dark.

Although, for other reasons, he would have rather preferred darkness.

5

After about another minute the last couple in the garden paid their bill and left.

Although Gorse had been gone more than four minutes, not the faintest suspicion of his treachery had crossed Esther's mind.

After about six minutes she began to wonder why he was so late.

When about eight minutes had passed, the waitress asked Esther if their tea was finished, and, if so, whether she might clear the table. Esther said that they had finished and that she might.

The waitress was a blonde, rather pretty, big, amiable girl of about twenty-eight.

'Your friend seems a long time,' she said cheerfully to Esther.

'Yes, he does,' said Esther, who was still not in any way alarmed.

'And they always say,' said the amiable waitress, 'that it's the girls that keep men waiting. *I* always say it's the other way about.'

Esther politely and smilingly agreed with her.

The table was cleared.

'Well, I expect he'll be along soon,' said the waitress, and, having put a bill on the table, she went into the inn.

Now all the tables were cleared, and Esther was alone in the garden.

6

When five more minutes had passed Esther became anxious – but not gravely so.

She had three theories with which she explained Gorse's absence.

The one she favoured most, for some reason, was that he had gone to the car to fetch something. Perhaps, telepathically, or by some subconscious means, she had sensed that he had walked in the direction of the car. She might even subconsciously have heard him do so.

Her other theory was that he had been taken ill while washing his hands. Her final theory was that he was, rather inconsequently and rudely, doing something the nature of which she could not guess but which he would tell her about when he returned.

The real solution to the mystery did not even cross her mind.

After five more minutes, still not suspecting the truth, she was alarmed, and, picking up the bill, walked towards the inn. At the door she met the amiable waitress, who saw that she was looking alarmed.

'What – ain't he come back *yet*?' she asked.

'No,' said Esther.

'What on earth could have happened to him?'

'I don't know. Perhaps he's gone to the car. That's what I expect he's done. I think I'll go and see, shall I?'

'Yes. Let's go and see,' said the waitress.

The waitress accompanied Esther from the back of the inn to the front for two reasons. In the first place, she knew that the bill had not been paid and dimly suspected that all this might be a swindle – a walkout. She had had experience of such things in her profession. In the second place, she was curious, and eager to help the clearly anxious Esther.

On reaching the front of the house the waitress said:

'Well – there's no car here.'

'No,' said Esther. 'He left it in a lane just near. Shall I go and see? It's very near.'

'Why did he do that?'

'Well, as a matter of fact, he said that if you drive up to a hotel with a swell car, they stuck on the price.'

'Well – *that's* nonsense, anyway,' said the waitress. 'At this place, at any rate.'

'Well – shall I go and see? It's only a minute's walk.'

'Yes. I'll come with you, shall I?' said the waitress, inspired by the same motives which had induced her to escort Esther from the back of the inn to the front.

On reaching the lane Esther at once saw that the car was not there.

'It's not there,' she said. 'It's gone.'

She was merely baffled by the mystery: she still did not suspect Gorse's treachery.

'Oh lord,' said the waitress. 'I hope he hasn't gone and hopped it.'

Now, and only because it had been suggested to her by another, a faint suspicion of Gorse's treachery came across Esther's mind. But she dismissed it from her mind.

'Oh no,' she said. 'There must be some explanation. He must have *moved* the car for some reason. He's probably back in the hotel. He said he was going to wash his hands. It struck me that he might have been taken ill or something in the bathroom. Shall we go and see?'

'Yes. Let's.'

'I'm sure there's some quite simple explanation,' said Esther.

'Do you know him well?' asked the waitress as they walked back to the inn.

'Well,' said Esther. 'Fairly well.'

'How long?'

'Oh – about three weeks, I suppose.'

'Well, that's not *very* long – is it? I don't want to put the wind up you – but it's not too long – is it?'

'No. I suppose it's not.'

'Where did you meet him – if it's not a rude question?'

'Oh – on the West Pier, Brighton.'

'You mean he picked you up?'

'Yes. You *could* put it that way.'

'Well – that's not as good as a proper introduction, is it?'

'No. I suppose it's not.'

By the time they had reached the inn Esther had had time to reflect upon the truth of the waitress's observation, and she was white in the face. The waitress saw this, and pitied her.

'Now – don't you worry,' she said. 'Even if he has gone, it's not the first time a man's walked out on a girl and left her to pay the bill.'

'Oh – I'd forgotten about the bill,' said Esther. 'And there's a lot more to it than that.'

'Is there? What?'

'Well – it's a long story.'

'Well,' said the waitress. 'Don't tell me now. I'll go and see if he's up in the bathroom, or anywhere else in the hotel. You come in here and sit down.'

She took Esther to a long, low, beamed room in which two residents were sitting.

These two residents were a married couple of the Anglo-Indian type.

'Now, you sit down here,' said the waitress, 'and then I'll come back to you. I don't expect there's anything to worry about.'

The Anglo-Indian couple had heard the waitress's reassurance, and, during the six or seven minutes in which Esther was alone with them in the room, they stared at her. They did this at times openly and rudely, and at times furtively, at times while pretending to talk to each other, and at times in silence.

The man, elderly and moustached, was particularly vulgar and cruel in this matter.

The waitress returned.

'No,' she said quietly. 'He's not in the hotel. Will you come with me? We'd better go to the manageress. I've told her about it.'

7

Esther followed the waitress into a small office. It had only a small window and was electric-lit, now and all the year round.

The manageress was a fat, dark, middle-aged disagreeable woman, who took an instant dislike to Esther's good looks.

'Well, young lady,' she said. 'You seem to have got yourself into trouble – don't you?'

'Yes,' said the ashen Esther. 'I'm afraid I have.'

The ashen face did not impress the disagreeable manageress.

'This is what comes from gadding about in motorcars at your age,' she said. 'How old *are* you – may I ask?'

'Just eighteen,' said Esther.

'Yes – so I thought. That's just seventeen, too, isn't it?' said the manageress. 'Well – young lady – I'm afraid you've got landed with having to pay the bill, haven't you?'

'But I haven't even the *money* to pay the bill,' said Esther. 'And there's more to it than that. You don't understand.'

Here the waitress cut in.

'Yes,' she said. 'You said there was something more. *What's* more?'

'Well,' said Esther. 'If he's really left me, he hasn't just left me to pay the bill. He's run off with all my money.'

'And is that a lot?' asked the manageress.

'Yes. A great lot,' said Esther.

'How much?' said the manageress. 'If it's not too rude to ask.'

'Oh, it's a terrible lot,' said Esther.

Even in her black predicament Esther retained a certain amount of pride. She simply could not name the real sum: it would make her look such a fool in front of this harsh woman.

'But *how* much?' asked the manageress. 'Of course you haven't *got* to tell me.'

'Well, it's all my *savings*, anyway,' said Esther, holding her own. 'Every *penny* of them. And they were a *lot*. My *mother* gave them to me, too.'

'Well, I wonder what *she's* going to say,' said the beastly woman.

'Yes,' said Esther. 'So do I.'

The manageress was now slightly appeased by the thought of Esther having lost all her savings, and adopted a slightly kindlier tone.

'Well, I'm very sorry for you, I'm sure,' she said. 'But what are we going to do about this bill?' How much is it? Can I see?'

Esther was holding it in her hand, and the manageress took it from her.

'It's three and two,' said Esther.

'Well, three and two's three and two, isn't it? How much *have* you got on you?'

'Nothing!' said Esther. 'Not even a copper! Look at my bag.'

The manageress took the bag from her.

'A very nice bag,' she said. 'Who gave you that?'

'*He* did.'

'Well – there's certainly nothing here. So what are we going to do?'

'I don't *know*!'

'Who are your parents? Where do they live?'

'In Brighton.'

'Where?'

'In Over Street. Near Brighton Station.'

'I don't know it. But are they on the phone?'

'No. Of course not! It's only half a slum.'

'Then there's no way of getting into touch with them?'

'No!'

'Well – I don't know *what* to say – I must say. It's all very difficult, isn't it?'

'And I haven't even got the money to pay my fare back by train!' said Esther. 'We're right out at Shoreham, aren't we?'

'Yes. We're very cut off here, I'm afraid.'

Here the agreeable waitress, who now deeply pitied Esther, again cut in.

'Excuse me, madam,' she said to the manageress. 'But I've got an idea.'

'Yes?'

'Well, madam. That bag of hers. It's worth quite a lot. If she'll leave it here – leave it with me – *I'll* find the money – the money for the bill, and the money to pay her fare back. Then, if her parents'll give her the money later, she can come back and pay me back, and I'll give her back the bag.'

'Well,' said the manageress. 'That seems fair enough.'

'Very well, madam. Shall I go and get the money now? It's in my room.'

'Very well,' said the manageress, and the waitress left the electric-lit room.

Esther had only to spend a minute alone with the manageress, who did not talk to her, but sat down and looked at letters on her desk.

The waitress returned, with a ten-shilling note in her hand, and addressed the manageress.

'Excuse me, madam.'

'Yes.'

'It's a long way to the station – ain't it? I was wondering if I might get Larry to drive her there. If we ought to charge her for it, it can all come out of the bag.'

'Yes. That seems all right. And I don't want to charge her. She's in trouble enough. Very well. You do that. And you'd better do it as soon as possible.'

They were clearly being dismissed.

'Thank you, madam,' said the waitress, and Esther, the erstwhile user of waiters at the Hotel Metropole, echoed the waitress and said, 'Thank you, madam.'

8

In the passage outside Esther said:

'Now I must give you the bag – mustn't I? And I can't thank you enough.'

'Well, I suppose you must,' said the waitress. 'And don't thank me. I'm only too glad to help. And then, later, when you've got the money, you can come back and get it – can't you?'

The waitress took the bag, and gave Esther the ten-shilling note. She also gave Esther a few small things from the bag.

'And I don't want the bag back,' said Esther. 'It hasn't got happy memories for me, but it may be luckier for you. You've been very kind to me, and I'd like you to have it as a present.'

The waitress protested, but Esther meant what she said, and never came back to claim the bag.

Thus Gorse had, indirectly, even deprived her of his one present to her, the bag.

9

When Esther and the waitress were outside, the waitress told her to wait while she found Larry, who was the man-of-all-work of the inn.

'He's very silly,' she said. 'But he'll drive you back to the station. And mind you don't give him a *penny* – even if he has the sauce to ask for it. I know old Larry. Promise?'

'Yes. Thank you.'

The waitress found Larry in a surly mood and, to make him hurry and behave himself, told him something of Esther's pitiful story.

In due course Larry appeared in front of the inn, and in due course Esther stepped into an old and cheap car – what Gorse would have called a 'tin Lizzie'.

Esther again thanked the waitress, said goodbye to her, and was soon being driven on the road to Shoreham Station, which was about three and a half miles away.

10

'Silly Sussex' is an old and well-known expression. Larry was about fifty-five, and indeed silly – so silly as to be quite evil.

The waitress had told him about Esther's misfortune, and he talked about it, with great relish, to Esther.

'Yes, you were *dished*, all right,' he kept on saying, and 'Yes – *you* were ditched.'

Esther, hardly listening to him, yet felt the evil of the man.

Larry, along with his incessant 'Yes, you were ditched, all right' or 'Yes – you were dished,' related some of his own experiences.

He told her that, as a child, he had had an experience roughly similar to hers.

For this, he said, he was given a 'good hiding' by his parents. He used this filthy expression several times – even temporarily dropping, for its sake, his 'ditched' and 'dished'.

He had noticed that Esther was a very pretty, very frightened girl, and he was being lascivious sexually.

As they approached Shoreham Station he asked Esther whether she was likely to get a 'good hiding' from her own parents. Esther did not answer him. She did not even properly hear him.

This angered Larry, and, on leaving her at Shoreham Station, he said:

'Well – what about a tip for the driver, miss?'

She said truthfully that she had only a ten-shilling note, and he left her rudely and in silence.

She had to wait over three quarters of an hour on the station for a train back to Brighton.

It was now getting dark. The carriage, in which she sat alone, was lit by incandescent gas. The train stopped at many stations, but no one came into her carriage.

During this journey home she was too stunned and numbed to suffer very much.

Chapter Two

I

That night the scene which took place between Esther and Mrs Downes was, perhaps, as painful a one as had ever taken place in a house in Over Street – and the houses of Over Street had had very many very painful scenes indeed enacted inside them.

Coming home in the train, Esther had decided that she could have tolerated having lost her entire fortune.

It was having to *tell her mother* which was so terrible!

She decided to do so as soon as possible, and did.

The scene began quietly, for Esther was still too stunned and numbed for tears or an emotional outburst. Her mother was at first quiet, too, for she was also stunned and numbed.

But at last the tears, the reproaches from the mother, the wretched explanations from the daughter, the recriminations from the mother, the anguished and passionate sobbing of the daughter, the anguished and passionate sobbing of the mother – all these began.

It was the sort of commotion which attracts the attention of children lying in bed, filling them, they do not quite know why, with hideous disquiet and fear.

The Downes children, Esther's little brother and sister, heard the commotion, and finally they were so alarmed that they came downstairs, the little brother opening the door of the sitting-room.

At this particular moment Mrs Downes and Esther were sobbing and crying inconsolably at the same time. Needless to say, this was the cue for the two children to start sobbing and crying, equally inconsolably: and the general din and hysteria were appalling. The children did more than cry. They yelled.

The children were at last got to bed, still crying. Then Esther and her mother went downstairs for some further sorrow, anger, explanations, and tears. At times, actually, it was Esther who became angry and reduced her mother to tears.

This scene might have gone on all night and into the morning. But Mr Downes was due to return some time after eleven, and in spite of all the hysteria, it had been decided that he must not be told.

When Mr Downes came in, therefore, Esther was in bed, by a magnificent effort controlling her tears lest she made the children cry again.

Mrs Downes put up an equally magnificent performance with her husband. But neither Mrs Downes nor her daughter had more than the barest semblance of sleep that night.

2

Esther, it need hardly be said, never recovered her fortune.

If she had been better advised, and had had better luck, there might have been a dim chance of her doing this.

If, for instance, at Ye Olde Wheatsheafe the manageress had been agreeable and sensible, or if the waitress had been sensible, the police might have been telephoned at once, and Gorse, conceivably, might have been intercepted before dark on his way to London. The car, after all, was conspicuous in colour and shape. But such a thing would not have been at all likely.

Then, if Esther had had better advice at home, it could have been just possible that Gorse might have at last been traced. But this again would have been most unlikely, for Gorse had not been so foolish as to neglect to cover up his tracks in every possible way.

The advice that Esther was given at home was as poor as it well could be.

The very poor, alas, do not usually behave at all wisely when they meet disaster of this sort.

Either they become angry, or even vindictive, and insist too much upon their rights, thus displeasing those who are trying to help them; or they sink into a state of hopelessness, and consequent apathy. The very poor, they believe, are the very poor, and it is useless to contend with the rich, their betters.

Mrs Downes was of the apathetic type. Mr Downes, though he was never told anything, would have been equally so. Esther herself was apathetic.

It must be remembered that in the veins of Esther and her father ran the blood of the runner, the consumptive follower of cabs. Inheritors of such blood are unlikely to fight boldly against a cheat or oppressor.

3

What Mrs Downes did was to consult her old friend – the ex-policeman, Mr Stringer. She could not have done worse.

Mr Stringer was elderly, and, in matters of law especially, pompous and a know-all. He really knew practically nothing about the law, and his little knowledge was in this case a fatal thing.

With her mother Esther had a long interview with Mr Stringer, who questioned her, thoroughly but foolishly.

Mr Stringer, like the manageress at the inn, did not like or approve of Esther's great beauty. He never had. He was not so bitter as the manageress, but it told against her.

Esther was to experience this disadvantage all her life, and always more than ever when she was in difficulties.

There is an absurd theory that juries take a favourable view of pretty women. Nothing could be further from the case. Juries, on the whole, take a suspicious and adverse view of pretty women.

Some of Mr Stringer's questions were to the point. Did Esther know the number of the car? Esther did not. This folly on Esther's part made Mr Stringer inwardly despise her more than ever.

Did Esther know the *make* of the car? Esther did not – but she described its colour and shape.

Did Esther know where the car was *bought*? Esther mentioned the man Gosling. This slightly encouraged Mr Stringer: but as there was no man Gosling, the clue was ultimately quite useless.

Did Esther know anything *about* Gorse? Esther did not. She did not even know his address in Hove. (This actually would have been of no use in tracing Gorse, for he had left a false address with his landlady.) Mr Stringer was made more irritable still.

Did Esther not know at least *something* about Gorse? Did she not know anything about his parents and upbringing? Esther thought. Then she said that she thought he lived in London, that his people were Army people, and that he had been to school at Westminster.

Her knowledge of his school again encouraged Mr Stringer a little, and he asked Esther if she knew any of his friends. She mentioned Ryan and Bell. And she knew Ryan's address.

This yet again encouraged Mr Stringer, but was finally of no value. (Inquiries were made at Ryan's lodging in Tisbury Road – but Ryan, in the flurry and misery of his departure from Hove, had left no address with his landlady.) And while he was staying with the landlady he had never given it to her. She trusted and adored him (as all landladies did) and the matter had been put off and off. Furthermore, Ryan did not know Gorse's address, as we have seen.

Oddly enough, the one who might have been of the greatest assistance was Bell. He had kept Gorse's letters, and knew Gorse's stepmother's address.

But Esther did not know Bell's address. Bell, who might have 'counted' now, had not 'counted' enough in the past.

Probably the best thing Mr Stringer could have advised would have been to tell Esther to seek an enterprising journalist on a local newspaper. There was, really, a 'story' – which might conceivably have found its way into the London newspapers. But such a thing never occurred to Mr Stringer.

And, even if it had, there would have been little chance of tracing Gorse. Gorse was 'lying low', as he put it, and had already told plausible lies to his stepmother, to whom he had given a false address, and with whom he did not intend to communicate, until the thing had 'blown over'. He watched the newspapers carefully for a matter of months. The thorough Gorse also dyed his hair black, and took off his moustache, and wore new clothes.

4

A feeble approach was made to the police, but this was done by the apathetic Mrs Downes, for Mr Stringer had by this time developed an agonizing attack of lumbago. The police were infected by Mrs Downes's apathy.

The towel was thrown in at a later interview between Mrs Downes, Esther, and Mr Stringer, who was in bed. At this interview Mr Stringer happened to ask Esther whether she had given the money to Gorse *voluntarily* (a word he liked). Esther replied, in a dazed way, that she had.

In that case, said the pompous know-all (who was still in considerable pain), there was really no sense in pursuing the matter. Even if Gorse was found, there was no redress in law.

Esther was at last forgiven by her mother. But on the night when the dreadful news had been broken, Mrs Downes, in her anguish and anger, had told Esther that she would never forgive her until her dying day – and that Esther had practically killed her mother.

These words stuck, and when Esther's mother died, which she in fact did a few years later, Esther always had a feeling that she had helped to kill her, and that she had never been forgiven. This notion haunted her all her life.

5

And so (apart from Esther and Gertrude) none of those five ever met again in Hove, or went on the West Pier.

On that Sunday evening – so terrible for Esther, so fruitful for Gorse – the West Pier, which had brought them all together, wore its own peculiar air of indifference about their departure.

This battleship – this sex-battleship – was on this Sunday evening more crowded than usual. Sunday evening was one of its best, and the season was at its peak. Many new curious acquaintanceships were made upon its resounding planks, and, as it grew dark, its secluded benches were used by many would-be lovers.

And, as it grew dark, Gorse, far away, was employing great speed in the use of his recently acquired car.

He had had the misfortune of having a breakdown on his way to London. This, before he had located the trouble in the engine, had delayed him nearly three quarters of an hour. He therefore had need of speed. He was late in his plans. He knew where he was going to leave the car in London for the night, and he did not want the place be be closed. At this place, he hoped, he was going to dispose of it at a great profit.

The car fancier's hopes were fulfilled. He sold the car, as he had promised Esther he would, at nearly double the price he had paid for it.

Gorse, as he drove, was deeply delighted by the superbly easy success of this – his first serious enterprise in his main profession in life – that of defrauding women.

But he was tired, and had to extract all the speed from the car that he could. Also, the breakdown had told upon his nerves.

There was, therefore, a set, ugly, hard, more than ever satanic expression upon the face of Ernest Ralph Gorse as he sped ahead – sped ahead to London, and to his very curious destination in life.

These words spoke — and when mother's mother died, which she had a few years later, as her drugs and affecting that she had helped to kill her — that she had never been forgiven. This never left her all her life.

And so, apart from Esther and Gertrude, none of those true ones had regrets. How, or where, were they?

On that Saturday evening — so terrible for Esther, so fruitful for Gorse — the West Pier, which had brought them all together, wore its own peculiar air of indifference about their departure.

The battlefield — the sea-horse-tap — was on this Sunday evening more crowded than usual. Saturday evening was one of the best, and the season was at its peak. Many new curious acquaintances were made upon its resounding planks, and, as it grew dark, its secluded benches were used by many would-be lovers.

And, as it grew dark, Gorse, far away, was employing great speed in the use of his recently acquired car.

He had had the misfortune of having a breakdown on his way to London. This, before he had located the trouble in the engine, had delayed him nearly three quarters of an hour. He therefore had need of speed. He was late in his plans. He knew where he was going to leave the car in London for the night, and he did not want the place to be closed. In this place, he hoped, he was going to deposit it at a great profit.

The car-dealer's hopes were fulfilled. He sold the car, as he had promised Esther he would, at nearly double the price he had paid for it.

Gorse, as he drove, was deeply delighted by the apparently easy success of this — his first serious attempt, in his major profession, in the art of defrauding women.

But he was tired, and had to extract all the speed from the car that he could. Also the tiredness worked upon his nerves.

There appeared, therefore, a very hard, more than ever relentless expression upon the face of Ernest Ralph Gorse as he sped ahead — ahead to London, and to the various dishonest undertakings ...

MR STIMPSON AND MR GORSE

Author's Note

All the characters in this book are entirely imaginary. So also are Mr Stimpson's Crossword Puzzles, the clues to which the reader is advised not to be beguiled into attempting to solve.

Contents

PART ONE

WIDOW OF A COLONEL

Chapter One

I

There are, clearly, in England and all over the world, countless Colonels with hard-working, valiant and enchanting characters. Why, then, is the thought or mention of a 'Colonel', purely in the abstract, faintly laughable, or even faintly displeasing, in some people's minds?

Why, for instance, did the eminent cartoonist, Low, make Colonel Blimp a Colonel, rather than a Captain, say, or an officer holding a different rank?

Colonel Blimp, of course, though laughable, was to a very large extent lovable. Many people, however, do not think of Colonels as being in any way lovable. Such people, on the contrary, can only picture Colonels either as moustached bullies bawling at men on parade grounds, or as uttering idiotic, outmoded and reactionary sentiments from the armchairs of Clubs. A progressive Colonel, to such people, is practically inconceivable.

Colonels are also famous for being 'retired'.

An ordinary man is permitted to retire in an aura of dignity and, often, of distinction – but such is not quite the case with Colonels.

'Retired' Colonels have, perhaps, brought about the faint ignominy attached to their retirement upon themselves. So many of them, for instance, have become seedy, inactive men committing the grave social error of permitting or encouraging themselves to be addressed as 'Colonel' long after they have left the Service in which they were never regular soldiers. Others – the rather self-consciously 'peppery', 'fiery' or 'choleric' type – attempt to use these attributes against servants or old ladies in the boarding-house in which they usually end their days.

There are obviously, however, innumerable meek, and possibly saintly retired Colonels in boarding-houses, and these have to suffer, in the general reputation of the world, for the folly of the others.

What, then, about Colonels' Wives? What about Mrs Plumleigh-Bruce?

2

It may be said that the popular prejudice against Colonels' Wives far exceeds that which is attached to their husbands: and it may be further said that this prejudice, amounting, often, to great dislike, is much more reasonable and easily understood than in the case of their husbands.

To begin with, the very conception of a Colonel's Wife brings waves of absurd thoughts about 'Tiffin', 'Pukka Sahibs', 'Chota Hasri', 'Indyah' and 'The Natives' surging into the mind.

This, of course, is grossly unfair; for Colonels' Wives are not, as is vaguely supposed, all 'Anglo-Indian'. Nevertheless, despite many noble, admirable or pathetic examples, Colonels' Wives form, on the whole, a very mixed class, and there are undoubtedly very many very objectionable Colonels' Wives.

3

Mrs Plumleigh-Bruce missed hardly a single characteristic appertaining to the worst sort of Colonel's wife. In fact, she was so true to this type that an author could hardly put her into fiction. She had only just enough wit to avoid naked, flaming 'Poona-ism'.

She was outwardly rather stout, and inwardly beyond measure arrogant. She was rude to her servants, insensitive, vain, and a social snob. She talked (it is hard to believe) about people who did not 'come quite out of the top drawer'. She talked (but this goes without saying) about 'Pukka Sahibs', 'The Natives', etc., and this without ever having been within a thousand miles of India. She talked about *Wallahs* – appending this word to members of the middle-class respectable professions – as in 'Solicitor-Wallah', 'Doctor-Wallah', 'Parson-Wallah', and so forth – but never, let it be noted, speaking of a Grocer-Wallah, Duke-Wallah, Draper-Wallah, or Earl-Wallah.

This Anglo-Indian word 'Wallah' was wonderfully suited both to her accent and voice. Into it she was able to project all the thick, drawling fruitiness of her affectedly indolent manner of utterance.

Mrs Plumleigh-Bruce's voice and accent were not by any means peculiar to herself, though in her these were probably slightly accentuated. They were, and still are, shared by an enormous class of women – what may be called the Plumleigh-Bruce class, or, more simply, the Plumleigh-Bruces. Another Galsworthy may one day write a Plumleigh-Bruce saga. Only the briefest sketch of them can be given here.

The Plumleigh-Bruces live, usually, in rather large and rather nice houses just outside villages or towns. Their lawns and tennis-courts are amazingly well-kept, and they keep dogs.

The Plumleigh-Bruces are always connected with the Army – though not necessarily with the Indian Army. Above all things it can be guaranteed that there is a *General* somewhere in the family. The General may be obscure or famous, a remote or close connection, but there he is. One cannot conceivably be a Plumleigh-Bruce without a General in the family.

The Plumleigh-Bruces of life are not exactly ostentatious, but, rather, quietly sure of themselves to quite a repulsive degree.

The Plumleigh-Bruce boys go to Public Schools and the daughters are usually somehow 'presented at Court'.

The men of this tribe (in which, of course, there are innumerable grades) are generally much less offensive than the women, and less easy to identify. The women can be spotted at once by an astute social botanist – and this, almost always, because of their voices and accent.

It has already been said that the Mrs Plumleigh-Bruce of this story spoke in a thick, drawling, fruity, affectedly indolent way – but this does not fully describe the flavour of her mode of speech, which was, really, excessively genteel.

The word 'genteel', in regard to speech, is normally associated with the thin, quick, clipped accent of the foolish, but perhaps struggling, West End shop assistant. Mrs Plumleigh-Bruce's accent, while remaining genteel, was exactly the opposite. It was rich, slow, and deliberate, and came forth from a mouth which moved much too much in an attempt to enunciate correctly every letter, vowel and syllable.

She put (like nearly all the Plumleigh-Bruces herein named after her) too much emphasis upon her 'H's'. If the servant shouted up to her that the man about the electric-light in the bedroom had called, she would not have replied rapidly and casually, as would the average 'educated' person, 'Oh – will you ask him if he'll come upstairs?' – the 'H's' here being almost completely dropped. She would have breathed the H's – saying, thoughtfully, lethargically, 'Oh – will you ask *Him* if *He'll* come upstairs?'

In other words, her accent, like that of the foolish shop assistant, was genteel because she was trying too hard.

If anyone had told Mrs Plumleigh-Bruce that she left anything in her accent to be desired or corrected she would either have laughed or been wild with anger – the first openly and when in company, the second secretly when alone.

Her pride in her knowledge of the grammar and correct usage of the English language almost equalled that which she took in her manner of pronouncing it. But here again she often made quite serious errors. She would talk, for instance, of things or people being 'aggravating' when her meaning was clearly 'irritating', and she would speak of demanding 'explicit' obedience from her servants.

As she alluded so often to people who did not come 'quite out of the top drawer', it is interesting to speculate as to what sort of drawer she thought she herself came out of. The top, surely, one would immediately imagine. But this would be to over-simplify matters. The Plumleigh-Bruce chest-of-drawers is a highly intricate one. In it the proletariat, or the tradesman class, occupy no drawer at all. But the 'genuine aristocracy' certainly does. Would Mrs Plumleigh-Bruce concede that she was in any lower drawer than the latter? She probably would – if and when she ever thought about the matter. And here, she was, for once, perhaps slightly underestimating herself, for the 'genuine aristocracy' has nowadays become by marriage so Plumleigh-Bruced as to be no longer fully itself.

As a faint extenuation of Mrs Plumleigh-Bruce's character it should be mentioned that she had had a very tricky upbringing. In addition to being a Colonel's Wife she was a Colonel's Daughter. Moreover both Colonels had been foolish, and both had been in the Indian Army.

She was, in point of fact, now a Colonel's Widow. Her husband, to whom she had been married only five years, had died shortly after the First World War. Her father and mother were also dead.

She was now forty-one, and, although rather plump, she looked frequently much younger. She was not totally unattractive. Indeed, by a businessman fresh from a Masonic Dinner, she was often thought ravishing.

She had tow-coloured hair, nice blue eyes, and a lascivious mouth. Her good teeth were slightly rabbity. The mouth and the teeth assisted her in, and accentuated, her mode of speech.

In 1928 she was living in a small house in Reading. One does not think of Colonels' Wives (or Widows) as living in Reading: there is hardly any more unlikely or unsuitable town.

She lived there, however, because she had little money, and because her deceased and only sister had bequeathed to her a small house there. She called this house a *pied-à-terre*.

The odd thing was that Mrs Plumleigh-Bruce did not at all dislike living in Reading. But this was to be accounted for by her intense absorption in the 'drawer' system.

No one, in Reading, in Mrs Plumleigh-Bruce's estimation, could imaginably come quite, or even at all, out of the 'top drawer'. She was therefore in a top drawer all by herself, and this pleased her insatiable vanity immeasurably. She looked upon herself as the eminent 'Lady' of Reading – and many residents took her at her own valuation. Businessmen in the town often alluded to her, without a trace of sarcasm, as 'The Lady of Reading' – or 'Our Reading Lady'.

Mrs Plumleigh-Bruce mixed with the more prosperous businessmen of the town.

She had, like so many Colonels' Wives or Widows, a great fondness for the company and flattery of men, and for the sake of these things she even went into Saloon Bars of public houses with such men.

She 'detested snobbery', and thought public houses 'great fun'. Also, without being in any way a heavy drinker, Mrs Plumleigh-Bruce did not find drinking a distasteful pastime – particularly as the drinks were always paid for by the men.

But she was fastidious in her taste about public houses, and the one she most frequented was The Friar. This was because its walls had recently been ye-olde panelled, and because there was a nook in it in which she could sit almost unespied by the populace, while holding a sort of Court for the prosperous businessmen.

It was in The Friar, in the year 1928, that she met and formed a friendship with the reddish-haired, reddish-moustached Ernest Ralph Gorse.

Anyone knowing the true character of Mrs Plumleigh-Bruce, and, at the same time, the true character of Ernest Ralph Gorse, would have decided that this friendship must prove an emphatically interesting one – indeed, a most exciting combination.

Chapter Two

For the benefit of those unacquainted with Ernest Ralph Gorse, it is now necessary to give a brief description of his character generally, his early background, and his youthful adventures and ventures. This will also be of assistance to those who already know about him.

Ernest Ralph Gorse, who was born in 1903, and whose mother died shortly after he was born, was the son of a rather successful commercial artist who, not very long after his wife's death, married an ex-barmaid – an extremely pleasant fat woman, who in her heart detested her stepson, but treated him not only fairly but indulgently.

Ernest Ralph Gorse belonged to a very seriously criminal type, and showed as much as a boy at his preparatory school.

At this school, which was in Hove and at which he was a day-boy, he was continually creating evil mischief purely for its own sake – and this was not only amongst his fellow schoolboys. He had the habit, for instance, when returning home from school on winter nights, of sticking pins into the tyres of any bicycles he could find in dark places.

He was also, at the age of twelve, suspected of having – on a summer's evening in the County Ground, Hove – tied a small girl to a cricket roller in an obscure shed, and of having robbed her of her money, a few coppers which she had in her purse.

A policeman in plain clothes called upon Gorse's headmaster about this matter. The headmaster was, for the sake of the reputation of his school, evasive with the policeman: but, like the policeman, he was, at the back of his mind, absolutely certain that Gorse was the culprit. Both were correct in the belief they held in common. Nevertheless, Gorse did not suffer in any way for this misdemeanour.

After this Gorse went to St Paul's School in London. Here he again created mischief, thought not of a technically criminal kind.

And here, also, he developed a remarkable taste for, and knowledge about, the Motor-Car. He had, at as early an age as that of sixteen, shady dealings with car dealers of dubious character in Hammersmith, which is very near to St Paul's School.

In 1921 he was once more in Hove on his 'holidays'. Here he mixed with two young men who had been at his own preparatory school – Peter Ryan and George Bell, and here he met Esther Downes, who was an unusually lovely and well-dressed girl who lived in a Brighton slum.

Esther Downes was picked up by the three young men on the West Pier. Ryan, a simple, good-natured, well-mannered boy – fell desperately in love with her. Gorse had no feeling for her, but found her beauty and good clothes social assets. He was then trying his wings in the art of frequenting opulent hotels, and he took her to drink cocktails at the Metropole.

In order to do this it was necessary to cut out Ryan. He succeeded in doing this by writing filthy anonymous letters, and by other abominable methods.

He discovered at a fairly early stage on this 'holiday' that Esther Downes had savings – enormous ones for a girl of her class. She had sixty-eight pounds fifteen shillings, which her industrious and ailing mother had given her, and which was kept in an old tin safe in an old tin trunk in her bedroom.

By employing the most astute trickery, which involved the use of a very smart red sports-car, he managed to deprive Esther Downes of every penny of her savings.

This was Gorse's second technically criminal offence, and he again escaped punishment.

In addition to robbing the wretched Esther Downes, Gorse sold, in London, the red sports-car at nearly double the price he had paid for it.

Since 1921 he had not actually done anything further for which the police could have arrested him. He had had no need to, for he had made a wonderful amount of money in reasonably honest speculation in cars. But the matter of necessity is really beside the point. Gorse loved trickery and evil for their own sakes, and, even if fabulously rich, would have indulged in both had he been taken by the whim to do so.

The motives of such a criminal as Ernest Ralph Gorse are only partially commercial, and their criminal behaviour comes and goes in waves – waves which, nearly always, increase in volume and power.

In years long after the events related in this book, people often argued as to whether Gorse (who was by then a famous figure) had 'any good' in him.

He had not any sort of good in him. He might have been just conceivably, and in a manner, insane – but evilly so – not pitiably. In spite of his worldly astuteness, he may have lived, perhaps, like so many outstanding criminals, a sort of dream-life. But, even if this were so, the dream was evil.

Moreover there was certainly nothing in his upbringing which could possibly account for his attitude towards life and his fellow-men.

He would have served, indeed, as a perfect model for, or archetype of, all the pitiless and not-to-be-pitied criminals who have been discovered and exposed in the last hundred years or so in Great Britain.

He had a touch of Burke and Hare of Edinburgh (though he was never a heavy drinker); he had a touch of Dr Pritchard of Glasgow; a touch of the multitudinously poisoning Palmer; of the strangely acquitted Miss Madeleine Smith; of Neal Creame, the Lambeth harlot-poisoner; of George Smith, the bath-murderer; of Frederick Bywaters, Ronald True, Sydney Fox, Frederick Mahon, Neville Heath and George Haigh.

And, added to this, he had a pronounced touch of one who thought never of murder but incessantly of money – the false and foolish claimant to the Tichborne Estate.

It was on a cold January night in 1928, at The Friar, Reading, that Ernest Ralph Gorse first met Mrs Plumleigh-Bruce.

Mrs Plumleigh-Bruce did not at once 'take' to him.

PART TWO

GORSE THE WATCHER

Chapter One

I

The Friar, as has been said, had only recently been ye-olded, and this had been lavishly done. It had also been enlarged, and it was one of the talks of Reading, where, in the main, it was looked upon with some awe by the public house amateur.

It occupied considerable space in Friar Street, Reading, which runs parallel to the main street, Broad Street.

Its principal feature was, of course, its dark-stained wooden panelling, with which the walls of all its bars were lined.

In its very long and large Saloon Bar was its *pièce de résistance*. This was an enormous 'Devonshire' fireplace, enveloping which was an enormous surround made of material resembling Portland Stone. Above this there were three shields upon which were brightly painted coats-of-arms.

This fireplace, which was in the centre of the long room and facing the bar itself, created, along with the panelling, a 'baronial' effect of the most painfully false character. But the Reading business barons in no way disliked it.

During the lunch-hour (lunches were given upstairs) the businessmen did not think much about their surroundings. They were too busy talking business, or telling dirty stories, or waiting with ill-concealed impatience or anger for other men to finish theirs so that they could tell their own. But in the evening, when the place was more empty, and lit with a coal-and-log fire, the businessman would look around him and be gravely pleased by the atmosphere.

The Friar was what, in those days, would have been called a 'posh' place.

The nook mostly occupied by Mrs Plumleigh-Bruce was at the end of the Saloon Bar furthest from the door, and was made a nook by a jutting partition, again of the dark-stained wooden panelling. There was another such nook nearer to the door, but this was more draughty and less intimate.

2

On the night upon which she first met Ernest Ralph Gorse, Mrs Plumleigh-Bruce was not in her usual place. Her nook had been occupied by a strange couple, and she was sitting on a high stool at the bar alone.

She was waiting for Mr Donald Stimpson, who was, most unaccountably, late. Naturally, she greatly disliked having to sit at the bar alone.

Her appointment with Mr Stimpson had been for six o'clock. She had arrived five minutes late. Ernest Ralph Gorse came into the bar at ten minutes past six, and sat on a stool rather near to Mrs Plumleigh-Bruce.

Apart from the strange couple, and the barmaid, there was no one else in the bar.

Gorse ordered a glass of beer and began to read an evening newspaper. While he did so Mrs Plumleigh-Bruce, who was sure she had never seen him before in Reading, observed him with interest.

Gorse was only twenty-five at this period, but he liked, for commercial and other reasons, to look considerably older. He pretended that he was thirty-one, and people believed that he was.

He had improved, both in his looks and his style of dressing, since his earlier days. At his preparatory school he had been a slim boy, with ginger silken hair which came in a large bang over his forehead, thin lips, a slouching gait, some freckles, an aquiline nose which always seemed to be smelling something nasty, and a nasal voice.

Now his nose only seldom, and when seen from certain angles, seemed to smell anything nasty. This was because he had managed to cultivate quite a powerful moustache.

His reddish hair was now of a thicker texture, and brushed backwards and kept in place by the discreet use of hair oil.

His moustache was, roughly speaking, of a 'tooth-brush' kind, and helped to give him the 'Army' appearance he was anxious to cultivate.

In certain carefully chosen quarters he passed as one who had been on active service in the 1914–18 War. He had awarded himself the rank of Lieutenant in this war – a Lieutenant in the Royal

Horse Artillery. In the quarters in which he put forth (and elaborated upon) this falsehood, he was believed.

He wore in these days a fawn-coloured 'trilby' hat, and, for the most part, dark blue suits which were well made. His shoes were expensive and always immaculately clean. So also were his shirts and ties.

He carried a rimless monocle not attached to any string in his waistcoat pocket, and this he stuck in his eye when he read in public, and on certain other occasions when people were present.

When he was younger his monocle had been made of plain glass. Now he had the sense to have a lens made, one suitable to a person with slightly short sight.

On his left little finger he wore a gold ring with a cornelian stone upon which was engraved the crest of a family to which he did not belong.

Mrs Plumleigh-Bruce, watching him, could not make him out at all – could find no 'drawer' to put him into. The 'top' she would certainly not concede to him, but, it seemed to her, he probably belonged to a higher class than that of the businessmen with whom she mixed – Mr Stimpson for instance.

She felt instinctively that, if she made his acquaintance, she would not be able to take the slightly or strongly patronizing attitude which she took always with other men in Reading.

And so, because of this, and because she was unable to place him, and because he was a stranger, her feelings towards him were on the whole hostile.

While Mrs Plumleigh-Bruce was watching Ernest Ralph Gorse, the latter was at the same time keenly examining Mrs Plumleigh-Bruce, and by more subtle methods than her own. While giving an imitation of reading his newspaper, he was looking at her reflection in the mirror behind the bar.

He found himself as interested in Mrs Plumleigh-Bruce as she was in himself; but this was not on account of any of those slightly mature physical attractions she had for certain men. He was too young for this, and, in any case, Gorse, as a rule, had little feeling for women in that way. Though he certainly at periods knew the meaning of sexual desire he was never in love with a woman during his entire life.

What interested Ernest Ralph Gorse were Mrs Plumleigh-Bruce's bearing and clothes. Her clothes were some sort of clue to her class, and her class, possibly, to her financial status.

The precocious young man at once perceived that she did not quite belong to Reading; and he surmised that she had been married and was no longer so. He quickly took in her wonderful complacency as a being generally, and he was sure that she was, because of this, gloriously susceptible to the right kind of flattery.

Mrs Plumleigh-Bruce seemed, in short, what Ernest Ralph Gorse would have called 'right up his street'. He decided to talk to her.

Like so many women with a strong liking for the company of men, Mrs Plumleigh-Bruce kept a dog, which was usually on a lead.

A dog on a lead is an instrument for coquetry of all kinds – particularly the more nauseating kinds. A dog, also, in public haunts, is often useful in causing an introduction to men.

Having made up his mind to speak to her, Gorse decided to make use of Mrs Plumleigh-Bruce's dog. He asked the barmaid for a packet of cheese-biscuits, which he had seen amongst the bottles behind the bar.

These were given to him. Then, still pretending to read his newspaper, which lay flattened out on the bar, he opened the packet of biscuits and began to munch one of them.

Then, making as much of a crackling noise as he could with the paper of the packet, he began to munch another.

The desired result was quickly achieved. Mrs Plumleigh-Bruce's dog – a liver-coloured spaniel – began to strain at its lead in the direction of Gorse, who feigned at first not to notice this, while making further luscious crackling sounds.

At last the dog's efforts to reach him became so obvious that they could hardly, in courtesy, be ignored. Gorse spoke to both the dog and its owner.

'Ah – I thought so . . .' he said, looking first mockingly at the spaniel, and then, amiably, at Mrs Plumleigh-Bruce. 'May I give him one – or is such a thing strictly "taboo"?'

Gorse's use and faint stressing, at this moment, of the word 'taboo', revealed his practically sixth-sensitive cleverness in the handling of certain women. 'Taboo' was, to Mrs Plumleigh-Bruce, a 'native' word, and Gorse, merely from looking at her for a few moments in a mirror, had suspected that such a word would please her. He almost knew already that she was connected with Colonels who had been in India.

Mrs Plumleigh-Bruce's opinion of Gorse at once improved because of his use of this word.

'Well,' she said, in her fruity, off-hand way. 'It is, actually . . . But I suppose one has to make an exception every once in a while.'

'Oh yes,' said Gorse. 'One can't abide by the strict Rules and Regulations all the time.'

Talking of Rules and Regulations, in the precise way he did, because it summoned up a picture of army discipline, was another clever touch, and one which further attracted Mrs Plumleigh-Bruce's friendly instincts.

Gorse now went up to the dog and gave it a biscuit.

'He'll make a dreadful mess on the floor, I'm afraid,' said Mrs Plumleigh-Bruce. 'And one's not supposed to bring a dog in here, anyway.'

'Ah yes,' said Gorse, looking ruminatively at the dog as it ate the biscuit. 'But then I imagine that he's especially favoured – isn't he? Or rather that you are?'

'Oh well – I don't know . . .' said Mrs Plumleigh-Bruce. 'Perhaps I *do* get rather special treatment in some ways . . .'

There was a pause during which Gorse gave the dog another biscuit.

'Are you a "regular frequenter", as they say, then?' asked Gorse, still looking dreamily at the dog. He had a motive in asking this. He was not going to waste any time on this woman if she did not live in Reading – if she were only staying in the town for a night or two.

'Oh yes,' she said. 'This is my favourite haunt, really. In fact very nearly my only haunt – when one comes to think about it.'

'You're a resident in this metropolis, then?' said Gorse, making assurance doubly sure. He was an extremely thorough young man in matters of this sort.

'Yes, I am,' said Mrs Plumleigh-Bruce. 'For my sins. I had a sister who left me a little house here, and somehow I never seem to have got out of it.'

'Why? Is it such a hateful place?' asked Gorse. 'I've only been here a few days myself, and I haven't had much time to look around.'

'Oh well – it has its advantages, I suppose. It's very easy to get to Town, for one thing.'

Mrs Plumleigh-Bruce had her own, markedly 'Plumleigh-Bruce' way of pronouncing 'Town'. She rounded her lips a little too much for the 'ow', and lingered a little too long on the 'n'. This did not pass Gorse by.

'But it's not really in my line,' she said, 'at all.'

'No,' said Gorse, now picking up his drink, and in the most natural way sitting on the stool next to Mrs Plumleigh-Bruce. 'I can understand that. No doubt it's a very excellent place – but the moment I saw you I thought that you must be – well – what shall I say? – not quite fitting in – rather a cut above it – if one's allowed to put it that way these days.' And, slightly lifting his chin, he looked at Mrs Plumleigh-Bruce through his monocle, at once appraisingly and approvingly.

Mrs Plumleigh-Bruce was in two minds about Gorse's approach. She liked his immediate recognition of her superior social standing in Reading. But, not being a complete fool in every way, she sensed a faint effrontery in his demeanour, his look, and his monocle. His as yet unidentified 'drawer' probably went further down in the chest. There was a pause.

'Do you go to Town a lot?' Gorse then asked.

'Oh yes. Quite a good bit. On business, and for a Show every now and again. The train service is simply wonderful in that way.'

(The Plumleigh-Bruces of life incessantly talk about 'Shows', and by this they mean theatrical performances in London – not in the provinces, where the word 'Theatre' suffices. There are, moreover, no other 'Shows' save theatrical ones.)

'Yes. I've heard the trains are very good,' said Gorse. 'Not that that bothers me very much, because I always get around everywhere by car – myself.'

Gorse here had gone too far. Mrs Plumleigh-Bruce at once felt that he was boasting about his car. If he had not thrown in the casual 'myself' like that it might have been better. Gorse, all his life, was unable to cure this sort of fault in his manners.

'Well – you're very lucky to have a car,' said Mrs Plumleigh-Bruce. 'I wish *I* had one.'

Gorse was aware that he had almost been snubbed, and hastened to rectify his error.

'Well, you wouldn't like mine,' he said. 'It's just about the most gimcrack affair you could find anywhere. However, it served its purpose in the recent little outbreak.'

He was alluding to the General Strike of 1926.

'What outbreak?' asked Mrs Plumleigh-Bruce, suspecting, without being absolutely certain of, his meaning.

'Oh – the outbreak of the Great Unwashed. The General Strike.

I was able to give a lot of people lifts, and all that, and to help in other sundry ways. In fact it was probably that that broke the little bus down. She was never worked harder in her life. Nor was I, if it comes to that.'

Gorse had now recovered all the ground he had lost. Mrs Plumleigh-Bruce had not enough sense or decency to have any feeling against the expression 'The Great Unwashed'. In fact, she used it frequently herself. Nor did she object to people calling their cars 'little buses'. And his attitude towards the General Strike not only pleased her; it very nearly excited her. Just as Gorse was incapable of sentimental love, so Mrs Plumleigh-Bruce was, in the ordinary way, incapable of any sort of intellectual passion. But the General Strike had had, and still had, the power to stimulate her intellect violently. She was not, as may be guessed, a friend of the working class.

'Oh – so you helped in the General Strike – did you?' she said, looking at him very much more warmly than before. 'Well – I'm glad to hear that.'

'Oh yes, I did my little bit,' said Gorse. 'I think nearly everybody did, really. I expect you did, too – didn't you?'

'Yes. I did,' said Mrs Plumleigh-Bruce. 'Though nothing very spectacular. Just secretarial work. Recruiting volunteers and all that. And it was wonderful how everybody rallied round.'

'Yes. It was – wasn't it?' said Gorse. 'And the old Bolshie certainly got what was going to him, for once.'

'Yes. He certainly did.'

There was now a silence, during which Gorse meditated as to whether or not it would be advisable to have fought in the 1914–18 War. Finally he decided to have done so. He was unknown in Reading, to which he had never been before, and in which he proposed (or had proposed) to stay only for a few weeks. He felt, therefore, quite secure from exposure.

'Yes,' he said. 'It was wonderful how everyone came up to scratch. But then, that's the Britisher all over – isn't it? He's as lazy as the devil until a real crisis comes; when it does come he's quicker off the mark than anyone on earth – whatever the inconvenience or trouble. Apart from all the bother, I know it cost *me* a pretty penny – hunting out the old uniform and all that.'

Gorse now hoped that Mrs Plumleigh-Bruce would inquire as to the nature of this uniform, but instead of this she only replied: 'Yes, it must.' And so he had to go on further.

'Reminded one,' he said, 'of the queer old days in France.'

'Why – were you in France?' said Mrs Plumleigh-Bruce, looking at him.

'I was,' said Gorse, sententiously and thoughtfully, and looking into the distance.

'Really?' said Mrs Plumleigh-Bruce. 'In the War?'

'Yes. I volunteered to play my little role in that little misunderstanding between ourselves and the Boche ...' Gorse now put on a faintly smiling and reminiscent, as well as thoughtful expression.

'Well, I must say that surprises me,' said Mrs Plumleigh-Bruce, who was now gazing intently at Gorse, who knew that she was doing this. 'I should have thought you were too young.'

'Yes ... I was. Definitely ...' said Gorse. 'But these things *can* be wangled – can't they? I'm not a wangler as a rule, but I think I was justified on that occasion ... In fact I managed to be on His Majesty's Service at the very immature age of sixteen ... and in France at seventeen. I suppose it was very naughty of me ...'

'Oh no – not naughty,' said Mrs Plumleigh-Bruce. 'Far from it.'

'What, then?' Gorse asked.

'Well – jolly sporty – I should say,' said Mrs Plumleigh-Bruce.

'Well – I suppose it was a fault on the right side,' said Gorse, and he again looked into the distance, as if weighing up the past. But he was not really doing this. He was weighing up Mrs Plumleigh-Bruce generally, and his own present age as one who had gallantly tricked his way into the 1914–18 War at the age of sixteen.

He liked Mrs Plumleigh-Bruce's use of the word 'sporty'. If she had said 'sporting' he would not have been quite so pleased. By the use of the former word instead of the latter, she had shown that she had exactly that sort of vulgarity upon which he could play. Gorse was, in his soul, incredibly vulgar. He could, however, mysteriously just distinguish the difference between one sort of cheapness and another – as in these two words. All this was part of his peculiar genius.

Gorse now believed that he had fully eradicated that slight feeling of hostility towards him which he had sensed in Mrs Plumleigh-Bruce. He even thought that he was well on the way to captivating her. He was right in both cases.

She had nearly finished her drink, and he was thinking of inviting her to have another at his expense. But at this moment Mr Donald Stimpson, the Estate Agent, entered.

Chapter Two

I

Ah – our Lady Joan,' said Mr Stimpson, hurrying up to Mrs Plumleigh-Bruce, whose Christian name was Joan. 'A thousand apologies for my remissness, madame.'

Mr Stimpson was a thick-set, moustached, virile, middle-aged man, of medium height, with a red face (redder now because of the cold outside), tortoiseshell-rimmed spectacles, false teeth, a heavy overcoat, a woollen scarf, gloves and a bowler hat.

Above all things Mr Stimpson was middle-aged. Merely to look at him was to think of middle age. Few other men in the world, of his years, which amounted to fifty-one, could have given forth this impression so strongly and quickly. He bounced with middle age; he had clearly been born, and would die, middle-aged, and, furthermore, he somehow seemed to glory in all this.

It is not easy to say exactly why or how he gave forth this overwhelming impression. One simply does not think of the age of countless other men of fifty-one. Perhaps it was because he was so intensely and overbearingly middle-class – in his social origins, in his profession, in his thoughts, and in his utterances. He was vehemently, formidably, almost dangerously 'middle' in every way.

'Well, you're certainly very late,' said Mrs Plumleigh-Bruce and, because of the presence of Ernest Ralph Gorse, there was an awkward silence, which Mrs Plumleigh-Bruce broke.

'Oh,' she said, 'I don't think you two know each other, do you? . . . This is Mr Donald Stimpson – and I don't really know *your* name – do I?'

She looked at Gorse, who replied. 'No, I don't think you do. It's Gorse, as a matter of fact. Ralph Gorse.'

'Oh – how-do-you-do, Mr Gorse,' said Mr Stimpson, and he snatched off his glove in order to shake hands with the stranger. He was a terrific and most adroit glove-snatcher-offer when being introduced to anyone, and his handshake was always warm to the extent of physical cruelty. He could tell the character of a man, he always said, by the way he shook hands with you: and nothing but near-violence suited his taste.

Gorse, who knew this type of handshaker, used almost as much strength with his own hand: but this did not, as had been hoped, please Mr Stimpson. Mr Stimpson loathed both the presence and the aspect of Ernest Ralph Gorse.

This was not because Mr Stimpson had enough wit even faintly to suspect that he was shaking hands with a criminal, or even with a dubious character. He detested Gorse merely because he was where he was – that is to say, in the immediate vicinity of Mrs Plumleigh-Bruce. He was afraid of a new candidate for her affections.

It would not be correct to say that Mr Stimpson loved Mrs Plumleigh-Bruce; although he often, particularly after business dinners, made love to her – either by verbal innuendo or in attempts to kiss her. He was, however, anxious to marry her.

As a widower of three years' standing, a snob, a social climber, a businessman, a boaster, and a subterraneously lecherous man, Mr Stimpson had every reason for seeking Mrs Plumleigh-Bruce's hand in marriage. The widower (as widowers so often do) wanted to marry again, the snob and social climber hankered for the outstanding 'Lady' of his circle in the town, the businessman thought she would be useful for his business as such, the boaster wanted her for both of the last two reasons, and the subterraneously lecherous man, after food and drink, found her by no means physically undesirable.

Mr Stimpson, in addition to all this, liked her small house – for its atmosphere, for its business possibilities, and for its maid's cooking. He rather liked the maid, too. He liked everything about Mrs Plumleigh-Bruce.

2

Gorse perceived that Mr Stimpson, in spite of the stupendous handshake, was displeased by his presence.

'Well,' he said, 'as you two had an appointment, I'm afraid I'm rather butting in – aren't I? So I'll go back to my newspaper, I think, if you'll forgive me.' He smiled at Mrs Plumleigh-Bruce, and moved as if about to return to the stool upon which he had originally been sitting.

'Oh no. Please don't go,' said Mrs Plumleigh-Bruce. 'We'd nothing private to talk about – or anything like that – had we, Donald?'

Mrs Plumleigh-Bruce gave forth this invitation to stay with more warmth than she might have used or than Mr Stimpson liked. There were four reasons for this. Firstly, she was anxious to annoy Mr Stimpson for being late. Secondly, she was flattered at having undoubtedly gained the attention of a decidedly 'young' man who did not even look what must be his age, and whose youthfulness must further annoy Mr Stimpson. Thirdly, she in no way disliked making Mr Stimpson jealous; for she at times seriously entertained the idea of marrying him, and therefore wanted to keep him as much at her feet as a man like Mr Stimpson was capable of being. Finally, she was genuinely interested in Gorse himself. Doubtful as she still was about the exact drawer he occupied, he was presentable and interesting, and he held the right ideas about serious matters, such as those of the General Strike and premature enlistment in the Army. And so she conveyed strongly to Gorse that she did not want him to leave them.

'No. Nothing private,' said Mr Stimpson, in an embarrassed way. 'Nothing private at all . . . Well – what are we all drinking? . . .' And he looked at Gorse as well as Mrs Plumleigh-Bruce, as if urging both to drink with him.

Gorse now saw that Mrs Plumleigh-Bruce would respect him, and desire his company in the future much more, if he withdrew. Also he was bored beyond measure by the notion of having to remain in the company of Mr Stimpson.

'No,' he said, therefore. 'I really won't stay, if you don't mind. I'll get back to my newspaper, if you don't mind. I'm not reading it just for pleasure. I've got quite a lot of work to do tonight.'

'Work?' said Mrs Plumleigh-Bruce. 'With a newspaper?'

'Yes,' said Gorse. 'Or rather study. I take great interest in the form and activities of a famous type of fast-moving quadruped, you see.'

'Oh,' said Mrs Plumleigh-Bruce. 'Horse-racing, you mean?'

'That's right,' said Gorse. 'And I have great schemes afoot just at the moment. So do you mind if I return to my re-searches?'

It happened that, as Gorse said this, the couple, who had been occupying the nook in which Mrs Plumleigh-Bruce usually sat, rose and left the bar. Mr Stimpson saw his chance.

'Well – if you've got *really* serious work to do – like *that*,' he said, facetiously, 'I suppose it wouldn't be *fair* to interrupt you. I also observe,' he added quietly to Mrs Plumleigh-Bruce, 'that our accustomed pew has been vacated . . . So what about sitting down properly, anyway?'

'Yes. You go and sit down,' said Gorse. 'I'll be quite happy here, concentrating for a bit.'

'Well, then,' said Mr Stimpson, looking hesitantly, first at Gorse, and then at Mrs Plumleigh-Bruce. 'What about it, Joan? If you go over I'll bring you fresh regalement.'

'Very well. It's certainly nicer over there,' she replied. 'Quite sure you won't join us?'

'No. I really won't,' said Gorse. 'Thank you very much all the same.'

'Very well, then,' she said, smiling at Gorse in a way which seemed almost to wink at him about Mr Stimpson generally. 'Well – *au revoir*, Mr – Gorse – wasn't it?'

'Yes. That's right. *Au revoir*, then.'

'*Au revoir*.' She went over to the nook, and there were now about thirty rather awkward seconds at the bar, during which Mr Stimpson ordered drinks for Mrs Plumleigh-Bruce and himself. Gorse helped out by pretending to look at his newspaper.

The drinks having been obtained and paid for, Mr Stimpson walked over in silence with them to Mrs Plumleigh-Bruce, and sat down next to her. Still no one else had entered the bar, and so, in the silence, Gorse could hear every word that passed between the other two.

'Well – where *have* you been?' he heard Mrs Plumleigh-Bruce say. 'I hope you've got a good excuse.'

'Oh,' said Mr Stimpson. 'Just Brushing Shoulders with the Nobility – as seems to be my wont these days.'

This remark gave Gorse such a start that he nearly lifted his eyes from his newspaper and looked over at Mr Stimpson. He succeeded in not doing this, but a close observer would have noticed that his head shifted a fraction of an inch upwards, as if he desired to read an item higher up on the page.

Gorse had not yet guessed, or even properly tried to guess, Mr Stimpson's profession, and he could not imagine how a man of this sort could conceivably 'brush shoulders' with the 'nobility'. Was it a joke, or a piece of sarcasm, on Mr Stimpson's part? For some reason Gorse rather fancied not. He beat around in his mind for a clue to the mystery, and listened more intently than ever.

'Oh, really?' said Mrs Plumleigh-Bruce. 'You mean Lord Bulford again?'

'No. Old Carsloe, this time,' said Mr Stimpson, with that droop of the mouth, and air of indifference, or even disdain, which a certain low-thinking type of man always adopts when alluding to a member of the peerage – particularly when he has recently met one of these. 'And then the old boy insisted on me having a cup of tea and a chat afterwards – and it's a long way away, as you know, and so I got late. So I hope that's a good enough excuse. It's business, after all, and very good business. So am I forgiven?'

'Yes. I suppose you must be,' said Mrs Plumleigh-Bruce. 'Business is business, after all.'

Gorse now experienced a sense of relief. He had greatly disliked the idea of someone he disliked 'brushing shoulders' with the 'nobility'. But now it had been made clear that it was merely a matter of business and that Mr Stimpson only got his shoulders brushed in this way in some kind of menial capacity. Gorse felt, too, that he had got nearer to placing Mr Stimpson's profession and social standing: and Gorse liked to place everybody. He guessed now that Mr Stimpson was some sort of Valuer, or Auctioneer, or Agent of some sort.

All the same, a nobility-shoulder-brusher was a nobility-shoulder-brusher, and, as such, not to be dismissed too lightly. Gorse realized that, if his friendship with Mrs Plumleigh-Bruce ripened, he had a more formidable rival in Mr Stimpson than he had at first imagined. And this thought, in its turn, made Mrs Plumleigh-Bruce a more formidable and attractive proposition, and strengthened Gorse in his resolution, hitherto rather vague, to become more fully acquainted with her.

He had seen at once, of course, that Mr Stimpson either consorted with, or desired to consort with, or desired to marry Mrs Plumleigh-Bruce. Even one much less brilliant at this sort of thing than Ernest Ralph Gorse would have seen as much.

Gorse now, while staring at his newspaper, made up his mind to listen to every word exchanged between these two. But here he met with bad luck, for, all at once, the Saloon Bar of The Friar became, it seemed, full of people.

This is the way of bars of public houses during the first half-hour or so of opening time. They will remain in a state of desultory, almost deadly quiet for a long while, and then, all of a sudden, burst into life. It is almost as though a small crowd of people had been loitering outside eagerly awaiting permission to enter. And then, directly permission has been granted, they come in, one after the other, with brightened spirits, eager to drink and highly loquacious.

Three busily talking men entered first, and these, merely by themselves, disabled Gorse from hearing more than an isolated word or so spoken by Mrs Plumleigh-Bruce and Mr Donald Stimpson. And a minute or so later, because of the influx of people, they were totally beyond Gorse's audible reach. Though he was still in a position to watch them, they were as remote from him as if they had been in another house – another city.

This remoteness from him – this sudden disappearance they had made, as it were, into another orbit – at once annoyed and enticed Gorse. For the orbit into which they had moved was now somehow a higher one than his own. Whereas they were together in a familiar place, he was entirely alone in an unfamiliar one. He was now, in fact, a solitary outsider. Five minutes ago he had been very much on the inside with an interesting woman.

These feelings were made even more acute by his noticing, about five minutes later, that Mrs Plumleigh-Bruce and Mr Stimpson had been joined by another man, who had sat down beside them.

This man was, like Mr Stimpson, middle-aged – but in no way overwhelmingly so. He was fair, and stoutish, and he wore a moustache. He looked like a 'gentleman', which displeased Gorse. Worse still, he looked like an ex-military man.

For the first time it occurred to Gorse that Mrs Plumleigh-Bruce might be married. All his instincts had told him, until this moment, that she was not, but now he had to give the matter thought. Could this military-looking man conceivably be her husband?

If such were the case, he reflected, he would probably abandon the pursuit of Mrs Plumleigh-Bruce. Women with husbands were never, for some reason, in Gorse's line, and a woman with an ex-military husband was practically out of the question, for, since he had, in this case, posed as an ex-military man himself, the danger of exposure would clearly be too great.

All the same, this man might easily be neither an ex-military man nor her husband. And so Gorse decided to remain in The Friar and see what happened, 'which way the cat jumped' as he would have put it.

3

When Mrs Plumleigh-Bruce had been talking to the two men for about ten minutes, Gorse, who had been aware that Mrs Plumleigh-Bruce had been looking over at him occasionally, decided that his pretence of looking at a newspaper was becoming hollow. He therefore, having ordered another beer, took a small notebook and pencil from his pocket and pretended to be making notes of an elaborate character. These, it was to be presumed, were racing notes, for Gorse continued, every now and again, to refer to his newspaper.

He was aware that this performance would not carry conviction for more than about twenty minutes, and he wondered how long Mrs Plumleigh-Bruce was going to stay at The Friar. It was his intention to follow her home, or to wherever she went next, when she left.

He decided that, if she did not leave soon, he would engage himself in conversation with someone.

Twenty minutes passed. The bar had now become very full, and Mrs Plumleigh-Bruce was still in the same place.

Next to Gorse, at the bar, and also drinking beer, there was now a young man of about thirty-six. This young man, who was between Gorse and the Plumleigh-Bruce nook, had, Gorse had noticed, on entering waved to Mrs Plumleigh-Bruce, who had waved back cordially. Gorse decided to engage him in conversation.

This was easily done, and soon the two were talking in a seemingly friendly way.

The young man was of medium height, hatless, emphatically good-looking, not at all well-dressed, and bearing the despondent air of one who works hard but fruitlessly. He did not look at all like an actor, but this he was. His name was Miles Standish, and he was running, at a loss so far, a small Repertory Theatre in Reading.

Gorse, who had a gift for rapidly discovering a person's profession, soon did so in this case, and he was much impressed.

Gorse, all his life, had a curious passion for the theatre, and a longing to be connected with it. This was to a certain extent because he greatly fancied himself as an actor.

Gorse was, of course, in the restricted and rather foolish sense of the term, a very fine 'actor'. That is to say, he could, in private, and particularly in private with women, put on an act, deceive, and create wonderfully the impression he desired to create. As an actor on stage, however, he was something worse than hopeless – he was embarrassing beyond measure.

He fancied himself as a light comedian, as an adept in 'Silly Ass' parts in which there was a lot of 'By Gad!', 'What?', 'Bai Jove!', 'Weallay!' and all that sort of thing.

But Ralph Gorse was no Ralph Lynn, and, in the few appearances he had succeeded in making upon the amateur stage he had been very far from successful. Once he had entered for a competition for acting in a provincial town – one in which he had to come upon the stage for ten minutes by himself. The audience was indeed provincial, and, as such, willing warmly to welcome the poorest exhibition. Nevertheless, Gorse was but feebly applauded, and most of the members of the audience blushed profoundly in their souls. But Gorse did not realize the type of reception given to him, and continued to believe vigorously in his capacities in this direction.

This belief was, perhaps, Gorse's sole concession to extreme vanity and exhibitionism – a funny Achilles' heel.

He was, too, attracted by the theatre for other reasons. At an early age he had become aware of its peculiar financial, social and psychological advantages. He knew that an enormous proportion of mankind feels, weirdly but indisputably, a stronger awe for the theatre than almost any other art or activity on earth. He knew that to get in on the inside, to be 'behind scenes' in the theatre, was to achieve a glamour completely out of proportion to that attached to almost any other profession. He knew that to give the average person free seats for the theatre (while pretending that such a thing was easy because one was intimately connected with it) gratified such a person a dozen times more than to give him the money for the seats. When anxious to flatter, cajole, or bribe people in the past, he had often himself bought seats at a theatre and then given them away with the pretence that he had come by them through inside influence and that they were of no use to himself.

He knew, in addition, that to be seen in the company of an

actress was to acquire prestige, or to be envied, or both. He knew, therefore, that it was wise to cultivate the company of an actor, for an actor might easily lead the way to an actress.

Accordingly, having discovered the profession of Miles Standish, Gorse became a very different sort of young man than he would have been with the type of stranger he usually encountered in a public house. He braced himself to exercise whatever charm he possessed – and this, with undiscriminating people, was often very considerable. Another motive for his doing this was his knowledge that Miles Standish was acquainted with Mrs Plumleigh-Bruce.

He completely failed, though, to charm Miles Standish. This hard-working young man – at once actor, producer, promoter, manager, and businessman – had a remarkable sense of people, and so far from being captivated by Gorse, he took an immediate dislike to him. He saw at once that Gorse was trying to flatter and please him, and he suspected that Gorse's motive in doing so was not at all straightforward.

Then Gorse did nothing to improve matters by beginning to talk about theatrical things in a much too easy, too confident, and too appallingly ignorant way. Miles Standish was inured to philistinism from strangers in this matter, but Gorse's philistinism – because of its boastfulness and false sophistication – got under his skin.

Finally Gorse offended the young actor by suddenly and most ungraciously drinking up a half-full glass of beer and leaving him with a polite excuse.

Gorse had done this because he had suddenly observed Mrs Plumleigh-Bruce and Mr Stimpson leaving the house.

Miles Standish had observed the same thing, and he felt certain that Gorse was, for some reason, following those two.

What the reason could possibly be was, of course, beyond him. But he was certain that it was in some way a base one – that Gorse was up to no good.

Miles Standish was, in fact, one of the select few first to suspect that Gorse was up to no good in life generally – that he was, possibly, destined to see the inside of prison bars.

4

Following people without being detected by the followed is, even in the dark, no easy business. Private (and even police) detectives more often than not make complete idiots of themselves at this task. Gorse, however, was one of the most gifted followers in existence.

When outside in Friar Street he saw Mrs Plumleigh-Bruce and Mr Stimpson, at about a hundred and fifty yards' distance, moving towards the eastern part of the town.

His fears were either that they would go into another public house or that they would take a bus. Without being exposed as a follower he could hardly enter one or the other after them.

But they did not do this. Instead they went, at a medium pace, and by ways which to Gorse seemed devious (but then he had not as yet found his bearings in the town) to a small dark road of what seemed to be recently built, semi-detached houses about eight minutes' walk away from The Friar. There were low double gates and small front gardens in front of these houses.

Mrs Plumleigh-Bruce stopped outside one of these houses, and then, after a pause, went with Mr Stimpson through the gate.

Then they both went to the porch of the house, whose hall and ground-floor room were lit.

Gorse had a feeling that Mr Stimpson would not go inside the house, and he was right. After less than a minute's apparently rather intimate conversation in the shadow of the porch, Mrs Plumleigh-Bruce went into the house and Mr Stimpson came brusquely back again through the double gate into the road and began to walk in the direction whence he had come. His air of brusquerie suggested, somehow, that he had kissed Mrs Plumleigh-Bruce.

Gorse succeeded, not without difficulty, in not being seen by Mr Stimpson, whom he continued to follow.

It soon became clear to Gorse that Mr Stimpson was returning to The Friar for another drink, and it is difficult to say exactly why he followed Mr Stimpson. Perhaps it was because he was a born follower, or perhaps he hoped to gain some further knowledge of Mr Stimpson's character by watching his back. Backs, even in the lamp-lit dark, give a good deal of information in regard to character.

Mr Stimpson walked less brusquely as he drew nearer to The Friar: and his shoulders, which had less than three hours ago been brushing against those of the nobility, began slightly to droop.

Gorse began to brood again upon Mr Stimpson's relations with the nobility, and he decided that, because of these relations, however slender or menial they might be, he would endeavour to make Mr Stimpson his friend.

One thing, he reflected, might well lead to another, if one was enterprising enough.

Both of these lamp-lit men in Reading – the followed and the follower – were social snobs. But whereas Mr Stimpson was a foolish, more or less superficial and lighthearted social snob, Ernest Ralph Gorse was a clever, profound, savage, bitter one.

Having watched Mr Stimpson re-entering The Friar, Gorse went into the Saloon Bar of a small public house in the same street. Here it was much more quiet, and, sitting alone over another glass of beer, Gorse gave himself up to calm, level musings – musings upon Mrs Plumleigh-Bruce, Mr Stimpson, the military-looking man, the repertory actor, and the problem of his possible dealings with any one or all of these during his stay in Reading.

It would have been impossible for one who knew Gorse only in his debonair and talkative moods (and in company he was seldom in any other) to conceive how long and deep a thinker the red-haired, slightly freckled young monocle-wearer was when he was alone.

PART THREE

PEBBLES, BRASS, SILK, VERSES AND ANECDOTES

Chapter One

I

Gorse, that night, had surmised that Mrs Plumleigh-Bruce's house was a recently-built and semi-detached one; and he walked past it next morning, at about ten o'clock, in order to verify his impression.

He had, last night, marked the exact house by counting lamp-posts.

His overnight impressions were entirely correct. Sispara Road, which branched off, to the left, from the main road leading to Oxford, was one containing nothing but semi-detached houses, all of which were built in roughly the same architectural style.

These houses were squat, two-storied affairs, round-looking because of their bow-windows on the ground floor, and with red-tiled or green-tiled roofs.

Their fronts had all been most oddly treated. It looked as though the builder had had some sort of infantile sea-side mania for shingled beaches, and that, to indulge this passion, he had, having covered the external walls with thick glue, used some extraordinary machine with which to spray them densely with small pebbles.

Gorse, passing quickly by on the other side of the road, noticed that there were brass plates on the pillars which supported the double gates in front of both of the houses immediately adjoining Mrs Plumleigh-Bruce's. He could not, of course, this morning, see what was inscribed upon these plates. Later he learned that one of them proclaimed that a seemingly very highly qualified Chiropodist practised within during certain hours, and that the other announced the residence of a Commissioner for Oaths.

In the front gardens of most of these houses there were, in addition to sundials, countless images of Gnomes, Dwarfs, Fairies, Goblins and Peter Pans – the inhabitants of Sispara Road having, it seemed, a strong turn of mind for the whimsical, the grotesque, and the beautiful, as well as for Oaths, Chiropody, Veterinary Surgery, Massage, Dentistry, and similar learned and healing professions.

2

Such, externally, was Mrs Plumleigh-Bruce's *pied-à-terre*, which bore the pleasing name of Glen Alan. (One of the houses next door bore the imposing name of 'Rossmore' – the other the lighthearted name of 'Deil-ma-Care'.)

Internally Glen Alan bore a strong aesthetic kinship (as did all the other houses in the road) to what was exhibited outside.

It was, to begin with, littered with pieces of brass, which had been moulded into almost every conceivable form of the whimsical, the grotesque, and the beautiful. Multitudinously sprayed pebbles outside a house nearly always indicate multitudinous pieces of brass inside.

There were brass trays, brass ornaments, and brass bells; there were brass pokers, brass shovels, brass tongs, brass coal scuttles, and brass toasting forks – all of these surrounded, of course, by brass fenders. There were brass ashtrays, brass candlesticks, brass paperweights, and brass jugs. Meals were announced by means of a brass gong.

In a clean and orderly household, such as Glen Alan certainly was, brass has to be cleaned, and only the cleaner, Mrs Plumleigh-Bruce's Irish maid, Mary McGinnis, could have given a full catalogue of all that went on in the way of brass inside this house. Mary – an extremely subdued but, in some ways, not at all unintelligent or unobservant girl in her twenties – would have been able to name the remotest brass cow, dragon, elephant, god, monkey, crocodile, lion, or snake in any room in the house.

Mrs Plumleigh-Bruce's sitting-room, in which she lunched, dined, and entertained, was, as may be guessed, the brassiest of all. The least brassy room was her bedroom.

This was exotic in quite another manner. Brass, indeed, had been almost completely banished from it, and whimsy and grotesquerie had been almost forsaken. Instead, sheer feminine be had been aimed at. In Mrs Plumleigh-Bruce's bedroom Silk, not Brass, reigned.

Mrs Plumleigh-Bruce's large bed (when it had been laboriously made by Mary) had an enormous rose-coloured silk coverlet which was surmounted at the bottom with a silk eiderdown, and at the top with a selection of round silk cushions. The dressing table (in front of which was a silk-covered stool) was draped with silk on runners, which were concealed by a pelmet made of the same material. There were silk lampshades, and the curtains were made of silky material. On Mrs Plumleigh-Bruce's silk-matted bedside table there was a telephone. This ugly black instrument had been most adroitly, fancifully, and enchantingly concealed by silk – that is to say, by a silken doll. This doll had a miniature china bosom, neck and head (the last being adorned with a wig of silver silk), and a vast silk crinoline, which covered the telephone. This crinoline, of course, did anything but assist Mrs Plumleigh-Bruce either in answering her telephone or in getting at it to use it. But for the sake of beauty it is necessary to suffer, and the crude, mechanical twentieth century was kept at bay.

Mrs Plumleigh-Bruce's silken bedroom was, undoubtedly, a room for dalliance – silken dalliance, indeed. Mr Stimpson, who had on a few occasions been permitted to enter it, but certainly not, as yet, to dally, found it (as he was meant to do) impressive beyond measure, opulently intoxicating, heady, dangerous, thrilling, unmanning.

Mr Stimpson liked being unmanned.

3

Mrs Plumleigh-Bruce considered that her maid-of-all-work, Mary McGinnis, had a much too easy life, as 'they all do nowadays': and it is not, really, a simple matter to understand how one woman, whose sole business in the day is to attend to the wants of no more than one other, could have anything but an easy life. Nevertheless, Mary's twelve or more hours of work a day, at a salary of twelve shillings a week, was far from being easy. For Mrs Plumleigh-Bruce, who prided herself upon being a 'martinet', and who demanded what she so unhappily but so frequently called 'explicit' obedience from her servants, made, in her deceptively lethargic, slow, and fruity-voiced way, ferocious use of Mary.

Mary's life was, in fact, a sort of unending corridor in a hideous, thick dream she could not shake off – a thick dream of brass, of silk, of cooking, of laying, clearing away, washing up, log-chopping, coal-getting, fireplace-preparing, fireplace-cleaning, clothes-washing, clothes-ironing, dusting rooms, turning out rooms, turning down beds, getting hot-water bottles, making beds, making midmorning coffee, making tea, making cakes and sandwiches and thin bread and butter, making herself look seemly in her uniform (provided) in the afternoon, external and internal bell-answering, and so on and so forth. And, stalking behind her in this corridor was always Mrs Plumleigh-Bruce, with her indolent, quiet, yet steamroller-like insistence upon 'thoroughness' and 'explicit' obedience. If Mary, for instance, having made the bed, put a single round cushion at the distance of more than an inch from its correct place at the head of the bed, she would be made aware of Mrs Plumleigh-Bruce's displeasure, and any sign of such displeasure terrified Mary – for it made her feel that she might lose her employment, and be thrown upon the world.

And yet Mary did not look upon her work as a hideous corridor in a thick dream. She had the profoundest respect, one might say veneration, for Mrs Plumleigh-Bruce – as well as for her methods of discipline, which she regarded as being entirely correct.

The shrewd, sensible, humane Mary was, perhaps, not totally sane about matters of this sort: her darkly poverty-stricken upbringing in County Galway in Ireland had at an early age stunned her, distorted her idea of humane behaviour as applied to the human race as a whole. She did not really look upon herself as one meriting, or as one who would be a fitting recipient of, compassionate treatment – though she never never thought about such things on a fully conscious level.

Mary did not think that she could conceivably find a better 'place' than the one she had with Mrs Plumleigh-Bruce. She regarded her wages as excellent, and, like the Reading businessmen, she took pride in her mistress as the 'Lady' of the neighbourhood.

Also Mary was strong, and, in a slim, rather gawky way, decidedly attractive. Naturally she looked about ten years older than her age; and her Irish teeth, of course, were in a bad way. Nevertheless the teeth which could be seen when she smiled were as yet presentable: her dark brown hair, eyes and face seemed, at moments, to be almost lovely; and, on her two afternoons off each week, which she spent with friends, she was often made aware of her charms.

These afternoons off, together with her attractiveness and the pride she took in working for an outstanding, a practically famous, local 'Lady', made her look upon her life as an enviable one.

4

Each day of Mary's enviable and unenvying life began at six o'clock.

At eight-thirty she entered Mrs Plumleigh-Bruce's silken sanctuary with a cup of tea, drawing back the silken curtains, causing the linen blinds to shoot upwards, and lighting the gas fire.

At nine-fifteen Mary again entered the room carrying Mrs Plumleigh-Bruce's breakfast on a tray.

At eight-thirty, when her tea was brought to her, Mrs Plumleigh-Bruce was usually sleepy, and sometimes irritable. But when her breakfast came in at nine-fifteen she was often in a strong mood for amiable conversation, or even playful wit, with her Irish maid.

Mrs Plumleigh-Bruce's notion of wit suited to an Irish maid would have been, to any sensitive listener outside, extremely agonizing, for she talked in what she believed to be an Irish accent, and Irish idiom, to Mary.

She amused herself, in fact, by talking *Oirish*.

Oirish may be considered as a language in itself, and Mrs Plumleigh-Bruce's *Oirish* was, in a way, perfect – for it lacked nothing. It did not omit 'Bedad', 'Begorrah', 'Faith', 'Sure', or 'Entoirely'. She would ask Mary if it was 'afther' being, doing, or getting something that she was ('that ye are'), and she often used the greeting 'Top av the morning' to Mary. She pronounced the word darling as 'darlint', delighted as 'deloighted', indeed as 'indade', what as 'phwat', and the words 'It is' as ''Tis'. She used such words as 'Colleen', 'Mavourneen', 'Paddy' and 'Macushla'. It was incredible.

Was the use of this abominably facetious *Oirish* an attempt, on Mrs Plumleigh-Bruce's part, to please, to ease the lot of her poverty-exiled maid? No – it was not. It was, on the other hand, a means either of patronizing Mary, or of making a fool of her. It was also a form of self-indulgence, and of Narcissism – self-indulgence because she greatly enjoyed displaying her virtuosity in *Oirish*, and Narcissism because, while talking it, she was all the time looking at herself, metaphorically, in a mirror, and profoundly admiring what she saw. While looking at Mary mockingly, quizzingly, a shocking sort of flirtatious, would-be-captivating *Oirish* twinkle came into her eye.

Mary herself did not notice this twinkle and did not really know what was happening. She did not get the impression that her mistress had gone practically mad, or even that she was making a fool of herself. She did not even know that Mrs Plumleigh-Bruce was imitating the accent and idiom of the land from which she, Mary, came. She took it all merely as one of the mysterious modes of behaviour of a class whose every deed and utterance were mysterious – almost beyond comprehension, but to be roughly identified and submitted to.

All the same Mary, on these occasions, was somehow aware that Mrs Plumleigh-Bruce was in a good humour – a better one than she was at any other time of the day. And this knowledge made her heart lighter, and show externally that it was.

Consequently Mrs Plumleigh-Bruce was given the impression that she was pleasing Mary beyond measure; and it was the remembrance of these almost daily little *Oirish* sessions with Mary which enabled Mrs Plumleigh-Bruce to boast, to her acquaintances, that she was 'great friends' with Mary, that she 'talked her own language', and that she treated her 'practically as an equal' (along with that demand for 'explicitness' in the matter of obedience).

5

This stoutish, silken Venus (as well as Lady) of Sispara Road, Reading, Berkshire, arose from bed at about eleven in the morning.

The time intervening between breakfast and this rising was spent in telephoning friends and tradespeople, and in reading.

Mrs Plumleigh-Bruce was a great reader. She called herself a 'voracious' one. (The word 'voracious' is applied almost solely to reading by the Plumleigh-Bruce class.)

But 'voracious' as she was, Mrs Plumleigh-Bruce was scholarly and highly fastidious here. No 'modern trash' for Mrs Plumleigh-Bruce, and scarcely any fiction. Mrs Plumleigh-Bruce specialized in History – French History, mostly.

'Glen Alan' French History was rather limited. It began and ended with Marie Antoinette.

In the character, life, death, looks and adventures of Marie Antoinette Mrs Plumleigh-Bruce was immeasurably interested. Mrs Plumleigh-Bruce, as has been said, was no friend of the People, so her attitude towards Marie Antoinette may be easily imagined. It was, in fact, one of admiration amounting to emotional adoration.

Mrs Plumleigh-Bruce fed this emotion by reading every popular, illustrated, and hysterically laudatory book about Marie Antoinette upon which she could lay her hands. Mrs Plumleigh-Bruce was certainly not, by nature, a book-buyer, but Marie Antoinette had almost made her one. She would order from London, and pay as much as fifteen shillings for, a book about her heroine.

As an authority upon Marie Antoinette she was, naturally, almost equally well versed in the French Revolution. And this caused her also to read any popular denigrations of such characters as Robespierre or Marat that came her way. And when she alighted upon a book about the Reign of Terror her feelings both for the *macabre* and for sentimental pity were given full rein at one and the same time.

At times Mrs Plumleigh-Bruce, day-dreaming in bed, almost imagined herself to be Marie Antoinette in person – the crinolined, white-wigged, 'eighteenth-century' doll (with a patch on its cheek) covering the telephone on her bedside table being of considerable assistance in creating this illusion.

Marie Antoinette, in fact, furnished whatever there was of poetry in Mrs Plumleigh-Bruce's soul. But Marie Antoinette had more mundane uses as well. By virtue of the extensive knowledge of History she had accidentally bestowed upon Mrs Plumleigh-Bruce, the guillotined queen was extremely useful in enlarging the vanity, the complacency, and even the sharply material calculations of the pseudo-Anglo-Indian woman.

Knowledge is power. So, also, is an assumed knowledge of Knowledge. To Mr Stimpson (as well as to other men) the latter was highly exhilarating and potent in its effect. Mrs Plumleigh-Bruce, it seemed to Mr Stimpson, was something more than a Lady. She read, she understood, she 'knew' History – an important branch of Knowledge. Therefore she was 'clever'. She read History because she was 'clever', and she was 'clever' because she read History. She had a 'brain'. She was, then, for a woman, most unusual – in one way at least fascinatingly above Mr Stimpson's head.

Mr Stimpson often boasted about Mrs Plumleigh-Bruce's 'brain' – to himself and to others.

Mrs Plumleigh-Bruce was fully conscious of Mr Stimpson's feeling of veneration towards her in this direction, and she exploited it to the full. She frequently gave him lectures – lengthy and to him quite intoxicatingly recondite – upon History.

Mr Stimpson had not as yet cottoned on to the fact that History began and ended with Marie Antoinette.

6

Having dragged herself away from her researches each morning, and having forced herself to rise, Mrs Plumleigh-Bruce put on a very provokingly exotic garment.

This, also, was silken, and was, in those days, called a 'Kimono'.

Mrs Plumleigh-Bruce's Kimono was made of pale blue silk, and, after the manner of Kimonos, it was covered with dragons, chrysanthemums, and other interesting and intricate matters.

In her Kimono Mrs Plumleigh-Bruce went gracefully to the bathroom and had her morning bath. Then she returned to her bedroom and dressed.

She was downstairs by about twelve o'clock.

She did not, at this time of day, use the sitting-dining-room, but a smaller room, which, next to her bedroom, she fancied most in the house. This room also, apart from the bedroom, was Mr Stimpson's favourite, and he fancied himself, in the event of his marrying Mrs Plumleigh-Bruce, using it a good deal.

It was, first and foremost, a room for a Man. It was 'tucked away': it contained a most serviceable roll-top desk, and it was mannish in other ways.

Mrs Plumleigh-Bruce cultivated, and in devious ways advertised to Mr Stimpson, the atmosphere of this room as one suited to the masculine spirit and habit. She alluded to it as a 'Study', as a 'Den', as a 'Snuggery', and as a 'Hidey-Hole'.

Some men, alas, are highly flattered by the notion of being provided with studies, dens, snuggeries or hidey-holes. It makes them feel that they are scholars, smokers, recluses, and clumsy lions.

This small room had a bow window facing the street, and two very small unopenable windows facing the side of the house next door. The two small windows gave little light, for, apart from their smallness, they were made of leaded stained glass which romantically depicted wave-and-foam-surrounded ships at sea.

In Glen Alan there were almost as many ships as there were pieces of brass. Nearly all of the parchment lampshades were ornamented with ships – or with ships' charts upon which ships were depicted. There were pictures of ships, including a reproduction of the seriously hackneyed 'Off Valparaiso', and there were two large models of ships – 'galleons' or 'caravels', of the sort that might be obtained from the firm of Liberty in Regent Street. Even some of the pieces of brass were ships.

There was only one reasonably pleasant ship in the house – a ship in a green bottle. But this had been relegated to the rubbish-heap – that is to say, to Mary's bedroom. And Mary herself did not think it particularly pleasing.

When she was in her 'Snuggery' Mrs Plumleigh-Bruce was brought coffee and digestive biscuits by Mary. These were put upon the desk – in front of which Mrs Plumleigh-Bruce sat upon a cushion in a swivel chair.

With her coffee Mrs Plumleigh-Bruce smoked her first cigarette of the day, and began to contend with the business thereof. She wrote letters, paid bills, or examined tradesmen's books – the last with extreme care in order to see that she had not been cheated either by the tradesmen or by Mary. Sometimes, she would ring a brass bell and question Mary closely about various items.

7

This morning, however, there was practically nothing to do, and Mrs Plumleigh-Bruce, over her cigarette, gave herself up to reflections of a mixed character.

The memory of Ernest Ralph Gorse soon entered, and at last almost completely dominated, her thoughts. In her mind's eye she saw him very vividly, and her mind's ear recaptured as clearly both his voice and the things he had said last night.

She wondered what he was doing in Reading, whether he would enter The Friar again, whether he would be staying long in the town, and, if so, where he was living or would live.

Thinking about him thus, in many different ways, and in relation to herself, one thing certainly did not enter her mind. She did not think of herself as his possible prey, or victim.

If anything, on the contrary, she thought of Ernest Ralph Gorse as her own possible victim – if not exactly prey.

Chapter Two

1

While Mrs Plumleigh-Bruce was thinking about Ernest Ralph Gorse, Ernest Ralph Gorse was thinking about Mrs Plumleigh-Bruce.

He was relieved from the necessity of wondering where she lived, for he had seen her house both by lamp-lit night and by day. And, having done so, he would have been glad to have given Mrs Plumleigh-Bruce information about his own present residence in Reading, for this was of a larger and more imposing kind than her own.

Ernest Ralph Gorse was now living in a three-storied house in Gilroy Road, Reading. Gilroy Road branched off from the Newbury Road, and, without being ostentatious, was much more imposing and delightful than Sispara Road. Its houses had been built in the late Georgian era, and had been reticently and decently numbered – not whimsically or impressively named as in Sispara Road – and there were no gardens or gnomes in front of them. Instead there were pleasant (and totally gnomeless) gardens at the back.

Gorse did not like the Georgian architecture of the house, for sprayed pebbles, front gardens and gnomes were actually more pleasing to his aesthetic tastes, and he looked upon Gilroy Road as being 'old-fashioned' in style.

Nevertheless, he realized that a very much higher social and economic grade of citizen dwelt in Gilroy Road than in Sispara Road.

Gorse neither owned nor rented this house, which he was occupying more or less by accident, for no particular reason, and rather reluctantly. It had been lent to him, along with its housekeeper, by an acquaintance of his – Ronald Shooter.

Ronald Shooter was, if in any business, in the car-business, and it was through this that the two had met, about two years ago. But Ronald Shooter, who was a little moustached man of about thirty-three, was not, truly, in any business; for, without ever being noticeably drunk, he drank from morning to night, and he had a good deal of inherited money of his own. For both of these reasons Gorse had made and cultivated the friendship. A friend with money, with people like Gorse, is naturally regarded as valuable, and one who drinks heavily is potentially more valuable still.

Gorse did not like Ronald Shooter at all. But then Gorse did not like anybody, and, actually, few people liked Ronald Shooter. The little man, in the drink in which he nearly always was, was bumptious, loquacious, an interminable teller of lewd anecdotes, a sordid womanizer, plainly conscious of the power of his money, and, all in all, a very serious bore. Gorse was his closest friend.

Only a few months ago Gorse and Ronald Shooter ('Ronnie') had taken together a fortnight's trip to Paris. Ronnie had insisted upon paying most of the expenses (he always embarrassingly insisted on paying for everything) and they had stayed at the Grand Hotel.

From this luxurious base they would emerge, each evening, to drink at *cafés*, and, afterwards, with the aid of guides, to visit brothels.

This trip had been, for the most part, exceptionally tedious to Gorse. For Gorse was not interested in Paris as a city; he did not like, and could only take little, drink; and, though he was by no means sexless, the level-headed young man did not like women in brothels.

However, he consoled himself with the thought that it was 'all in a good cause' – that is to say he was, by acting as companion, listener, and adviser, getting himself further and further into the good graces of the well-to-do, the lavish Ronnie.

On the trips to brothels Gorse, who acted as manager and negotiator, could, had he wished to do so, have pocketed for himself a lot of Ronnie's money. But he elected to do precisely the opposite. He had used his level head to save Ronnie's money – to preserve him from exploitation. He haggled about terms on Ronnie's behalf, and, in the sober mornings, would often present Ronnie with francs which he had either secreted or retrieved – thus greatly impressing his friend. Gorse always had both the wisdom and the self-restraint to look far ahead in cases of this sort.

On this trip Ronnie had met, and had been captivated by, a Canadian prostitute, and he had made promises to live in an apartment in Paris with her.

Gorse had thought that Ronnie, on his return to England, would not fulfil these promises; but he was wrong. Ronnie was already back in Paris and was living in an apartment, which he had rented for three months, with the Canadian girl.

Before returning to Paris Ronnie had been confronted with the problem of what to do with his house and housekeeper in Reading. He had, therefore, suggested to Gorse that he should live there – free of any charge unless Gorse cared to pay the housekeeper's wages.

Gorse had not particularly liked the idea, but, still with an eye to the future, had simulated great pleasure and gratitude.

And there were, in fact, many things to be said in favour of this exile in Reading. In the first place it was difficult to object to living in a house with a housekeeper already provided. Then Reading was very near London, and Ronnie had made it plain that Gorse was under no obligation to remain in Reading all the time – that he could spend as much time in London as he wished.

Then Gorse had a feeling that Reading might be a happy hunting-ground for a car-speculator – new and interesting territory. And on top of this the house in Gilroy Road was impressive – the first that Gorse, who had hitherto only lived in lodgings, had ever occupied. And an impressive house is not without its uses in the selling of cars.

Gorse had, however, as yet kept on his room in London, intending to see the lie of the land in Reading before deciding how much time he would spend there.

Having spent a few days of loneliness in Gilroy Road, Gorse had begun to hanker to return to London, and had even made up his mind to return and remain there for periods as long as were permissible during Ronnie's absence in France.

But having met Mrs Plumleigh-Bruce, and the interesting set by which she seemed to be surrounded, and having seen her house, he was now strongly inclined to make Reading his base for a month or two.

2

As he walked this morning – he was a great walker and did most of his thinking while he walked – Gorse wondered whether Mrs Plumleigh-Bruce would be in The Friar again this evening. He rather suspected that she would not, and he decided that, even if she were there, it would not be advisable to go into the place himself.

He had, he fancied, made quite a strong impression upon the woman last night, and he believed that the right moment had already arrived, if not actually to display indifference, at least not to show any too great enthusiasm in the matter of meeting her again.

That evening, however, he was tempted to reconsider his decision. For, happening to pass The Friar on his way to a cinema, at about six o'clock, he observed the fair-moustached military-looking man of the night before entering; and this somehow gave him the impression that Mrs Plumleigh-Bruce was, or would be, in there also.

He was still not certain as to whether the military-looking man was her husband, and his anxiety to solve this problem once and for all was, he now found, very strong.

He, therefore, did not go to the cinema, but to the small public house in which he had ruminated at such length last night. Here he ordered a glass of beer, and, sitting down, tried to make up his mind about his correct tactics in the next half-hour.

Chapter Three

I

The military-looking man had in fact been a military man. He had joined the Army during the 1914–1918 War and had risen to the rank of Major. He was known, and liked to be known, as Major Parry.

Major Parry was fifty-five, and, like Gorse's friend Ronnie, he drank and talked and thought about women in a silly way too much.

This was largely because, unknown to himself or to anyone, he was undergoing a change of life – what is now well known as menopause. This agitating condition was then, and by an enormous amount of people still is, supposed to be confined to women; but nothing in fact is further from the case. Though the physical and mental symptoms are less obvious, men are victimized by this disorder as much as women, and often with as serious, or more serious, consequences. Men constantly run away from their long-married and virtuous wives under the influence of this disorder.

In moral character and intellect Major Parry would have been, in a normal state, almost certainly Mr Stimpson's superior: but just at present he was not. He was a good deal lower in his thoughts and utterances, and thus lost favour with Mrs Plumleigh-Bruce, upon whom, despite the fact that he was married, he had eager designs.

He was, tonight, the first of Mrs Plumleigh-Bruce's court to enter The Friar. He ordered a large whisky and took it over to the vacant Plumleigh-Bruce nook. Then, having glanced briefly at his newspaper, he took out a pencil and a piece of paper from his overcoat pocket and began to scribble and think deeply, and then scribble, and think deeply again.

2

Major Parry was the victim of another misfortune besides the one already mentioned. Three years ago he had had the bad luck of having an Armistice Day Poem accepted, and spectacularly printed, on the front page and in a black frame, by a Reading newspaper.

This had made him almost a local celebrity, and he was deeply anxious to maintain his fame (and earn another three guineas) by writing another November the Eleventh poem in honour of the glorious dead.

Another poem, sent in the year before last, had been rejected: but he had had a most polite letter from the editor of the paper encouraging him to try his hand at the glorious dead next year: and by now the thing had become at once a hobby and a small obsession with him.

Diffident of his powers, and fearing the humility of another rejection, he had submitted nothing last November; but he had set his mind to the task of perfecting, during the winter and summer months, something for 1928.

Major Parry, who had somehow as a boy developed a small talent for rhyming, prosody, and even poetry of a sort, had several opening lines for his poem in his mind. His favourite, for the last three weeks or so, had been the mournful but simple:

> 'They are gone, they are gone, they are gone'

which was to be followed, probably, by a half-austere, half-ironical:

> 'Is it worth, then, thinking on'

But here the Major was in doubt. Did this line scan, and, if so, did it express the sort of tragic lilt he was aiming at? It would be all right if the reader would pause before and after the 'then', but the commas did not properly intimate that he should do this, and one could hardly use dashes. ('Is it worth – then – thinking on.') For this reason the Major favoured:

> 'Is the matter worth, then, thinking on.'

He liked this, but, unfortunately, the solution of one difficulty only raised another. For his third line was pretty well decided on. It would be:

'Those who anguished as they shone'

or something like it. But talking about 'the matter' threw everything out. 'Is it worth, then, thinking on Those who anguished as they shone' was perfectly in order, but 'Is the matter worth, then, thinking on Those who anguished as they shone,' certainly was not.

What about (Major Parry wondered, as he gazed at his piece of paper in the Plumleigh-Bruce nook in The Friar), 'Is it worth then thinking, thinking on?' Rather a nice, dreary and sort of Irish lilt, perhaps?

He would have to think about it and decide later. Of one thing he was fairly certain – the fourth and last line of the first stanza – that which followed 'Those who anguished as they shone.' This must, almost certainly, be:

'On Flanders Field?'

Major Parry was not particularly pleased by this line in itself. It was, he felt, a trifle banal and hackneyed. But its one great advantage outweighed any considerations of this sort. The Major was determined to make the last line of each stanza rhyme with the last line of each of the others, and the rhymes for the word 'Field' were not only magnificently plentiful, but richly appropriate, suggestive, and helpful to the poet.

There was, for instance, 'yield' ('Yet did they yield?'). Then there was 'sealed' ('Whose Fate was sealed'). Then there was 'healed' ('Whose wounds now healed'). And then there was 'steeled' ('To battle steeled').

Four absolute beauties you could simply conjure with. But there were, if necessary, many more. There was 'appealed' (to God . . .), 'revealed' (Light was . . .), 'shield' (Their safest . . .), and 'reeled' and 'wheeled'. You could depict Battle as having done either of the last two.

There were, even, if the worst came to the worst, 'peeled', and 'congealed'.

'Peeled' didn't seem to be much good to the Major, who simply couldn't think of anything more dramatic or stately to peel than apples, oranges, or bananas. But 'congealed' might do. One might suddenly go all realistic and congeal blood. Or, if that was going too far, mud.

Then if one came to think about it, there was 'pealed' spelt with an 'a' as opposed to an 'e'. Bells, of course. And 'heeled' was not completely to be dismissed. The heeled boot of the Hun and all that. 'Boots harsh (grim? crude?) and heeled'.

And what about 'Weald'? Sussex Weald. All earthy – and where the simple sort of ploughman chaps came from. 'From Wold and Weald' for instance.

You could, really, go on for ever, of course. And the real point was that 'On Flanders Field?', though slightly cheap, was the only possible last line for the first stanza.

It also had another advantage apart from that of providing such a fine crop of rhymes. It introduced a locality – the name of a place – Flanders – and the Major was anxious to use other names of specific places. Particularly, if it were possible, Passchendaele.

Mention of Passchendaele, he felt, would be most inspiring. It was not only a sonorous, slow, grim and romantic word in itself. It furnished almost as many rhymes as 'Field'. There was 'fail' ('Shall we then . . .?'). There was 'bewail' (Who shall . . .?). There was 'gale' (Midst War's great . . .). And 'pale', and 'dale', and 'veil', and 'hail', and 'quail', and 'flail', and 'nightingale', and 'grail' (holy, naturally), and 'vale', and innumerable other smashing ones.

But *not*, of course, 'jail', or 'male', or 'rail', or 'sail', or 'stale', or 'tail', or 'nail', or 'pail', or 'ale'. Although you *might* perhaps use 'nail', if you wanted to go all religious and do something about The Crucifixion. That involved nails, and, so as to get them into the singular, you could talk about 'Each and every nail' or 'Each piercing nail', or something like that.

Next to Passchendaele, the Major was tremendously anxious to use Ypres. But here, when it came to rhyming, he was totally stumped. In fact all he could think of, miserably, was Pepys. But the name of the famous diarist was neither a true rhyme to Ypres, nor, if you came to think about it, in the smallest way suited to the subject being dealt with.

The Major suddenly perceived that his mind was wandering, and that he must stick to essentials. He had got quite a good rough sketch of his first stanza: now he must get on to his second.

He wanted this to begin in the same mournful, repetitive way as the first, and he had already invented a first line for it which, he thought, could hardly be bettered. This was:

'They are fallen, they are fallen, they are fallen!'

But here again the rhyme problem was hideous. It was, in fact – or so it seemed to the Major at the moment – worse than hideous: it was insurmountable.

Come now, there must be something, thought the Major: and, as he went on wretchedly searching his mind, the most impractical and fantastic notions entered the Major's head.

There *was*, for instance (if you could only *somehow* break into an old-fashioned, foolish, foppish accent), 'appallin'' or, even, 'appallen', using an 'e' to make the rhyme more perfect.

The Major, who was tired, and whose whisky (his fourth this evening) had slightly affected his brain, now dreamily – and, because dreamily most ludicrously – began to extemporize.

'They are fallen, they are fallen, they are fallen,
It really was most, *most*, most, *most* appallin'.'

Or:

'The slaughter, really *was* you know, appallin'.'

Then there was 'mauling'.

'They got an absolutely *awful* maulin'.'

Or:

'Those lads – good God – they got a frightful maulin'.'

And, of course, there was 'callin'.'

'Can't you hear yet, their voices callin', callin'?'

Or:

'Their sacrifice to Heaven high was callin'.'

There was, even, a treatment of 'stone-walling'.

'Grit, *grit*, pluck, *grit*! They *stuck* at it – *stonewallin'*!'

Or:

'On sticky wicket – there they were – stonewallin'!'

Or:

'By Jove, *one* art they knew, those boys, *stonewallin'*.'

And then there was 'crawling'. ('No whine from them, no whimperin', no crawlin''), and 'bawling' ('Just listen! Hear the Sergeant Major bawlin'!'), and 'stalling' ('No engine *there* was coughin', kickin', stallin'').

To say nothing of 'galling' ('The situation really was most gallin'').

Because of his intense anxiety and seriousness about his poem, the tired Major, in this whiskyfied rhyme-and-line reverie, had, as yet, completely failed to notice that he had entered the realms of pure idiocy, and it is really doubtful whether he would ever have done this – at any rate this evening.

But unfortunately, at this moment, Mr Stimpson entered the Saloon Bar, and, while ordering a beer at the bar from the barmaid, brusquely interrupted the Major's distressed trance with a hearty greeting.

'Evening, Major!' cried Mr Stimpson, and the composer replied, 'Hullo, Stimpson', and put his pencil and piece of paper back into his pocket.

Chapter Four

I

Having been given his beer, and having taken a sip at it, so that it would not spill as he walked, Mr Stimpson went over to Major Parry, and sat down beside him.

'Well, Major,' he said, with great cheerfulness. 'What's the news with you?'

'Not a thing. Dull as ditch-water. What about you?' replied the Major, and there was a pause.

2

Businessmen – all over the world, in the remotest provinces and the mightiest capitals – do not, on the whole, like each other at all.

Major Parry did not like Mr Stimpson, and Mr Stimpson did not like Major Parry.

Major Parry was not, of course, strictly speaking a businessman. He was enormously and doggedly military. Nevertheless, like so many ex-officers, he mixed almost exclusively with businessmen, and, in general habit and manner of thought, he certainly was one at heart. His little, rather pathetic, school-acquired gift for versifying need not be taken into account. When Major Parry met Mr Stimpson businessman met businessman, and there was mutual dislike.

Why, then, do provincial businessmen constantly 'foregather', as they would put it, in their leisure hours?

The reason is that they are too useful spiritually to each other to refrain from doing so: they cannot do without each other. The very law of their being compels them to find someone upon whom they can unload their funny stories – the 'latest', the 'One About the . . .'

Just as *Oirish* is a language in itself, so what may be called 'One-Aboutism' is an art in itself – perhaps the only one which really stimulates people like Mr Stimpson and Major Parry.

The art of One-Aboutism, however, does not consist, as might be thought, mainly in the discovery and clever narration of the stories. These are hardly listened to, and are only perfunctorily laughed at, by the other One-Aboutist. The real art lies in succeeding in not being *out*-One-Abouted – in beating down, by astuteness, quickness, personality, and, if necessary, sheer vocal power, your rival One-Aboutist – in telling, in short, more and longer stories within a given time than anyone else present.

In those days of 1928 the now outdated Limerick was still much used, and, before Mr Stimpson had been sitting more than two minutes with Major Parry, he had asked the latter whether he had heard the one about the Young Lady of Leicester.

Major Parry was in the unfortunate position of being unable to say that he had, and so he had patiently to listen to, and at the end manage to heave out a fairly presentable laugh at, the singular and, indeed, nauseating predicament of the Young Lady of Leicester.

Then the Major smartly counter-attacked with a Young Parson (about whom he had only heard that morning in another public house), from Brixham.

(Parsons, Vicars, Rectors, Old Ladies, Young Ladies, Old Men and Young Men are almost the only prominent or active citizens in Limerick-land.)

This amazingly quick *riposte* from the Major naturally displeased Mr Stimpson, but he also managed something quite reasonable in the way of a laugh. Then, in order rapidly to subdue his opponent, he said, 'Yes. That's a good one. And that reminds me of the story of the policeman in the tram. Know it?'

The expression, 'And that reminds me', is constantly employed by the more ruthless One-Aboutist, and it is, on nearly every occasion, an absolutely lying expression – a flagrant device. The Young Parson from Brixham bore not the faintest resemblance, either in his character or his unusual experience, to the Policeman in the Tram. Therefore it was quite impossible for the one to have reminded Mr Stimpson of the other: and Mr Stimpson was hitting below the belt. Such technical fouls are, however, regarded by these *raconteurs* as more or less part of the game, for which no sort of Queensberry Rules has yet been invented.

The Major knew nothing about the Policeman, and so had to listen to Mr Stimpson describe his adventures in the tram – which, being extremely intricate, took at least three minutes in the telling.

The story of the policeman's adventure, as well as being involved, was of a sexual nature. Nearly all such stories are. Those which are not either deal with the processes of bodily elimination, or, felicitously killing two birds with one stone, deal with these processes and sex at the same time.

Major Parry listened for the three minutes with feigned pleasure, sniggering appreciatively at the indicated moments, and laughing aloud at the climax.

He found the story almost insufferably lengthy, tedious, and, because he did not really see the point of the climax, practically incomprehensible. Indeed, had not Mr Stimpson employed a certain look, certain gestures, and a certain rising and as it were goodbye-saying tone of voice – all of which could be easily recognized as showing that the end of the story had come – the Major would not have known that this had happened and that his cue for laughter had been given him.

The story of the Policeman 'reminded' Mr Stimpson of yet another story, which he related.

Of this the Major did at least see the point, but he did not think it in the smallest way funny. To his mind, it was, if such a thing was possible, as boring as the previous one.

Nevertheless Major Parry did not fail to take a mental note of this story. This was because stories of this kind, with people like Major Parry and Mr Stimpson, are capable of undergoing strange – it would not be going too far to say mystical – metamorphoses. When listened to, they are hideously dull. But if, having been heard, they are borne in mind for a few days by the sufferer, and if, after a few days, the opportunity arises of his relating them in different company, then they are no longer dull. On the contrary, they are now quite, or very, or even uproariously or hilariously funny to the narrator, who is wounded bitterly if their richness – the last drop of the cream of the jest – is not appreciated to the utmost. The Major, almost certainly, would before long be telling this story of Mr Stimpson's elsewhere.

3

After a while the flow of story-telling – or rather Mr Stimpson's flow, for he was easily the Major's master in this art, and succeeded in finishing three stories and two Limericks up – came to an end.

They talked of other matters, including that of the weather, which was remarkably warm and muggy for the time of year.

The Major then complained that he was too warm at the moment, and he rose to take off his overcoat. As he did this, he asked:

'And is our Lady Joan gracing this hostelry tonight?'

'Yes,' said Mr Stimpson, with a rather funny look in his eye. 'I think she is . . . At least she *said* she was . . .'

'In which case,' said the Major, 'the atmosphere will be somewhat warmer still, I fancy. What?'

'Yes. I suppose it will . . .' said Mr Stimpson, and the look in his eyes became even funnier, and more evasive, than before.

Mr Stimpson's look must be explained.

Some months ago, before the Major had begun seriously to nurse and nourish designs upon Mrs Plumleigh-Bruce, and before Mr Stimpson had begun to entertain the idea of marrying her, Mrs Plumleigh-Bruce had not been treated at all respectfully in conversation between Mr Stimpson, Major Parry and other men.

Although acknowledged as the Reading businessman's outstanding Lady, she had, at that time, in fact been the subject of many joking, suggestive or lascivious remarks and innuendoes. She had been alluded to, to quote the less vulgar expressions used, as a bit of goods, the goods, a nice (or scrumptious) piece of skirt, hot stuff, and 'nice work if you can get it'. It had even been suggested that such work might not be at all difficult to get, and facetious bets had been made as to who would get it first.

But the days of such talk were, for Mr Stimpson at any rate, very much in the past. One's possible future wife cannot be spoken of in this way.

Therefore, when Major Parry, thinking of her as hot stuff, had suggested that the atmosphere would be warmer still when Mrs Plumleigh-Bruce entered, Mr Stimpson had been both embarrassed and displeased.

The Major had, in fact, in the existing circumstances, practically 'spoken Lightly of a Woman's name': and to do such a thing as this is one of the worst possible social crimes in the delicate minds of limerick-and-story tellers of Mr Stimpson's type.

Such people are exquisitely fastidious, and, therefore, easily shocked in matters of this sort. (To tell a dirty, or even only slightly *risqué* story, in the presence of what they so often call 'The Sex', is only next, in caddishness and bestiality, to speaking Lightly of a Woman's name.)

The Major, being already married and having never even thought of marrying Mrs Plumleigh-Bruce, had, of course, no notion that she had recently become a Woman to Mr Stimpson – least of all one whose name could not be spoken lightly of. And so, in no way conscious of what he was doing, he continued to torment and embarrass Mr Stimpson.

'Yes,' he went on. 'As hot as jolly old Hades, in fact. At least them's *my* sentiments. I don't know about yours. What?'

'No, I don't know either really, I suppose,' was all that Mr Stimpson could manage to reply.

'Well, you ought to,' said Major Parry. 'I noticed you managed to obtain the privilege of escorting her home last night. And that's not the first time, either – unless my senses have deceived me. Or *have* they deceived me?'

'No,' said Mr Stimpson. 'I suppose they haven't – really.'

'No. So I thought,' said the Major. 'And how did *that* go?'

The Major, although he had not as yet any conception of the fact that, in Mr Stimpson's eyes, Mrs Plumleigh-Bruce had almost become a woman about whose name it was highly improper to speak lightly, was all the same aware that something of some sort was going on between these two; and he was highly interested in the exact character of the relationship. As he himself in his own way strongly desired Mrs Plumleigh-Bruce, this was only natural.

He had noticed that Mr Stimpson had lately been more and more frequently given the privilege of escorting Mrs Plumleigh-Bruce home from The Friar, and one or two remarks and conversations between these two in his presence had revealed quite clearly that Mr Stimpson had more than once entered Mrs Plumleigh-Bruce's house.

As to the matters of the length of such visits, and the exact depths of Glen Alan into which Mr Stimpson had penetrated, and the capacity in which he had been received therein – these were matters of conjecture to the Major.

Was it possible that Mr Stimpson had already secretly managed to acquire that nice work which, it had been agreed, it might not be at all difficult to get?

The Major thought this unlikely, but he was determined to probe the matter, and so he had now said, in reference to Mr Stimpson's confessed escorting-home of Mrs Plumleigh-Bruce: 'And how did *that* go?'

'How do you mean – how did that "go"?' said Mr Stimpson, after a slight pause, and looking keenly at the Major through his thick-lensed spectacles.

'Well, how did it go?'

' "Go?" How?'

'I mean *Go*,' said the Major, doggedly, and, after a brief pause, added, 'I mean for instance, did our Lady Joan issue an invitation to enter her abode?'

'No, I just left her at the front door – that's all.'

'Really?' said the Major. 'You didn't go further than that?'

'No,' said Mr Stimpson. 'No further than that . . .'

There was a pause in which the two men looked at each other – Mr Stimpson resentfully, the Major, in his innocence of the real situation, jovially, rallyingly, yet inquisitively. The thick lenses of Mr Stimpson's spectacles disguised his resentment, and so the Major had no qualms in proceeding with his lighthearted yet increasingly suggestive cross-examination.

'When I said "further",' he said, 'I didn't mean Geographically further.'

'What, then?' said the nettled Mr Stimpson. 'Historically?'

'Yes,' said the Major. 'Historically, if you like. I thought perhaps you'd been making History with our Lady Joan – our Lady Joan of Arc.'

'What sort of History?' said Mr Stimpson. 'I don't follow you.'

'Oh – a little amorous history, perchance,' said Major Parry, who, because he was talking about History, dropped into 'historical' language. 'Thou hast not, peradventure, made successful suit, or attempted such, with our illustrious Maid of Orleans?'

'Oh, no, nothing of that sort,' said Mr Stimpson. 'Believe me.'

'If Maid she may be termed,' said Major Parry. 'It seemeth to me very mightily otherwise. Doth it not so with you – after our now somewhat lengthy acquaintanceship with her?'

'I don't know . . .'

'Nay?' said the Major, whose whisky was now noticeably affecting him. 'I wot then, that thou'rt but little acquainted with the Sex, after all. In fact, to employ common parlance, I should say she's crying out loud for it.'

Really, thought Mr Stimpson, this is absolutely insufferable. But what could he do? He knew that the Major intended no offence, and that he himself had brought this misfortune upon himself by, at an earlier date, speaking in just the same way about Mrs Plumleigh-Bruce. He decided that he must somehow change the subject: but, for the life of him, at the moment, he could think of no subject to change to, and so he just murmured, 'Do you? . . .' and the Major marched inexorably and terribly on.

'I do,' he said. 'In fact yelling the place down for it.'

'Oh – come now . . .' said Mr Stimpson.

'Well,' said the Major. 'Such are my views, at any rate . . . However – it seems that I'm mistaken about your own relations with the brave and noble girl from Orleans. Thou hast not, so thou assurest me, as yet waged amorous battle with her?'

'No. I haven't . . .'

'Nor pierced her valiant armour? What?'

'No,' said Mr Stimpson, still beating around in his mind for another topic of conversation. 'Certainly not . . .'

''Twould be without much difficulty pierced, methinks,' said Major Parry with mock sententiousness.

The situation had now reached a point at which the exasperated Mr Stimpson was nearly out of his mind, and, possibly, he would not have been able to control himself if, at this moment, a young man had not entered the bar and ordered a bitter from the barmaid.

The young man was Ernest Ralph Gorse. His curiosity about the Major's relationship with Mrs Plumleigh-Bruce had won the day.

4

Mr Stimpson, who, as we know, had the night before hated both the presence and aspect of Ernest Ralph Gorse, now found both pleasing.

Normally he would have either cut the young man or given him a curt greeting from a distance. Now, because of the intense suffering Major Parry was inflicting upon him, he took a totally different line. He caught Gorse's eye, and waved to him, and said, or rather shouted, cordially, 'Hullo! . . . Good evening!'

Gorse returned the greeting in the same words, and in the same spirit, and sat down on a stool to read his newspaper. But Mr Stimpson would endure no such unsociability.

'Come and drink it over here,' he said, employing the same half-shout. 'And let me pay for it.' (Gorse was at this moment paying the barmaid.)

'Well,' said Gorse, picking up his glass of bitter and walking towards Mr Stimpson and the Major. 'I'll bring it over, but I've paid for it already. How are you?'

'How are *you*?' said Mr Stimpson, warmly, and he introduced Gorse to the Major, and Gorse sat down with both of them.

PART FOUR

GORSE THE FORTUNE TELLER

Chapter One

I

The enormously imperturbable Gorse was not always immune from fear, and he now found himself decidedly afraid of the Major, who might be Mrs Plumleigh-Bruce's husband, and who, if he were the ex-military man he seemed to be, might easily expose as false his pretensions, made last night to Mrs Plumleigh-Bruce, to having served in France during the 1914–18 War.

This fear of the Major was not lessened by the fact that the latter, as soon as Gorse was seated, began to look at him in a keen and protracted way.

In fact the Major, who was rather uncouth in the matter of staring at people, was only wondering, quite naturally, who the hell this reddish-haired young stranger was, and why Mr Stimpson had so eagerly summoned him over to the practically sacred Plumleigh-Bruce nook. But Gorse, equally naturally, did not interpret the Major's look correctly; and it even occurred to him that Mrs Plumleigh-Bruce had told her husband (the Major) about the young man she had met last night who had got into the Army at the age of sixteen, and that the Major, having seen him, did not believe a word of it, and meant to examine him closely about the matter.

For all these reasons there was now a long and uneasy silence between all three. Gorse, being least at ease of all three, at last found this silence so unendurable that he was spurred into breaking it, and he banally resorted to the weather. He said that he thought that the evening was warmer.

'Warmer?' said the Major. 'It certainly is. In fact it's damned muggy and unseasonable. In fact I've just taken off my overcoat, with that blazing fire and all . . . I don't know why you two don't take off yours. I know my old friend Stimpson always sticks to his like a leech, but I should've thought you're young enough to be more Spartan, Mr – Gorse – was it?'

Gorse still did not like the way the Major was looking at him. Nor did he like the suggestion that he should remove his overcoat. Nor did he like the rather brusque and military '– Gorse – was it?' All three made him feel that the Major was inviting, if not almost ordering him, to enter the witness-box and undergo examination.

'Yes. That's right. Gorse,' he said, and added, feebly employing a small joke which he normally, when asked about his name, brought forth with a certain gusto. 'Not Furze. Or Broom. Or Bracken – or Heather, or anything like that . . . And I think I *will* take your advice, and doff the dear old outer garment, cloak or mantle.'

He rose, and took off his overcoat in yet another silence. Now his nerve was returning. This was probably because there had luckily come into his mouth the words 'doff the dear old outer garment, cloak, or mantle', and they had given him confidence. Gorse, all his life, was in the habit of employing, in speech as well as in writing, a style which was a hideous, wretchedly imitative mixture between those of Jeffery Farnol and P. G. Wodehouse. His monocle encouraged this style. And the style encouraged the wearing of his monocle. It was all part of that 'Silly Ass' act in which he took such pride.

He also employed, at times, the ridiculous pseudo-Elizabethan or 'historical' style of speech which the Mr Stimpsons and Major Parrys of life so often employed – a style of speech closely related to his own Jeffery Farnolism.

He was now almost completely himself again. If the Major meant to put him through it, he felt, he was ready for it.

Having briskly and neatly folded his overcoat, he put it on the seat beside him, and, sitting down, faced the two middle-aged men, who were still silent, but no longer, to Gorse, formidably so.

'Well,' he said, hitching his trousers cleverly in the manner of a monocle-wearing Wodehouse character. 'I seem to be somewhat making myself at home – don't I? Aren't I butting in a bit? Haven't I interrupted some momentous confab betwixt my grave and venerable masters? What?'

He looked, first at the Major, and then at Mr Stimpson.

2

'No,' said the thickly-lensed Mr Stimpson rather shiftily. 'We had no subject in hand meriting further discussion, I fancy. You're most welcome – I assure you.'

'What?' said Gorse. 'No ponderous matters concerning the affairs of this, our state – our realm?'

At this he snatched out a high-powered gold cigarette case from his hip pocket, and without a word offered a cigarette to both – Mr Stimpson politely rejecting the offer, and the Major accepting it, thus further easing Gorse's mind.

There was a cheap mode, in those days (even more popular than in these) never to say 'Thank you' when accepting a cigarette. The Major did not say 'Thank you', and this friendly and knowing lack of courteous gesture pleased Gorse even further still.

'Well,' said the Major, tapping his cigarette on the table, while Gorse tapped his own upon his gold cigarette case. 'I don't know about affairs of state. It was more a question of a state of affairs, if anything.'

'And may I ask the purport of such question?' asked Gorse. 'Or would that be intruding? Wilt thou not tell me the matter engrossing thee?'

He went on tapping his cigarette, and so did the Major. Gorse did this rather nervously – the Major ponderously.

Then Gorse produced a brilliant silver cigarette-lighter from his waistcoat pocket, and flicked on a light for the Major.

Both cigarettes having been lit, Gorse took the initiative.

'A state of affairs, you said?' he said. 'Come now – wilt thou not disclose thy story, e'en unto a stranger?'

'Well,' said the Major, puffing at his cigarette. 'It's a very old story – a very old story indeed. In fact it's the oldest story in the world.'

'Ah,' said Gorse. 'Then I think I can guess. You're alluding – I take it – to what our friends across the English Channel, which I myself have only so recently crossed, would term *L'Amour*. Correct?'

'Yes. Quite correct,' said the Major. 'So you've just come back from France, have you?'

'Yes. Only a few weeks ago.'

'Really? . . . Where did you go?'

'Nowhere,' said Gorse, 'but Gay Paree. And gay enough I found it, in all conscience.'

'You did – did you? It's such a long time since I've been there myself that I wouldn't know.' Here the Major again showed curiosity on his face as he looked at the bold and puzzling young stranger. 'What were you there for – business or pleasure?'

'Pleasure,' said Gorse. 'Three weeks' undiluted pleasure – such as only Paris, as no doubt you're aware, can provide.'

Gorse, as we know, had had, in fact, an almost intolerably wearisome fortnight with his friend Ronnie in Paris. But he had been sharp enough to observe that the Major's eyes had lit up at the mention of 'Gay Paree' – and that to talk of pleasure, in the 'Parisian' sense, would both stimulate and impress the man.

'So you strolled along the Bois de Boulogne,' said the Major, quoting the old music-hall song, 'with an independent air – did you?'

'*Most* independently,' said Gorse. 'And not solely along the Bois de Boulogne – either. In fact I indulged my fancy in several other places – believe it or not.'

'The music-halls? . . . The *Folies Bergères*, and all that? . . .' suggested the Major.

'Yes. The *Folies Bergères*, and a good deal *more* than that,' said Gorse. 'I'm sure I needn't tell *you*, sir, that in that gay city there are many other Halls, and haunts, in which even more enticing things than Music are provided. Or does Music come first with you in life?'

'No,' said the Major. 'Music's an also-ran, as far as I'm concerned, and particularly when I'm in Paris. And you certainly needn't tell *me*. But didn't it cost you a pretty packet of money?'

'Yes. It did indeed cut into the good old wad a bit,' said Gorse. 'It has to, if you do things properly – and I'm sure you'll agree it's wise to do things properly on such occasions, and in such a wicked city as Gay Paree. Isn't that your experience?'

Gorse was playing up this 'Gay Paree' business for two reasons. In the first place he was certain that he was obscurely exciting, as well as plainly impressing, the Major. In the second, he felt that, by keeping the conversation on this topic he would soon solve the problem about the Major which concerned himself and his possible future dealings with Mrs Plumleigh-Bruce. In fact, he rather fancied that he had solved it already. If the Major were Mrs Plumleigh-Bruce's husband he would not, Gorse fancied, talk (at any rate in a public house which his wife entered) in so eager and easy a way about the pleasures of brothels in Paris. ('And you certainly needn't tell *me*,' the Major had said only a moment ago.)

However, Gorse knew that there are hardly any limits to which certain married men will not go when drinking in public houses in male company; and so he was still in doubt about the Major's relationship with Mrs Plumleigh-Bruce.

'Yes . . .' said the Major. 'You've certainly got to do things properly, or you're asking for trouble. Though perhaps you're safer in Paris than anywhere else.'

This did not help Gorse with his problem. It might merely be that a middle-aged man was giving a young man advice. Gorse decided to try a more direct, local attack.

'However,' he said, 'where were we? Weren't you saying that you were discussing a state of affairs – a state of affairs concerning the old, old story? And wasn't I inquiring what the story was?'

'Were you? . . .' said the Major, vaguely – vaguely because in his thoughts about Paris he had lost the main thread of the conversation.

'Why yes. Surely. Wasn't I, sir?' said Gorse, now appealing to Mr Stimpson, who had been sitting all this time in silence and with a glum and fishy look on his face.

Mr Stimpson, now forced into the conversation by Gorse, had been looking silently glum and fishy because he had not been liking the conversation between Gorse and the Major.

Mr Stimpson, without ever having visited Paris, had never taken to the idea of it at all. He thought of it, of course, only as a city of sin – and, though he had more than once sinned, both in thought and in deed, in England, he was envious of that sort of sin, abstruse, elaborate, yet facile, which (so he had gathered) went on in Paris.

And this upright, fastidious and patriotic man, naturally, did not have any fancy for those people who ate frogs, and to whom he alluded, mostly, as 'The Frogs'.

Over and above all this, Mr Stimpson was, just at this period, in a strongly puritanical mood.

Provincial businessmen contemplating marriage are more often than not in such a mood. Purity suddenly overwhelms them. The women they are about to marry must, in the course of nature, be immeasurably pure, and meaning to remain so for the rest of their lives. Therefore they, the businessmen, are under an obligation to go in for purity themselves. Impure behaviour must not be indulged in, and impure thoughts must not be thought, and impure utterances must not be made. Even other people must not speak in the smallest way impurely. (There is, of course, a sort of Special Treaty, or Dispensation, in regard to the narration of impure anecdotes or limericks.)

However, Mr Stimpson had now been directly questioned by Gorse about the main thread of the conversation, and he had perforce to answer.

'Why – yes,' he said. 'I believe you were . . .'

'Well, then,' said Gorse, looking at the Major again. 'Can't you tell me something about this particular example of the old, old story? Or would it make my juvenile ears blush?'

'No. I don't think so,' said the Major. 'We were only discussing a Certain Lady, that's all. And she's not even one you'd know about, unless I'm wrong. I mean you wouldn't unless you're a resident of Reading and a frequenter of this hostelry. And you're not either, are you?'

'Well,' said Gorse. 'Yes and no. I'm probably only what you'd call a bird of passage in Reading – but I've already frequented this pub. In fact I did so last night. Didn't I, sir?' He again appealed to Mr Stimpson.

'Yes,' said Mr Stimpson. 'Quite correct.'

'And as for ladies, "certain" or otherwise,' the audacious Gorse continued, 'let me see now. I don't know that any have come my way at all . . .' He affected to pause, search his memory, and suddenly remember. 'Oh yes! I have met one. Only last night, and in here. That's again correct, isn't it, sir?'

'Yes,' said Mr Stimpson, now deeply regretting having, to save himself torture from the Major, spoken to Gorse this evening. 'That's right.'

'And very charming she was,' said Gorse. 'not at all "certain", as I saw it. Or "uncertain" one might say. In fact she seemed to me a lady, in the true sense of the word, from top to toe.'

The bold, shrewd Gorse was now both pumping and flattering the two men – mitigating, or disguising, the pumping by the flattery. Mr Stimpson – to him clearly either Mrs Plumleigh-Bruce's pursuer or paramour – could not be anything but pleased by what he had just said. Nor could the Major who, in Gorse's mind, still might conceivably be her husband.

'Why,' said the Major, addressing Mr Stimpson. 'Has our young friend here met our Lady Joan?'

'Yes,' said Mr Stimpson, and looked at Gorse. 'We had a little chat at the bar last night – didn't we?'

'Really,' said the Major. 'How interesting . . . And what did *you* make of her, Mr Gorse?'

This query from the Major enabled Gorse to make up his mind once and for all that Mrs Plumleigh-Bruce was not the Major's wife. Further, the way in which the Major had put the question – his underlining of the word 'you' combined with a faintly amused and disdainful expression in his eye – made Gorse suspect that the Major in no way put Mrs Plumleigh-Bruce on a pedestal of any sort – rather the contrary in fact. And so he now hedged with both men.

'Well, I didn't really have time to make anything of her,' he said, and went on to another matter which had slightly puzzled him. 'By the way, I notice you alluded to her just now as "Lady" Joan. Is she in truth an entitled lady of quality – or did you speak in jest? I don't even know her name – with a handle attached to it or otherwise.'

'No, it's only a little joke,' said the Major, 'and her name's Plumleigh-Bruce – Mrs Plumleigh-Bruce.'

'Married, or widowed?'

'Widowed,' said the Major. '*Long* widowed.'

He was again somehow suggestive in the way he stressed the length of her widowhood, and Gorse did not fail to notice this.

'We always call her our Lady Joan, for some reason,' the Major continued. '"Our Lady Joan of Arc" is my own usual appellation.'

'Oh yes?' said Gorse. 'But surely the widowed Mrs Plumleigh-Bruce, your Lady Joan of Arc – could not be the same Certain Lady who was under discussion when I appeared on the scene?'

'That's all *you* know,' said the Major. 'In fact I think we were discussing a little question of her armour – weren't we, Stimpson?'

'Her armour?' said Gorse. 'Now I'm afraid I don't follow you.' (But he did.)

'Well, we were just wondering whether it could be pierced, that's all,' replied the (to Mr Stimpson) vilely vulgar and ostentatiously lewd Major. 'And, if so, how easily.'

'Oh yes?' said Gorse, quickly glancing from one to the other. 'And what conclusions did you come to – if any?'

'Well, *I've* got *extremely* decided views,' said the Major. 'But my friend Mr Stimpson here seems to be in doubt. Don't you, Donald, my boy?' (Mr Stimpson's Christian name, it will be remembered, was Donald.)

Mr Stimpson, who would now willingly have physically wounded the Major, could only reply: 'Yes. I am. Certainly.'

Gorse perceived that the man would have liked physically to wound his friend. He hesitated as to whose side he should take, and, in order to satisfy his curiosity by the light of the sparks he might make fly, he decided to encourage the Major.

'Well,' he said. 'The proof of the pudding is in the eating – isn't it?'

'Yes,' said the Major, going from worse to worst. 'And what we all want to know is whether anybody's *eaten* the pudding yet, and, if so, who it is that's done the eating.'

'Yes. I see . . .' said Gorse. 'Though I suppose it's a little impolite to allude to so charming a lady as a pudding – isn't it?'

The Major now achieved the miracle of going from worst to worse than worst.

'Well, I don't know about that,' he said. 'She is a bit puddingy, if you look her all over and come to think about it . . . Didn't *you* notice certain traces of avoirdupois, Mr Gorse?'

'Well, my meeting was so brief that I hardly noticed,' said Gorse, deciding to make the sparks fly further and faster. 'But she certainly struck me as no skeleton, shall I say?'

'Not,' said the Major, 'that I have any particular objection to puddings. In fact puddings are rather in my line, on the whole . . . But perhaps I've got curious tastes.'

'Well,' said Gorse, in a detached way, 'I don't really know . . .'

'You *will*, young man,' said the Major, 'when you're older. The older you get the more puddingy you like them. I was like you when I was young. But when you're more advanced it's the extra pound of flesh you want – believe me. What think you, my silent friend, Mr Stimpson?'

There was a pause.

'By the way,' said Mr Stimpson. 'You know that Mrs Plumleigh-Bruce is coming in here tonight. In fact any moment now.'

Mr Stimpson seemed to think that the announcement that Mrs Plumleigh-Bruce was soon to appear in their midst, was near, would somehow scare the Major, make him drop the subject. But he was mistaken. Nor did the Major (though his whisky had now gone violently to his head) miss Mr Stimpson's pompous use of 'Mrs Plumleigh-Bruce' instead of the easy and familiar 'Our Lady Joan'.

'Oh – so "Mrs Plumleigh-Bruce" is – is she? So much the better. We can then more closely scrutinize the pudding – see exactly how puddingy Mrs Plumleigh-Bruce is. Plumleigh's rather a good word, by the way. Makes you *think* of puddings. Plum Puddings. *Delicious* plum puddings – what?'

The Major drank off the little whisky which remained in his glass. 'Well – what about all of us having another drink while we await the serving of the pudding – what?'

At this moment, most alarmingly to the Major, the pudding was within less than three yards of himself.

Mrs Plumleigh-Bruce, though arrogant in manner, was an exceedingly quiet and unobtrusive intruder into rooms or into company. Mr Stimpson, even, had not observed her entrance into the bar. This soft, supremely dignified unobtrusiveness was, perhaps, part of the woman's inner arrogance.

'What *are* you men talking about?' said Mrs Plumleigh-Bruce, with gracious humour. 'Puddings? What on earth do you know about puddings?'

Chapter Two

The three men rose – the Major giving a brisk military salute to the woman who had so recently figured in his imagination as a plum pudding.

Mrs Plumleigh-Bruce, who had not heard enough of the conversation to know that she had been compared to something you stick holly into at Christmas, all the same sensed that there was something slightly funny in the reception she was now given by Mr Stimpson, Major Parry and Gorse.

She was inclined to put this down, however, to shyness – shyness caused by the presence of the stranger, Gorse. And, in any case, she quickly dismissed any such suspicious thoughts, for she was, though she would never have admitted it to herself, delighted beyond measure to see Gorse. She had thought, during the day, that the interesting young man had possibly gone out of her life for ever. Now he was in her very own nook – her web, as it were.

Mr Stimpson, Major Parry, and to a certain extent Gorse, were, needless to say, in a state of grave embarrassment, which they tried to conceal as well as they could.

Mrs Plumleigh-Bruce had brought her 'bloody dog' (as both Mr Stimpson and Major Parry, for once in agreement, always secretly thought of her spaniel) with her, and the settling-down and insincere flattery of this animal delayed, for a few moments at least, the tactful management of the pudding question.

But soon enough the dog was settled, and the pudding was there again.

What on earth was to be said, and how was it to be explained away? Everything depended, of course, upon how much of the conversation Mrs Plumleigh-Bruce had heard, and this was completely unknown.

The whole matter, perhaps, might be tactfully dropped. But this was risky. Moreover, Mrs Plumleigh-Bruce did not herself permit this.

'Well. Do go on,' she said, having sat down. 'What were you saying about puddings? And what do you think you know about them?'

Gorse came to the rescue.

'No,' he said. 'We weren't professing to *know* anything about them. We were just talking about them. We were, in fact, mundane as it may seem, having a lengthy discussion, as to what would be our favourite meal, if we were given *carte blanche*. And we were going through it course by course. The Major here had arrived at plum pudding – hadn't you, sir?'

'That's right,' said the Major. 'I'm all for it.'

'Every day?' said Mrs Plumleigh-Bruce. 'Or just at Christmas time?'

'Oh – every day,' said the Major. 'In fact three time a day if necessary.'

'Oh – you detestably coarse man,' said Mrs Plumleigh-Bruce, employing, as she so often did, what she imagined to be a sort of Marie Antoinettish flirtatiousness. 'It's *just* what I'd've thought of you.'

She was not usually flirtatious with the Major, who, she considered, did not deserve such a compliment. But flirtatiousness, though directed apparently towards one man, may be in fact aimed at another. She was, in reality, at this moment, flirting with Ernest Ralph Gorse.

'Well,' said Gorse. 'We weren't only talking about eating – we were talking about drinking – having another spot, in fact. Yours is a whisky, I think, Major – and yours is a beer, I think, sir, isn't it?' He then, as he rose, turned from Mr Stimpson to Mrs Plumleigh-Bruce. 'And yours, I fancy – unless there's any variation from last night, is a Gin and It – No?'

There were now the usual claims from the men as to whose 'turn' it was to pay for the round, and Gorse succeeded in establishing his own.

'There's plenty of time after this,' he said. 'Besides, the situation simply demands a drink all round on me tonight. My researches, last night, into the form and qualities of the equine quadruped richly rewarded me – believe it or not. So if you'll all remain seated I shall now play the role of *garçon* and bring you the sustenance as specified.'

At this he went over to the bar and ordered drinks from the barmaid.

While waiting for these he wondered what sort of impression he had made upon Mrs Plumleigh-Bruce with the shots he had fired. He had shown himself as one casually lavish in the matter of paying for drinks; he had (lyingly, of course) intimated that he had won a good deal of money on today's Racing; he had done this in what he considered a most gracious and well-worded little speech which included the French word *garçon* (he had used *carte blanche* earlier on, and he intended to use his recent trip to France as much as possible when he had rejoined her); and, best of all, he had flattered Mrs Plumleigh-Bruce by remembering what she had been drinking last night.

Gorse fancied that at least one of these shots must have gone home.

In fact, all of them had.

Gorse ordered a large Gin and Italian for Mrs Plumleigh-Bruce and himself, a pint of bitter for Mr Stimpson, and a large whisky for the Major. He carried them over, in two journeys, to the Plumleigh-Bruce nook.

When he was seated again, Mrs Plumleigh-Bruce protested against his having ordered a double, as opposed to a single, Gin and Italian: but Gorse said, 'Well, you know, I really don't think it'll bring you to ruin,' and then, after he had been thanked by all for the drinks, and there had been a rather awkward pause, he said, 'Well – here's jolly old How, and all that. And what have you all been discussing in my absence? The problem of the perfect repast – as before?'

The others – all of whom were now looking, almost staring, with great curiosity at this perhaps over-bold and over-generous young stranger – replied that they had not.

'Not that it's not a most fascinating subject,' said Mrs Plumleigh-Bruce. 'May I ask your ideas?'

'Well – it's difficult to say,' said Gorse. 'But of one thing I'm certain. I certainly wouldn't go to England for it.'

'Where, then?' said Mr Stimpson. He spoke rather sharply, for whereas Mrs Plumleigh-Bruce was emphatically intrigued by Gorse's personality, and the Major found it puzzling but by no means intolerable, Mr Stimpson was liking it less and less. This was largely because he had already sensed that his possible future wife was decidedly interested in the young man. He was also quite certain that Gorse was yet again going to allude to the unvisited yet deeply envied and hated France.

'Oh,' said Gorse. 'France. Where else? I'm afraid English cooking isn't at all in my line. Is it in yours?' He looked at Mrs Plumleigh-Bruce, amusedly and knowingly.

'No,' said Mrs Plumleigh-Bruce. 'It certainly isn't – if I had my way. But don't tell my Irish maid that. She does try so hard – poor thing.'

'The deadly secret shall not be revealed,' said Gorse. 'However, I'm sure you'll agree that French cooking is really the only possible thing. Don't you?'

Before Mrs Plumleigh-Bruce could reply, Mr Stimpson cut in quickly.

'Including,' said Mr Stimpson, 'frogs?'

The jaws of the man suffering so acutely from Gallophobia were now set hard, and his tone was quite savage. Gorse took advantage of this by adopting a particularly urbane, and therefore gently reproachful, tone.

'Why, yes, I can't say I exclude the frog – though it's not a delicacy I go in for regularly. May I ask *your* opinion on that much discussed matter?' said Gorse, again addressing Mrs Plumleigh-Bruce.

'No,' she replied. 'I entirely agree with you. There's a lot to be said for the frog.'

Mrs Plumleigh-Bruce had never actually eaten a frog. Indeed the idea of doing so nauseated her. But she was aware that those who would seem sophisticated must profess delight, or at any rate not disgust, in frog-eating, and so, in order to hold her own with Gorse, she had as good as said that she had indulged in this experiment.

Major Parry, who himself had never eaten a frog, was now more candid than Mrs Plumleigh-Bruce, and admitted that he had not, but that he would not have any objection to doing so. He then made the well-known, agonizingly stale remark about the resemblance between the flavour of a frog and that of a chicken.

Mr Stimpson had now been made a fool of, and his spectacles did not prevent him from showing as much on his red, moustached face.

Mrs Plumleigh-Bruce who, it must be remembered, often entertained the notion of marrying this man, saw that frogs must not be rubbed into Mr Stimpson, and that she must help him out.

'However – one can't survive on frogs only – can one?' she said.

'And we still haven't come to your perfect meal – have we? What would you begin with – anyway?'

'Well – if I had my way, I'd begin with nothing but the best,' said Gorse. 'But then, if I had my way, which I haven't, I'd have nothing but the best all round – food, cars, clothes, everything. It's an economy in the long run – don't you agree?'

'Yes,' said Mrs Plumleigh-Bruce. 'I certainly do . . . but how would you start this meal of yours?'

'Oh – pâté, prawns, oysters, and all that,' said Gorse. 'And I'm on remarkably friendly terms with lobster soup – if correctly made.'

'Yes. I adore lobster soup, I must say,' said Mrs Plumleigh-Bruce.

'Oh – and then I was forgetting caviare,' said Gorse. 'Caviare, above all.'

Mrs Plumleigh-Bruce felt that it was permissible to dispute the merits of caviare. Her husband once, in the presence of, and with the support of, a senior officer, had done so. She therefore decided to do the same thing with Gorse. She was now in the position of finding it quite difficult to hold her own with this young man – a type of experience she had not encountered for a long while anywhere – least of all in Reading.

'Well – I'm not so certain about caviare,' she said. 'I'm afraid I rather waver in that direction.'

'Oh – do you?' said Gorse, and Mr Stimpson, having himself eaten caviare, and encouraged by Mrs Plumleigh-Bruce's seeming hesitation, saw a chance of recovering lost ground.

'Tastes like cart-grease to me,' he said, grimly. 'Ball-bearings soaked in cart-grease.'

'Oh, Donald,' exclaimed Mrs Plumleigh-Bruce. 'Do not be so horribly vivid and lurid. You're worse than Leonard.' (Leonard was Major Parry's Christian name.)

The words 'horribly', 'vivid' and 'lurid' (in addition to suiting Mrs Plumleigh-Bruce's low-toned, studiously mouth-projected and fruity voice to perfection) were, she felt, taken together and used one after the other, impressive, clever, and charming – charming in her own particular manner. She had even practised, in the privacy of her bedroom – both mentally and vocally – the use of these three words in combination, as a girl of another era might have practised 'Stewed prunes and prisms'. She was very satisfied by the rendering she had just given, and wondered whether Gorse had been charmed.

Gorse had not. Women, in any case, never charmed Gorse – at any rate conversationally – and, in this case, he perceived that Mrs Plumleigh-Bruce was being abominably affected. He decided, in the near future, to play upon, by seeming to be ravished by, any further affectations of the same kind. And he observed, among other things, that both Mr Stimpson and Major Parry had been captivated by her words and voice at this moment. Gorse was advancing rapidly with what now seemed almost certainly to be his Reading holiday-task – Mrs Plumleigh-Bruce.

'Yes,' Mrs Plumleigh-Bruce went on. 'I must say I *am* in two minds about caviare . . . However – what would you choose to follow?'

'Well,' said Gorse. 'We mustn't overlook our dear old friend the omelette – particularly our friend when cooked in France and nearly always our enemy when cooked over here – don't you agree?'

'I certainly do,' said Mrs Plumleigh-Bruce. 'The French are absolutely superb at omelettes – aren't they? . . . But do go on. You're simply making my mouth water with all these delicacies.'

'I'm sorry,' said Gorse. 'I suppose I've been spoiled by my recent sojourn in Paris.'

'Oh. Really?' said Mrs Plumleigh-Bruce. 'Have you been to Paris lately, then?'

'I have indeed,' said Gorse. 'And very reluctant I was to return to my native land – I can tell you – though I hope I'm being in no wise unpatriotic.'

'No. You must find it a very dismal contrast – between Reading and Paris,' said Mrs Plumleigh-Bruce, looking at him. 'And from what you told me about yourself yesterday evening, one could hardly call you unpatriotic.'

Gorse knew exactly to what she was referring. She had in mind his (imaginary) service in France during the 1914–18 War and his (actual) activities among the ranks of those opposing the working class in the General Strike of 1926. But he feigned complete ignorance.

'Well, I hope I'm not,' he said. 'But what makes you so certain, after my remarks concerning my country's culinary efforts, about my patriotism?'

'Oh – only what you were telling me last night.'

'Oh. Really? What was that?'

Gorse was aware, of course, that the tricky moment had come. Now he was in danger, possibly, of being exposed as an impostor by the military man sitting opposite to him. (He had no fear of Mr Stimpson.) However, he had worked out a long while ago, and had again gone over in his mind only this morning, the details of his regiment and general record in his invented military experiences in France. Gorse, who as a boy at school had had a tremendous predilection for uniforms and war, knew almost as much about Army matters as he did about cars. Also he had pumped, and by pumping flattered, his loquacious friend Ronnie Shooter, about his military adventures in France, and he had decided that, if ever questioned too closely about his own spurious career as a soldier, he would impersonate, in retrospect, Ronnie. Now, too, he was conscious of being in a good mood, and felt that he could hold his own with the Major, or, if that became too difficult, cunningly dodge the subject.

'Well – your joining up and all that,' said Mrs Plumleigh-Bruce. 'I hope I'm not revealing a secret. *You* told it to me, anyway.'

'Oh,' said Gorse. '*That* . . .'

'What?' said the still aggressive Mr Stimpson. 'Did you join up? When?'

'Yes,' said Mrs Plumleigh-Bruce. 'And he managed to do it at the age of sixteen. That's right, isn't it, Mr Gorse?'

'Yes. Correct enough,' said Gorse, and here, as Gorse had expected, the Major cut in.

'Good Heavens,' he said, 'you weren't old enough for that – were you? I mean even if you got in at sixteen – were you?'

Gorse noticed, with pleasure, that the Major's look and tone, so far from being suspicious and hostile, were credulous and flattering.

'I was, though,' said Gorse. 'Of course, I looked a lot older than my age in those days. Just as, so it seems, I look a lot younger than my age nowadays. How old would *you* take me to be at the moment?'

The Major looked at him.

'Oh,' he said. 'Twenty-two – three – four. Just possibly five.'

'And you?' Gorse asked Mrs Plumleigh-Bruce.

Mrs Plumleigh-Bruce did not know whether Gorse wanted to look older or younger than his years. She thought older, probably.

'Well – possibly twenty-five,' she said. 'But I certainly wouldn't like to bet on it.'

'And you, sir?' said Gorse to Mr Stimpson.

'Yes,' said the crudely spleenful Mr Stimpson. 'I'd say you're a good twenty-five.'

'Well – you're nearest,' said Gorse, 'but you're all hopelessly out. I'll be thirty within a matter of weeks.'

'Well – I certainly'd never have thought that,' said the Major.

'No. Nobody does. And I can never make up my mind whether it's an advantage or not. I suppose it's very nice to be thought so extremely juvenile. On the other hand, when it comes to business matters, I often fail to be treated with the respect which I consider due to my years.'

'Well,' said Mrs Plumleigh-Bruce. 'I certainly think you ought to be treated with respect. Anyone who wangles his way into the Army at the age of sixteen should be treated with the profoundest respect, I should say. And you were in France, too, weren't you?'

'I was,' said Gorse, sententiously, ruminatively, and retrospectively, looking into the distance. Things were now getting decidedly warmer, and this distant look served to conceal the fact that he was thinking quickly in preparation for the cross-examination which he felt certain was coming.

'Really,' said Mr Stimpson. 'Were you in France? Where?'

Mr Stimpson was proving much more suspicious and difficult than the Major, but Gorse still was not in the least afraid of him.

'In many and varied places,' he replied.

'And in an active capacity?' the Major, who had only served in an administrative capacity and had not been to France during the war, now asked.

'Well,' said Gorse. 'For long periods not at all as active as one could wish. But extremely lively – I can assure you. However, I came out completely unscathed.'

'And what outfit were you associated with?' The Major certainly was now looking quite keenly at Gorse, but, Gorse surmised, in a respectful and marvelling rather than doubting way.

'The Gunners,' said Gorse. 'The Royal Horse Artillery – to be precise.'

'And did you get a commission?' asked Mrs Plumleigh-Bruce. 'You certainly must have deserved it.'

'Yes,' said Gorse. 'I did finally achieve the rank of Lieutenant.'

'And were you in any of the big shows?' asked the Major.

'Yes. I was present at more than one – I must say.'

'Do tell us,' said Mrs Plumleigh-Bruce.

'Now – I really mustn't become reminiscent, you know,' said Gorse. 'If there's any reminiscing to be done, I'm sure that's up to the Major.'

'No,' said the Major. 'I had an extremely dull time. In fact, hard as I tried, I never actually crossed the Channel. So it's for you to hold forth – if anyone.'

'Well, *I* think it'd be better if no one did,' said Gorse. 'To *begin* with these stories are always extremely boring to everybody – except the participant . . .'

'And to go on with?' said Mr Stimpson, who simply could not control his rage.

'And to go on with,' said Gorse, imperturbably, 'one doesn't really like – at least *I* don't – digging up these things. There are some things one wants to forget – and most of all when drinking in cheerful company. I know some people simply can't resist pouring forth their war experiences – but that's not my line at all. And I know a lot of other fellows – particularly those who went through the worst of it – who feel just the same. I'm sure *you* can understand that – can't you – Mrs Plumleigh-Bruce?'

'How on earth did you know my name?' Mrs Plumleigh-Bruce was surprised into asking.

'Well – I have to admit that I was making inquiries about it before you came in. I hope you don't think it impudence. It was really a compliment – I assure you.'

'And taken as such,' said Mrs Plumleigh-Bruce. 'I assure *you*.'

'Well, I'm glad to hear that.'

Gorse now saw that this rather stupid, rather plump woman was falling for him, hook, line, and sinker, and that he must not, at present, go too far – particularly in front of the two men who were so clearly enslaved by her.

He looked at her, seeking the cause of this enslavement, and wondering whether he himself could be attracted by her physically in any way in the future. Such a thing, he now thought, was not absolutely inconceivable. Plumpish she certainly was, but the Major, inspired by whisky, had certainly gone too far even in facetiously comparing her to a plum pudding. She had very nice, friendly, sparkling eyes, a good skin, and a lascivious mouth, which was, to Gorse, not spoiled by the rather rabbity teeth. Gorse, like many other men, had a liking for rabbity teeth. Also, affected as they were, and as he knew they were, he did not altogether dislike her low, 'musical' voice and fruity accent.

Gorse was not, it must be remembered, seeing the Mrs Plumleigh-Bruce whom her maid Mary saw during most of the day. With Mary the eyes were narrower and meaner, the mouth was sulky and malicious rather than lascivious, and the voice, while remaining affected, was coolly commanding in a most objectionable way.

But now Mrs Plumleigh-Bruce was dressed in her very best clothes, and 'got up to kill' – to kill Ernest Ralph Gorse, actually – though, while dressing this evening, she certainly would not have admitted this. Nor did Gorse suspect any such thing.

'Well,' said Mrs Plumleigh-Bruce. 'You certainly seem to have crowded a lot into your twenty-nine – or as you say nearly thirty – years.'

'Yes. I think I've managed to see a bit of the world – one way and another, and in its various aspects.'

'And what on earth brought you to Reading?' asked Mrs Plumleigh-Bruce. 'Surely *that's* not a very desirable aspect of life to want to see?'

'What's wrong with Reading?' said Mr Stimpson.

'Now, then, don't be foolish, Donald,' said Mrs Plumleigh-Bruce. 'You're not at your best when you're pretending to be so violently provincial.'

Once again, in her queenly, low-voiced snubbing of Mr Stimpson, Mrs Plumleigh-Bruce was flirting with Gorse.

'Well, I *am* provincial,' said Mr Stimpson. 'I don't go gadding about on the Continent and all that. I'm too busy. And even if I weren't I doubt if I would. It's not in my line, as it happens.'

'Don't mind him, Mr Gorse,' said Mrs Plumleigh-Bruce. 'But tell me – how did you manage to land up in Reading?'

'Yes,' said the Major. 'It's certainly a pretty awful hole – taken all in all.'

'Well,' said Gorse. 'It was purely by chance, as a matter of fact. I have a friend – he was doing Paris with me, by the way – and he's lent me his house here, along with his housekeeper.'

'That sounds very generous of him,' said Mrs Plumleigh-Bruce.

'It is,' said Gorse. 'But then he's absolutely rolling, wallowing in money – and so I suppose he can afford to be generous.'

Here Gorse, having greatly exaggerated the wealth of his friend in Paris purely for the sake of impressing Mrs Plumleigh-Bruce, had a sudden inspiration.

'And there's a little more to it than that,' he added. 'He's bored stiff with the house himself – he's got a lot of property and houses all over the place – and he wants me to buy it from him – lock, stock, and barrel. Whether I shall or not remains, of course, to be seen . . . However, that's why this bird of passage has alighted in Reading, and proposes to stay here until he's made up his mind.'

Gorse, all his life, had, when lying, the gift of sudden inventions and inspirations of this sort. It was largely because of this gift that, when he was ultimately a nationally famous figure, people often said that he had a 'genius' of a perverted and evil kind. Such people were, perhaps, right.

This particular little fiction about his friend wanting to sell the house in Gilroy Road, which had entered his mind seemingly purely by accident, was destined to have most serious and interesting consequences in his dealings with Mrs Plumleigh-Bruce.

Chapter Three

'When you say,' said Mr Stimpson, still in a bellicose and cross-examining mood, 'that your friend's got property all over the place – do you mean all over the place in Reading, or just all over the place everywhere?'

Knowing as much about house property in Reading as, perhaps, anyone else in the town, Mr Stimpson had a faint hope of catching Gorse out, or, at any rate, of showing his superiority in at least one branch of knowledge or sophistication.

'No, not "all over the place in Reading", – just all over the place – all over this island – this "precious isle set in a silver sea", or whatever Shakespeare calls it.'

'And where's the house – if it's not a rude question?' said Mr Stimpson, asking a rude question.

'Gilroy Road,' said Gorse. 'Know it?'

This made Mr Stimpson sit up. It gave him, indeed, almost as much of a shock as he had inflicted upon Gorse last night when he had alluded to the brushing of his shoulders against those of the nobility. For Gilroy Road was, Mr Stimpson knew, possibly the most distinguished road in Reading. In Gilroy Road dwelt the most affluent, the most old-fashioned, and the most gently born residents of the town.

Mr Stimpson, like Gorse, did not at all like the 'old-fashioned' Georgian architecture of Gilroy Road: but it was, all the same, a road which had to be taken very seriously by an Estate Agent.

'Really,' he said, hardly endeavouring to conceal that he was astonished. 'Gilroy Road? Yes . . . I certainly know it.'

The Estate Agent had now displaced the snubbed and envious man.

'Yes, I know Gilroy Road all right,' he went on. 'And a very interesting little bit of Reading it is.'

'Why so interesting?' said Gorse. 'They seem to be asking a pretty stiff price for the houses there, and I haven't quite been able to find out why – as yet, at any rate. They're nice and spacious and large and all that, but they seem to be a bit too old-fashioned to me – both outside and inside.'

'Oh,' said Mr Stimpson, now almost completely forgetting his animosity towards Gorse in his interest in the subject in hand. 'That's the mystery. They *are* old-fashioned – you're right. In fact I doubt if I'd want to live in one if you paid me. But our view isn't shared by everyone, I can tell you. In fact, they're asking for more money for a house in Gilroy Road than you'd believe – believe me.'

'I certainly do believe you,' said Gorse. 'In fact I have every reason to – from personal experience.'

Gorse had noticed the change in Mr Stimpson's mood, and decided to make friends with him.

'Tell me – what sort of price would *you* say was reasonable?' he asked.

'Well. I wouldn't say it was reasonable,' said Mr Stimpson. 'But I can give you a rough idea of the price . . . You certainly wouldn't get one, freehold, under two thousand five hundred, and three thousand pounds'd be nearer the mark.'

'That,' said Gorse, 'is exactly what I've found – somewhat to my surprise. In fact that is just about where I am at the moment, in my present negotiations – or rather contemplated negotiations.'

'Well,' said Mr Stimpson. 'If you got one for twenty-five hundred you wouldn't be a loser, I can assure you.'

'Again you reflect my own sentiments, and what I've gathered elsewhere. But it still remains a bit of a mystery.' He turned to Mrs Plumleigh-Bruce. 'Do *you* know Gilroy Road?'

'No,' she replied. 'I've never heard of it, as a matter of fact . . .'

'Oh, come now, surely you have, Joan,' said Mr Stimpson. 'You must know it. It's where Sir Charles Wharton lives. In fact I've pointed it out to you.'

'Oh, yes,' said Mrs Plumleigh-Bruce. '*I* remember . . . I remember the road at any rate. I just didn't know it was called Gilroy.'

'Sir Charles Wharton?' said Gorse. 'Now – who is he? . . . My friend Ronnie never told me about him . . . Knight, or Bart?'

'*Bart*, believe it or not!' exlaimed Mr Stimpson. 'Of course he's got a house in London as well, but he was born in Gilroy Road, and he's stuck on to the place. Sentimental, I suppose. He's pretty old. How he got born there I wouldn't know. But there's a lot more to Reading than you'd think – I mean anyone who'd just seen

Broad Street and Huntley & Palmer's, and just that . . . Yes. We Boast a Baronet in our Midst – believe it or not.'

Gorse was, secretly, as delighted by the Baronet as Mr Stimpson was. For, as he was at present occupying a house in Gilroy Road, he could now himself Boast a Baronet, not only in a vague Midst, but as a near neighbour. Everything seemed to be falling into his hands.

'I wouldn't be surprised,' said Mr Stimpson, 'if Sir Charles hadn't helped to put the prices up. A Bart – and he's none of your new creations – he goes back pretty well to the Conqueror, as far as I can gather – gives a sort of *cachet* to the place, I suppose. Now I'm breaking into French myself. But that's the word I want, isn't it?'

'Yes. That's the word all right,' said Gorse, as if politely attempting not to be too patronizing to Mr Stimpson in front of Mrs Plumleigh-Bruce. 'It's incredible, isn't it – the length to which snobbery goes – even in these days. So I'm living within a stone's throw of a Baronet! I must see that I behave myself! But, joking apart, you don't think twenty-five hundred too much to pay for a house in Gilroy Road?'

'I certainly don't,' said Mr Stimpson. 'In fact I think you'd be extremely lucky if you got away with it at that.'

'Well, I'm very grateful for your advice, and I'll think about it, and very likely act upon it.'

Gorse now thought the time was ripe for the further subduing of Mrs Plumleigh-Bruce by asking about her own small dwelling-place. He again turned to her.

'And where do *you* live?' he asked her. 'Are you in as august a position as myself, or more humble – or perhaps very much more august?'

'Oh,' said Mrs Plumleigh-Bruce. 'Very much more humble.'

'I find that hard to believe,' said Gorse. 'But stranger things than that happen in life nowadays. May I ask where it is?'

'Oh – it's off the Oxford Road,' said Mrs Plumleigh-Bruce. 'Just a quiet little row of semi-detached houses. My chief reason for living in it is that it was "bequeathed" to me by my sister. It bears the remarkable name of Sispara Gardens.'

'What-ara?' said Gorse.

'Sis,' said Mr Stimpson. 'Sispara. It's a funny name.'

'It certainly *is* funny,' said the Major. 'Funny in two ways. It always makes *me* think of *Cas*cara – in fact.'

'Oh, Leonard,' said Mrs Plumleigh-Bruce, rebuking (half in order still to flirt with Gorse) the Major for this allusion to the then enormously popular aperient. 'You really are abominable. What am I to do with you – you atrocious man? And you've made that particular little joke at least a dozen times before.'

'Have I?' said the Major, meekly. 'I'm sorry . . .'

'However,' said Gorse. 'What's in a name? The point is whether Sispara Road's comfortable and convenient. Is it?'

'Well – it's not too bad – in its own way, of course,' said Mrs Plumleigh-Bruce. 'But I've never looked upon it as anything more than some sort of temporary *pied-à-terre*, really.'

'Well – I trust it's not so old-world in style as Gilroy Road. And that all, or nearly all, modern conveniences are supplied – running h. and c. – reasonable amount of min's walk to Station or bus. And telephone, and all that?'

The last-named convenience – the telephone – was the one in which Gorse was interested.

'Yes. Running h. and c.,' said Mrs Plumleigh-Bruce. 'But I'm afraid my maid Mary frequently allows it to run cold just at the wrong moments. And it's quite ten minutes' walk to the Station.'

'And the telephone?' asked Gorse, permitting himself to look in a rather suggestive way at Mrs Plumleigh-Bruce – as if he might telephone her himself in the near future. He had meant not to go any further with this sort of thing in front of her two admirers. But he had to find out whether the woman was on the telephone. Meetings in The Friar would, if he meant seriously to tackle and pursue Mrs Plumleigh-Bruce, clearly not be enough.

'Oh yes,' said Mrs Plumleigh-Bruce. 'I've got a telephone.'

'And are you in the book?' asked Gorse, with the same look. 'Or do you keep it secret from the world?'

'No,' said Mrs Plumleigh-Bruce, interpreting his look exactly as Gorse had wished she should, and giving him a by no means uninviting glance in return. 'It's open to the public gaze.'

There was now, almost, a secret understanding between the two – the subtle but familiar telephone-pact which is revealed in the eyes of those who desire to become more privately or intimately acquainted with each other.

Gorse saw that his two rivals had both smelt the possible existence of such an eye-pact, and he hastened to do his best to destroy their suspicions.

'I asked you,' he said, 'because I'm not in the book myself as yet – naturally. And if I'm *going* to take the house I'll certainly have to be. Tell me – can it be done fairly quickly, or do you have to wait for months and months?' he was addressing all three – but particularly the now almost tamed and friendly Mr Stimpson.

'Oh no,' said Mr Stimpson. 'It shouldn't be long. It's a question of luck, really – whether you're inserting it at just the right time. But you ought to get to work as soon as possible, if you *are* going to stay here.'

'And the question is,' said Gorse, ponderously. '*Am* I? Would *you*?'

'Well,' said Mr Stimpson. 'It really all depends on –'

But Mr Stimpson was prevented from finishing what he wanted to say.

For at this moment, Mrs Plumleigh-Bruce, meaning to get a handkerchief out of her bag, accidentally spilt her glass of Gin and Italian with the sleeve of her coat. The drink went over the table, on to her hand, and on to her skirt.

Just as Gorse's unpremeditated lie about his contemplated purchase of a house in Gilroy Road was to have a serious and intricate effect upon his future dealings with Mrs Plumleigh-Bruce – so was Mrs Plumleigh-Bruce's accidental upsetting of her drink, at this moment, also fated to have considerable influence upon these dealings. They were, at any rate, expedited by the small accident.

Chapter Four

I

'Oh – how appallingly clumsy of me!' said Mrs Plumleigh-Bruce, but, before she had got the words out of her mouth Gorse had snatched the handkerchief displayed in his front pocket, and was himself wiping her skirt.

Gorse's handkerchief was immaculately clean and made of the finest Irish linen. Mrs Plumleigh-Bruce noticed this.

'Oh – thank you so much,' she said. 'And you really shouldn't spoil your handkerchief.'

'Never mind about the handkerchief,' said Gorse soothingly, as he dabbed at her skirt in a modest yet expert and very thorough way. 'It's sticky stuff – Gin and It – and particularly sticky when taken externally. Also quick measures are advisable in such a case . . . There . . . I don't think there'll be much of a stain now – or at least nothing that a little petrol won't remove . . . And I see your hand's wet. Come along now. Let's deal with that, and then we'll replenish your glass . . .'

Gorse took her hand and began to wipe it.

'I feel just like a nursemaid,' he said.

'And I feel just like a very naughty little girl,' said Mrs Plumleigh-Bruce.

Gorse was, for the second time, breaking his resolution not to proceed with his enticing of Mrs Plumleigh-Bruce in front of the two men. But Gorse seldom let a gift-opportunity simply handed to him on a plate, as this had been, go by – and he was determined not to do so in this case. His flirtation with Mrs Plumleigh-Bruce (particularly after her 'little girl' stuff) was now flagrant, but he did not care. He meant, indeed, to press it further.

Having wiped the palm of Mrs Plumleigh-Bruce's hand, he went on to wipe the table, saying, while doing this:

'That's a very interesting hand, by the way. Or palm, rather. But then I suppose you don't believe in the science of the palm. I personally do – believe it or not.'

He was now putting his soiled handkerchief into his overcoat pocket.

'What do you mean?' said Mrs Plumleigh-Bruce. 'Fortune telling?'

'Yes. If you like to put it that way. Character reading, anyway. Perhaps it's the same thing.'

'You mean you think you could read my character by looking at my palm?' said Mrs Plumleigh-Bruce.

'I certainly do. And I *will*, if you like, moreover . . . However, the immediate business in hand is to replace your drink. You had hardly any of that one – so shall it be the same again?'

'No,' said Major Parry, rising. 'This is my turn. What are you all going to have?'

Mr Stimpson said he would 'stay out'. Mrs Plumleigh-Bruce said that, well, she *would* have a *small* Gin and It. Gorse said that he would go over to beer again – a half of bitter.

The Major went to the bar to get the drinks, and Mr Stimpson, taking another sip at his beer, looked intently at his possible future wife and Gorse. This look did not bother Gorse at all. He was on top of his form.

'Well,' he said. 'What about this hand of yours? Shall I have a try?'

'Well, you can have a try,' said Mrs Plumleigh-Bruce. 'Though I don't really believe in a word of it, myself.'

'Very well, then, let's try – shall we?'

He took her hand without any sort of hesitation, and there was a pause, as he gazed at it.

'Well,' said Mrs Plumleigh-Bruce, who, particularly because of Mr Stimpson's look, was by no means at her ease, 'can you discern my future? . . .'

'Well,' said Gorse. 'Your *immediate* future, at any rate. You are going to be brought, by a soldierly man, a small Gin and Italian . . . But we must go deeper than that – mustn't we?' And he gave a very fine imitation of one who is really quite serious about what he is doing.

Gorse, when he ultimately achieved great fame, had many stories told about his 'fortune telling'. Journalists, as well as more serious writers, nearly always mentioned it.

The cheaper journalists enlarged upon this alleged gift. One of them said that it was 'a pity he couldn't tell his own'. And his alleged 'Hypnotic eyes' were nearly always mentioned along with his power of deceiving women by pretending to look into their future.

Gorse had neither the gift of hypnotism nor that of looking into the future. In regard to fortune telling, all he had was common sense, shrewdness and bravado.

To one who has these qualities, nothing is easier than making women (and men) believe that their characters, pasts and possible futures are being explained and exposed with almost uncanny intuition. Treated properly, sceptics often become near converts about 'fortune telling' – in which art Gorse was, though spurious, certainly very capable indeed.

Gorse had discovered that this art was, like all arts, though difficult in a way, enormously simple – that it really relied mostly upon simplicity.

He had a few simple rules.

Having roughly summed up the character of the one who is having her or his hand held, you first of all very deftly pretend that you are much more interested than you thought you were going to be. Then, after a pause of the right length, you say, 'You're disappointed in some way,' or 'You haven't got from life *just* the thing you wanted,' or both. Men, as well as women, always agree with both of these hypotheses.

Then you seem to be even more interested still. Also puzzled. And then you say: 'Yes – there's some *frustration* somewhere – I can't quite *get* at it . . .'

This also is universally agreed with.

Then, when you are dealing with a woman, you say, with a little giggle: 'Well – I'm afraid there's been a *man* in your life – in fact very much *more* than one . . .' (The most hideous, jealous, malicious and neglected spinster will unfailingly rise to this.)

Then you say: 'I may be wrong, but I'd say you're in *slight* money troubles – or at any rate money complications . . .' (Agreed again by all.)

Then, having said: 'Of course this is the most fascinating thing *ever* . . .' you say: 'Not only have there *been* a lot of men in your life – there's one coming *into* it, before many moons – unless I'm gravely mistaken.'

Such were Gorse's usual openings – all of which he now, and in the order named, employed upon Mrs Plumleigh-Bruce, who, while holding on to as much as she could of her scepticism, became very fascinated indeed.

2

The Major returned with the drinks.

'Oh, you've started, have you?' he said, alluding to the couple who were holding hands. 'Has he already disclosed the mysteries of your future?'

'No,' said Mrs Plumleigh-Bruce. 'He's really only more or less dealt with things as they are, so far, and I must say he hasn't been far out. Now let's get to the future – shall we? What about this "man" who's coming into my life, for instance?'

'No,' said Gorse, as if this did not at the moment interest him. 'I'll come to him in due course. Let's stick to generalizations for a little – shall we?'

'Very well,' said Mrs Plumleigh-Bruce, with half-mocking, half-serious meekness.

'Well,' said Gorse. 'One thing's extremely clear . . . You're an easy-going person on the whole – *very* easy and long-suffering – but when you're taken advantage of you're an extremely formidable opponent. In fact, I certainly wouldn't like to be up against you, myself.'

'Wouldn't you? . . .'

'No. Definitely not.'

Gorse for a moment wondered whether he was going too far with this drivelling flattery, but then decided that he was not. He was, after all, in exceptionally foolish company, and both the Major and Mr Stimpson seemed to be pleased by, rather than jealous of, this gross praise of the woman by whom they were both so enchanted.

'Well? . . .' said Mrs Plumleigh-Bruce.

'Well – although you like taking things easily, you're extremely fastidious.'

'In what way?'

'Oh – about the house . . . I mean I wouldn't like to be a servant of yours. I mean I wouldn't like to be one unless I did the work very thoroughly indeed. I should say that everything has to be very much "just so". Am I correct?'

Gorse knew he was on doubtful ground here. But he would have been willing to bet that Mrs Plumleigh-Bruce fancied herself as a 'martinet', and the suggestion could do no harm, anyway.

'Yes,' said Mrs Plumleigh-Bruce. 'I rather think you are. I think my maid Mary would be slightly inclined to agree with you, anyway.'

'Yes. So I thought,' said Gorse, who thought it would be wise, at this moment, to mix just a little bitterness with this odiously sweet treacle. 'And I'm not sure it's a virtue, really.'

'Oh – really? . . . Why?'

'Well – it's quite clear that you like all the best things in life – food, clothes, drink, etcetera . . .'

'Well – why shouldn't I? Don't we all?'

'Yes – but that's beside the point, really. The point really is,' said Gorse, again pretending to giggle, 'that you're very much like me, and a lot of other people, if it comes to that. In fact, to put it bluntly you're just a tiny, *tiny* bit lazy.'

'Well, I suppose I am,' said Mrs Plumleigh-Bruce. 'But then again – aren't we all, if we have the opportunity?'

'Certainly. That goes without saying. But has one the right to demand everything perfect from those who attend upon us, if we're lazy ourselves? Personally, I'm absurdly easy-going with servants. I err on the other side, probably.'

'Well, you may be right,' said Mrs Plumleigh-Bruce, 'but I don't think my Mary would really agree with you. In fact she and I are tremendous friends – aren't we, Donald?'

'Yes,' said Mr Stimpson. 'I certainly haven't noticed any dissatisfaction in that quarter.'

'But all the same,' said Gorse, 'I expect she knows all about it when things aren't done properly.'

'Yes,' the low-voiced Mrs Plumleigh-Bruce conceded. 'That's true enough. But it's all done just by delicate hinting. I've never had to have her really on the mat ever since she's been with me. Of course she's a very good girl. But go on. What about this future? What about this "man" who's coming into my life?'

'Ah – the man . . . Yes . . . Now let's see . . . Well – I'm not sure he's not already *in* your life. Or, again, he may be someone who's going to take a much more serious part in your life than he has hitherto.'

Mr Stimpson fell for this like a load of bricks.

'Young – or old?' asked Mr Stimpson.

Gorse now had to decide quickly whether he should make himself, Gorse, the man, or further flatter Mr Stimpson by suggesting that it was he who was being mystically discussed. He compromised.

'Neither . . .' he said. 'Of course, it depends upon what you consider young or old.'

'Well,' said the almost savagely middle-aged Mr Stimpson. 'Middle-aged, perhaps?'

Here Gorse thought that a good time had come for him to produce his monocle. Doing this also gave him time to think.

'Ah – we must go more deeply into this,' he said, and, still keeping Mrs Plumleigh-Bruce's hand in his own, he took a sip at his drink, brought his monocle forth from his waistcoat pocket, neatly stuck it into his eye, and said, 'Now – let's see . . . Yes – conceivably middle-aged . . .'

'Dark or fair?' said Mr Stimpson, who was dark.

'Just a moment,' said Gorse. 'Now I look more closely, I think I can perceive *two* men. I hope I'm not seeing double. I haven't drunk enough for that . . . One's dark and verging on middle age – the other's fair and a bit younger.'

'And who's going to win the day with the lady?' asked the Major, who, as Gorse had intended, thought that the fair and slightly younger man might be himself.

'Ah – I'm afraid that's beyond my powers of divination. And I don't even know for certain that either of them are actually going to *try* to win the day,' said Gorse. 'And I expect you think that all this is nonsense – don't you? I do myself – sometimes. Anyway, I think we've had enough – haven't we?' He looked at Mrs Plumleigh-Bruce, smiled at her, released her hand, took another sip at his beer, and put his monocle into his waistcoat pocket.

'When you say you think it's all nonsense "sometimes",' said the Major, 'do you mean that at other times you don't?'

'Yes. That's exactly where I stand, really. There are times when I think it's anything but nonsense. I've been almost forced to.'

'And who taught you this magic art?' asked Mr Stimpson.

'Well – that was rather odd. It was in France, actually – during the war – when I was on leave in Paris. I ran into a most extraordinary little man in a café. I don't know how it was, but we somehow became friends, and he initiated me into the secrets. I think he was half spoof and half genuine. I've never made up my mind. All I know is that he made absolutely weirdly true predictions about myself, and that since I've tried to practise his art I've made astonishing forecasts about people – I mean astonishing to the people, and astonishing to myself.'

The extraordinary little man whom Gorse had met in Paris was nearly always used by Gorse when he looked at women's palms. He existed only in Gorse's elaborately inventive mind.

'Well,' said Mrs Plumleigh-Bruce. 'You haven't really made any "forecast" about me – have you? Apart from two rather vague men who are going to enter my life . . . All you've done is to tell me something about my character – and I must say you've got remarkably near the truth . . . What I want to know is whether I'm going to be *happy* or not? Am I?'

'Yes, of course you are.' Gorse looked at her again. 'Or as happy as anyone can be. And one hasn't got to look at your hand to tell you that.'

'Really? . . . Why not?'

'Because you simply radiate happiness, in your own way.'

There are few people in the world, Gorse knew, who take violent objection to being told that they radiate happiness.

'Well,' said Mrs Plumleigh-Bruce, modestly, 'that sounds very nice – but I certainly never thought of myself in that light.'

'Or rather you radiate happiness for other people. And that means that in the long run it radiates back upon yourself – doesn't it? Don't forget I used the words "in the long run".'

'Well – I only hope you're right,' said Mrs Plumleigh-Bruce, and there was a pause in which she was so pleased that she was unable to conceal from her face the look of a cat who has less than a minute ago eaten a canary.

The perfect moment had arrived, Gorse perceived, to leave. He had not only pleased Mrs Plumleigh-Bruce. He had, he fancied, by no means displeased either of her middle-aged admirers.

And he was entirely correct. Major Parry was looking forward, in a rather coarse way, to basking quite gloriously in the rays of Mrs Plumleigh-Bruce's happiness. Mr Stimpson, more purely, had practically made up his mind to marry the woman on the spot.

It was Gorse who, in effect, had radiated happiness.

And so, Mrs Plumleigh-Bruce being in the telephone book, it was time to go – to radiate an air of indifference or aloofness – to radiate doubt, in the minds of his listeners – particularly Mrs

Plumleigh-Bruce's, of course – as to whether the radiator would ever be met again.

Gorse looked at his wrist-watch and was most surprised by the time.

'Good Heavens,' he said. 'I must be going.'

'Oh – for Heaven's sake don't do that,' said Mr Stimpson, who was, just at present, at the young criminal's feet. 'I owe you a drink, anyway.'

'Well – perhaps that matter can be adjusted at a later date,' said Gorse, as he rose, and drank off the remains of his beer quickly. 'But go I must. *I* certainly won't radiate happiness with my present housekeeper, Mrs Burford, if I'm late for the meal she's preparing for me with such scrupulous care at Gilroy Road. So I must buzz off. Will you forgive me?'

'Yes,' said Mrs Plumleigh-Bruce. 'We'll forgive you. But we hope we're going to see you again sometime.'

'Well, so do I,' said Gorse. 'But I suppose that's rather in the lap of the gods. In fact *everything* seems to be rather in the lap of the gods with me, just at present . . . However, I do hope we meet . . . Cheerio!'

He looked and smiled at all three, waved, and left them.

When he had gone into the street all three began to talk about Gorse. When he was in the street Gorse began to think about all three.

PART FIVE

KIMONO

Chapter One

I

'An' sure,' said Mr Stimpson, ''tis a greatly pretty girl you're afther lookin' this mighty evening.'

Mr Stimpson was speaking to Mary McGinnis, Mrs Plumleigh-Bruce's maid, in Mrs Plumleigh-Bruce's brassy hallway, at about nine-forty-five, three evenings after the evening upon which Gorse had told Mrs Plumleigh-Bruce's fortune. He had dined at 'Glen Alan' and was just leaving.

Mr Stimpson, who had himself often dabbled in *Oirish* on his own account, had lately, because he had listened to Mrs Plumleigh-Bruce using it on Mary, himself been spurred into trying to brush it up.

But Mr Stimpson was by no means fully at home with this language. The word 'greatly', for instance (in his sentence ''Tis a greatly pretty girl you're afther lookin' this mighty evening'), does not really belong to *Oirish* at all. Nor does the word 'mighty' as used in his 'this mighty evening'. They were both pure inventions of his own – innovations which no serious student of *Oirish* would permit.

Mary, who had just helped Mr Stimpson on with his coat, was as puzzled as she was when submitting to her mistress's *Oirish*, but did at least understand that she had been called pretty.

'Thank you very much, sir,' she therefore said, modestly.

'*Noth* at *Arl*!' said, or rather cried, Mr Stimpson, who was genially translating, for Mary's sake, the English 'Not at all'. And then he gaily and gently pinched Mary's cheek.

The man had had too much to drink, and he had always had a dim notion that pinching young girls' cheeks was somehow all part of being *Oirish*.

'Top av the evening to you,' he added. 'Well, it's going that I must be afther – entoirely.'

Mrs Plumleigh-Bruce, who was in the hallway watching all this, did not at all like what was going on.

She was aware that Mr Stimpson's *Oirish* was not only grossly incorrect but imitative of her own: she was aware that her imitator had drunk too much, and that Mary was probably aware of the same thing: and she did not like his pinching Mary's cheek.

She put the last down to his having taken too much to drink. But here she was mistaken. Mr Stimpson, apart from wanting to be *Oirish*, had certain other motives, as will be seen.

'Well, then, it's top av the evening to yourself, as well, it seems,' said Mr Stimpson, taking his gloves from his overcoat pocket, and looking rather defiantly at Mrs Plumleigh-Bruce, who was here even further revolted by the hopeless ineptitude of Mr Stimpson's *Oirish*. 'Top av the *morning*' was, of course, altogether in order, but 'Top av the *evening*' was absolutely ridiculous.

Mr Stimpson, if he had been wiser, would have stuck to *Scotch* ('Wheel mon', 'I Dinna Ken' etc.) or *Welsh* ('Indeed – Gootness – Whateffer!' etc.). He was quite good at these languages, and with them did not offend either Mrs Plumleigh-Bruce or his business friends – nearly all of whom talked *Oirish*, *Scotch*, and *Welsh* – as well as a certain amount of *American* ('Aw – shucks!', 'Say Bo' etc.).

'Well – goodbye,' said Mrs Plumleigh-Bruce, in a more frigid tone than she had employed with Mr Stimpson for a long time.

Mr Stimpson, who had put on his gloves, did not notice the coldness in her voice, snatched off a glove in the finest Stimpson manner – a glove-snatcher-offer's hit for six, as it were – said 'Goodbye, madame,' kissed Mrs Plumleigh-Bruce's hand, leered at her, and left the house.

Mrs Plumleigh-Bruce returned to her sitting-room, which was filled with Mr Stimpson's cigar smoke – and sat down on her sofa to think.

Unlike Ernest Ralph Gorse, Mrs Plumleigh-Bruce very seldom thought intently for any length of time. But tonight Mr Stimpson (as well as, oddly enough, Ernest Ralph Gorse) made it seem necessary. She put a cigarette into her long, black cigarette-holder, and lit the cigarette, in order to assist herself in rising to the occasion for thought.

2

Because Mr Stimpson had been so recently with her, and for so long a time, and because he had behaved so uncouthly, she thought first about him. She could come to Gorse, whom she had still not seen since the fortune-telling episode, later.

Mr Stimpson, this evening, on the sofa on which she was now sitting, had made love to her.

There was, of course, nothing unusual about his doing this. But this evening he had been much bolder in his approach. He had kissed her and leered and talked at her at much greater length and with much greater strength than ever before.

She had, in one way, been considerably interested in and gratified by the comparatively prosperous Estate Agent's more audacious attitude. But there was a debit as well as a credit to what had gone on.

On the credit side were, mostly, the things he had said rather than done. He had, she believed, come nearer this evening to a straightforward verbal proposal of marriage than he ever had in the past. She tried to recall his exact words.

'You and I were made for each other – *are* made for each other, Joan,' he had said, either breathlessly or passionately (she could not tell which) after a protracted kiss. And to this she had replied '"Were"? or "are"?'

'Are' somehow suggested the notion of marriage much more than 'were', and she had wanted to make sure that he had corrected himself.

'Are!' he had said, vehemently. 'You know it.'

'In what way?' she had then tried. 'Tell me . . .'

'In *every* way,' he had said. 'You *must* know. I mean the whole *hog*.'

Mrs Plumleigh-Bruce had been (and still was) mystified as to the exact nature of Mr Stimpson's Whole Hog which, for some weeks now, had been appearing in his conversation.

How whole was this puzzling allegorical animal? And, even if it were wholly whole, where did it lead to in life? To marriage – or to sordid sin in Sispara Road, Reading?

And so she had then braced herself to force Mr Stimpson to give a much clearer picture of his own conception of his own Hog.

'When you say "whole" hog,' she had said, 'what do you mean, exactly?'

'You *must* know what I mean,' said the agitated leerer.

'I don't, you know . . . I really don't . . .' said Mrs Plumleigh-Bruce. 'Do you mean you want to "live" – with me . . .?'

'Of course I do. To all eternity – as far as I'm concerned.'

But there are different ways of dwelling in eternity.

'But in what way?' she persisted. 'I mean in what capacity?'

'In *every* capacity,' said Mr Stimpson.

'Yes – but in *what capacity*?' said Mrs Plumleigh-Bruce.

Mr Stimpson – the cautious Mr Stimpson, nearly always as cautious when he had taken drink as when he had not – here hesitated. He had spotted that Mrs Plumleigh-Bruce had spotted that there were all sorts of whole hogs, and many different ways of inhabiting eternity, and he was not willing to commit himself to any greater accuracy.

'Oh – *every* capacity,' he said.

But 'every' is a word which may be used elastically.

'Yes – but such *as*? . . .'

'Such as *everything*,' said Mr Stimpson, attempting to use his vehemence to disguise his ambiguity, but, of course, not succeeding, and hardly hoping to do so.

'Yes – but what does "everything" mean?' said Mrs Plumleigh-Bruce. 'And what do you mean when you say "live"?'

'Why – LIVE!' said Mr Stimpson, feigning a sort of impatience. 'What else should I mean?'

But impatience did not serve Mr Stimpson's purpose any better than vehemence.

Mrs Plumleigh-Bruce realized that she would get no more out of Mr Stimpson by the more or less delicate methods she had used so far. Now she must either drop the matter or come completely out into the open with 'Do you mean live as man and wife – or what?' or something like that.

She very nearly took this course, but something held her back.

She felt, really, that she could not possibly humiliate herself so far.

It must be remembered that Mrs Plumleigh-Bruce, the daughter of a Colonel, and the widow of one, despite her often entertaining the notion of marrying him, looked upon the Reading Estate Agent with considerable contempt – contempt generally, but most of all social contempt.

Mr Stimpson was removed very far indeed from the top drawer. Furthermore, he could not even be classed as 'One of Nature's

Gentlemen'. Nature had neglected to polish Mr Stimpson in any way – and, in the event of marriage, no such excuse could possibly be used with any of those remaining acquaintances of Mrs Plumleigh-Bruce who were on the Colonel level. Harsh, self-seeking, bustling Estate Agency – not kind, disinterested and placid Nature – had moulded Mr Stimpson's character and manners. He was not at all the sort of man to introduce in those circles from which Mrs Plumleigh-Bruce considered she had, on account of her exile in Reading, almost fallen, and to which she was anxious to return.

Therefore, Mrs Plumleigh-Bruce felt that she could not conceivably lower herself by being the first to hint at marriage. And, of course, if she did so and received any sort of rebuff, the situation would be unbearable.

However, she decided to have one more shot at delicacy.

'I do wish you'd explain yourself properly,' she said. 'I really don't understand you.'

At this Mr Stimpson decided to hide behind facetious flirtatiousness combined with further physical approaches. The two usually went together in Mr Stimpson's theory and practice of love-making.

'Don't you – you damned fascinating little devil?' said Mr Stimpson, leering more horribly than ever. 'I'll bet you do . . . I understand *you*, at any rate. I can read every little thought that goes on in that fascinating little head of yours. I even know what's going on in it just at this moment.'

'Do you?' said the actually rather large-headed Mrs Plumleigh-Bruce, momentarily hating Mr Stimpson intensely, but nonplussed. 'What?'

'*This*,' said Mr Stimpson, and he lunged at her to kiss her in a very much more clumsy and revolting manner than usual.

At this Mrs Plumleigh-Bruce was as near to losing her temper violently as so smug and complacent a woman could be.

She thrust him away from her, and he said in a surprised way, 'What's the matter?'

'Nothing's the matter,' said Mrs Plumleigh-Bruce, regaining her composure. 'But don't you think it's time you went home? It's after half past nine.'

'Well – you often let me stay till ten – or after – don't you?'

'Yes. But I'm tired tonight, and I want you to go. It's not as though we were talking sense of any sort.'

'*I* thought we were talking great sense. I don't follow you.'

'Well – don't *try* to follow me. Just do as I tell you and go, will you, Donald?'

There was a look in Mrs Plumleigh-Bruce's eye which Mr Stimpson had never seen before, and which he did not like. Also his physical advances had never been repelled in exactly the way they had a moment ago, and he did not like this, either.

Normally he would certainly have been cowed or made uneasy by this change in her manner – but tonight he was in a different sort of temper generally – one which requires explanation.

3

The odd thing was that, had Mr Stimpson not been in this altered mood, this evening's session with Mrs Plumleigh-Bruce might well have ended in a proposal of marriage, and its immediate or tactfully delayed acceptance. But Mr Stimpson was not, in regard to Mrs Plumleigh-Bruce, at all the same man he had been three nights ago.

Mr Stimpson had, in fact, got above himself. Or he had at any rate got above his previous more timid self. And this had been brought about, paradoxically enough, by that conversation about Mrs Plumleigh-Bruce – which he had at the time so blackly hated and despised – with Major Parry.

The Major, by speaking so coarsely and cheaply about Mrs Plumleigh-Bruce and by suggesting that Mr Stimpson had possibly won her favours in the fullest way, had, after Mr Stimpson had had time for reflection, put ideas into his head.

A piece of impudence on the Major's part had, indeed, been transformed magically into a piece of flattery.

What, thought Mr Stimpson, if Mrs Plumleigh-Bruce were, after all, a woman about whose name it was permissible, or even correct, to speak lightly?

And, if such were the case, did it not follow that it was permissible, or even correct, to treat her lightly – amorously trifle with her?

And had not Major Parry clearly intimated that he imagined that Mr Stimpson, if he had not already trifled with her in such a way, was clearly the principal man in the running for such a thing? And was there not an enormous amount of truth in the Major's suggestion?

Brooding upon the matter, Mr Stimpson had suddenly been visited by a vision of a glorious feather in his cap.

In his life hitherto he had seen himself, had taken pride and almost revelled in himself, as a hard-working, average human being. He was very fond of calling himself 'just a simple plodder'.

Now, out of the blue, had come a startling, violent picture of himself as anything but a plodder. Instead he saw himself as a potential dog – a lad – a lady-killer – a *dasher*. Without ever having heard of Casanova he almost pictured himself as the possible Casanova of Reading. He imagined an event which would simply ring through Reading. What if the Lady of Reading became, not his wife, but his acknowledged mistress?

Mr Stimpson – the snob, the social climber, the boaster and subterraneously lecherous man – had all at once perceived that he might satisfy his snobbery, his social climbing, his boasting and his subterraneous lechery in a much easier and more magnificent way than he had dreamed of before. And on top of all this he would be saving *money*.

He was awe-inspired by, he trembled before, the audacity of his own vision; but the very fact that he was so afraid in a manner fortified rather than softened the businessman's determination to pursue his design.

Thus it was that Mr Stimpson had, this evening, adopted, towards Mrs Plumleigh-Bruce, a very different manner from the usual one.

Mr Stimpson was, of course, very easily influenced by popular expressions. And if they served his purpose they practically hypnotized him.

Mr Stimpson was now closely mentally wrapped up in the matters of marriage, love and seduction – and two famous slogans governed his mind. These were 'Love 'em and Leave 'em' and 'Treat 'em Rough'.

And so, on being rebuked and almost dismissed by Mrs Plumleigh-Bruce tonight, he had decided to treat her rough, and at any rate give the appearance of perhaps loving and leaving her.

And so when Mrs Plumleigh-Bruce had told him to go, he had at once obeyed her, and, in drink and defiance, spoken a tremendous amount of *Oirish* to, and pinched the cheek of, the maid Mary McGinnis.

4

Mrs Plumleigh-Bruce, not having the faintest idea that she was being treated rough and loved and left, was, naturally, bewildered, and, in order to assist herself in the solution of the puzzle, put yet another cigarette into her black cigarette-holder and lit the cigarette and puffed away in that nauseatingly affected way she always did in the presence of men. No man was present, but Mrs Plumleigh-Bruce was seldom able to drop her affectations even when alone.

As she smoked and thought in front of the embers of her densely brass-surrounded fire, Mrs Plumleigh-Bruce gradually began to entertain thoughts that Mr Stimpson would not do – would not do at all.

At the moment she hated him physically more than she had ever hated any other man. And this was saying a lot.

Mrs Plumleigh-Bruce disliked men physically almost as much as she disliked the working-class spiritually.

Money, this nasty woman decided, wasn't everything.

5

Thinking of Mr Stimpson led Mrs Plumleigh-Bruce into thinking about Ernest Ralph Gorse.

This young man had not turned up again at The Friar. Nor had he fulfilled the eye-telephone-pact he had made with her when she last saw him there.

In fact it seemed to her that Gorse must be written off. He had probably gone back to London. Or dashed off to Paris. He clearly had money.

And so perhaps money (Mr Stimpson's) was, after all, something.

She had no sooner had this thought than she heard her telephone ringing.

She had an extraordinary feeling that Gorse was telephoning her.

Though no runner, Mrs Plumleigh-Bruce almost contrived to run up to her bedroom to answer the telephone.

She snatched off the Marie Antoinette doll and said, 'Hullo?'

A nasal voice replied, slowly, 'Hullo . . .'

She wondered whether this voice belonged to Ernest Ralph Gorse.

It did.

Chapter Two

I

Gorse, when dealing in a predatory way with men or women, always liked to telephone them late at night, or at any rate as late at night as he thought advisable.

It was, he found, likely to frighten them – or, failing that, to catch them unawares, if only because of their sleepy or fatigued condition.

And women were often intrigued. They would be surprised but excited – pleasantly shocked. Gorse would often telephone women as late as or later than midnight.

With Mrs Plumleigh-Bruce, Gorse had struck one of his finest successes in this direction. He could not have caught her at a better moment. She was surprised, excited, pleasantly shocked, and tremendously relieved to know that the odd but highly interesting young man had not left Reading, or forsaken the eye-telephone-pact made at The Friar.

In addition to this Mr Stimpson's recent revolting behaviour gave the reddish-haired head of Gorse a kind of golden halo.

'Hullo. Who's that?' she said.

'Oh, is Mrs Plumleigh-Bruce there, by any chance?' said Gorse.

'Yes. Speaking . . .'

'Ah,' said Gorse, 'I thought I recognized your voice . . . But I don't expect you can recognize mine – can you?'

'I'm not sure,' said Mrs Plumleigh-Bruce, who was by now absolutely sure. 'But I have just a vague idea . . .'

'Well – do you want me to give you a hint? Or shall I save time by telling you outright?'

'I think you'd better tell me outright – hadn't you?'

'Very well, then, the name's Gorse. Ralph Gorse. Ralph or Rafe – whichever you prefer. And I think we met in An Certain Hostelry, not so long ago.'

Mrs Plumleigh-Bruce took no exception to Gorse's foolish and vulgar way of describing The Friar. She rather liked it.

'Oh – yes,' she said. 'I remember it very well.'

'Oh, well, I'm glad of that ... However, the point is, do you prefer Rafe or Ralph? I'm sure you'll have to use one or the other, sooner or later.'

It suddenly occurred to Mrs Plumleigh-Bruce that Gorse, like Mr Stimpson, had had too much to drink.

'You sound very gay tonight,' she therefore said. 'And it's very late to phone – isn't it? I hope you haven't been hitting it up – painting the town red, or anything like that.'

Gorse's whole tone changed.

'No. Believe me not. No gaiety. Anything but. That was all bluff,' he said, as if utterly exhausted, but bravely fighting his own condition. 'In fact I'm absolutely worn out. And as for being gay I can only tell you I'm absolutely miserable. And that's why I've telephoned you. I know it's horribly late at night, but I felt I simply had to.'

'But what's the matter?'

'Well, the point is, really, what *isn't* the matter ... I'm just off the train after the most appalling day in London any man's ever had, and I rang you up to ask you if you could help me.'

'But what's the trouble?' asked Mrs Plumleigh-Bruce. 'And how on earth can I help you?'

'Well – the trouble's business trouble. But I'll get over that all right. In fact I'm pretty certain I'll come out on top in the long run. But the run's been a very long one today and I'm feeling depressed and completely done in.' Gorse's voice now became, in a restrained way, quite piteous. 'And that's where you can help me, if you will, and if you can. Will you?'

There was a pause.

'Yes. Of course I will. If I can ... But how?'

'Oh, just let me come round and talk to you – let me spill out a few of my woes. Hold my hand for a little.' Gorse's tone became that of one wearily attempting humour. 'I mean figuratively, of course – or metaphorically or whatever the word is.'

There was another pause in which Mrs Plumleigh-Bruce half doubted, and half believed in, the sincerity of Gorse's voice and intentions.

'Yes. I'd like you to,' she said. 'But when?'

'Now,' said Gorse, with noble simplicity and directness. 'I expect it's impossible. In fact I expect you've gone to bed or that you've got people there. But I thought there'd be no harm in asking. I never did find any harm in asking for anything. *Have* you gone to bed, and *have* you got people there?'

'No,' said Mrs Plumleigh-Bruce dubiously, and added, slightly defensively, 'except for my maid, Mary.'

'Well, then. If you're still up, and if your maid's still up, would there be any impropriety in my looking in just for a little while? Or is it all too much of a crashing bore?'

'No. Of course it wouldn't be a bore. But I don't know that *I'd* be of much help.'

'Well, then. You don't know enough about yourself.'

'In what way? I don't follow you.'

'Well, I told you about yourself when I read your hand. Didn't I tell you that you radiate happiness – for *other* people at any rate?'

'Why, yes. I believe you did . . .'

Mrs Plumleigh-Bruce, who, in fact, envied or loathed practically every member of the human race with whom she did or did not come into contact, had, nevertheless, been fancying herself as a radiator of universal happiness ever since Gorse had endowed her with this gift. She had been much nicer to Mary (who had had to listen to more *Oirish* than ever) and she had put on a playful, tolerant tone even with tradespeople.

'Well,' said Gorse. 'I'm afraid it's a bit like begging – but after the day I've just had I'd like to bask – for however short a time – in the good old beams I mentioned the other night. You radiate comfort, too – although I suppose comfort and happiness are roughly the same thing – on the spiritual level anyway. And comfort's what I want. So may I come round for a bit?'

'You're being very flattering, you know,' said Mrs Plumleigh-Bruce, now having a strong notion that the young man was making love to her, and not disliking the notion at all.

'I *am* being flattering,' said Gorse, firmly. 'But that doesn't mean I'm being insincere. I know I've many faults, but insincerity isn't one of them. It isn't, really. Anyway, the point is that I can hardly wait to see you again. So may I come round now? Just give me judgement, oh wise – and fair – Portia. I promise you I won't take it ill, like Shylock, if you refuse.'

Being called a fair, as well as a wise Portia, went to Mrs Plumleigh-Bruce's head. She had no doubts now that Gorse was making love of some sort to her, and she found herself almost delighting in his love-making.

'Very well. I pronounce sentence,' she said. 'You may come. But not for long. Because I'm rather tired, and I can't keep Mary up much longer. Do you know where I live?'

Mrs Plumleigh-Bruce brought out these words in the most glorious 'Plumleigh-Bruce' manner. Her 'You may come' was superb. It was lady-like, fruity, and regally indolent beyond measure. Mrs Plumleigh-Bruce was endeavouring to use every ounce of 'charm' she believed she had. An intelligent outsider would have found this 'charm' quite nauseating. Gorse was not nauseated. He was merely pleased – for he knew that things were going very much his way with this easily flattered woman. For him she was, at the moment, a sitting bird – sitting almost idiotically.

'Yes,' he said. 'I know where you live all right. I've found *that* out.'

'Really? . . . How? . . .'

The charmer laboriously and seductively breathed the 'H' of the word 'How' and pronounced its 'w' with fantastically rounded and luscious lips.

'Well,' said Gorse. 'You told me you were in the telephone book, and so I looked you up without very much delay. You live at Glen Alan, Sispara Road – don't you? And I've found out where Sispara Road is.'

'Have you? . . . HoW? . . .' sighed the delicious Portia.

'Well – just by asking people . . . However – that's beside the point. The point is that you've given me permission to call – isn't it? So may I? I can do it in about ten minutes – or even less, I think. So may I come round?'

Mrs Plumleigh-Bruce told Ernest Ralph Gorse that he might come rOWnd, and they rang off.

Then Mrs Plumleigh-Bruce at once found Mary, and asked her, hurriedly and apologetically, to make fresh coffee and tidy the sitting-room as much as possible. She explained to Mary that she had had an important telephone call, and that she had to see a man on a matter of urgent business at once.

This deceptive woman was, for some reason, never very good at lying, and Mary saw something in her mistress's eye which made her guess that she was not telling the truth. However, Mary did not show that any such suspicion had crossed her mind, and she immediately did what she had been told to do.

Then Mrs Plumleigh-Bruce went up to her bedroom again in order to make herself look as attractive as she possibly could.

She had not taken much trouble with Mr Stimpson tonight, and she did not think that the dress she was wearing was adequately or correctly enticing. She wondered whether she had time to change it – and, if so, into what she should change.

She had, all at once, a startling but most exciting inspiration.

Her *Kimono*! What if she entertained her late visitor in her Kimono?

Did not his lateness justify such a thing? And would not the wearing of a Kimono make the hour seem later than it was, and therefore more alluring, bewitching, intriguingly 'fast'?

And she could change much more rapidly into a Kimono than into another dress, and thus, probably, be given time to arrange the sitting-room (the 'scene', she was really thinking), exactly to her liking.

Yes – she would wear her Kimono – and that was *that*!

2

Mrs Plumleigh-Bruce was downstairs, in her Kimono, five minutes before Gorse arrived.

She arranged the sitting-room with great care – improving upon Mary's work. She removed every sign of her recent entertainment of Mr Stimpson. She brought forth, from the cupboard, brandy, whisky, and port, in decanters. (Mr Stimpson had been drinking beer.) She poked and tidied the fire and beat and changed the places of the cushions.

Mary, meanwhile, was making fresh coffee in the kitchen. Mary was considerably interested in what was going on. Her mistress had had, perforce, to let her see the Kimono, and Mary knew that this garment had never before purposely been worn when a man called. The lateness of the hour – combined with the Kimono – slightly scandalized Mary. A Kimono somehow did not go with what Mrs Plumleigh-Bruce had called urgent business.

Mrs Plumleigh-Bruce, waiting in the sitting-room for the ringing of the bell, was fully as scandalized as Mary – possibly more so. She was now afraid of what she had done.

Was she losing 'caste'?

She was also a little bit afraid of Gorse himself. Indeed, it even crossed her mind, because of the lateness of the hour, her Kimono, and the fact that she had only met Gorse twice, that he might be in some way slightly dangerous, and she was glad that Mary was in the house.

Then she asked herself, 'In what way dangerous?'

Then it crossed her mind that she might be entertaining a thief, a raper, or swindler. Or even a potential slayer!

She then dismissed, or tried to dismiss, these thoughts as absurd. She had, she decided, been reading the sensational newspapers too much recently.

The door-bell rang, and she heard Mary go to the door.

A few moments later Gorse entered the room.

The moment she had greeted and shaken hands with Gorse she was completely reassured.

Any thoughts of him as a thief, a raper, a swindler, or a potential slayer fled from her mind.

Mrs Plumleigh-Bruce, however, was shaking hands with one who was all these things.

Furthermore Gorse was to be, in reality, a slayer.

Chapter Three

I

The future slayer's manner, as he sat down in the armchair offered him, was charmingly exhausted, wistfully grateful. Mrs Plumleigh-Bruce fell a hundred per cent, or more, for his exhaustion and gratitude. She almost bustlingly offered him whisky, brandy, port and coffee.

He accepted coffee and brandy. He thought it wise to take the most expensive drink. It showed that he was 'used' to things, and it flatteringly implied that his hostess was equally so. The neat brandy and black coffee, taken at the same time, gave forth, he thought, an air of worldliness.

He said nothing, of course, about her wearing of her Kimono. He took it easily for granted. Nevertheless he saw that she fancied herself enormously in it, and he made a point of looking at it as though he shared her enthusiasm. (Actually his first thought about it had been 'My God!' Though his own taste was far from being good, Gorse disliked dragons and chrysanthemums surrounded and grown all over with fusses on blue silk.)

'Ah –' he said, when his coffee and brandy had been put on a small table behind him. 'Just what the doctor ordered. *Un café et une fine*.'

Thus Gorse reminded Mrs Plumleigh-Bruce of his recent trip to France and displayed his knowledge of the French language.

But Gorse was a poor linguist, and he pronounced the '*et*' as 'eight'. Thus, as students of French will know, he had not said, as he had wished, 'A coffee and liqueur brandy' but 'A coffee *is* a liqueur brandy'.

Mrs Plumleigh-Bruce, whose knowledge of French was worse than Gorse's, had no knowledge that she had been given the bewildering information that a coffee is in reality a liqueur brandy – and the Marie Antoinette in her was delighted to have heard French spoken in her presence.

'Well, now. Tell me. How can I help you?' she said, crossing her legs and putting one arm over the back of the sofa on which she sat. 'You certainly look very tired, poor thing. Tell me. What's all the trouble?'

She was astonished by the effrontery of her own 'poor thing'. But the whole atmosphere – the late hour – the Kimono – the charm, the dejection, the brandy-drinking and French-speaking of her guest – had simply forced it from her. Also it must be remembered that just at this period she was radiating universal happiness and comfort. Nothing could keep her off it.

'Oh – what I told you over the phone,' said Gorse, looking sadly into the fire. 'Business, business, business . . . But I'll get over it all right, I can assure you. It's the incessant wrangling that gets you down – wrangling with people who don't keep their word. But I suppose that *is* business. Do *you* know anything about business?'

'Not the *first* thing,' said Mrs Plumleigh-Bruce, gaily. 'I'm a complete ignoramus in that way, I'm afraid.'

Gorse's eyes left the fire and were turned sharply – but not with noticeable sharpness – upon Mrs Plumleigh-Bruce.

Was the woman speaking the truth? There could, of course, be no better news if such was the case. And, looking at her, he very much inclined to the view that it was. He had always suspected that she was, generally speaking, a dupe of the first water for someone like himself, but he had feared that she might have some sort of 'head' for business matters.

'Really? . . .' he said. 'I should have thought you were pretty shrewd in that way. I shouldn't have thought you'd be easy to do down.'

'Oh, no. I'm not easily done down,' said Mrs Plumleigh-Bruce. 'In fact anybody who tries to do me down always finds, I think I can say without fail, they're very much done down themselves.'

That (Gorse's thoughts were, as he looked at her) is all *you* know, and we shall see what we shall see.

'But I don't know anything about business details and all that,' said Mrs Plumleigh-Bruce. 'In fact you could call me, in that way and perhaps every other way, a complete fool, really.'

Gorse did not say, 'It seems to me as though you certainly could do both,' but this was his thought.

'Well,' he said. 'Perhaps you're very well out of it. Money-making's a sordid, grabbing affair on the whole. But money's got to be made.'

'And are *you* good at making it?'

Gorse pretended to look back on his past as a money-maker. Then he smiled faintly, and tapped the table beside him with his forefinger.

'Touch wood. Yes,' he said. 'Very much so. In fact you could almost say that everything I touch, in a small way, seems to turn to gold. Or a lot of silver and coppers at any rate.'

'Well. I wish *I* had the gift,' said Mrs Plumleigh-Bruce, looking at him and almost completely believing him. 'Or that you could bestow it on me.'

'I'm certain I could bestow it on you. But it's not really a gift. It's only common sense and hard work. Hard work, and, on the whole, very silly work. I'm not particularly keen on money, really – are you?'

'Well,' said Mrs Plumleigh-Bruce. 'I wouldn't go as far as that. It has very important uses, hasn't it?'

'Yes. But I mean money in *itself*. Some people just chase it for its own sake – not for the realities it helps you to get. Money isn't really a reality – is it?'

'Well – I'm not so sure. What would you call a real reality?'

'Oh . . . Health, and love, and fresh air, and freedom, and a clean conscience, and a thousand other things that bring genuine happiness.'

Gorse, speaking slowly, had, with the most adroit indifference, slipped in love between health and fresh air, but, as he suspected, Mrs Plumleigh-Bruce had done anything but miss the inserted word.

'Yes, I suppose you're right,' she said. 'And which would you call the most valuable of the realities you've mentioned?'

'Oh health, of course, first. Because without that you can't do or enjoy anything. And next, I suppose, love. In fact all *I* want to do is to settle down peacefully with the woman of my choice . . .'

There was a pause, in which Mrs Plumleigh-Bruce wondered whether she dared to be so bold, and then decided to be.

'And have *you* found the woman of your choice?' she asked.

There was another pause in which Gorse again seemed to be looking into his past, and also his present. It would not be advisable, he thought, to hand her what she was asking for – the acknowledgement that he was not committed – on a plate, and so he held the pause for as long as he could, and when he at last spoke, his tone was slightly dubious and enigmatical – perhaps just denying the literal sense of his words.

'No,' he said. 'Still searching – searching . . . And I think you'll admit it's a pretty difficult search. And a pretty difficult choice.'

'It is indeed,' said Mrs Plumleigh-Bruce.

'And how do you stand in that direction?' asked Gorse. 'If it's not a rude question, have you brought yourself to making any choice?'

'No,' said Mrs Plumleigh-Bruce. 'I'm quite fancy free, just at the moment.'

'But not without a great deal of fanciers, I fancy?' said Gorse, smiling charmingly.

'Oh – I don't know about that . . .' the Lady and Venus of Sispara Road modestly replied.

'Oh – come now . . . Now I believe you're fishing for compliments. You mustn't forget I've observed your hand.'

'Well, you've said that's probably all nonsense, haven't you?'

Gorse ignored this.

'And I've observed *you*, too . . . And I've also had the opportunity of observing you in the company of men.'

'Well? And what did that tell you?'

'It told me very plainly that you're very far from being unattractive to men – very far indeed. I have eyes in my head, you know.'

'Well – even if you're right,' said Mrs Plumleigh-Bruce, remembering the odious behaviour of Mr Stimpson less than an hour ago, 'it's really more a question of whether I'm attracted to them – isn't it?'

'Oh, yes. Of course. *Cela va sans dire.* All the same I can still tell you that though you may have other troubles you'll have no trouble in *that* direction.'

'Well – you're very flattering about me,' said Mrs Plumleigh-Bruce. 'But you didn't come round here to talk about me – did you? We're here to talk about you and your troubles – aren't we?'

'Oh – they're so sordid – I don't really want to talk about them,' said Gorse. 'At any rate *now*. You know, it's so peaceful here, I've completely forgotten them. That's really why I wanted to come round. I told you you radiate happiness and peace. And somehow, looking at you now, I feel you're not at all the person to talk about filthy lucre to. It'd be rather like counting out your silver in a cathedral – if you see what I mean . . .'

Gorse glanced at her to see if he had succeeded in making a woman swallow a cathedral. He believed that she had almost digested it already.

'Well,' she said. 'You're still very flattering . . . But I do agree that money matters are very sordid. I've always found them so, at any rate – little as I know about them.'

'And the more you know about them, the more you'd find out about it, believe me . . . You know, I suppose it's a weird and rather awful thing to say – but do you know what I sometimes feel . . .?'

'No . . . What?'

'Well, I sometimes feel that I'm fed up with civil life – with all its damned pettiness. I feel that I'd – well – I'd like to be back in the Army again. I certainly don't want another war, and I'm certainly not a blood-thirsty person – but all the same that's what I sometimes feel. Can you understand it?'

'Indeed I can,' said Mrs Plumleigh-Bruce. 'And I know a lot of other men who feel the same way.'

'Yes. I believe there are . . . I can't personally say I had a nice time "over there". In fact it was very unpleasant and very perilous. But one's got to realize that people degenerate, and that there're the perils of peace as well as the perils of war.'

'Yes. I see what you mean,' said Mrs Plumleigh-Bruce, very much impressed by his epigram.

'At least,' Gorse continued, 'one was doing something, *serving* something, over there. Now one's only doing things for oneself and serving oneself. Helping oneself to what one can get of little bits of metal . . . Well, I suppose it's got to be done, but I've got a bit of metal that wouldn't fetch anything on the market, but it's worth more to me than all the King's coinage – all the coin of the realm.'

'Oh. What's that?' said Mrs Plumleigh-Bruce, looking at him, and guessing what was coming.

'Oh – a little trinket for services rendered to the King. Rendered, not taken.'

'You mean a medal?'

'Yes. A Military Cross, actually,' said Gorse, still looking into the fire. 'But as I said, it has very little value on the money market.'

'Good Heavens!' Mrs Plumleigh-Bruce was stunned, but not incredulous. 'Did you get an M C?'

'Yes . . . Why do you seem so surprised?'

'Well – it's a pretty high honour – isn't it? What did you get it for?'

'I don't know why on earth I'm telling you about all this, you know . . .'

'No. Go on. Do tell me.'

'Well, for certain very obvious reasons,' said Gorse with a sly, yet winning smile, 'we were, I regret to say, retreating from certain positions, and I managed to carry an extremely badly wounded man for about a quarter of a mile to a place of greater safety. Thank Heavens he was a small man and a pretty light weight, or I couldn't have done it. But he was fearfully shot up – poor fellow . . .'

'Well, I think that's wonderful, and that you ought to be very proud.'

'Oh – I don't know . . . These things are tremendously a question of luck, you know. Thousands of other fellows did the same sort of thing, and much better, but didn't get any award . . . It's a crude thing to say but the whole point is that you've got to be *seen* doing things like that – and that's where the luck comes in. I can assure you there were many unnoticed deeds of valour which have been lost in oblivion. So perhaps there's not so much in the medal itself. I often think I get more satisfaction from the letters of gratitude I get from the man and his parents. They're very humble folk, and they live in Middlesbrough, of all places. I go up and see them sometimes – they're too poor to come down here – and I'm regarded as a sort of hero. It's all very touching, but an awful bore to have to go up to Middlesbrough. That *is* heroic!' The tired Gorse again smiled.

'Well, I think it's absolutely wonderful,' said Mrs Plumleigh-Bruce. '*Wonderful* . . .'

2

Gorse had not previously awarded himself a Military Cross, but his richly inventive imagination had often caused him to long to do so, and he had ready the full story of his method of acquiring it.

He was aware of the dangers entailed – of the fact that the matter could be checked up on by anyone hostile or suspicious. That was why he had until now abstained from this luxury. But Mrs Plumleigh-Bruce simply asked for it, and he had found the temptation wholly irresistible.

Also, should any enemy get to work, he had, he believed, all the answers ready.

He was not, however, willing to let the story go any further than Mrs Plumleigh-Bruce, and so he now hastened to insure himself against such a thing.

'I can't conceive why I'm telling you all this,' he said. 'And you won't let it go any further, will you?'

'But why not? I should've thought you'd've been proud of it. I don't see any sense in being *too* modest.'

'No. You don't understand. People're odd. They think you're boasting or something. As I said, I can't imagine why I told *you* – except that you're the sort of person who simply invites confessions, somehow. But you realize it *is* a confession – that what I've told you is in the confessional – don't you? You realize that you're bound by vows not to disclose it to another soul – don't you?'

Mrs Plumleigh-Bruce had by this time not only swallowed and digested the cathedral. She had become a cathedral – with all its holiness, hangings, and furniture. She was, therefore, necessarily a confessional-box as well.

'No,' she said. 'If you want it that way, you can certainly rely upon *me*.'

'Yes. You haven't got to tell me that,' said Gorse, and there was a silence in which he thought that the time had approached at which it would be advisable to withhold any further stimulation of Mrs Plumleigh-Bruce's vanity. It would now be wise, he decided, to stimulate, instead, her financial greed.

3

'Anyway, I can assure you I'm not *really* a hero in any sense of the word,' he said. 'In fact I'm not sure that I'm not a bit of a crook, on the whole – believe it or not.'

'Well – I don't find it easy to believe.'

'Well – I'm what they call a "fast worker" anyway. And I'm not at all averse to the material things of life, as you know. And in spite of all the things I've said against money I've absolutely no objection at all to raking it in – and using all my wits in the raking. I've got quite a strong gambling streak, too. Have you?'

'No,' said Mrs Plumleigh-Bruce, quite truthfully. 'I can't say I have, really . . . And in what way do you like to gamble?'

'Oh – horses, mostly – as I've told you. I suppose I do it mostly for the fun of the thing – but I've found it very profitable fun. Don't you ever put money on a horse?'

'No,' said Mrs Plumleigh-Bruce, again truthfully. 'Hardly ever, except on the Derby and things like that. And then I always have to get somebody to do it for me. And I generally lose. I don't know the first thing about racing, but personally I'm a believer in the old saying that you can't beat the book. Aren't you?'

Gorse once more looked into the fire to think. 'No. I'm not,' he said. 'I think the book *can* be quite easily beaten – but I think you've got to know how to set about it.'

'And how do you do that?'

'By knowing the right people,' said Gorse. 'I don't believe in any of these silly "systems" or anything like that. But if you know the right people and put in a few hours of intelligent study every other day – you saw me doing it the other night, by the way – I believe the book, or the bookmakers – not a crowd I like – are quite easy to beat. Anyway, I did it in a big way the other night, and I've every intention of doing the same thing tomorrow. By the way, do *you* want to be put on to something good? I'll do it for you, if you like.'

'Something good. Do you mean what they call a "dead certainty"?'

'No. There's no such thing as a *dead* certainty . . . Well – just think about it. There wouldn't be any betting on a race if there was. But there's such a thing that's as near a dead certainty that it makes practically no difference. If you know the right people – that is.'

'What do you mean by the "right" people?'

'Well – some of them are very high up, and some of them, I regret to say, are very low down. I've got a foot in both worlds.'

'And you think you know this nearly dead certainty tomorrow?'

'I don't *think* I know – I *know* I know – or *will* know tomorrow.'

'What's the name of the horse? And where's it running?'

'It's the Bramford meeting,' said Gorse, 'and the first race. Two o'clock. But I can't give you the name of the horse just at the moment. It might be one of two – *Lazy Boy*, or *Stucco*. And it might be yet another. And just *conceivably* I won't bet at all. That'll all be ascertained by yours truly early tomorrow morning.'

'And you're so sure, if you do bet, that it's going to win?'

'So sure that I'm willing to put money on it for you, and to guarantee now, if it loses, to pay you back the money myself. That's fair enough – isn't it?'

'No – it's absurd. It's heads I win tails you lose. In fact I couldn't do it. And, really, you know, I don't like betting.'

'Oh come now. Have a little flutter – although this could hardly be called a "flutter". It's just a way of making easy money.'

Mrs Plumleigh-Bruce was silent as she reflected.

'Well, I don't know what to say . . .' she said.

'Well – perhaps I shouldn't persuade you if you don't like that sort of thing. But you'll regret it tomorrow evening when you read the newspaper.' Gorse broke off to laugh at himself. 'You see I *am* a crook, after all, as I said! Or at any rate a tipster. Aren't I?'

'Don't be absurd . . .'

'But I am, you know. Because racing, on the whole, is a crooked business, and I've got to admit that I'm employing, more or less, crooked means, or rather dealing with more or less crooked people. On the other hand I'm only removing money from even more crooked people, and that pleases me a lot. It also puts my conscience almost completely to rest. Wouldn't it yours?'

'Yes. Of course it would. But all this is simply Greek to me. I don't know how you set about it all.'

'Yes – I can understand that. And it's all much too long and complicated and silly to go into, really.'

Gorse was speaking the truth. What he had been talking about, suggesting, was certainly much too long and complicated and silly to go into – above all silly – and would not have borne any sort of critical examination. Gorse was merely throwing forth a wordy mist of horsey wisdom with which to deceive an ignorant woman.

'Very well,' said Mrs Plumleigh-Bruce. 'I'm game for a little flutter. How much shall I put on? Two and six – five shillings, or something like that?'

'*Five shillings!*' Gorse exclaimed. 'Good Heavens, no. If you're not going to go further than that it's not worth anyone's while. I'm not expecting big odds, you know. In fact I don't expect more than three to one – if that . . . You don't want to rope in seven and sixpence or something like that, do you? . . . Oh, no. Let's say five pounds – or leave it alone.'

'Five *pounds*!' said Mrs Plumleigh-Bruce. 'But I can't afford to risk five pounds. I'm not a rich woman, you know.'

'All the more reason for enriching yourself. And it's not really a risk, and, as I've said, I'm willing to insure you against any loss.'

'And, as *I've* said before, I couldn't possibly let you do that . . . No. Really. Five pounds is too much for me. Really it is.'

'Oh, come now. Now you're not speaking like yourself. Unless I've mistaken you – and I'm quite sure I haven't. In this world one's got to do things in the right way – and that means the big way – or not at all, hasn't one? If one does things in the small way – in the Reading way, if I may say so – one never gets anywhere. And, although chance has brought you temporarily to Reading, I know you're not the type of person who does things in the Reading way, the silly, fiddling, petty little middle-class way.'

Gorse, when defrauding women, all his life took this line about doing things in the big way. (He had used it most successfully with the wretchedly ambitious slum-beauty, Esther Downes, at Brighton.) It was a line which shamed and flattered his victims at the same time, and was therefore almost irresistible. Mrs Plumleigh-Bruce, though much older than Esther Downes, was, nevertheless, like her, both shamed and flattered. All the same, she still tried to hold out.

'Yes. You're right there, certainly,' she said. 'But I still say five pounds is too much for me. And I haven't got all that ready cash in the house, anyway.'

'Nobody's asking for ready cash,' said Gorse. 'As I've said, I'll put the money on for you, and take the rap myself if you lose.'

'And I've said I certainly wouldn't allow it. It's absurd.'

'Very well,' said Gorse, looking at her in a quizzing way. 'Let's make a compromise. You write me an IOU now for five pounds – and if the horse goes down, I'll come on you like an extortionate money-lender for my due.'

'Well – that'd be *slightly* more reasonable.'

'Not "slightly more" reasonable. Absolutely reasonable . . . Very well, then, let's settle for that. Shall we? Come along now. Be a sport. I know you are one at heart, but be one now. I'll think very poorly of you if you're not. Actually it's not a very "sporting" thing to say, but I swear to you that in this case you've simply got nothing to *lose*. In fact it hardly *is* sport.'

Mrs Plumleigh-Bruce was again silent, as she turned the proposition over in her mind. She saw that there was, indeed, not such an awful amount to lose – particularly as Gorse had suggested an

IOU. She had not liked the idea of parting with five pounds in cash. It had, indeed, crossed her mind that Gorse might disappear with it into the blue. But an IOU was a different matter – and the more so because Gorse had said he would not, and to her mind obviously would not, insist upon its being honoured.

Over and above this she fundamentally trusted Gorse, and believed that his horse would almost certainly win. Had he not won last night? And when he had said he would think very poorly of her if she was not a 'sport' Gorse had got at her in two ways. It had filled her with an intense longing to show that she was something more than fully a 'sport'; and it had filled her with the fear that, if she did not show herself one in front of this affluent visitor to Paris (who had joined the Army at the age of sixteen, won the Military Cross, been active with his car against the enemy in 1926, and was now dwelling in an imposing house in Reading) he might think so poorly of her that he would drop her altogether. In spite of his fortune-telling and eye-telephone-pact he had already shown a curious coolness and indifference towards her by making no further effort to meet her for a matter of three days, and he might do the same thing again – only this time permanently.

And would not an arrangement about betting prevent such a thing? Would it not, on the contrary, assure his quick return to her – cement their friendship?

All these thoughts, taken in conjunction with his slightly wearied charm, and the cosy, Kimono lateness of the hour, made her suddenly make up her mind to take the risk.

'Well – I must say it all sounds very tempting,' she said.

'It is, indeed, very tempting,' said Gorse, who saw clearly that he had achieved what he wanted, and so feigned half to withdraw. 'But for Heaven's sake don't let *me* persuade you. If you've got a real hatred of betting, you stick to your guns. One should never go against one's own instincts. That's *one* of the things I've learnt from life, at least. Well – which shall it be? "To bet or not to bet, that is the question" as our friend Hamlet might have said.'

'To bet,' said Mrs Plumleigh-Bruce. 'Definitely. But you've got to let me give you the IOU.'

'Oh – *must* we go through that formality?'

'Yes. We certainly must. And I'd like to do it now.'

'Very well, then. If you must you must, I suppose. But don't let's make a fuss about it.' Gorse began to fumble in his breast-pocket and brought out some letters. 'Here you are. Just jot it down on the back of one of these. Here we are.' He had selected a letter and was glancing at its contents. 'Yes. This'll do . . . Have you got a pen? Here's one if you haven't.' He produced an extremely expensive fountain pen from the same pocket, and rose and went over to her, folding the letter. 'Now – you just write it on the back of that, and all's in order. And while you're doing it I'd like to go and wash my hands if I may – to be excused, as we used to say at school. May I be excused?'

'Yes. You may be excused,' said Mrs Plumleigh-Bruce, in her own rich, regal way. 'The bathroom's just at the top of the stairs . . . There's a light on up there, I think. But I've no idea how you write out these things.'

'Now – surely you do,' said Gorse leaning over her, and putting the pen into her hand in a way which, like his earlier fortune-telling, established direct physical contact. 'All you've got to do is write "IOU" in capital letters, and then five pounds in numerals, and then again in words. And then sign it. Haven't you ever seen an IOU?'

'Yes. I have, as a matter of fact, but I've somehow forgotten the exact thing you do. Never mind. I think I can manage . . .'

'Very well, then, you do your best, while I leave you for a moment or two. And if you've done it wrong I'll tell you when I come back. *Au revoir*.' And Gorse left the room.

Gorse had two objects in making this excuse to leave her alone.

Chapter Four

I

Gorse, it may have been noticed, had a remarkable gift for killing two, or even three, birds with one stone. One of the birds he had in mind at the moment was a quick exploration of as much of 'Glen Alan' as he could; the other was his desire to leave Mrs Plumleigh-Bruce alone, so that she should have time to unfold and read the letter on the back of which she was to write the IOU. He had not the faintest doubt that she would do this, and the letter, used before for roughly similar purposes, had seemed casually, but in fact most carefully, selected from his pocket.

One of Gorse's settled habits was to steal any sort of headed notepaper which he thought might be useful to him – notepaper from private houses, from business and solicitors' firms (the bigger and better-known the house and firms the better) – and from West End clubs. The notepaper he had just left in Mrs Plumleigh-Bruce's hands came from the Bath Club, Dover Street. He had managed to gain an invitation to enter this club by means of a prospective deal with a car (imagined by himself) with one of its members – and, by telling a hasty lie, he had managed to gain access to and pocket the notepaper without any difficulty.

On the headed sheet which he had given to Mrs Plumleigh-Bruce he had written a letter in a disguised hand. Gorse never attempted to be a great, but was always a competent, forger.

The letter began with 'My dear Ralph', ended with 'Yrs. ever', and was throughout of a jovial and intimate nature. Thus Gorse was demonstrating to Mrs Plumleigh-Bruce that he was on jovial and intimate terms with a member of the Bath Club.

2

On leaving the sitting-room and mounting the stairs, Gorse had no difficulty in spotting which room was the bathroom. But he played to himself the role of an absent-minded or undiscerning young man, and made straight for what he felt certain was Mrs Plumleigh-Bruce's bedroom.

Here the wool-gatherer switched on the light, boldly because innocently. Then, seeing that the room was in fact Mrs Plumleigh-Bruce's bedroom, and unoccupied, he had a good look round. He was highly pleased by the silken opulence and femininity of the room – pleased, of course, commercially, not artistically or amorously.

He then boldly switched off the light and went to the bathroom. This also was to his satisfaction from a commercial point of view. About half a minute later he returned downstairs to the sitting-room.

'Well,' he said. 'Done your homework?'

'Yes. I think that's all right – isn't it?' said Mrs Plumleigh-Bruce, handing him back his fountain pen and his refolded letter.

Gorse glanced at the I O U.

'Yes. Perfect,' he said. 'We'll make a sharp businesswoman of you yet.' He sat down again in the armchair, putting the Bath Club letter casually back into his pocket, and speaking humorously. 'And now you're in my clutches – aren't you? I've only to pretend I've backed the wrong horse – and I can come round and claim five pounds.'

Mrs Plumleigh-Bruce giggled. 'Yes,' she said. 'I never thought of that . . .'

'You should think of everything when dealing with a crook like me . . . You obviously don't know the ways of crooks at all . . .'

'No. I must say I don't . . .'

Gorse became serious again.

'Well – I've been more or less forced to myself. You see, there're enough of them about these days – everywhere. It's the aftermath of the war, I suppose . . . However, I hope you're confident about your own safety in the little transaction we've just made – provided the horse comes in – that is.'

'Oh, yes. *I'm* satisfied enough. But I don't think that my bank manager would approve. He's very much against speculations of any kind.'

'Oh – so you're on friendly terms with your bank manager? Is he in Reading or London?'

'Reading . . . Yes. We're on very good terms. He's a funny little man but I quite like him. He gives me advice about my investments. He's very nice, really.'

'Well – if you've got a credit balance – *all* Bank Managers are nice, really. It's their job. The trouble about Bank Managers is that they're usually too conservative.'

'How do you mean – conservative?'

'Oh – I don't mean conservative politically. I wouldn't mind that. In fact I'm a dyed-in-the-wool Conservative myself from that point of view. And am I right in suspecting that you are, too?'

'Yes. I certainly am.'

'Yes. So I thought. But I meant conservative in another way – from a money point of view. I know it's their business to give absolutely safe and sound advice – but some of them carry it too far – particularly in the provinces. They get stuck in the mud, and won't give advice against the most reasonable changes or shiftings of investments. Thus losing a considerable amount of completely sound and honest profit to the holder. No. He's trustworthy enough, your provincial bank manager – but he's as dead as mutton, usually. Personally, I bank in the City – where I think one should bank – at Coutts. And I'm also a friend of the Manager there, like you. And he's a very live wire, for a bank manager anyway. None of them could be called *really* live wires, of course. You've got to go to the Stock Exchange for that – and I've got an extremely sound man in that direction.'

'A stockbroker, you mean?'

'Yes. I'm afraid to say I dabble a good bit on the Stock Exchange. It's rather like horses with me. But I don't know why I say I'm "afraid". I've done extremely well out of it up to date.'

'Well – I'd certainly be "afraid". All that sort of thing's beyond me, and I leave it strictly alone,' said Mrs Plumleigh-Bruce.

Gorse had been both pleased and displeased on learning about Mrs Plumleigh-Bruce's investments. On the one hand it seemed to prove for certain that she had a certain amount of money behind her; on the other hand investments, with a bank manager of her own guarding them, might be difficult to dig out of her.

He had thought it wise to plant a seed in her mind by at once disparaging her provincial bank manager, and speaking of the City and the Stock Exchange: but here, he thought, the matter had better be completely dropped for a little.

'Yes,' he said. 'And I think you're wise to leave it alone. You've got to know your way around if you go in for that sort of thing. Putting five pounds on a horse is a very different thing from playing with large sums on the market. One's a bit of fun – a bit of sport – the other's quite a serious business – believe me.'

'Yes. I'm sure it is . . .'

There was now a long silence in which both, finding nothing to say, looked into the fire. Gorse looked at his watch.

'Well,' he said. 'I suppose I must be going. It's quite late and you said you were tired.'

'Oh no. Do stay and have another drink, or cigarette or something – won't you? I'm feeling quite lively now.'

'And I'm feeling quite soothed,' said Gorse, looking at her. 'As I predicted I would. But all the same, I do think I'd better go. I don't know what your maid Mary'll be thinking.'

He rose, and warmed his hands at the fire.

'I wouldn't bother about Mary,' said Mrs Plumleigh-Bruce. 'She doesn't think at all. I'm afraid she wasn't trained for thinking, poor girl.'

'All the better for her,' said Gorse, turning from the fire, and looking at her. 'But I must go. Really I must. And I can't thank you enough for letting me come round. As I said, I'm feeling completely soothed, and all my troubles seem to have vanished into thin air.'

'But you haven't really *told* me about your troubles,' said Mrs Plumleigh-Bruce, rising, and looking, with a shyness which was half genuine and half flirtatious, at her visitor.

'No. I know I haven't,' said Gorse, putting his hands behind his back with an air of one using will-power in order to refrain from flirting with her, or, even from attempting to kiss her. 'In fact all I've done is talk about myself – and a bit of my past – and a lot about racing – and to give you a tip, which you've taken, and to get an IOU from you, which *I've* most ungraciously taken . . . All the same, as far as I'm concerned, I've got even more than I hoped for.' He was walking towards the door. 'It'd be funny if the horse falls down, after all, and you lose your money, wouldn't it? And horses do fall down, you know – particularly over the sticks.'

He opened the door, indicating that she should join him in the hall.

'Well,' said Mrs Plumleigh-Bruce, joining him in the hall. 'I'll just have to keep my fingers crossed. By the way – how and when will I know what's happened? I don't even know the name of the horse – do I?'

Gorse began to put on his overcoat in a leisurely way.

'Do you take an evening paper?' he said.

'Yes. The *Evening News* . . .'

'And what time does it come?'

'Oh – about five-thirty to six.'

'Well, I'll know what we're on a long while before that – so I can telephone you or send you a message in the morning – or at any rate early in the afternoon. Then you'll have to wait breathlessly for the *Evening News*. It's rather fun – don't you think – waiting breathlessly?'

'Mm . . . I'm not so sure about that,' said Mrs Plumleigh-Bruce, and went on to ask the question which now interested her most. 'But if all goes well, or ill, how will I meet you again, anyway? I've either got to pay you five pounds or collect my winnings, haven't I?'

'Yes. You've certainly got to collect your winnings, anyway.' Gorse was slowly putting on his scarf. 'And if it's a question of winnings we ought to celebrate a little. So what about meeting at the good old Friar at about six-thirty? Then we can drown our sorrows in drink, at any rate, if we've lost. I may tell you I'm putting on a great deal more than five pounds myself. So what about it? About six-thirty at The Friar?'

'Yes. That'd suit me.'

'Very well. The Friar it shall be . . . Six-thirty . . . Well – I must be off. And I really can't thank you enough for having me round. I only wish I could do something for you in return – I don't mean just by putting you on to a winner.'

Gorse was putting on his gloves.

'Well – if the horse wins,' said Mrs Plumleigh-Bruce, 'it'll be a question of me having to think of doing something for *you* in return – won't it? And I can't think of anything at the moment. Can you?'

Gorse fiddled with the button of his glove, and pretended to be thinking for a moment.

'Well,' he said, 'as a matter of fact, you can. It's only provided the horse wins of course. If it doesn't, you must cast me out.' He smiled at her. 'But I think you *could* help me – give me your advice – about a small matter.'

'Yes. What is it? Do tell me. What small matter?'

'I should have really said quite a large matter,' said Gorse, flicking his wrist, thoughtfully and gently, with his other glove. 'And one I know pretty well nothing about. I've just been telling you about a lot of things I *do* know about. But it might be possible to change parts, and for you to tell me something I feel certain *you* know about.'

'Yes? What is it?'

'Oh. About houses . . . One house in particular, really. I mean that house in Gilroy Road. I simply can't make up my mind about it. I can't make out whether it's really a property – whether I'm on to a really good thing or not.'

'But *I* don't know the first thing about the value of houses,' said Mrs Plumleigh-Bruce.

'Yes. That may be – about their value in money – from just a crude masculine point of view. But what I'm wanting is a *woman's* angle. Because that's the only thing that counts in the long run. Women are the only people who know how to run a house, and if a house *can* be run comfortably. I have a feeling that this one can't – although it may be going for a song. But I don't want to sing a song for a white elephant, and that's where you could help me. *Would* you?' Gorse looked at her appealingly.

'Of course. But how, exactly?'

'Oh – just by coming round and looking at it – going over it thoroughly, and casting around that deadly searching eye that only a woman has – employing that awful instinct that belongs to the female sex alone. I have an idea you'd be able to spot all the snags, and then make up my mind about it once and for all. So will you? Couldn't you come to tea or something one day? It'd be perfectly respectable. Old Mrs Burford – that's my housekeeper – she'd be there. And she makes, I may say by way of tempting you, just about the most heavenly scones you've ever tasted. So do come one day, will you?'

'Yes. Of course I will. Whenever you like.'

'Well – I'd like to say tomorrow – but actually tomorrow's Mrs Burford's afternoon off. And anyway we've fixed up six-thirty at The Friar – either to drown our sorrows or celebrate. But what about the day after? Anyway we can discuss it when we meet tomorrow. It's really very good of you . . . Oh – and by the way, about tomorrow . . .'

'Yes. What? . . .'

'Well, is this rather – er – unorthodox visit of mine to you, so late in the evening, supposed to be official? I mean – is it to be mentioned in front of anyone else we might meet in The Friar?'

Mrs Plumleigh-Bruce thought for a second or two, and then, remembering Mr Stimpson's alcoholically defiant air earlier, decided to be defiant herself.

'Yes,' she said. 'Of course. Anybody can know. There's been nothing wrong about it – has there?'

'Certainly not. In fact I hope, if the horse wins, there'll be everything very much right. I only asked you because you know how people gossip in these provincial towns – don't you? But I might have known you're above even thinking of such things, as *I* am . . . Well – now I really *must* be off. Goodbye, and thank you again.'

Gorse, who, unlike Mr Stimpson earlier in the evening, had put no glove on his right hand to snatch off (as Mrs Plumleigh-Bruce noticed), shook hands gracefully with Mrs Plumleigh-Bruce, and a few moments later had left the house – a silent house in which Mary had gone to bed, and in which Mrs Plumleigh-Bruce, returning to the sitting-room, had a lot to think about – Mr Stimpson, Gorse, Military Crosses, being a Cathedral, and the possibility of having lost five pounds.

She could hardly believe she was likely to win any money, and she was still, somehow, dimly suspicious and afraid of Gorse – or at any rate of the, to her mind, slightly too dashing and monied way he did things.

PART SIX

GORSE THE TEMPTER

Chapter One

1

The next evening Mr Stimpson was the first to occupy the Plumleigh-Bruce nook at The Friar.

Owing to his having been partially inebriated as well as defiant last night, Mr Stimpson had made no appointment to meet Mrs Plumleigh-Bruce. He had been tempted, during the day, to telephone her, but, as a lustily thriving lover and leaver and treater of them rough, he had resisted the temptation.

2

Mr Stimpson, like Major Parry, had suffered a small misfortune about a year ago – a misfortune, very much like Major Parry's, derived from unexpected success. He had solved a crossword puzzle set by a well-known national evening newspaper, which had presented him with a guinea and mentioned his name. This had been, rather feebly, used in defence against Major Parry's front-page, black-framed Armistice Day Poem, and had rather upset his life. Like Major Parry, Mr Stimpson desperately wanted to repeat his performance. He had a faint suspicion that Major Parry was secretly having another go at the glorious dead, but he was not certain of this. At any rate Major Parry had obviously not had any luck for the last two years, and so he might, Mr Stimpson thought, have decided to retire from the ring – from the black frame. In which case, if Mr Stimpson could only solve another crossword puzzle, he would be on equal terms with the Major. In Mr Stimpson's reckoning, two solved crossword puzzles in a national paper were well worth one Armistice Day Poem in a local one.

Unhappily, Mr Stimpson was no good at all at crossword puzzles. He was, in fact, much worse at them than the Major was at his poems. He had solved the one he had by dogged patience, luck, and, mostly, by obtaining the assistance of acquaintances in public houses and elsewhere. But he had grimly determined not to surrender, and, whenever he had the time, he had a go at one of the beastly things.

What faced him tonight was even more beastly than usual, and he had got practically nowhere with it. He was faced by a few black and a lot of white squares, underneath which had been printed the following objectionable, sly, whimsical gibberish:

Across

1. *Cartographer's business.*
8. *Lowland reels perhaps.*
9. *Diverges.*
10. *Flies at sea.*
11. *False.*
14. *Boredom.*
15. *Many of these make one.*
18. *Jenny – me when me met. (Leigh Hunt)*
19. *Mean Lady (Anag.).*
21. *Of course.*
23. *Northern 'lights'.*
24. *Both ways.*
25. *Illuminated.*

Down

1. *Shy girls do this.*
2. *Extremely small.*
3. *Rigid.*
4. *Not permitted.*
5. *Latin for scales.*
6. *Plant leaps (Anag.).*
7. *Lonely talk.*
13. *Unrealized.*
14. *19 across would like this.*
16. *Fruitful.*
17. *Perhaps.*
18. *Beginning.*
20. *Rough justice.*
22. *More than edible to unbelievers.*

Well, some of these seemed to be more or less in the bag. Take 1 Down for instance: 'Shy girls do this'. That must be 'blush' . . .

But no – it *wasn't*! 'Blush' was only five letters, and six were required. Shy girls do this . . . Shy girls do *this* . . . Blush. What was another word for 'blush'? What *was* blushing? It was going red in the face. Red. Hullo! What about 'Redden'? How many letters in 'redden'? One, two, three, four, five, *six*!

But be careful, now. Don't mess up the white squares with pencil until you're certain. What *else* did shy girls do? Smirk. Simper. Oh

God – 'simper' was six letters, too. Better leave it for the moment, and try something else.

'Cartographer's business', 'Lowland reels', 'Diverges'. All beyond him at the moment. (He didn't even know what a Cartographer was, but he could look it up in his Cassell's when he got home.)

'Flies at sea' – a long one – nine or ten letters. Flies at sea, Flies at sea, Flies at *sea* . . . Hullo! *Hydroplane!* Surely he was home here. Hurrah! Brilliant! Check up on the number of letters. Hydroplane. One, two, three, four, five, six, seven, eight, nine, *ten*. It looked as though it would fit. Now check on the number of white squares. One, two, three, four, five, six (things were looking good), seven, eight, *nine* – blast it!

Check again on squares and hydroplane . . . No. No good . . . What on earth sort of thing, then, flew at sea? There were millions of flies on the river – there was fly-fishing – but what about the sea?

Wait a minute! What about flying fish?

What about *porpoises*? Didn't porpoises fly out of the water, or sort of jump out of it at any rate? It could be *called* flying, and porpoises looked about ten letters . . .

No. No good. Caught again. Even if porpoises flew, the clue was 'flies', not 'fly', and so only one porpoise would be flying. And one porpoise would never run to be ten letters, surely.

Mr Stimpson checked up (in a purely academic spirit, for he knew now that he was getting nowhere) on his lonely porpoise . . . Yes. Two letters short.

What about trying the Anags. Sometimes he got these in a flash.

'Mean Lady' . . . Mean Lady, Neam Ydal, Dylad Name . . . Dynamo? No. Dynamaled? No such word, but you must try out everything. Named Yal? Named Lay . . . *Damnedly*? Yes, surely! . . . No. Too many 'd's' and not enough 'a's'. And anyway there probably wasn't such a word. 'Damnably' there certainly was, but 'Damnedly' would almost certainly not be in Cassell's.

The other Anag., then – 'Plant leaps'.

Pleasant? No. Pleasance? Unpleasant? No . . . Slant-something? Nap-something? *Pale*-something. *Ape*-something.

No. 'Plant leaps' was worse than 'Flies at sea'.

Perhaps 'Flies at sea' was a pun. Flies. Things you swatted. See. Vision. Flies obstructing the view. See. Holy See – flies in a church or something, or on a Bishop or something . . . Top C. A soprano trying to hit the top C. – flying at it. *Soprano!*

No. Caught again! Soprano was only seven.

This was getting absurd. 'Simper' and 'redden' were as yet his only hopes. Better go for the *really* easy ones.

After much morose mental lurking around Rough justice, Perhaps, Beginning, Many of these make one, Rigid, Extremely small, Both ways, and Fruitful, Mr Stimpson at last alighted upon what he thought were two dead certainties. These were 'lit' for a three-letter 'Illuminated', and 'untrue' for a six-letter 'False'.

He was pencilling these in, with a feeling of frustration and compromise rather than elation, when he was joined by Mrs Plumleigh-Bruce.

As he rose to greet her he hastily put away the newspaper and pencil into his overcoat pocket. He was as anxious to hide his continued preoccupation with crossword puzzles from Mrs Plumleigh-Bruce, as he was anxious to hide it from the poem-writing Major. Until he was again successful with one, he wanted to hide it from all the world. That was why he never now sought advice on clues from any kind of acquaintance, and, as a consequence, never got within even a reasonable distance of solving a problem.

3

Mr Stimpson had been so absorbed by hydroplanes and blushing girls that he had completely forgotten Mrs Plumleigh-Bruce, and the situation in regard to her. He was not, therefore, for a moment, particularly surprised or pleased to see her. He simply welcomed her politely, ushered her into her usual seat (her throne, one might say), and went over to the bar to get a Gin and It, together with another beer for himself.

When he was at the bar, however, and waiting for the drinks, he came to his senses, and realized that a remarkable, and remarkably gratifying, thing had happened.

Last night he had given her no invitation to join him in The Friar. She never, so far as he knew, went into The Friar without an invitation. And yet here she was, seemingly following him in, seeking his company.

What could this indicate but a triumph for himself? Was it not evident that his tactic last night had succeeded brilliantly – that loving and leaving them and treating them rough were now proved to be incomparable slogans? Good Heavens, he thought, the Lady of Reading, the famous Lady Joan, so far from having taken offence, seemed to be practically chasing him! Women, this original thinker decided, were Funny Creatures. All they needed was Handling . . . As he returned with the drinks he complacently braced himself to the most agreeable task of Handling her.

But, when he had sat down beside her, he somehow had an instinct that she was for some reason not in any sort of mood to be Handled.

This was not because she was in any way disagreeable. Rather the contrary. She was, perhaps, more pleasant to him than usual, and she was, it seemed to him, in a state of internal happiness and excitement which she was not, in spite of an effort, quite able to subdue. He could not in any way account for this mood. He only knew that it was certainly not one of 'chasing' him. It looked, really, as if she had been chasing something else, and had captured it.

Mrs Plumleigh-Bruce's mood, if only Mr Stimpson had the requisite knowledge, could have been easily explained.

During the middle of the afternoon she had received a written message from Gorse, in which, among other things, he had named the horse which he had backed on her behalf – *Stucco*.

She had waited in anguish for her evening newspaper, rushing into the hall to get it, opening it dizzily, and, having seen that *Stucco* had won, at 4–1, returning to the sitting-room in a condition of dazed and almost delirious pleasure.

Those who back horses regularly have little idea of the emotion which is awakened in the breasts of those who, having in their lives hitherto only put a little money on big events (and usually lost it), all at once have the experience of winning money on an everyday race. And in this case Mrs Plumleigh-Bruce had won what seemed to her an enormous amount of money – twenty pounds. (She kept on thinking of it as twenty-five, including her stake in her winnings, as the inexperienced so often do.)

With such inexperienced people, who never even glance at Racing pages or news, the very obscurity of the race furnishes the major part of the excitement and pride they take in having found and backed its winner. To win on the Derby or the Grand National – that is nothing, mere racing froth and frivolity. Everybody around you has had a bet, and won or lost. But to have picked the winner of a race which most people have never even heard of – this is indeed getting behind the scenes, sends one soaring above the trivial class of the amateur punter.

Such people, carrying their evening newspapers announcing the news about with them (as Mrs Plumleigh-Bruce was now), somehow feel that they are themselves in the news – in the limelight of print. They almost look upon themselves as celebrities. They are in the 'know', too, which is almost as good as, or perhaps better than, being in the news.

And, because they are in the 'know', they feel enormously clever, shrewd, and far-seeing – even if, as Mrs Plumleigh-Bruce had, they have obtained their information entirely fortuitously, and have supported it reluctantly.

Delicious gratification, in fact, floods in upon them from every conceivable side. And, today, Mrs Plumleigh-Bruce had further cause for gratification.

Along with his afternoon message about the horse, Gorse had sent Mrs Plumleigh-Bruce flowers – six or seven very fine chrysanthemums. Both these and the message had been despatched from what was recognized as easily the finest florist in Reading.

4

Gorse had not, in fact, put any money on any horse, either on Mrs Plumleigh-Bruce's or his own behalf. Instead he had caused, by means of an early-morning telegram, a Hammersmith friend of his, who attended every race-meeting, to telephone him and give him the result of the two o'clock race. He had then hastened to the florist.

It may be wondered why he had gone to all the trouble – why he had not waited until he had found the winner of the race by ordinary methods, and then announced to her that he had backed the winner.

This was all part of Gorse's life-long technique with women – that of submitting them to as much suspense and relief as he possibly could. Relief was his main object – but for this suspense was necessary. In a state of wild relief women would agree to almost anything he proposed.

5

Mrs Plumleigh-Bruce, then, sitting with Mr Stimpson, was not only bathing in the luxurious complacency of a successful racing expert: she was bathing in relief, and in the pleasure and vanity – which she could not, however much she tried, restrain – derived from having received such delightful flowers from so young a man.

She had entered The Friar at 6.33. Gorse had said 'about' six-thirty. She would, normally, have arrived five minutes late – but her happy impatience had made her cut off two minutes – a favour never conceded to any other man. She was disappointed, as Gorse had meant her to be, not to find him there already, but she fully consoled herself with his use of the word 'about', and was, indeed, radiating true happiness without any effort or self-consciousness.

Mr Stimpson, the Handler so fresh to Handling, found himself puzzled (and of course completely unable to do the smallest thing in the way of Handling), when confronted with this odd, agitated, but obviously joyous mood in Mrs Plumleigh-Bruce.

He hoped it would simmer down after a bit. But it did not, and when two or three minutes had passed Mr Stimpson became very seriously annoyed by it. He tried to control this annoyance, but at last could do so no longer.

'You seem to be very cheerful about something tonight,' the ungracious man, the thwarted Handler, said at last. 'What's happened? Some good news? Somebody left you a fortune or something?'

'No,' said Mrs Plumleigh-Bruce, with a sparkling, teasingly satisfied look. 'Not a fortune. But I *have* come into an extremely nice little bit of money, as a matter of fact . . .'

This scared Mr Stimpson out of his wits.

He had no idea what she meant, and it occurred to him that she might have suddenly inherited money – and done so in quite a big way. This would be awful. He knew something of her financial situation, which was not at all a good one, and, in his heart, he knew that his one hold over her was his own money, his financial soundness, acumen, and growing prosperity.

As if a switch had been suddenly turned off, in the next few moments the recently-lit but warm electric fire of Mr Stimpson's imagination – his dreams of becoming the Casanova of Reading – began to fade, go white. Even his red face became almost visibly whiter.

On the other hand, Mr Stimpson, thinking intensely, managed quickly to find the switch of some secondary lighting. If Casanova was down, Mr Stimpson reflected, the idea of marriage could come up – could be resumed. And, if she had inherited money, marriage was all the more desirable.

'Really? . . .' he said. 'And what do you mean by "quite a little"?'

'Oh – *quite* a little,' said Mrs Plumleigh-Bruce mischievously.

'But what does "quite" mean? These things are relative, aren't they?'

'Just what I said. *Quite* a little. In fact I might say quite a *lot* – for somebody like myself at any rate.'

Mr Stimpson was more frightened than ever.

'But where did it come from?' he asked. 'Have you inherited money, or something? I mean, how did you come by it?'

'Ah,' said Mrs Plumleigh-Bruce, who intended to keep him guessing as long as possible, partly because of her high spirits, and partly to revenge herself upon the man who had kept her guessing and behaved so uncouthly last night. 'That'd be telling.'

'And you won't tell me?'

'I'm not so sure. Why should I? . . . By the way,' said Mrs Plumleigh-Bruce, showing more astuteness than was usual with her, 'you seem to be looking very miserable at the thought of my having got some money. I should've thought you'd 've wanted to congratulate me.'

'But of course I want to congratulate you. But how can I until I know how much it is, and how you came by it?'

'I don't see how I came by it really has anything to do with it,' said Mrs Plumleigh-Bruce. 'The point is, I've got it.'

Here she looked at the door. It had suddenly struck her that she had not as yet got the money, and that her doing so depended entirely upon Gorse. What if Gorse – the still faintly suspect young man – had decamped? What if he had decided to keep for himself the twenty pounds he had made? What if he did not want to pay up? Such a thing would, indeed, make her look foolish – idiotic.

She had looked quite a few times at the door before, and Mr Stimpson had noticed it. This last look stung the highly irritated man to comment.

'Why do you keep on looking at the door?' he asked.

'Was I? I didn't know I was.'

'Are you expecting all this wonderful money to come through the door, or something?'

He had, of course, accidentally, hit the nail on the head.

'Well,' said Mrs Plumleigh-Bruce. 'Such a thing *could* happen, you know . . .'

Mr Stimpson experienced considerable relief. Only a comparatively small sum of money, probably in cash – not an inheritance – could possibly come through the door of the Saloon Bar of The Friar.

'You know, I do wish you wouldn't be so mysterious, Joan,' he said, in a much less irritated tone. 'Do tell me. Won't you? I believe you're enjoying keeping me guessing.'

'Perhaps I am,' said Mrs Plumleigh-Bruce. 'Perhaps it's a secret.'

'Oh well, if it's a secret you'd better not tell me. Is it a secret?'

'No. It's not a secret,' Mrs Plumleigh-Bruce relented. 'Or it's a very open secret, anyway.'

'How open?'

'Well – it's free for everybody to see. It's in the newspaper, as a matter of fact.'

'The newspaper!' Mr Stimpson again had horrible forebodings of some spectacular inheritance.

'Yes. In fact, you can look at it, if you like. There you are.' She gave him her newspaper. 'You'll find it on the back page.'

As with all successful punting fledglings, the incessant looking at and showing of the evening newspaper were the peak-points of Mrs Plumleigh-Bruce's happiness.

'I don't follow you. Where am I to look?' said Mr Stimpson, happy at any rate to have observed that Mrs Plumleigh-Bruce's picture was not on the back page. 'Do help me out.'

'Look at the racing.'

'Yes. What about it?'

'And look at the winner of the two o'clock at Bramford.'

'Yes . . . Yes . . . *Stucco* . . . What about it?'

'Well – I've backed it, that's all. And it's come in at four to one.'

'Good Heavens,' said Mr Stimpson, now perfectly happy again – so happy that he was almost happy for Mrs Plumleigh-Bruce, who, he imagined, had for some reason put two bob or something on the race. 'Well. I never knew you went in for betting, Joan. Good for you. How much did you have on?'

'Five pounds.'

'Five *pounds*! *Pounds*, did you say?'

'I did.'

'Joan – have you been going mad? Five pounds on a *horse*?'

'Yes. Why not? After all,' said Mrs Plumleigh-Bruce, in her smugness almost quoting Gorse word for word, 'in this world one's got to do things in the right way – and that means the big way – doesn't it? . . . And look at the result. I've won twenty pounds – instead of just a few shillings.'

'But I never dreamed you went in for this sort of thing.'

'I don't – as a rule . . .'

'No. So I thought. Then somebody must have put you up to it.'

'Perhaps they did . . .'

'I'm sure they did. Come along now. Who was it? Or is that a secret, too?'

'No. That's not a secret of any sort, really.'

Mrs Plumleigh-Bruce had made up her mind to be absolutely candid about Gorse's visit last night. She had had his permission to do so, and, in addition to the fact that it was the safest course to take, it would almost certainly make Mr Stimpson very jealous indeed, and so, in its turn, make herself much more desirable in his eyes. Then, fired by jealousy and desire, Mr Stimpson might, before long, become much more explicit about his Hog. It might, indeed, turn out to be not only whole, but wholly estimable and matrimonial.

'Well, then, don't keep me waiting,' said Mr Stimpson. 'Who was it?'

'Only the newcomer in our midst. He certainly seems to know something about horses.'

'Oh . . . *Him* . . .' said Mr Stimpson. 'So *he* gave you the tip . . . But how on earth did you get it from him? I haven't seen him for about four days. I thought he'd vanished.'

'Yes. So did I, rather. But he's only been to London, and so far from vanishing he turned up last night as large as life.'

'Last night? When?'

'Oh – after you left.'

'How do you mean? Did he phone you or something?'

'Yes, he did phone me as a matter of fact. But after that he came round to see me.'

'Came round!'

'Yes. He was frightfully miserable, poor boy. He'd had a simply awful day in London, haggling over business. And he asked me to give him a little bit of comfort, by talking to me, and I simply didn't have the heart to refuse him.'

'And did you give him "comfort"?' said Mr Stimpson, not unsuggestively.

'I hope I did. I gave him a drink and some coffee, anyway, and although he was only with me about half an hour, he seemed to be in a much happier frame of mind when he left.'

'And he gave you a tip about a horse in among?'

'Yes. So my good deed had its reward, you see. He's a funny young man. He seems to be amazingly worldly-wise, and yet fearfully pathetic and dependent, at the same time. He sent me some flowers this afternoon. It's just a tiny bit embarrassing to tell you the truth.'

Mr Stimpson was in too stunned a state at the moment to feel jealousy.

'Well,' he said. 'Flowers and visits late at night *do* seem a bit embarrassing. You don't, by any chance, think he's "smitten", do you?'

Mrs Plumleigh-Bruce seemed to deliberate on this question.

'I sincerely *hope* not,' she said at last. 'I certainly haven't encouraged it, if he is. There's quite a considerable difference in our ages, isn't there?'

'Yes. There is. But funnier things than that happen in life, you know. And I'm sure you'll agree with me. I hope you're not going to turn into a baby-snatcher.'

Mrs Plumleigh-Bruce again deliberated.

'No. I don't think there's much danger of that,' said Mrs Plumleigh-Bruce, and then turned the screw a little further on Mr Stimpson. 'And yet, you know, although he's so young in years, he's so amazingly grown-up in everything he does. And everything he's done, too. You'd be surprised by the things he told me about himself last night.'

'Oh – what was that?'

'No,' said Mrs Plumleigh-Bruce, who had in mind Gorse's Military Cross. 'That was in the confessional.'

'What, something discreditable?'

'Oh, no. Very much the opposite. But I just happened to promise to keep it secret. I don't know why he wanted me to, and if he gives me permission I'll be only too happy to reveal it. And I'm sure he will, if I ask him . . . By the way, I'm wondering why he's not here now, to tell you the truth. We arranged to meet about six-thirty, and it's much more than that, isn't it? True, he only said "about" six-thirty.'

'Yes,' said Mr Stimpson. 'But here he is, if I'm not gravely mistaken.'

Gorse had entered.

Gorse went to the bar and ordered a drink with the pretence of not looking at the Plumleigh-Bruce nook.

Then he stuck his monocle into his eye, and, apparently with its aid, saw that Mrs Plumleigh-Bruce and Mr Stimpson were present.

Then, looking at Mrs Plumleigh-Bruce, he lifted his head with an air of restrained pleasure and mock 'I told you so' conceit. Then he put his monocle back into his waistcoat pocket, and paid for his drink.

Then he brought his drink over to the other two, with the mock-strutting gait of one who was highly pleased with himself, and said, 'Well – how *are* we all this evening?'

'We're *extremely* well,' said Mrs Plumleigh-Bruce, 'and I think we have rather good cause to be, haven't we? You and I, at any rate.'

'Yes, I must say there isn't *too* much rotten in the state of Denmark just pro tem,' said Gorse, sitting down opposite Mrs Plumleigh-Bruce and Mr Stimpson.

'No,' said Mr Stimpson. 'You two seem to have been doing pretty well for yourselves, as far as I can gather.'

'Oh – so you've been told about our little excursion into the realms of chance, have you?' said Gorse. 'Not that it was really chance. It was as near to a dead certainty as you could get in this uncertain world.'

'I only wish *you'd* been there a little later, Donald,' said Mrs Plumleigh-Bruce. 'And then you could have been put on to it. I know you're very flourishing, but I don't expect you'd turn up your nose at getting twenty pounds – would you?'

'No, I –' began Mr Stimpson, but Gorse cut in.

'What did you say?' he said, raising his chin and looking intently at Mrs Plumleigh-Bruce. 'Twenty pounds?'

His intent and serious look might easily be interpreted as a look of alarm: and Mrs Plumleigh-Bruce was alarmed. There was a pause.

'Well,' said Mrs Plumleigh-Bruce. 'That's right, isn't it? It *is* twenty pounds – isn't it? I put five pounds on it, and it came in at four to one. That makes twenty pounds, doesn't it?'

'Oh no,' said Gorse, maintaining his steady look. 'Not twenty pounds.'

Gorse was playing at suspense and relief again.

'But it *did* come in at four to one – didn't it?'

'Yes. It certainly did.'

'Then what's the trouble?' said Mr Stimpson. 'That's twenty pounds all right, isn't it? Unless I'm a Dutchman.'

'Then I'm afraid you *are* a Dutchman, Mr Stimpson,' said Gorse, producing his gold cigarette case, and taking out a cigarette. 'The sum's not twenty pounds, I can assure you.'

'What then?' said Mr Stimpson.

'Twenty-five,' said Gorse. 'A clear twenty-five. A quarter of a century, in fact.'

'No,' said Mr Stimpson, glad to be able to argue in a business-like way on Mrs Plumleigh-Bruce's behalf, this having been, for a long while, another of his holds over her. 'You don't mean a *clear* twenty-five – twenty-five clear profit. You're not thinking of the original stake – are you? That's not part of the profit.'

'Agreed. All the same,' said Gorse, 'I still say a clear twenty-five.'

'Well – it beats me,' said Mr Stimpson.

'It does me, too,' said Mrs Plumleigh-Bruce.

'It's very simple,' said Gorse. 'If you'll only think for a little.'

'Well,' said Mr Stimpson. 'No amount of thinking's going to make *me* see it differently. Unless I've cracked up on my simple arithmetic.'

'No. You haven't done that, but it's still very simple. I backed *Stucco* each way – that's all.'

'Oh – I see!' said Mr Stimpson. 'Why didn't you say so before?'

'Oh – I don't know. I somehow thought it was taken for granted, I suppose . . . Oh yes, I was on to *Stucco* for a place as well. I told you only last night,' said Gorse, addressing Mrs Plumleigh-Bruce, 'that you've got to do these things in the big way – didn't I?'

'Yes. I believe you did,' said Mrs Plumleigh-Bruce, after a pause. 'We were certainly agreed on *that* matter.'

With these words Mrs Plumleigh-Bruce was trying desperately to cover up her tracks in front of Mr Stimpson. Only a few minutes ago she had spoken to Mr Stimpson about the necessity of doing things in a big way – and this as if she had been expressing her own life-long opinion. Now Gorse had made it seem that she had cribbed dreadfully – that her opinion, indeed, so far from being life-long, had only been acquired last night.

Mr Stimpson was not fooled by her suggestion that there had last night been a spontaneous, mutual agreement between Gorse and Mrs Plumleigh-Bruce on this method of procedure in life. He was pleased to have found her embarrassed by the accidental disclosure, and, in order to regain a little more power over her by further embarrassing her, he did not drop the matter.

'Yes,' he said, looking at her meaningly. 'That was just what you were saying a few minutes ago, wasn't it?'

Mrs Plumleigh-Bruce, aware, like Gorse, that Mr Stimpson had scored, changed, or rather returned to, the subject.

'Well, then – that's simply wonderful, isn't it?' she said. 'Twenty-five pounds! I can't believe it. And I don't really think I ought to take it from you just on the strength of that IOU . . .'

'Oh – here it is, by the way,' said Gorse, taking the piece of Bath Club notepaper, and handing it to her.

'And what do I do with this?' she asked. 'Keep it, or tear it up?'

'I wouldn't bother about anything till you've got your money,' said Gorse, facetiously.

'And when do I get that?' said Mrs Plumleigh-Bruce. 'You know you're making me most horribly greedy and commercial, and I can hardly wait to grab the money. When do I get it?'

'Ah,' said the indomitable salesman of suspense. 'That's the question. I don't actually square up accounts with my bookmaker until the end of each month, and that's a long way away.'

'Oh dear,' said Mrs Plumleigh-Bruce, pouting and shaking her hands with kittenish impatience. 'Have I got to wait all that time? Oh – poor, greedy little me!'

Gorse noticed that Mrs Plumleigh-Bruce was not much good as a kitten. He felt that it would be better if she stuck to her slow, royal, fruity stuff. All the same, he managed to seem to be fascinated.

'No,' he said, in a kitten-stroking voice. 'Not all that time. But I'm afraid I can't give it to you this evening, I haven't got it on me. In fact, I'm afraid you'll probably have to wait until the day after tomorrow . . . And that brings me to another matter, by the way . . .'

Gorse's serious look and tone again frightened Mrs Plumleigh-Bruce.

'What matter?' she said.

'I'm afraid I've got to go to London,' said Gorse. 'And that right soon.'

'How soon?' asked Mrs Plumleigh-Bruce. 'And for how long?'

'As soon as this very evening that ever was, I'm afraid,' said Gorse. 'And it'll be for two nights at least. In fact I think I'll buzz off after this drink. I hate driving a car with more than one drink inside me. It's not that I can't – but if anything *did* happen in the way of an accident, the policeman smells it on your breath and draws false conclusions.'

'Oh dear. What a pity,' said Mrs Plumleigh-Bruce. 'What on earth's happened? Some further business crisis?'

'No. Just the culmination of the crises I told you about last night. And I think all's well. But I've got a nine-thirty visit tomorrow morning with a very tough customer in Kensington, and I want to be up in good time and have my head clear for it. So I'm making the journey tonight. And then, tomorrow evening, I've got yet another visit, at the King's Hotel in Piccadilly, with a much more pleasant customer – still business, but a friend. And so that means I'll be two nights away altogether.'

'Oh dear,' said Mrs Plumleigh-Bruce.

'You know, *that's* funny,' said Mr Stimpson. 'I've got to go to London myself tomorrow on business. And I'm staying up for the night, too. I'm staying with my sister, out Richmond way.'

'Well – that's a coincidence,' said Gorse, thinking quickly. 'And are you going to be *very* busy?'

'Oh – no. Not as busy as all that. In fact I ought to be through by tea-time.'

'Well,' said Gorse. 'In that case – couldn't we meet?'

'Why, yes. I don't see why not. But where? And when?'

'Well – what about the King's?' said Gorse. 'I expect you know the very nice cocktail bar there – down below. And if my business goes through as expected I'll be in a mood for gaiety – even for painting the town red – or at any rate a mild pink.'

Mr Stimpson had indeed heard of the King's Hotel – which was a very large and well-to-do Hotel almost opposite the Lyons 'Pop', which Mr Stimpson mostly used when bent on gaiety or relaxation in the West End. Mr Stimpson had always regarded the King's as above his mark – financially and socially – though he had never done more than glimpse enviously through its revolving doors.

Mr Stimpson had also heard of the downstairs cocktail bar at the King's, which was well-known for furnishing facilities for making the acquaintance of an expensive type of prostitute – too expensive and too frightening for Mr Stimpson. Mr Stimpson always went for Wardour Street.

Mr Stimpson made a trip to London about once a month, in fact doing business and staying with his sister at Richmond. But with these duties he combined, or had until recently combined, pleasure: and he had in the past seldom appeared in his sister's house, of which he had the key, until midnight or afterwards.

In his last few visits, however, he had been back in time for an evening meal with his sister. This had been because of that fierce attack of purity which had overtaken him ever since he had first seriously thought of marrying Mrs Plumleigh-Bruce.

But now, with his changed attitude towards Mrs Plumleigh-Bruce, purity was on the wane. Indeed, impurity was very much on the up and up.

Therefore, when Gorse suggested a meeting at the King's, Mr Stimpson was very interested indeed. If such a meeting came off he would not only, because of a companion, be able to enter the King's without social fear: he would be exploring fascinating avenues of improper behaviour.

This young man Gorse, he decided, certainly had something to him. He went to France, won big money on horses, and had a general air which Mr Stimpson in a way envied and in a way admired.

'But aren't you doing business at the King's?' he asked Gorse. 'And won't you have a friend there? I don't want to butt in or anything.'

'No,' said Gorse, having noticed the gleam of happy anticipation in Mr Stimpson's eye. 'I don't expect the business'll take more than half an hour at the outside. And then I'll probably be alone. And even if I'm not – who cares. The more the merrier. What about it?'

Gorse had always suspected that Mr Stimpson was the sort of man who made occasional visits to town in order secretly to pursue paid women. His aggressive middleness of age and class made it almost transparent. Gorse had also wondered whether he might, somehow, take advantage of Mr Stimpson's secret, if it existed.

And the gleam in Mr Stimpson's eye now almost assured him that it did.

Gorse had formed no precise plan as to how he might exploit the Reading man's guilt in London, but that he could do so, in one way or another, he had no doubt.

Gorse, strangely enough, was never a direct blackmailer. But he was, when it suited him, a tale-teller, and a careful hoarder (or brilliant inventor) of the shameful secrets of others.

Mr Stimpson, it must be remembered, was Gorse's enemy and rival in the case of Mrs Plumleigh-Bruce. He was formidable too – for he had marriage and money to offer, a long acquaintanceship with Mrs Plumleigh-Bruce, and a business head with which to advise and protect her. Mr Stimpson, in fact, would sooner or later have to be moved from the arena – or at any rate reduced to impotence therein.

'Well,' said Mr Stimpson. 'That sounds all right to me. In fact it sounds a *complete* bit of all right.'

Gorse's ability to make everybody and everything centre around himself was, indisputably, phenomenal. Along with Mrs Plumleigh-Bruce, Mr Stimpson himself was now seeking his favours.

Not only was Mr Stimpson enormously relishing the idea of visiting the King's Hotel, Piccadilly: he was getting his own back, taking it out on Mrs Plumleigh-Bruce. She, a few moments ago, had adopted the attitude of having the red-haired young man almost pathetically in tow. But now he had been snatched away from her, and practically belonged to Mr Stimpson. Mr Stimpson of course was not able to exercise any sort of feminine control over Gorse, but a masculine bond, in the present circumstances, was, really, considerably stronger. His meeting with Gorse at the King's introduced a wonderfully monied, 'all-boys-together', London, West End atmosphere – something which Mrs Plumleigh-Bruce might put into her pipe and smoke.

'Well, then – that's fine,' said Gorse. 'What time shall we meet? Seven o'clock? You know the bar, I take it?'

'Oh yes. I know the bar,' said Mr Stimpson, who did not, but who had learned that it was 'down below' and, confident of his ability to find it, was not going to betray his ignorance in front of Mrs Plumleigh-Bruce. 'And seven o'clock'd do fine.'

'Very well, then. Seven o'clock it shall be,' said Gorse. 'And then, the next morning, I can run you down here again in my car, if you like. Or are you motoring up?'

Gorse was certain that Mr Stimpson had no car, and, in order, Cardinal-like, to keep the balance of power, he had given a point to Mrs Plumleigh-Bruce.

'No,' said Mr Stimpson, knowing that Mrs Plumleigh-Bruce was regaining a little ground. 'I haven't got a car as a matter of fact. Not just at the moment at any rate.'

'Well, then,' said Gorse. 'You must let me run you back . . . And talking of running, I ought to do a bit now, myself. I've laid on a meal with my landlady in London, and I mustn't keep her up. Also I want an early night.'

'Oh, come on,' said Mr Stimpson. 'Have another drink. I owe you one from the other night, anyway.'

'Yes. Do stay and have *one* more,' said Mrs Plumleigh-Bruce.

'No. I really won't . . . And the repayment of the drink can be done tomorrow night at the King's – can't it? . . . No,' said Gorse, drinking off his drink, and rising and buttoning his overcoat. 'Rules are rules. And particularly when you're driving. Thanks very much all the same . . . Very well, then. Seven o'clock – King's Bar – downstairs – tomorrow evening. And the evening after that perhaps we'll *all* meet again.' He looked at Mrs Plumleigh-Bruce. 'I'll arrange to have your money by that time, at any rate . . . Well – goodnight, both.'

He smiled and waved at Mrs Plumleigh-Bruce and Mr Stimpson, and walked, in an erect, rather hurried, military way from the Saloon Bar of The Friar.

The two he had left were, on the whole, despondent, though they had no reason for unhappiness. Mrs Plumleigh-Bruce should have still been rejoicing at her winnings; but owing to the sudden departure of Gorse, and his meeting tomorrow with Mr Stimpson, she was not. She was gloomy.

Her gloom infected Mr Stimpson, and at last damped his pleasure in the thought of his meeting with Gorse tomorrow evening.

They spent an uneasy half-hour over another drink, and then told lies in order to escape from each other.

Chapter Two

I

The next day Mr Stimpson, while going about his business in London, vacillated most uneasily between the ideals of purity and impurity.

And the problem, he knew, would, almost without doubt, confront him in a concrete form in the evening.

Had Mr Stimpson taken Gorse seriously as a rival in the pursuit of Mrs Plumleigh-Bruce, purity would have won the day. He would have 'fought' for Mrs Plumleigh-Bruce, and sustained himself in the battle with the knowledge of his own white, Galahad-like behaviour. He was sure that the France-visiting Gorse was not the type of young man who would allow purity to enter into his calculations at any time.

Mr Stimpson rather fancied the idea of 'fighting' for Mrs Plumleigh-Bruce. As a self-styled 'plodder' he took great pride in his pedestrian, indefatigable qualities – and would not at all mind a situation in which he would be able to exercise his 'grim' or 'dogged' determination.

But Mr Stimpson was quite unable to think of Gorse as a rival. Gorse was too young, to begin with – the discrepancy between his and Mrs Plumleigh-Bruce's years making the notion of an affair (or marriage) between the two seem quite absurd. Mrs Plumleigh-Bruce was, after all, too sensible to make that sort of a fool of herself.

Gorse, in addition, was too lighthearted and worldly, too much a man about town, to dream of any such thing.

Gorse, bored in Reading, might, of course, be in a small way 'smitten' by Mrs Plumleigh-Bruce, but such a thing clearly presented no danger.

Therefore, during at least half of the time he gave to reflection on the theme, it seemed to Mr Stimpson that the situation had not really been changed in any way by the appearance of Gorse at Reading. And so renewed impurity in London was entirely in order.

Mr Stimpson, when looking at things from this angle, so far from being made jealous by Gorse's interest in Mrs Plumleigh-Bruce, experienced, in anticipation, the pleasures of vanity. If Gorse was indeed a little 'smitten', then here was the possibility of yet another feather in Mr Stimpson's cap – Gorse being the feather. If the Lady of Reading became Mr Stimpson's acknowledged mistress, a highly presentable and slightly 'smitten' young man hanging around made her more enviable a capture than ever.

Thinking on these lines, Mr Stimpson permitted himself happily to indulge in a gentle, almost sentimental pity for the young man.

This, in its turn, made him like Gorse more and more, and to look forward to the Mrs Plumleigh-Bruce-ousting, 'all-boys-together' meeting at the King's Hotel with very great relish.

Mr Stimpson was in the vicinity of the King's Hotel a full hour before the time of the meeting, and had two pints of beer at a public house before meeting Gorse. Mr Stimpson always drank more in London than in Reading, and, in this case, he wanted to fortify himself for the coming ordeal of passing through the portals of the large, imposing hotel.

Over his beer Mr Stimpson's attitude towards Gorse grew even more warm and deliciously patronizing. The 'old plodder' decided, if the opportunity arose, graciously to give the 'young shaver' a 'wrinkle' or two.

Mr Stimpson, in his rather excited mood failing to allow for the conventional five minutes by which the public house clock was fast, found himself outside the King's Hotel about seven minutes before seven o'clock.

He had no intention of going in too early. He meant, on the other hand, to be at least five minutes late – so that he might find Gorse already there.

Middle-aged provincial businessmen are often as shy, or shyer than, young boys. The thought of entering and being alone in the downstairs cocktail bar of the King's – the bar with the reputation it had – was too much for Mr Stimpson.

He therefore took a stroll in the neighbourhood for about twelve minutes, interesting himself by glancing at what went on on one or two of those pavements best known at that time for bringing about encounters desired by businessmen bent on illicit and rapid pleasure.

2

What Mr Stimpson was able to see early in 1928 was very different from what he would have seen today – and, from his own point of view, very much more satisfying.

Prostitution, in fact, was just then approaching its heyday – the collapse of the 1926 strike having put the working class into a mood of dejection, apathy and submissiveness, which, taken in conjunction with increasing national unemployment, had thrown more dejected, apathetic and submissive women upon the West End streets than, perhaps, ever before.

Many of these women or girls were quite desperate. On the other hand many others – more beautiful, lucky, or experienced – were by no means desperate, for there was a lot of money about. Taken all in all, though, the supply of street-women far exceeded the demand, and street-women thronged certain streets of the West End.

In 1928, in fact, it was almost impossible for any sort of man to walk given streets, at given times, without being ferociously accosted, sometimes by more than one woman or girl simultaneously. And such streets rang with the cries of 'Hullo, darling', 'Where are *you* off to, darling?', 'How are you, dear?' or the 'Where you go, dar*leeng*?' of the French in Old Bond Street (Old Bond Street had long ago been conquered, and is still held, by the French).

Because it was not yet seven o'clock, and because of the rather superior nature of the area in which he was walking, Mr Stimpson was not actually accosted this evening.

Nevertheless, Mr Stimpson saw, particularly when he was in Vigo Street and in Sackville Street, much that interested him.

3

He was six minutes late for Gorse when he went timidly, hat in hand, through the revolving doors of the King's Hotel.

He was fortunate enough to see at once, in front of him at some distance, an electric-lit arrowed-sign saying 'COCKTAIL BAR' – the arrow pointing to somewhere downstairs.

He found the Bar – and Gorse waiting for him.

The Bar was practically empty, and Gorse was standing at one end of the bar by himself.

He was smoking a cigarette and wearing his monocle and an extremely impressive dark blue 'lounge' suit. He was, in this suit, noticeably and gracefully 'lounging' against the bar, and, though he waved and smiled at Mr Stimpson, this did not disturb his poised, calm, cool demeanour.

Chapter Three

Gorse, when lounging at one end of an expensive bar, nearly always wore a monocle and looked like a curious, undistinguished mixture between Bertie Wooster and Satan.

An astute observer would have been more impressed by the moustached-satanic, rather than the monocled-Wooster, aspect of the young man, and would have realized that he was looking at a character by no means unformidable.

Mr Stimpson was not an astute observer, and at the moment even less so than usual, because of his uneasiness at his first entrance into the well-known, well-lit, glittering, thickly-carpeted bar. The fact that Gorse was there, indeed, made the young man seem quite angelic – certainly not satanic.

Nor did Mr Stimpson observe, in the first few minutes of talking to Gorse, that he had been tempted by Satan, in the person of Gorse, and had succumbed. He had, however.

For Gorse had ordered for Mr Stimpson an extremely strong cocktail. This was on the bar beside his own drink, and both had a most pleasant, green, frothy appearance. But Gorse's drink, though it resembled Mr Stimpson's externally, had practically no alcohol in it. He was, therefore, deceiving as well as tempting Mr Stimpson.

'I've taken the liberty of ordering a drink for you,' he said. 'In my view it's the very best they provide here – but if you don't like it, I'll order something else, and drink it myself . . . I often think it's a pity they don't like you drinking good old beer in places like this – don't you?'

Mr Stimpson did not like cocktails, but, by these last words of Gorse, was of course shamed into readily accepting what Gorse had provided for him. The Tempter tempts with shame very often.

'No,' said Mr Stimpson. 'That looks like just what I wanted. But now you're *two* drinks up on me. I mean I owe you *one*, already, as I said last night.'

'Plenty of time,' said Gorse, smoothly.

'Well, here's how,' said Mr Stimpson, and 'Here's how,' said Gorse, and they both drank.

Gorse noticed with pleasure that the inexperienced Mr Stimpson took a large amount of his cocktail with his first mouthful.

It was Gorse's ambition to make Mr Stimpson drink too much tonight.

And, if possible, he would make him fully and uninhibitedly drunk.

If Mr Stimpson drank too much he might disclose many secrets – secrets about the nature of his relationship with Mrs Plumleigh-Bruce, and his real attitude towards it. Mr Stimpson might also, if tactfully handled, disclose such secrets about his own private life as Gorse might, by repeating them deftly to Mrs Plumleigh-Bruce, use against the Estate Agent.

Then, if Mr Stimpson could be led into really serious and really uninhibited drinking, the result might be the disclosure of even more shameful secrets, and also something better still – the performance of some shameful act, which Gorse might witness.

'Your friend not here?' said Mr Stimpson.

'No,' said Gorse, whose friend was fictitious. 'He hopped off just before you came in.'

'And how did business go?'

'Fine,' said Gorse. 'Couldn't have been better. I'm through with all my difficulties and everything's fixed up beautifully. So I'm in a mood for frivolity and gaiety . . . And how did *your* business go?'

'Oh – mine was just ordinary plodding routine.' Mr Stimpson took another large mouthful of his cocktail. 'I'm only a plodding sort of chap, you know. Not a gay spark – like you.'

This early, personal and rather sentimental confession made Gorse suspect that Mr Stimpson had been drinking before he had entered the King's Hotel, and that drink had already slightly affected him.

'Well – I don't know that I'm much of a gay spark,' said Gorse. 'And, by the general look of you, I should say you've done a good deal better out of straightforward plodding than I have in my line . . .'

There was a pause. Then Mr Stimpson, having taken another sip at his drink, looked at Gorse and said, 'Tell me, old man, what *is* your line, exactly? That is if it's not a rude question. If it is, don't *tell* me, but just tell me *off*!'

Because of the premature 'old man' and the premature question, Gorse was now certain that alcohol had affected Mr Stimpson's head.

'No. It's not a rude question at all,' he said. 'But it's rather a difficult one to answer, because I've got so many little lines. What I was dealing with just now – with my friend, who's given me such satisfaction – was about wireless sets – or rather parts. I've got quite a lot of money in that line. But then I hope to take a lot of money out. There *is* money there, you know. In fact I think it's still only in its infancy, and that if you can get in on the ground floor there's a packet to be made.'

'I've no doubt of it,' said Mr Stimpson.

'And then cars is another line of mine – the one I like best, I suppose. I suppose, really, you'd call me a sort of all-round speculator. Do you go in for speculation of any sort?'

'No. I just go jogging along the good old middle path. No fancy stuff for me. Not that I'm not interested in speculation. I always was. What other lines do you indulge in, may I ask?'

Gorse saw that the moment had arrived to change the conversation. His recently revealed speculation in wireless parts had been as fictitious as the friend who, having given him such satisfaction on the matter, had just 'hopped off', and Gorse had not worked out any other fictitious form of speculation.

'Oh – they're much too many and involved to go into,' he said. 'And for Heaven's sake don't let's talk about business tonight. We're on pleasure bent, I trust. I know I am, anyway. Tell me, don't *you* feel that way, when you get out of Reading for a night?'

'I certainly do,' said Mr Stimpson, his mental vision already roving back in the direction of Vigo and Sackville Streets. Gorse guessed roughly where his mind was, but did not want the man to start anything of that sort just at present. Gorse wanted first to do some solid digging – or rather unearthing – on the Plumleigh-Bruce soil.

'And what happened to *you* two last night?' he asked. 'Did you make a night of it?'

'No. Anything but. We just had another drink and both went off home like the respectable citizens that we are – or we're supposed to be.'

'Meaning you're not, really?' said Gorse, with a sly confidence-inviting twinkle in his eye.'

'Well,' said Mr Stimpson, 'that's a question I'd find difficult to answer, really.'

'You mean about yourself, or Mrs Plumleigh-Bruce?' said Gorse, with the same sort of look, perhaps slightly slyer.

'Both, I'd say. It depends on what you mean by respectability, really, doesn't it?'

'You mean to say,' said Gorse, speaking ostensibly in jest, but in fact taking the bull by the horns, 'that you don't look upon Mrs Plumleigh-Bruce as the height – the very cream – of respectability?'

'Ah now,' said Mr Stimpson. 'That'd be telling, wouldn't it?'

'Yes, I suppose it would . . . All the same, something in your eye tells me that there's a story to tell – and that you're the one to do the telling – if there's anybody.'

Gorse, with his wonderful sense of timing, had been watching Mr Stimpson's reactions to alcohol closely, and had hit upon the exact moment in which to put forth a suggestion which at another time might have given offence.

The plodder in Mr Stimpson had suddenly changed into the dog.

'Yes. I wouldn't be surprised if I could tell a thing or two – quite a thing or two . . . Now tell me, old man (or should I say young man?) . . . You're a newcomer to the scene, with a fresh eye. What're *your* impressions of our Lady Joan?'

Mr Stimpson, though speaking in beer-and-cocktail boldness, was honestly seeking the truth. He respected the sophisticated London, Paris-visiting, horse-race-winning young man's judgement, and he wanted to know whether he thought of Mrs Plumleigh-Bruce gravely, as he, Mr Stimpson, had once done, or lightly, as he had recently been trying to do.

'In what way?' said Gorse. 'Physically, intellectually, or morally?'

'All three,' said Mr Stimpson. 'Go on. Begin at the beginning. Physically, for instance?'

'Well. That's hard to say. I'd say that she was tremendously attractive – to a certain type of man. But then there're so many types of men, aren't there?'

'Yes. And so many different ages. Is she attractive to you, for instance?'

'No. Not in that way,' said Gorse, after thinking carefully. 'Not at all in that way.'

'You mean,' said Mr Stimpson, 'she's a bit too long in the tooth for the likes of a young man like you. Come on now, young man. Out with it. We're all lads together now, you know.'

'Long in the tooth? You mean she's got slightly prominent teeth? I don't mind that, and she's got a lovely mouth.'

'No. I *don't* mean that – and you ought to know it. I mean too long in the *tooth* – to old, to put it plainly. For someone of *your* age, at any rate.'

'No – I wouldn't say that. It's just that, although I can see her attractions, I just don't think of her in that way. It's funny.'

Gorse was hedging, for he knew that this conversation would almost as certainly be repeated to Mrs Plumleigh-Bruce by Mr Stimpson, as it would, in an edited or elaborated form, be repeated to her by himself. Having built up Mrs Plumleigh-Bruce as a radiator of universal happiness, a comforter, and a cathedral, it was necessary to stick to his guns. The woman must remain, somehow or other, pretty holy. And also nothing must be said against her physical attractions.

'I don't think it's funny,' said Mr Stimpson. 'I think it's only natural, in someone of your age.'

'Well, maybe it's that,' said Gorse. 'I can only say again that I never think of her that way . . . I feel – it may be a silly thing to say – that it'd be a sort of – well – sacrilege.'

This at once slightly nettled and absolutely delighted Mr Stimpson. He was slightly nettled because Mrs Plumleigh-Bruce – if truly sacred – could not, perhaps, be treated in the light way for which he had lately been making mental preparations. On the other hand he was absolutely delighted at being told she was sacred. If he married her, it suited him down to the ground. If he made her his mistress it was just as good. And then, remembering the countless deep kisses which had taken place at Glen Alan, his bosom swelled secretly with the pride of the violator – the masculine, worldly-wise snatcher of veils from the temple. If only the poor young man, the 'smitten' Gorse, knew what had gone on at Glen Alan! The thought that Gorse did not – that the neophyte merely admired, or, conceivably, worshipped, from afar – added to his delight. Indeed his heart was so filled with sudden, gushing, alcoholic pity for the now almost pathetic Gorse, that he could not refrain, having taken another sip at his drink, from gushing.

'You know, I *like* you, young man,' he said. 'I did the first moment I saw you.'

'Well,' said Gorse, 'that's a very nice thing to be told . . . But what on earth do you like in me?'

'I like the way you speak about Women,' said Mr Stimpson. 'I like the respectful way you speak about them – as you did just then.'

'But surely there's nothing particularly likeable about that,' said Gorse, assuming the charming, puzzled demeanour of one who was little more than sixteen years old. 'It's only right to respect them – or to respect the right kind – isn't it?'

'Yes. Certainly. Of course it is,' said Mr Stimpson, whose soul was growing larger and larger. 'But it was the way you did it. It was so youthful – so straightforward and youthful – that's what I liked.'

It may be thought strange that Mr Stimpson's soul could get so large, so quickly, on the strength of two pints of beer and the better part of a single strong cocktail.

Gorse, in fact, who did not know what he had been drinking, imagined that he must have had a good deal more than he had in fact had.

The explanation was, however, that Mr Stimpson had been drinking heavily with business friends at lunch-time. And it is a well-known drinking law that heavy lunch-time drinking can be extremely treacherous. Its effects, having lain seemingly more or less dormant during the late afternoon, are often suddenly resurrected, released as by the pulling of a trigger, and given a sort of fresh, augmented, wild potency, by merely a few drinks taken again in the early evening. Many a man who has drunk heavily at lunch-time will become quite absurdly, excitably, and, to his friend, inexplicably drunk over only a small amount of alcohol thrown down his throat at such a time.

'Well –' began Gorse, but Mr Stimpson would not let him go on.

'Ah, youth, youth, *youth* . . .' said Mr Stimpson, looking into the distance. 'So confused, so poetical, so *happy* . . . What wouldn't I give for *my* youth again.'

'But surely there's not all *that* difference in our ages,' said Gorse.

'Oh yes, there is, and you know there is. I'm middle-aged – nearer an old man than a younger man. I'm just a middle-aged old plodder . . . Well – I suppose it has advantages. You know your way around, and you're treated with more respect . . . And that's *another* thing I like about you, my boy.'

'Oh – what's that?'

'*Respect,*' said Mr Stimpson, finishing off his drink and looking Gorse straight in the eye. 'I like the respect you show to your elders. It came out only the other night, in the way you called me "Sir", if you want to know. You don't get much of that sort of thing nowadays, and it doesn't mean much, but I liked it.'

The sardonic Gorse was here tempted to say 'Well, I'm very glad to hear it, sir,' but decided not to go to quite such lengths, for the time being at any rate. So he said merely, 'Well, I'm very glad to hear it.'

'Not that it *means* anything,' said Mr Stimpson. 'Good Heavens, *I* don't want any of your silly "sirring". You and I are out on the spree, now – just a couple of lads together . . . And so what about another drink? Same again? I don't know what that was, but it was very nice. So shall we have the same again? You do the ordering, and I'll do the paying. Go on.'

'Right,' said Gorse, and spoke to the barmaid, who was near, and with whom he was on friendly terms. 'Can we have the same again, Pixie?' he said. 'Just exactly the same again?'

And here, unseen by Mr Stimpson, he gave the barmaid a look, which was in effect a wink, and which intimated that Mr Stimpson was to be given a powerful drink once more, while Gorse would remain content with another weak one. The barmaid fully understood Gorse. She had done things like this with him before.

'Yes . . . Respect . . . Respect,' said Mr Stimpson, almost as if he were reciting, as they waited for the drinks. 'And respect for Women, too . . . You stick to it – stick to it. Maybe you'll learn things later that'll shatter your illusions – maybe you won't . . . But stick to it while you've got it. There's nothing like respect for Women – nothing. Treat every one of them as Sacredly as you'd treat your Mother – that's my advice to you.'

Here Gorse saw that he must not overdo, or allow Mr Stimpson to overdo, this sacred stuff. If he did, he would clearly be unable to extract any sharply material information about the relationship between Mr Stimpson and Mrs Plumleigh-Bruce. Nor must he allow Mr Stimpson to get too drunk too quickly.

'Do you mean you've personally had your illusions shattered?' he said, hoping that this might lead to a more solid and earthly level of discussion.

Mr Stimpson paused heavily, and swayed slightly.

'I fear I have,' he said at last. 'Yes. I fear I have. Yes, many's the castle I've built in the air that's fallen about my head like a pack of cards. *Many*.'

'But not with the right sort of woman, surely?' said Gorse.

Mr Stimpson, perhaps blinded and confused by a kind of snow-storm, or blizzard, of cards from castles falling about his head, suddenly switched from pure idealism to fearful cynicism.

'Is there such a thing?' he asked. 'I wonder. If there is, name her.'

'Well,' said the audacious Gorse. 'What about Mrs Plumleigh-Bruce, for instance?'

Mr Stimpson again paused.

'No women are goddesses, you know,' he said. 'They've all got feet of clay, somewhere . . . I could tell you things that'd surprise you . . .'

'Could you?'

'Yes. I could indeed . . . Pretty girl,' said Mr Stimpson, alluding to the barmaid, who had just put the new drinks in front of them, and gone off to serve another customer.

'Yes. She is. Very pretty,' said Gorse.

'Where's she gone to? I haven't paid,' said Mr Stimpson, fishing in his trouser pocket.

'Oh – she'll come back. She and I usually square up at the end.'

'Yes. Very pretty,' said Mr Stimpson, looking at the barmaid from a distance. 'Very pretty indeed.'

'But – I suspect – with feet of clay,' said Gorse, in order to lead back Mr Stimpson to Mrs Plumleigh-Bruce. 'There I'd certainly agree with you – in fact, I know it for a fact. But a barmaid in the King's Hotel isn't the same thing as a Mrs Plumleigh-Bruce, I imagine.'

'Isn't she?' said Mr Stimpson, who had now made a complete *volte-face*, and who, swelled out with new cynicism, took a large mouthful of his new drink.

'I don't know. Is she? I certainly don't think she'd be so easy-going with men as the beauty serving us yonder. In fact, I wouldn't say that she'd be easy-going at all, in that direction.'

'Really? . . . That's all you know.'

'Well,' said Gorse. 'You surprise me, I must say . . . I mean, she's an attractive woman, and no doubt a lot of men want to – well – kiss her, and all that. But I should think she's pretty adamant even about that sort of thing.'

'Would you? . . . You'd be surprised.'

'But how do you know?'

'How do you think?'

'From personal experience, you mean?'

'I do.'

'Well – there's no harm in kissing. It's an attractive woman's due after all. She looks upon it as a sort of homage. But I don't expect the lady in question – and she's obviously a lady in every sense of the term – lets matters go further than that.'

'Oh, no,' said Mr Stimpson. 'I don't mean she goes the Whole Hog, or anything like that. But she certainly kisses, I can assure you. And *how* she kisses – believe me. Oh boy! – as our American friends say. She goes the limit there all right! She goes the whole hog when it comes to kisses. And she might go the whole hog altogether, if treated in the right way. "Wimmin is funny critters" as the old countryman said . . . They only want a bit of handling, you know, my boy.'

Gorse's nature was not a delicate one, but he was slightly nauseated by Mr Stimpson's astonishingly quick leap into this sort of vulgarity and lack of reticence. Gorse, who drank, who was only able to drink, little himself, was always repelled by drunkenness.

He was happy, though, in having obtained, with such astonishing rapidity, as much as he wanted to know about Mr Stimpson and Mrs Plumleigh-Bruce, and as much conversational material to repeat to the latter as he could desire. It hardly needed editing or elaborating.

Mr Stimpson had said that she was long in the tooth, that she had feet of clay, that he could 'tell' Gorse some things about her, that he had kissed her, that she had returned such kisses in a violent 'Oh boy!' way, and that she might, if properly handled, 'go the whole hog'. What more could one want?

'Well,' he said. 'I must say you surprise me. But I should think she'd be pretty fastidious, whatever she did. It wouldn't happen just with any man who came along. After all, she's a lady.'

'Oh no . . . No Tom, Dick, or Harry for her. And she's a lady all right, from the top of her fingers to the tip of her toes. *Breeding*, old boy, that's what she's got. It sticks out a mile.'

'It certainly does.'

Gorse had now to decide on his next move with this foolish man. He had succeeded, according to plan, in getting him drunk and in making the required disclosures. Bur now his second plan had to be put into operation. This was, as has been said, to make Mr Stimpson even more fully and uninhibitedly drunk and so indulge in shameful behaviour.

But here Gorse had to be careful. If Mr Stimpson became too drunk he would be incapable of any sort of behaviour.

PART SEVEN

ODETTE

Chapter One

I

The main characteristic of people like Mr Stimpson is their extraordinary ability, mentally and morally, to eat their cake and have it too. After which they consume it.

They will bathe gloriously, firstly in the Sacred, and then (without any sense of inconsistency or knowledge of the transition) burst into the Profane – and will leap back from the Profane to the Sacred in the same way.

Mr Stimpson had exemplified this splendidly tonight with Gorse in his lightning jump from almost scout-masterly idealism into swaggering worldliness.

In the same way, such men will turn, at a moment's notice, from the keenly shrewd to the lusciously sentimental, and from the grasping to the giving – though they seldom give away much materially.

Again, they will, as rapidly, and with one and the same man, turn from the obsequious pursuit of favours or patronage, to the boastful giving of favours (or talk of it) and a patronizing attitude. In accusing the Jews of doing this they are very black pots calling grey kettles black.

Tonight Mr Stimpson had nervously entered the King's Hotel willing to seek worldly knowledge from Gorse, but only a little time had passed before he was lavishly bestowing worldly knowledge upon the latter.

After another quarter of an hour two further drinks for both had been almost finished by both, and Gorse was still being patronized, and Mr Stimpson was now, to use his own expression to Gorse, Seeing through Gorse like a *Book*.

2

This magnificently transparent Book had appeared upon the scene because Gorse, slightly embarrassed by Mr Stimpson's loud voice, had dropped his in the hope of infecting Mr Stimpson with his own more seemly tone. But Mr Stimpson had taken this for dejection on Gorse's part, and had, with spirituous cunning, discerned its cause.

'*You're* looking very glum,' Mr Stimpson had suddenly said. 'What's the matter?'

'No. I'm not glum,' said Gorse. 'What should make you think I am?'

'Oh yes – you are. Don't try and fool me,' said Mr Stimpson. 'I can see through you like a *Book*. I can, you know.'

'And what can you see?' Gorse asked.

'The Green-Eyed God,' said Mr Stimpson. 'Ever heard of him? He's there all right. The Little Green-Eyed God.'

'You mean jealousy?' Gorse asked.

'I do,' said Mr Stimpson. 'I can see through you like a *Book*.'

'But jealousy about what?'

Gorse was trying to look as much like an easily read (and jealous) Book as was possible, for the results of Mr Stimpson's violent perspicacity, if revealed, might give him some clue as to Mr Stimpson's real thoughts about him – and it would be useful to know these.

'About a Certain Lady,' said Mr Stimpson. 'You're a bit smitten with her – aren't you? Go on. Admit it.'

'Well,' said Gorse. 'Perhaps I am a little. But in a very humble and reverent way.'

'There you are! I told you so!'

'And what do you mean by jealousy?' Gorse asked.

'Well, perhaps I shouldn't've said jealousy,' said Mr Stimpson. 'I ought to have said disappointment. I've gone and shattered your illusions about the lady, haven't I? Don't try and deny it! I can see through you like a Book, old boy.'

Gorse was already getting rather impatient at having to look and behave like a Book, particularly as Mr Stimpson kept on looking and slightly nodding at him, through his thick-lensed spectacles, as if he were turning page after page of it with delicious comprehension. But Gorse, as usual, curbed his impatience.

'Well,' he said. 'I suppose what you said did come as a bit of a shock.'

'I know it did. I can see through you like a Book. A *Volume*, my boy!' said Mr Stimpson, as if a Volume were something very different from and much easier to read than a Book.

There was a silence in which Gorse tried to look like a Volume.

Mr Stimpson was now not only enjoying his superiority over and patronage of Gorse. He was, after the way of his type, enjoying to the full a splurging belief in his own fiction. He had now got Gorse exactly where he wanted him – a worshipper from afar of Mrs Plumleigh-Bruce. And no doubts assailed him as to whether or not Gorse in fact stood in the place assigned to him. This self-deceiving self-assurance, this psychological grabbing of everything in every way, was partially attributable to drink, but mostly to the provincial businessman mentality mentioned above.

'Yes – like a *Volume* . . .' said Mr Stimpson, swaying visibly as he ruminated. 'And perhaps I did wrong. It never does to shatter illusions. I did wrong. You're only a kid you know, for all your cleverness. One should never shatter illusions.'

'Well,' said Gorse. 'On the other hand, it's no use living in a dream world – is it?'

'No. Never shatter illusions. Never,' said Mr Stimpson, with an air of severe admonition, as if it had been Gorse who had committed this error. 'Never *do* it.'

Gorse, without replying, nodded humble but hearty agreement, as one who, enlightened by a master, has decided never again to shatter illusions.

Mr Stimpson had, it will be seen, had his cake, eaten it, and consumed it. He went on to munch it.

'No,' he said. 'Keep your eyes on the stars.

> "Two men looked out of prison bars,
> One saw the earth. The other saw the stars."

That's a poem. My old Mother taught me that – God bless her – and I've never forgotten it. See the stars, my boy! See the stars!'

At this there was a very moving Old-Motherly silence, in which both seemed to be looking upwards from a cocktail bar to the stars. Neither was, however. Gorse was wondering how he was going to keep this man from getting incapably drunk, and Mr Stimpson expressed his real thoughts by asking, in a secretive, confidential, but alarmingly sudden way, 'Where's the Gents' here, old boy?'

Gorse told him what he wanted to know, and Mr Stimpson left the bar.

Gorse took advantage of his absence to put his own weak drink in place of Mr Stimpson's and into Mr Stimpson's drink he poured powdered Aspirin from a folded piece of paper. This was taken from his waistcoat pocket. When the far-seeing Gorse saw a night of drinking ahead of him he nearly always took the precaution of carrying powdered Aspirin about with him. He did this for his own sake, in the belief, derived from a conversation with a chemist's assistant, that the sedative held drunkenness at bay. But tonight the position was reversed: he was defending not himself but his companion from drunkenness.

He hoped that, when Mr Stimpson returned, he might be more sober. Mr Stimpson, however, was a good deal less sober.

He showed, on the contrary, in his gait as he moved towards Gorse, that intense upright sobriety which always indicates its polar opposite, and he at once returned to the Book, which, seemingly, was on his brain.

3

'Yes,' he said, laying his hand ponderously on Gorse's shoulder. 'A Book. I saw through you like a Book . . . No one's ever saw through a book as I've sawn through you.' He was conscious of some verbal or grammatical error in what he had just said, and he hastened to rectify it. '*I* saw through you. . . *I* saw. . . I'm a saw-mill, in some ways, when it comes to sawing. Not that I get *sore*. Oh *dear* me, no!. . .'

'Well, I hope you're not sore with me,' said Gorse.

'Sore with you! God forbid,' said Mr Stimpson. 'I *like* you. I liked you from the moment I saw you. We're lads together tonight. We're going to be lads. Are we or aren't we?'

Though Mr Stimpson had in mind nothing particular in what he had just said, Gorse saw his chance, and leapt to it.

'Yes,' he said. 'I'm game if you are.'

'Game for what?' said Mr Stimpson, momentarily more than ever confused.

'Game for anything,' said Gorse, with a knowing look. 'Game for games – what?'

Knowing looks always strike home with inebriated men – who are, of course, the most knowing on earth, and who will often force themselves into a sort of self-restraint in order to do credit to their own knowingness.

Mr Stimpson braced himself. He saw Gorse's meaning, and his mental vision again wandered back towards Vigo and Sackville Streets.

'Games where?' he asked.

'Well – there's only one sort of game that I know of around these parts,' said Gorse. 'It's one of the oldest games in the world, and we're right bang in the middle of where it's played most.'

Here Mr Stimpson took fright. He thought that Gorse was alluding to the King's Hotel – and this was not in the Wardour Street adventurer's line at all. It was too 'flash', dangerous, and intimidating because above his head. Also Mr Stimpson was, just at that moment, rather less interested in encounters with women than in drinking and conversation – in seeing and sawing through people.

Also he did not want to give away to Gorse that he ever embarked upon such enterprises. If he decided to do so later, he would somehow shake Gorse off.

'Yes. It's old enough,' he said. 'And dangerous enough, too. *And* expensive.'

'But all nice things are dangerous and expensive, aren't they?' said Gorse.

'*You* know a thing or two, young man – don't you?' said Mr Stimpson. 'Be careful you don't know too much.'

'I certainly know my way around this part of the world, anyway,' said Gorse. 'And if *you* don't, I'll be only too happy to show you.'

'No,' said Mr Stimpson. 'Not for me. It's all right for a young chap like you – but it's different for me . . . You're a gay young spark with all those things in front of you – and quite right too. But I'm just a silly old plodder – that's all I am.'

'Really? That's not how you strike me at all, you know,' said Gorse. 'In fact you give me exactly the opposite impression, and I bet *you* could give *me* a wrinkle or two, if you cared.'

But this piece of flattery, to Gorse's surprise, entirely failed. Mr Stimpson had stopped seeing and sawing and had gone mad about plodding. And plod he meant to.

'No,' he said. 'I'm just a plodder. I plod along. Plod, plod, plod. That's me . . . I'm nobody. I'm just a *clod*, perhaps . . .'

'Oh – don't say that,' said Gorse, but Mr Stimpson was adamant about his own cloddishness.

'Yes, just a clod. That's what I am. A clod that clods.'

Gorse here observed, with some consternation, that Mr Stimpson was entering that comatose, rhyming phase known to experts in inebriation. The man, in fact, was practically asleep on his feet, and talking in his sleep.

'A clod that plods. Nods,' said Mr Stimpson, and nodded.

Gorse was silent, wondering whether it would soon be necessary either to abandon Mr Stimpson or have him removed from the hotel.

Suddenly, however, like a snorer who wakes himself with his own snore, Mr Stimpson stood at attention and shot out a sharp observation – so sharp that it seemed almost to be trying to bring a mentally wandering Gorse to order.

'A nod's as good as a wink to a blind horse,' he said, most aggressively. 'Is it, or isn't it?'

Gorse agreed that it was, but did not like Mr Stimpson's quarter-deck voice and manner.

'Or a horse is as good as a wink to a blind whatever-it-is. Or isn't it? . . . It's all the same, isn't it?'

Gorse again concurred.

'I suppose you think I'm drunk,' said Mr Stimpson, having gazed at Gorse with glassy penetration for a long while. 'But I'm not, you know. I may be a plodder, but I jog along all right. I can take my drink all right. I may be a silly old buffer – but I jog along. And sometimes I go the whole hog.'

'Do you?'

'I do. Wasn't that what we were talking about?'

'Yes. It was.'

'Yes. I knew it was. I may be just an old buffer, but I remember things all right.'

'And so you go the whole hog sometimes, do you?' said Gorse.

'I *do*. Although I'm just an Ancient old Buffer. Who *said* I didn't?'

Gorse welcomed this less comatose and much more combative mood, but realized that he must not permit Mr Stimpson to become too violent. The thing to do was to let Mr Stimpson – the vigorously, almost vindictively, self-styled old buffer – let Mr Stimpson Anciently Buff, plod, nod, jog, and be a clod to his heart's content – but to do so in the direction into which Gorse was anxious to steer him.

'Well,' said Gorse. 'It's sometimes just the old plodders who go the whole hog a good deal more than the rest – isn't it? Or that's my experience.'

'And your experience is correct,' said Mr Stimpson, mollified, but not wholly so.

Gorse realized that he was now dealing with a child (very young people bear an amazing resemblance to very drunk people) and Gorse was good with children. He certainly did not like them, but they liked him. The same thing applied to dogs, and that this should have been so was regarded as a strange paradox by those who wrote about Gorse later. There was, however, no paradox. The powers of mystical discernment popularly attributed to dogs and children are in fact practically non-existent.

'Yes. Give me the plodders,' said Gorse. 'Give me the plodders, all the time.'

Mr Stimpson, suddenly and capriciously, that is to say childishly, more sober, now saw a chance of doing what Gorse did so often and so well – killing two or three birds with one stone. He could, he thought, if he played his cards correctly, plod, jog, go the whole hog before long, and get worldly advice into the bargain.

'Yes,' he said. 'I'm a plodder all right. But sometimes we old plodders get into a bit of a rut, you know.'

'What about?'

'What we were talking about. Going the whole hog. How'd *you* set about it in these parts, for instance? You know your London better than me, perhaps. I've been jogging along in Reading for a bit too long, I sometimes think.'

Mr Stimpson still had in mind Vigo and Sackville Streets. What he had seen there earlier in the evening had impressed him as something a good deal better than his familiar Wardour Street; and, in his present alcoholic audacity, he was anxious to try out new territory. At the same time he was afraid of the unknown.

'How do you mean – "these parts"?' said Gorse. 'Exactly?'

'Well – not so far from here. I saw some pretty spicy things round in Sackville Street just before I came in here, as it happens.'

'Yes, Sackville Street's all right,' said Gorse. 'But one can do better than that.'

'Really? Where? How?'

'Well – one can go farther afield without walking much further – into foreign lands, as it were, if it suits your taste. Of course, you must remember I've just returned from Paris.'

Mr Stimpson recoiled, both with fear and repulsion, at this, and became more sober still. Gorse was obviously alluding to Frenchwomen.

'Oh,' he said. 'You mean the Frogs – do you? No. No Frogs for me. Sorry, old man. You like 'em, don't you? But Frogs aren't up my street.'

'They aren't up mine, really,' said Gorse. 'But they have their uses – the female of the species have, at any rate.'

'No, thanks. No fancy stuff for me. I don't go in for fancy stuff. I've never tried it, and I don't mean to start it.'

'Really,' said Gorse. 'You mean you've never been with a French girl?'

'No. And never mean to,' said Mr Stimpson, swilling off the remainder of his aspirin-powdered drink. 'Come on, let's have another of these.'

By good fortune and raising his voice he caught the attention of the barmaid, who was now very busy, and gave the order.

'Well,' said Gorse. 'I think you're missing something. You get better value for your money, even if you do have to pay a little more for it.'

Gorse had a reason for pressing a French rather than an English woman upon Mr Stimpson.

Gorse was always very popular with prostitutes, with whom he mixed only socially, and who liked him. (In later days there were many West-End women of the streets who hotly defended him.)

His popularity here was easily explained. His assured sense of social superiority made him very much at ease with such women, who, because of their low educational level and somewhat debased sense of humour, were pleased, or even delighted, by his dashing air, his monocle, and the 'Silly Ass' act in which, with them, he was able to indulge to the full. 'Hullo, girls!' or 'Hullo, old things!' or Hullo, old beans!' were his cries when entering their haunts, where he was thought of as a 'card' a 'one', and, though foolish (perhaps *because* foolish) a 'gentleman'. A 'public-school' voice and a monocle are regarded as symbols of a 'gentleman' in such credulous circles. But he was also thought of as a 'real gentleman'. For he was generous with his money, made no amorous advances, and frequently went out of his way to do one of these girls or women a 'good turn' – such as lending her money (usually repaid), or giving her a lift in his car.

Gorse was not totally disinterested here, for he knew that all sorts of uses and contacts might arise from such friendships. He was also, in his precocious way, aware of that almost drivellingly sentimental loyalty and generosity which is part of the looseness of these loose livers. He knew that, should he ever be in trouble, financially or criminally, help would be gushingly forthcoming. However, it may be said that, on the whole, he liked their company for its own sake.

Recently Gorse had taken to frequenting a small café in Mayfair in which mostly Frenchwomen resorted late at night, and where he was already a popular figure.

He knew exactly where these Frenchwomen walked, and was anxious to make Mr Stimpson walk amongst them.

He might thus, not only do another 'good turn' to one of his café acquaintances: he might be able to learn the exact locality of the adventure upon which Mr Stimpson was, obviously, determined to embark. Furthermore, he might be able, afterwards, to learn the nature of the adventure in detail.

And so Gorse risked incurring the displeasure of Mr Stimpson by boldly praising the French.

4

New drinks were brought: Gorse, though severely lectured, stuck to his guns about the French, and Mr Stimpson, swallowing another furious mouthful, turned his back on Gorse to look around the crowded room, and became, in a flash, deliriously drunk again, and was in his delirium converted to the French and the whole world. He liked the world. He liked everything that was in it.

'Frogs – eh?' he said, turning again to Gorse. 'All right then – frogs it shall be. If *you* want frogs – *I* want frogs. Lead me to 'em – worthy varlet . . . Always believed in trying everything once. Lead on, sirrah! On, knave! On! "Charge, Chesters, charge, on, Stanley on!" were the last words of Marmion. Excuse my French. Poetry . . . Sir Walter Scott – the old bastard. Bart, too. Learned him at school. Bloody bore, if you ask me. However, lead on, noble lord . . .'

'Very well,' said Gorse, now aware that people were looking at and listening to his companion. 'We'll go directly we've paid. But I suppose we must do that . . . Pixie . . . How much do we owe you?'

He put his hand to his hip pocket, but Mr Stimpson would have none of this.

'Oh no,' said Mr Stimpson. 'Oh *dear* me no . . . Oh *dear* me no . . . Me . . . *All* me. *Only* me . . .' He produced a wallet from his breast pocket.

'But you can't pay for all the drinks,' Gorse protested.

'Me were the words I *used*,' said Mr Stimpson. 'And Me were the words I *meant* . . . Me. Simple word. Second person singular – or plural – or accusative. It doesn't bother me. *Accusative* . . .'

Mr Stimpson then said that he wasn't Accusing anybody, and found himself in difficulties with the money in his wallet. Gorse aided him, extracting two pounds from the wallet, which he managed to get back into Mr Stimpson's pocket, and he gave the barmaid the notes.

While the barmaid got the change Mr Stimpson went on saying that he had accused nobody, and that nobody had accused anyone, that there was too much suspicion in the world. Everybody accused everybody else and what was wanted was Trust.

He then called Gorse his Trusty Companion – his Trusty Companion of the Bath – and picked up the change from his two pounds from the counter.

Gorse, using the same methods as those which he had adopted with his friend Ronnie Shooter in Paris not long ago, allowed Mr Stimpson to pay without protest. In the morning he would remind Mr Stimpson of the debt, and insist on repaying it.

Mr Stimpson, however, did not know that, in a place of this sort, a barmaid should be tipped, and this error Gorse could not allow. He winked at his friend Pixie, and gave her two and sixpence from his own pocket.

'Well, then,' he said. 'Off we go – what?'

'Fine. Off we go. Off . . . Lead on, then, good my page,' said Mr Stimpson, and, having put his arm on Gorse's shoulder, gave Gorse a chance to assist him from the bar, and up the stairs.

Mr Stimpson took the stairs in a very silent and serious spirit. With his arm around Gorse he leaned over them, looking at them intently, not like a man walking up them, but like a General (in a third-rate picture or illustration depicting military headquarters at the most desperate moment of battle) fiercely scrutinizing maps and making dramatic decisions.

'All right,' he said, when he had gone through all the maps, and was on the ground floor. 'All right.'

As if with these words dramatically announcing that the battle had been won, he dispensed with the assistance of Gorse's shoulder, and made for the revolving doors.

These he reached in reasonably good order, and, preceding Gorse, got through very finely. When Gorse had joined him in the street, though, he wanted assistance again, and put his arm, with an affectation of pure affection, around Gorse.

'Nobly done, good mine page,' he said. 'Now whither?'

'You just follow me,' said Gorse. 'I'll show you whither.'

'Whither thou goest I shall go too,' said Mr Stimpson, 'and thy people shall be whither thou goest . . . Frogs, I fancy.'

'Yes,' said Gorse. 'But you mustn't call them that, you know, if you meet one.'

'Why not? They *are* Frogs, aren't they?'

'Well – one's got to be tactful, hasn't one?'

'Tact? Very well. Tact it shall be,' said Mr Stimpson, as they walked along in the direction of Dover Street. 'Tact with Frogs . . . Tact with Frogs . . .'

There was a silence, and then Mr Stimpson said, 'Tact with *Logs*,' and, receiving no reply from Gorse, said, 'Tact with Cogs.' He was now rhyming-drunk again, but, since he was walking reasonably steadily with Gorse's support, Gorse did not mind this.

'Tact with *Hogs* . . .' said Mr Stimpson. 'Tact with *Hogs* . . . Tact with Dogs . . . Tact with *Cogs*. Cogs. we're all Cogs in a Great Machine, you know. Aren't we?'

'Yes,' said Gorse. 'That's all we are.'

'Tact with Fogs,' said Mr Stimpson, and then went, in an orderly way, through the whole alphabet from beginning to end – mentioning, laboriously, Tact with Bogs, Cogs, Dogs, Fogs, Gogs, Hogs, Jogs, Kogs, Logs, Mogs, Nogs, Pogs, Quogs, Rogs, Sogs, Togs, Vogs, Wogs, Yogs, and Zogs.

Doing this took him some time, and because of the mental concentration demanded by the feat, he was again more sober when he had finished.

Indeed, by the time they had reached (and at Gorse's instigation turned up) Dover Street, Mr Stimpson was walking without Gorse's aid, and had returned to Frogs, and was complaining of their absence.

'All right – just wait a bit, and follow me,' said Gorse, but no sooner had he said this than, to Gorse's annoyance, the matter was taken out of his hands.

The familiar 'Where you go, dar*leeng*?' was heard from a doorway, and Mr Stimpson stopped.

5

Gorse was annoyed because he had not as yet got Mr Stimpson into the exact quarter he wanted, and he did not know the woman who had accosted them. He was upset in his managerial capacity. He would have liked, indeed, to have led Mr Stimpson on, but Mr Stimpson, having heard the accent of a Frenchwoman, would not be led on.

The Frenchwoman – a short, dark, rapacious-looking woman – in moving from the doorway had in fact ignored Mr Stimpson and addressed herself to Gorse. But Mr Stimpson did not realize this.

'Ah-ha!' said Mr Stimpson, and bowed low, adding, 'Madame!'

'I give you a nice time?' said the Frenchwoman, now rather confused and addressing both. 'You have nice time with me?'

'No,' said Gorse. 'Not for me. Definitely not for me. And I'm afraid my friend here's a bit beyond it.'

'Beyond eet? He drink too much? Ah, poor Monsieur!' She looked at Gorse. 'Then I give him nice time and he get better – no?'

'No. Really –' began Gorse, but now Mr Stimpson was controlling the situation.

'Drunk too much?' he said. 'Beyond it? Who said I've been drinking too much?'

'No. Of course you not drink too much. So I give you nice time? No?'

The woman, Gorse saw, was now turning against himself. So also was Mr Stimpson, whose momentary recovery was remarkable and bulldoggish. Gorse thought quickly, and decided to keep on the right side of both.

'No,' he said to the woman. 'We really are a bit beyond it, you know. But if you could take us both back for a cup of black coffee – we might get better. What about it, darling?' He winked at her, as if to call attention to his friend's state. 'Strong black coffee – that's the thing. *Café noir. Très fort*. Agree?'

The woman looked at both, trying to make up her mind.

'I'll make it worth your while,' said Gorse. 'You needn't worry about *that* side of it.'

At this Mr Stimpson suddenly lurched sideways, and assisted the street-walker in making a decision. She had seen from Gorse's wink and promise that he was sober and presumably reliable, and she had seen from Mr Stimpson's lurch that he was spectacularly drunk. The proposition, in fact, looked exceedingly promising to her. Drunk men are lavish with money, and should this one prove aggressive or parsimonious, she had a protector in Gorse. She took Gorse's side at once, winking back at him. At the same time she took a patronizing attitude towards Mr Stimpson, going up to him.

'Ah – poor old thing,' she said. 'You drink too much. You come with me. Odette – she makes you well. She gives you coffee and makes you well. She gives you nice time. She gives you what you want. The poor old thing – he drink too much wine. Odette make him well.'

As they moved on she kept up this chatter, which displeased Gorse, while apparently delighting Mr Stimpson, who was now silent. Gorse did not like the mixture, in this woman, of rapacious looks and skittish talk. But there was nothing to be done.

Odette lived quite near, and they were soon mounting the many stairs leading to her flat. Mr Stimpson again made General's maps of stairs, and at this Odette was even more offensively skittish than ever as she assisted him.

They entered her flat, which had two main rooms – a bedroom and sitting-room – and a kitchen and a bathroom.

All of these were highly characteristic, in their furnishing and atmosphere, of such a woman's flat. The kitchen was dirty and disordered: the walls of the bathroom were peeling around a rusting bath. There was a large doll on the bed of the bedroom – whose walls displayed provocative drawings of girls, along with a crucifix bearing a plaster image of a crucified Christ. In the sitting-room there were statuettes of nude girls, two more dolls, and religious pictures. In brief – the familiar rust, dolls, dirt, girls, and emblems of piety everywhere. These flats change hands incessantly, collecting the symbols of the different moods of their occupants, nearly all of whom are constant at least to religion.

Mr Stimpson was fairly easily persuaded to lie down on the bed, while Odette went into the kitchen with Gorse to make black coffee.

Here terms were discussed, and Odette found that she was dealing with a very much more sharp (yet calm and knowledgeable) antagonist than she had expected. There was, indeed, haggling –

the usual weary, dreary haggling amidst surroundings of dirt, dust, dolls, girls, and emblems of piety – in which Gorse used Mr Stimpson's drunkenness as a weapon, claiming that two pounds was reasonable compensation for a cup of black coffee and less than an hour of Odette's time.

During this contest Gorse went into the bedroom and found, to his delight, that Mr Stimpson was fast asleep. He removed Mr Stimpson's wallet from his breast pocket, and, having put it into his own, he returned to the kitchen.

Here he reported that Mr Stimpson was asleep, and said that he would fetch his own car, which was in a garage not far from where they were, and take him away.

Having been given two pounds, which Gorse extracted from his own hip pocket, Odette allowed him to leave the flat in order to get his car.

Gorse was away less than twenty minutes.

When he returned he found that the hopeful Odette had been attempting to restore Mr Stimpson to a normal condition – arduously but ineffectually. Mr Stimpson was less than half awake on the bed, and the only words he was capable of bringing out (or apparently knew) was *Frogs* . . . He answered all queries as to his condition and capability of moving with this word.

He was at last made to rise, however, and at last left the flat with Gorse. The disgruntled Frenchwoman, who in Gorse's absence had, needless to say, searched Mr Stimpson's pockets (in vain), nearly slammed the door in their faces.

Gorse, having got Mr Stimpson into his car, managed to extract the address of his sister in Richmond, and drove him to it.

Mr Stimpson was, perhaps, fully able to enter his sister's house without assistance. But Gorse insisted upon aiding him – aiding him, most skilfully, to sway rather than to walk properly. The frightened sister – a widow of about sixty – was more than grateful to Gorse, who helped her to get Mr Stimpson to bed, and who asked her her telephone number. He wanted, he said, to telephone Mr Stimpson in the morning, to see that he was all right.

The grave, sober, sane, tolerant young man then drove back to his West Kensington lodging – in the grave, sane, sober, tolerant spirit which characterized him.

Chapter Two

1

Mr Stimpson, next morning, was given a handsome breakfast in bed by his sister, but he did not want to eat it at all.

He wondered what he could do with it, and even contemplated making a plausible mess of his plates, and then enclosing eggs, bacon, porridge, toast and marmalade in some newspaper, and hiding these ingredients in his suit-case – this in order not to offend, and to preserve his dignity in front of, his sister.

But, alas, he had left his suit-case at Paddington Station yesterday morning, meaning to pick it up later in the day. He remembered this much about yesterday – but little else.

He was saved, temporarily, from much gloomy plotting of this sort by the announcement, made by his sister from outside a knocked door, that he was wanted on the telephone below.

Dressed only in the shirt and dressing-gown in which he had been put to bed last night (the dressing-gown had once belonged to his widowed sister's husband) he went, slipperless, downstairs to the telephone, and was greeted by a jovial voice.

2

'Hullo,' said Gorse. 'And how are *we* this morning?'

'Oh . . . Hullo . . . I'm all right,' said Mr Stimpson, who did not exactly take to Gorse's obvious 'you' implied by his underlining of the word 'we', and who decided to be defiant. 'I'm in the middle of breakfast, as a matter of fact.'

Thus a slipperless man, dressed only in a shirt and a borrowed dressing-gown, endeavoured to give a picture of an orderly, respectable citizen having breakfast, as it were, *en famille*.

'Enjoying it?' said Gorse, again with offensive jollity.

'Yes. Fine, thanks,' said Mr Stimpson. 'How are *you*?'

Mr Stimpson, because he was as yet hardly able to remember a single thing about last night, had a faint hope that Gorse might have been drunk too, in which case his underlining of the 'you' would be striking back and home.

'Fine,' said Gorse. 'In the pink. But there's a spot of bother.'

'Oh. What's that?'

'Well – I've been on the phone this morning, and it looks as though there're still some snags in my business and that I'll have to stay up another night. And that means that I can't run you down in my little bus to Reading, I'm afraid.'

'Oh . . . *That's* all right,' said Mr Stimpson, overjoyed at the thought of not having to meet Gorse or being driven down to Reading. The thought of the latter almost made him vomit. 'I can get along fine.'

'But I'll tell you what,' said Gorse. 'I've got most of the morning free, and I can call for you in the car and take you to Paddington.'

'Oh, no. Don't bother. I can easily get there. It's very nice of you – but don't bother.'

'No. No bother at all. I'd like it,' said Gorse. 'And there's another more important reason for seeing you, too, if it comes to that.'

'Important? . . . What? . . .'

'I've got some money of yours, and I'd like to hand it back.'

'Money?' said Mr Stimpson, taken completely unawares. 'What money?'

'Well – a walletful of it. I managed to save it from the wreckage last night. Haven't you missed it yet?'

Mr Stimpson tried to think and remember quickly, but was unable to do so, and could only say feebly, 'No . . .'

'Well – I didn't *think* you'd remember the episode, as a matter of fact,' said Gorse, and was silent so that this might sink in.

It did so, frightening Mr Stimpson horribly.

'Oh . . .' was all he could manage, and then he decided that he must see Gorse as soon as possible in order to get information about this forgotten episode, which Gorse, by using a particular tone of voice, had made sound extremely sinister. 'Well . . . Yes . . . Well, if you could come over here and give me a lift to Paddington, it'd be very nice. And we could have a chat.'

'Yes,' said Gorse, mercilessly. 'Compare notes . . . By the way I can't imagine why I didn't stick the wallet back into your pocket last night, when I got you home. But in states of confusion like that one forgets these things.'

'Yes,' said the sick, cold, slipperless, and almost trembling Mr Stimpson. 'I know . . . What time'll you be along, then?'

'Ten-thirtyish suit you?'

'Yes. That'd do fine.'

'Fine. Cheerio, then. See you ten-thirty.'

'Cheerio.'

They rang off and Mr Stimpson went upstairs again. In the wreckage of his spirits – the wreckage, it seemed at the moment, almost of his whole life – he forgot entirely about the matter of deception in regard to his breakfast, and concentrated fiercely upon the mental reconstruction of his behaviour last night.

He took a bath, hoping that this might help him.

3

When Gorse called at ten-thirty Mr Stimpson was dressed and ready for him, had regained a certain uneasy, shifty dignity with his sister, and was a little more composed in his mind.

He now remembered a good deal about last night – but how he had lost his wallet, and in what sort of 'episode', were beyond him.

The breezy Gorse rang the bell as a telegraph boy might, and Mr Stimpson opened the door, wearing his overcoat and hat, and shut it after him.

'What?' said Gorse. 'No luggage?'

'No,' said Mr Stimpson, walking down the pathway of his sister's suburban villa. 'That's at Paddington Station.'

'Paddington Station? Why on earth there?'

'Well,' said Mr Stimpson. 'I meant to collect it last night. But things went a little awry, didn't they?'

He had not as yet made up his mind as to what attitude to take with Gorse about last night – whether he should be stubborn, light-hearted, or contrite. Gorse, similarly, though he had started off by treating Mr Stimpson pretty roughly on the telephone, was in two minds as to how far he should go with such treatment. He was certainly going to maintain and use the hold he had acquired over Mr Stimpson, but he did not want to make an enemy of the man. It might be wiser to use last night as a means of deepening the friendship. As they entered Gorse's car and drove away, both, therefore, were hedging.

'So you've got some money of mine, I gather,' said Mr Stimpson.

Mr Stimpson was compelled to open the necessary discussion by the sheer force of his curiosity about the 'episode'.

'Yes. All safe and sound,' said Gorse, and was silent so as to make Mr Stimpson come to him again. Mr Stimpson did so. He now felt that confession and contrition were the best lines to take.

'You know, it's a weird thing,' he said. 'But I simply can't remember a thing about losing it. What happened?'

'Well, you wouldn't remember it,' said Gorse, after a pause. 'Because you were deep in the arms of Morpheus at the time. It was most skilfully stolen from you, actually.'

'Stolen. Who stole it?' said Mr Stimpson, his heart nearly missing a beat at the thought of having fallen amongst thieves as well as loose women last night.

'*I* did,' said Gorse.

'*You?*'

'Yes. But that was just to see that no one else did. You got yourself in with a very crooked and dangerous little lady last night, you know . . . Can't you remember "Odette"?'

'Oh – that was her name, was it? Yes, I remember. But what do you mean, *I* got in with her? It was you who wanted us to pick up a Frog – wasn't it? I was all against it from the beginning – wasn't I?'

'Yes. But you changed your mind. And when once you did change it, there was no stopping you, and you lost your powers of selection. One's got to be very fastidious when dealing with French dishes in the West End of London, and your choice couldn't have been worse, I'm afraid. However, I stuck with you and got you out of it, in the long run, at the cost of two pounds. Believe me, it was cheap at the price . . . I also took the precaution of pinching and concealing your wallet on my own person while you were asleep. And so, as there wasn't any money to be found on you, our charming little "Odette" let us go. Otherwise it might have been a very nasty business. She was quite ready for blackmail and intimidation of any kind. I know the type.'

Theft, blackmail, intimidation! . . . The Reading businessman became almost faint with horror.

'And, of course,' Gorse added, taking a corner sharply in order to make Mr Stimpson feel even fainter still, 'very much worse dangers than that.'

Gorse was hinting at venereal disease, and Mr Stimpson knew that he was doing so. He searched his mind frantically to remember whether he had had any sort of physical contact with the woman. He could not recall anything of that sort – in fact he was almost willing to swear that there had been none. But doubt – black, lurking, nagging doubt – sickly mistrust of one's own memory – is the main symptom of the malady of the morning after the night before, and Mr Stimpson pathetically sought assurance from a witness as to what exactly had happened.

'Well, anyway, there was no danger of *that* in *this* case, was there?' he said.

'How do you mean?' said Gorse.

'I mean – well, nothing Took Place, or anything of that sort – did it? I just went to sleep, as far as I can make out. Didn't I?'

'Well – I don't know,' said Gorse, hooting impatiently at an obstructive vehicle in front of him.

'But you were there – weren't you? You must know.'

'Yes. But I wasn't there all the time. I had to leave you for about three quarters of an hour to get the car to bring you home. When I came back you were sitting up in bed drinking coffee, attended upon by our loving "Odette".'

'Oh – no – there was nothing of that sort, I'm *sure* of it. Quite sure of *that*,' said Mr Stimpson, as if to assure himself by auto-suggestion, and there was a long silence as the car approached the thronged Chiswick High Road and Mr Stimpson continued unconsciously to attempt to employ the methods of the then still popular M. Coué.

4

Gorse, having glanced at Mr Stimpson, and having observed that he was already, as had been intended, suffering horribly from venereal disease, thought that it was time to change his attitude.

'Well,' he said. 'We had a jolly good time while it lasted. You can't always strike it lucky all the evening. No harm done, and no regrets – that's what *I'd* say.'

Gorse's 'No harm done' uttered in an authoritative, bracing, doctor-like tone, at once cheered Mr Stimpson. Sufferers from mornings after nights, in the weakness of their anxiety, are absurdly easily susceptible to outside suggestion.

'Yes,' said Mr Stimpson. 'No harm done and no regrets. That's always been *my* slogan . . . All the same, it'll be a very long while before I indulge myself in *that* way again.'

'Oh – don't say that . . . One can't keep on the straight track all the time, and a little of what you fancy does you good, *I've* always been told.'

'Yes. Perhaps you're right. But perhaps I'm getting a bit too old for that sort of thing.'

Mr Stimpson had now practically thrown off venereal disease, and was concentrating on another matter – that of ensuring absolute secrecy from Gorse about what had happened last night – absolute secrecy, in particular, in the case of Mrs Plumleigh-Bruce – indeed plain lying.

Needless to say, the recent sufferer from venereal disease had swung wildly over from the ideals of impurity and adventure to those of purity and marriage, and would, had she been present, probably have been willing to propose marriage to Mrs Plumleigh-Bruce without delay.

'So you're not coming down tonight?' he tried. 'Our Lady Joan'll be mighty disappointed, methinks.'

'Yes. And I owe her some money, too,' said Gorse. 'If you see her, will you tell her I'll be down tomorrow, and that I'll give it to her then? Will you be seeing her?'

'Yes. I expect so. I can telephone her at any rate . . . But if I meet her, and she should ask for a description of last night's revels – what description am I to give?'

'Well, we met and had a few drinks at the King's . . .'

'Yes. And then . . .?'

'And then, I should say, we went off quietly to our respective homes. Wouldn't you?'

'I certainly would,' said Mr Stimpson. 'And can I rely on you to relate the same tale?'

'You certainly can,' said Gorse. 'Women don't quite see these things as men do . . . And a woman like Mrs Plumleigh-Bruce least of all . . . There's nothing I detest more than lying – and particularly with someone as clean and straight as she is – but – well – I'm afraid we men are made of a rather lower mould generally, and there *is* such a thing as discretion.'

'There is. Beyond a doubt. Then I may rely on your discretion?'

'Absolutely and completely. You needn't have any trouble on that score.'

'By the way,' said Mr Stimpson. 'I seem to remember talking a lot of drivel about Joan last night.'

'Really . . . When?'

'Oh – early in the evening. Don't you remember?'

'No. Not a word of it. What did you say?' said Gorse, casually.

Mr Stimpson looked at Gorse in order to see whether his casual air was assumed. He believed that it was not. He therefore took an audacious line.

'Oh – I don't know,' he said. 'I seem to remember getting a bit sentimental, one way and another.'

'Well – I can't remember it, but there's no harm in that – is there? I'm a bit sentimental about her myself, if you want to know the truth.'

'Are you? *How* sentimental? You don't mean you're "smitten" by her – do you?'

'Why, yes,' said the candid Gorse. 'I should say that's just what I am, really.'

'Really? You don't mean you're in love with her, or anything like that – do you?'

'Good heavens, no – not in love. I wouldn't dare to be. She's much too above my head – in years and other ways. But I can pay homage from a distance, and I love talking to her and all that. Don't you?'

The credulous and greedy Mr Stimpson, not content with having thrown off an abominable malady and having obtained an oath of secrecy from Gorse, resumed his habitual trick with the cake, and began to indulge in the delicious pleasure of praising the virtues of the woman of his choice.

'You can bet I do,' he said. 'You don't know that woman, my boy. She's got everything. She's a lady through and through – she's got what I'd call poise – she's attractive – and she's as clever as they're made. And when I say clever I mean it in the real sense. I mean she reads. Reads and thinks. In fact she's above *my* head I can tell you – when it comes to reading. You wouldn't guess the books she goes in for.'

'Really? What sort of books?'

'Oh – History, Marie Antoinette, French Revolution and all that. What she doesn't know about History's absolutely nobody's business, I can tell you. I wish I knew a quarter of it – that's all I can say. She's got *intellect*, that woman. That's what I admire in her.'

'Yes. I can well believe you,' said Gorse. 'But you're not a little "smitten" on her yourself, by any chance, are you?'

'Well – I suppose even that's not impossible,' said Mr Stimpson with a smirk in his voice.

'Well, if you are – good luck to you,' said Gorse, changing gears in the Chiswick High Road. 'You've certainly got a prize worth winning. By the way, you don't object to *my* friendship with her, do you? It's very innocent, I can assure you.'

'*Mind* it! *Mind* it! Don't be absurd, old boy. I *admire* it. She's as near a goddess as they're made – so why shouldn't you pay her obeisance? I know that *I* do.'

Gorse saw that Mr Stimpson, talking about goddesses, was just about to enter the semi-lachrymose state of one who had drunk too much the night before, and thought it advisable to stop this nonsense.

'By the way,' he said, 'I haven't given you your money back yet.'

Mr Stimpson became less lachrymose.

Chapter Three

I

Shortly after six that evening Mrs Plumleigh-Bruce heard her telephone ringing. She ran to the Marie Antoinette doll, certain, for some reason, that it was Gorse who was telephoning. She was therefore bitterly disappointed when she recognized Mr Stimpson's voice, saying, 'Hullo, Joan, how are you?'

'Hullo,' she said. 'How are you?'

'I'm all right,' said Mr Stimpson. 'Are you stepping forth tonight?'

'Well – I haven't really thought about it,' said Mrs Plumleigh-Bruce, who had been thinking of little else during the last hour. Practically Gorse's last words to her, the evening before last, had been, 'And the evening after that perhaps we'll *all* meet again,' and, though no firm arrangement had been made, Mrs Plumleigh-Bruce, often looking at the chrysanthemums she had received from Gorse, had been confident that she would receive a telephone call, if not a message, during the day.

'Well – what about it?' said Mr Stimpson.

'Where are you phoning from?' she asked.

'I'm at the good old Friar. Coming along?'

'Are you all alone, then?' she asked, seeking to discover whether Gorse was with him.

But Mr Stimpson saw through her seemingly disinterested, almost solicitous query. He knew that it was Gorse that she was after, so that she could collect the money she had won on the horse *Stucco*. And so, being anxious to see her, he was not going to give away the fact that Gorse was not, and would not, be present.

'Yes – at the moment,' he said. 'But that won't last long. I seem to have got in here very early. Anyway, the point is, will you join the merry dance?'

Mr Stimpson had been most wily in speaking of 'the merry dance'. It suggested the presence of the gay, dashing Gorse most vividly.

'Very well,' said Mrs Plumleigh-Bruce. 'I'd like to.'

'Fine. How long will you be'

'Oh – about half an hour. I've got to get ready and all that,' said Mrs Plumleigh-Bruce, who was entirely ready and could have been at the Friar within ten minutes.

'Fine. Hurry up, then,' said Mr Stimpson, and they said goodbye and rang off.

2

Mrs Plumleigh-Bruce had said 'about half an hour', and, if she had thought she had been going to meet Mr Stimpson alone, she would not have been at The Friar until three quarters of an hour later. But with Gorse it was a different matter. He was, she had been compelled to learn, a slightly elusive as well as forthcoming young man, and, if she was too late, he might easily have disappeared. She therefore made a compromise and was at The Friar within five and twenty minutes.

She found Mr Stimpson sitting and thinking gloomily by himself.

Since the morning Mr Stimpson had had several recurrences of venereal disease – the sharpest of these being at tea-time. This had brought him in despair to The Friar as soon as its doors were open. A pint of beer, as expected, had slightly reduced both the likelihood and severity of the malady, and by the time Mrs Plumleigh-Bruce had arrived Mr Stimpson was deep in repentance as to the past, and in burning resolution as to upright behaviour in the future.

Mrs Plumleigh-Bruce was, of course, highly disappointed at not seeing Gorse with him, but hoped that he might turn up before long. She concealed her disappointment as well as she could – but not successfully – from Mr Stimpson, who went to the bar and got her a Gin and Italian.

When he returned, in order to conceal her disappointment more fully, Mrs Plumleigh-Bruce made an effort to be particularly cheerful and gracious with him.

'Well,' she said. 'And how did you get on in the great gay City? Not led astray, I hope.'

'No,' said Mr Stimpson. 'Very dull on the whole. Very much as usual.'

'What? Not lured by the gay night lights?' said Mrs Plumleigh-Bruce.

She was, of course, fishing for information about the manner in which he had spent, not his day, but his evening with Gorse.

Mr Stimpson noticed that she was doing this, and decided to keep her waiting. It would, he thought, do her good. Although, at the moment, he was in no way jealous of Gorse – was, on the contrary, feeding his own vanity of Gorse's admiration for Mrs Plumleigh-Bruce – he was slightly annoyed at her too flagrant interest in the young man.

'No. Not lurid in any way,' he said. 'The lights of Reading are good enough for me. And how have *you* been keeping?'

'Oh – just the same.'

Mrs Plumleigh-Bruce saw that Mr Stimpson was withholding information either out of obstinacy or foolishness, and that if she was to get what she wanted, she must slightly humiliate herself. She did so.

'And did you go to The King's?'

'Oh – yes. We went there . . .'

'And how did that go?'

'How do you mean "go"?'

'Well – *go*,' said Mrs Plumleigh-Bruce, now infuriated by the maddeningly obtuse, or deliberately irritating, Mr Stimpson. 'I mean what *happened*?'

'What "happened"?' said Mr Stimpson, infected by her own irritation, and – in the condition of general exhaustion and touchiness caused by his drunkenness last night, his possible disease, and his remorse – not at all inclined to take things sitting down. 'What *should* happen? Nothing *happened* that I know of. An Elephant or anything didn't walk in, if that's what you mean.'

'I didn't imagine that an Elephant walked in,' said Mrs Plumleigh-Bruce. 'I simply –'

'Well, one certainly didn't,' said Mr Stimpson, interrupting her. 'You'd've read about it in the newspapers if there had, I imagine.'

'I'm not *talking* about Elephants,' said Mrs Plumleigh-Bruce, to which Mr Stimpson quickly rejoined, 'I didn't say you were. Why have we suddenly got on to Elephants?'

'Well – you *started* them,' said Mrs Plumleigh-Bruce, flicking ash irritably from the cigarette in her holder.

Mr Stimpson looked at the angry woman who had, after last night, been reinstated as his proposed wife – and, having looked at her, decided that he would certainly think twice about the project of marrying her. 'Lady' she might be, but he certainly wasn't going to get tied up with an irritable, dominating bitch.

For a moment Mr Stimpson was seeing the Mrs Plumleigh-Bruce whom her maid Mary saw most of the day – the narrower and meaner eyes, the sulky and malicious rather than lascivious mouth. And he was hearing the coolly commanding rather than rich and fruitily seductive voice.

Mr Stimpson was aware that her accusation was correct – that he had indeed started Elephants – but his mood was such that he was willing to irritate her further by pretending that she had. Having captured her for the first time in a more unfavourable light than ever before, he was eager, for the sake of experiment, to make the light worse still.

'*I* started Elephants?' he therefore said. '*I* didn't start them. I'm not *interested* in Elephants.'

'Really,' said Mrs Plumleigh-Bruce. 'This is absolutely childish, Donald. If you've just dragged me out to talk about Elephants, I might just as well go home.'

'Well, let's keep our sense of humour, at any rate,' said Mr Stimpson.

'Yes. Let's. By all means,' said Mrs Plumleigh-Bruce. 'I was only asking you if you had a nice time at The King's, you know. Surely there's no harm in that.'

Her more placid and peace-making tone had been so suddenly adopted that Mr Stimpson was easily able to discern its cause. She was determined to get back to Gorse. He supposed it was about time he gave her the bad news.

'Well, I had quite a nice time,' he said. 'But nothing spectacular. Just a few drinks and we both went our ways.'

'And how was our young friend?'

'Oh – he was in very good form, as usual . . . Oh, and by the way, he asked me to give you a message.'

'Really? What about?'

'He hoped to be in tonight, but he couldn't make it. He said I was to say he was sorry – that's all.'

'Oh. Really . . .?' said Mrs Plumleigh-Bruce, and, in her acute disappointment, she swallowed nothing. This empty gulp she attempted to conceal by quickly taking a sip at her cocktail, but Mr Stimpson was not deluded.

'He's kept in London on business or something,' said Mr Stimpson. 'And I was to send his apologies.'

'Well,' said Mrs Plumleigh-Bruce. 'There was no need to apologize. There wasn't any fixed arrangement, was there? Or *was* there?'

'I can't remember,' said Mr Stimpson, who, having administered full punishment, had now completely regained his temper, and was sorry for the woman. Twenty-five pounds was twenty-five pounds, after all, and he could understand her childish feeling of frustration at this further delay in receiving so novel and glittering a prize.

'But anyway,' he said. 'He told me to tell you he'll be down tomorrow – and that he can give you the money he owes you then.'

'How do you mean by "down"? In here or where? Or what?'

'I don't know. That was left vague. In here, I should think. Anyway that was the message.'

'Oh, well – it doesn't matter much, does it?' said Mrs Plumleigh-Bruce. 'No doubt he'll get into touch.'

Because he was now sorry for the rather subdued Mrs Plumleigh-Bruce, Mr Stimpson turned his thoughts to marrying her again, and, though he was neither jealous nor afraid of Gorse, he thought that it would do no harm to put in a word against him in order to enhance his own value as a candidate for her hand.

'He's a funny young man,' he said. 'Isn't he?'

'Well – I don't really know him . . . How "funny"?'

'Well. Flighty, let's say. A bit of a gad-about, wouldn't you say? That's the impression I got in London, at any rate.'

'You mean you wouldn't trust him?'

'Oh – good Heavens, no. He's all right at the bottom, I'd say. But just a bit of a butterfly, that's all. Not like yours truly, at all. Yours truly's probably a bit *too* steady. He's been pretty steady to you, anyway, hasn't he, for a pretty long time, now?'

'Yes,' said Mrs Plumleigh-Bruce after a pause. 'I suppose he has.'

Her flirtatious pause, and the flirtatiousness conveyed in her deliberate manner of speaking as she looked down her nose, put ideas into the vacillating and changeable Mr Stimpson's head. Why not have some more drinks and make love to her as usual?

'Come on, Joan my dear,' he said. 'Drink that off. I feel in the mood for a few tonight – don't you?'

Mrs Plumleigh-Bruce at once detected her companion's new

mood, and as rapidly made up her mind that it was not her own tonight, and that she would have none of it.

She looked at her watch, was surprised at the time, stubbed out her cigarette and said good Heavens no, she must fly. She had given Mary permission to go to the pictures this evening, and had arranged to be home for her meal at a quarter past seven at the latest.

Mr Stimpson then began to argue with her, making many plausible, and indeed logical suggestions that Mrs Plumleigh-Bruce should telephone Mary and dine with himself in a restaurant in Reading.

But Mrs Plumleigh-Bruce remained adamant, and this threw Mr Stimpson into a very bad temper again. This, in its turn, threw Mrs Plumleigh-Bruce into a temper, and she said No, she really must go at once – really.

Then Mr Stimpson began to fish for an invitation to dinner at Glen Alan the next evening, but Mrs Plumleigh-Bruce, feeling that she had a lot to think about and that she must keep herself free for Gorse tomorrow evening, made further excuses, which increased Mr Stimpson's rage.

'Well – I can't see you home,' he said. 'I've promised old Parry I'll be in here tonight. He ought to be in here now, in fact. And I can't very well let him down – can I?'

Mrs Plumleigh-Bruce said No of course he couldn't, and she rose. Mr Stimpson, controlling his rage, accompanied her to the door, and said goodbye to her with reasonable cordiality in the street.

Then, on re-entering The Friar he obtained a large Gin and Italian at the bar, took it over to the Plumleigh-Bruce nook, and sat sulking . . . Take the bitch home – Trust *him*!

Mr Stimpson had, in fact, no appointment with Major Parry, and was only fearful that the talkative man might appear. All he wanted to do was to sulk, and think and drink.

Such were the last gloomy effects of Mr Stimpson's hopeful journey to London. He had two more drinks, sulking and thinking deeply over them.

He then decided that he must take his mind off himself and his problems, and, getting his evening newspaper and a pencil from his pockets, he looked at the clues of the Crossword Puzzle.

He saw:

Across

1. Mollified.
7. Follows suit.
9. Bean.
10. A picnic.
11. Reviled. (Anag.)
13. Affirmation.
15. Spirit.
16. Slow to anger.
19. Sagging.
22. Obviously.
24. Only one in five escapes.
25. Recedes.
26. The end.
27. Elderly female found this bare.

Down

2. Displeasing to actors.
3. Game.
4. Wraith.
5. Emollient.
6. Euphemism for theft.
8. Rodent.
12. Shrewder than bees.
13. Complicated.
14. Headquarters.
17. Snakes' Paradise.
18. Celebration.
20. Sought place in sun.
23. '– is for remembrance' (Shakespeare)

But persons, words or things Mollified, Following Suit, Displeasing to Actors, Sagging, Slow to Anger, or Euphemistic for Theft, did not take Mr Stimpson's mind off himself. In fact they seemed only to drive him back upon himself.

Over his last drink, however, he managed, angrily, to solve the Anag. *Reviled* with *Deliver*. But then he became even more angry at realizing that Relived would do as well, and then less angry because the last letter of *Deliver* was an 'r' and this fitted in with the three-letter 8 down – *Rodent* – obviously *Rat*. Then, with the last sip of his drink he solved *Elderly female found this bare* with *Cupboard*, walked out of The Friar, and made for home.

He tried to console himself with the thought that he had got three anyway. But he was not truly consoled.

For a crossword puzzle man, he knew, cannot thrive on *Deliver*, *Rat*, and *Cupboard* alone.

PART EIGHT

GORSE THE REVEALER

Chapter One

1

Looking back on it afterwards, Mrs Plumleigh-Bruce believed she could recall exactly the moment at which she decided that she might just, just conceivably succumb to Gorse's proposals of marriage – his proposals of marriage, that was to say, if they were repeated, and if they were indeed proposals of marriage.

She was sitting drinking coffee and brandy with him after dinner at Glen Alan, and they were talking about Mr Stimpson.

It was three weeks after the latter's disastrous trip to London, and, somehow or other, this journey had come up in the conversation.

Or, rather, Mrs Plumleigh-Bruce imagined that it had come up somehow or other. In fact it had been steered into by Gorse, who, having done so, had said, with a reflective sigh, 'Oh dear – it's a pity our Mr Stimpson, for all his sterling qualities, hasn't really reached the years of discretion – isn't it?'

'How do you mean?' said Mrs Plumleigh-Bruce. 'I should have thought he was the most discreet, steady-going person – too steady-going, if anything, in fact.'

'Would you?' said Gorse, looking into the fire, and his tone of scepticism, combined with that of one who could tell much if he wished so to do, interested Mrs Plumleigh-Bruce beyond measure.

2

Mrs Plumleigh-Bruce had, in fact, been for a long while interested in this trip of Mr Stimpson's to London, having a feeling that a great deal more had happened than she had been told about.

She had felt this even during her meeting with Mr Stimpson on the evening of his return: but a few evenings later the feeling had grown into a conviction.

On that evening the four of them – herself, Mr Stimpson, Major Parry, and Gorse – had all met at The Friar, and it had been Mr Stimpson who had by his own stupidity put the conviction into her head.

Having mentioned their meeting in London, since when Gorse and Mr Stimpson had not seen each other, he had said to Gorse, 'Well, it was nice to have had a nice quiet evening in the gay city the other night – wasn't it?'

The mere forced use of the word 'quiet' would have aroused Mrs Plumleigh-Bruce's suspicions in any case. But Mr Stimpson had not been content with this. He had faintly underlined the word, and, in pencil, drawn some inverted commas around it.

Worse still, he had looked at Gorse with a sort of bulldoggish leer which the simplest-minded observer would have interpreted as a broad wink.

In extenuation of so much folly on Mr Stimpson's part, it may be said that he thought it was necessary to convey to Gorse that he had already told Mrs Plumleigh-Bruce that the evening had been a quiet one – and to remind Gorse, in case he had forgotten, that there had been a pact between them that this was to be the story told by both.

But later on Mr Stimpson had gone far beyond possibly excusable folly. He had descended almost to idiocy.

'Yes,' he had said to Gorse. 'We'll have another nice quiet bachelor evening together in London one of these days.'

At this, of course, Mrs Plumleigh-Bruce lost any shred of doubt she might have maintained that Mr Stimpson had been up to nonsense of some sort. She had always suspected that Mr Stimpson, on his visits to London, indulged in furtive adventure of some sort.

But what about Gorse? Was not he also involved? This matter was, really, more interesting than that of Mr Stimpson.

For, as she sat, three weeks later, drinking coffee and brandy with him at Glen Alan, Mrs Plumleigh-Bruce was very much more interested in Ernest Ralph Gorse than Donald Stimpson.

After Gorse's sad, sceptical 'Would you?' Mrs Plumleigh-Bruce was quite unable to control her curiosity.

'Why yes,' she said. 'I would. Wouldn't you? You know, you look as if you wouldn't – somehow . . .'

'Do I?'

'Yes. In fact you look as though you could say a lot of things if you wanted to.'

'Do I? . . . Well – even if I could, I wouldn't.' Gorse looked at her quizzingly. 'So I think this is where we change the subject – isn't it?'

'No. Why change it? It's extremely interesting. I mean the subject is – not Mr Stimpson. Go on. You mustn't start something and not go on with it.'

'Did I start something?'

'Yes. Of course you did. You know you did. Come along, now. What makes you think Donald Stimpson hasn't reached the "years of discretion" as you put it?'

Gorse was silent.

'No,' he said, at last. 'There are certain things one just doesn't reveal: I've no particular feelings of respect or friendship for Donald Stimpson, but he's done me no harm, and there *is* such a thing as honour amongst men – as well as amongst thieves. Particularly men out on the spree, as on *that* occasion.'

'Why? Were *you* out on the spree that night?'

'Me? Oh dear me no. Believe me – it was most dreary. Now – do let's change the subject – shall we?'

'No. You started it, and I think it's only fair that you should go on with it.' Mrs Plumleigh-Bruce here adopted her queenly, fruity, semi-joking tone. 'I shall be very angry with you if you don't, you know.'

'Well, then, I'm afraid you must be angry. Though God forbid that,' said Gorse, and then, after another long pause, added, 'It'd be different, of course, if you and I stood towards each other in the relationship I've been proposing recently . . .'

3

This, Mrs Plumleigh-Bruce realized, was probably Gorse's third proposal of marriage.

She thought quickly – her mind reviewing the almost incredible landscape of her last three weeks with Gorse, and the two proposals, if such they were, which stood out as peaks in the novel and exciting scenery.

The first proposal had been over drinks at The Friar shortly after she had been over and had tea at the house he occupied in

Gilrov Road. Then he had said, talking of the house, 'Or perhaps it might be yours – as well as mine,' and dropped the subject.

The second proposal had been a week or so ago, over brandy and coffee at Glen Alan. Then they had been talking about Life, and he had said, 'Unless yours and mine were one, you know,' and again the subject had been dropped.

There had then been a half-proposal when he had kissed her. This he had done in a gentlemanly, reverent way (and again in the sitting-room), saying immediately afterwards, 'I'm sorry. But I don't do that sort of thing unless I'm taking things very seriously, you know,' and yet again no more had been said. Mrs Plumleigh-Bruce doubted whether this 'counted'.

Now he had just spoken of a relationship he had been 'proposing' recently. The very word 'proposing' suggested a proposal. And it was exactly at this moment (she thought afterwards) that she decided that she might, just, just conceivably succumb to his proposals of marriage if and when he renewed them.

4

Three proposals and a half, then, thought Mrs Plumleigh-Bruce, looking at Gorse looking into the fire. But none of them direct, demanding direct compliance or rejection. And so modesty demanded that she should again ignore what he had said.

Intense feelings of curiosity about Mr Stimpson (and his evening in London with Gorse), however, were at conflict with the demands of modesty, and curiosity momentarily won the day.

Therefore, in order to entice Gorse into revelations about Mr Stimpson, she said, 'How do you know that we might not come to stand in that relationship?'

After a pause Gorse threw his cigarette into the fire and looked like one who wanted to jump from his chair.

'Do you realize what you've just said?' he said.

'No . . . What?' Mrs Plumleigh-Bruce looked down her nose – an affectation she had employed a great deal with Gorse in the last three weeks.

'Do you realize you've given me some hope – or a little morsel of it, anyway?'

'Have I? . . .'

'Of course you have. You know you have. In fact if you weren't what you were, I'd say that you're leading me on. Come now, Joan, admit that you've given me a tiny morsel. I don't mind how tiny – as long as it's there.'

Curiosity should now, Mrs Plumleigh-Bruce thought, collaborate with modesty. Both (it seemed to the vain woman) would benefit.

'Well,' she said, looking even more concentratedly down her nose. 'Perhaps a teeny-weeny. And perhaps it's wrong of me. And anyway that sort of thing wants a lot of thinking about, doesn't it?'

'Of course it does.'

'So shall we go back to where we were?'

'Yes . . . Where were we? I'll do whatever you say. I'm an extremely patient person. Where were we?'

'We were talking about Mr Stimpson not having reached the years of discretion. I rather doubt whether *you* have, if it comes to that. But tell me about Mr Stimpson. Go on.'

Gorse looked at her, as if confused and almost maddened, for a long while.

'Joan,' he said, sententiously. 'Have you ever heard the story of Samson and Delilah?'

'Yes.'

'Well. I'm certainly no Samson, but it seems to me you've got a very strong touch of Delilah.'

'Why? . . .' said Mrs Plumleigh-Bruce, and, because Gorse was silent, added a deliciously throaty 'Wherefore? . . .'

This silly complacent fool, thought Gorse, will develop adenoids and a permanent squint if she goes on looking down her nose and talking like this.

But this was none of his business. The point was that the late Cathedral and radiator of universal happiness was now Delilah, and extremely wicked. He strove to make her wickeder still.

'Well – you're only asking me to betray secrets,' he said. 'In other words, you're only twisting me round your little finger. But after what you've said, after that little morsel you threw me, I'm willing to do your bidding . . . Anyway, my conscience isn't very much disturbed. It's only a very silly and very absurd and sordid little secret. And I know I can trust you in every way. I know you're "Steel-true and Blade-straight", as Stevenson said . . . "Steel-true and Blade-straight, The Great Artificer Made My Mate". That's what he said of his wife, you know.'

Gorse, who had accidentally come across these words only a few days ago while browsing in the Reference Room of the local Public Library, had memorized them with the dimly formulated object of using them at some time upon women. He had had a curious fleeting notion that if you could only convince women that they were Steel-true and Blade-straight, you could make them, before long, and for your own purposes, as malleable as plasticine and as crooked as hair-pins.

But just at this moment he feared he had gone a little too far. If Mrs Plumleigh-Bruce became Steel-true and Blade-straight on the spot (and he feared she had) she might forbid him to disclose the secrets concerning Mr Stimpson which she was so anxious to hear and he was so anxious to disclose. He should, perhaps, have kept her as Delilah and not tried to have forged a sword.

His Delilah, however, as her next remark revealed, was by a piece of good fortune a spectacularly clever sword-swallower.

'Well, you can certainly trust me. You know that,' she said, clearly having thrust right down her throat, and enjoyed to the utmost, the sword, without suffering the smallest internal damage or letting it in the smallest way interfere with the business of cropping the strong man's tresses. 'But if it's all so absurd and silly, I don't see why you shouldn't tell me. Go on. Tell me your silly story. I hope it's not too sordid.'

'But what do you want to know, exactly?' said Gorse.

'Oh – just what happened that night.'

'It's not so much what happened,' said Gorse. 'It's the way it happened, I suppose. There are ways and ways of doing things, aren't there?'

'You mean ways of drinking, for instance?' said Mrs Plumleigh-Bruce, who had seen Mr Stimpson foolishly drunk more than once, particularly at Christmas time.

'No. Not drinking,' said Gorse, heavily. 'Though that certainly came into it – most strongly. I mean other things really . . .'

'What things?' said Mrs Plumleigh-Bruce, now thrilled at the thought of having her darkest suspicions fulfilled.

'Oh, *things*,' said Gorse. 'The things men do . . . All the sinful lusts of the flesh, and all that. The things they do particularly when they've been drinking, and particularly when they're in the West End. I don't think I need explain myself further – do you?'

'No. I don't think you need, really . . . And so he'd been drinking heavily, and then pursued – "all the sinful lusts of the flesh", as you put it?'

'You seem to know a lot about him. It sounds almost as if you were there yourself.'

Gorse had been visited by a sudden fear that Mr Stimpson had made some sort of confession to Mrs Plumleigh-Bruce – in which case the present conversation would lose half its potency.

'Yes. I think I know a lot about him,' said Mrs Plumleigh-Bruce. 'In fact a good deal more than he thinks I know.'

'But how? He doesn't ever *talk* to you about that sort of thing – does he?'

'Oh – good Heavens, no. It's just that I've always had an instinct, that's all . . . And so there was drinking and – the other thing – that night, was there? And did you partake of these pleasures?'

'Now. Don't be absurd. Didn't I say I didn't? In fact I found it all incredibly dreary . . . Mind you, I don't want to set myself up as a plaster saint in any direction. Don't get that into your head. In fact, in my early roaring twenties I've done a lot of things that – well, I was going to say regret – but I don't know that I *do* regret them. They're all part of one's growing pains and you have to get that sort of thing out of your blood. And you'd be a prig if you didn't do what everybody else in your circle does . . . But as I said, it's the *way* you do it – that's what matters.'

'And Donald Stimpson did it all the wrong way?'

'He certainly did, in my view. In fact first of all he got objectionably drunk, and then betook himself to the most objectionable quarters to satisfy his other desires. There was no stopping him.'

'But how do you know about that part of it? Unless you joined him?'

'I *did* join him.'

'Really. Why?'

'I kept with him so that I could look after him. And it was a good thing that I did. I was able to save him a little matter of something like fifteen pounds. Although, perhaps, it'd've been better if he'd lost it. It might have taught him a lesson. Although, again, you can't really teach that sort of a man a lesson. They just never learn from experience. That's what I meant when I said he hadn't really reached the years of discretion.'

'But how on earth did you save him fifteen pounds?'

'Oh – I took the precaution of removing his wallet during a period when he was half asleep, so that an extremely low but extremely determined young lady didn't get at it.'

'But surely she wanted some money – for "services rendered", as they say.'

'Yes. And I gave her two pounds. And that was a good deal more than she was worth, I can assure you.'

'And were the "services rendered" for that amount?'

'That I can't say for certain. I'd hardly be standing by and watching it happen, would I? The only thing was that I did have to leave him alone with her for about three quarters of an hour while I dug out my car from a garage, so that I could take him home to his sister at Richmond. And what happened in the interim I'm afraid I can't tell you.'

There was a pause, as Gorse looked at her looking into the fire.

'Yes,' said Mrs Plumleigh-Bruce. 'It's just what I always thought, you know.' And there was another pause.

'Anyway,' said Gorse, 'it's all very trivial, as I said. Men are men, and that's that. Or at any rate a certain type of man is a certain type of man, and though I certainly hope I'm not personally that type, I suppose one's got to make allowances. I really think that that little episode wasn't as bad as what went before it.'

'You mean his drinking. I've seen him drunk myself, before now.'

'No – not exactly his drinking . . . It was what he *did* in his drinking – or rather what he said . . .'

'You mean he used a lot of bad language?'

'Oh dear no. I'm used to that. It was the way he revealed himself – the things he *gave away* . . . I could hardly listen to him, I was so disgusted . . . But then, of course, there's no stopping a drunken man. Especially when he's with another man. He'd be different with you . . . I mean, a man . . .'

Mrs Plumleigh-Bruce here, rather brusquely, interrupted Gorse's discourse in order to focus upon its two vital words.

'*Gave away?*' she said. 'What did he give away? Things about himself – or about other people?'

'Both,' said Gorse. 'A drunken man always gives *himself* away in any case.'

'And what did he say about other people? What sort of other people?'

'Oh – all sorts . . .' said Gorse.

'But who? Anyone in particular?'

'Yes.'

'Who?'

'You,' said Gorse. 'In fact it was you more than anyone else. That's what made the whole thing so horribly embarrassing and revolting.'

'Really,' said Mrs Plumleigh-Bruce. 'This is extremely interesting. Go on. What did he say?'

Gorse took a sip at his drink, lit a cigarette, put his elbows on to his knees, looked into the fire, and said, 'Joan . . .'

To which Mrs Plumleigh-Bruce, herself nervously snatching at a cigarette from a box beside her, replied, 'Yes . . .'

There was a silence while Mrs Plumleigh-Bruce lit her cigarette.

Then 'You've been asking me a lot of questions. Now I want to ask you one,' said Gorse. 'You needn't answer it if you don't want to – but may I ask it?'

'Yes. Of course you may. Go on.'

'Well – has there ever, at any time, been anything "between" you and Donald Stimpson?'

'What do you mean by "between"?'

'Well – has he – kissed – you, or anything like that?'

'Yes. He's kissed me.'

'And you've allowed it?'

'Yes. I suppose I have. I've put up with it, anyway.'

'Oh Joan,' said Gorse, still looking into the fire. 'How *could* you? . . . You know you'll make me think he's right in what he said. You *have* got feet of clay.'

'Did he say that?'

'He did.'

'And what do you imagine he meant?'

'I don't know. I only know he said he could "tell" me a lot of things about you if he wanted to.'

'You don't mean he suggested – you don't mean . . .'

'Oh, no. I've got to be fair to him. Drunk as he was, he didn't go as far as that. He wouldn't have dared to, for one thing.'

'Why not?'

'Well – if he had, there'd've been a very unusual little scene in the most respectable precincts of The King's Hotel.'

'What scene?'

'I'm afraid Mr Stimpson would have found himself flat on his back from a blow well and truly delivered by Mr Gorse. I can stand a good amount of drunken drivel, but one has to draw the line somewhere – hasn't one? No – he didn't go quite as far as that. However, he did say that you had feet of clay, and he did say that he had kissed you. I thought it was drunken drivel at the time – but now it seems that he's right.'

'Well, you'd know he's not right, and that it was drunken drivel, if you knew the circumstances. You can't slap a silly man's face just for trying to kiss you every now and again, you know. Can you?'

'No. You can't. In fact, if you could, I'd've had my own slapped – wouldn't I? Don't think I don't know all that you must have to put up with from men all the time. I'm not a fool, you know.'

Mrs Plumleigh-Bruce, who had, in fact, not been kissed by any man, apart from Mr Stimpson, in the last four years, here looked down her nose again – seeing, beyond her nose, multitudinous kisses from multitudinous men, welcome and unwelcome.

'No. I'm not fool enough to blind myself in that way,' Gorse went on. 'All the same, one does get a bit of a shock, in the circumstances, when one knows the man – and what sort of man he is . . . But I knew you'd tell the truth straight out like that. "Steel-true and Blade-straight", as I said . . . You see, I'm always right about you . . . Don't bother, I'll get over it.'

'There's nothing to get over in *that* case, I can assure you,' said Mrs Plumleigh-Bruce. 'But tell me, did he say anything else?'

'Oh – he drivelled on. It was half complimentary – half abusive.'

'Abusive?'

'Well – it seemed abusive to me. But then I'm prejudiced, as you know.'

'But what *did* he say?'

'Do you know, I can't remember properly? . . . I wasn't really listening, of course . . . Oh – yes, there *was* one thing – one fantastic expression he used . . . Now what on earth was it? . . . Oh yes! *I* remember! It'll make you laugh, if I tell you.'

'Go on. Tell me.'

'He said you were "long in the tooth",' said Gorse. 'For some reason I've never personally heard the expression – as applied to a human being, anyway – and I didn't even know what he was talking about at first. I thought he meant that you have slightly projecting teeth. And as a matter of fact you *have* – very slightly – haven't you? . . . It's all part of the fascination . . . But then I got his meaning.'

'And what did you say when he said I was "long in the tooth"?'

'I thought he meant what I was thinking of, and I agreed with him, I'm afraid. In fact I said I thought you'd got one of the loveliest mouths I've ever seen on any woman. And I meant it, needless to say. That rather took him aback, I'm afraid. But don't think I descended to gossiping about you with him. It just came from me spontaneously . . . He must have seen that, because a moment afterwards he asked me whether I was "smitten" by you.'

'And what did you reply to that?'

'I replied that I wasn't – that I didn't think of you in that way. I said that I thought it would be sacrilege. And I still do. At least I do in a way. But three weeks have passed since then – haven't they? And in those three weeks maybe I've been guilty of sacrilege – both in thought and deed . . . But we'd better not go into all that at the moment . . . Now, what *else* did he say? There was another weird expression . . . They do get hold of some funny words, these funny men . . . Oh yes! He said that women only wanted "handling", and that if you were properly "handled", you'd probably do *something* – now what *was* it? It meant go to extremes. Go to the limit. Go the whole – way or something – what on *earth* was it? . . .'

'Hog?' asked Mrs Plumleigh-Bruce, with a terse air.

'Hog!' said Gorse, triumphantly congratulating Mrs Plumleigh-Bruce on her capture of the word. '*Hog*. That was the word. Aren't they wonderful – these people?'

'And what did you reply to that?'

'I've forgotten. You must remember I wasn't really listening to the man. If I'd realized his implication at the time, there might have been trouble. However, let's drop Mr Stimpson, shall we?' Gorse looked at his wristwatch. 'It's a very dull subject, and if I'm going to keep our pact not to scandalize Mary and go home by ten forty-five as promised, we've only a few moments left to talk about more edifying things in – haven't we?'

The time being less than five and twenty to eleven, there were actually more than ten minutes left in which to talk, but Gorse, seeing from her general look and bearing that Mrs Plumleigh-Bruce was now wholly preoccupied with rage against Mr Stimpson, had made a deliberate error when looking at his wristwatch. It would be well, he thought, to leave her alone in her present mood and with her present thoughts. By his doing this, he felt, a totally ineradicable hatred against Mr Stimpson would be almost assured. He believed he had said neither too little nor too much.

He was right. Mrs Plumleigh-Bruce furiously wanted to be left alone with her furious thoughts.

So much was this so that all the Delilah went out of her, and she said, 'Well – it *is* rather late – isn't it? And I *am* rather tired, I must say.'

Gorse jumped to his feet, with a slightly martyred, yet brave, disciplined and soldierly air.

'Very well, then,' he said. 'No edifying conversation. I'll be off. I can see you're tired.'

'For Heaven's sake don't think I'm turning you out,' said Mrs Plumleigh-Bruce. But she rose.

'No. I don't think that,' said Gorse. 'And even if I did I wouldn't mind. You've given me enough – you've said enough – for one night. You might spoil it if you said any more.'

'What have I said? What have I given you?'

'Oh – just that little morsel – that little particle of hope. You know what I mean all right. And it's really more than a morsel with someone like you. Because you're not the sort of person who leads people on – unless I'm a very bad judge of character.'

'I certainly hope I'm not. And I certainly hope I haven't led you on. But do you realize I hardly know you? Do you realize how short a time it is since we first met? It's a very short time, you know.'

'I know exactly. It's three weeks and five days, if you want it exactly. Two days off a month. Do you think I'd forget a thing like that? But what may be called a remarkable three weeks, I fancy . . . I don't expect they're as clear to you as they are to me. Now – don't say any more, and let me see myself out as usual.' He kissed her fraternally on the cheek. 'If you said any more you'd be bound to spoil it. Goodnight, Joan. A ring in the morning – also as usual. I'll go to my thoughts, and I'll leave you to yours. Goodnight.'

Within ten seconds Gorse was outside the room (the door of which he had closed with a semi-conspiratorial quietness all his own) and within a minute Mrs Plumleigh-Bruce had heard the last sound of his car, as it turned from Sispara Road into the Oxford Road. And within two minutes Mrs Plumleigh-Bruce, having lit another cigarette, was alone with her thoughts and thinking them with remarkable intensity.

Chapter Two

1

Contrary to Gorse's (and her own) expectations Mrs Plumleigh-Bruce's thoughts soon turned from Mr Stimpson to Gorse himself, and to the 'remarkable' three weeks he had just mentioned.

Her fury against Mr Stimpson melted in thoughts of the gentle, protective, upright, amorous (and yet so reticently amorous) Gorse. With such an admirer in attendance upon her, Mr Stimpson became merely crude and despicable – swinish – something beyond the pale.

The three weeks which Gorse had mentioned had indeed been 'remarkable' – to Gorse, perhaps, even more than to Mrs Plumleigh-Bruce – and a brief account should now be given of them.

2

Thinking it advisable still further to exploit, just at present, his gift of causing and using the emotion of relief in women, Gorse had not returned to Reading on the day promised in the message he had given to Mrs Plumleigh-Bruce through Mr Stimpson on the morning after Mr Stimpson's calamitous night. He let another day – a Thursday – go by.

Nor did he communicate with Mrs Plumleigh-Bruce in any way until Friday evening.

Then he telephoned her at about a quarter past six. Mary told him that she was out, but would be returning to dinner at half past seven. Gorse did not leave his name, but said that he would ring again in about an hour's time.

Gorse rightly guessed that she was round at The Friar with Mr Stimpson. She had intended not to see Mr Stimpson until she had heard from Gorse, but his continued absence and silence had put her into a small panic about the money owing to her. She now practically regarded those deliciously lucky winnings more or less in the light of solid property which she had held for years, and she had a sense of being temporarily deprived of this property – or even robbed.

She had, therefore, during the day of the evening on which Gorse telephoned her, accepted an invitation to meet Mr Stimpson at The Friar. Mr Stimpson had telephoned her during the afternoon, and she had accepted because she had a feeling that Gorse might be also present, or that Mr Stimpson might know something about his continued absence.

Mr Stimpson was, however, as puzzled as herself, and gained renewed favour in her eyes by virtue of his constancy seen against the background of Gorse's elusiveness.

Because he was again in favour Mr Stimpson, who, as on the night before last, desired either to take her out to a restaurant or to return to Glen Alan for dinner, managed to make her drink larger quantities of Gin and Italian more quickly than usual. But he overreached himself and did not succeed in having dinner with her. Mrs Plumleigh-Bruce suddenly felt her head swimming, and felt that she must get home – be alone at home – as soon as possible. She also had a feeling that Gorse might have telephoned her or be telephoning her. She made polite excuses.

Mr Stimpson escorted her home, kissed her in the porch, and left her. Her head was no longer swimming.

No sooner had she entered Glen Alan than Mary informed her, in a rather frightened way, that a 'gentleman' had rung and that he had said he would ring again soon. This made Mrs Plumleigh-Bruce's head swim again, but with pleasure and excitement rather than Gin and Italian Vermouth.

A few minutes later the telephone rang, and twenty minutes later Gorse, having been invited to take 'pot luck', was in the Glen Alan sitting-room drinking champagne with Mrs Plumleigh-Bruce.

The champagne had been brought by Gorse so that they might 'celebrate' Mrs Plumleigh-Bruce's victory on the turf, and Mrs Plumleigh-Bruce – having told Mary to delay the 'pot luck' (a cold meal from which a good deal of the luck had been eliminated, and into which a good deal of discretion had been quickly thrown during the time intervening between Gorse's telephoning and arriving) – took a glass of champagne with Gorse, half reluctantly and half with delight.

Gorse, who saw that she had had too much to drink, nevertheless managed to make her take yet another glass before eating. This he did by bemusing her, at exactly the right moment, with the sight and sound of fresh pound notes taken from his pocket. No one in England could make more delicious, fresh, crisp noises with fresh pound notes than Gorse.

By the time the pot luck was served Mrs Plumleigh-Bruce was hilarious – so much so that Mary (at whom more fantastic *Oirish* was flung than had ever been heard at Glen Alan before) noticed her hilarity, and suspected its cause. Gorse, in order to sustain the general tempo, indulged in a little *Oirish* himself, and made Mary take a small wine-glassful of champagne back into the kitchen with her.

After Mary had cleared away and brought the coffee, Gorse had persuaded Mrs Plumleigh-Bruce to drink brandy with him. The meal had now allayed Mrs Plumleigh-Bruce's slightly too sharp hilarity. But this had been replaced by a deep, deep elation, and a very beautiful faith in life, and in the cleverness, kindness and grace of her visitor.

Gorse having asked what she was going to do with her winnings, and Mrs Plumleigh-Bruce having told him that she had no idea, the subject of money generally was embarked upon. Gorse took an extremely cautious attitude towards money.

He was, indeed, in spite of the success they had been and still were celebrating, severely and admonitorily cautious. It was as if he were afraid that success might go to her head.

Mrs Plumleigh-Bruce, listening to him in a gin-champagne-supper-coffee-brandy haze, soon became shrewdly yet sublimely cautious. Indeed, leaning back on the settee, and looking at her worldly-wise visitor, she bathed in caution.

While thus bathing, on Gorse's delicate prompting, she disclosed something of the nature of her own investments to Gorse, throwing around them a sort of beautiful, rose-tinted mist of caution.

Finally, and again at Gorse's instigation, she became so cautious that she could not resist jumping out of her caution-bath and dragging her investments back into it in order to play with them. In other words, she left the room and withdrew (from the desk in her 'Hidey-hole', 'Study', 'Den', or 'Snuggery') a list of her investments, and showed them to Gorse.

Gorse, having stuck his monocle into his eye, now changed the mood of caution into one merely of serious concentration upon the document in his hands.

He then began, slowly, to be unable to refrain from giving forth a faint giggle at some of the items he was reading. Others he seemed to take more seriously.

Mrs Plumleigh-Bruce, watching the monocled but austere young man closely, was disconcerted by these giggles. Did they denote delight in her caution, or scorn at her lack of it? At last she was compelled to ask him if he thought anything was wrong.

To which Gorse replied (while he still looked in a preoccupied way at the document) that No, there was certainly nothing *Wrong*. It was all just a little bit too *Right*.

This struck fear into the soul of Mrs Plumleigh-Bruce, who, naturally, was terrified by the thought of anything which was a little bit too Right. She had visions of an evil or fearfully ignorant adviser (her Bank Manager) and pictured herself in an almost immediate state of penury.

'You know,' said Gorse. 'You really ought to have someone who knows his business to keep an eye on this sort of thing. Tell me, what sort of man is your Bank Manager? You were telling me about him the other night – weren't you?'

A sort of despairing yet resigned tone used by Gorse in putting this question threw Mrs Plumleigh-Bruce into greater panic than ever.

'I've always thought him very helpful and nice,' she said, feebly. 'Why? Does anything make you think he isn't?'

'No. But it's the helpful and nice people who land one into such trouble in this world, isn't it?' said Gorse, and then, putting his finger on another item in the document he was holding, he added, 'Good God! The man ought to be *prosecuted*.'

He flung the document upon his lap, took his monocle out of his eye, and gazed in astonishment at Mrs Plumleigh-Bruce, who said, 'What do you mean? You don't mean that everything there's not perfectly safe – do you?'

'What do you mean by "safe"?' said Gorse, realizing that he could hardly extract any further drop of anxiety, even of the minutest kind, from his hostess, and that the time had come for her to drink her draught of relief. 'Safe? Of course they are. You're as safe as houses, believe me.'

'Well – I'm glad to hear that,' said Mrs Plumleigh-Bruce. And (as if it were her draught of relief) she took a sip at her brandy.

'In fact you're so safe,' said Gorse with jovial sarcasm, 'that you're only losing about a half – or at any rate, a quarter – of what ought to be your income. However – that's your business. It's none of mine.'

During the next ten minutes Mrs Plumleigh-Bruce endeavoured to make her own business Gorse's – but he would have none of it. He didn't like, he said, advising other people about their investments. All he wanted to say was that, if she got proper advice, she could nearly double her income – that was all.

He then feigned tiredness, seeming to suppress a yawn – a suppressed yawn which was so perfectly timed that it made Mrs Plumleigh-Bruce, who was genuinely tired, yawn as well, and in less than a quarter of an hour he had left Glen Alan in a rather indifferent, and perhaps slightly rude and abrupt way.

Mrs Plumleigh-Bruce went to bed in a disturbed frame of mind.

She was disturbed by thoughts about her investments, by Gorse's sudden slight indifference and abruptness, and by the knowledge that she had drunk too much. She hoped, as she went to sleep, that she would feel better about things in the morning.

So far from feeling better next morning, Mrs Plumleigh-Bruce, waking much earlier than usual at the hideous summons of stale gin, champagne, and brandy, felt very much worse, and Gorse, later in the morning, made use of this.

3

Waking early on the Saturday morning, Mrs Plumleigh-Bruce had, naturally, a headache, but she looked upon this as the least of her miseries. She was conscious of having made a fool of herself in front of Gorse, and a fool of herself in front of Mary. She also remembered her general indiscretion – particularly her impulsive disclosure of her investments. She remembered, too, Gorse's rather hasty and cool departure, and thought that this might have been due to his displeasure or boredom at her looseness of behaviour.

Mary had no *Oirish* thrown at her that morning; nor was Marie Antoinette studied in bed after breakfast. Instead of this, Mrs Plumleigh-Bruce smoked three cigarettes in bed – with her an almost unknown thing – and gave herself up to melancholy brooding.

Gorse, last night, so far as she could remember, had made no mention of a future meeting, and this increased Mrs Plumleigh-Bruce's melancholy.

When, therefore, at about ten-thirty, the telephone rang, and, the doll having been snatched off it, she heard Gorse's nasal 'Hullo? . . .' she was made relieved and happy beyond measure.

She had already made up her mind as to what line she should take with Gorse about last night. She would boldly admit that she had had, or feared she had had, one 'over the eight', and had been a little 'squiffy' (the feminine Plumleigh-Bruce word for inebriation, and, pronounced as 'Squiffeh', suiting this particular feminine Plumleigh-Bruce's voice and accent to perfection).

She did this, and Gorse at once took advantage of her mistake in doing so. Instead of 'pooh-poohing' what she said, he took an 'Oh, well, we all have to sin some time' attitude, which aggravated Mrs Plumleigh-Bruce's distress and humiliation, and gave Gorse, temporarily, almost complete mastery over her. He told her that he knew exactly what she wanted, and asked her if he might bring it round that morning. He would not disclose the nature of his remedy, and Mrs Plumleigh-Bruce, less eager for physical alleviation of her condition than for his mere company, the chance to reinstate herself as a sober, well-bathed, well-groomed, well-dressed, disciplined, dignified woman, invited him to come round at twelve o'clock.

Gorse, accordingly, came round at twelve, and was received in the sitting-room. His remedy for Mrs Plumleigh-Bruce's condition was a bottle containing ready-prepared gin cocktails – the 'hair of the dog that bit you'. The pleasant-shaped bottle, with frosted-glass somehow suggesting ice and coolness of mind, was enticing without at first enticing Mrs Plumleigh-Bruce. She was shocked at the idea of drinking in the morning and might well have refused to do so had not Gorse somehow managed to put in a remark about the necessity of being able to 'take one's oats'.

To members of the Plumleigh-Bruce tribe there is, perhaps, no more horrible suggestion to be made than the one that they are unable to Take their Oats. They would be willing not to play with straight bats, not keep their chins up, let sides down, lose caste, and all the rest, rather than show this atrociously unpukkahish weakness. Mrs Plumleigh-Bruce, therefore, was soon taking her oats, and liking it.

She was persuaded to drink two cocktails, and after that she went out to lunch with Gorse at the best restaurant in the town, where she drank wine and brandy.

In the evening they went to The Friar and drank with Mr Stimpson and Major Parry.

Mr Stimpson was told neither about the 'pot luck' they had taken last night, nor the drinks and lunch they had taken that morning. Mrs Plumleigh-Bruce, telling Gorse that she had not allowed Mr Stimpson to dinner the night before, made him promise not to reveal these things. Already, although no word had been spoken against either Mr Stimpson or Major Parry, there was a pleasant feeling of mildly conspiring against the two provincial men.

It was at this meeting in the evening at The Friar that Mr Stimpson had made those idiotic references to his 'quiet' evening in London with Gorse – thus putting violent suspicions into Mrs Plumleigh-Bruce's mind.

At this meeting, too, Gorse contrived to make Mrs Plumleigh-Bruce drink more than she thought she was drinking, and more than was good for her.

Gorse allowed Mr Stimpson to see her home, he himself being happy in the knowledge that he had a secret arrangement to call on her the next morning at twelve. Indeed he almost forced Mr Stimpson, who was in a lazy mood, to see her home – thus further charging with an electric air of conspiracy and naughtiness his relationship with Mrs Plumleigh-Bruce.

Gorse was round at Glen Alan next morning at twelve o'clock and both were drinking prepared gin cocktails from the frosted-glass bottle by a quarter past twelve.

Gorse felt, on this second morning of successfully tempting her to drink, that he had, as it were, really weighed anchor with this woman, and that the voyage had begun.

He was right. From that morning onwards there were few mornings during which he did not drink cocktails at Glen Alan, and this curious combination between these two curiously ill-assorted people began to develop, in outline, signs of that finally almost weird aspect it was to assume.

Chapter Three

I

Both Gorse and Mrs Plumleigh-Bruce were aware of the slight weirdness of what was happening – Mrs Plumleigh-Bruce supinely and apathetically, Gorse more consciously.

To begin with, Gorse, who was seldom at a loss with any woman, before long found himself in some ways a little out of his depth with Mrs Plumleigh-Bruce, and he decided to be cautious. He did not like being cautious with women.

His next move, with another sort of woman, would have been to exploit social and money snobbery to its utmost.

But with Mrs Plumleigh-Bruce (he sensed just in time) this move would be a bad one to play too quickly or too obviously.

Paradoxically enough, seen in a certain light the Plumleigh-Bruce tribe, though snobbish, is not snobbish – either monetarily or socially. It is too complacent to be so.

It will talk about people not coming, or (worse still) coming, out of the top drawer – it is drawer-conscious to an agonizing or revolting degree – and yet remains, in many ways, not snobbish.

Towards the industrial lower classes it is not even snobbish in any way. Its emotions towards these are those simply of bitter class-hatred. Towards the agricultural lower classes its attitude is condescending and patriarchal rather than snobbish: towards the middle trading classes it is merely disdainful: and towards the upper class – which it meets occasionally at bazaars, fêtes, flower-shows, etc. – its feelings are strangely neutral. It does not really think about the upper class – it does not compare itself with it, and, while vaguely revering it, it makes little or no attempt to enter it or mix with it.

And the Plumleigh-Bruces are, with one exception, never social climbers.

The one exception lies in the direction of the Army. Here the mothers and daughters climb frantically, and the fathers and sons do the same thing – though less frantically because they simply regard doing so as the main business of their lives.

It has been said earlier that, with the Plumleigh-Bruces, there is always a *General* somewhere in the family. The General, it has been said, may be obscure or famous, a remote or close relation or connection, but there he is. A Plumleigh-Bruce without a General is not fully a Plumleigh-Bruce.

Our Mrs Plumleigh-Bruce herself had quite a good General within a reasonable distance. Her late husband's sister had married a man whose uncle was a General – General Sir George Matthews-Browne. Sir George, whom Mrs Plumleigh-Bruce had never met, and who was now dead, had received little publicity in the press during his lifetime, but he was good enough for Mrs Plumleigh-Bruce, who, sooner or later, in any social acquaintanceship she struck up with anyone, would drawlingly mention him. She had also acquired a photograph of this General, and put it into a silver frame on her mantelpiece.

Gorse, before long, was told about this General (who was made to seem much more nearly connected to Mrs Plumleigh-Bruce than he was), and he was considerably thrown out by him.

Gorse was thrown out because he had a General of his own up his sleeve – one whom he would, in the ordinary course of events, have played at this stage.

Gorse's General was both a false and true one – and Gorse had acquired him by a piece of wonderful good fortune. The General was false in that he was in no way related to Gorse, true in that he had in fact existed until a few years ago.

Indeed, General Sir Trevor Gorse had done more and better than exist. He had obtained, during a brief period, considerable publicity over a small but bloody civil-military encounter in India a few years after the 1914–18 War. General Gorse of Assandrava was never any rival, from a publicity point of view, to General Dyer of Amritzar, but all the same the press, during a 'silly' season, gave him a good deal of attention, and his countless foolish relations often endeavoured to put him on a level with the notorious Dyer.

Ernest Ralph Gorse, reading about him, and knowing that Gorse was by no means a common name, felt almost overwhelmed with his good luck. He decided without hesitation to unite his own family with that of the General, and he cut out from the newspapers every paragraph or photograph of the latter that he could find.

These cuttings, the most impressive of which he went to the extent of obtaining in duplicate or triplicate, he preserved carefully and cleanly, while making up his mind as to the precise nature of his kinship with the General.

Finally he decided to vary this according to the company in which he found himself, and, hitherto, he had only used the General on three or four occasions, on only one of which, and then in low company, had he made the military hero his uncle. The General, he felt, was too fine a property to be expended frivolously or indiscriminately.

On his first meeting with Mrs Plumleigh-Bruce he had realized that she would be exquisitely susceptible to his General – indeed so exquisitely (and therefore inquisitively) susceptible, that the greatest caution would have to be used. He had, therefore, bided his time.

On learning, over morning cocktails at Glen Alan, of Mrs Plumleigh-Bruce's General – General Sir George Matthews-Browne – Gorse applauded himself warmly for his own reserve. He had very nearly sprung General Sir Trevor Gorse too early. Now, obviously, Sir Trevor must be held in reserve, or even abandoned. There were serious perils in throwing a General against a General, and, in any case, it would be unwise to make the atmosphere too Generally all at once. It would be infinitely shrewder to let, or cleverly make, Mrs Plumleigh-Bruce entirely exhaust her mantelpiece General – extend her mantelpiece General-communications to the fullest extent – and then hurl in his own with annihilating force.

2

And so Gorse, who at the same time was beginning to realize that Mrs Plumleigh-Bruce was not, as he had thought, an all-round social snob, decided altogether to abandon the exploitation of social snobbery just at present.

Herein lay another curious feature of the Gorse–Plumleigh-Bruce combination, for Gorse, unlike Mrs Plumleigh-Bruce, was a deep, burning, embittered social snob. Social snobbery, indeed, may conceivably have been his one true passion in life. Probably it far exceeded his love of money, which, perhaps, derived only from his ambition to appease his social aspirations.

And, next only to social snobbery, was Gorse's passion for anything to do with the 'Army'.

From early boyhood he had had a passion for military things

and military uniforms, and, as the years passed, he had completely dropped his real parentage (his father had been a quite successful and in some circles quite well-known commercial artist) and turned his 'people' into 'Army People'. He had assisted himself in the task of robbing Esther Downes by impressing her with these 'Army People', and, since then, having spread the fiction so much, he had come almost mentally to accept this sort of thing himself.

He had, as has been seen, used it upon Mrs Plumleigh-Bruce on his first encounter with her, giving himself a romantic career in France in the 1914–18 War – and this (because such a thing was by now part of his being) without the slightest strain and practically believing what he was saying. (Later this passion for the 'Army' was to become almost pathological with Gorse, and to cause him to masquerade in uniform in the West End of London and elsewhere.)

And yet, here, with Mrs Plumleigh-Bruce, he was dealing with one who was paradoxically not only less snobbish generally than most women, but, disconcertingly, the genuine daughter and widow of a Colonel.

He saw that he must watch his step, and, while doing so, listen to Mrs Plumleigh-Bruce and perhaps learn from her.

There was no harm, however, in continuing to play upon her cupidity, and so he now began to draw her attention to the house he occupied in Gilroy Road.

3

On the afternoon of the Tuesday following the Friday upon which she had been admittedly 'Squiffeh!', Mrs Plumleigh-Bruce went most sedately to tea with Gorse at the house lent to him at Gilroy Road.

The scones were, as he had promised at an earlier meeting at Glen Alan, indeed delicious: the housekeeper was respectable and respectful: and the house made a deep impression upon Mrs Plumleigh-Bruce.

For all her brass, maps, and ships at pebble-sprayed Glen Alan Mrs Plumleigh-Bruce knew at once that 21 Gilroy Road was, as a residence and in its furnishings, on an enormously higher and more solid level than her own.

She knew, perhaps, in her heart of hearts, that her own brass, maps, and ships were more or less defiance – whistling in the decorative dark; and the more Gorse (humbly seeking her advice in room after room, beseeching her to agree that the place was hopelessly old-fashioned, and pointing out every defect he could find or imagine) the more she was impressed. She told him as much.

After tea they walked to The Friar, and here Gorse made his first strange 'proposal' with his 'Or perhaps it might be yours – as well as mine' – quickly dropped.

Mr Stimpson had entered almost immediately after this, and Gorse had made a point of boldly and immediately disclosing the manner in which Mrs Plumleigh-Bruce and himself had spent the afternoon.

He asked Mr Stimpson if he would do him the same favour as Mrs Plumleigh-Bruce had done – that was to say, take a look over the house – and he made Mrs Plumleigh-Bruce and Mr Stimpson discuss the details of the house earnestly – Mrs Plumleigh-Bruce undertaking the describing, and Mr Stimpson undertaking the listening and nodding and abstruse commentary, and both getting rapturously above the head of the silent, pathetic seeker after knowledge – Gorse.

All three were very much annoyed when joined by Major Parry – who was talkative and not interested in house-property – decidedly mundane.

Later in the week Gorse made his second 'proposal' with his 'Unless yours and mine were one, you know' after a discussion, at Glen Alan, upon Life, and early in the next week he had kissed Mrs Plumleigh-Bruce and assured her of the seriousness of his kiss.

In the week following Gorse had appeared at Glen Alan one morning in an extremely luxurious Vauxhall car which, he said, he was contemplating buying, and some days later, having covered considerable mileage in rambling and talkative drives in the country in this car, he had persuaded Mrs Plumleigh-Bruce to transfer five hundred pounds from a deposit account she held at the bank into a current account.

Finally, he had decided that the time had come to betray the secret of Mr Stimpson's night in London, and to make it absolutely clear to Mrs Plumleigh-Bruce that he desired to marry her. And, doing both at one sitting in the manner described, he had left her, in her sitting-room, to the intensity of her thoughts by the ashes of her fire.

4

The luxurious Vauxhall, the transfer of the money, the betrayal of Mr Stimpson's secret, and the proposal of marriage, were all cards played excellently and characteristically by Gorse.

But his ace of trumps, the General, had as yet been withheld.

PART NINE

THE DIARIST

Chapter One

I

The painful fact must now be revealed that Mrs Plumleigh-Bruce kept a diary.

Worse still – in order to throw in their only true light Mrs Plumleigh-Bruce's real feelings about Gorse and his behaviour from the moment she first met him until she decided that she might, just, just conceivably, marry him, it is necessary to give extracts from this exceedingly embarrassing document.

Mrs Plumleigh-Bruce had, in fact, kept a diary most of her life – but only intermittently. Although in reality an inveterate diary-keeper, for long periods she would completely forget that she was one or even that she had ever kept one. But then, for some reason, the urge would return.

Two days after Gorse's revelations about Mr Stimpson, and his (as it seemed) firm proposal of marriage to herself, Mrs Plumleigh-Bruce's instincts subtly informed her that diary-time had come round again. And, happening to discover, in a Reading bookshop, a brown, suede-bound book containing blank pages, and upon the brown suede of which had been stamped, askew at the top and in gold, the simple but inviting words 'My Thoughts' – she had bought it with the intention both of thinking thoughts and making them endure within the brown suede.

The book had been intended, no doubt, for the use of schoolgirls – but Mrs Plumleigh-Bruce did not realize this. Nor did her style have any of the directness, pathos or simplicity of many schoolgirl diarists.

For, in the last seven years or so, Mrs Plumleigh-Bruce had begun strongly to fancy herself as a potential 'writer' (she meant, she had confided to Mr Stimpson and others, to 'write a novel one of these days') and those who acquire this fancy, without having the ability to write, are seldom either direct, pathetic or simple. Mrs Plumleigh-Bruce's more recent diaries, therefore, had been, from the point of view of style, below the level of the average schoolgirl.

Also she made the mistake of adopting several different styles – sometimes as many as three in the same entry, and just as they suited her whim. In all these styles, however, four tricks were always cropping up – the use of alliteration, the use of exclamation marks, the use of inverted commas around words for no discernible reason, and the use of Wardour Street English gone mad. Also she was infatuated by a stupid use of the word 'very'.

The opening words of her first entry in the brown-suede diary were written in bed after Mary had brought her breakfast, and were, after she had given the date, cleverly instilled with a feeling of drama.

2

'Morning – of another day!' she wrote, in a paragraph all by itself.

The dash and the exclamation mark, of course, were what gave these words their dramatic and intriguing quality. It was as though days were rather unusual things, that days, in the normal course of life, did not necessarily follow days, and, somehow, that days did not always begin with mornings. She had made it clear, in fact, that something most interesting, if not alarming, was afoot.

'Morning,' she repeated, and then got into the narrative. 'Irish Maid Marian has left my room, leaving me with my thoughts – and my breakfast!'

(The dash and the exclamation mark here indicated not drama, but humour.)

'My thoughts! Round and round they go! In and out, to and fro, backwards and forth!

'Usually I chat with Irish Maid Marian at this time of day – chaff her and cheer her – cheat the churlish hour by asking and advising her about her childish concerns. But this morning Maid Marian was dismissed without a word, and here I am with my thoughts, committing them – seeking relief from very anguish of mind – to these pages.

'My thoughts. What shall I do? Whither shall I turn? What

woman, ever, was in such woeful or wildering pass! Shall I or shall I not? Do I or do I not? Yes or no? Aye or Nay?

'I am loved. Yes, it seems that I am truly loved. But do I love? "Ay – there's the rub". And, did I love, have I the *right* to *love*?

'"He" is so young. "He" seems, at times, hardly more than a boy. And yet, at others, so worldly and mature.

'How has it all happened? It is less than a month ago since I first met him. I "took" to him at once, and he (as I now know to my very cost) indeed "took" to me!

'How shall I describe him? He is tall, fair, slim, and has a well-groomed, well-tubbed appearance. He wears a small moustache – the relic, no doubt, of his days in the Army. (He "wangled" his way in at the age of sixteen, by the way, and was endowed with the Military Cross for his services!)

'He has a cultured voice, an easy manner, tact, humour, and an "air" – all the things so sadly missing in the "gentlemen" I meet in Reading. He is a man of the world, too. When I first met him he had just returned from Paris, and he speaks French fluently.'

Mrs Plumleigh-Bruce, who had heard Gorse use only a few French expressions, who did not know anything whatsoever about his abilities in this direction (and knew that she did not), nevertheless could not resist making Gorse speak French fluently. There is a sort of woman who is intoxicated by the word 'fluently' in regard to their friends' skill in languages: it gives them, themselves, a vicarious, warm, superior, fluent feeling.

'He has money,' Mrs Plumleigh-Bruce went on, 'and he obviously knows how to handle it. Indeed – this "boy" is already handling mine! (He won me, by the way, twenty-five pounds by putting me on to a "good thing" at the races soon after I had met him, and now he is "keeping an eye" on my investments.)

'He runs a large Vauxhall car, and, on his own admission, "likes the good things of life".'

Mrs Plumleigh-Bruce, as in the case of Gorse's fluent French, could not refrain from making him 'run' a 'large Vauxhall car', although she knew, from his own lips, that he had only been driving it for about a week, that he had not paid for it, and was merely contemplating buying it.

Mrs Plumleigh-Bruce, of course, like most diary-writers of her kind, although seemingly making a detached statement, was in fact doing something else as well. She was writing a letter to an imaginary woman friend – a friend who was, occasionally, so disagreeable as to be almost an enemy – and with whom, therefore, it was necessary to hold one's own. With Gorse's fluent French and large car Mrs Plumleigh-Bruce was, as it were, tossing her head disdainfully at this friend, at whom, throughout, she was making incessant 'digs'.

'And do not I?' she continued, alluding to the good things of life. 'Alas, I know only too well that I do. I am, I often think, quite hopelessly spoiled, and I know full well that "he" would fain spoil me. There would, if I did what he asked – come now, let's be blunt and say if I "married" him – certainly be no lack of "the good things of life".

'Am I "commercial"? Am I a "gold-digger"? Have ever such thoughts entered my mind since first I knew, for certain, that he would, if he could, make me "his own"? I sometimes think so.

'Nay – out o' the thought! I am, at least, something of what he thinks I am. "Steel-true and blade-straight" he called me only the other night. For all his worldly wisdom my "boy" has strange "flashes" of poetry.

'Are we not, then, perfectly matched? Am I not worthy of him as he is of me? Sometimes I think that nothing shall stand in my way.

'And yet, and yet, and *yet*! Ever and anon creeps in that fatal "and yet"! The disparity of our ages – my doubts concerning my own feelings. Do I love him? Have I ever loved any man? Am I capable of love? 'Tis sometimes a matter of doubt, in very truth.

'Now, from sundry familiar sounds below, I gather that it is time for me to "raise me from my couch". Should I not, Maid Marian will be impatient. Strange – how we are the "servants" of our servants! Yet so it must be, it seems.

'Maid Marian? Doth *she* languish and fret and doubt, as I do, o'er some dashing "Robin Hood" of her own? No doubt she doth. However, I must to my ablutions – or, in common parlance, my bath. Oh well. So let it be! Heigh-ho!'

At this, Mrs Plumleigh-Bruce, having rather unexpectedly found herself roaming in Sherwood Forest, closed her first entry in her diary, and went to her bath.

3

Drunk men sometimes show their drunkenness with lightning suddenness. Having been quite silent for a long while, they will all at once spring from their chairs, wrap themselves in floor rugs, balance things on their heads, use a falsetto voice, put their hands on their hips and imitate women, etc.

In very much the same way certain women, stimulated by the admiration of a man, will suddenly let it go to their heads, and behave, to themselves and to the man, with totally unbalanced vanity and coquetry. The next entry in Mrs Plumleigh-Bruce's diary, made next morning, showed that she was entering this phase of intoxication.

'Another day!' was the startling and astonished opening cry of Mrs Plumleigh-Bruce's entry.

It seemed as though the regular workings of the solar system were beginning to have some peculiar effect upon her nerves.

This morning, however, the temperamental writer was out of Sherwood Forest, and in the world of commerce.

'"He" came round yesterday morning for cocktails, and we talked, for once, business – just commonplace dreary business.

'And yet "he" has the gift of making even "business" interesting, and I ended up feeling quite excited. It seems that he has been put on to "a good thing" in the City, and is anxious for me to join him in "playing the market".

'He himself is investing heavily and was anxious that I too should have a little "flutter".

'I was certainly not averse to this, but was certainly dumbfounded when I learnt that by "a little flutter" he meant no less than two hundred pounds!

'Indeed, in my all-pervading hatred of business and "speculation" I argued with him for a long time, but he would not hear of my investing any smaller amount. It would not, he said, be worth while, and there was no sense in doing that sort of thing unless one does it in the "proper" way.

'I still argued, however, and seeing my reluctance, he at once dropped the matter. He never "forces" matters like this – that is what is so winning about him. He seems, at times, to have an almost uncanny insight into my temperament, and to know that it is useless to attempt to "force" Joan Plumleigh-Bruce into any line of action! – that she is a "tough proposition" and cannot be persuaded into anything against her will.

'But – poor boy! – he looked so sadly crestfallen! He could not disguise it! It was obvious that he had so wanted me to take a part in his speculation and share in its success – that he wants to link his life, in every way, with mine – even "financially".

'At last my heart melted and I said I would "reconsider" the matter. I said that I could certainly not invest the amount he had suggested, but that I might "put in" a smaller sum, if he would give me time to think about it – and that I would give him my decision in the evening, when he came to dinner.

'And sure enough, after dinner, *his* will prevailed, and the stubborn Joan meekly followed his instructions in writing out a cheque for fifty pounds!

'And in doing this I do indeed feel myself more closely linked with him than ever. So much so that I ask myself if I have done wrong!

'Is this the "thin edge of the wedge"?

'Will I, at last, find myself inextricably bound to him?

'The investment – some sordid thing to do with "Chromium" or something – I have a note of it downstairs in my desk – is, as he calls it "safer than houses". One stands nothing to lose, and a good chance of reasonable gain in what he calls a "quick return". I trust him explicitly in business matters, but all the same in my feminine soul I hope the return will indeed be "quick"!

'After all, he "made" twenty-five pounds for me over "Stucco", and so, even if the "worst came to worst", I stand to lose only twenty-five pounds. In fact, if one works it out, I stand to lose absolutely nothing!'

Here Mrs Plumleigh-Bruce had tripped up on her simple arithmetic.

'And then he looked so boyishly happy, on my acceding to his request! Indeed so much so that I could not refrain from giving him a chaste kiss on his forehead!

'After which, needless to say, business was temporarily forgotten!

'Not that he took the smallest advantage, as most men would, of my impulsive, maternal gesture. He looked at me as if merely dazed with delight – so boyish! Indeed, looking at him standing there, I could not refrain from patting his cheek and making the exclamation "Boy!"

'This seemed to both "nettle" him and yet please him at the same time, and later, as we sat on the settee (I allowed him to hold my hand, which was all he attempted) I could not help "twitting" him with the ignominious expression "Boy!"

'Then, suddenly realizing I was in fact talking to a highly experienced man, and recalling his record in the war, I changed the epithet to "Soldier Boy!"

'He then accused me of mercilessly "*vamping*" him! *Was* I?

'I have something of the devil in me, perchance.

'But still he took no advantage of my "devilment", if such it was. Once, only once, did he kiss me. This was after I had said I intended to call him "Boy", or "Soldier Boy", from henceforth.

'His kiss was strange – something unknown to me before, and indeed refreshing to one who is used to the miserable muddled maulings of men. It was reserved, reticent, reverend. It was as though, indeed, I am in very truth a "little tin god" – or should I say "goddess"? – to him.

'He does not kiss me – he has *never* yet kissed me – in what I call "that way". He seems to know instinctively that I do not like being treated in "that way" at all.

'Soldier and man of the world that he is, he is curiously ethereal in some ways. Is it possible that here his nature matches mine? Is it possible that he, like myself, does not *think* in "that way"?

'Men have called me "frigid". The accusation has been hurled at me so often that I have almost come to believe it true. It has worried me.

'And yet what if I have found one who thinks not after such manner? – one who reveres what the world so contemptuously calls "frigidity" – one who is, in that coarse sense of the word, "frigid" himself? – one who worships at the shrine of Pure Beauty and High Companionship rather than the lewd and lecherous lust of those such as whose name I shall not allow even to sully these pages.'

Here, obviously, the wretched Mr Stimpson was being lashed at by Mrs Plumleigh-Bruce's merciless pen.

Although Mr Stimpson – now made a pale, almost colourless figure by Gorse – did not enter her thoughts very much these days, Mrs Plumleigh-Bruce, occasionally remembering what he had said to Gorse, would get into uncontrollable rages with him.

'"Hogs" indeed!' continued Mrs Plumleigh-Bruce, in her sudden angry confusion of mind most unjustly thinking of Mr Stimpson, not as one who had merely suggested going the whole hog with her, but as one who had accused her of being a hog herself. 'Is it not *they* who are the hogs? Is it not *they* who have "feet of clay"?'

Appeased by this outburst Mrs Plumleigh-Bruce became more calm and elevated.

'Did not Plato exist?' she asked. 'And Socrates, what of him? Is there no such thing as Platonic relationship? And is it not possible that I have found one who sees eye-to-eye with me on this matter most vexed?

'And, if such were the case, would I not cast a different eye on the proposal he makes – an eye even more favourable than now it is? Certes, 'twould be a blessed boon.

'And so to my ablutions.'

By 'ablutions' Mrs Plumleigh-Bruce meant her bath, and by 'Platonic relationship' and 'blessed boon' she meant a conceivable relationship with a prosperous young man in which, though married to him, she would seldom, if ever, have to fulfil the normal sexual obligations of marriage – perhaps the highest earthly good conceivable by women diarists of this kind.

4

In Mrs Plumleigh-Bruce's next entry there were no exclamations either against or about the solar system, to whose regularity and order she seemed to have become inured; and she began, instead, on a light, Restoration note with:

'Yesterday evening to the play, where we were vastly entertained!

'"Boy" (N.B. I am calling him "Boy" quite naturally already!) took us all in his car – the five of us – D. S., L. P. and wife, "Boy" and myself.'

(D. S. and L. P. were the initials of Donald Stimpson and Leonard Parry – the Major.)

''Twas the small theatre – "The Kemble" in the Oxford Road – run by young Miles Standish – our young acquaintance of The Friar. We had the best seats in the house, and, owing to "Boy's" influence, free of charge.

'"Boy", it seems, is interested in things theatrical – about which he knows much and in which he likes to "dabble" – and he is putting money into the little "Kemble" – hitherto, I gather, running at a loss or barely making a profit. "Boy" tells me that it could be made a "property" if run in the correct way, and that all it wants is "putting on its feet" in a businesslike manner. Poor young Miles

Standish is hardly businesslike (he does not look it anyway) and so luck seems to have come his way.

'Both going and returning I sat in the back with D. S. and Mrs Parry – the latter seeing to it that her husband sat in the front with "the driver" – this obviously to keep an eye on me to prevent anything "taking place" between her spouse and myself in the darkness of the car!

'She had some justification, for, as I know to my cost from a certain episode the Christmas before last, the Major is not to be trusted in the back of a car! He made, on that memorable occasion, the most crude advances to me, thinking they were undetected by the others, and Mrs Parry was not going to permit a recurrence of such a thing!

'How she hates me – that thin, spinsterish, dried-up woman! And yet what have I done? Is it my fault that I undoubtedly attract men – that they make, willy-nilly, these monstrous attacks on me when given the chance? Is it my fault that I have been compelled to learn that I have that indefinable quality – "*It*"? – a gift more embarrassing than flattering in most cases, as I would like to assure her – who is so insanely jealous of it. Even at the theatre she saw to it that I was as far removed from poor L. P. as possible.

'The play? Trash. The acting? Good. Young Miles Standish should go far if given the chance, and it seems as though, if "Boy" should take him up, he may yet find his way into the "West End" – that "Mecca" of the struggling actor.

'When the curtain had fallen, owing to "Boy's" influence, we all went round "behind the scenes". A fascinating and disillusioning experience – the tawdry paste-board scenery, the smell of grease and glue – the thick "make-up", the powder and pomades of the play-actors in their pokey little dressing-rooms!

'I have often been told that I myself was "cut out" for "the boards" – maybe with some truth, for I could certainly have acquitted myself better than the so-called "Leading *Lady*" last night – but, seeing these "merry mummers" – these puppets from the other side of the "peepshow" – I felt grateful that I never succumbed to the temptation to try my hand in this direction.

'We were all treated with the greatest deference, however – this, no doubt, being again due to "Boy's" influence as a prospective "backer".

'In the car going home I was forced to sit next to D. S. – who has, by the way, a streaming cold, which I have no doubt I shall catch. I do wish people would not inflict their sniffing proximity upon others when in this condition. Faugh – the fellow was very offence!'

5

The solar system was still kept at bay in Mrs Plumleigh-Bruce's next entry, from which the Restoration spirit had also disappeared. Instead there was a feeling of breathless, hothouse intrigue.

'Last night, bringing roses, he came.

'I chid him for his extravagance, but knew how useless it was.

'It was after I had dined, and Mary's evening off. We were both in childish playful mood – relieved, perhaps, by the absence of Mary – and I made him help me arrange the roses – a few of which I took up to my bedroom (they lie on my dressing table as I write) – allowing him, for the first time, to enter these "hallowed precincts".

'My bedroom – intensely feminine and furnished, I flatter myself, a little more than fairly well – is my favourite, and I wondered how it would affect him.

'How different was his attitude to that of D. S. who, needless to say, always thought it beseeming, whenever he was permitted to enter it, to smear my sanctuary with leering and lewd approach.

'He looked round him shyly, strangely, as though ardent, eager, with ethereal awe. Then, without a word, he followed me out.

'In the more "prosaic" sitting-room we resumed our playful talk over coffee. Now I always call him "Boy" (or "Soldier Boy") and he has taken, in gleeful impudence, to calling me "Bunny"! This is a reference to the shape of my mouth. He once told D. S. by the way, that I had the "loveliest mouth he had ever seen on any woman".

'I fear that before long I was mercilessly "vamping" him yet again! Poor boy – he simply asks for it! And, as he never takes advantage of it, I simply cannot resist the temptation to tease and torment him.

'I know it is wrong but can woman ever flee from her own femininity? I am but human. Besides, in a way, I know he likes it!

'Then suddenly, we became very serious, and solemn, and talked about "*That*". How it happened I know not, but I suppose I led him into it. His boyish burning eyes, combined with that strange, severe, solemn self-restraint, puzzled me, and I had to find the answer. I did.

'He said that he does not really feel "that way" about me. He says (as he has said before) that it would be "sacrilege". He said that he has never really, in his heart of hearts, felt "that way" about any woman – that he has a higher ideal. He said that he has betrayed that ideal in the past, but that with me things were different – that in me he had found the "perfect blend" – what he had always sought and waited for – the blend of the spiritual, the mental, and the physical.

'He said that my "beauty" at moments "fascinated, bewildered, maddened" him, but that he was content to let it remain thus. He said, at last, that if only I should consent to marry him, I would not be bothered in "that way" unless it was my own desire.

'Then, imploring me to marry him, the poor boy almost completely broke down. He flung his head on my lap and seemed to almost sob.

'What was I to do – what say? At last, stroking his head, I whispered to him "My Soldier Boy" and reminded him that he was, after all, a Soldier.

'At this he pulled himself together and apologized.

'He said I had "taken the spine out of him" completely. Then, trying to throw off his emotion, he assumed a forced jocular tone and said "Well – what about a good stiff brandy?" He got one for both of us, and we talked gallantly about trivial matters before he left.

'Is it true? Is he indeed one of those rare beings who, in his own words, are content to worship from a distance, from afar?

'Or is he deluding himself? Wily Daughter of Eve that I am, I fear that he is. Should I marry him, would not "that way", ere long, become uppermost in his mind? We women see deeply and look ahead.

'But, whatever the outcome, Eve must bathe. And so to my bath.

'Ah, well. The future will look after itself. And if it does not, who cares? Not I, I vouch, verily. Ho-la! then, and to my bath!'

Chapter Two

I

A foolish journalist, writing long afterwards about Gorse, said that he 'played incessantly upon the vanity, greed, and folly of women'.

The journalist was foolish, but he was here not totally inaccurate. To have spoken a more entire and exact truth he should have said not that Gorse played upon, but that he had the supreme gift of stimulating, the vanity, greed, and folly of women. These qualities having once been fully stimulated, it was hardly necessary for Gorse to play upon them: they practically played themselves.

The journalist might also have added that one of Gorse's finest gifts lay in his quick instinctive recognition of vain, greedy, or foolish women. The wretched Esther Downes might with some justice have been called all these things, though her age and the circumstances fully excused her, as they certainly did not with Mrs Plumleigh-Bruce.

The vanity, greed, and folly of Mrs Plumleigh-Bruce 'Heigh-hoing' and 'Ho-laing' to her bath, had now, clearly, been stimulated to excess, were indeed violently over-active, and Gorse had, henceforth, little more to do than play a quietly encouraging and passive part.

Gorse, later, had the pleasure of reading Mrs Plumleigh-Bruce's diary. She was unaware that he had done so, but there were, in fact, hardly any documents belonging to Mrs Plumleigh-Bruce which Gorse did not somehow gain access to and read.

Gorse's pleasure in Mrs Plumleigh-Bruce's sprightly outpourings did not derive from his sense of humour: for Gorse – though gay, debonair, and full of jokes – was, like Mrs Plumleigh-Bruce, entirely without humour.

He saw nothing particularly funny even in her style. His pleasure arose, rather, from the profound satisfaction with which he was able to retrace, step by step, the absurdly easy success of his psychological and other devices.

She had, to begin with, simply gobbled up his premature

enlistment in the Army, his Military Cross, and his Parisian sophistication. (Gorse was a little worried on reading that he spoke French 'fluently', for he feared he might have to live up to this.)

Then she had swallowed, seemingly without any difficulty, a rather difficult mixture to put down any patient's throat – the mixture of belief in his 'boyishness' and a belief in his astuteness, prosperity, and solidity as a businessman.

But he had done it. ('He has money and he obviously knows how to handle it. Indeed this "boy" is already handling mine!')

Gorse had been rather surprised by the facility with which he had made her remove five hundred pounds from a deposit to a current account, and he put it down to the fact that he had not really any formulated motive in making her do so. It was not, as yet at any rate, any part of his major plan, and so he had not been forced to be in the smallest way too persuasive.

He had also been surprised by the ease with which he had made her put fifty pounds into his imaginary 'good thing' in the City.

He had originally intended that she should refuse to invest anything, and that he should look 'crestfallen' because of her refusal. But when she had offered him a cheque, made out to himself, for fifty pounds, he had thought it best to take it. He had now recovered, he realized, the money which he had given her on the mythical bet on *Stucco*, and was twenty-five pounds in hand. This twenty-five pounds ought, he thought, roughly to cover his general expenses in dealing with her.

Gorse took no self-congratulatory pleasure in her blithe creation of him as one who 'ran' a large Vauxhall car. This had been child's play.

The car, in fact, belonged to his friend Ronald Shooter, still safely in Paris, and had been lent to him along with the house and the housekeeper in Gilroy Road.

Here, however (as was not the case in making her invest money), Gorse had a definite design in mind.

Gorse had also liked the internal evidence given of the relish Mrs Plumleigh-Bruce had taken in his imaginary interest and monetary speculation in the small local repertory theatre – 'The Kemble'.

Gorse, as has been said earlier, liked the theatre both for its own sake and for the curiously strong effect an assumed esoteric knowledge about it – an assumed power 'behind the scenes' – had upon human nature.

He had, therefore, gone to some trouble in cultivating the acquaintance of Miles Standish, to whom he had spoken on his first night at The Friar.

The young actor, it will be remembered, had not liked Gorse at all at this first meeting. He had, in fact, suspected that Gorse was up to no good in life generally, and that he was possibly destined to see the inside of prison bars.

Struggling young repertory actors, however, have no objection to being backed financially, and when Gorse, in subsequent talks, suggested that he might do this, Miles Standish, without exactly altering his view of Gorse, was not so foolish as not to listen to him.

Gorse talked in a big way, and was extremely plausible – and plausible, for once, not of his own volition.

For Gorse, with the slightly 'silly ass' air which his monocle bestowed upon him, did look, in fact, like a typical vain and foolish backer of plays.

Young Standish, indeed, soon began to take Gorse most seriously as a possible backer – looking upon him, in the remote recesses of his mind, as a perfect example of this sort of 'sucker'.

Not that Miles Standish was being in any way dishonest or meaning to take advantage of Gorse. Struggling young repertory actors believe too fervently in themselves and their prospects ever to entertain the conscious thought that their backers can suffer – or, at any rate, the thought that their backers can suffer in anything but a noble cause.

2

But, above all, Gorse, in reading Mrs Plumleigh-Bruce's diary, was pleased by the internal evidence it gave of his success as a 'boy' – a boy being 'mercilessly vamped', 'twitted', and 'curiously ethereal in some ways'.

He had sensed, at an early stage, that Mrs Plumleigh-Bruce was all but sexless, and as soon as he had got really to grips with her, he had set to work to achieve the paradoxical feat of stimulating – along with her greed, vanity and folly – her sexlessness. She was, he thought, quite vain, foolish and greedy enough to have this trick played upon her.

It was rather difficult, he had found at first, to be burning with subdued physical passion and curiously ethereal at the same time, but after a while, with her aid, the task had become easy.

And so he had permitted himself to be sadly crestfallen, vamped, twitted, wrongfully encouraged, maternally and impulsively kissed, dazed, nettled, allowed to hold her hand, bewildered, reserved, reticent, reverend, teased, tormented, ardent, eager and awed, to Mrs Plumleigh-Bruce's heart's content.

As he was in no way physically attracted towards the woman, and she was in no way physically attracted to him, it suited both (he reflected philosophically) down to the ground.

PART TEN

DEBATE

Chapter One

I

They are at rest, they are at rest, they are at rest

or *They are at rest – rest – long long ago at rest.*

The Major, sitting alone in the Plumleigh-Bruce nook at The Friar, at about six-fifteen, was again grappling with November the Eleventh.

Of the two lines the Major fancied the latter – 'They are at rest – rest – long long ago at rest'. As opposed to the other it had a sort of onomatopoeic, marching lilt (Left – left – Left, right, left) which he had been anxious to introduce for a long time.

But one moment. *How* long, to be precise, *had* they been at rest? The Major had to face the fact that it was hardly ten years, taken all in all. Was that long, long ago? It wasn't. But one mustn't fuss. It was long enough – damn it. Get on with it for Heaven's sake.

What did you do with them now they were at rest? He had some ideas for rhymes, but they somehow didn't get him anywhere. There was 'jest' (Fate's grim . . .) and there was 'lest' (We shall not forget them . . .). But we shall not forget them lest *what*? Lest something rather awful happens to us, presumably – but the Major beat his brains in vain for any sort of majestic retribution rhyming with 'rest'. Best? Zest? Guest? Messed? Confessed? Test? Pest? West? Crest?

The Major thought he would leave this for the moment and consider another stanza whose opening line had come to him only this morning while shaving.

They have fled – they have fled – they have fled.

Now – surely – if he could not do something, perfectly simple, with 'bled', 'dead', and 'Poppies red', then his gift had altogether deserted him.

Nevertheless the Major, after five minutes of intense concentration, and after having considered 'bed' (earthy), 'fed' (worms), 'led', 'head', 'said' ('twas or 'tis), 'wed' and 'dread' – had made no progress of any sort.

This was all very infuriating, and the Major, to console himself, re-read a stanza, probably the concluding one, which he had composed last night, and which he believed definitely would do, with a little touching up.

Shall we, then, fail those who did not us fail
Amidst the splintering tumult of War's gale –
At Ypres, at Arras and at Passchendaele –
And did not yield?

There were only two little bits of trouble here. He wanted to underline the 'us'. But how could you do this without using italics? An impermissible device, surely?

And he did not like the two 'dids' – 'did not us fail', and 'And did not yield'. The last line, because of this, was a hopeless anti-climax, was it not?

The Major worked for another five minutes, this time with greater success, indeed almost with inspiration. Had he got it?

Shall we, then, fail, those who did deign to fail,
Amidst the splintering tumult of War's gale –
At Ypres, at Arras, and at Passchendaele –
Nor dreamed to yield?

This, the Major thought, was pretty well perfect, and he was particularly pleased at having at last got in Ypres and Passchendaele. He was a little worried about the order, in time, of the scenes of action – Ypres, Arras, and Passchendaele. But he could look this up – and what did it matter, anyway?

So pleased was the Major with himself that he began, foolishly, to dally with improvements on what he considered almost perfection.

What about making it *Mars'* great gale instead of War's? And what about the *screaming* tumult, the *thundering* tumult, the *moaning* tumult?

Mr Stimpson at this moment entered the bar and, greeting the Major, ordered his beer from the barmaid.

The Major, putting away pencil and paper, prepared to talk to the man, angry at being interrupted in a fine creative mood.

2

'Well, you're a stranger all right,' said the Major. 'Very nice to see you. How are we, now we're on our feet again?'

Mr Stimpson was indeed a stranger, not having entered The Friar, or seen the Major, for more than two weeks.

Two days after the night upon which all five – Mrs Plumleigh-Bruce, Major and Mrs Parry, Mr Stimpson and Gorse – had gone to the theatre, Mr Stimpson's ('Faugh – the fellow was very offence!') cold had developed into influenza, and he had been forced to take to his bed.

Very nearly three weeks, indeed, had passed since Mr Stimpson had seen either Mrs Plumleigh-Bruce or Gorse, and he had come into The Friar on this, his first evening out – with the vague hope of meeting them. He had given a lot of thought, during his illness, to these two, and had imagined, correctly, that they had been into The Friar a good deal.

His impulse, on sitting down beside the Major, was at once to ask about 'Our Lady Joan' (whom he had once or twice telephoned from his sick-bed) but pride withheld him from doing so.

Instead he asked the Major, as usual, about the news generally, and before long they were, again as usual, One-abouting each other.

A man who has lain in bed for a fortnight must not only necessarily be rather weak physically (and therefore less agile mentally and vocally than usual); he has also not been in a position to have heard ones about anybody at all – certainly not the 'latest' – and, one-aboutedly speaking, he is impotent, atrophied.

The Major, sensing his late tormentor's weakness, took cruel and horrible revenge. Stocked with a fortnight's Ones About – all fresh from the oven of businessmen's lunch-time conversation over drinks – he struck mercilessly at Mr Stimpson – beginning with the One About the Page Boy and the Bishop, the One About the Shop Assistant at Selfridge's who had a Cold, the One About the Young Plumber of York (limerick), and the One about the Old Gentleman who had Climbed Mount Everest.

This Old Gentleman 'reminded' the Major of the One About the Hypnotist who went to Blackpool, who, again, reminded him of the Old Lady who went to Tussaud's, who, yet again, reminded him, firstly of The Centipede with a Wooden Leg, secondly of The Girl in the Lift, thirdly of the Old Man of Cape Peele (limerick again), and, finally, of The Chairmender who Went to Buckingham Palace.

Mr Stimpson, now totally deflated, feebly attempted to make the Chairmender who went to Buckingham Palace remind him of The Billiard-Player who saw a Ghost in Bed, but not being able fully to recall the anecdote, he fumbled at its beginning, and was smashed to pieces by the Major, who had no qualms in interrupting him, with the One About the New Chauffeur and the Duchess, and the One About the Piano-tuner who was Taken to a Night Club in Montmartre.

Mr Stimpson made no further attempt to retaliate, and the Major, seeing his complete and pathetic exhaustion, had pity on him and related no further anecdotes.

They spoke of other matters, and before long Mr Stimpson asked after 'our Lady Joan'.

'Oh – she's all right,' said the Major.

'Been in here a lot?' asked Mr Stimpson.

'Yes. Quite a lot,' said the Major. 'Mostly with young what's-his-name. They seem to be getting very thick – those two.'

'What do you mean by "thick", exactly?' Mr Stimpson could not resist asking.

'Oh – they just seem to be going about a lot together. He's still gadding about in that huge great Vauxhall of his, by the way. How he gets all his money – that boy – I don't know – but he certainly knows how to find it somewhere.'

'Yes. It beats me, too,' said Mr Stimpson, who had given this matter much thought during his illness, and who was not as happy about the friendship between Gorse and Mrs Plumleigh-Bruce as he had been. He had not minded, indeed he had, as is known, enjoyed Gorse's worshipping Mrs Plumleigh-Bruce from afar on the old basis. But worshipping from afar in a large Vauxhall car, and in Mr Stimpson's absence, was less pleasing.

'Well – how are you?' said the Major, changing the subject. 'And what on earth did you do with yourself in bed all that time?'

'Oh – read a bit – and thought,' said Mr Stimpson. 'Thought

mostly. I was pretty bad at one time, and one gets thinking, you know – thinking seriously.'

'Yes – I suppose one does. And what did *you* think about?'

'Oh, Life, and one's soul, and one's past, and one's future, and all that.'

Mr Stimpson, like most people who are seldom ill, had seriously entertained during his illness the thought that he was going to die, and had, indeed, been looking into the matters of his soul and the universe with more care and at greater length than he had for years.

'That's bad,' said the Major. 'Nobody ever got anywhere by thinking about their soul.'

'Well – one's got to think about it some time, hasn't one?'

'Has one?' said the Major. 'I never did. *Why* has one?'

'Well – one's got to meet one's Maker – or Creator, or whatever you care to call it – sooner or later, I take it – hasn't one?'

'Has one?' said the Major, heartily. 'I don't really see why.'

The Major, it may be said, was not only constitutionally unreflective and determinedly irreligious (Armistice Day poems excepted); he was, at this period, sharply anti-clerical as well – this owing to his hated wife having recently come under the influence of a popular local clergyman and having taken to going to Church at unusual and highly inconvenient hours. He was therefore in no mood for this sort of thing from Mr Stimpson, who, however, rashly persisted.

'Don't be silly,' he said. 'One's got to believe in Something – hasn't one?'

'Has one?' said the Major, rudely. 'What?'

'Well – *Something*, that's all,' said Mr Stimpson. 'There's got to be a Reason somewhere – hasn't there? There's got to be a First Cause, you know. You can't get away from that, at any rate.'

'Can't you?' said the Major, more rudely still. '*I* can.'

'Well, then, you're cleverer than most people,' said Mr Stimpson, faintly beginning to lose his temper. 'Who Caused *you*, for instance?'

'My mother and father, so far as I know,' said the Major.

'Yes. And who Caused them?' asked the shrewd logician. 'May I ask?'

'You certainly may. My grandfather and grandmother. And a very nice old couple they were too. Though the old boy used to drink like a fish.'

'Of course, now you're simply trying to treat serious matters in a spirit of levity,' said Mr Stimpson.

'A spirit of what?'

'Levity was the word I used,' said Mr Stimpson, heavily.

'That's a new one on me,' said the Major. 'I've heard of Spirit Levels, of course. In fact I've used them. But Spirits of Levity aren't much in my line. However, you were talking about my grandmother and grandfather. Go on.'

'I was *not* talking about your grandmother and grandfather,' said Mr Stimpson with great testiness, for his temper was growing rapidly worse. 'I –'

'Then who were you talking about? That's what I thought you were talking about.'

'I was talking about *Things*. I was talking about the First Cause!' said Mr Stimpson, and added, more quietly and sardonically, 'Your grandmother and grandfather weren't the First Cause, you know.'

'I didn't say they were. I certainly *hope* they weren't anyway,' said the unchastened Major. 'Go on, then. What *is* the First Cause?'

'The First Cause of *Things* – the First Cause of the *Universe*. May I ask who you imagine First Caused the Universe?'

'Ask me another,' said the Major. 'Who?'

There was a pause.

'Look here,' said Mr Stimpson, trying to regain his composure. 'Who makes a Watch?'

'A watch-maker, I presume.'

'Very well, then,' said Mr Stimpson. 'There you are.'

'Where?' asked the Major.

'Well – if a watch-maker makes a watch – the First Cause made the Universe – that's all.'

'Why?'

'Really. This is absurd,' said Mr Stimpson. 'If you can't see –'

'I really can't see what watch-makers have got to do with the Universe,' said the Major, interrupting Mr Stimpson again. 'And even if they have, who made the watch-maker who made the watch, and who made whoever it was who made the watch-maker?'

Mr Stimpson decided to dodge this.

'And who,' he said, 'keeps the Watch Going? Can you tell me that?'

'The mainspring, I take it. Or it always did when I was a boy.'

'Precisely. The Mainspring. I'm talking about the Mainspring of the Universe. I couldn't have put it better myself. And who winds and regulates the Watch? It doesn't wind and regulate itself, does it?'

'I don't know. Why shouldn't it? You haven't been reading Paley's Evidences, or anything like that, have you?'

Mr Stimpson, who had never heard of Paley's Evidences, implied that he had by replying that he didn't see what Paley's Evidences had to do with it, and that all he wanted to know was Who Started it all.

'All what?'

'The Universe!' shouted Mr Stimpson in his anger. 'Who starts a *car*? It doesn't start *itself* – does it? Even *you* couldn't make a car start by itself – could you?'

'Well – I could if I had a self-starter,' said the Major. 'And anyway I always get other people to start the cars *I* go in. That's one of the advantages of not having a car of one's own, and travelling in other people's.'

'Are we talking about Cars?' said Mr Stimpson, with an extremely deceptive air of calm. 'Or are we talking about the Universe?'

'I don't know,' said the Major. 'We were talking about my grandmother and grandfather not so long ago. So what *are* we talking about? Cars, or my grandmother and grandfather, or the Universe? Or Watches?'

'We were talking about the *Universe*,' said Mr Stimpson. 'Cars and Watches are completely irrelevant.'

'Irrelevant or irreverent?'

'Irrelevant,' said Mr Stimpson. '*And* irreverent. Both.'

'Oh dear,' said the Major. 'I know what you're trying to talk about.'

'What?'

'God,' said the Major. 'I've seen it coming on for a long while.'

'And may I ask,' said Mr Stimpson, in his rage thinking that the longer he made his words the icier they would be. 'May I ask what Harm there may Accrue in peacefully discussing so major a topic as that of the first Creator and Originator of the Firmament in which it so *happens* that we *happen* to dwell – in other words, the Deity?'

But the Major was not frozen. He had, however, now lost his own temper too.

'No harm at all,' he said. 'But it so "happens" that I "happen" to think that it "happens" to be silly to "happen" to talk about the Deity – as you "happen" to put it – in a public house and over quiet drinks.'

At this ridiculing of his use of the word 'happen', Mr Stimpson completely lost control. Having taken another sip at his beer, he banged down his glass on the table, and said, with a livid air of resignation:

'Very well. *I* don't mind. It doesn't bother *me*. It's the old story. "The Fool hath said in his Heart" . . . Yes. The Fool hath said in his heart . . . I needn't go on . . .'

'Meaning I'm a fool?' said the Major. 'Go on. Say it.'

'I'm neither saying nor meaning anything,' said Mr Stimpson. 'I'm merely *thinking*.'

'Well – if you're not saying or meaning anything, why go to the trouble of saying it?'

'Oh dear,' said Mr Stimpson. 'The Fool hath said. The Fool hath said . . . Oh – dear. Oh dear . . . Dear me . . .'

The voices of both were now raised, and other people in the Saloon Bar of The Friar (which was still empty enough for the overhearing of conversations at almost any distance) realized that a terrible row about God was going on between two men. These people stopped talking and listened eagerly.

Unfortunately for these listeners, at this moment Mrs Plumleigh-Bruce and Ernest Ralph Gorse entered the bar, and gaily greeted the two angry men.

Chapter Two

I

Because of Mr Stimpson's recent illness – because he had not been seen for so long, and his call at The Friar tonight was a surprise one – the greetings were much gayer and noisier than usual, and an apparently happy quartet completely took the stage previously occupied by two dangerously angry adversaries.

The listeners to the latter soon, but with intense annoyance and disappointment, resigned themselves to what had happened – the fact that a bitter religious war had been replaced by a smiling and loquacious reunion – and, after watching and listening with faces which made no attempt to conceal their unhappiness, returned to talk, in a lifeless way, to each other once more.

Before long, however, Mrs Plumleigh-Bruce and Gorse, who were in exceptionally high spirits, began to notice that these were not shared by the two men, who, when the first necessity for superficial cordiality had passed, sank back into a condition of sullen and smouldering contemplation of their recent dispute.

So obvious did this become at last that Mrs Plumleigh-Bruce, who was in even higher spirits than Gorse, was so bold as to remark upon it.

'You two seem to be very quiet tonight,' she said. 'Is anything the matter?'

'No. Nothing's the matter,' said Mr Stimpson giving, as he always did, the show away. 'Nothing's the matter at all. Nothing.'

'Now then, Donald, I know you,' said Mrs Plumleigh-Bruce. 'Come along now. What is it? Or is it just depression after flu?'

'No. Nothing like that. My friend here and I have just been engaged in a slight argument – that's all.'

'Really. What about? Have you been quarrelling? What's the argument? Come along, Leonard,' she said, addressing the Major. '*You* tell me.'

'Oh. It wasn't anything, really,' said the Major. 'I've just been having Paley's Evidences and Watches thrown at me, that's all . . . It doesn't bother *me* . . .'

At this injustice all Mr Stimpson,s anger returned. Nor was he able to subdue it in the smallest way.

'*Me* throw Paley's Evidence and Watches at *you*!' he exclaimed. 'That's a good one – I must say – from someone who threw Paley's Evidences at me.'

'*I* didn't throw Paley's Evidences,' said the Major.

'What did you do, then? *I* didn't start Paley's Evidences – did I? You started them – didn't you?'

'No – I didn't start them. I just mentioned that you might have been reading them – that's all. And you certainly started throwing Watches.'

'Really,' said Mrs Plumleigh-Bruce. 'What *is* all this about?'

'To say nothing of Cars,' added the Major.

'Look here,' said Mr Stimpson. 'If a man can't mention Watches and Cars without being accused of throwing them at people – things have come to a very strange pass.'

'What *are* you two talking about?' said Mrs Plumleigh-Bruce.

'It's all perfectly simple,' said Mr Stimpson. 'I just happened to mention that somebody has to make a watch and somebody has to start a car – but he doesn't agree with me. What do *you* think?'

'Well, of course, somebody has to. But what are you arguing about?'

'Yes. *I* know someone's got to start cars. But all I was asking,' said the Major, 'was who started the starter, and who started the starter of the starter, and who started the starter of the starter of the starter? That's simple enough, isn't it?'

'Oh – I see,' said Gorse. 'You've been getting on to first causes, I take it.'

'To *The* First Cause,' said Mr Stimpson. 'The First Great Cause – that's all. In which, odd as it may seem, it so occurs that I chance to believe in. That's all.'

'And for which I got called a fool for daring to not believe in. Yes. That's all.'

'I did *not* call you a fool,' said Mr Stimpson.

'What did you call me, then?'

'I said The Fool in his Heart,' said Mr Stimpson. 'Saying The Fool in his Heart isn't calling somebody a fool – is it? It's just saying The Fool in his Heart – isn't it?'

The two were now once more calling attention to themselves, thus renewing the hopes of the outside listeners – and Mrs Plumleigh-Bruce, noticing this, cut in.

'Well it all sounds very foolish to me,' she said. 'Let's change the subject – shall we?'

'Willingly!' said Mr Stimpson, with passionate eagerness. But it was easy to see that the man was not passionately eager to do so.

2

In about three minutes' time, Mr Stimpson, having been questioned solicitously about the details of his illness, and his present state of health, by Mrs Plumleigh-Bruce, was more or less appeased, and (the Great First Cause, Watches and Cars rapidly occupying a more distant and diminished place in his thoughts), he returned to what had been very much in the forefront of his mind during the last fortnight – Mrs Plumleigh-Bruce and Gorse.

'Well – don't let's go on about me, and my ailments,' he said. 'What have *you* been up to – the two of you? Gadding gaily about, I take it?'

At this a rather curious look (not unnoticed by Mr Stimpson) took place between Mrs Plumleigh-Bruce and Gorse, who were both silent for about two seconds longer than they might have been.

It was as though, Mr Stimpson thought, they had news of some sort to break, and that neither knew who should do the breaking.

Mr Stimpson – always more shrewd and sensitive about matters concerning Mrs Plumleigh-Bruce than about most others – was correct in his surmise, and it was Gorse who undertook the announcement of the news.

'Yes,' he said, with a joviality which did not deceive Mr Stimpson. 'Gadding gaily and giddily about. And *she* is going to gad, so far as I can gather – egad even more gaily and giddily than ever, before many moons.'

'Oh – really? In what way, and in how many moons?' said Mr Stimpson, looking intently through his thick-lensed spectacles at Mrs Plumleigh-Bruce, who was therefore obliged to speak.

'Well, before *any* moon, really,' she said, with a nervousness almost entirely foreign to her. 'In fact the day after tomorrow to be precise.'

'And whither gaddest thou, pray?' said Mr Stimpson, noticing her nervousness and trying to increase it. But here Gorse took over again.

'She gaddest to the gay city – so far as I learn,' said Gorse. 'To the Metropolis – to the very centre of gadding and gaiety. Is that not so?' He appealed to Mrs Plumleigh-Bruce.

Gorse's 'So far as I learn' and 'Is that not so?' augmented rather than removed Mr Stimpson's general suspicions, and he made up his mind to get at the truth by blunt questioning.

'Oh – really?' he said. 'And for how long?'

'Oh – about a week,' said Mrs Plumleigh-Bruce.

'And where are you staying?'

'Oh – where I always do – the good old "in-laws" at Wimbledon. Very little gadding there.'

'And what makes you suddenly decide to do this?'

'Oh – one's got to make a change,' said Mrs Plumleigh-Bruce. 'And they've been asking me for so long I can't very well go on refusing.'

'And you?' said Mr Stimpson, turning ruthlessly to Gorse. 'Are you gadding at the same time?'

'Oh – dear me, no,' said Gorse. 'I'm staying more or less put.'

'More?' said Mr Stimpson, most unpleasantly. 'Or less?'

'*More*, on the whole,' said Gorse, in a detached way. 'Though I'm not saying that I propose to stay absolutely put. In fact I hope to be in London myself for a night or two at least. In which case couldn't we *all* foregather? Couldn't we have another drink at The King's or something? And then do something a little more exciting afterwards than we did previously?'

At this Gorse looked Mr Stimpson in the eye in a way which Mr Stimpson did not like. The reminder of that evening in London, in fact, together with this look, had the effect Gorse desired. Mr Stimpson, knowing what Gorse could reveal, dropped his cross-examining manner at once.

'Well,' he said. 'It might not be a bad idea. But what sort of thing?'

'Oh – a show – or something like that,' said Gorse.

'Yes. Sounds all right to me,' said Mr Stimpson, meekly, and here the conversation was changed.

3

Not a word of it, *not* a *WORD* of it, thought Mr Stimpson, lying awake in bed just after three o'clock next morning.

He knew what they were up to. *He* knew what they were up to all right.

Those two were going gadding about London together.

He knew what they were up to all right. *They* needn't think they could try and fool *him*.

He saw the whole thing, from beginning to end, through and through.

But Mr Stimpson, even in the horrible clarity of the black fourth hour of the day, was seeing the thing neither from beginning to end nor through and through – for he was unaware that Gorse and Mrs Plumleigh-Bruce proposed to spend a week in London together at the same hotel, that Gorse had several times proposed marriage to Mrs Plumleigh-Bruce, and that Mrs Plumleigh-Bruce had finally (and less than twelve hours ago) accepted Gorse's proposal joyously.

PART ELEVEN

GORSE OF ASSANDRAVA

Chapter One

I

Having worked herself up to 'Ho-lahing' to her bath in that last entry, Mrs Plumleigh-Bruce seemed to have been infected by the romping, fickle, carefree spirit of her own words, and had neglected her diary altogether from that time until nearly two weeks afterwards.

But three days before she went with Gorse into The Friar and was cross-examined by the sceptical Mr Stimpson, she had felt an impulse to resume it.

The cause of this impulse revealed itself at an early stage in the entry.

The solar system was, apparently, still slightly exercising Mrs Plumleigh-Bruce's mind – but this time less because of the regularity of its motions than because of its having suddenly speeded up.

'Day follows day in maddening whirl!' she began. ''Tis – how long? – near a fortnight surely – since I last put pen to my paltry thoughts on paper!'

The day-whirled woman then sharply contradicted herself.

'Nothing has happened,' she continued. 'All goes on as before – except that D.S. has caught influenza, and has "taken" to his bed. I thought that night at the theatre that such might be his fate.

'I wish the man no ill, but must say that, in my present predicament, his "room" is somewhat preferable to his "company". For "Boy" is ever-present and I have long been fearful of some clash between these two. "Boy" cannot bear the man after those remarks he made concerning me, and "Boy", for all his outward calm, has a fiery spirit.

'And D.S., too, had he been present to witness to what extent these days "Boy" dances daily attendance on me, might well have been spurred to jealousy. For after all the man loves me – in his brutish, boorish way.'

Now Mrs Plumleigh-Bruce revealed her real motive in resuming her diary, which was, at times, it will be remembered, also an imaginary letter to a disagreeable woman friend with whom it was necessary to hold one's own, or to snub. From this woman friend there was a piece of news too glorious to be withheld.

Mrs Plumleigh-Bruce did not disclose this news crudely. She cleverly pretended to have forgotten about it, and then, more or less by a happy chance, to have remembered it.

'What, then, has been happening since I last covered these pages with my scrawl?' she wrote. 'Let me see.

'Ah – yes! A morsel of mighty interest! And that gleaned only yesterday morn!

'"Boy", it seems, is a close relation of the famous *Gorse of Assandrava*! He is his nephew! When I say "is" I should say "was", of course, for the great soldier, alas, as all know, is no more.

'It is funny how many people have not heard of "Gorse of Assandrava". They forget so easily. I myself was somewhat "vague" about him, but as soon as "Boy" mentioned him – which he did quite casually and by accident – I remembered the Assandrava "episode" and the General's heroic firmness and decisiveness in that "gruelling" dilemma.

'"Boy" was surprised by the intense interest I showed, and brought, in the evening, sundry "cuttings" he had preserved from old newspapers, and "illustrated weeklies", recalling the story and giving pictures of the General – to whom, by the way, "Boy", if one looks closely, bears a likeness most remarkable!

'I told "Boy" that he should indeed be proud, and asked him why he had not told me before. He seemed to think there was no reason for him to have done so. "Boy" is curiously reticent in some ways. He does not believe, as I have learned time and again, in "putting his goods in the shop window".'

Here Mrs Plumleigh-Bruce, having crushed her woman friend with wonderful delicacy yet thoroughness, suddenly began to talk to herself in a manner much too candid for the eye of anyone – least of all any woman friend.

'One can be too reticent, I sometimes think, for I have to admit that this belated "disclosure" in some ways put "Boy" up in my estimation – made me see him in quite a "new light" indeed!

'Although I have often subtly "pumped" him, "Boy" has always been very reserved about his "forebears" – to such an extent that I have even sometimes thought that he has a "skeleton in the cupboard", or that he secretly felt that he might lose favour with me by being forced to reveal that he does not emerge from – well, what shall we say? – *quite* the top drawer?

'And (I must 'fess to my shame!) I have sometimes had faint, fleeting doubts concerning this myself.

'When I first met him I was in doubt about him. His bearing and voice were, of course, vastly superior to anything I have met amongst men in this town (with the exception perhaps of L.P.) – but for a long while I wondered whether he was really in any way "our sort".

'He seemed, then, as I remember, a little too "dashing" – too "fresh" as I believe they call it nowadays – too "knowing" in the wrong way – and this in spite of his brave and brilliant record in the War.

'It was, perhaps, his voice that slightly "put me off". Every now and again a slightly "common note" seemed to creep in to an otherwise perfect gentleman's accent.

'On knowing him better, though, I discerned that this was simply because he speaks in a slightly "nasal" way – that it is merely a very minor physical defect which gives him, every now and again – so seldom that I now barely, if ever, notice it at all – that rather "common" note.

'And now I have discovered, out of the blue, that he is the nephew of Gorse of Assandrava! Verily, he hath put me myself to shame! We both now, it seems, have "Generals" in the family! – but, before General Sir Trevor Gorse even General Sir George Matthews-Browne, of whom I have been so proud, seems a mere nobody! Indeed, *I* shall have to take to minding *my* "p's" and "q's" in front of the "Boy".

'Yesterday evening, having extracted so much from him I deftly "pumped" him further about his "family". They have all, he said, in a vivid expression, "Followed the Drum".

'He calls again at twelve today. And so, to make myself seemly in Milord "Boy's" eyes, M'Lady "Bunny" goeth yet again to her ablutions!'

2

'A strange day yesterday,' Mrs Plumleigh-Bruce wrote next morning. 'From the moment "Boy" came for cocktails in the morning there was a curious electrical atmosphere. I could see that he was excited, and before long I as usual "dug out" of him what it was.

'It seems that he is now in a position to acquire the house in Gilroy Road for the sum of £2,500 – "lock, stock and barrel" – this meaning furniture and everything.

'He showed me a letter from Paris from his friend "Ronnie" confirming this, but making it clear, in a friendly way, that the transaction must be "speedy" or that it would fall through.

'"Ronnie", so "Boy" tells me, has been living a very "wild" life in the gay city – (apart from other things he is an inveterate gambler at "the tables" it seems) and is at the moment in "sore straits" for ready cash. Consequently he is letting the house, which he never liked, go for a "mere song".

'"Boy" asked my advice, and I, having been to tea at the house and thoroughly overlooked it more than once, could not possibly advise against the proposition. (D. S. himself – and he should certainly know if anyone did – has said that it would be a "smashing" bargain at £2,500 – then not thinking of the furniture.)

'But then "Boy's" mood changed. He became somewhat silent, and, for him, almost "sulky". But (once again) I "dug out" of him the cause of his change of mood before long!

'He said that he knew that he had a bargain, but that there were plenty of other bargains going, and he didn't particularly want a house in Reading – "Unless – well . . ."

'I knew perfectly well what he meant by that "Unless – well", but all the same this devil in me (will I ever cure it?) made me ask him what he meant by the words.

'Then "Boy" showed a mood I have never witnessed in him before. He said, not angrily, but with unusual firmness, that I knew perfectly well what he had meant. He had meant unless I was going to marry him.

'He then talked to me, very quietly, but still very firmly, like a "Dutch Uncle" for some time! He repeated that there were plenty of other bargains in house-property, in which he had speculated a lot in the past, and that although this particular one was certainly a "smashing" one, if it went through, money was not everything, money for its own sake never meant anything to him, and that he did not want to buy a house in this part of the world unless something lured him and tied him to it. He was really a London man, where all his ties were.

'Also, he said, he did not really like taking advantage of his friend Ronnie in his present low financial position.

'He then said that he was not "proposing" to me there and then, and reminded me (truthfully enough!) that for nearly a fortnight he had made no attempt to "press" me. But, he said, there had to be limits, and the limit was very nearly reached.

'At this I asked him, somewhat flippantly, how I could either reject or accept his proposal if he had made none for so long a while!

'He smiled at this, but replied that I knew perfectly well that his "proposal" had always been there, as firm as rock, and that he had only been waiting for the smallest "sign" from me for him to make it again. He had given me many a chance, he said, to make this "sign", but I had not given it. (The truth!)

'He then said that I was something of a "delayer" and a "coquette" (how well he knows my character!) – but that he was not the sort of person who could put up with that sort of thing too long. He might have "taken" it from another sort of woman whom he loved lightly, but that with me, whom he loved so differently and more deeply than ever before, the matter was different. I must not think that because he was able to hide his feelings under a gay exterior, they were not "burning him up" within.

'In short, he said, he had to have an answer – Yes or No – and that before the end of the week, and that *that*, he was sorry to say, was very little short of an ultimatum!

'Should the answer be "No" he knew what he would do. He would return to London at once and never be seen in Reading again.

'He would forget that he had ever been to Reading. He would certainly give up the project of buying the house in Gilroy Road. By doing so he knew that people would think him a plain fool for "losing a chance of a lifetime", but he did not care. He said that his buying it would involve his coming to Reading constantly, and this he would not do. All the associations would be too unutterably painful, and he might run the risk of running into me.

'Besides, he said, the very house was now so closely linked, in his mind, with myself – that it would be anguish even to enter it. The house, he said, *was* me. It was I who had first advised him about it from a woman's point of view, and that while he was listening to my advice, and every time I had been there, it was me, and only me, whom he had dreamed of dwelling in it as his wife. He said I must have known this. (I *had* guessed as much!) He wanted it to be *mine* – in every *way* mine. He wanted everything he *had* to be mine, he exclaimed.

'I remained silent as he went on fervently in this strain. Then, controlling himself with an obvious effort, he suddenly became lighthearted again and gave me another drink.

'Only once did he refer again to the matter during that sitting. Then he said, lifting his glass, "Well – here's to the jolly old ultimatum!" But although he spoke lightly, I could see in his eye he was in deadly earnest, and thinking his own thoughts.

'At this moment he reminded me physically more than ever of his "illustrious relation" – and made me think that there must have been much in common between General Sir Trevor and Ralph Gorse. He is not to be played with.

'Heavens! It is nigh on a quarter to twelve, and I must get up!'

Here Mrs Plumleigh-Bruce left her diary, which she resumed later in the day.

3

'Tea-time,' she wrote at about five o'clock, 'and here I am scribbling again! 'Tis but to beguile the burdensome hour, for "Boy" is in London today on business, not returning till late at night, and thus leaving his "Bunny" to her own resources!

'I feel strangely lost and melancholy without him – I am surprised how much – and would find, even, the company of D. S. less distasteful than usual. But not only is he still down with flu – there would indeed be "ructions" should "Boy" learn that I had met him in his absence and without leave!

'All day "Boy's" "ultimatum" of yesterday has been on my mind. "Before the end of the week", he said. Did he realize, when saying it, that I am now left with *only two days*!

'Yes – if I know his character he knows only too well! Just as, if I know his character, I know there can be no further dallying with him. He once said, talking of some business matter, that "one doesn't deliver an ultimatum twice". He said that it would not be an *ulti*matum if one did.

'Is he, then, holding me up at pistol point? Is he playing upon his knowledge of what I should feel should I give him a "Nay"? Does he know – perhaps only too well – that should he return to London next week, never to see me again, I should be the wretchedest woman on earth?

'Yes – there I have admitted it! – It has come out at last!

'Let it be faced. "Boy" has given "colour and richness" to my life such as I never dreamed would come my way. Still I have doubts about the depth of my love – still I fret and fluster over the disparity of our ages – and yet I know now that life without him, in this dark and dreary town (the rain pelts down outside by the way!) would be barren, empty, a very desert.

'No. "Nay" I cannot say! Then what else but the fearful "Yea"! He has me trapped – has he not?

'Or is it "bluff"? Should I still "dilly and dally", as he has well-nigh accused me of doing, would he really depart? Would there not still be subtle means of "bringing him to heel" – of "keeping him within my web"?

'No. "Bluff" of that sort is not in his nature. It is not written on his face. Sir Trevor did not "bluff" on that famous day at Assandrava. Would Ralph, on this?

'"Pistol point", then, it seems to be. But is he not justified? 'Tis long since he first "proposed". Have I not, in fact, "dallyed and dillyed" with him, dangled him, like a very paper puppet, on playful string?

'And have I not, in my heart of hearts, *enjoyed* doing so? Am I *not* a "coquette" as he says? He sees deep into my nature, without ceasing, it seems, to yet worship the ground I tread on!

'Then at lunch yesterday – (taken, as usual, at the little Italian Restaurant, still struggling so bravely in this mediocre town which concentrates its mind on hard cash rather than good cooking) – at "Belloto's" – where the proprietor, "Mario", ushers us always to our own corner table, and treats us already somehow (these Italians are so shrewd in matters of this sort!) as though we were newly married or betrothed! – then at lunch "Boy" sprang yet another surprise – in truth a most puzzling and perplexing proposition!

'It seems that business will keep him in London nearly all of next week, and he did no less than ask me to join him there – staying at the same hotel as his own – near Victoria Station – nothing less grand, if you please, than the Buckingham! At first I thought he was joking, but I soon saw that he was quite serious.

'He asked what harm there could possibly be? The hotel was big enough for both of us, he said; and that I, if necessary, could have a room in one wing and he in another – a mile away in a hotel like that! Thus he tactfully made it clear that he was not "suggesting" anything (the thought *had* flashed across my mind!) and that I would not be "compromised" in any way.

'Then I asked him how he thought I was going to afford to stay at a place like the Buckingham, and pointed out that I was not a millionairess.

'He replied that he knew indeed I was not – but that that didn't mean one need not "go on the spree" once in a while. Particularly, he added, meaningly, if there was something to "celebrate".

'I ignored this only too obvious hint!

'Then he said that he knew the manager at the Buckingham, and that he could assure me that I would "get out" – even if I stayed for the whole week – well under ten pounds.

'Thus again he showed his tact – in the way he took it for granted that I would, in the present circumstances, "pay my own way". (Another man – D. S. for instance – would have thought it befitting his masculine grandeur to offer royally to pay the whole bill himself. It is these subtle little "touches" which reveal the inner "gentleman".)

'And, sure enough, before long, he had me myself seriously entertaining the idea. I am still. What harm *could* there be, and would I not like a "good time" in London for a week?

'But the proviso! "*If* there was something *celebrate*?" Sometimes I think that I am in "Boy's" web rather than he in mine – that *he* tempts *me* rather than I tempt him!

'*IF!*

'Come now, Joan Plumleigh-Bruce – let us weigh the "Pros and Cons". Which first, then?

'The "Cons". Get the worst over first – square up to them in proper style – ("steel-true and blade-straight" as he has always called me).

'Well – the first can be said in plain enough English. *Do I love him enough? Do I?* And, if I do not, would it be fair to *him*?

'Then – our ages. What would the wagging tongue of the world say to this? Would it accuse me of being a "baby-snatcher"? Would it say that I have enmeshed him – that I am "after his money"? Not that I care – or ever cared – a jot for the world's opinion, and nor does "Boy". I have posed the problem to him and he has laughed it to scorn. But what might he think *later*?

'Then – my *liberty*. I have a fierce, proud, independent spirit – it is carried to a fault in me – and should I again, at this age, submit to the "yoke" of wedlock? Would it "work"?'

Having thus frankly stated the 'Cons', Mrs Plumleigh-Bruce proceeded to undo her brave work by arguing against them in such a manner as to turn them, almost (if not entirely), into 'Pro's'.

'And yet – what *is* love?' she asked. 'Is it not *giving* rather than *taking*? If it is in my power to give "Boy" deep, deep happiness (and this I do not doubt) is it for me to withhold it? He told me, early in our acquaintanceship, before he knew anything about me, that I naturally "radiate happiness" to all and sundry, and, if he is right, if indeed I have this gift, should I not bestow it on one who can appreciate it to the full – one who thirsts for it? Surely this would be "fair" enough to him – indeed more than fair – in fact only right and good?

'It would be different if the physical side were uppermost – either in his mind or mine. Then the matter of our respective ages would verily "loom large". But between "Boy" and myself, is it not utterly beside the point?

'And am I as "mature" and unattractive as all that? Many men think not!

'Then, my independence. I have this strain deeply, I know, but am I not really – strange contradiction – also dreadfully dependent – at times yearning to lean on another? To this day I do not know whether I am dominant or really seek dominance. Would "Boy" dominate me, or would I dominate him? He once said that "I ought to be taken in hand". Well, I might let him think he was "dominating" me, but little would he know (devilish offspring of Eve that I am!) who was "pulling the strings"!'

Having thus neatly arranged and adjusted the 'Cons', Mrs Plumleigh-Bruce began to examine the 'Pro's'.

'And now to the "Pro's".

'No one, I think, ever has, or ever could, accuse me of being commercial, but it would be absurd to say, at this stage of my life, that I am loftily "above" financial considerations of any kind. I would marry "Boy", if so I willed, were he a penniless beggar and I had to support him – but all the same I cannot help taking our respective financial positions into account, and in this case it seems that it is I who am, comparatively, the "beggar-maid"!

'An assured income – the "right" sort of house in the "right" sort of place – proper servants in place of one struggling Irish maid (not that in any event would I ever discharge my faithful Mary!) – frequent visits, if not a *pied-à-terre*, in Town – a large Vauxhall car at my disposal – what "beggar-maid" would look with haughty disdain upon the thought of such material pleasures?

'Yes – even his car seduceth me – let it be said! I should like to see the expressions on Pam and Roger's faces as I drove up in it, married to the nephew of "Gorse of Assandrava"! A slight difference, I think, to Lieutenant Roger Braithwaite, recently "invalided" (such is their story) from the Indian Army!'

Pam and Roger were a married couple, related to Mrs Plumleigh-Bruce by marriage and particularly detested by her owing to what she believed was their aloofness or disdain.

Mrs Plumleigh-Bruce, carried away by this thought, now went on to imagine the 'expressions' she might possibly observe on the faces of several other people as they saw her alight from the large Vauxhall car with the nephew of 'Gorse of Assandrava' as her husband. Indeed, she became so carried away by this ravishing theme that she at last completely lost her original one – that of the 'Pro's'.

'Ah, well,' she concluded, 'who shall say? The rain still pours down outside – it is near seven o'clock, and I must scratch and scribble no more. Whatever befalls, I only know I feel drear and dead without my "Boy" (where is he, I wonder?) and I mean, believe it or not, to have a cocktail at this moment all by myself! Have I ever done this before? Am I "taking to drink"? Anyway I shall drink a solitary toast to tomorrow, and to "Boy's" return.

'Tomorrow he calls at twelve as usual, and has promised, by the way, to take me, in the afternoon, for another drive. And to where – think you? To see what he calls the "haunts of his childhood". In other words to "Gorse of Assandrava's" one-time abode, just outside Lingbourne! It is within fifteen miles of Reading, he says, and is now inhabited by his other uncle, the General's brother – his uncle George – a Brigadier-General himself.

'For "certain reasons" we are not to "call" – we are merely to "observe from a distance", "Boy" said over lunch yesterday.

'To this moment I do not know what he meant, but the drive should certainly prove interesting!'

Chapter Two

I

'*Interesting!*' wrote Mrs Plumleigh-Bruce, alluding, two mornings later, to the final word in her diary. '*Interesting!*

'It is said, I believe, that we British are famous all over the world for our gift of "understatement"!

'Well – it is done – it is over! It has happened. One Joan Plumleigh-Bruce is the "betrothed" of one Ernest Ralph Gorse.

'There it is. That is all! Somewhat "interesting", I think!

'How did it happen? Shall I ever forget? It is stamped indelibly on my mind, and there it will remain for ever.

'And yet there was nothing "dramatic". It simply happened. Hardly any words were spoken. We simply drove on in silence.

'And yet what were our thoughts in that long silence! I could see that he was controlling his excitement only with the greatest force of will-power. And I? Well, I was strangely cool, calm, collected – uncannily so, it almost seemed.

'Perhaps this was because I had instinctively predicted so well what was coming, and, in my innermost soul, had known what my answer must be.

'He called here at twelve in the morning, and we had our usual "cocktails". Yet again the atmosphere was somehow "charged" with "electricity".

'I asked him about how he had got on in London, about his business affairs – but he seemed disinterested – distracted. He kept on looking at me in a way I have never seen before, and his answers were "perfunctory" – sometimes little more than "monosyllabic".

'The "ultimatum" was coming! When would it be delivered? It was like a very thunderbolt hanging over our heads!

'In my nervousness I chatted wildly of this and that, trying desperately to "make things go". And, at last, my efforts succeeded. By the time we went off to lunch he had "rallied" and we were both talking as gaily and foolishly as a couple of children.

'Lunch at "Belloto's" – at our usual table with Mario hovering!

– and then off in the car to Lingbourne to "observe from a distance" the "haunts of his childhood" – in other words the Brigadier-General's house just outside Lingbourne – "Grasswicke".

'I asked him what his mysterious "reasons" were why we should only "observe from a distance" and he replied that it simply was that I didn't know his Uncle George!

'The Brigadier-General, it seems, is well over sixty, and something of an eccentric and recluse. Also, something of a "martinet".

'"Boy" told me that, when you knew him, he was a charming and gracious old gentleman of a really old-world type – but that his "eccentricities" and "ways" had to be obeyed in every particular!

'He has, "Boy" said, a hatred of three things – what is known in the family as Uncle George's "three C's" – Cats, Cars and Callers!

'He is *afraid* of Cats, and will either run a mile from them, or even produce an airgun and aim at them from upstairs windows! – he *detests* Cars, which he looks upon as an abominable modern invention of the Devil! – and with casual Callers he is hardly able to be *civil*! He also dislikes the Telephone, and, if one wants to visit Uncle George, "Boy" said, one has to write a formal letter about three weeks ahead! Then he is charm and hospitality itself.

'It took us about half an hour to reach "Grasswicke", which is a few miles beyond Lingbourne, and I was amazed when I found we were entering by Lodge gates! It is a very Estate!

'We passed in the car through this "right-of-way" (another of the Brigadier-General's *bêtes-noires*!) and slowly approached the house itself.

'As "Boy" drove along, at a seemly speed, he pointed out various haunts and "nooks" where he had played as a boy, and then we stopped at the best spot from which the House and Gardens could be seen – having backed and turned the car, in order that, "Boy" said, we could "make our escape" in case the old boy was in the Gardens or on the prowl!

'And what a lovely place – Elizabethan in period, with certain slightly later "restorations", and all mellowed by time to the perfect old English Country House – the ancient yet perfectly kept lawns with cedar trees leading up to the lovely façade of the back of the house – tennis and croquet lawns at a further distance – and a glimpse of the romantic old stables and a kitchen garden further away! Though we were seeing it at the worst time of year, and it now had a "deserted" look, its peace and loveliness sank into my being. It is from such places that the very "salt of the earth" have sprung – to do their duty – and some to die – in the far-flung corners of the earth.

'I could see that "Boy" was himself moved as he quietly cast his reminiscent eye over the scene, and he was silent as we drove back towards commonplace, commercial Reading.

'Then, when we had passed through the gates again, he stopped the car, and, looking back, pointed to a small church in the distance. I knew it was coming, and, sure enough, it came!

'"Well," he said, resuming his usual gay air. "That's where all the Gorses have been buried and married since time immemorial. How would you like to be married there, with Uncle George as best man and with his blessing?"

'I hardly know what I replied, and he covered my embarrassment by going on gaily.

'"To say nothing of the blessing of all his blessed relations," he said. "Although they're a very nice lot really – even if some of them are a bit too grand and stuffy for *me*."

'I was still silent, and then, without looking at me, he said, very quietly and thoughtfully –

'"Well. Which is it to be? Yes or No, Bunny? Here's the good old ultimatum, I'm afraid."

'There was a pause, and I said I did not know what to say. He said he would help me then. Let us try both. Was it "No"?

'"No," I stammered feebly, after another pause.

'At this he himself was silent. Then he said, "Well, that means Yes, you know, Bunny." He put his hand on mine. "Now. Don't say any more at the moment or there may be an emotional scene in the middle of the peaceful English countryside. Let's go back to tea – shall we – or Mrs Burford'll be getting into a state."

'He took his hand away from mine, and we drove on.

'Then believe it or not, there was complete silence for something more than five minutes!

'And that was *that*!

'Only when we had passed through Lingbourne again did we begin to speak – about indifferent matters – and only when we were approaching the gloomy precincts of Reading did he say, "By the way, you know you're leaving this God-forsaken town, and coming to London with me next week?"

'I was taken aback by this, and let him know that I was, but he said that I could not go back on a promise. I ventured to doubt whether it was a promise, but he swore that I had promised to "celebrate" – *IF*. I suppose I had.

'Then tea, with Mrs Burford's wonderful scones as usual, at Gilroy Road.

'A sweet old thing – Mrs Burford! Does she "guess"?

'"Boy" and I agreed that everything should be kept secret from everybody for the time being – but that perhaps Mrs Burford should be the first to know. At present she isn't even aware that the house, if all goes through, will have changed hands in a few days' time. "Boy" said that his friend "Ronnie" in Paris had insisted that it should be "broken gently" to the poor old thing. She is an old "retainer" who has "kept house" there for years, and it might come as a shock.

'"Boy" said that he would like to keep her on or "take her over". By this he meant have her somewhere else, for, he says, he does not *really* want a house in Reading *permanently*. Buying the house is only another of his "speculations" – though probably the luckiest he has ever struck, and he has other ideas.

'All this almost whispering over "cocktails" taken after Tea at No. 21 – lest Mrs Burford should overhear!

'I asked him what his ideas were, and he said a flat in town and a house in the country – somewhere, if possible, very near "Grasswicke" (he had an actual place in mind). For all his "roots" were there, and that he knew I would captivate the Brigadier-General. What did I think?

'The notion certainly seemed attractive enough to me, but then we agreed that it was absurd to discuss all that sort of thing just at present. There is my own house to be thought of, and Mary, and Mrs Burford. He said that it was quite clear that I had "captivated" *her* already.

'Then, over a *third* cocktail (I am drinking far too many cocktails these days, but has not this very upheaval and earthquake in my life warranted it!) the spirit of mischief got into both of us, and we decided to go to the "good old" Friar where chance, mere *chance*, had brought us together!

'At The Friar we met L. P. and D. S. – the latter just up from his sick-bed. The two men had been arguing about something and were most *surly*! However, I soon "thawed them out" and then D. S.

began to "cross-examine" me about my visit to London, which "Boy" had revealed.

'Knowing what we knew, "Boy" and I could hardly keep our faces straight, or from giggling or laughing outright! – particularly as D. S. obviously had some suspicions of some sort at the back of his mind and adopted quite a "bullying" manner.

'But "Boy" came to my rescue, and after a while he adopted a much milder tone.

'Talking of angels! – D. S. (if "angel" he may be called!) has this moment rung up! It seems that his "daily" is now down with "flu", obviously caught from himself, and he has asked me, if I was going away on Monday, whether my Mary could not "help him out". He said that he would pay her full wages while I was away, if she would come to him, and it seems a fair enough proposition. At any rate I told him I would think about it, and we rang off.

'Poor D. S.! I feel, at this stage, almost deeply sorry for him. If only he had an inkling of what has gone on and will go on!

'How will the news be broken to him, and how will he take it?

'Poor man. I suppose he loves me after his brutish fashion. I suppose he might have made, in his own way, a "worthy" husband.

'He will not, I fear, at all like having been "cut out" by a mere "youngster" like "Boy"! – who does not seem to think I am "long in the tooth" or that I have "feet of clay"! Well, the man must learn. The hard way, I fear.

'Heavens, Mary has knocked without, and I must up.'

2

Gorse's reflections, on reading these later entries, were of the same sluggishly satisfied and entirely humourless nature as had characterized his reading of what had preceded them.

He had enjoyed (without laughing at) the airy 'dear-me-I-almost-forgot' way in which she had introduced the General ('Let me see. Ah, yes! A morsel of mighty interest!'). And he had enjoyed his physical likeness to General Gorse ('if one looks closely').

He had not, however, liked her coy ''fessing' to having had at one time secret doubts about his having emerged from *quite* the top drawer, and he had intensely disliked reading that she had at times thought he gave forth a 'common' note.

Here Gorse was struck at what was, perhaps, his most vulnerable point, for this otherwise almost horribly realistic young man was not only bitterly ambitious socially – he was at times almost idiotically vain in this direction.

Moreover, the suggestion that he would not 'pass' in any circle whatsoever was an assault upon him, as it were, professionally – upon the pride he took in the art of his life.

Gorse was almost as incapable of real anger as he was of real humour, but, on coming across Mrs Plumleigh-Bruce's most candid words, he stopped reading for a moment and his sluggishly satisfied expression changed into something slightly more lively and thoughtful.

In fact Gorse never forgave Mrs Plumleigh-Bruce for this passage in her diary, and he was, at the last, to be a good deal less merciful with her than he might have been had she not written it.

However, as he read on, Gorse greatly relished the success of his 'ultimatum' and her weighing of the 'Pro's' and 'Cons', and he noticed the speed and deftness with which she had turned the 'Cons' into 'Pro's', while leaving the latter intact.

The 'Pro's', he observed, were really very few in number – probably capable of being resolved into four constituents only – his promise of virtual sexlessness in the case of marriage, his money, his car, and his General.

But this almost elementary piece of psychological chemistry had flown like wildfire to the childish woman's head.

Each of the four constituents, he realized, made each of the others more potent and credible. The car, naturally, gave credibility to the money, the money gave lustre to the car, the General gave glorious colour to both, both gave substance to the General, and the promise of virtual sexlessness in marriage undoubtedly made all even more splendidly tempting than they would have otherwise been. The grasping widow wanted absolutely everything and believed she was going to be given it.

The General, of course, had been Gorse's *coup de grâce*, and, though thrown in last, was really the base, or yeast, of his composition. Sometimes Gorse wondered whether he could have dispensed with the General.

The General, however, was a dangerous element, and Gorse, before using him, had taken considerable pains in further research in regard to his soldier-uncle. This had been done in the Reference

Room of the local Library, where Gorse had alighted unexpectedly upon the General's brother – the Brigadier-General. The latter in fact lived in the house a few miles beyond Lingbourne to which Gorse had taken Mrs Plumleigh-Bruce (having himself, beforehand, made two exploratory and thoughtful journeys there in his car).

Gorse, realizing fully how dangerous an element the General was – particularly if used in combination with his brother – had held him back until practically the last moment.

The General, and his brother, he had decided, must be used only at the beginning of the final stage – indeed within two days, at the most, of the final delivery of his 'ultimatum'.

After that Mrs Plumleigh-Bruce must be swept away to London, and, under his eyes, given no time or opportunity to think or inquire about anything – least of all Generals.

Gorse (who had not then read anything of Mrs Plumleigh-Bruce's diary) had been a little nervous on that drive to 'Grasswicke', and he had therefore been more delighted than he had expected to have been at its romantic outcome.

The final stage of this Reading adventure, Gorse believed while driving Mrs Plumleigh-Bruce back from 'Grasswicke' into Reading, had now been passed. The rest was child's play, merely a matter of going through certain easy, necessary, and perhaps rather boring motions.

And, sure enough, the necessary motions were very easy indeed. They were better. They were so easy as to be amazingly exhilarating.

PART TWELVE

LADY PUPIL

Chapter One

I

The vast Buckingham Hotel – slightly modernized downstairs and in its bedrooms, but giving forth an air of a museum or mausoleum in its considerable acreage of staircases and passages above – catered mostly for birds of the briefest passage. This was because it was in the Buckingham Palace Road and so extremely close to Victoria Station.

It had, however, a regular clientele, mostly of elderly people with memories, who dined in the old-fashioned Restaurant rather than in the modern Grill, and liked its thickly carpeted, hushed, mausoleum-like quality above.

In all three of these ways – in its modernity below, its dim and dignified spaciousness above, and its countless birds of passage mingled with a sedate and faithful clientele – it bore a certain resemblance to the famous Hotel Metropole in Brighton, where Gorse had years ago robbed Esther Downes.

Here Mrs Plumleigh-Bruce and Gorse arrived on a Monday afternoon in time for tea.

Gorse had engaged a small single room for himself, and a large double-bedded room (on the same floor and at about a distance of two hundred yards) for Mrs Plumleigh-Bruce.

Gorse, having unpacked and walked from his own room – along a corridor so high and hugely silent that he was aware of the sound of the clanking of the key in his hand against the uncouthly ponderous and savagely serrated piece of metal to which it was attached – had tea in Mrs Plumleigh-Bruce's more spacious and opulent room.

Gorse and Mrs Plumleigh-Bruce made the latter's room more or less their headquarters during their stay in the hotel. On the first evening they had drinks there and, instead of going out, dined in the old-fashioned Restaurant.

2

Those two, even on their first night, made a marked impression upon the regular and for the most part elderly diners in the Restaurant, and, later, the more they ate there, the more marked, and the more displeasing, did this impression grow.

And this applied to nearly all other public places they visited in which they could be studied.

For those two were not the couple they were in Reading – either to the outside world, or in their own eyes.

In the provincial town the few people who had watched or known them together had either given them little thought, or had grown used to the slight oddity of their companionship. In London things were different.

Londoners, seeing or listening to them for the first time, found this couple not only slightly odd. They found them slightly, or even decidedly, repellent.

Mrs Plumleigh-Bruce had, as is known, become entirely used to Gorse's flamboyant and rather 'common' manner – so much so that she did not notice or think about it. The observant Londoner was not thus blinded, and found Gorse's monocle and youthful bravado highly distasteful – particularly when he was seen with the obviously much older woman. Such an observer thought of Gorse at his real age – that of twenty-five – and of Mrs Plumleigh-Bruce at her own – that of forty-one.

Mrs Plumleigh-Bruce had also become entirely used to what she called in her diary the 'disparity' of their ages (while being completely deluded as to the full extent of this disparity). She thought of 'Boy' as being in his thirties, and she also believed that she might be taken as being no more than thirty-five.

Then again, the moment they entered London, both began to behave in an entirely different and more loose and excited manner.

Gorse, though Mrs Plumleigh-Bruce did not notice it, became much more dashing and 'common' than he had ever been in Reading, and Mrs Plumleigh-Bruce became much more girlish, flirtatious, and audibly talkative. Gorse noticed this, and of course encouraged it, for the more excited and silly he could make her, the more he was pleased.

Hence arose the very unpleasant impression they made upon the average observer, who could not make out which of the two was the more offensive or culpable. Was it the swaggering and foolish and slightly 'common' young man? Or was it the woman, who could not exactly be called 'common', but whose unbecomingly girlish manner and loquacity made her fully as unattractive as her escort?

And what was their relationship? Were they about to be married, or living together out of wedlock? And, whatever the case was, who was the seducer? Had a middle-aged woman, with money, ensnared a foolish young man? Or was a predatory young man exploiting a matured and moneyed woman?

There could, of course, be no doubt that there was something of some serious sort between them. It was revealed in their eyes, their talk, their gestures – the whole impudently intimate and self-assured aura they cast forth.

Dining in the evenings in the sedate Restaurant of the Buckingham Gorse soon developed the habit, after dinner, of holding Mrs Plumleigh-Bruce's hand over the table, and looking swimmingly into her eyes, while she looked swimmingly down her nose.

This disturbed the other diners, as well as the staff, very much indeed – elderly women residents of the hotel exclaiming 'Really!' and using such epithets as 'nasty', 'disgusting', 'horrible' or 'unhealthy'.

One such embittered woman went so far as to say that Mrs Plumleigh-Bruce 'ought to be flogged'.

'Boy' and 'Bunny', however, did not dine very often at the Buckingham.

It was Gorse's business not only to maintain but to increase Mrs Plumleigh-Bruce's general state of excitement, and this he did by taking her to theatres ('shows'), dinners and suppers at West End restaurants, and to night-clubs – all in such a way as to make her drink the greatest amount of which she was capable without realizing she was doing so.

At the theatres, restaurants, and night-clubs they made, of course, much less of an impression than at the Buckingham. All the same they succeeded in making an impression.

Indeed they succeeded in being an outstandingly distasteful couple in nearly every place to which they went.

Chapter Two

I

Very early in this uncanny sojourn in London Gorse got down to that he called to himself 'business'.

In the afternoons it was his habit to take Mrs Plumleigh-Bruce for long, circuitous drives in the car to places like Virginia Water, Hampton Court, and Maidenhead. He thus further excited and exhausted her, and so made her more readily susceptible to the drinks she took in the evenings.

On one of these evenings, having rather mysteriously absented himself from her on the pretext of 'business', Gorse returned to Mrs Plumleigh-Bruce's room at about seven o'clock in what she called in her diary 'jubilant mood indeed!'

He was now, he said excitedly, the owner of No. 21 Gilroy Road, and he flourished at her two large sealing-waxed envelopes, intimating that they contained deeds and documents.

In his haste to get a drink for both, and because of the necessity to leave her room immediately in order to lock up, in his own room, just at the moment, the precious titles to his new property, his showing her of the contents of the envelopes was finally somehow overlooked and forgotten.

On returning to her room he had further good news to break – though, according to Mrs Plumleigh-Bruce's diary, '"Boy" most mercilessly made me verily grind my teeth with vexation!'

He had, it seemed, 'sold out' and made well over a hundred pounds on the investment into which he had originally urged her to put two hundred pounds. And because she had been so timid in putting in 'only fifty' her own gain amounted to something less than ten pounds.

'Boy' insisted, however, that she should have the full ten pounds – 'a round sum if but a paltry one', as he put it, and he made her accept two five-pound notes from him then and there.

Later that evening, Mrs Plumleigh-Bruce – insisting on 'paying her way for once', went with Gorse to another night-club, where she drank so much that she had almost to be assisted home and to bed.

But the next day, over further cocktails, she had rather hysterically revived by lunch-time, and Gorse took her for another long drive in the country in the afternoon.

During this drive Gorse announced that his buying of the car now looked as though it was 'out'.

This was a pity, for he had longed to give it to her as a wedding present.

If he bought it, he said, on top of having bought the house in Gilroy Road, he would be practically penniless. His practical pennilessness would be evanescent, of course, since the house in Gilroy Road could be sold at an enormous profit in due course.

But at present it looked sadly like 'no car'.

As Gorse's methods with Mrs Plumleigh-Bruce have been so often demonstrated and illustrated before, it would be wearisome to give in detail the conversation about the car which took place between the two.

It need only be said that Gorse slowly made it clear that, if a loan of five hundred pounds were forthcoming, the car would be his – or rather Mrs Plumleigh-Bruce's – and that Mrs Plumleigh-Bruce tentatively offered to lend Gorse this sum, or part of it.

Nor need it be said that Gorse at first hotly rejected her offer. But later, over drinks in the evening, he thought better of his sterner attitude in the afternoon.

In fact he was visited by a sudden inspiration.

She would have, after all, the *car itself* as security! The moment it was bought (and she could witness its buying), she could put it (if she wanted!) into any garage of her own choice (a secret one if she wished!) and just hang on to it!

By seven o'clock that evening Mrs Plumleigh-Bruce had offered to lend Gorse the five hundred pounds now in her current account.

This offer, again, was firmly rejected.

Though there was no real harm in it, Gorse 'did not like' doing things this way. He had no intention of starting his married life in debt to his 'Bunny'. But then came another inspiration.

What if 'Bunny' put the money into a Joint Account from which they could both draw?

'Boy' would probably not have to touch it, and, if he did have to do so, for incidental expenses, Bunny would be consulted. In fact,

'Bunny' temporarily would have to 'dole out' money to the great financier – 'Boy'! A strange reversal of the situation, but perhaps it would be 'jolly good' for him!

Before midnight the matter was settled, and the next morning Gorse obtained three specimen signatures from Mrs Plumleigh-Bruce as well as her signature to a cheque for five hundred pounds. He then left her to open a Joint Account with her at his own Bank – a Joint Account from which either could draw separately, and in which there was already money of his own amounting to over two hundred pounds.

'Boy' returned shortly after midday, and, over cocktails at the new Cocktail Bar of the Buckingham, showed 'Bunny' a printed document she had to sign, and also a new chequebook from the Bank in which they were both now banking.

'Bunny' signed the document in a state of delight and bemusement caused by the newness and strangeness of the new and strange chequebook, which bore the opulent and imposing address of Cavendish Square.

Gorse was aware of the childish delight people take in new, unblemished chequebooks from new Banks. (They get a curious notion that they are in some way beginning their financial life again with a clean sheet.)

The rattled-out new cocktails in the new Cocktail Bar, taken together with the new chequebook from the new Bank, made Mrs Plumleigh-Bruce think practically nothing at all about the document she signed.

Two days later, Gorse – having enticed Mrs Plumleigh-Bruce into a delicious defiling of her new chequebook with a small sum – asked her to telephone the bank as to the exact state of their Joint Account. This she did, and was told that it stood at £723 5s 11d.

From Gorse's point of view all was over now. There were hardly any more necessary motions to go through.

He almost regretted having to do no battle of any sort with Mrs Plumleigh-Bruce about the five hundred pounds, and, brooding in his bed, it occurred to him that, had she only shown some sort of resistance, he might have done better.

She might, after all, have nearly or even completely forced him to marry her – and was marriage to her such a bad idea? Why had he limited himself to five hundred pounds?

Gorse (as yet unmarried) all his life took a very light view of this bond, and he was keenly anxious to see America, to which he had always made up his mind to go if he was forced into marrying anyone undesirable.

However, the infatuated woman had proved herself totally unable to face the idea of parting with the luxurious Vauxhall car.

Gorse, who had by now read her diary, imagined that her vision of the 'expressions' on people's 'faces' on seeing her drive up in this vehicle, with the nephew of Gorse of Assandrava as her husband, had simply been too much for her.

And so, as they had come his way so absurdly easily, he thought he had better settle for the five hundred pounds, and go through the final necessary motions.

2

Even the final necessary motions, so far from being tiresome, Gorse found as exhilarating, or even more exhilarating, than those which had preceded them.

Gorse just at this period was, possibly, in the heyday of his existence. Exuberant in his youth and an assured knowledge of his gifts, he was enjoying nearly every moment of his life. And, with a zest for such things which later was lost, he was enjoying the Buckingham, the motor-driving, the theatres, and the night-clubs. Also, at this period, he had more money than he ever had later, and saw great riches coming his way.

These hopes somehow never materialized. Soon after his relationship with Mrs Plumleigh-Bruce his fortunes did not exactly decline but were only kept at the same level by serious exertions on his part. Finally, when his fortunes did decline, his confidence in himself declined also, and with his confidence his skill.

Gorse, robbing Mrs Plumleigh-Bruce, made the mistake of thinking there were countless other and richer women waiting to be defrauded in roughly the same way.

Thus Mrs Plumleigh-Bruce, by her quite exceptional silliness and credulity, almost certainly had an adverse effect upon Gorse's career.

He was never to find another Mrs Plumleigh-Bruce, and, because of this, a sense of frustration and disappointment slowly began to tarnish, and, at last, to corrode his belief in himself. And this, in its turn, caused him to take to more crude, criminal, and violent methods with women.

3

In the days that followed Gorse made Mrs Plumleigh-Bruce write out a few more small cheques, for small pleasures, on their Joint Account. He also, with her sanction, cashed two small cheques of his own on this Account – which was now seen by both in the light of a further sentimental 'bond' between them.

Gorse remorselessly kept up the drives in the country, the theatres, the night-clubs, and the drinking necessarily attendant upon such outings.

The young man, as has been said, was enjoying these things to the full; but the mature and over-excited woman slowly began to tire seriously.

Finally she reached such a stage of exhaustion and over-excitement that she could hardly be said to be in full possession of her senses, as Gorse observed from reading her diary, in which, perhaps because of her over-excitement, she still wrote either last thing at night, or first thing in the morning.

Gorse had discovered her diary on the afternoon of their third day in London. On that afternoon Mrs Plumleigh-Bruce had visited some of those relations whose 'expressions' she was so anxious later to see, and Gorse, who from the earliest possible moment had established the precedent of keeping or asking at the Reception for the keys of both of their rooms, had entered hers in order to explore it thoroughly. He had found little to interest him apart from the suede-covered *My Thoughts* – which she kept hidden beneath clothes in the lowest drawer of her chest of drawers. Thereafter, whenever other opportunities arose, he took a glance at it.

Seeing from her diary that she was tiring, and that she was secretly anxious to go home before he had achieved all he desired in the neatest way possible, Gorse, in the last few days, threw in further pleasures, excitement, and enticements to keep her going. He began to make her drive the car (she could drive a car after a manner, and soon, under his tuition, which was kind and clever, was handling the Vauxhall with great skill and pride): he took her to two places in Bond Street to choose an engagement ring, but would consider nothing cheap, and saw to it that both should indulge in heavenly deliberations before making a purchase; and he casually promised to take her, and a few evenings later did take her, to meet Leslie Rodney and Joan Farrell (the then extremely famous married actor and actress) in their dressing-rooms at the Coburg Theatre, in Shaftesbury Avenue, after Gorse and Mrs Plumleigh-Bruce had seen the play.

Gorse had obtained an introduction to this couple through Miles Standish, who had all his life known and had at one time been on long tours with the now highly publicized couple. Standish had given this introduction with much reluctance, but could not risk offending his potential backer with a refusal.

Before taking Mrs Plumleigh-Bruce to the Coburg, Gorse had first visited Leslie Rodney and Joan Farrell after a matinée with his letter of introduction, and so, in front of Mrs Plumleigh-Bruce, he was able to give an impression of being on easy, if not familiar, terms, with the two celebrities, who, because of this false familiarity disliked and distrusted Gorse almost as much as did Miles Standish. But they showed all the outward cordiality which their profession and distinguished position demanded. (Mrs Plumleigh-Bruce came out of the stage door entranced with delight and awe at their 'simplicity' and 'naturalness'.)

And during all this period Gorse engaged Mrs Plumleigh-Bruce in incessant discussions as to when and where they were to be married.

Although he wanted to be married at the church at 'Grasswicke', with the Brigadier-General's blessing and all that, he chafed at the delay which such a thing would cause – the 'reading of the banns, etc.' – and favoured an immediate marriage at a Registry Office in London. After all, he was not 'religious' – or, at any rate, not religious in that way.

But here the more romantically-minded 'Bunny' restrained her impetuous 'Boy', and at last made him agree to marry her at 'Grasswicke'.

('What a tussle I have had about it all!' she wrote in her diary. 'But as usual, after adroit handling, poor "Boy" gave in! How little he knows how he is being "handled". Will this be the "pattern" of our married life? It will, methinks privately – but "mum's the word", and he will probably never know what is taking place for his own good!")

'Boy' and 'Bunny' spent, in all, twelve days at the Buckingham – 'Bunny', on the last day, returning to Reading by herself; this owing to an obligation on 'Boy's' part to attend a 'Sparktone' meeting in the City. ('Sparktone' was the name of the wireless firm in which he had much money, and of which he was a Director.)

Their parting, however, was to be of the briefest and most stimulating kind.

'Bunny' was to take her courage into both hands and drive ('little me all alone?') the Vauxhall back to Gilroy Road.

Here she should arrive at about two-thirty at the latest, and then, with the aid of Mrs Burford (who had been telephoned), she would prepare tea and await the arrival, by train, of her 'lord and master' at about four, or earlier.

This would give Mrs Plumleigh-Bruce a further chance of 'captivating' Mrs Burford, who was (both now agreed) a 'dear old soul' to whom the '*News*', both about the real ownership of the house, and the impending marriage, it would only be fair to break soon.

'And by the way,' shouted Gorse – amidst the noise of the starting engine (and of an electric drill – at that period a much discussed and hated innovation – at work about fifty yards away) – as he saw Mrs Plumleigh-Bruce off in a side-street near Buckingham Palace Road, 'you know this is yours now – don't you?'

'*What's* mine?' cried the deafened Mrs Plumleigh-Bruce.

'Oh – only the car,' Gorse replied, putting his mouth near to her ear. 'I paid for it yesterday – and all's signed and sealed, and your property entirely. So take care of your own property – won't you? Off you go!'

Gorse moved away and waved, and off a slightly stunned Mrs Plumleigh-Bruce went – driving her car towards Reading with just that extra *finesse* in accuracy, timing and patience which distinguishes a new car-owner from a normal car-driver.

Gorse, who had so patiently and cleverly taught Mrs Plumleigh-Bruce to drive the Vauxhall, forgot, for the moment, the divinely new Sunbeam two-seater, which had become his property only yesterday (and which had been immediately behind the Vauxhall while he was saying goodbye to Mrs Plumleigh-Bruce), and watched her until she was out of sight.

He thought well of his lady pupil.

PART THIRTEEN

GORSE THE ABSENT

Chapter One

I

Foolish, vain, greedy, lethargic, affected, mouthingly arrogant, and for the most part unpleasantly dishonest in mind Mrs Plumleigh-Bruce certainly was, and all these qualities, taken together, might have been said to have added up to a species of serious evil in the whole. Nevertheless it would be hard to say that she entirely merited the evil which descended upon her that afternoon and evening.

This lady owner-driver of a Vauxhall car arrived at 21 Gilroy Road, Reading (now the property of her future husband), at about three o'clock, and was let in by Mrs Burford, the dear old soul whom Mrs Plumleigh-Bruce had so captivated, and who would almost certainly be employed by her after her marriage.

To fill in the time before 'Boy' arrived at four (or earlier), Mrs Plumleigh-Bruce further captivated Mrs Burford by going down to the kitchen for the first time, asking how the delicious scones were made, and entering into a womanly and woman-to-woman conversation about the house generally. In doing this she was unable quite to conceal a prematurely possessive, patronizing and employing manner – a manner which Mrs Burford did not fail to notice and which she thought mysterious as well as slightly insolent.

2

Mrs Burford was far from being the dear old soul romantically created in the roseate conversations of the betrothed couple.

In spite of her professional grey hairs, soothing manner, cosiness, stoutness and spectacles, the housekeeper ruthlessly took monetary advantage of her absent employer – Mr Ronald Shooter – bullied and nagged and constantly changed the young girls whom she employed to help her run the house, had countless acquaintances to tea, drank stout with them at Gilroy Road and in public houses, gossiped, dwelt upon or predicted every sort of local misfortune or scandal, and denigrated friend and foe alike while predicting or loftily contemplating such disasters.

Gorse (to whom she had always been as sweet as honey) she disliked because he was an intruder and possible spy or reporter on behalf of her employer; and she had been even sweeter to Mrs Plumleigh-Bruce, whom she disliked even more than Gorse.

The gifted scone-maker, in brief, was not at all the sort of person to sustain, encourage, fortify or soothe Mrs Plumleigh-Bruce in the evil which fell upon her that afternoon and evening.

3

At about a quarter past four, Mrs Plumleigh-Bruce, having temporarily parted from Mrs Burford, began to look out (through the gracious bow-windows of the spacious and well-furnished sitting-room) for Gorse, who should, unless his train was late, have already appeared.

Dusk was descending, and in its grey, hazy light, Mrs Plumleigh-Bruce took great pleasure in surveying the stately outlines of the Vauxhall car.

Had she been alone in the house Mrs Plumleigh-Bruce would probably have experienced not the faintest feeling of apprehension when, at half past four, Gorse had still not appeared.

But because of the nearness of Mrs Burford a faint irrational uneasiness came over her – or rather stole up to her from the kitchen below.

There was, possibly, a logical psychological cause for this seemingly illogical uneasiness in Mrs Plumleigh-Bruce. The woman below had, undoubtedly, a sixth sense for impending disaster.

Disasters falling upon others were, after all, the very breath of the housekeeper's being.

The late arrival of anyone would at once put the thought of disaster into her mind – the thought would rapidly develop into a distant hope, the distant hope into a yearning, and the yearning, finally, into a state of excitation in which the woman became inspired – a prophetess.

At half past four this final prophetic stage had certainly not been reached, but some of the preliminary symptoms were doing something more than mystically stirring within Mrs Burford: they were mystically being conveyed, in the hour of dusk, and with its aid, to the waiting woman upstairs – conveyed in the sound of slightly impatient footsteps, in the rather noisy opening and shutting of oven and other doors, and in the distant but peculiarly audible rattle of cutlery and crockery.

Taking a sudden dislike to the dusk and to the noises below, Mrs Plumleigh-Bruce switched on the electric light. But this only made her feel a good deal more dreary and slightly more apprehensive than before. Also she was dimly disturbed on noticing, as she drew the curtains to, that the lamps in the street were already lit – for this announced the unmistakable arrival of evening, or even of night.

Four-thirty being the time arranged for tea, Mrs Plumleigh-Bruce forced herself to wait until a quarter to five before calling to Mrs Burford from the top of the basement stairs. This she did under the pretence of being merely solicitous about the scones and in no way disturbed by the lateness of the arrival of the temporary master of the household.

But Mrs Burford, by this time almost in her yearning stage of hideous prediction, would not permit any such evasion, and, treating the matter of the scones most lightly, said: 'He *is* late – isn't he?'

Mrs Plumleigh-Bruce here pretended that she herself took this lateness in as light a spirit as Mrs Burford had taken the matter of the scones, but then made the grave mistake of saying that 'he' might have missed the train, and would be on the next one. This was playing into Mrs Burford's hands.

Mrs Burford said, accurately, that even if 'he' had missed the intended train, the one after it should be in by now, and that 'he' should be here by now.

This agitated and dismayed Mrs Plumleigh-Bruce, and Mrs Burford, seeing this sign of weakness on her face in the light of the basement stairs, at once took further advantage of Mrs Plumleigh-Bruce. She dropped the vague and rather self-conscious 'he' and, having repeated that the tea and the scones were of no consequence, added, humorously, and just before turning resignedly from the bottom of the basement stairs to her kitchen: 'Yes, *your* gay young man's *certainly* got behind in his time!'

Mrs Plumleigh-Bruce naturally regarded this as being abominably familiar, and, on returning to the drearily electric-lit sitting-room, decided, as she listened to every footstep in the lamp-lit street outside, that she would almost certainly not 'take on' Mrs Burford after her marriage.

Matters were then made worse for Mrs Plumleigh-Bruce by the telephone ringing.

The telephone was just at the top of the basement stairs and Mrs Plumleigh-Bruce, certain that it was 'Boy' calling to explain his delay, cried joyously down to Mrs Burford, who was half-way up the basement stairs, 'All right, Mrs Burford, I'll take it!'

The telephone call was, however, a case of one of those wrong numbers whose wrongness takes a very long time in being argumentatively (and at last angrily) revealed, and Mrs Plumleigh-Bruce, having known all the time that Mrs Burford had been listening on the stairs, had to cry down, 'All right, Mrs Burford. Only a wrong number!'

Then Mrs Plumleigh-Bruce returned to the sitting-room in a state of fierce irritation with Mrs Burford, and serious anxiety about Gorse, which, after listening to more footsteps in the lamp-lit street outside, she at last decided she must control. She went yet again to the top of the basement stairs, and told Mrs Burford to bring up the tea. There was no sense in waiting and spoiling the scones.

Mrs Burford, bringing in the tea and scones, had now very nearly reached her inspirational phase, but, fearing disappointment, she concealed her condition with further insolent humour.

'Well,' she said, putting Mrs Plumleigh-Bruce's tea in front of her. 'It looks as though your young man's gone and deserted you – doesn't it? – *good* and proper!'

'Well,' replied Mrs Plumleigh-Bruce, also affecting humour in order to conceal her emotions. 'Even if he has, he's left me a very nice car, just outside!'

'Well, he's left you Mr Shooter's car, at any rate!' was the retort of the gay, cosy, dear old soul, as she went to the door.

Mrs Plumleigh-Bruce very nearly let Mrs Burford close the door behind her without making any reply. But something made her say: 'What do you mean – "Mr *Shooter's* car", Mrs Burford?'

4

'Why, just Mr Shooter's car, madam,' said Mrs Burford, respectfully and meekly, and to this Mrs Plumleigh-Bruce replied, What do you mean – Mr Shooter's car? It was Mr Gorse's.

Well, it wasn't, madam, said Mrs Burford, and Well, it *was*, said Mrs Plumleigh-Bruce – because she knew for certain that it was.

Well, Mrs Burford didn't know *how* Mrs Plumleigh-Bruce knew for certain it was, as she (Mrs Burford) happened to know for certain it wasn't – unless Mr Shooter had sold it to Mr Gorse, which wasn't very likely.

And here Mrs Plumleigh-Bruce completely lost her nerve and her temper, and said that recently *other* things had been changing hands – including housekeepers, even.

And then, naturally, the storm broke.

Chapter Two

During a lull in the storm, it did not take long for Mrs Burford to prove that neither the house nor the car belonged to Mr Gorse.

She went upstairs and showed Mrs Plumleigh-Bruce a letter she had received from Mr Shooter from Paris only yesterday morning. This letter, which was in a totally different handwriting from the one Gorse had shown Mrs Plumleigh-Bruce, by a happy coincidence covered both matters. As well as speaking of returning in a fortnight's time to 21 Gilroy Road, in a manner which made it abundantly evident that he was not conscious of having sold the house to Gorse, Mr Shooter mentioned both Gorse and the car, jovially 'trusting', that 'our friend' was using both the house and the car, 'to say nothing of the housekeeper', in a 'fitting manner'.

Mrs Burford then supplemented this evidence firstly by telling Mrs Plumleigh-Bruce that she could there and then ring up Mr Shooter's solicitors in Reading, who for years had done all the business concerning the house, and secondly by naming the garage in Reading where Mr Shooter always kept his car. The owner of the garage was a personal friend of Mrs Burford's, and would explain that the car had only been lent temporarily to Gorse.

But what did it matter? Mrs Plumleigh-Bruce had not, by any chance, lent or given any *money*, or anything like that, to Mr Gorse – had she?

Mrs Plumleigh-Bruce then made her inevitably ghastly evening at least three times more ghastly by admitting that she had.

The inspired prophetess at once changed into an inspired interpreter of past history.

She had always *known*. She had known it from the *beginning*!

The moment she had clapped eyes on that young Mr Gorse she had known!

She had never liked him. She had *never* trusted him. *She* had never been taken in by his so-called 'gentlemanly airs'.

Then, watching Mrs Plumleigh-Bruce growing whiter and whiter in the face, the inspired interpreter turned into a glorious, divine, Christ-like comforter and sustainer, taking control of the entire situation.

Almost with physical violence she compelled Mrs Plumleigh-Bruce to sustain herself with tea, while she made the necessary telephone calls to Mr Shooter's solicitors in Reading, and to the owner of the garage in which Mr Shooter kept his car.

Then, again almost using physical compulsion, she forced Mrs Plumleigh-Bruce to talk on the telephone to Mr Shooter's solicitors, and to the garage-owner.

Both confirmed Mrs Burford's assurances in a manner which left no conceivable doubt in Mrs Plumleigh-Bruce's mind as to their genuineness and accuracy.

The garage-owner – a Mr Berry – asked with some anxiety about the present whereabouts of the car, and Mrs Plumleigh-Bruce said it was outside the house. Mr Berry suggested that he should come round and call for it, and Mrs Plumleigh-Bruce agreed.

Mr Berry said that he would be round in about twenty minutes, but did not appear until about three-quarters of an hour later.

Mr Berry, though kindly, was a gloomy and tactless man, who made more inquiries and comments than he should have done with a woman in so tragic and humiliating a predicament. And, on departing, having put Mrs Plumleigh-Bruce through the black shame of removing her luggage from the car she did not own into the house Gorse did not own – he suggested that it was, surely, a matter for the Police, and that at once.

This threw the prophetess, the interpreter of history and divine consoler, into yet another sort of ecstasy – a police-ecstasy of the most violent kind. She was the personal friend of an authoritative police officer in Reading, and she insisted that he should be telephoned at once.

But here Mrs Plumleigh-Bruce just managed to restrain her, though she had first to become hysterical and had almost to use physical compulsion herself with her comforter, guide and friend.

Mrs Plumleigh-Bruce did this for several reasons. She felt she could bear no further humiliation that evening: she was too feeble to undergo further questioning, and she still felt that Gorse, though he had lied about the car and the house, might not have robbed her financially. That could only be ascertained by telephoning the Bank about their Joint Account next morning.

Over and above this, Mrs Plumleigh-Bruce had already an instinctive feeling that she would never apply to the police. The risk of the hideous public exposure of her folly and infatuation which such a thing might entail would (she dimly foresaw) be too great.

Instead of telephoning the police Mrs Plumleigh-Bruce telephoned Glen Alan to speak to Mary. (She had intended to do this at tea-time, probably to say that she and Mr Gorse would be in to dinner.) To her surprise there was no reply from Glen Alan.

Then Mrs Burford insisted on Mrs Plumleigh-Bruce drinking brandy, and again tried to make her telephone the police, urging that she ought, at any rate, to have the advice of a *Man* at once. Didn't Mrs Plumleigh-Bruce know a *Man* she could go to?

Slightly stimulated by the brandy, Mrs Plumleigh-Bruce realized that she did indeed want the assistance of a Man, but she could think of only one – Donald Stimpson.

Could she swallow her pride, she wondered, by going to him and telling him all? Might he not forgive her? Might he not even forgive her and marry her?

At this moment of her life the idea of marriage – as a refuge and means of restitution of her lost pride before herself and the world – was immeasurably desirable to Mrs Plumleigh-Bruce.

Over a second brandy she decided to telephone Mr Stimpson, if possible meet him, and confess all.

But there was no answer from Mr Stimpson's number. He was, Mrs Plumleigh-Bruce guessed, almost certainly round at The Friar.

Then, in order to escape from the hateful house, and the hateful housekeeper's presence, Mrs Plumleigh-Bruce said that she must go home. Her maid Mary, she said, would be getting anxious about her.

Mrs Burford asked what she was going to do about her luggage, and Mrs Plumleigh-Bruce, almost running out of the house, replied that she would send Mary or 'somebody' (she hoped Mr Stimpson) round for it 'later'.

She did not intend to return at once to Glen Alan, but to go to The Friar in the hope of meeting Mr Stimpson.

The Friar was nearly half a mile away, and on her way she was caught by a sharp shower of rain.

On arriving at The Friar she found only one friend – Major Parry.

Chapter Three

I

The Major was exceptionally drunk and exceptionally inspired.

He had got drunk in the morning on the strength of some staggering news imparted to him by Mr Stimpson (who had also taken a lot to drink) and his evening drinks had (as they had with Mr Stimpson on that night in London) flown like wild-fire to his head and rendered him practically insane.

He was inspired because he was drunk, and drunk because he was inspired. He had got his rhyme for 'fallen!' ('They are fallen, they are fallen, they are fallen.')

His miraculous solution of his long-standing problem did not look at all good to the Major next day. But tonight it was all as simple as pie!

He was suddenly going to change the rhythm, go into inverted commas, and brackets, and give a grim yet intensely exciting picture of a sort of foppish but magnificently exuberant sort of ex-public school leader in battle itself. Thus:

'(Just listen! Isn't that the Major callin' –
In accents loud – yet cool and calm and drawlin'?
"Come on now lads – just stick at it! Stone-wallin'!
No whimpering – no whining now, no crawlin'!
Nothing's too bad for *us* – *nor* too appallin'!
It's *they* – not us – that's goin' to take the maulin'!
What's wrong with death? Adventure most enthrallin'!")'

And so on and so forth. He'd work it out properly tomorrow, but the idea was simply terrific.

Perhaps he shouldn't make it a Major, because he was a Major himself and they might think he was trying to advertise Majors and being conceited. But that could be changed tomorrow, too.

As he put his pencil and paper away and sat back in a daze of delight, Mrs Plumleigh-Bruce entered.

2

In her state of distress, Mrs Plumleigh-Bruce was quite unconscious of the Major's present condition.

The Major, however, even in the dizzy mist of alcohol and military realism surrounding him, at once suspected that she was in a state of distress, and somehow pulled himself together and asked her what she would drink.

On her asking for brandy, his suspicions were confirmed, and, on returning with the brandy, he asked her outright if anything was the matter.

Mrs Plumleigh-Bruce replied that well, as a matter of fact there was, quite a lot really, and that she was anxious to see Donald Stimpson. Had he been into The Friar this evening? Or did the Major know whether he was likely to be in?

To this, the Major, looking at her in an odd way, and giggling, replied, Well, no, and what with all these goings-on of his it looked as though he wouldn't be quite as regular a frequenter as usual.

The odd look, the giggle, and the curious remark were not taken in by the distraught woman.

The Major then asked if *he* could help. Come along now, what was it all about?

Then Mrs Plumleigh-Bruce, having looked at the Major, had a sudden impulse to tell a 'Man' something of the truth.

She said it was a very long and complicated story, but the point of it was that it looked as though she had been 'done out of some money' by 'our young friend'.

'What – not young Ralph Whatsisname?' asked the Major, to which Mrs Plumleigh-Bruce had to reply Yes.

The Major then asked Where, When, How? And how *much* money?

And Mrs Plumleigh-Bruce, beginning by telling him half the truth, soon found herself telling it almost in its entirety.

In her relief at finding that the Major showed no signs of being either a prophet, an interpreter of the past, or a rhapsodist of any sort, she told him about her recent trip to London, the house in Gilroy Road, the car, and the Joint Account.

'But why on earth a *Joint* Account?' the Major exclaimed, and before long Mrs Plumleigh-Bruce had half confessed that she had half contemplated marrying Ernest Ralph Gorse.

The Major saw without difficulty that this was in fact a full confession, and said that something must be done at once. He mentioned the Police, and False Pretences and all that, and went to the bar to get Mrs Plumleigh-Bruce another brandy and a large whisky for himself – as if doing this was obviously the quickest and most efficient way of getting to the Police.

But, on returning to her, the silly, excitable, but kindhearted and in many ways sensitive maker of verses saw that Mrs Plumleigh-Bruce was in no mood either for the Police or for drinking any more brandy.

He therefore told her that she had better go home at once, and, with his aid, look at things in a new light in the morning. He would escort her home.

Mrs Plumleigh-Bruce agreed to this, and the Major, having rapidly drunk his own large whisky, as well as (in a waste-not-want-not spirit) Mrs Plumleigh-Bruce's brandy, took her out of The Friar.

On the walk back to Sispara Road in the lamp-lit darkness Mrs Plumleigh-Bruce noticed that the Major had suddenly become very inebriated. He was, in fact, staggering – at moments reeling. But the Major's staggering and reeling were so infinitely preferable to Mrs Burford's prophesying that Mrs Plumleigh-Bruce was scarcely offended by it.

Glen Alan was reached, through dense rain, at about eight-thirty.

The house was dark, and Mary, mysteriously, was not in the house.

The Major knew exactly why Mary was not in the house, but he did not reveal his knowledge to the agonized woman. Instead he put the lights on for her, 'stoked' the fire (which was nearly in ashes) and, promising help early next morning, blundered away into the darkness and rain.

3

It was not until Mrs Plumleigh-Bruce had poured out another brandy for herself and was sitting by the slowly kindling fire, that she noticed that Mary had left a letter for her in a conspicuous place on the sitting-room table.

She thought at first that this must be a brief note explaining her servant's absence. But, on opening it, she found that it was an eleven-page letter.

Mary, though an intelligent girl, spelt and wrote so badly that Mrs Plumleigh-Bruce could hardly be bothered to read it. She simply glanced at some of its phrases, weakly trying to make some sense out of its illiterate but passionate ramblings.

'*Left everything in Apple Pie Order Madam,*' she read, and '*would never Let you down*', and '*You have always been So Good to me*', and '*Would never let you down and Have left everything in Apple-Pye order I trust*', and '*He says it would be unsuitable for me to Continue under such circumstances*', and '*I hardly know wear I am*', and '*surely it would be unwise for me to refuse such an offer as I am only a poor girl and it is a chance of a lifetime I know you will agree and so do all my friends*', and '*I dred to meet You it is such a strange Contradiction in all ways*', and '*there is only a little while now*', and, finally, '*I am still your humble and obedient and devoted servant in every way and only wish to serve you and will Help out whatever he says whenever you Only ask me and I remain your*
Respectful and gratful Servant,
Mary McGinnis'.

It was only when Mrs Plumleigh-Bruce had at last gone to bed (and was re-reading this letter, under the silk-shaded electric light and in the comforting presence of her silken Marie Antoinette doll) that she realized that her maid Mary McGinnis had left her and would be marrying her friend Mr Donald Stimpson very shortly.

PART FOURTEEN

SISPARA ROAD

Chapter One

I

Never, to the end of her days, could Mrs Plumleigh-Bruce in the smallest way understand the mad event which, along with her personal tragedy, made it absolutely necessary for her to leave Reading almost at once and for ever – Mr Stimpson's marriage to her maid Mary.

But Mr Stimpson's motives were really very easy to understand.

Mr Stimpson had always, even while making love to Mrs Plumleigh-Bruce, looked on Mary in a highly libidinous way, and, on her coming to work for him, his carnal desires completely overcame him.

Then, during Mrs Plumleigh-Bruce's absence in London, Mr Stimpson made some inquiries about Gorse's whereabouts. He telephoned 21 Gilroy Road, and was told by Mrs Burford that Mr Gorse was at the Buckingham Hotel in London, and would probably be there for about a fortnight.

Then, with mounting suspicions having telephoned the Buckingham Hotel and ascertained that both Gorse and Mrs Plumleigh-Bruce were staying there, the Estate Agent had not the slightest doubt that the two were living together in the large hotel in sin – sin which, he somehow felt, would almost certainly be later redeemed by marriage.

Thus, his sudden violent carnal desires towards Mary coincided with almost equally violent desires for revenge upon Mrs Plumleigh-Bruce and Gorse.

The two things together, however, might still not have made him make the spectacular move he did, had he not, one morning, accidentally run into a journalist on a local paper, and said to him, half in joke, that he was thinking of marrying his maid, who was 'by the way, the most perfect cook in Reading or anywhere'.

The journalist sensed at once that Mr Stimpson was speaking only half in joke, and spoke of the 'wonderful story' it would make, of Mr Stimpson's delightful 'originality and courage' should he take such a step, and of the enormous publicity which he would like to give it locally.

The journalist toppled Mr Stimpson over into seeking Mary's hand in marriage. The Mr Stimpsons of life are excited almost as frantically by the idea of large local publicity as by the idea of the fulfilment of their carnal desires, or the sweetness of revenge.

2

The trouble was Mary herself.

This chronically and incurably obedient girl, shocked beyond measure by the proposal, entreated Mr Stimpson, almost on her hands and knees, not to make her do such a dreadful and ridiculous thing.

But her temporary employer and master was absolutely adamant. With sudden proletarian fervour he himself doggedly visited and entertained Mary's many friends, and made them his supporters.

The distressed, weak Mary was told that she was missing 'a chance of a lifetime', that if she married the Estate Agent she would become a 'lady', and that she need never do a 'hand's turn' ever again. Also she could support her mother in Ireland.

Under extreme pressure from Mr Stimpson and his working-class supporters, and for the sake of her mother, Mary at last gave in.

About only one thing was she herself adamant. She was a Roman Catholic, and insisted upon being married in a Roman Catholic Church.

Mr Stimpson pleaded with Mary about this matter, but was quite unable to shake her, and so, as rapidly as possible, he embraced the Roman Catholic faith. This caused delay, as he had to go through quite a lot of tuition and examinations about the nature of, and one's earthly obligations to, the First Cause.

But he got a lovely big picture of himself and his bride in the paper, and he soon found himself very happy in his new faith (more so than Mary) and they were, on the whole, an unusually happy couple.

This curious sort of thing is constantly happening in provincial towns.

Chapter Two

I

Major Parry telephoned Mrs Plumleigh-Bruce on the morning after the evening he had seen her home in the rain, and could hardly get any sense out of a stupefied voice.

He suggested coming round, and (Mrs Plumleigh-Bruce feebly agreeing) was at Glen Alan by ten-thirty.

Mrs Plumleigh-Bruce was white, not made up, and in her Kimono. She had wretchedly been attempting to make herself, and make herself drink and eat, some coffee and toast, and the sitting-room in which she received her guest was made even more bleak and sordid than it might have been by this scrappy unfinished meal on a tray and the dust and ashes of last night's fire.

Mrs Plumleigh-Bruce had long ago lost any ability she ever had for housework of any sort, and this morning she was, of course, quite incapable of putting up any sort of decent performance in this direction.

Mrs Plumleigh-Bruce apologized for the 'state' the place was in and explained that Mary had left her. The Major then said that he knew already that this had happened, and had only not told her last night in order not to distress her further.

'It's all the funniest business *I've* ever heard of,' said the Major. 'And I only hope they'll be happy, that's all. But I doubt it – don't you?'

'Yes. I do,' said Mrs Plumleigh-Bruce, and, the Major, seeing that Mrs Plumleigh-Bruce, who had obviously been crying a great deal, might easily cry again, changed the subject, and it was not alluded to again.

The Major, then, in duty bound, had to speak of action being taken in regard to Gorse.

Mrs Plumleigh-Bruce said that she didn't see that there was any action to take. She had opened, of her own free will, a Joint Account with Gorse – one from which they were both permitted to draw – and so she had virtually given the money to Gorse.

Nevertheless the Major argued that it must be a case of getting money by false pretences, or something like that, and urged her to apply to the police or see a solicitor (his own) at once.

Then Mrs Plumleigh-Bruce suddenly recalled that she did not as yet know for certain that Gorse had taken any money from her, and the Major, realizing that this was not utterly impossible, said that the Bank must be telephoned; and he himself undertook to do the telephoning.

But this was a long and arduous task and one which the Major was not able to complete by himself. Before giving information the Bank required details which only Mrs Plumleigh-Bruce could provide, and she had to go to the telephone.

It was finally ascertained that the rather weird sum of £8. 3s. 11d. stood to the credit of the Joint Account of Mrs Plumleigh-Bruce and Ernest Ralph Gorse.

After this telephone call Mrs Plumleigh-Bruce broke down. She began to cry, and fled from the Major in order to conceal her tears. She was heard by him sobbing in the Study, Den, Hidey-Hole or Snuggery.

When she at last recovered she rejoined the Major in the sitting-room.

Here the Major again began to talk of resorting to the law, but Mrs Plumleigh-Bruce would still not hear of it. Everything would come *out*, she kept on repeating, everything would come *out*.

Even if there were any redress on the score of 'false pretences', or anything, she would have to explain the nature of these pretences – her folly and credulity about the house and the car, her ridiculous acceptance of Gorse's proposal of marriage, her Joint Account with him, and her stay with him in London. Imagine, she argued, how it would *look*!

Gorse was nothing more nor less than a young and possibly dangerous criminal. That was all he was. And he was a criminal of whom she was *afraid*. She said, truthfully, that she had always been a little afraid of him. And how could she, Mrs Plumleigh-Bruce, ever hold her head up again in the world if she were involved in a criminal case of *that* sort?

The Major saw that there was a lot of truth in all this, and, because she was already breaking into tears again, decided to delay pressing her any further until she was more composed.

After a while, Mrs Plumleigh-Bruce, having looked around the sordid sitting-room and at the uneaten breakfast, found her misery beginning to turn more towards the loss of Mary rather than the loss of her rich young lover, her money, and her self-respect.

She had to have *someone* to help. Who was she going to get, and how was she going to set about it?

Here the Major was at a loss, and could only suggest that his wife might help. In fact, why not let his wife come round now? She could tidy up, and take charge generally, while Mrs Plumleigh-Bruce went to bed. That was where Mrs Plumleigh-Bruce certainly ought to be.

Then Mrs Plumleigh-Bruce, in a panic, asked the Major whether he had told his wife about this.

The Major swore that he had not breathed a word of the matter to his wife. But, of course, he had told her the story in full detail last night.

Then Mrs Plumleigh-Bruce made him swear, on his sacred word of honour, that he would never tell his wife, or anyone. And the Major, rather uneasily, did this.

He then continued to urge bringing in his wife to help, and Mrs Plumleigh-Bruce at last consented.

The story to Mrs Parry was to be merely that Mrs Plumleigh-Bruce was indisposed by fearful and prolonged neuralgia, and had suddenly lost her maid during this period of suffering and practical collapse.

The Major, not being on the telephone, was unable to telephone his wife, and so was compelled to leave Mrs Plumleigh-Bruce in order to fetch her.

He was glad that he was compelled to do this, as he was thus able to explain to his wife, on the way back to Glen Alan, that his wife knew nothing about the Gorse business and that Mrs Plumleigh-Bruce was merely suffering from fearful and prolonged neuralgia and had suddenly lost her maid during this period of suffering and practical collapse.

Mrs Parry, who hated Mrs Plumleigh-Bruce as much as Mrs Plumleigh-Bruce hated her, was extremely exhilarated by the task set her, and was kindness itself to Mrs Plumleigh-Bruce.

Though rather base, Mrs Parry was not as base as Mrs Burford, and, on the strength of her exhilaration, brilliantly disguised her inner happiness.

She made Mrs Plumleigh-Bruce go to bed, brought her Bovril

and toast, tidied up the sitting-room and kitchen, and set about the task (over the telephone) of getting Mrs Plumleigh-Bruce a new maid or help.

She left Mrs Plumleigh-Bruce in the afternoon to sleep with the aid of Aspirin, and she called again in the evening to cook a light meal, which Mrs Plumleigh-Bruce managed to eat.

Suitable domestic help at Glen Alan was not found until two days after this – two days in which Mrs Plumleigh-Bruce's neuralgia grew slowly better (so that she came downstairs) and in which she was visited regularly by the Major and his wife.

The Major, whenever he was (with his wife's exhilarated permission) alone with Mrs Plumleigh-Bruce, still urged action being taken about Gorse, but Mrs Plumleigh-Bruce would still not consent to this.

The Major, undoubtedly, behaved remarkably well and selflessly with Mrs Plumleigh-Bruce. This was probably because she had now lost nearly all her physical attractions in his eyes, and, with this complication gone, he was able genuinely to pity her.

She had not become less physically attractive to him because he had seen her so pale, and puffy-eyed, and slatternly and miserable. He could have looked to the future and got over that.

She had become less desirable because two other men, Gorse and Stimpson, had made it plain that they had no desire for her.

This woman was not desired, in fact, at the moment, by any man – and women, in such a pass, mysteriously lose every capacity they have for creating such desire.

Unto those who have, it shall, uncannily, be given. Unto those who have not, it shall, uncannily, be taken away.

2

Mrs Plumleigh-Bruce, despite the Major's sustained but kindly pressure, never resorted to the law about the abhorrent young man who had tricked and plundered her.

All she did was to beseech the Major somehow magically to 'hush it up', and to help her leave Reading as soon as possible.

But the Major, who had already revealed everything to his wife, was unable to hush it up.

And, with the aid of the inexhaustible Mrs Burford, who was enormously powerful locally, this strange scandal somehow reached nearly every quarter of the town and became, very nearly, a legend therein.

And Mr Stimpson's astonishing marriage to Mary (with the picture of the wedded pair in the paper) of course made matters a hundred times more fascinatingly complicated, and so worse for Mrs Plumleigh-Bruce.

Sispara Road itself was on to it very soon. Mrs Plumleigh-Bruce's next-door neighbours – the Chiropodist and the Commissioner for Oaths (living respectively at 'Rossmore' and 'Deil-ma-Care') – had been closely watching Mr Stimpson, Gorse, and the Vauxhall car coming and going for a long time; and, as soon as the news filtered through, the Chiropodist and the Commissioner (with the industrious support of their wives) spread it all along the whole row of pebble-sprayed, gnomed, brass-infested houses – from 'Rossmore' and 'Deil-ma-Care' to Strathcairn, Mon Repos and Lyndhurst – and thence to Greenways, to Grass Holme, to Colombo, to Ivydene, to Montrose, to Cranford, to 'Kismet', to Belle Vue, to 'Chez-Nous', to Champneys, to 'Wee Ben', to Seafield, to Val Rosa, to 'Ourome', to St Alban's, to Loch Corrib, to Mansfield, Sandbourne and all the rest.

Mrs Plumleigh-Bruce was fully aware of what was going on, and, with the Major's assistance (after two months of intense suffering), at last let Glen Alan and found refuge in Worthing, Sussex.

She first of all stayed at a small hotel there, and then took over a small maisonette in the upper part of a small grey house in a small grey road from which one could walk to the Worthing sea just within ten minutes.

What Gorse had done, for about six months, improved Mrs Plumleigh-Bruce's character, manners and accent wonderfully.

But the monocled young man's fine endeavour was at last lost.

For gradually Mrs Plumleigh-Bruce began to forget her humiliation and, coming out of retirement, to sit for longer and longer periods in shelters on the sea-front at Worthing.

And there she struck up acquaintances who were all, before long, acquainted with her relationship to the General – General Sir George Matthews-Browne.

And Mrs Plumleigh-Bruce's rich, regal, mouthy, throaty, fruity, haughty and objectionable voice became a recognized noise in the wind and desolation of the hopeless and helpless sea-front.

PART FIFTEEN
COLEOPTERA

Chapter One

1

That afternoon Gorse, having watched Mrs Plumleigh-Bruce going off in his friend Ronald Shooter's Vauxhall car, stopped to survey her gift to him, the ravishingly new Sunbeam, and then, because he was so intoxicated by the sight of this, he did an unusual thing. He returned to the Buckingham Hotel and drank a glass of port.

He lingered over the drink, happy in the thought that he had plenty of time on his hands.

But at last, having paid his bill and having gone to the Porter's desk and asked for his luggage to be brought down from his room, he returned to the Sunbeam and drove it up in front of the great hotel. His luggage was put into the car, and he drove off.

Gorse had no exact idea as to where he was going to drive, but for some reason felt that somewhere in the middle of England would be the best and safest place for him for the time being.

Gorse found himself quite inadvertently using to himself the word 'safest', and he wondered why it had come into his head. For he had, really, no feeling of being in any way unsafe.

2

Gorse, particularly with women he was defrauding, always talked at great length and with much apparent erudition about the finer points of the 'law', but in fact he knew next to nothing about it.

In this case he was quite certain that the 'law' could in no way distress or annoy him, and he had no intention of changing his name or employing any busy devices in the way of concealment or flight.

In the first place he was confident that no proceedings would be set in motion against him by Mrs Plumleigh-Bruce. He predicted that she would take precisely the horrified and hopeless attitude that she did.

In the second place, even if she did otherwise, he was not in the smallest way afraid of any action she might take.

He was not only prepared to swear black and blue that she had given him the five hundred pounds as a present: he rather relished the idea of being called upon to do so.

In such circumstances, he felt, he would be able (as he put it to himself) to 'take it out' of the 'silly bitch' in 'no uncertain manner'.

He had, he saw – with the aid, paradoxically, of his own crime – severely compromised Mrs Plumleigh-Bruce by staying so ostentatiously with her at the Buckingham. Should she 'start anything' in regard to his crime he would be willing to swear that he had lived with her there under conditions of the extremest sexual intimacy. And he knew that the world would believe it.

The five hundred pounds with which he had bought the Sunbeam car (he would swear) had been a present for 'services rendered' to a woman more than fifteen years older than himself.

In other words, Gorse was prepared to pose as what was, in the stupid, excited late twenties of this century, a much more publicized and talked-about type than it is now – a *gigolo*.

Great odium, of course, was then attached to this word by the public, but Gorse was not the type to fear popular odium. He also knew that much greater shame was borne by the employer of the *gigolo* than by the *gigolo* himself – and that this was a sort of shame which Mrs Plumleigh-Bruce would be less able to endure, perhaps, than any woman in England.

In fact, he 'had her every way', so far as he could see.

Even if he was sought by the police, he thought he was not at all likely to be traced.

The car was his own, bought and paid for in an entirely straightforward and honest deal (honest, that was to say, as between himself and the dealer) in Great Portland Street. He therefore had no intention of refraining from using it, henceforth, wherever and whenever he wished. He was prepared to flaunt it.

3

Gorse, musing thus, was taking a remarkably inconsequent attitude.

If the police were active the car could in fact be traced by means of the cheque written out to the dealer, who could give its description and number. And the oaths, black and blue, which he was willing to swear about his relationship with Mrs Plumleigh-Bruce might not have stood up to keen, thorough or fierce examination.

Gorse's glass of port made him feel more inconsequent than he might have been, and as soon as he was in the Sunbeam his peace of mind became, for a character normally so alert and perspicacious, almost fatuous.

He was, perhaps, stupefied by the pleasure he took in driving his new car to nowhere in particular in the unexpectedly warm and sunny February afternoon.

The fact that he was running in a new car, which had not to be injured by being driven at a speed of more than twenty-five miles an hour, added to his sense of slow, god-like calm.

4

All this inconsequence – which he had shown, really, from the very beginning to the very end in his dealings with Mrs Plumleigh-Bruce – Gorse was never to experience again.

After this Gorse slowly lost his inconsequence. He began to think – to think before, during, and after the commission of his crimes. He became, therefore, less of an artist and less successful in his art – like a painter who nags at perfection in a picture until he is distraught, or a writer who thinks about the intricacies of meaning, grammar or syntax until he nearly goes mad.

Too much thought is bad for the soul, for art, and for crime. It is also a sign of middle age, and Gorse was one who had to pay for the precocity of his youth in the most distasteful coin of premature middle age.

Chapter Two

1

Gorse, driving slowly to nowhere in particular in the middle of England, thought of himself as very much the master of himself and of his car. But he was the deluded victim of both – particularly of his car.

In his attitude towards his car, though, he was not making an error in any way peculiar to himself. It was one shared by the owners of the multitudes upon multitudes of other cars which he met or which overtook him on his way.

For it was just about at this period that these vehicles, so strongly resembling beetles if seen from the air, finally took complete control of the country, the countryside, the villages, the roads, the towns and the entire lives of the human beings who dwelt or moved therein.

Gorse was, one might say, on that sunny February afternoon, driving unconsciously not into the middle of England – but into the middle of the hideous Land of Coleoptera (the rather sinister name for beetles used by serious students of insects).

2

When Gorse was born, in 1903, these machines were not distinguishable as Coleoptera. They were rare, explosive, laughably crude and high in stature, constantly breaking down, and objects resembling, on the whole, absurd and lovable grasshoppers rather than beetles.

But slowly, as they multiplied, they changed their shape and greedily clung closer to the earth which they were at first merely to infest but at last completely overrun.

By the time Gorse had reached his majority they were recognizable as beetles.

There were large, stately, black beetles – small, red, dashing (almost flying) beetles – and medium-sized grey, blue, white, brown, yellow, green, orange, cream, maroon, and black, black, black and again black beetles.

Soon after Gorse's majority the beetles got into a great state of confusion. They began to run into and seriously obstruct each other.

Because of this there was a sort of beetle-revolution – a battle not between beetles and beetles but between beetles and men. In this rather bloody revolution the beetles demanded, and succeeded in easily obtaining, from men, what they considered justice and order for themselves.

Men, having surrendered unconditionally, set to work (not unlike the unhappy builders of the Pyramids) laboriously and carefully to satisfy the demands of their crawling yet pitilessly exacting new rulers. The beetles were not magnanimous in victory.

Vast new roads had to be made for the convenience or pleasure of the beetles; open spaces were set aside for them in the smaller towns in the country; and in the larger towns the most complicated buildings (in which the beetles, when seeking rest, could dive underground or go spirally upwards to floor upon floor) were erected.

Thus there in due course appeared a vast slave-army, spread all over the country, of harassed but sedulous attendants upon beetles.

There were beetle-physicians, beetle-hospitals, beetle-nurses, beetle-feeders (by means of tubes), beetle-washers, beetle-oilers, beetle-watchers, and beetle-guides.

The watchers and guides were sternly made to wear smart uniforms and to salute any passing beetle; and, in private houses, beetles were given private bedrooms, in which, if the weather was cold, they were solicitously covered with rugs.

There were tens of thousands of men who spent many hours of the day (or night) lying supinely underneath beetles and examining their greasy intestines by the light of torches.

All this went, not inexcusably, to the heads of the conquering race. They multiplied further, took further advantage of the conquered, and went further afield.

Dizzy with success – doctored, nursed, fed, washed, oiled, watched, guided – they entered into a mad round of dissolute pleasure. They went to race-meetings, tennis-tournaments, theatres, horse-shows, dog-races, golf-tournaments and so on and so forth.

In these open-air places (at golf-tournaments for instance) they bore an ugly resemblance to swarming bees. And in such swarms they still got into frantic muddles and obstructed each other – Ford arguing with Hillman, Alfa-Romeo with Bentley, Swift with Sunbeam, Talbot with Wolseley, Alvis with Buick, Cadillac with Fiat, Essex with Chrysler, Hispano-Suiza with Citroën, Austin with Bean, Daimler with Hupmobile, Lagonda with Lincoln, Morris-Cowley with Humber, Morris-Oxford with Studebaker, Vauxhall with Triumph, Standard with Riley, Packard with Singer, Rover with Bugatti, Star with Beardmore, Rolls-Royce with Armstrong Siddeley, and Peugeot with Invicta – to say nothing of obscure conflicts between the Amilcar, Ansaldo, Arrol-Aster, Ascot, Ballot, Beverley Barnes, Brocklebank, Calthorpe, Charron, Chevrolet, Delage, Delahaye, Erskine, Excelsior, Franklin, Frazer-Nash, Gillett, Gwynne, Hotchkiss, Hudson, Imperia, Italia, Jordan, Jowett, Lanchester, Lancia, Marmon, Mercedes, Opel, Overland-Whippet, Panhard-Levassor, Peerless, Renault, Rhode, Salmson, Stutz, Trojan, Turner, Unic, Vermorel, Vulcan, Waverley and Willys-Knight.

But there their slaves were, exhausting themselves in giving them intricate but necessarily bawled instructions as to the manner in which they might extricate themselves from their difficulties. (Beetles were always and still are very bad and slow at going backwards.)

In the nightmare of Coleoptera only two sorts of beetle retained any dignity or charm. These – the lumbering Omnibus and Lorry – were very large, very helpful and for the most part smooth-tempered. Furthermore they killed men, women and children very little. (All the other beetles had begun to kill men, women and children at a furiously increasing pace – practically at random.)

3

Gorse, then, whose whole character and aspect were, really, of a very beetly kind, knew as little of what he was doing as of where he was going.

(In fact he ended up that day in a medium-sized Commercial Hotel in Nottingham.)

Other beetle-owners (that is to say, beetle-slaves) who overtook or met Gorse on his way, at least knew where they were immediately going, and had a very rough unconscious idea as to their ultimate destination on this planet. They imagined that they would one day, having worn their lives out in beetle-service, die, more or less painfully and slowly, in bed. And most of them did.

But the red-haired Gorse – the reddish, reddish-moustached, slightly freckled beetle-driver, driving slowly into the era of the all-conquering beetles – did not have even this trivial advantage in unconscious foreknowledge.

For he was to die painlessly and quickly. And he was not to do this in bed.

But the red-haired Gossel – the reddish moustache, slightly faded, the beetle-lover, slowing slowly into the era of the all-comprehending beetles – did not have even this trivial advantage in such regions for knowledge.

For he was to die painlessly and quickly, and he was not to die in bed.

UNKNOWN ASSAILANT

Chapter One

1

Ivy Barton, a Chelsea barmaid, was on Sundays able to stay in bed an hour later than on weekdays. This she relished very much.

She did not, however, use the extra hour for extra sleep. Her mother brought her a cup of tea and a newspaper – the *News of the World* – and she read.

One Sunday morning, early in the year 1933, she came across an item dealing with a matter of robbery with violence.

A working girl, it seemed, had been tied to a tractor in the country (somewhere in Norfolk not very far from King's Lynn) and had been robbed of about twenty pounds. She had, after some time and with difficulty, released herself from the tractor: but by this time her 'unknown assailant', as the *News of the World* described him, had escaped. The police were searching for him.

Ivy Barton was not particularly interested in this piece of news, which was not given much space by the famous newspaper, and at which she only glanced rapidly. She merely vaguely wondered how and why a working-class girl had had as much as twenty pounds upon her at the time.

But she would have been a good deal more than interested had she known two facts – the fact that she had met and conversed with the 'unknown assailant' ony last night, and the fact that she was going to meet him again within the next twelve hours.

2

Ivy Barton was a decidedly foolish but very good and lovable girl.

She was twenty-eight years of age, dark, birdlike and vivacious – much too vivacious, even for a barmaid, whose business it is, of course, to be sprightly in manner.

In her unnecessary vivaciousness she revealed but one aspect of her foolishness, which derived, possibly, from an ingrained and totally ineradicable habit of obedience to everybody and everything.

This frame of mind had, beyond doubt, been originally instilled into her by her father – an ex-gamekeeper under whose roof she still lived.

The moustached, ageing, thin, grey-haired, round-shouldered Mr Barton was also foolish – but not in a lovable way. He was a harsh, vain, grasping and embittered man. Because of these faults in his character he had at long last been tactfully dismissed from an excellent position on a very pleasant country estate in Cheshire.

To all trespassers, guilty or innocent, gamekeepers nearly always seem to be brusque or harsh. All that, however, is probably part of a gamekeeper's business, just as it was part of Ivy Barton's business to be almost fulsomely cordial. But Mr Barton had always been gratuitously savage to those trespassers who had been momentarily within the scope of his authority.

Because he had been grasping he had made money. And he would, of course, not admit that he had been tactfully dismissed from his employment. He had dismissed his employers, and come to live in Wynch Street, Fulham, of his own free will. He told Wynch Street (here quite truthfully) that he had always wanted to live in London.

The great town had not made him any happier.

Without actually beating Ivy in early life much more than an average gamekeeper beats his daughter, he had succeeded, by means of constant ferocious nagging, in subduing her utterly – in making her much more hopelessly compliant and foolish generally than she might have been.

But he had failed to make her like himself – unlovable. His behaviour, on the contrary, had only made her more simple-minded, and therefore lovable, than she would have been naturally.

3

The name of the 'unknown assailant' was in fact Ernest Ralph Gorse, but, just at this time, he was masquerading under the name of 'The Honourable Gerald Claridge'.

Ernest Ralph Gorse was a very serious criminal.

Ivy Barton, from the first, thought him charming – a 'real gentleman'. And Ivy often boasted that she could 'tell a real gentleman the moment she saw him'.

The public house in which Ivy worked was geographically but not spiritually in Chelsea. It was in a backwater north of the King's Road and within five hundred yards of St Luke's Church.

Chelsea proper is, as is well-known, despite its countless normal inhabitants, the favourite London resort of those who are obvious failures or of those who are obviously going to be failures before long.

The failure is nearly always of an 'artistic' kind.

This was not always so. Very many writers and painters who have made a serious mark in the world have lived in Chelsea. It is such people, however, who have caused considerable confusion in the district, into which hundreds upon hundreds of young exponents of the arts have flocked in the hope of emulative or imitative success.

Some of these are humble and pathetic beyond measure. Others are extremely arrogant and ostentatious. Perhaps it might be said that the members of both types are to be pitied. Nearly all of them are very poor, and borrow too much money, and drink too much out of despair or bravado. Chelsea is a sort of borrowing and alcoholic Bloomsbury. Bloomsbury, on the whole, prefers financial integrity and cocoa.

Because she worked in a backwater, Ivy Barton was hardly aware of what went on in the public houses quite near to the one in which she was employed. She knew that there were some 'funny ones' in the locality – that was all.

The name of the house in which Ivy worked was The Marlborough, and most of her work was done in the Saloon Bar.

That Sunday evening 'The Honourable Gerald Claridge' came in at about eight o'clock.

Because there were few customers about she was able to talk a great deal, and in the most friendly and interesting way, with the red-haired, nasal-voiced, slightly freckled, monocled young man of thirty.

Before he left The Marlborough he casually, as it were accidentally, – seemingly coming across it accidentally in his pocket – gave her his card. This disclosed the fact that his address was that of a well-known West End Club and that he was what Ivy called 'an Honourable'.

Both disclosures were meant to put Ivy into a state in which she might be knocked down by a feather – and they did.

Chapter Two

1

Ivy, a week or so later, told her mother about her remarkable new acquaintance, with whom she was now even more friendly. And her mother, almost as impressed as her daughter had been by the card, was unable to resist showing it to her husband.

Mr Barton, although he would not admit it, was really as much intrigued as his daughter and wife. He disguised his feelings with an air of indifference and scepticism.

But his attitude of scepticism was never, at any moment, sincere. Had it been so he would have looked more closely into the matter of 'The Honourable Gerald Claridge'.

Mr Barton, as an ex-gamekeeper, knew quite a lot about 'titles', and he could easily have gone to his local Public Library – of which he was quite senselessly and purely out of a grasping spirit a member – to find out more about the name of Claridge.

Had he done so he might have been saved much trouble.

Instead of taking this precaution, however, with most unusual politeness he invited his daughter, one evening after tea on her evening off, to have a talk with him alone in the sitting-room of his rooms in Fulham.

Ivy was delighted by this suddenly most courteous invitation from her harsh father.

2

That was a very strange, indeed almost an uncanny interview.

Mr Barton began with sustained indifference and scepticism. But he was still strangely polite to his daughter.

He asked her who *was* this Mr Claridge? Was he a gentleman?

'Oh yes,' replied the still rather terrified Ivy. 'He's *that* all right. In fact, he's got Eton and Harrow written all over him.'

Mr Barton saw no absurdity in this notion – that of a man who had first of all gone to Eton, and then to Harrow, and who revealed, simultaneously and unmistakably, the stamp of both schools in his demeanour. On the contrary, he fully understood Ivy's meaning – though he was not willing fully to accept Ivy's extremely high estimation of the man.

He then asked Ivy 'how far it had gone'.

'Well,' said Ivy, 'he certainly seems very interested. As a matter of fact he's asked me to go out with him, or if he can come round and see me here.'

'Come round and see you here *alone*?' Mr Barton asked.

'Oh no,' said Ivy. 'Come and see me with you and Mums. He says he'd like to meet you both.'

Mr Barton was here decidedly dumbfounded and bewildered. The man from Eton and Harrow, if he had spoken the truth, clearly had no immediately evil designs upon Ivy. But why should such a man want to visit an ex-gamekeeper and his wife living in a very poor street in Fulham?

'You've got to be careful of these people, you know,' said Mr Barton, speaking with very much greater wisdom than he knew. 'Why should he want to come here? It's not much of a place, is it? You don't think he's got a real fancy for you, or anything like that, do you?'

'I don't know,' said Ivy. 'He might have. Anyway, he looks at me and talks to me as though he does – I must say.'

Mr Barton here looked intently at his daughter, trying, not for the first time, accurately to appraise her potentialities in the way of attracting men. As usual, he failed. He knew that Ivy, without being pretty, had in the past had one or two admirers, of whom he had not approved, and who had all finally disappeared: but this was all he knew. And looking at her was never of any assistance to him.

It occurred to him this evening that Ivy might be a good deal 'deeper' than he had imagined. What if, unknown to himself, she had the ability seriously to ensnare men? She had, after all, obtained a position as a barmaid; and a barmaid, in Mr Barton's estimation, ran second only to a chorus-girl or an actress in matters of glamour and fast behaviour. Because of this he had originally almost forbidden Ivy to work at The Marlborough.

In those days of 1933 the now outmoded fashion of peers marrying chorus-girls still survived. Why, then, should 'The Honourable Gerald Claridge' not have designs upon a barmaid?

Because he was an ill-natured man Mr Barton's impulse was still to maintain his scepticism and do all in his power to damp Ivy's obvious interest in Mr Claridge. But something held him in check.

'And he really wants to come round here?' he asked.

'Oh yes,' said Ivy. 'He's most insistent about it – and wanting to meet you and Mums.'

'Perhaps he just wants to find out what it's like,' said Mr Barton. 'And he might be pretty disillusioned – mightn't he?'

'No. I don't think so,' said Ivy, unusually firm in her defence of her new friend. 'I told him we were only humble people, and he said what on earth did that matter? He said he hated snobbery more than anything. He said he'd had enough of that from his own family.'

Here it occurred to Mr Barton that Mr Claridge might be the 'black sheep' of some powerful family. He nearly said as much to Ivy.

But again something held him back.

The truth of the matter was that both his curiosity and vanity had been strongly stimulated – mostly his vanity. The thought of entertaining, in his own home, and on reasonably equal terms, a member of a class to which he had once been entirely subservient, was extremely pleasant.

The 'black sheep' hypothesis did not deter him at all. On the contrary it rather encouraged him.

And here his greed was at work. Black sheep were, to his mind, almost certainly either unwise, degenerate or gullible sheep, and so 'something might come of it'. He did not know what – but something.

'Well – there's certainly no harm in his coming round here if he wants to,' he said, imitating an air of condescension. 'In fact I'd like to see him. When does he want to come?'

'Well – we didn't fix a date. I was waiting to ask you,' said Ivy. 'But he said he'd be in at The Marlborough tomorrow night, and we can fix it then, I suppose.'

'Very well. You do that. He's very welcome, as far as I'm concerned,' said Mr Barton, and he changed the subject, questioning Ivy, with a totally unprecedented cheerfulness and consideration, about her other personal affairs. Ivy responded with totally unprecedented loquaciousness and frankness. She believed, for the moment, that she might have misunderstood her father's character. Ivy was very easily swayed, and responded instantaneously to kindness of any sort from anyone.

All the time they were talking, however, there was a funny, thoughtful glint in Mr Barton's eye as he looked at his daughter. The man was speculating shrewdly as to the 'something' which might conceivably arise from this acquaintanceship with the Honourable Gerald Claridge, and he was in fact hardly listening to his daughter.

That glint in Mr Barton's eye – along with his unusual courtesy, and Ivy's talkative (though still half-frightened) happiness – was what made the interview, in its small way, so uncanny.

Chapter Three

I

Ivy was given her afternoon and evening off from The Marlborough on Thursdays. On the evening of the Thursday following that on which she had had that rather uncanny interview with her father, she brought the Honourable Gerald Claridge round to Wynch Street, Fulham, at about six-thirty. The interview that followed was even more uncanny than the other.

It took place in Mr Barton's sitting-room – a clean, gas-lit room, engagingly overcrowded with such pleasant furniture, hangings and pictures as may still be found in a few country cottages.

Mr Barton, on the whole, detested and despised his own furniture, which came from the cottage he had once inhabited on the estate in Cheshire. The only piece of which he was really proud was his large wireless set – in fact the only abomination in the room.

Mr Barton, before the Honourable Gerald Claridge arrived, had been much exercised in his mind as to how he should address the young man. In spite of his decided preference for an urban rather than a rustic way of living, Mr Barton was politically a most reactionary Tory, and was vindictively, and constantly vocally, anxious that everyone should know and keep their place.

Should he not, then, address the Honourable Gerald Claridge as 'Sir'?

Finally he decided to leave this matter in abeyance until he had seen his guest.

Almost as soon as he had done this he decided to use the word 'Sir'.

He saw, in the gaslight of his sitting-room, a slim, reddish-haired, reddish-moustached, quite tall and decidedly well-dressed young man. Mr Barton had no doubt that he was looking at a 'gentleman'. He was not absolutely certain that he had Eton and Harrow written all over him but was very much inclined to that opinion.

So 'Sir' it should be.

2

The trouble was that the Honourable Gerald Claridge at once began the interview by addressing Mr Barton as 'Sir'.

'How do you do, sir,' he said, as, breezily and yet with a diffident smile, he shook Mr Barton's hand. 'I'm very glad we've met at last.'

It took a lot to make Mr Barton look or feel silly, but this opening did so.

'How do you do, sir,' said Mr Barton feebly, and he tried to smile back. But Mr Barton was not good at smiling and was at a complete loss.

Ivy came to the rescue, inviting Mr Claridge to sit down in the best armchair in the room.

Mr Claridge was about to accept this invitation, but, just before doing so, hesitated.

'But isn't this *your* chair, sir?' he said. 'I'm sure this is yours – isn't it?'

'No – it's not mine in particular,' said Mr Barton, although it was. 'And this one's just as comfortable.'

'Sure?'

'Yes, sir. You sit there and I'll sit here.' Mr Claridge sat down, and Mr Barton sat down in another armchair facing Mr Claridge. 'But can't I give you something in the way of refreshment, sir?' he went on, after a pause. 'I'm afraid we haven't got much very interesting, except what you see there.'

Mr Barton pointed to a small table, near Mr Claridge, upon which two bottles of wine and wine glasses had been set out on a tray. One bottle contained elderberry wine and the other dandelion wine. These wines had been made by Mrs Barton, who was an adept in concoctions of this sort. Mrs Barton, a neurotically timid woman, had absolutely refused to meet Mr Claridge, but had hoped that this contribution might further the success of the meeting.

'And what *do* I see there?' said Mr Claridge, drawing his monocle from his waistcoat pocket and looking at the tray on the table. 'Well – at a superficial glance, it looks excellent to me.'

Mr Barton was pleased by the monocle, not because he was foolish enough to think that the wearing of a monocle was a sign of one who had Eton and Harrow written all over him (as Ivy almost did), but because he thought that it was a sign of foolishness, of foppery, of a 'silly ass'. And the thought of the Honourable Gerald Claridge as a 'silly ass' not only made his interest in his barmaid daughter more credible: it gave further sustenance to Mr Barton's hopes that something might arise from all this – in other words that the Honourable Gerald Claridge might without difficulty be ultimately exploited in some way or another.

'Well, it's not what you'd call a man's drink, certainly,' said Ivy, 'it's just some wine my mother makes. But it's very nice if you don't mind a soft drink.'

'I can think of nothing nicer,' said Mr Claridge. 'Do let me have some. Perhaps you'll pour it out with your own fair hands. Will you?'

'Don't know about fair,' said Ivy, and began to pour out some elderberry wine for Mr Claridge, Mr Barton and herself.

'Well – this is a very nice little place you seem to have here,' said Mr Claridge, as Ivy busied herself. 'Very nice indeed.'

'Well that's very good of you to say so, sir,' said Mr Barton. 'But it's certainly not what I'd like myself.'

'Isn't it? Then what sort of thing would *you* like, sir?' said Mr Claridge.

Mr Claridge – that is to say Ernest Ralph Gorse, the 'unknown assailant' about whom Ivy had read in the *News of the World* only two Sundays ago – now saw that this double-sided 'sir' business was becoming very ridiculous indeed. But he did not at the moment know how to put an end to it.

'Well – I'd like something a lot more modern – not all this country junk,' said Mr Barton. 'Wouldn't *you*, sir – if you were in my place?'

Gorse emphatically agreed with Mr Barton. (Their tastes in furnishing were, in fact, very much the same.) But of course he could not say as much, and he compromised.

'Well I don't know . . .' he said. 'But I suppose one's got to keep up with the times.'

'You're right there, sir, and this is just as far behind the times as you could find. Don't you agree, sir?'

Here Gorse decided to dodge the issue by audaciously attacking the 'sir' problem.

'You know, you mustn't call me "sir", sir,' he said, smiling charmingly. 'That's for me to do – surely – isn't it?'

'What – out of respect for my grey hairs, you mean, sir?' said Mr Barton.

'Well – I don't know about grey hairs, exactly. There're a lot of quite young people with grey hairs, aren't there?' said Gorse. 'All the same, I'm sure you know what I mean. Don't you?'

'Well, perhaps I do, sir . . . Very well, then, I'll call you Mr Claridge, sir – if that suits you.'

'It suits me perfectly . . .' Ivy was handing Mr Claridge his drink. 'Ah, thank you very much, Ivy. This looks extremely delicious.'

'Well – I hope you think it tastes delicious,' said Ivy. 'It won't make you very gay. It's only an old-fashioned country drink.'

'And what could be better than something old-fashioned and from the country?' said Gorse.

There was a pause, as Ivy gave her father a glass of elderberry wine. Because of this pause, Mr Barton was given time to collect himself, and he saw that he had now been given his first opportunity of seeking information about the Honourable Gerald Claridge.

'Are you a country gentleman, then, Mr Claridge?' he asked.

3

All his life Ernest Ralph Gorse, in spite of his astonishing astuteness generally, was capable of absurd, seemingly totally inconsequent, blunders.

In assuming the name of 'The Honourable Gerald Claridge', which he had only done in the last week or so, it had never even occurred to him to invent any sort of family to which this imaginary character belonged, or any background from which he had emerged.

Therefore, at this moment, he had no idea whether he was a 'country gentleman' or not.

Gorse, however, when it caught up with him, was usually able to redeem this strange and incurable flaw in his mental make-up by quick thinking and audacity.

He knew that at the moment he was talking to an ex-gamekeeper. Therefore it would be fatal to pose as one with any knowledge of the country. And so he replied:

'No, sir. I'm afraid I'm very much of a town-bird. Much too much, I sometimes think. No . . . I'm afraid bars and theatres are more in my line than birds and trees.'

Gorse speaking of bars and theatres, with a monocle in his eye, made the naïve Mr Barton at once think of chorus-girls and champagne. And this confirmed his impression of Gorse as a 'black sheep' or 'a silly ass'.

'Yes,' said Ivy, who was now sitting on a small chair with her own glass of elderberry wine, 'you know a lot about the theatre, don't you?'

'Well, you have to,' said Gorse, 'if you're interested in it from a financial point of view, as I am.'

'Why – have you got money in the theatre, then, Mr Claridge?' asked Mr Barton.

'I have indeed, sir,' said Gorse. 'In fact I've got the greater part of my money tied up in it.'

'And you find it a profitable business?'

'Well – and I have so far, I must say,' said Gorse. 'Of course the profit really comes from solid bricks and mortar – from rent – more than from the shows themselves. The shows themselves can be pretty risky things, as no doubt you know, sir.'

Mr Barton was not particularly pleased by the solid bricks and mortar and rent. Was the Honourable Gerald Claridge (who had now removed his monocle) less of a fool than he seemed – a shrewd young financier, conceivably, rather than a fool?

'No. I don't know the first thing about it,' said Mr Barton. 'I like going to the theatre well enough but I've never what you call been "behind scenes" in my life.'

'What – never been "behind scenes"? Well – we must remedy that.' Gorse smiled. 'That is if you're interested, of course, sir.'

'Neither have I, if it comes to that,' said Ivy. 'Only behind the bar – that's me.'

'Well, then – you've both missed something, I can assure you,' said Gorse. 'Not that there's really anything to it. But it ought to be done once in a lifetime.'

'Why,' said Ivy. 'Could you get us in through the stage door somewhere?'

'I certainly could,' said Gorse. 'Though personally I usually prefer the pass-door. You know what I mean – the pass-door from the auditorium to the back?'

'No. I've never heard of it,' said Ivy.

'Well, then – you must let me introduce you to it . . . What about it? Let's all three of us go to a show one evening, and then go round behind afterwards. I can fix it all up free, gratis and for nothing. And wouldn't your mother like to come, too?' said Gorse, addressing Ivy.

'I'm sure she would,' said Ivy. 'And you would, too, Dad – wouldn't you?'

'Yes. I must say I'd like to see what goes on behind. I like to get behind and see the workings of everything.'

Mr Barton spoke like a highly disinterested scientist – a Sir Francis Bacon, with all knowledge as his province. But in fact he was anything but disinterested. Both his commercial and emotional instincts had been awakened. On the commercial side he was delighted by the notion of getting something free, gratis and for nothing; and he also felt that such a visit to a theatre would help to cement an acquaintanceship with a most interesting and possibly affluent young man. On the emotional side he was excited merely by the idea of being taken 'behind scenes'. Mr Barton was certainly not a boyish character on the whole, but Gorse's offer had succeeded in bringing into being a quite puerile enthusiasm.

Along with this his vanity saw an opportunity of being richly fed. He pictured himself boasting to his friends, in the public houses he frequented, about the experience promised by Gorse – boasting both in anticipation and retrospect.

It was, really, at this moment that Mr Barton completely succumbed to Gorse's personality, fell, as Gorse would have put it, 'hook, line and sinker'. (The foolish, chronically obedient and credulous Ivy had of course done this already.)

Gorse had no difficulty in seeing that Mr Barton was already captivated, and had been easily victimized by a trick which he, Gorse, had used a great deal in his life – that of luring people by an assumed inner knowledge of the theatre.

Those with some experience of the theatre often find it hard to believe with what awe masses of people regard this medium, both from an artistic and social point of view. To be given free seats for the theatre gives such people the acutest happiness – one which amounts almost to delirium when they are taken 'behind scenes'.

Why this should be so, why so many people should be more excited by being permitted to see some of the inner workings of the theatre rather than being taken over a glass factory, say, or a biscuit factory, remains a mystery. But there it is, and Gorse, at an early age, had probed and played upon this mystery.

Gorse, that night, did not remain more than three-quarters of an hour at Wynch Street.

At about quarter past seven he suggested that Ivy and her father (and mother, if she wished) should go with him to a local cinema.

Mr Barton, in spite of Gorse's pleading, could not be prevailed upon to accept the invitation – but he was most insistent that Ivy and Gorse should go.

'No, not for me,' he said. 'But you two go and enjoy yourselves.'

After this he kept on saying 'No – you two go and enjoy yourselves', in a rather meaning way – thus already beginning to be slightly familiar with, and so slightly to patronize, Gorse.

It was, of course, extremely unwise either to be familiar with or to patronize Gorse.

It was, indeed, unwise, or even dangerous, even to know him. But Mr Barton could not have been expected to have had any suspicion of this.

Chapter Four

I

Nearly all writers about Gorse, in later years, referred, with an air of incredulity, to the credulity and folly of those whom he victimized.

It is fair to suppose, though, that very many of these writers, had they themselves had dealings with him, would have behaved in very much the same way.

The two best biographers of Gorse were undoubtedly G. Hadlow-Browne and Miss Elizabeth Boote – though both made grave errors, factually as well as psychologically. Both were what are popularly called 'criminologists', with several books (and prefaces to books) on criminals to their credit. Miss Boote, who had also written a well-known novel founded upon a famous crime, was more serious in her approach to her subject than Hadlow-Browne, who was inclined to a humorous attitude which occasionally degenerated into facetiousness. Nevertheless he probably hit the nail on the head more truly and often than Miss Boote.

'But fortunately for people like Gorse,' wrote Hadlow-Browne, 'the powers of self-deception in mankind are limitless. It is because of self-deception, rather than deception, that the Statue of Liberty has in the past so frequently been sold to private individuals. Self-deception, in fact, is probably the quality which most clearly distinguishes *Homo sapiens* from the rest of animal creation. Animals deceive, and are deceived, but of self-deception they are as guiltless as small children . . .

'The self-deceiving Mr Barton', Hadlow-Browne went on, a few paragraphs later, 'seems to have been vanquished, from the very first meeting, by the charms of the monocled "Honourable Gerald Claridge".

'They met first of all at the public house in Chelsea called The Marlborough, where his daughter Ivy worked as a barmaid.'

Here, as we know, Hadlow-Browne (himself something of a self-deceiver) was indulging in factual inaccuracy. He proceeded (another fault of his) imaginatively to build upon a false foundation.

'The English public house, as is well known,' he wrote, 'is a meeting place for all types. Class distinctions vanish and all men, "over a pint", thrash out the problems of the day on an equal and amicable footing.'

Here, Hadlow-Browne, of course, disclosed his lack of knowledge of public houses.

'Mr Barton, warming to the young stranger over the beer brought to their table by his daughter Ivy (*sic*), saw nothing in the smallest way odd in this presumable scion of some great family seeking either his own friendship or that of his daughter. They talked of country matters (*sic*), politics, sport, and all those other trivial and engrossing matters which engage the minds of men in their leisure hours.'

At this point Hadlow-Browne forsook fiction and hit, as he so often did, the nail on the head.

'Of one thing, however,' he wrote, 'Mr Barton neglected to talk. He seems to have made no inquiries as to the family of which "The Honourable Gerald Claridge" was a member – an oversight which he was to regret.

'Finally the talk turned, as it does in most classes of society, to the theatre. Mr Barton was much impressed to learn that his well-born young friend was interested in this from a commercial point of view, and before long Mr Barton found himself contemplating himself in the conceivable role of "backer".

'The reader may well be surprised that a comparatively poor man – an ex-gamekeeper living in a humble Fulham back-street – could ever have been induced to have aspired to play such a part. And it is, indeed, difficult fully to appreciate the plausibility and almost hypnotically persuasive powers of Ernest Ralph Gorse.

'All details are not fully known. In any case, as we have already described at considerable length the methods normally used by Gorse when duping his fellow creatures, it would be tedious as well as needless to describe those with which Mr Barton was beguiled. We may be certain that they were very much the same as those which brought the widowed lady in Reading, the Haywards Heath dentist, the Rugby watchmaker, and, first but not least, the unhappy Esther Downes, all to such unhappy passes.'

2

Hadlow-Browne, with his mixture of inaccuracy, accuracy, facetiousness and shrewdness, is of service to us here.

To those acquainted with the character and history of Ernest Ralph Gorse it would, indeed, be 'tedious as well as needless' to describe his methods – particularly those he employed with Esther Downes of Brighton and Mrs Plumleigh-Bruce of Reading. And those unacquainted with Gorse's character may be satisfied with Hadlow-Browne's remarks about Gorse's powers of exploiting self-deception in others.

Although, as we know, Mr Barton did not 'first of all' meet Gorse at The Marlborough, he did in fact meet him there, and did in fact there talk of 'country matters, politics, sport and all those other trivial and engrossing matters which engage the minds of men in their leisure hours'.

But this was after Gorse had taken Mr Barton and his daughter, on the Thursday night following that on which the three had first met, to the Empress Theatre in St Martin's Lane.

3

If any doubts had ever existed, in the minds of either Mr Barton or his daughter, about the authenticity of Gorse's statements about himself, they were permanently dispelled that evening at the Empress, when, in the interval, he introduced them, in the bar, to Lord Lyddon, who gave them a drink and talked to them.

Lord Lyddon (authentically Lord Lyddon) was a morose but good-natured young man of thirty-five, who drank too much by himself during the day, but who cheered up in company, and seldom failed in good manners.

At an early age he had been exaggeratedly 'stage struck'. He had indeed in some ways resembled a member of that long-extinct type, a 'Johnny-at-the-Stage-Door' or a 'Johnny-in-the-Stalls'. But his interest in the theatre had not been confined to actresses: he had been intrigued by it financially and had put money, not without success, into quite a few plays.

On inheriting money he had ventured much further in this direction with much less success: and at the time of meeting the Bartons he was quite seriously financially embarrassed.

The revue at the Empress, called *Reaching for the Moon*, was losing a great deal of money weekly.

Lord Lyddon was, in a not immediately noticeable way, good-looking, but his face was prematurely rather lined, and there were streaks of grey in his fair hair.

If he had thought about the matter he would have found that on the whole he disliked Gorse, who had thrust himself upon him, but whom he had no reason actually to distrust.

Gorse was not masquerading as 'The Honourable Gerald Claridge' with Lord Lyddon, to whom he had given his correct name. He was, however, posing as a monied young man, a potential backer, and one who could without difficulty obtain substantial backing from other sources. For this reason Lord Lyddon tolerated his company, which he might otherwise have politely dodged.

Gorse, in introducing the Bartons to Lord Lyddon, was, without at first realizing it, once again making one of his absurd and seemingly inconsequent blunders. Known as Ralph Gorse to Lord Lyddon and as Gerald Claridge to the Bartons, his pretensions might easily have been exposed both to the Bartons and Lord Lyddon. But it was done on the spur of the moment – for he had not known for certain that Lord Lyddon was going to be in the bar – and Gorse had the sort of mind which would certainly have found some acceptable explanation.

Owing to the poor business being done by *Reaching for the Moon*, the small Circle Bar in which they met was almost empty, and Lord Lyddon, dressed in a dinner jacket (for he had a social engagement later which needed one), and sitting alone, was glad to have someone to talk to.

He could not make out what sort of people the Bartons were. Mr Barton, who was neatly dressed in a dark blue suit with an unbecoming stripe and of poor material, reminded him of a gardener at a wedding. If Mr Barton had worn a sprig of heather in his buttonhole the resemblance would have been perfect. Instead of this Mr Barton wore the metal badge of some obscure, parochial, and, one might be sure, abominably reactionary organization. Ivy reminded Lord Lyddon of what she was – a modest and good-natured barmaid.

Mr Barton was much more at ease than his daughter with Lord Lyddon, whom he at once, rather ostentatiously and too often, began addressing as 'My Lord'. Mr Barton, as we know, was a bitter and unyielding advocate of everyone knowing and keeping their places.

Ivy, overwhelmed at being presented, in such circumstances, to a 'Lord', gazed in a frightened way at him, and called him, to begin with, 'Sir'.

On Lord Lyddon's recommendation Mr Barton and his daughter missed two numbers of *Reaching for the Moon*, and sat in the bar over a second round of drinks, which were paid for by Gorse.

This was, undoubtedly, the most memorable and exhilarating evening of Ivy's life.

To talk and drink, to be, although at present in front of the house, 'behind the scenes' with those who had originated, those who actually engineered and dominated the 'scenes', to whom they were an everyday matter – this would have been more than enough for Ivy. But that one of these godlike beings should have been a good-looking 'Lord', and the other (though through familiarity with the idea she had now almost forgotten this) an 'Honourable' – this was almost too much.

Ivy, unlike her father, was entirely free from social snobbery; but, again unlike her father, she was the victim of excessive naïvety about matters relating to social position.

She had always gathered that members of the 'aristocracy', and, even, of 'Royalty', 'The King and Queen' themselves, were, in private life, 'probably just like us, really'. Nevertheless, to sit with and watch and listen to a 'Lord' obviously being just like us really (and Lord Lyddon, who had at once sensed Ivy's goodness, simplicity, and lack of social snobbery – as well as, perhaps, her naïvety about social position – went out of his way to talk to her mostly, and most pleasantly) was delightful to an extent which brought her almost to heavenly happiness.

When the second round of drinks was finished the four returned to the auditorium, Lord Lyddon having said that there was a number which he himself wanted to see and which he thought the visitors might like to see.

This number had just begun; the auditorium was in darkness; and so they stood at the back of the Circle to watch it. Lord Lyddon, next to Ivy, leaned against the barrier dividing them from the back row.

Ivy was so conscious of his thus standing next to her in the glowing darkness that she could hardly take in what was happening on the stage. She looked, instead, mostly at the backs of the people in the seats in front of her.

'And these,' was her thought, 'have all *paid* for their seats! And they are, naturally enough, seated in them and intently watching the performance! But I, Ivy Barton, have not paid for a seat, and, with Lord Lyddon next to me, am observing these earnest, these almost foolishly earnest people who *have* paid!' If this was not going 'behind scenes' she'd like to know what was! Her whole attitude and values, towards the theatre and, at the moment, life generally, were readjusted, transformed, radiantly transfigured.

It was, indeed, almost chilling to the spirit when the number ended and she and her father were able to return to their seats and sit amongst other theatre-goers as if they themselves were mere theatre-goers. But she knew that Lord Lyddon and her friend were behind her, either still watching the performance or again in the bar, where she and her father were to meet them at the end of the performance, when they were to be taken 'behind'.

The curtain fell for the last time; they met Lord Lyddon and Gorse in the bar: and then were taken down to the deserted stalls, and through the pass-door, and on to the stage.

This was the first time that Ivy had ever been upon a stage, and she gazed about her with all that eager curiosity and enchanted disillusionment which such initiates often experience. There was a lot of banging, talking and fussing going on on the part of the stage-staff, and Lord Lyddon got into conversation with a carpenter about a technical matter. When this was finished he made a point of coming up to Ivy and showing her some of the mechanical contrivances of the stage – the flats, the battens, the gleaming switchboard, the 'flies', the 'grid' far above. Lord Lyddon was shrewd enough to see that he was giving Ivy a feast of pleasure, perhaps because he was a 'Lord' and certainly because she had never before been on a stage, and he went all out for it. He did this largely because he was a naturally good-natured young man, and largely because it is part of human nature to enjoy being the first to explain mysteries, and the workings of contrivances, to others.

After this the four went behind the stage into the gloomy stone passages containing the doors of the fiercely-lit dressing-rooms. Actors and actresses (to Ivy fantastically and almost frighteningly painted) were walking about, and Lord Lyddon either greeted in passing or stopped to have a word with these wanderers. To one of them, a star well-known by name to Ivy, he introduced herself and her father.

Lord Lyddon then intimated that he had to be elsewhere, and said goodbye to them, shaking hands and expressing the hope that he might see them again. He said 'Well, goodbye, Ralph' in a friendly way to Gorse, for the first time disclosing the genuine and potentially incriminating Christian name. But, in the excitement of the moment, neither Mr Barton nor his daughter noticed this.

Gorse then escorted them through the stage door, and along a passage, to St Martin's Lane, where he stopped a taxi. In this he took them both home to Wynch Street, Fulham.

Gorse, in parting from them, was aware that he had fulfilled their keenest anticipations. And he was aware that, in doing so, his own anticipations in regard to his future dealings with them had also been as good as fulfilled – that, as he put it to himself, the matter was 'pretty well in the bag'.

Chapter Five

I

The next evening, Mr Barton, entering the small public bar of the public house to which it was his habit to go nearly every evening, had a gleam in his eye and on his countenance which boded ill for those whom, therein, he habitually bored to distraction.

He was, of course, going to relate his adventure of the previous night.

But, as is so often the case with foolish, boastful men, he was indirect in his method of boasting. He disdained the exhibition of any simple pleasure or pride in the description of his experience: it was necessary to enlarge his triumph by the pretence that he did not regard it as such, that it had been a trivial occurrence all in the day's work, and only worth mentioning because it arose accidentally in the midst of other conversation.

His proper task was gently and adroitly to originate the conversational accident. But because he was totally unable to control himself Mr Barton rushed to surmount this difficulty within a minute of entering the bar. He began, indeed, with the barmaid, from whom he obtained his half of mild-and-bitter. Looking at his glass, he asked her, with forced joviality, whether she had mixed the two beers in their correct proportions, to which she naturally replied that so far as she knew she had.

'You can't fool *me*, you know,' he said. 'As it's my habit to go backstage, I know what goes on behind.'

This opening, which he had roughed out on his short walk to the public house, was not only idiotically crude and inaccurate: it was totally incomprehensible to the barmaid.

The barmaid, unaware that she was being invited to enter, as a listener, into a discussion of the world of the theatre, merely replied: 'Well – I think you'll find that's pretty well the same as usual.'

Mr Barton, nettled by the consciousness of having bungled, made matters worse by further crudity.

'Yes, as it's my *habit* to go backstage,' he said, making his inaccuracy even more deplorable by underlining the word 'habit', 'I know what takes place behind all right.' And he took a sip at his beer, hoping for an answer which might show that he had struck home.

The barmaid, however, now leaning her elbows on the bar and looking dreamily into the distance, made evident her sustained impenetrability only too clearly by simply, and absent-mindedly, replying with a monosyllable. All she said, in fact, was 'Yes . . .'

This irritated Mr Barton.

'What do you mean?' he said, '"*Yes*".'

'Why,' said the barmaid, still looking into the distance, '"*Yes*". That's clear enough, isn't it?'

'Yes – but what do you mean by "Yes"?'

'What I said,' said the barmaid. '"Yes" just means "Yes" – doesn't it? Or it did when I was at school. I'll say "No" if you like.'

'"*I* don't want you to say "*No*",' Mr Barton sharply returned.

'Very well, then,' said the barmaid, 'I'll say "Yes".'

Mr Barton here suspected that the girl was being intentionally insolent.

'And I don't want you to say "Yes",' he said. 'All I was asking was what you *meant* by "Yes".'

'Ask me another,' said the barmaid. 'How did all this begin, anyway?'

Seeing a chance to return to his opening, and still achieve his end, Mr Barton controlled his anger.

'I was just talking about me having been backstage,' he said, quite calmly. 'And all you said was "Yes".'

'Well – that's a good enough answer, isn't it?'

'It would be if it meant anything. But what *does* it mean?'

'It means "Yes, you've been backstage" – doesn't it? I can't see anything difficult about that.'

It is not inconceivable that the barmaid, having been half-consciously aware from the beginning that Mr Barton was anxious to boast to her about something, was adopting this opaque, perhaps too strictly logical, attitude on purpose. And, as she disliked Mr Barton intensely, she was not likely to abandon strict logic for the sake of sociability.

Fortunately for Mr Barton, because the bar was so empty, this conversation had been overheard by an elderly taxi-driver sitting at a table in a corner of the small bar. This man was kindhearted, and his feelings towards Mr Barton were those of friendly contempt, rather than dislike.

'So you've been backstage, Mr Barton, have you?' he said. 'Well, come and sit down and tell us all about it.'

Though it was kindly intended, the condescension implicit in this invitation did not escape Mr Barton. This was not at all what he anticipated when he had come round here tonight.

Nevertheless, the invitation had to be accepted, and, with a polite greeting, he took his beer over to the table in the corner.

'It doesn't matter being a *backstager*,' said the taxi-driver. 'As long as you're not a *back-number*, that's the thing.'

This banality, of which Mr Barton would have been perfectly capable himself, Mr Barton regarded as supremely banal. Also it seemed to him that the desired line of conversation was again in danger of being dodged. He had not come round here to talk about back-numbers. He had come round to talk about his remarkable adventure yesterday evening, which had included meeting Lord Lyddon and culminated in going backstage.

'No. I hope I'm not a back-number,' he said, sitting down. 'Saw enough numbers last night, though – and some of 'em pretty spicy ones.'

After this things got a little better for Mr Barton, because he became a little more natural and less indirect with the aid of the kindhearted taxi-driver, who allowed him to describe his evening yesterday at some length.

But soon other acquaintances of Mr Barton entered: the taxi-driver had to leave: everything went wrong again: and from then on went from bad to worse.

Mr Barton was making the same sort of mistake as so many people make about curious dreams they have had in the night – that of imagining that because such dreams are vivid to themselves they will also be vivid to other people.

Being given free seats for a theatre, meeting Lord Lyddon there socially, being escorted to the back of the stage by him, meeting actors and actresses in passages and then being taken home in a taxi – all this was even more vivid, curious and exciting to Mr Barton than a remarkable dream. To Mr Barton's acquaintances, however, his experience did not in the smallest way come to life. Consequently it seemed to them both commonplace and dull, or, even worse, irritating.

Indeed, to many of those to whom he succeeded in narrating it, it was entirely exasperating. This was because of Mr Barton's laboriously indirect method of introducing the theme to each of his acquaintances, a method which revealed at once that his object was to boast as well as bore. And Lord Lyddon, so far from inducing amazement and awed delight in Mr Barton's listeners, caused only resentment. One listener, a retired milkman, went so far as to say 'Who the hell's *he*?' and, on being told that he happened to be *Lord Lyddon*, that was all, said that he thought Mr Barton had said Lord Lytton, who had written *The Last Days of Pompeii* and *Quo Vadis* – both highly interesting novels. Then someone said that it wasn't Lord Lytton who wrote *Quo Vadis* but somebody else, he couldn't remember the name at the moment – Somethingwinks or something. To which the retired milkman replied that he could have sworn that it was Lord Lytton who wrote *Quo Vadis* because (here the milkman was illogical) it was all about Early Christians and lions.

Thus Lord Lyddon was completely erased from the picture by Lord Lytton, and a discussion on theatre-going and a member of the peerage was replaced by one on literature and history.

And, on each occasion Mr Barton introduced Lord Lyddon, Lord Lyddon was somehow almost immediately, and most astutely, submerged in the most unexpected topics having absolutely no bearing whatsoever upon Lord Lyddon – Football Pools, for instance, Greyhound Racing, the Wireless, Wages, Pigeons – even Alarm Clocks and Christian Science.

The total result was that Mr Barton, instead of spending a delightful evening as the centre of attraction, spent a horrible one in which he was deliberately jostled even further from the centre than usual, and, in his frustration and humiliation, drank more than he usually did, with worse effect.

Finally he left the public house in a fury, and, as he walked homewards, decided that they were a silly lot in there and that if he had any sense he would never mix with them again. They were 'beneath' him, and they were 'ignorant'.

In fact his acquaintances had shown that they were anything but ignorant, particularly in the matters of Mr Barton's character and ruses as a bore and snob. And an underlying consciousness that such was the real case added to Mr Barton's bitterness.

It was perhaps this evening's bitterness which led to the final bitterness which tipped the scales in making Mr Barton invest money unwisely.

He was to do this, later, in no small way out of motives of revenge. His acquaintances had not allowed him to talk. But money, he knew, talked. It did this without external assistance, flooring any crude opposition.

2

Ivy's allusions, in the public house in which she worked, to her evening at the theatre were in direct contrast to her father's, both in the methods she used and in the success she achieved.

Because she was simple-minded, and therefore direct, she caused not the smallest irritation.

Indeed, in spite of something approaching garrulousness at moments, she was listened to either with pleasure, interest, or entirely friendly envy. She was even definitely encouraged to talk – both by the sophisticated and the unsophisticated. And Lord Lyddon, so far from being rushed out of the way by Lord Lytton or other cruelly irrelevant topics, was permitted to shine in all the glamour she attached to him. The news that he had carried himself 'just like us, really' the unsophisticated heard with plain satisfaction and approbation, the sophisticated with a more complicated satisfaction in Ivy's pleasure.

3

Oddly enough it was Ivy who, in her credulity and simplicity, did a thing which her suspicious and complicated father did not do, but might have been expected to do. She went to the Public Library and looked up Lord Lyddon in Debrett.

She did this, needless to say, purely out of naïve and joyous curiosity. And joy she certainly derived from it. She was made so happy that she copied out almost everything the book contained about Lord Lyddon – his antecedents, brothers and sisters – even some of the wives and husbands of the brothers and sisters. She took a note of his 'motto', and had she been a more capable draughtswoman she might easily have made a copy of his 'crest'.

At the same time she looked for the name of Claridge. Her

failure to find this did not disappoint her, though. Under the Lyddon item there had been so many members of his family bearing different names, that she decided that her friend's father need not have been called Claridge.

She showed this ardent transcription to her father who, not unnaturally, ridiculed her for compiling it. He was not totally uninterested in it, however, for one of two of the names recalled memories of visitors to his employers during his days in Cheshire.

Chapter Six

1

It was on the Thursday following that on which she had met Lord Lyddon that Gorse proposed marriage to Ivy, and as her feelings were governed mostly by sheer terror, it would be impossible to say whether she was made happy or unhappy. She was, really, numbed by terror.

The offer was made on a seat in the Temperate House in Kew Gardens at about three in the afternoon. Ivy had managed to get the whole day off by means of a reciprocal arrangement she had more than once made with another barmaid at The Marlborough.

2

Though paralysed by fright, Ivy was not taken completely by surprise. The Honourable Gerald Claridge had, for the last three weeks, been making such remarks and innuendoes as, in ordinary circumstances, an ordinary girl could only regard as the precursors of such a proposal.

But the circumstances were not ordinary. The Honourable Gerald Claridge was an 'Honourable', and Ivy was a barmaid. Ivy had, therefore, discounted all that he had been suggesting as being manifestly absurd, mere fooling on his part, gay, aristocratic philandering. Much of her reading of fiction had informed her that it was the habit of the aristocracy to indulge in trifling of this kind. Normally she would, on the principles outlined in the fiction she had read, have disapproved of such a thing (though, really, she was temperamentally almost incapable of disapproving of anything). But with Gorse she could not apply these principles. Though in other matters he was gay enough, his approach here was not a gay one: it seemed, rather, as profoundly earnest as it was profoundly mysterious. It must be remembered that Gorse was, after all, a decidedly profound young man, and Ivy, in spite of her stupidity, somehow sensed this – realized that the laws applying to most men could not quite be brought to bear upon him. In this instinct she surpassed herself and got as near to the real Gorse as she ever did.

On that Thursday Gorse called for her at Wynch Street in his sports car and drove her to Richmond, where they had lunch at a small Italian restaurant not far from the Station. Here he insisted upon her having a cocktail, and wine with her food. Ivy did not like drink, which nearly always made her feel, instead of merry, either pleasantly or unpleasantly 'swimmy'. By the end of lunch she was over-hot and hopelessly 'swimmy' and was most happy to get out into the fresh air and walk, at Gorse's suggestion, to Kew Gardens.

The fresh air to some extent revived her, but the rest of the afternoon, because of the wine she had had at lunch, was dream-like. It was neither an agreeable nor disagreeable dream – simply peculiarly unreal and bewildering in its novelty.

The day was cold, windy, and grey, and to enter the sudden, warm quiet of the enormous Temperate House gave Ivy aesthetic as well as physical pleasure.

It was, to her, like being in the Crystal Palace and the lush green tropics at the same time – very strange. It was practically empty, apart from a few distant gardeners; and the beauties of the plants and flowers were quite incredible – weird. The fact that she was in here seeing them with an 'Honourable' was weird. Everything was weird.

Everything was, in fact, so weird, that when Gorse, in a quiet seat in one of the side aisles, quietly made his proposal she at first hardly regarded his having done so as being more odd than anything else.

She was conscious, at that moment, mostly of the remarkably heavy, fluttering noise, almost a thudding noise, made by the wings of a very small bird hopping and flying near them: of the glowing effect (resembling the poet Marvell's golden lamps in a green night) of the golden, red, yellow, white, pink blossoms against the hugely dark and dense green foliage: and of the gentle hissing of a small hose being used by a gardener in the distance. Then she pulled herself together.

'Well – when are you and I going to get married, Ivy?' had been all he had said, and she stared at him.

'What *do* you mean?' she said at last, showing her complete unaffectedness of character by making no pretence not to have heard exactly what he had said.

Gorse repeated his question, and she replied, still staring at him, 'But you couldn't marry *me*.' And Gorse asked her why not.

'But you *couldn't*,' said Ivy, and for the next ten minutes or so nearly everything she said began with 'Buts', all of which were gently, generously, and logically dismissed by the one who was asking for her hand.

It would not be easy to say precisely whether Ivy, that afternoon, accepted Gorse's offer, or rejected it, or played for time. She was too frightened to accept it, she was too compliant to reject it, and she had neither the character nor skill to play (or even ask) for time. By the time they had left the Temperate House, and were walking back to Richmond to have tea, the position was still quite nebulous.

3

On this walk back they talked of other matters. Gorse, taking her arm, had to do most of the talking, for Ivy was too preoccupied to say anything.

It was characteristic of Ivy, during this walk, that she took absolutely none of those minute, intangible, almost imperceptible 'advantages', exhibited none of those *nuances*, in the way of coquetry, possessiveness, or, even, incipient domination, which, in the case of most women in such cases, appear stealthily but with quite painful rapidity (within half an hour, for instance) from their ubiquitous lurking-places in the feminine soul. In only one matter did she make a womanly request, which her suitor granted. He had suggested that they should have tea at a well-known hotel at the top of Richmond Hill. She was bold enough to ask if they might not go to such a 'swell' place, but to somewhere less exacting – a Lyons, A B C, or Express Restaurant in the town. They went to an Express.

This had marble-topped tables and, without being crowded, an air of bustle and of middle-class and semi-proletarian reality which, along with her tea, put new life into Ivy. Her brain cleared, and, when the topic came up again, she was able to put forth, more cogently than she had in the exotic atmosphere of the Temperate House, her objections to Gorse's proposal, whose complete sincerity and seriousness she did not doubt for a moment.

'But it'd mean I'd be a *Lady*' she protested. 'Or try to be.'

To this Gorse naturally replied that he had always taken her for a lady already. What on earth did she mean?

'And it'd mean I'd be an "*Honourable*" – or something – wouldn't it?' she said, hardly able to bring the word out, and looking into his eyes almost frantically.

Gorse replied that this would be so. But what did that matter? The only thing that mattered was whether she loved him enough or not – wasn't it?

Here he had raised an interesting point. Ivy certainly did not love Gorse. Nor was she likely to do so in the future. Ivy was on the whole a sexless girl – more than usually so – and, although she had had admirers, no one had as yet stimulated whatever capacity for physical love there might have been latent in her. No one, in fact, had tried very hard.

Gorse was fully aware of this. It was, actually, one of his original reasons for making up his mind to rob Ivy financially. Gorse nearly always chose almost sexless women for this purpose. It gave him much less trouble: and, because his own sexual advances were so mild, it really gave the women much less trouble. It suited both parties.

'But just think of me being an "Honourable"!' said Ivy, looking into the distance. 'It's absurd!'

'Very well, then,' said Gorse. 'We'll drop the "Honourable" completely if you like. *I've* never liked it, and it's very easy to drop.'

Here Ivy, by her thoughtful expression as she gazed into the distance in the silence that followed, revealed that she was subject to human contradiction. If she was *going* to be a Lady, she was thinking, if she had simply *got* to be a Lady (and he seemed to be quite adamant about it), she might just as well be an 'Honourable'. In fact, in such circumstances, she would *prefer* to be an 'Honourable'!

This, so far from being a manifestation of any social ambition on Ivy's part, was a mixture of common sense and childishness.

She was, of course, unable to disclose such a thought to Gorse, who, however, could see perfectly well what was going on in her mind.

Gorse at this moment was not troubled, as another adventurer might have been, by compassion for her puzzled anxiety. He was troubled only by boredom. He had not the smallest doubt that she would accept his proposal (if, indeed, it had not by implication been accepted already), and all he wanted was to go through, as soon as he could, all the very easy motions needed today, and then to get away from her.

Gorse never had any objection to a sitting bird. This one, though, was almost tiresomely vulnerable. He had foreseen that she might be, and had engineered a reasonably early escape by an excuse made earlier in the day.

As the argument continued, though, he was made in a manner grateful to Ivy for making the easy motions demanded from him even easier than they might have been.

Ivy did not, as so many girls to whom he had made the same proposal in roughly the same way, harp upon the tender emotions and intricacies of love and marriage. She did not, for instance, say that they had had no time to Know each other yet; she did not make an idiot of herself by telling him that she wondered whether she would be able to Give enough to him; she did not express doubts as to whether she would be Worthy of him; she did not ask any of those drivelling questions as to When he First Knew, or Made the Decision etc., etc. He had suffered severely from this in the past, having found that even sexless girls like their bit of Romance as much as, or even a good deal more than, experienced and normally sexed women.

As a matter of fact Ivy, modest as she was, did not really have any doubts that she would be Worthy of, or Give enough to him. Though she understood little about it, she took the marriage bond with the intensest seriousness, and, in her uncomplicated way assessing her own character without any neurotic misgivings or distortions, she was convinced that in the ordinary way she would make the best sort of wife. Her trouble here was the position, the difference in their classes, her manifest inability to rise to his, and the absurdity (along with the absurd delight) of being an 'Honourable' herself.

'Well, it's certainly very *kind* of you,' she said at last, still looking pensively into the distance. 'And I don't know *what* to say.'

In saying that she did not know what to say she did not mean that she did not know whether to say Yes or No. In view of the overwhelming compliment he had paid her, she would have regarded such a thing as grossly discourteous. She meant simply that she did not know what to say.

Gorse knew all this and, seeing that he might now soon make his escape, replied:

'Well – don't say anything more at the moment, darling (here he had called her 'darling' for the first time and she looked at him with quick surprise) – and as we've finished our tea let's go and get this blasted telephone call of mine over – shall we?'

4

The excuse he had made earlier in the day in order to dodge boredom in the evening had been that he had to make a telephone call at about five o'clock. On this call would depend whether he would be able to spend the whole evening with Ivy or not. It was, he had said, a matter of the utmost importance. There were 'great matters in progress' in his business affairs, and there was a man he had to see as soon as he possibly could for a long interview.

This invention had the added advantage of preparing her mind for the fraud he intended soon to perpetrate upon her.

They walked back to the Station through the shop-lit and cheerfully busy Richmond High Street. In the Station, asking her to wait outside, Gorse went into a call-box and, by closing its door, surrounded himself with that silent, fiercely bright and rather uncanny illumination and atmosphere behind glass which callers in such boxes habitually exude.

Ivy, watching him, in her heart hoped that the result of his call would mean that they would have to part. She was mentally exhausted, and, feeling that further conversational effort was beyond her, she wanted to be by herself.

When he came out she was not disappointed in her hope, though she had to respond to his exclamations of regret, irritation and distress with some show of sorrow on her own part.

Gorse said that, to make matters worse, he was in a hurry. The man he had to see, who had a house by the river at Shepperton, had his lawyer with him at that moment, and if Gorse could get there at once the three of them could have a 'confab', and probably get everything settled with unforeseen expedition. He thought he could get there in the required time in his car. How was Ivy to get back?

Ivy said that she could easily take a District train to Sloane Square, and urged Gorse to go at once. But Gorse would not hear of such a thing. He bought her a ticket, and a newspaper for her to read in the train, and then a platform-ticket for himself, and went with her on to the platform to see her off.

They had to wait for a train for a matter of seven uneasy minutes, walking up and down the platform together.

Ivy was deeply reluctant to return to the matter so closely concerning them both, but at last forced herself to ask him something which she regarded as being of immediate and serious importance.

'Then am I to tell my father about it all?' she asked, suddenly, and in a desperate tone.

'All what?' said Gorse, disingenuously.

'Well,' said Ivy. 'All "it". *You* know what I mean.'

As Gorse was reflecting upon his answer the train came in.

'Ah – here we are,' said Gorse. 'Now what would suit you? Here?' He took her arm and led her to the door of the carriage.

'But *am* I to?' she said, in a kind of panic before getting inside.

'Oh, *that*,' said Gorse, looking at her hurriedly yet affectionately. 'Well – what do you think?'

'I don't know. It's for you to say.'

'Well. It doesn't matter – does it? But I'll tell you what. Let's keep it just as our secret for a little, shall we, darling?' (His second 'darling'.)

'Yes. If that's what you say.'

Yes. Let's keep it as our secret – just for fun – shall we?' He looked at her again, and then at the train. 'Well – time and tide and trains wait for no man – so I suppose this is goodbye . . . Well – I'll be in tomorrow at The Marlborough, usual time . . . Well, goodbye, darling.'

He kissed her on the cheek, looked at her affectionately yet again, smiled while raising his hat, waved and walked away.

All this had been done with a haste for which there was no necessity. Richmond being a terminus, Ivy's train was not due to go out again for some minutes. Both were aware of this, but both were only too glad to take advantage of the urgency of the moment invented by Gorse.

Gorse went at once to his car and, well pleased with himself, drove straight back to his lodgings in London.

He was certain that Ivy would not tell her father about his proposal: but he was on the whole indifferent as to whether she did or not. It was, really, the father more than the daughter whom he hoped to plunder, and the news of his engagement to the latter, if divulged to the father at the right time later, might, he believed, be of assistance.

Ivy, left alone in the brightly lit, empty compartment of the electric train, was immeasurably relieved to be alone, and tried to begin to arrange her thoughts.

She realized that she was companionless for the entire evening, with nothing to do, and for a moment wished she could go to her work. Then she reflected that she had plenty to think about, and that it was good for her to be alone in order to do so.

Gorse's having talked of keeping it 'just as our secret for a little while' had made it seem obvious that she had fully consented, and Ivy was at the moment too overwhelmed by the weird unreality of the situation to arrange her thoughts.

Slowly the compartment began to fill with other travellers, who, by their brisk, newspaper-reading, matter-of-fact air – which somehow seemed rather brutally to intimate to Ivy that they were certainly neither 'Honourables' nor in any danger of being faced by such a predicament – only intensified her own sensations of unreality and isolation.

Then the train began to make mysteriously intermittent throbbing noises, as if it could not make up its mind whether to start or not, and this also, by suggestion, increased her own feelings of indecisiveness and doubt.

It was a relief when this train did at last make up its mind, and also when at each station it picked up more and more passengers.

By the time Hammersmith had been reached many passengers were strap-hanging in a deafening roar not affecting the general newspaper-reading. But Ivy, though she had been given a newspaper, did not so much as look at it. With her hands on her bag in her lap, and sitting slightly forward in her seat, she simply stared ruminatively at nothing.

One watching her fixed expression would have thought of it as anything but a happy one. It was less like that of a barmaid who had recently had a proposal from a socially eligible young man, than that of a concentrating child – a child who had lately, in the midst of high spirits, been suddenly snubbed, and who was seeking to understand the nature of the error it did not doubt it had made. Or she might have been someone a short while ago inexplicably dismissed from some employment in which she had hoped beyond measure to succeed.

It was, above all, in its self-distrusting, self-effacing, self-abasing confusion and intensity, an excessively piteous expression – almost agonizingly so in view of the fact that in her thoughts about Gorse, her own feelings, and her own future, it did not cross her mind for a single instant that he was not as serious, as desperately serious, as herself.

Chapter Seven

I

Although she was not to tell her father, Ivy wondered that evening whether it would be permissible to tell her mother, and after a struggle with herself decided that she must not do this until she had asked Gorse if she might do so.

By the next day Ivy's natural resilience of mind had overcome the first wretchedness of its bewilderment. As soon as she was back at work she was beginning to look upon what had been a total unreality as an unforeseen reality which she had to face.

But, although she thus healthily adjusted herself, she never, in her entire dealings with Gorse, fully lost her sense of their basic unreality. In this one respect the foolish Ivy, in the humility of her foolishness, was less deceived by Gorse than many more astute girls and women had been and were to be.

In the next few weeks Gorse came to The Marlborough regularly, and took her out on Thursday afternoons and evenings.

At the pictures he would hold her hand, and on seeing her home at night he would kiss her in the street. Ivy, who had been kissed by men before, neither liked nor disliked this.

He still asked her to keep 'it' as their secret for a little, but, in a general way, most adroitly managed to keep away from much concrete discussion of 'it'. This, as he knew, entirely suited the timid and still frightened Ivy.

He in a manner made excuses for the lack of intensity of his physical advances by throwing much blame upon, and pretending to be exasperated by, the fact that she had at present to work all day – and also by posing as an idealist. He told her that he was no doubt silly and old-fashioned but that he did not believe, as most of his friends seemed to do, in full sexual intimacy before marriage, which, he said, he regarded as a sacrament. Ivy, though she did not admit it, did not know what sacraments, exactly, were, but she was glad that there existed such things to protect such women as herself in such circumstances.

Gorse, having learned from Ivy that she had been at Debrett about Lord Lyddon, had now invented some sort of background and family for the Honourable Gerald Claridge. He did not mention to Ivy his father's alleged title or name (though he was ready to do so if it was forced from him) and he alluded to his relations vaguely as 'all that Claridge lot'. Ivy showed no curiosity, and felt remarkably little. It was all beyond her understanding and part of the general unreality of the situation. Gorse was aware, though, that there were certain difficulties ahead in this direction.

He talked to Ivy a good deal about his business affairs, inventing richly, and within three weeks of their visit to Kew, having ascertained that she had almost exactly fifty pounds of her own, he asked her if she would like to invest money of her own in the theatre.

This would be in a project into which both Lord Lyddon and himself were putting money. He said that it was, in fact, 'a sure thing', though he warned her that there was, technically, no sure thing in any form of financial investment.

Ivy looked upon this proposition as being all part of the uncanny world into which she had been suddenly swept, and astonished Gorse by putting up practically no resistance at all.

Ivy was curiously disinterested in money, even in her own savings, which she had put by reluctantly and simply because her mother had told her that it was the correct and necessary thing to do. They bored her, and she could think of nothing nicer than taking them out of the Post Office and using them in the more glamorous way to which Gorse said they would be put.

She was even disappointed when Gorse said that if she did any such thing she must certainly first tell her father that she was doing so. She asked him if just telling her mother might not suffice, but Gorse was adamant. He said that women knew nothing about business, and he would never allow such a thing. And, if she was given paternal consent, he would of course have to see her father about it.

It would also be advisable, he said, if she, or her father, saw Lord Lyddon about it too.

Ivy therefore screwed up her courage and had another interview with her father, dreading a flat refusal. She found her father, however, remarkably non-committal.

The truth was that Mr Barton, who did not care for his daughter in the smallest way, had absolutely no interest in her savings, apart from mildly resenting the fact that she had any. The only thing which would have aroused his interest and pleased him, indeed, would have been her losing them through her own folly.

He was immediately flattered by Gorse's rectitude and respect in making her come to him for advice. And the knowledge that he would have to meet Gorse again before giving his consent, and afterwards, perhaps, to meet Lord Lyddon about it, went at once to his head. He said that he would be glad to have a talk with Gorse, whose uprightness of character he commended to Ivy.

At this interview, he also again asked Ivy, politely, what was 'going on' between herself and Gorse. Ivy did not disclose the proposal of marriage, but replied, quite truthfully, that she 'didn't really know'. She said that Gorse certainly seemed to be 'very attached' to her, and on her father asking whether she thought it was 'serious' she said Yes, she thought it was, rather – she couldn't make it out, really.

She thus left her father as mystified as herself, and, as in his first discussion with her about Gorse, he looked at her, trying to assess her possibilities in the way of attracting men. He had noticed Lord Lyddon's most attentive politeness to her at the theatre, and he was inclined to think that he had previously underestimated her in this matter.

In dismissing her he repeated, in a condescending way, that he would be glad to see the young man whenever he liked to come round.

2

Two evenings later Gorse came round to Wynch Street and saw Mr Barton. Ivy was working, and so they were alone together in the sitting-room.

Mr Barton was not at first at his ease, but with the aid of Gorse soon became so, and before long was exhibiting almost as much condescension in his manner as he had with Ivy.

He praised Gorse for his correctness and wisdom in coming to see him: and Gorse replied that he would never have dreamed of doing otherwise. Though the matter was only a trivial one, it was one concerning business, and Mr Barton, he was sure, knew what women, however charming, were like in business.

Gorse continued gently to stress the triviality of the whole thing, saying that he had only suggested it as a means of giving Ivy pleasure. Although, in his view, she would be likely to double or triple her investment, because of its smallness it could hardly bring her in much more than useful pin-money.

On the other hand, Gorse said with a smile, she had nothing to lose, for certain obvious reasons about which he expected Mr Barton already knew.

Here Mr Barton thought he understood, but feigned ignorance of the other's meaning.

'Well, sir,' said Gorse, 'I imagine you must have been having a pretty shrewd idea of where the land lies in that direction – haven't you?'

Mr Barton now simulated a sort of semi-knowledge, and Gorse added, 'Well, sir. I'm sure you know what I mean. I mean you must know that I'm hoping before very long – well – how shall I put it? – well – to be in a position where I'll be responsible for any little debts or losses she may incur. You surely must know that, sir.'

'Well, I hope I keep my eyes open as well as anybody else,' said Mr Barton. 'But as a matter of fact I didn't know it'd gone quite as far as that.'

'Oh, yes – quite as far as that,' said Gorse. 'But that's another matter I'd like to go into with you at another time. Amongst other things you'll be wanting to know all about my family, and all that. But that can wait. This is just a small money matter I want to get your approval about.'

Mr Barton was glad to dodge immediate discussion of the other matter, for he had been taken aback and wanted time for thought. It seemed to him that the Honourable Gerald Claridge had, in effect, just told him that he was soon going to ask him for his daughter's hand in marriage. And such a thing, with all its implications, was too bewildering for clear thought at the moment.

Gorse went on to explain the nature of the theatrical enterprise into which he was entering with Lord Lyddon, and before long said, as if half joking, that it would really be much more sensible if it had been Mr Barton, rather than his daughter, who was making the investment.

Mr Barton did not wholly dismiss this as a joke, and Gorse added that he did not see why it could not be 'wangled'. Lord Lyddon would, of course, have to be consulted.

He used the words 'We'd have to go and consult Lord Lyddon, of course,' – thus hinting at another meeting, *à trois*, with Lord Lyddon.

Before Mr Barton had time fully to absorb this by no means displeasing suggestion, Gorse said that it would also probably be necessary to see a Mr Kayne, who was also concerned in the enterprise.

He went on to say that Mr Kayne was, really, of more importance and substance in the enterprise than Lord Lyddon. Mr Kayne was a man from the North, with a business shrewdness and solidity of the most reassuring kind. He had demonstrated this by the very great wealth he had accumulated, from the humblest beginnings, in Walsall. If anyone had his head screwed on the right way it was Mr Kayne of Walsall.

Gorse, in fact, would like Mr Barton to meet him in any case, for he was very much a 'character'. In spite of his financial success and possessions he had remained completely unspoiled and natural. He never forgot any of his old friends from the days of his early poverty, treating them with as much respect and geniality as he bestowed upon his more opulent and imposing acquaintances of the later years. He was, in fact, entirely free from any sense of class-distinction. When in London he lived in a large flat in a Mayfair block, to which Gorse often went. Gorse would like to take Mr Barton there one evening.

Mr Barton, as Gorse had intended he should be, was deeply impressed by Mr Kayne. Indeed, the mixture of Lord Lyddon and this Mr Kayne almost at once slightly unbalanced him. He had a sudden vision of entering, or half entering, by a piece of ridiculously good luck, a circle of very great wealth and opportunity. Such pieces of good luck did, after all, sometimes befall men: and Mr Kayne's genial Northern simplicity and complete lack of snobbery, as described by Gorse, in addition to removing any fear he might have had in the thought of meeting him, brought both the rather ethereal Lord Lyddon and the rather mysterious Mr Gorse somehow nearer to earth.

In less than five minutes, in fact, Mr Barton was remarkably anxious to meet this Mr Kayne in his large Mayfair flat, and he conveyed as much to Gorse, trying to conceal his eagerness and maintain his dignity by the pretence that his interest in Mr Kayne would reside mostly in his being a 'character'.

It may be said that Mr Barton, at the time of this talk with Gorse, had not as yet in any way recovered from the injuries to his soul inflicted upon him in the public bar of The Unicorn – the public house he frequented in Wynch Street. The wounds had, indeed, festered and become more infuriating. In the monied Mr Kayne (because money talked) he pictured possible alleviation.

Having thus got the man more or less eating out of his hand, Gorse reverted to the small matter of Ivy's investment, and was soon given the paternal consent he sought.

The fact of the matter was that, having no interest in it save a slightly resentful one, Mr Barton was more than willing to offer up Ivy's money in order to meet Mr Kayne.

Chapter Eight

I

An unusual feature of the situation just at this time was that Gorse had not in a single essential detail spoken a falsehood.

There was in fact an enterprise of the kind he had described (which was simply one of backing a new musical play) and, as well as Lord Lyddon, there was in fact a Mr Kayne interested in it.

Furthermore, Mr Kayne had been most accurately described by Gorse.

Mr Kayne – a large, stout, red-faced, grey-haired, grey-moustached man of sixty – had first met Gorse about three months ago in the Cocktail Bar of The King's Hotel, Piccadilly. They had got into conversation accidentally and were now on friendly terms.

Mr Kayne, though by no means a fool, in no way distrusted Gorse. It was very difficult for him, when in London on holiday, to dislike or distrust anybody. On such occasions he was always too determinedly enjoying himself and enjoying other people.

In London this successful, rich, good-natured and simple man was in a sort of dream-land; and when Gorse had introduced him to Lord Lyddon the colour of the dream he was then enjoying had been considerably intensified.

Gorse, as well as many others, took Mr Kayne for the sort of successful businessman from the North who might easily be plundered in the South. But Mr Kayne did not belong to this type. Being himself absolutely honest and devoid of greed, he was the least likely person to be the victim of any sort of financial trickery.

He was keenly aware of the power of money, and he knew that he was more or less paying for the company he sought and found in London.

Though ravished by the charms of the theatre, he had few illusions about the chances of solid profit to be extracted from theatrical enterprises. But this did not prevent him from liking to put his money into them. He had money enough, and, as in the case of the friends he made in London, he was willing to pay for the delightful and exciting world to which such investments introduced him.

He was, really, both a naïve and astute man, and one who had never ceased to be grateful for the good fortune which had lifted him from his cruelly harsh and bleak early life. He was, indeed, so happy, every day of his life, about his own money, that his geniality towards others sometimes degenerated almost into sentimentality – but never into stupidity.

Without distrusting Gorse he thought him, with his monocle, a bit of a 'queer fish' – but then he thought that nearly all Londoners were rather queer fish.

When Gorse asked him if he might bring Mr Barton to his flat in Mayfair, he at once acquiesced.

Accordingly, four days after Gorse's interview with Mr Barton, Mr Kayne was at the front door of his flat, at six o'clock in the evening, welcoming both warmly.

2

Mr Kayne felt even less distrust for Mr Barton than he did for Gorse. He did not even think he was a queer fish. On the contrary Mr Barton, with his semi-peasant, semi-proletarian appearance (in the blue suit which had made Lord Lyddon think of a gardener at a wedding), was a type which Mr Kayne could readily recognize and understand, and he went out of his way to make himself agreeable to him.

Gorse had prepared the way for this meeting by telling Mr Kayne, again accurately, all that he knew of Mr Barton's origins and mode of life. He had added, less truthfully, that Mr Barton had, he believed, a somewhat pathetic desire to invest in a very small way in some sort of theatrical enterprise, and that he, Gorse, could not resist attempting to fulfil for him this childish ambition.

Mr Kayne, having no reason to disbelieve this story, liked Gorse all the better for wanting to make such an attempt with such a man.

To Mr Barton this meeting, which took place in the sitting-room of the opulent Mayfair flat, might have seemed too gorgeous to be wholly credible had not the glowing and unmistakable authenticity of Mr Kayne's personality made it absolutely real.

The furniture, the rich red silken hangings, the silver cigarette-lighting novelties, the glittering decanters on the tray for drinks, the pictures, the coal fire and the rich carpet – all these, in the centrally-heated hush of the sitting-room, beyond measure delighted and dazed Mr Barton, who thought of his usual evening visits to the sawdust on the floor of the public bar of The Unicorn in Wynch Street.

He accepted a whisky from Mr Kayne, who of course gave him a vast one, and looked about him in an almost childishly awed way which Mr Kayne did not fail to observe, and which made him more genial and vigorously 'homely' in his manner than ever.

In such surroundings Mr Barton had never in his life before been treated so firmly as an 'equal' (even Lord Lyddon had somehow not quite done this), but he made no attempt to behave as one. He called Mr Kayne 'Sir' and, although he soon became less ill at ease, his manner remained deferential to the end.

In the general good humour and warmth of the occasion the business matter which had brought the three together was only mentioned once, and briefly at that.

This was when Mr Kayne, to fill in a pause, said, in his ugly, yet (because it came from himself) singularly attractive, Walsall accent:

'So you're coming into business with us, are you, Mr Barton?'

To this Mr Barton replied, Well, he had *thought* of doing so, in a very small way, and Mr Kayne replied, jokingly:

'Well – I'd give it a *lot* of thought, if I were you! They'll probably diddle you – Lord Lyddon and this young chap here. They've got *me* in their clutches all right. In fact, I'm in it up to the neck, and I don't see how I can back out now!'

'Well – it's still not too late, Frank,' said Gorse, in the same spirit of humour. And then Mr Kayne, looking at the slightly puzzled Mr Barton and feeling that his joke might not have been taken as such, and fearing that he might be slightly tarnishing a humble man's naïve pleasure, in the kindness of his heart hastened to rectify any wrong impression he might have given.

'No,' he said, in a serious tone, to Mr Barton. 'You're safe enough. In fact you're on to about as good a thing as you really could be – as far as I can make out. And I know something about this sort of thing – believe me.'

What Mr Kayne really meant was that, in view of the grave uncertainty of theatrical adventures, this one seemed to be as good a one as you might find. But his words had not conveyed this to Mr

Barton. They had, on the other hand, seemed to express Mr Kayne's own complete belief in the solidity and possibilities of the enterprise. (Mr Kayne might have chosen his words more carefully had he thought that Mr Barton proposed to invest more than twenty pounds, or some such amount, which, if lost, he would willingly pay back out of his own pocket.)

Gorse saw that, from his own point of view, exactly the right thing had been said and exactly the right impression made upon Mr Barton. He therefore quickly changed the subject.

Soon Mr Barton and Mr Kayne found that, as they had both lived so long in adjoining Midland counties, there were many people and matters about which they both knew, and about which it was delightful to have a discussion. Mr Barton was given another (vast) whisky, and the two warmed to each other, with Gorse almost being excluded.

In their talk Mr Kayne made an even deeper impression upon Mr Barton by unwittingly disclosing that he was indeed a man of great substance. Gorse, realizing this, was only too glad to be left out of the conversation.

Mr Barton wisely refused a third whisky and in due course was escorted – along with Gorse, who was also leaving – to the front door, where Mr Kayne strongly urged him to visit the flat again, writing out the telephone number on the back of an old envelope.

'We three conspirators must keep together,' he said, himself made a little over-cheerful by the whisky. 'And I hope young Tommy Lyddon'll come along next time, too.'

To be classed familiarly as a 'conspirator' with a member of the aristocracy and of the plutocracy at the same time was exceedingly gratifying to Mr Barton, who, by the time he was out in the fresh air, had begun to feel the full effect of the whisky, to which he was unaccustomed. As Gorse drove him back to Wynch Street in his car, the normally sober man was drunker than he had been for a long time. On Gorse asking him his opinion of Mr Kayne, he revealed his condition in a lyrical way.

'A heart of *Gold*,' he said. 'It sticks out a mile. That man's got a heart of *Gold*.'

'Yes. I agree,' said Gorse. 'And he's not only got a heart of gold. He's got a purse of gold too. And the two don't often go together.'

'Yes. *He's* a brick all right,' said Mr Barton. 'A *Gold* Brick. That's what he is. A gold *Brick*.'

Gorse, saying that he himself was going to see Ivy at The Marlborough, dropped Mr Barton outside his home. But Mr Barton was in too excited a mood to go inside, and as soon as Gorse had disappeared he made his way to the public bar of The Unicorn.

On his way there the golden joy of his admiration for Mr Kayne was replaced by renewed black resentment against his acquaintances in The Unicorn.

He decided vindictively to tell them nothing of his visit to the palatial Mayfair flat. He had a feeling that, just as Lord Lyddon had somehow got lost in *The Last Days of Pompeii* and similar grotesque irrelevancies, so Mr Kayne might lead to sugar-cane or something, and thence to sugar-crops, or groceries, or any of those other vile and mundane matters discussed by the ignorant.

His acquaintances, therefore, noticed a hostile look in his eye as he entered. They also noticed that he had been drinking, and one of them jovially asked where he had been.

'Oh, I've *been* somewhere,' he replied. 'I've *been* somewhere, all right.'

As this provoked curiosity, he was again asked where he had been.

'Ah,' said Mr Barton, cunningly. 'Where? That's just the question – isn't it? Where?'

It was here pointed out that it was, of course, the question. And so where *had* he been?

To which Mr Barton replied, with mordant sarcasm: 'Oh – *nowhere*. Nowhere at all. That's plain enough, isn't it?'

It was anything but plain to his listeners, who, however, dropped the matter.

But Mr Barton, burning with desire to go on having savagely been nowhere, would not allow the matter to drop. He ordered a pint of stronger beer than usual, and, in order to re-establish the fact that he had been nowhere, perversely repeated that he had been somewhere. Yes, he'd been somewhere all right. If anybody had been somewhere, he had.

He was then asked if he had been, perhaps, to Buckingham Palace to see the King.

This at any rate gave him the chance to say that he had been nowhere again. Absolutely nowhere – that was where he had been.

He had, in all, four pints of the stronger beer on the strength of his bitterly mysterious visit, and when the house closed he was seriously drunk. He was, however, again lyrical, and his wife, assisting him to undress, was compelled to listen to wildly wandering and unintelligible talk about hearts of gold, bricks of gold, bricks with hearts of gold, hearts with bricks of gold, golds with hearts of bricks, and, even, half-bricks with halfs of gold.

He then showed truculence by threatening to throw half a brick at anyone who contradicted him, but redeemed himself with unexpected wit and alertness of mind (on his wife complaining that he was 'hicking') by saying that they were Gold Hicks.

Not Seymour. Gold.

He expressed his complete confidence in his wife's ability to differentiate between the two things. One was a well-known actor. The other was not.

He pointed out that thus to differentiate was in no way difficult, but of serious importance.

Chapter Nine

I

It now seemed to Gorse that the situation was sufficiently mature for him to set in motion the final machinations in his dealings with Ivy and her father, and these necessitated a talk with Lord Lyddon, who, two days later, accepted, rather reluctantly, an invitation to drink with Gorse in the Cocktail Bar of the King's Hotel.

At this meeting Gorse again splendidly revealed a gift he had had all his life – that of killing two (or three or four or five) birds with one stone.

He spoke of Mr Barton's pathetic desire to be a theatrical 'backer' in a small way, and of Mr Barton's meeting with Mr Kayne. He extracted from Lord Lyddon a promise that he, too, would see Mr Barton about the matter, and, finally, he prevailed upon Lord Lyddon to open a small joint banking account with himself.

Lord Lyddon, though he somehow disliked Gorse at the back of his mind, had no reason to be suspicious of him, and he had been most impressed and delighted (as most people were) by Mr Kayne, to whom Gorse had recently introduced him in the Mayfair flat. Naturally he was also keenly interested in Mr Kayne as a backer, and felt indebted to Gorse for making the introduction.

He was slightly taken aback when Gorse asked him about the joint account, and at once relieved when Gorse said that all he himself needed to put into it was ten pounds at the outside.

He remained mystified, however, and politely asked Gorse his reasons for wanting such a thing.

'Oh – it just gives me a very good Handle,' said Gorse. 'If you'd had to deal with these lads from the North as much as I have, you'd know what I meant all right.'

'How do you mean – exactly – a Handle?' Lord Lyddon asked.

'Well, it sort of puts me into a genuine financial associationship with you – or partnership – or whatever you like to call it – if you see what I mean.'

'But why,' asked Lord Lyddon, half suspecting what Gorse's answer would be, 'would that give you a Handle?'

'Because you're a Noble Peer of the Realm, my boy,' said Gorse. 'That's all. It's a pity, but you've no idea what it means to people like Frank Kayne, however nice they may be.'

Lord Lyddon did not at all like being called a Noble Peer of the Realm, and he did not particularly like being called 'my boy' by the monocled Gorse. Nevertheless, he thought he could see Gorse's point, and before long he consented.

Lord Lyddon was too absent-minded at the time to realize either that he was making himself a party to a very minor species of false pretences, or that, if such pretences were desirable, they could easily be made by Gorse merely telling people that he was in financial partnership with himself.

'Of course,' added Gorse, jokingly, 'you'll have a cheque-book along with me, and you'll be able to rob me of all – or a lot of it – if you suddenly decide to decamp.'

It happened that Lord Lyddon had on him at the time a cheque for twenty-six pounds odd made out to himself. He showed this to Gorse, and asked him if it would serve the purpose. Gorse said that it would, but that the amount far exceeded what he wanted. Lord Lyddon, however, endorsed the cheque and insisted that he should take it.

2

G. Hadlow-Browne, in writing of Gorse afterwards, was not a believer in the popular theory that he used hypnotism, or had 'hypnotic eyes'. About this episode, though, he wrote, with his usual mixture of accuracy and inaccuracy: 'Believers in Gorse's so-called hypnotic powers may well feel that their theories are to some extent substantiated by the fact that at this meeting Gorse, immediately and apparently without the slightest difficulty, inveigled Lord Lyddon into opening a joint account with him.'

In fact, in view of Lord Lyddon's absent-minded, distrait, and rather bored mood at the time, there was nothing in the slightest way surprising in what happened.

After the cheque had been handed over, more drinks were taken, and Gorse returned to the matter of Mr Barton. He then asked Lord Lyddon what he thought of his daughter, Ivy, and, in a burst of confidence, confessed that he was hoping to marry her.

Lord Lyddon was able to say, with complete truthfulness, that he had thought her delightful. At this Gorse showed great pleasure and expatiated upon her goodness.

He said that Lord Lyddon might think it an odd match, but that he believed that, apart from his affection for her, she was the perfect type for someone like himself. He had had, he said, a rather too gay and exciting life, and he believed that she had exactly the sort of personality to steady him.

Her being a barmaid was actually a great advantage, too, for his real ambition had always been to settle down and buy and run a small public house in the country. He regarded this as the ideal life.

This dream of semi-bucolic, semi-alcoholic peace and simplicity was much in vogue at that time, and Lord Lyddon had himself often wished that he himself could live in such a way. He grew more friendly to Gorse as both enlarged in detail upon the advantages of this mode of existence – one which, since those days, has been proved, by the harsh experience of many amateur pioneers, to be rather more like hell than heaven on earth.

Over further drinks Gorse again thanked Lord Lyddon for consenting to see Mr Barton. He said that he was naturally anxious to please his future father-in-law by assisting him in his simple-minded ambition to dabble in the world of the theatre.

'But do point out that there *are* risks,' said Gorse. 'I don't think they're very grave in this case, or I wouldn't be putting what *I'm* putting into it. In fact I think the old man stands to win quite a lot in his small way. And even if things should go wrong I can see that he doesn't lose. All the same he ought to be told that there's no such thing as a certainty in this business – as *I* know well enough – although I've done well enough out of it, I must admit.'

This led Lord Lyddon to ask Gorse how he had first become interested in the theatre, thus enabling Gorse to insure himself against a minor possible danger.

He told Lord Lyddon that he had got into the business more or less accidentally, by more or less accidentally becoming an actor. He had, indeed, a stage name, by which he was still mostly known by most of his acquaintances. He had had to take a stage name because of his parents' disapproval of the theatre.

The history of his coming by this name had been rather amusing. He had chosen it because his first part – a 'silly ass' one in a foolish forgotten play done by a small unsuccessful repertory company long ago – had been that of 'The Honourable Gerald Claridge'.

'My God – what a lovely name!' said Lord Lyddon, delightedly.

Lord Lyddon meant, of course, that it was anything but a lovely name. He meant, on the contrary, that it had struck him as being a decidedly ridiculous name. And this both baffled and offended Gorse, for it was his own creation, and he believed it to be as good a name as could be found – a 'lovely' name, in fact.

He showed something of this on his face, and Lord Lyddon, sensing he had made a mistake, hastened to rectify his error.

'Of course,' he said, 'it's a splendid actor's name—if you come to think of it. Gerald Claridge ... Yes ... it couldn't be better really.'

'Well – that's what I thought, anyway,' said Gorse, still unable to conceal something of his chagrin, for he had invented the name not as an actor's name but as one savouring of the highest aristocratic connections.

'Yes, you're quite right,' said Lord Lyddon, seeing the need further to rectify his error. 'It's got a sort of star quality, when you come to think about it. I only thought it was funny with the "Honourable" in front of it, and so gorgeously typical, in a silly play. But in real life and without the "Honourable" it's about as good as it could be.'

Gorse was still not entirely appeased by Lord Lyddon's explanation, but he managed to master his emotions and to take the displeased expression off his face.

'Oh, yes,' he said. 'Absurd in a play but all right in real life. Some of my old friends still go on ragging me by calling me "The Honourable Gerald Claridge", though. It's sort of stuck.'

He had now, he felt, fully insured himself against the danger he had foreseen, and, with permission to open the joint account and a cheque with which to do so in his pocket, he again warmed to Lord Lyddon.

They parted on the friendliest terms.

Chapter Ten

I

The name of the musical play in which Ivy was investing, and into which Mr Barton had been tempted to put his money, was *You and Me.*

The day after Gorse's interview with Lord Lyddon there appeared in an evening paper, accidentally and prematurely, some advance publicity about this play.

This was of great service to Gorse, who bought half a dozen copies of the newspaper.

One of these he gave to Ivy at The Marlborough, at the same time asking her to give it to her father along with a message from himself.

Delighted as Ivy was by the press paragraph, she had, as always, to brace herself to speak to her father, and tackled it that evening after her work, going boldly into his sitting-room and showing him the newspaper.

Mr Barton was profoundly impressed by what he read, but of course did not show his feelings to Ivy. He only said, in effect, Very interesting – but what about it?

'Well – you see, *he* asked me to show it to you,' said Ivy, 'and to give you a message.'

In front of her father she could somehow only allude to her strange wooer as 'he', but Mr Barton knew to whom she was referring.

'Oh – what did he say?' he asked.

'He said,' said Ivy, speaking rapidly, 'he's spoken to Lord Lyddon, and that if you're interested, he thinks it can be managed – but he'd like you to go and see Lord Lyddon about it yourself.'

Here Mr Barton, try as he might, was quite unable to conceal a look of pleasure and complacency. Thus to be invited to meet Lord Lyddon privately, and above his daughter's head, was too much even for this most stony of men.

'Well,' he said, almost smiling, indeed very nearly giving forth a little chuckle in his pleasure at the prospect. 'I don't see any harm in going and seeing him, anyway. But when's the meeting to take place?'

'He said the sooner the better,' said Ivy. 'And if he could come round here tomorrow about six o'clock and see you, he could talk to you and fix it up.'

Mr Barton, with most amicable graciousness, gave his consent to this, and Ivy left him to his thoughts.

Since last seeing Gorse with Mr Kayne, Mr Barton had more or less made up his mind to put money, if he was given the chance, into *You and Me*. The glamour of Lord Lyddon, and the solidity of Mr Kayne, the manifest authenticity of the one as a peer and of the other as a shrewd and prosperous businessman – all these had been working together in his mind to bring him to the decision.

The paragraph in the newspaper added further reality, and also further grandiosity, excitement and romance to the project.

He read it again and again, and decided to take it into The Unicorn as soon as he possibly could. He had an idea he could make them sit up in there at last, and this with a vengeance.

2

Mr Barton's interview with Lord Lyddon, two evenings later, was so odd in character that it might have been called weird.

It took place in the Circle Bar of the Empress Theatre, where the two had met before, and while the curtain was up on *Reaching for the Moon*.

A more ill-assorted couple, meeting under the particular circumstances in which they met, could hardly have been found in any case. But their difficulties had been increased ten-fold by Gorse's previous promptings to both. He had asked Lord Lyddon almost to discourage Mr Barton in his ambition to speculate, or at any rate to point out the not inconceivable risks entailed. And he had told Mr Barton that he must express to Lord Lyddon the utmost enthusiasm and gratitude for being given this opportunity. He had hinted to Mr Barton that Lord Lyddon was doing him an almost unprecedented favour in 'letting him in', and that anything but a display of a keen desire for this might hurt or offend Lord Lyddon, and make him change his mind.

Added to this, both, in anticipation, were afraid of the meeting –

Mr Barton because he was aware of being socially out of his depth, and Lord Lyddon roughly for the same reason, as well as the knowledge that he had, as it were, a 'piece' to say to the ex-gamekeeper. It was because of this that he had arranged the interview to take place in the bar of the theatre. Here he felt at home and he could informally have and offer the man a drink.

Mr Barton appeared, promptly on time, again in the suit which so strongly reminded Lord Lyddon of a gardener at a wedding. He himself was in a dinner jacket and drinking at the bar when Mr Barton was brought up by an attendant.

Mr Barton accepted a drink and sat down at a table with Lord Lyddon, who talked about the weather, and then raised his glass, saying 'Well – good health and all that,' to which Mr Barton replied, 'Good health, my lord.'

There was then an awkward pause, in which both were aware of the distant singing of the chorus of *Reaching for the Moon*, and which Lord Lyddon at last forced himself to break by coming directly to the point.

'Well,' he said. 'I hear you're thinking of coming in on this little adventure of ours.'

'Yes, my lord,' said Mr Barton. 'I was, really. And I gather you've said you've no objection. It's very kind of you, my lord, I'm sure.'

'Well, I don't know that it's kind of me,' said Lord Lyddon, with the most pleasantly sardonic and rather weary smile which so often came upon his face. 'Nobody objects to financial support of any kind, do they? Not that you're coming in in a very big way, I take it – are you?'

'Well, it depends on what you mean by a big way, my lord. It certainly wouldn't be a big way by your standards.'

'Yes – that's all very relative, of course,' said Lord Lyddon, getting ready to do his duty. 'But what I mean is you're not risking your all, are you? Because that wouldn't be at all wise, you know.' He again smiled.

'Oh, no, not my all, sir. Certainly not that.' Mr Barton smiled back.

'Have you done anything like this before?' said Lord Lyddon, looking at Mr Barton in an endeavour to discover his true motives.

'No, my lord. I haven't actually. No.'

'Well, if you had, I can only tell you that you'd know well

enough by now that it's not the sort of thing to put your *all* into. In fact, it's only fun if you've got a little money just to play with, and have a flutter. Is that what you're doing?'

'Yes, my lord, I suppose that's really just what it is, really.'

'And you really *want* to?' said Lord Lyddon, determined to do his duty thoroughly.

'Oh *yes*, sir,' said Mr Barton, remembering Gorse's instructions.

'I mean there *are* risks,' said Lord Lyddon. 'You do know that – don't you?'

'Oh yes, my lord. I know that. And that's just what Mr Claridge said.'

It did not escape Lord Lyddon's notice that Mr Barton had alluded to Gorse as Claridge, but he thought nothing of it. If Lord Lyddon had mentioned the name of Gorse first, some complications might have arisen. Gorse had known that he was taking certain risks in bringing these two together alone, but he had a dozen different answers ready should he be later questioned by Mr Barton as to the discrepancy between the two names.

'Well, as long as you realize there *are* risks,' said Lord Lyddon, 'that's all right.'

'But it's not *all* risks, is it, sir?' said Mr Barton. 'Or people like you and Mr Kayne and so on wouldn't go in for it, would they?'

'Oh, good lord, no – anything but,' said Lord Lyddon, not wanting to dishearten the man. 'In fact, I certainly wouldn't be in it myself if I didn't think that I'm on to about as good a thing as could be. All I meant was that there *are* risks, and that it's not the sort of thing to go in for unless you've got a little money to play with. And you say that's what it is in your case?'

'Yes, sir. That's how it is with me.'

'Oh, well, that's all right. And you certainly get fun for your money.' Here curiosity overcame Lord Lyddon. 'But tell me, if it's not a rude question, what sort of amount of money do you feel you yourself have just to play with?'

'Well, it's rather difficult to say, sir,' said Mr Barton, and there was a pause in which the other looked at him. It had occurred to Lord Lyddon, who had a quick sense of people, that Mr Barton might be of that tenacious, calculating, and grasping character which, in fact, he was. In which case, in spite of his gardener's suit, he might easily be a decidedly well-to-do man.

Mr Barton had hesitated in giving an answer to the question

asked him because pride, caution, and avarice were at this moment at strife in his soul. Caution urged him to underestimate the sum: pride urged him to suggest a lordly one to Lord Lyddon, and here pride was in a manner assisted by avarice. For Mr Barton was, at heart, convinced that he was by a piece of wonderful good luck on to a really good thing, and he was genuinely afraid that he might lose his chance of being permitted to invest his money if he mentioned too ridiculously small a sum or showed any pusillanimity.

'Yes, sir,' he went on. 'It's rather difficult to say, isn't it? Not very much more than a hundred, I should say, or perhaps something like two, would be just about the mark.'

'Well, there's a lot of difference between one and two, isn't there?' said Lord Lyddon, again smiling and meaning to suggest that one hundred would be a very much better idea.

Mr Barton, however, took the smile to mean exactly the opposite.

'Well, then, let's say two, sir,' he said. 'Or even a bit more.'

By making this rash statement to Lord Lyddon, Mr Barton condemned himself to lose, to Mr Gorse, at least one hundred pounds more than he might have lost.

3

While Mr Barton had been hesitating over his answer, both men had been hearing the sound of clapping coming through, in a muffled way, from the auditorium of the theatre.

This meant, as Lord Lyddon knew, that the first interval had arrived, and that the bar would very shortly be full of people.

Suddenly the door of the bar was opened violently (those who first enter theatre bars during intervals usually do so with seemingly unnecessary violence) and this first intruder was one of Lord Lyddon's friends – a virile yet strongly effeminate young man in an evening jacket who had evidently not met Lord Lyddon for some time, and who at once came over to greet him.

'*Tommy!* My dear *boy*!' he cried. 'How lovely to find you here!'

This gusty greeting made things even more difficult for the ill-at-ease pair. Nor did Lord Lyddon's attempt to introduce Mr Barton to his friend make things any easier. The young man was puzzled by Mr Barton's appearance, and, though polite, was made momentarily silent by embarrassment.

In the resilience of his virile effeminacy, however, he quickly recovered himself and began praising what he had just seen of *Reaching for the Moon* with the slightly exaggerated fervour common to his type. Mr Barton saw that it was time to go, and when the young man, promising to return, had gone to the bar to get a drink, he said to Lord Lyddon: 'Well, sir. I think I had better go.'

'Oh, don't go,' said Lord Lyddon. 'This is only the interval, and we can go on talking afterwards. And wouldn't you like to see some of the show again?'

But Mr Barton was in fact anxious to go, and could not be persuaded. He could not, however, dissuade Lord Lyddon from escorting him down the stairs to the comparative quiet of the *foyer*, where they had a small conversation before saying goodbye.

'Well, then,' said Lord Lyddon. 'That all seems to be fixed up, doesn't it? But I've made it clear that you're not certain of making a fortune – haven't I?'

'Oh yes, sir,' said Mr Barton. 'And I'm very grateful to you for seeing me, sir.'

'In fact,' said Lord Lyddon, with a final smile and a twinkle in his eye as they shook hands, 'you've been warned – and if I were you I'd keep right out of it!' He then held the door back for Mr Barton, who went through the door saying, 'Thank you, my lord. Good-night, my lord,' and out into the street.

Thus Mr Barton had been told to keep out of it both by the gracious and friendly peer, Lord Lyddon, and the hard-headed and extremely prosperous businessman, Mr Kayne.

And thus was finally cemented his decision to go into it.

4

Apart from his embarrassment in the bar, one of Mr Barton's reasons for wanting to leave it had been his desire to get to The Unicorn, before it was too late in the evening, and begin retaliatory and punitive operations at the best possible moment.

Coming straight from Lord Lyddon, and with the paragraph from the newspaper, only two days old, in his pocket, he felt that his assault would be weakened if he delayed.

His acquaintances in The Unicorn, seeing him in his best suit again, again asked him where he had been, and one of them remarked that he seemed always to be 'dolled up' nowadays, thus giving an excellent lead to Mr Barton, who said that a man had to doll himself up when he went to theatres and was engaged in theatrical speculation.

This remark was too concrete and interesting to be ignored, for the frequenters of the Public Bar were all keenly interested in financial speculation of all sorts. Also they felt that Mr Barton, although a boaster, would not be a complete liar as to matters of fact. He was therefore questioned – questioned in a slightly inimical and challenging way, but questioned. He was thus enabled to produce the paragraph in the paper, which at once made a deep impression upon all. It was handed round and read with care. Such is the searching power of the press in the obscurest haunts of the biggest towns or remotest villages of every country.

This paragraph, indeed, was so successful that Mr Barton had, that evening, hardly any need to use his other two deadly weapons – his interview that evening with Lord Lyddon and his earlier meeting with Mr Kayne. These two characters were mentioned only briefly, for Mr Barton, having at last gained an audience, wisely decided to keep them in reserve.

That evening, undoubtedly, Mr Barton did make the scoffers sit up with a vengeance, and, in the malicious magnanimity of victory, even bought beer for those especially humiliated.

Chapter Eleven

Gorse, having had reports both from Lord Lyddon and Mr Barton about their meeting, now felt that he should apply himself to the task of rounding up this little matter neatly within three weeks at the outside.

An irksome preliminary to this was the necessity of making love to Ivy more seriously. He did this, pressing her to give him a date for marriage as soon as possible. This, as he had expected, brought forth surmises from her about what his 'family's' reactions would be, and also, at last, almost direct questions as to who his 'family' were and where they lived.

Having thus caused these questions to be put he was able to give her his carefully prepared replies at a time chosen by himself. He gave a few names but still hid behind further references to 'all that Claridge lot', with whom, he said, he was not, at present, on good terms, largely because of his connection with the theatre, of which they disapproved. He said, though, that he had a delightful aunt, who lived in Berkshire, whose favourite he had always been, and to whom he had confessed his desire to marry Ivy, and also his desire to settle down in a country public house. He showed her a letter he had had from this aunt upon the matter.

Ivy, who had of course been terrified by Gorse's sudden pressure for immediate marriage, was very much relieved by this letter, which, of course, had been invented by Gorse and written by him in a disguised hand.

He had said that his aunt was not 'all snobby like the rest', and the letter proved that she was indeed not. She wrote that she was delighted by the news, that she had thought for a long while that her nephew should marry and settle down, and that his notion of doing this in a public house in the country seemed ideal. And, naturally, his future wife's knowledge of the business would be of enormous practical value here.

She asked if she might meet what she called his 'intended', and invited them both to stay a night or two with her in the country. The accommodation she could offer was, as he knew, not very 'grand', but she was sure she could make them both comfortable.

She ended her letter by alluding, as if in answer to some remarks made by Gorse, to the attitude his family might take. She agreed that some of the very 'stuffy' ones might at first take a foolish attitude, but this did not matter, and they would soon come round anyway. The others (she mentioned one or two Christian names) would certainly not be so foolish, and he could rely upon her own warm support.

This letter had a 'cosy' quality generally which almost completely removed Ivy's social fears, but she remained afraid.

The real truth was that, although she had no suspicions of Gorse, although she liked him, she did not love him, did not properly understand him, and did not really want to marry him.

She consulted with her mother, largely confessing her doubts and showing her the aunt's letter. Her mother said, wisely, that if Ivy went and stayed with the aunt she would know her own feelings better.

Her mother also, with Ivy's permission, showed the letter to Ivy's father, and he again had a talk with Ivy in his sitting-room.

It was at this point that Mr Barton, had he shown any reasonable paternal consideration, might conceivably have saved his daughter and himself from the disaster threatening both.

His word carried fantastic authority with Ivy, and he might have extracted from her an admission of her inner reluctance to marry Gorse, and have advised her earnestly to obey her own instincts.

He might at any rate have caused a delay, and thereby had some opportunity to find out more about Gorse's real antecedents and background.

But Mr Barton, when not actually resentful of Ivy for one reason or another, was constitutionally absolutely indifferent to her, and, just at the moment, remarkably indifferent about Gorse.

The erstwhile rather formidable 'Honourable', the man with Eton and Harrow written all over him, had become more or less of a nonentity in the lime-lit scene of Lord Lyddon, Mr Kayne, and Mr Barton's forthcoming investment in the theatre in association with both.

All he did was to give Ivy permission to go and stay a night or two with the aunt.

In other words he did not care a jot either about Ivy or Gorse. He had a strong feeling that their relationship would not fully materialize (in the same was as so many of Ivy's other relationships with men had not materialized) and he did not care.

Since his last meeting with Lord Lyddon, and his victory at The Unicorn, this foolish man's greed and vanity had gone wild – particularly his vanity. This was so much so that even what he had of worldly judgement had been seriously affected.

He had by this time again seen Gorse at Wynch Street, and had given him a crossed cheque, made out to Lord Lyddon, for two hundred pounds. He knew that, in writing it out in favour of Lord Lyddon, there could be no possible danger of fraudulence, and, though he would have done it, he was secretly rather glad that Gorse had not asked him to make it out to himself.

By this time, also, Ivy, with Gorse's assistance, had withdrawn her savings of fifty pounds from the Post Office in pound notes which she kept, on Gorse's advice, in a trunk in her bedroom.

She would willingly have given Gorse this money, about which she was still ridiculously indifferent, but he would not allow her to do so. He said that in due course she should start a proper account at a bank, as she was now, as it were, in business of her own – business from which he hoped she was going to make profit before long.

And so, a few days after Gorse had obtained Mr Barton's cheque, Ivy, having been given two days' leave of absence from The Marlborough, set off with Gorse in his car for a visit to his imaginary aunt in the country.

On Gorse's advice she carried with her, in a small attaché case, the fifty pounds which had been in her trunk, Gorse having said that he did not quite like the idea of her leaving it in a bedroom in which she would not be sleeping.

The attaché case was put with his own luggage in the boot of the car.

They set off from Wynch Street at a quarter past eleven in the morning.

The day was unusually warm and sunny for the time of year, and they drove in a leisurely way in the direction of Reading – drove into the last afternoon they were to spend together – a long, hideous, indeed one might say bestial one.

Chapter Twelve

I

Writing about Ernest Ralph Gorse, many years afterwards, the well-known novelist and student of crime, Miss Elizabeth Boote, got into trouble with the press because she had been slightly out of her depth, and thus caused countless others – writers of editorials, leading articles, sensational articles, and, above all, writers of letters to the newspapers to get very much further out of their depth than Miss Boote herself and to flounder hopelessly.

There would have been even more casualties by complete intellectual drowning than there actually were had not these tricky waters been suddenly editorially drained by a spectacular breach of promise case brought by an usherette of a Worthing cinema against a world-famous tennis star.

Miss Boote may be easily forgiven for getting out of her depth, for all she had done was to succumb to a most alluring temptation – that of discussing the ultimate responsibility of a criminal for his crimes – and she had suggested, in an advanced and liberal way, that every criminal, even the most abominable, must in the long run be fully forgiven because fully explained.

She had, really, unwittingly embarked upon the whole problem of evil and its origin, and this was biting off more than very much more experienced and astute philosophers than herself could hope to chew.

She had said that Gorse would, finally, have to be comprehended and forgiven, but that he would be amongst the last to be granted this forgiveness. She then made certain comparisons and comments which infuriated the more backward sections of the reading public.

She said, for example, that, compared with the odious Gorse, George Haigh and Neville Heath had exhibited 'a certain charm, kindliness, generosity and dash'.

Naturally this did not appeal to those whose pleasure it was to think in terms of 'blood-drinking monsters', 'human vampires' etc.

She went on to say that, in the matter of purely repulsive, sustained, and thorough-going evil, Gorse belonged to a sort of upper class. Only such characters as Brides-in-the-Bath Smith, she said, or Sydney Fox, or Neill Cream were his equals.

She had in mind, in particular, his life-long habit of writing filthy anonymous letters and of abandoning women with entirely gratuitous cruelty.

She did not actually mention the case of Ivy Barton, which perhaps she might have thought provided the finest example of all of his characteristic manner of abandonment.

There was no need, that afternoon, for Gorse to take Ivy out in his car. He could have had her money without the slightest difficulty in many other, comparatively merciful, ways.

Furthermore, he already had her father's money, for he had removed it all from the joint account he had with Lord Lyddon. All that he now had to do was to get Ivy's money in a simple way and abscond.

In this case he did what he did, really, less from a desire to be cruel than simply from force of habit.

He was by now so used to employing cars in order to leave women he had successfully robbed and who had therefore become nuisances, that it did not occur to him in the case of Ivy to do it in any other way. What he did with her was, in fact, a case of sheer absent-mindedness.

But then Gorse by this time was already beginning to show signs of his premature loss of touch.

Gorse had had no intention of that afternoon being long, hideous and almost bestial. He had meant it to be short and delightfully easy.

2

Ivy and Gorse arrived at Reading at about half past twelve.

Gorse, suggesting that they should have lunch in the town, left his car outside the small park which lies, roughly, between the famous Reading prison and the railway.

Ivy was surprised at his leaving the attaché case containing her money locked in the boot of the car, and she was bold enough to say as much. What if the car were stolen?

Gorse smiled at her naïvety. If anything, he said, he wished that the car might indeed be stolen. It was insured for a sum very much in excess of its actual worth, and he and Ivy would profit greatly by such a theft.

Ivy completely accepted this explanation, and felt slightly ashamed of her own ignorance and smallness of mind.

What *was* important, said Gorse, was her handbag, containing what he called all her 'womanly paints, powders and cosmetics', and what was more important *still* was a brief-case of his own, which held documents and cheques of 'truly great moment'. Even the insurance of the car could not cover the loss of these, he said.

Ivy believed every word of what he said.

Gorse then, with the brief-case under his arm, took her to a warm, smallish public house nearby, where he prevailed upon her to have two glasses of Gin and Italian. He then took her to the Station Hotel to have lunch.

Ivy was very much impressed by the grandeur of the hotel, and with her lunch and wine.

When Gorse suggested that they should return to the car and drive on to his aunt's house Ivy was as giddy and confused with cocktails and wine as she had been on the afternoon during which Gorse had proposed marriage to her at Kew.

3

'Well – it's *not* been stolen, you see,' said Gorse as they approached the car.

He then suggested that they should have a small walk, and 'a bit of a sit-down', in the small park outside which the car was standing.

Ivy was only too glad for an opportunity to get some fresh air.

Gorse then said (truthfully) that he knew Reading very well, and, pointing out some buildings of interest, he took her round to the railway side of the park before entering it.

As he escorted her to the War Memorial in the centre of the park he said that he would have to leave her in order to 'wash his hands' before long. He would have done this at the Station Hotel if he had had any sense.

But there was no hurry.

They sat down facing the War Memorial (on the top of which there was an enormous lion and around which were inscribed the names of the fallen) and Gorse, talking peacefully, smoked a cigarette. He was feeling very much at peace with all the world.

When he had finished his cigarette he said that he must leave her for a minute for the purpose he had mentioned, and he rose.

'*You* keep that – will you?' he said, alluding to the all-important brief-case, which had been lying on the seat beside him. 'Only don't let anybody run away with it – will you?' He smiled. 'And don't run away yourself, either – if it comes to that! I mustn't lose you both at the same time, you know. That'd be just about the end of everything.'

'No,' said Ivy, smiling back at his pleasantry. 'It'll be safe enough with me.'

'Well, so long,' said Gorse. 'Won't be a jiffy.'

He left her, strolling easily in the direction of the entrance by which they had entered.

He could not, at that moment, have been more easy or more leisurely in his mind. Nor could Ivy. The whole business, therefore, for Gorse, should have been almost deliciously easy and leisurely.

But about a quarter of a minute later something – something she was hardly aware of and certainly could not name – began to stir at the back of Ivy's simple mind.

Chapter Thirteen

I

It is not impossible that stupid people are in some ways, at some moments, more clever than those more mentally alert.

Those who spend most of the day thinking and calculating have their minds full of one thing after another; those whose minds are more or less vacant are, perhaps, more susceptible than thinking people to impressions rather than thoughts.

As Gorse strolled away Ivy was not really thinking of anything. She was simply conscious of certain things – of the little park made bleak and grey by winter, of the huge lion and the names on the War Memorial, of the leafless trees, of the small, bandless bandstand not far away, of the sound of trains from the railway, and of the strangeness of her present situation and her relationship with Gorse generally.

She was, finally, conscious of two other things – of Gorse's recent remark about not running away, and of the brief-case which he had left with her and which lay, rather obtrusively and uncomfortably, along with her handbag, upon her lap.

The thought of not running away then, quite naturally, brought into her mind the notion of people who did sometimes run away from others, and this brought into her mind an episode at The Marlborough about a year ago.

2

A man, one evening shortly after the house had opened and was completely empty, had come in with a woman and had drinks at a table in a corner of the large Saloon Bar. The woman Ivy could scarcely remember, but she remembered the man because he had been slightly drunk when ordering the drinks and because of what happened afterwards.

What had happened was this. The woman had left the man, telling him that she wanted to telephone a friend and that she would return in a few minutes, and she had left her handbag on the table at which she had been sitting with him.

About a quarter of an hour had then passed, and the woman had, rather mysteriously, not returned.

Then another five minutes had passed, and Ivy's immediate employer, the proprietor's wife (thought of by Ivy, of course, as 'the Governor's wife'), having observed the man looking lonely and slightly disturbed in the corner of the deserted Saloon Bar had jocularly called over to him: 'What – gone and walked out on you – has she?' To which the man had made an appropriate, good-natured and seemingly unworried reply.

Then, in the Saloon Bar into which no other customer had as yet entered, nearly ten more minutes passed.

Because the woman had still not returned, this passage of time had been peculiarly nasty, eerie, uncanny, silent, and also embarrassing, for Ivy, the man, and the Governor's wife.

The latter had been at last unable to stand this any longer, and had called over to the man:

'Well – she *does* seem to have gone and left you – doesn't she!'

'Well,' said the man, 'if she has, she's gone and left her bag with me, anyway. So I'm pretty well insured against loss.'

'Oh, that's an old trick,' said the Governor's wife. She still spoke as if she were joking, but she was really quite seriously concerned, knowing well that this was in fact a trick often played upon men by women of dubious character.

The man asked her what she meant, and in reply she said, yet again as if in joke, that she had wondered whether perhaps he had given his lady friend any money recently.

The man then replied, with an unmistakable look of fright, that that was exactly what he had done.

Now the joke was over. The bag was looked into and found to contain nothing apart from a soiled handkerchief and a much used lipstick.

It turned out that the man had picked up the woman, whom he had never met before, in the street only a short while before entering The Marlborough with her, and had given her three pounds on the strength of her promise to allow him to spend the night with her in her flat. She must have put this money into her overcoat pocket.

On the Governor's wife explaining, in a soothing and knowledgeable way, that this was indeed quite an ancient ruse, the man had taken his loss and humiliation with very good grace, had had another drink, and then left The Marlborough. Before going he insisted on leaving the bag with the proprietor's wife, as what he called 'a souvenir of a sucker'.

The Governor's wife had kept the bag in a drawer for a few weeks, and had then asked Ivy if she would like it.

Ivy had at first accepted the offer, but, on being given the bag, found that, because of its associations, it repelled her immeasurably. She did not like even holding it. In doing so she felt she was like the man – being tricked, left.

At last she said as much to the Governor's wife, who fully understood her feelings and who put the bag back into the drawer, where it had been forgotten by Ivy, until this moment.

3

This long-forgotten episode was of grave disservice to Gorse that afternoon. It was, in fact, a piece of unusually bad luck for him. Taken in combination with a slight error in psychological judgement it brought havoc into his plans.

His small psychological error had been in speaking, to such a girl as Ivy, about not running away – in facetiously asking her not to run away from himself.

To a woman just a little less foolish it might have inspired a sort of serene confidence (as he intended that it should) that he was not likely to run away himself.

With Ivy it merely brought up an unpleasant picture of one person running away from another.

And, on top of this, in order to inspire further confidence, he had left his obtrusive brief-case in her lap.

Quite suddenly, as she waited dreamily for Gorse to return, Ivy found this brief-case an object of extreme repulsion. She was, subconsciously, associating it with the bag which the Governor's wife had given her and which all her instincts had forbidden her to keep.

A few moments afterwards her feelings leapt startlingly from the subconscious into the conscious, and she found herself almost throwing the brief-case off her lap.

Then she began to think consciously and concentratedly, and panic struck her with great force.

Here Gorse again was unlucky simply on account of Ivy's stupidity. Another girl, in such circumstances, would have almost certainly begun to argue with herself, to talk herself out of the absurd fear which had suddenly overtaken her. But Ivy, being so silly, was incapable of sustained or logical argument against any person or proposition. Least of all could she argue against fear.

Gorse had now been absent about four minutes. This was not Ivy's notion of a 'jiffy'.

She examined the brief-case, and noticed the cheapness of the leather – as cheap as that of the handbag which she had, nearly a year ago, been hardly able to hold. It was mysteriously cheap.

4

Then, in a huge wave, the whole, long, oppressive mysteriousness of Gorse – his being an 'Honourable', his proposing marriage to a barmaid, his car, everything – flooded over and into her soul. In something like a frenzy, she jumped to her feet.

She tried to assemble her thoughts sensibly, but was unable to do so. All she knew was that she must get rid of this filthy brief-case as soon as she could, and that in order to do this she must get back to her base, which, at this moment, was the car.

She had noticed, as she and Gorse had strolled into the park, another entrance much nearer the car than the one he had chosen. She made for this very rapidly, looking back, every ten seconds or so, at the War Memorial, in case Gorse should be returning to it.

Anyone watching her might have thought her slightly demented, which, indeed, she temporarily was. But there was no one to watch her.

Just before leaving the park Ivy actually began to run towards where the car had been left. She was running, first of all, towards a corner from which she knew it might be seen.

On turning the corner she saw the car.

She also saw Gorse, with his back to her, sitting in the driver's seat. She continued to run.

Gorse, just about to drive comfortably and quietly away, saw, in his mirror (he had two of these) Ivy running towards him, although she was then quite a hundred yards away from him.

He at once climbed, in a very leisurely way, out of the driver's seat and, with the greatest indolence, went to the bonnet of his car, and began to open it.

Ivy, seeing this, stopped running, and began to walk towards him. She did this as slowly as she could – at last almost ridiculously slowly.

5

The slowness of Ivy's walk gave Gorse even more time to think than he needed.

It had always been his principle and habit – when caught out in a lie or faced by an unexpected crisis – to behave with the utmost deliberation. This was why he had (on seeing the Lilliputian Ivy in his mirror running tinily towards him) made no attempt to drive away from her, but, relying upon his instincts, almost as much as Ivy just had upon hers, climbed out of his car in order, in a spirit of pure scientific inquiry, to examine its engine.

The sight of his slow, absolute imperturbability almost completely took the wind out of the sails both of Ivy's panic and suspicions.

She realized that she had made a fool of herself, and began to try to think of excuses for having returned to him in this extraordinary way. She worked out a few of these before going up to him and saying 'Hullo – here I am again – you see!'

Gorse, who had, needless to say, been intently listening to each of her approaching footsteps, and, although apparently absorbed in abstruse technicalities regarding his machine, almost seeing her from some obscure corner of one of his eyes, lifted his body from his work and looked at her with surprise. But his astonishment was of the calmest and most genial sort.

Gorse was not as yet as angry as he was to become later because the shock of Ivy's return had atrophied his feelings, as had also his knowledge of the necessity to behave calmly. And so his good temper completely convinced Ivy, and made her feel more than ever that she had made a fool of herself.

'Well,' said Gorse. 'What on earth are *you* doing here? I thought we'd arranged to meet back there.'

'Yes. I know,' said Ivy, slightly breathless on account both of her recent running and of her embarrassment. 'But I wondered where you'd got to. I'm sorry.'

'Not at all. Very nice to see you, anyway,' said Gorse, bending once more over the intricacies of his machine. 'But why did you wonder where I'd got to? I hadn't been very long, had I?'

'Well, you'd said you'd just be a jiffy, and I got worried,' said Ivy. 'I'm sorry.'

'You mustn't say you're sorry, darling. It's very flattering for me to know you worry about me so much . . .' Gorse suddenly stood erect and looked at her and spoke to her in a decidedly quick and frightened way. 'By the way, you've got my brief-case, haven't you?'

'Yes. It's here,' said Ivy, showing it to him.

'Oh – well, that's all right,' said Gorse, again bending, and at his ease. 'I must say it'd've been too bad if you'd left that behind.' He paused, and then began his explanation. 'But really, you know, I couldn't have been away more than three minutes. And all I did was to come back to take one of these beastly digestive pills I'm supposed to take directly after lunch. I forgot it as usual, needless to say. Like one?' He produced a phial of white pills from his pocket and showed it to her. 'No. I thought you wouldn't.' He put the phial back in his pocket and went on with his mechanical work. 'And while I was at it I thought I'd better warm up the old bus.' (Gorse, although he had tried all his life to educate himself, had never got out of the unfortunate habit of alluding to his cars as 'old buses'). 'Like all other old ladies she doesn't like being left out in the cold too long, and she's been making a little pinking noise this morning that I haven't quite liked . . . But anyway, I couldn't have been away more than three minutes – could I?'

'Well – it seemed a lot longer to me, I must say,' said Ivy.

'And you couldn't have said anything more flattering, darling,' said Gorse. 'Now – I have a fancy we've cured that little bit of trouble. Let's see.'

He shut the bonnet, went round to the driver's seat, climbed into it again, started the engine, and revved it, noisily and intermittently, for about half a minute. Then he let it tick over gently.

'There you are,' he said. 'Perfect. Listen. Sweet as a pea again.' He switched off and looked at her. 'Now, darling, shall we resume our little promenade in the park, or shall we proceed gently on our route to Aunt Bella?'

'I think we might just as well be getting on,' said Ivy. 'Don't you?'

'Right you are,' said Gorse. 'Hop in – and off we'll go.'

At this moment Ivy was so relieved, after her panic in the park, to be with Gorse and his delightful car again – so reassured by his genial and unhurried talk (she had been particularly impressed, incidentally, by his sudden anxiety about his brief-case) – so convinced of the authenticity of his elaborate foolery with the car – so ashamed of having been so silly, and of her silliness generally – so grateful for his slow, charming, chivalrous forgiveness – and, finally, so happy, after the brief but appalling terror she had endured, merely to have company, and the company of a man and her wooer at that – that she probably felt, as she got into the car beside him, a much deeper affection for him than she had ever known before.

Indeed this emotion was so strong that, when Gorse started the car and they began gently to move towards his aunt's home in the country, she did something she had never done before. She voluntarily slipped her hand through his arm, and rested her body against his – did something which in her idiom was known as 'snuggling'.

'You know, I really think you were afraid I was going to run away from you, darling,' said Gorse. 'But you were wrong. If anything, it's I who've got the terror that you'll run away from me – one of these days.'

'Oh no,' said the exuberant Ivy. 'You haven't got to bother about that. You don't know what you've let yourself in for. You'll have trouble in getting rid of *me*, I can assure you.'

With these alarming words she 'snuggled' even more closely to Gorse, and at this moment the dormant but wild fury and resentment in Gorse's soul began slowly to awaken.

Chapter Fourteen

I

In justice to Gorse it must be conceded that, on this grey, rather warm winter's afternoon, he had a formidably difficult task on his hands – that of taking a young woman of twenty-eight, with whom he was fictionally in love, and to whom he fictionally believed himself to be engaged, to stay with a fictional aunt in a fictional house in a fictional part of the countryside.

And matters were not made any easier by his beloved, for the first time during his courtship, showing genuine affection, even love for him, 'snuggling' up to him, and telling him that she could assure him that he would have trouble in getting rid of her.

There was, of course, a ghastly kind of humour in the situation. But Gorse, almost devoid of humour even of the simplest kind, was certainly incapable of perceiving a point so extremely *recherché* and inverted as this.

His fury began to take proper shape after he had shaken off the traffic problems of Reading and they were more or less in the countryside.

The extraordinary intensity which his fury was ultimately to reach (and Gorse did not often succumb to rages of any sort) could be accounted for in many ways.

It would have been a great blow to his pride, in any case, to have encountered, as he had here, the first failure of his life in the art of abandoning a woman more or less exactly according to his own plan. But this disaster was aggravated a hundred-fold by the type of woman who had brought it about – possibly one of the silliest in the world, and certainly quite the silliest he had ever personally known.

The sitting bird had had the effrontery not only to elude his gun but to come round behind his back and peck savagely at his neck.

Furthermore it was still on his shoulder, and in a position to peck very nastily again.

Instead of doing this, however, at the moment it was showing signs of the utmost affection and a determination to stay on his shoulder for the remainder of his life.

Things might have been a little better if only Ivy had been clever and pretty. In such a case he might have accepted temporary defeat and, perhaps reluctantly half admiring her, invented some lie in order to defraud her and shake her off at a later date. But Ivy was not clever and pretty. She was silly and hideous – idiotic and *repulsive*! *Repulsive!* (His fury rose as he repeated this word to himself.)

Added to all this Gorse was enduring a sensation which overtakes even entirely humane people. An ordinary man or woman often begins to feel a bitter hatred, a sense of abominable detestation, against some living thing he or she has failed to kill instantly – an animal or insect – a mouse, a bird, a beetle, a moth – even a bluebottle or a fly.

Such, then, were Gorse's emotions, and the causes of his almost uncontrollable fury, which, because he had to control it, made him more furious still.

2

Another deplorable feature of this last drive of theirs together was that Ivy, having to her surprise come near to loving Gorse for the first time, and being soothed and made slightly sentimental by the peaceful countryside through which they were passing, felt that she must show still further her new affection, that she must show him that she was willing to 'give' more to him than she had heretofore. Consequently – more voluntary, and more emphatic, 'snuggling'.

But her doing this was deplorable, really, only from the point of view of an imaginary humane and pitying outsider watching Ivy. To Gorse it was convenient. 'Snuggling' involves, necessarily, long, dreamy silences and these suited Gorse admirably. They enabled him to hide his violent rage behind apparently responsive silences; and they gave him time to think.

While giving Ivy the impression of taking her to his aunt he was in fact wandering quite aimlessly about the countryside, which he knew very well.

It was only after they had been driving together for nearly an hour that Gorse hit upon a concrete plan, and began to drive with a definite aim in a definite direction.

Chapter Fifteen

I

Gorse, though normally rather sexless, had bouts of great physical passion, and when these came upon him he was mostly stimulated by what is (on the whole foolishly) known as a perversion.

He liked to tie women up in order to get the impression that they were at his mercy, and he also liked to be tied up by women and to feel that he was at theirs.

It is foolish to call this a perversion because, as every serious student of the general psychology of sex (who would be supported by any prostitute, or keeper or frequenter of brothels) knows, it is merely a rather emphasized form of the sadistic or masochistic element underlying every physical relationship between man and woman, or, if it comes to that, man and man, or woman and woman.

Gorse was, therefore, not to be blamed simply because of this so-called perversion. What made it objectionable in Gorse was the highly distasteful way in which he indulged in it. But then Gorse exhibited bad taste in almost everything he did.

While driving Ivy towards the sinister destination he had in mind he was certainly not influenced by any sort of carnal desire. Ivy had never meant anything to him in that way, and now this bird on his shoulder and at his neck was so unutterably loathsome to him, spiritually and physically, that such a thing was absolutely out of the question.

It had occurred to him, though, that he might harness the technique he had so often used for pleasure to the harsh business of ridding himself of Ivy's detestable proximity.

In other words, he had decided that he would tie Ivy up, in an isolated spot which he knew well because he had used it more than once for pleasure, and thus free himself from her.

To do such a thing, he knew, required considerable forethought and skill in the preliminary stages. And so, while Ivy 'snuggled', he began slowly to make a careful plan. At last it was made to his satisfaction.

Soon after he had made it he said to Ivy that he thought he heard a noise in the back of the car. She said, 'What? Again?'

To which he replied, 'No. I don't mean the front. I don't mean pinking. I mean at the back. Amongst the luggage. Something's wobbling. Can't you hear it?'

'No. I can't hear anything,' said Ivy, in her dreamy state hardly attempting to do so.

'Well, I certainly can,' said Gorse. 'But we'll soon put it right.'

He drew the car smoothly up to the side of the road, looked at Ivy lovingly, kissed her (it was the first kiss she had had from him which she had in any way liked, and the last she was to get), climbed out of the driver's seat, and went to the boot of the car, which he unlocked and opened while Ivy remained seated in front.

While she looked absent-mindedly at the scenery in front of her he made noises behind her resembling those of a man rather irritably adjusting luggage.

He was in fact taking, from the bottom of the boot, the long length of a rather thin cord, the cord of a window-sash, which he had often used for the gratification of his so-called perversion.

Having made a slip-knot at one end of this he put it into his overcoat pocket.

He then re-locked the boot, returned to the driver's seat, and smoothly drove forward to his destination, which was less than three miles away.

'Well – we're not far away now,' he said a minute later. 'Are you ready to face our dear old Aunt Bella?'

This query at once made Ivy more alert, and she began to tidy her hair, and powder her nose, in a mirror taken from her handbag.

She had never done this in front of him before, and her doing so now, for some reason, made Gorse so angry that he could hardly keep himself from hitting her.

'You haven't got to be in such a hurry,' he said, getting some of his spleen off in this way. 'Because before we actually go into the house I want to take you somewhere just near it. I've got a surprise for you. Would you like a pleasant surprise?'

Ivy said that of course she would. What was it? To which Gorse replied, logically, that if he told her it would no longer be a surprise.

He went on to say that he wanted to give her something, and

that he wanted, for sentimental reasons, to do it on one exact spot, and no other, near his aunt's house. He had spent so much of his early youth on this spot, romantically dreaming and hoping for happiness – a happiness which he believed was now, miraculously, almost within his grasp.

'Here we are,' he said, as he stopped the car on the upward incline of a remote Berkshire lane. 'I'm afraid it's rather a steep climb. But even the climb's romantic to me.'

He pointed to a sharply rising, densely shrubbed, wooded little hill, immediately on their right.

'And when I've given you what I want to give you,' he said, 'we can look over the top and have a peep at Auntie's house before we enter her presence.'

The thought of looking at the aunt's house before going into it made Ivy very happy.

'I never minded a climb!' she said, in a sprightly way, and they both got out of the car.

'I'm afraid we'll have to take the brief-case,' said the careful Gorse, taking it out of the car. 'I'm afraid it's not a very romantic thing to take with one on a purely romantic excursion – but there we are.'

He then made her walk, in front of him, up a difficult, leaf-strewn path on the thickly-wooded little hill – a path which he knew and remembered well.

Ivy, as she walked ahead of him, wondered what she was to be given. She imagined that it was to be an engagement ring, which, rather unaccountably, he had never spoken of giving her before.

She was on the whole mostly interested, however, in the peep at the aunt's house which had been promised her.

The climb up through a leafy, overgrown track in the wood soon made Ivy breathless, and she was glad when he said, 'Here we are, darling.'

She turned and saw him looking, nostalgically, around him.

Then he put the brief-case on the ground, and his hands into his overcoat pockets.

'Pretty secret and secluded spot – isn't it?' he said.

'Yes,' said Ivy.

And indeed it was possibly one of the most secret and secluded spots to be found in Berkshire at that time of year.

'This was where I used to hide away, and do all my thinking and dreaming,' he said.

While still seeming to look around him with a kind of awe, he was actually manoeuvring skilfully in his overcoat pocket with the sash-cord. Then he looked lovingly at Ivy again.

'Very well, then,' he said. 'Now for your surprise. Shut your eyes and hold out your hands.'

'Hands?' she said. 'Or hand?'

'No. Both hands. I want to give you two things, really. And mind you shut your eyes tight. You won't get anything if you open them before I tell you.'

Ivy did as she was told, screwing her eyes up tightly.

2

Gorse took his time as, watching Ivy's eyes closely, and making a noise with his shoes on the dry leaves beneath them, he withdrew the long sash-cord from his pocket and arranged the slip-knot gently around the wrist of Ivy's right arm.

This was a curious moment, and a moment of great curiosity, for Ivy.

She was determined to keep her word and not open her eyes, and to aid herself in doing this she screwed them up even more tightly.

She was keenly conscious of the sound of the dry leaves being spasmodically stirred by Gorse's shoes, and she was aware that something was being put around her wrist. She thought that, perhaps, he was giving her a bracelet of some sort. It was certainly not an engagement ring, which would go on the left hand anyway. Perhaps the ring would be his second gift – saved up for the last, as it were.

She then felt something soft going over her left wrist and she began to be puzzled. Was he giving her two bracelets?

In a manner of speaking, Gorse was doing exactly this, as Ivy, the next moment, was sharply to discover.

Holding her right wrist at first gently, he suddenly held it firmly and violently wrenched the slip-knot tight. Then, still holding her right arm with his left hand he wound the sash-cord twice around her left wrist. Then he forced her wrists together and began to wind the cord savagely round both.

As he went on winding he said, rather breathlessly and very rapidly, 'You'll be all right if you don't make any noise, my little clinging Ivy! But if you make any noise you'll be far from all right! You remember that. See?'

Ivy, having opened her eyes, was in much too dumbfounded a state to make any noise. She was, indeed, too dumbfounded even to be frightened.

She simply watched Gorse winding the sash-cord around her wrists.

Then he stopped doing this and looked at her, in complete silence. Gorse was slightly embarrassed by her own silence. He was, at the moment, in a much more panicky state than herself.

'Well – why don't you say something?' he asked, with great irritation.

'What do you want me to say?' said Ivy, with a calmness and simplicity which enraged Gorse even further.

There was a pause.

'My god! What a *face*!' said Gorse, forced into being merely abusive. 'I wish you could see your own silly little hooked-nose face! . . . Go on. Sit down! I want to talk to you.'

'Where am I to sit?' asked Ivy.

'Where you are. Underneath you. It's comfortable enough – isn't it?'

Ivy managed, with his aid, to sit down on the leaves, which were entirely comfortable.

Gorse, keeping the unused remnant of the sash-cord in his hand, sat down beside her.

'Now I've got you on the lead, my girl – see?' he said.

'What are you going to do to me?' said Ivy, still entirely undisturbed.

Gorse lit a cigarette. This, together with Ivy's amazing imperturbability, made him much calmer.

He smoked nearly half of the cigarette before he spoke to her again, and when he did so he was almost completely himself again.

He then gave her a quiet, quite short, most lucid and most authoritative little talk.

He made no allusions of any sort to their past relationship or to his motives in having done what he had just done. He simply gave her instructions as to what she was to do in the next half-hour.

These instructions were simple enough, for all she had to do was to remain exactly where she was after he had left her. But, he pointed out, if she failed to obey these instructions to the letter she would suffer in a sort of way he did not care to mention. Perhaps she would understand.

Ivy did not understand. Nor, really, did he. But Ivy said, 'Yes. I'll do what you say,' and he replied, 'You'd better. Believe me, my darling clinging little Ivy.'

Then Gorse did a weird and yet perhaps very characteristic thing. He felt in his breast pocket for his wallet, and produced from it a cutting from a newspaper.

The cutting was from the *News of the World*, and the matter dealt with was the case, already known to Ivy, of the girl who had been tied to a tractor and robbed of her money not far from King's Lynn.

He put the cutting into Ivy's trussed hands and made her read it aloud to him.

He did this largely to frighten her into obedience after he had left her, but mostly to appease his great vanity. He was fantastically proud of this reference to himself (as 'the unknown assailant') in the famous newspaper, and at last he was able to show it to someone to whom he could identify himself as the unknown assailant.

When Ivy had finished reading it aloud, which she did in a voice which was at last beginning slightly to tremble, she said: 'Yes. I've read that before. It's from the *News of the World* – isn't it?'

This pleased Gorse beyond measure. His eyes lit with delight.

'Have you?' he said, unable to refrain from smiling with happiness as he looked at her. 'Well – *I'm* the "unknown assailant". You didn't know *that* – did you?'

'No. I didn't,' said Ivy. 'But I read it in the *News of the World*. I remember it well.'

'Well,' said Gorse. 'So you know the sort of person you're up against now. So don't get up to any funny tricks when I leave you. Which I'm now going to do.'

He rose.

'No, I'll do what you say,' said Ivy.

'You'd better. I'll be watching you, you know, in my own way. And I said half an hour. I see you've got your wrist-watch – so you can time it all right.'

He threw the remains of the sash-cord on to the leaves beside her.

'Yes,' said Ivy. 'I can time it all right.'

'And you can get free all right when the time's up? There aren't any knots there, you know,' said Gorse, looking at her trussed wrists with some concern. It had occurred to him that she was so unutterably silly that she might not be able to free herself when the time came merely by the process of simple unwinding – in which case she might get into some sort of panic, and never leave the wood alive. He certainly did not want a dead body on his hands.

Also he was so delighted by her having previously read his piece in the *News of the World* that he now quite liked her again, and was almost anxious to help her.

'Yes. I can get free all right,' said Ivy, and added, with quite genuine gratitude, 'Thank you very much.'

Gorse smiled at this.

'Not at all, madame,' he said. 'The pleasure's been all mine.' He raised his hat. 'Well . . . *Eauvoir*, madame . . . French for goodbye, you know. Or roughly . . . Oh – and by the way, you might give my love to your father when you see him, and thank him for letting me hop off with his two hundred pounds . . . Well – goodbye. And you're sure you can get free?'

'Yes. Goodbye,' said Ivy. 'And thank you very much indeed.'

Gorse hesitated, and then, picking up his brief-case, he turned and began to walk down the difficult, leaf-covered track, leaving Ivy to her thoughts.

Chapter Sixteen

I

As she heard Gorse retreating down the leaf-strewn, leaf-sodden, arduous track, and, a little later, start his car and drive out of her life, Ivy's thoughts were of an astonishingly uncomplicated nature.

She was simply trying, desperately hard, to remember something – namely, whether Gorse had, in his instructions, given her permission to release her hands before the half-hour was up. She knew she was to stay exactly where she was, but she simply could not recall whether or not she was to do so with her hands bound.

At last she decided that she had better be on the safe side, and so she made no attempt to free herself.

Then she realized, with something of a shock, that she had made no note of the exact time at which he had left her, and felt that she should somehow apologize to him for her remissness. How, after all, could she know when she might leave if she did not know the time at which she had been left?

Not without difficulty, she raised her hands and managed to look at her wrist-watch. She was not quite sure whether she was allowed even to raise her hands, but she thought that this must, surely, be permissible. She noted the time, which was just after half past three, and decided that, again to be on the safe side, she would pretend that it was only half past three. Then she could go at four.

She had no more idea than Gorse had of the meaning of his remark that he would be watching her in his 'own way', but she had not the slightest doubt that he would be doing this.

2

All this mental drivelling on Ivy's part was only in a small way attributable to severe shock. It could mostly be put down to the wretched girl's irredeemable stupidity.

When talking, at a later date, about the next half-hour, Ivy would always say that it 'seemed like an eternity'. But here she was merely repeating, parrot-like, a familiar cliché.

The time really went quite quickly for her, for she was so intensely absorbed by her problems.

In the first ten minutes she was earnestly working out what she was allowed to do and what she was not – such matters as to how much she might move or adjust herself in order to be more comfortable entering into her calculations. In the following twenty minutes the full horror and agony of her situation as a whole began slowly to dawn upon her.

She was, during this last period, first of all appalled by the loss of her clothes and the various accessories in her suitcase – all of which had been her 'best' because of her having had to visit Gorse's most kind but for all that still most formidable and impressive aunt.

Then she was very seriously dismayed by the complete loss of her savings – her fifty pounds in cash. On this head she was, perhaps, more bitterly unhappy on behalf of her mother, who had made her make them, than on her own behalf.

The thought of her mother brought into her mind the thought of her father, and this thought brought, for the first time since Gorse had left her, real terror into her soul.

For not only had she lost her own savings, she had lost two hundred pounds of her father's.

Although she should have reflected that her father had lost his money entirely voluntarily, Ivy did not think in this way at all. She had been instrumental in bringing her father and Gorse together: therefore his loss of two hundred pounds was absolutely her own fault.

What would he say? What would he *do*?

Would he beat her? Would he turn her out of the house for good? She pictured him doing both in the most violent way. (Ivy had a vivid and elaborate imagination when it came to anything to do with her father.)

How was she to face her father again? How, if it came to that, was she to get back home in order to face him? She had left her handbag, with her little money (about seventeen shillings) in it, in the car in which Gorse had just driven away.

The more she thought of the difficulty, the virtual impossibility, of getting home, and the more she thought of what her father would do to her if she did, the more acutely terrified she became.

In this state of mounting terror she spent the last five minutes of the half-hour in which she had been told to remain exactly where she was.

Indeed, she was so frightened that she neglected to look at her wrist-watch to see if the time was up until it was three minutes after four.

There was, as Gorse had predicted, no difficulty in releasing herself from the sash-cord, though, because she was naturally silly and now in a panic, she made the task unnecessarily complicated.

She found, when she at last came to the slip-knot, that Gorse's violent wrenching of it had caused a nasty contusion on the skin of her wrist.

Her innate sense of tidiness and economy made her wind up the sash-cord, and take it with her as she began her journey down the track.

This was even more difficult to descend than ascend, and Ivy's terror and haste made it triply difficult.

At one point she turned her ankle, amongst the deep leaves, very badly; and she nearly fainted from the pain and from the thought that she had either sprained or broken it.

But the pain and faintness at last subsided and she made her way successfully to the lane.

Her one thought now was to get to a main road of some sort. On such a road she might ask for help, and along such a road she might reach a railway station of some sort.

Although she knew that she had no money with which to pay her fare to anywhere, she still felt that a railway station was the first place she must somehow reach.

Then she remembered that she had, at any rate, her wrist-watch, for which she had originally paid thirty shillings a year or so ago. Surely someone would advance her a little money on this.

She could recall, roughly, the latter part of the route by which Gorse had brought her to the lane in which she was, and she knew that they had come from a main road not much further than a mile away, and which she should be able to find without much difficulty.

Before long she saw the main road beneath her in the distance, and she took heart.

Having reached level ground she had to walk through a very long narrow road, with hedges and bleak ploughed fields on either side of her, in dead flat country.

Before reaching the main road she did not pass or see a single person. She did, though, on this narrow road, pass one of those isolated cottages which are so often seen standing, seemingly for no conceivable reason, in the wastes of flat countrysides.

It simply did not occur to her to knock at the door of this cottage in order to seek help.

The walk along this narrow half-mile road, did, truthfully, seem metaphorically to be 'an eternity', but Ivy, in relating her story later, forgot it altogether.

On at last reaching the main road Ivy saw and read sign-posts, but they meant nothing to her. She turned to her left.

She was in fact within three miles of Pangbourne, to which she was advancing and where there was a station.

Every now and again a car passed her and she thought of attempting to stop one.

Finally she determined to try to do so, and she did try.

But the gesture of appeal she made, as the first two cars flashed by her, were too unemphatic and made too late. It is doubtful whether the owners of the cars, even if they would have stopped, realized that this was what she desired.

After a third hopeless attempt she decided to give up trying. She must speak to someone walking on the road. There were very few.

She passed a fierce-looking, rapidly-striding man wearing gaiters, a mackintosh, and a bowler hat. But he was so fierce-looking, and walking so quickly, that she did not dare to address him.

Then she passed what seemed to be a hedge-cutter. This elderly man was not in any way fierce, but he turned from the hedge and stared at her with a dumb, prolonged interest which made Ivy think that he was either surly or hostile. And so she passed without speaking.

She then passed two elderly ladies who were gossiping to each other violently, and who obviously, it seemed to Ivy, belonged to what she would call the 'church-going' class. As such they were, manifestly, out of the question.

Ivy was, by this time, desperately beginning to wonder whether she would ever have the courage to speak to anybody.

But then Stan Bullitt, on his bicycle, mercifully rode into Ivy's life.

Chapter Seventeen

I

Stan Bullitt's bicycle was unusual. It was painted red. His clothes also were unusual. He wore a blue uniform (with red piping on the coat and trousers) and a cap very much like a postman's.

Stan Bullitt was employed by the General Post Office to deliver telegrams – a telegram boy.

Ivy had the courage to stop him for more than one reason. He was riding his bicycle very peacefully, and this was in delightful contrast to the cars which she had attempted to halt. He was young (he looked about sixteen) and therefore not as awe-inspiring to Ivy as the wayfarers she had feared to approach so far.

More important still, he was in a uniform of sorts. It had been in Ivy's mind for a long while that she should, in her abominable predicament, seek the aid of a policeman – who would, to her mind, naturally be in uniform. Here was somebody in a uniform. Here was somebody who, simply because he wore a uniform, was in some sort of position of authority.

Ivy had to screw up all her courage before she managed to accost him.

'Excuse me!' she said, gazing passionately into the boy's eyes.

Stan Bullitt, having looked at her and passed her, slowly applied the brakes to his bicycle and most gracefully alighted from it.

He then turned and, walking with his admirably managed machine towards Ivy, said:

'Yes, Miss?'

His tone was at once respectful, composed, and faintly dictatorial, as befits one who is accustomed to bringing either bad, middling or good news to countless types of people, and waiting for an answer.

He was not six feet, but he seemed almost as tall as this to Ivy. He was slim, and he had grey, shrewd eyes, and rather fair hair and a slightly freckled complexion.

'Could you help me?' said Ivy. 'I was wondering whether you could possibly help me.'

The shrewd grey eyes of the adolescent had already observed the sash-cord still held, rather ridiculously, in Ivy's hand; and now they were looking, with more than average intentness, into the wretched, bewildered, brown, bird-like eyes of the distraught girl of twenty-eight.

'I was wondering where the nearest station was,' said Ivy. 'Could you possibly tell me?'

Stan Bullitt's eyes again wandered to the sash-cord before he replied.

'Well, the nearest's Pangbourne, Miss,' he said. 'But that's a good way away.'

'How far?' said Ivy. 'I want to get to the nearest station, you see.'

Stan Bullitt at once noticed that she had repeated herself unnecessarily, and this, added to the fact of her holding the sash-cord in her hand, made him think that he was possibly talking to a madwoman. But it also occurred to him that she might be seriously upset on account of some recent accident.

'Well, it's a good three miles,' he said, looking into her terrified, shocked eyes again. 'Have you got to get there quickly, then?'

'Yes. I'd like to get there as quickly as possible,' said Ivy. 'Could you tell me how to do it as quickly as I can?'

There was a long pause, during which Stan Bullitt still looked into her eyes, and during which he realized that he was certainly dealing with a 'case' of some kind – either with a female lunatic or with the victim of some tragedy which had taken place not very long ago.

'Excuse me, Miss,' he said at last. 'But are you in any kind of trouble?'

'Yes. I am. I'm afraid I *am*!' said Ivy.

The kindness of his tone had brought tears at last into her terrified brown eyes.

'Yes, Miss,' said Stan Bullitt in an even, level-headed, and rather pompous way. 'I can see that you are. You're in grave trouble – aren't you?'

Ivy held back her tears as well as she could, but she could not.

'Yes!' she said. 'I'm in *grave* trouble! And I want some help! Can you help me?'

She turned away from him and began to cry into her hands.

The wise Stan Bullitt let her cry for a few moments.

When she turned to face him again, he smiled gently at her.

'Well, there's no need to turn on the waterworks,' he said. 'That doesn't get anybody anywhere – does it?'

'No!' said Ivy, looking passionately into his eyes again, and more or less controlling her tears.

'The point is,' said Stan Bullitt, 'where you want to go to – isn't it? And the point is to get you there, isn't it? That's all that matters – as far as I can see. Where *do* you want to go?'

'I don't *know*!' said Ivy. 'I ought to get back to London, really. But I can't even pay my fare! I've only *got* my wrist-watch! Look!'

In showing him her wrist-watch she revealed the contusion, now blackening, upon her wrist.

'Where did you get this, then?' said Stan Bullitt, taking her hand and looking at her bruised wrist above the watch.

'Oh – it's such a long story!' said Ivy. 'It's such a long *story*!'

'Well,' said Stan Bullitt, still gently holding her hand. 'Every story has to come to an end at some time – doesn't it? And sometimes it has a happy ending – doesn't it?'

'Yes!' said Ivy, as he went on examining her wrist.

'The point is to *make* the happy ending – isn't it? And the only way to do that is to *do* something about it – as far as I know . . . Now let's see what we *can* do . . . Do you want to get back to London in a hurry?'

'Oh no,' said Ivy. 'I don't really *want* to go back there at all!'

'Good,' said Stan. 'Then I know exactly what we can do. You're going straight back to my grandmum's. It's not so very far.'

'But how can I *get* there? It's all so *lonely* here,' said Ivy.

Stan Bullitt released her hand in as gentle a way as he had held it.

'Oh – we'll soon see about that,' he said, more dictatorially again. 'There'll soon be a car. In fact I think I can see one coming now. Now – you wait there and see.'

Leaving Ivy at the side of the road he walked into the middle of it with his bicycle.

He had been right in thinking that he had seen a car approaching them from a distance. As it gradually approached he said to Ivy:

'I'd come with you – only I'm not off the job yet. But all you've got to do is to go to my grandmum's. Bullitt's the name – Bullitt – like what you have in a gun. And when you get there, say Stan sent you. Just say that and you won't have any trouble. I'll give you the address in a moment.'

The approaching car, an open one, was now within a hundred yards of them. Stan put up his hand to signify that it was to stop. He had not the slightest doubt that it would.

It is not possible actually to force a car to stop. Nevertheless, Stan's confidence was completely reasonable. In any case it is most difficult to run down a boy standing bang in the middle of the road with a bicycle. And when the bicycle is painted red and the boy wears a blue uniform, with red piping on it, it is practically impossible.

There is always something impressive of some sort about any uniform, but the uniform of a telegram boy – who may be bringing tidings of deaths, births, disasters, joys, weddings, funerals, and a hundred other kindred urgent matters – such a uniform cannot be disregarded, least of all when the one who is wearing it is standing in the middle of a narrow and lonely country road with his bicycle.

Stan Bullitt was fully aware of his power, and he did not hesitate to show, in his general demeanour as he raised his hand, his inner knowledge of the strength of his position.

The motorist stopped. (He did not want to do this, but, after all, he thought, there might somehow be a telegram for *him*.)

'Excuse me, sir,' said Stan Bullitt, rather as if he had a warrant for the arrest of the motorist. 'Could you help me over a small matter?'

'Yes, certainly,' said the motorist. 'What's the trouble?'

'This young lady's in a little bit of trouble, sir.'

Stan Bullitt went on as though he were warning the motorist that anything he said might be taken down in writing and used as evidence.

'I would be very much obliged, sir,' he said, 'if you could kindly assist by conducting her to my grandmother's house. It's not much more than two miles or so away – and on your route, I think. Would you oblige, sir?'

The handcuffs were now firmly fastened on the wrists of the unhappy motorist, who replied, meekly, 'Yes. Certainly.'

'Thank you very much, sir,' said Stan, less firmly, as if acknowledging his appreciation of the fact that the man had agreed to come quietly. He turned to Ivy.

'Now,' he said. 'Will you come in beside this gentleman, Miss?'

He opened the door of the open car for Ivy, and she got into the seat beside the driver.

Stan Bullitt then produced, with the quickness of a *prestidigitateur*, a pencil and a notebook, and wrote down his grandmother's and his own address.

'There you are,' he said, handing a slip of paper to Ivy. 'Mrs Bullitt, Three Old Mill Lane, Little Bedmonton. And just say that Stan sent you. That's all you've got to say. Remember that – won't you? Stan. And then she'll look after you until I get back.' He spoke to the driver. 'You'll find it very easy, sir. If you go straight ahead it's the first village you come to, and if you stop at the church at the fork of the road she'll be able to find her way all right.'

He then again saw the sash-cord which Ivy was still holding.

'I think you'd better let me take that,' he said, and took it from her. 'Well, I'll be seeing you before very long. And Grandmums'll look after you in the meanwhile.' He spoke again to the motorist. 'Thank you very much, sir. I'm very much obliged indeed. Thank you.'

The motorist, realizing that he had been dismissed, quietly said, 'Not at all' and resumed, with Ivy beside him, his journey.

2

The motorist, a surly, moustached, heavy, middle-aged, middle-class man, who was himself a motor salesman, did not speak to Ivy as they began their drive together.

He had by now had time to recover from the shock of Stan Bullitt's tremendous personality, and was beginning to resent having to give this woman a lift. He did a lot of motoring and it was his principle never to give casual lifts to anybody.

Ivy, it goes without saying, did not dare to speak.

And so the two did not exchange a word with each other until the church at Little Bedmonton was reached. Then the motorist, stopping the car said: 'Here we are, I think. Can you find your way all right?'

'Yes. He gave me the address. I've got it here,' said Ivy. She got out of the car. 'Thank you very much indeed. I'm very much obliged, I'm sure.'

'Not at all,' said the motorist, ungraciously: and he drove on.

Ivy had no difficulty in finding her way, without making any inquiries, to Three Old Mill Cottages.

The Old Mill Cottages (of which there were only five) were

thatched and whitewashed. She knocked on the door of Number Three, and did not have to wait long before it was opened by the telegram boy's grandmother.

Mrs Bullitt was a stoutish, apple-faced, grey-haired, spectacled, kindly, meek woman of sixty-five. She appeared to be almost as frightened of Ivy as Ivy was of her.

'Excuse me,' said Ivy. 'I was told to come here. I was told to say that Stan said I was to come here before he came back. He said that if I said Stan had told me it'd be all right. Is it all right?'

Here Mrs Bullitt looked rather more frightened than before.

'Oh, yes,' she said. 'If Stan said so, of course it's all right. Will you come in?'

Ivy was then taken into a small, warm, dark, delightful room, with a coal fire. It was furnished in roughly the same way as her father's sitting-room in Wynch Street. She was made to sit down in an armchair.

'Will you have a cup of tea?' said Mrs Bullitt. 'I was just going to have mine.'

'Oh – thank you very much,' said Ivy. 'Thank you very much indeed.'

Mrs Bullitt, stoking the fire and putting on the kettle for tea, thought she must make some sort of polite inquiry.

'So Stan sent you, did he?' she said. 'How did you meet him? Or do you know him?'

'Oh, no. I don't know him. I just met him by accident,' said Ivy. 'I was in the road, you see.'

'In the road?' said Mrs Bullitt, in a puzzled way which made Ivy think that she must make some sort of explanation.

'Yes. In the road,' she said. 'And he was very kind to me, and he said that you'd look after me until he came back.' She then forced herself to add: 'I'm in trouble, you see. I'm in serious *trouble*.'

Her having blurted this out made her begin to cry again.

Now tears, particularly when poured forth in conjunction with the notion of a forthcoming cup of tea, were exactly – indeed quite gloriously – up Mrs Bullitt's street. She lost all her fear of Ivy in an instant, and was warm and wise beyond measure.

'That's right,' she said, 'you have a cry. Then we can have a nice cup of tea and talk about it. There's a remedy for everything, you know. At least, that's what I've always found. You go on crying, darling, and we'll soon have the tea.'

Being called 'darling' made Ivy cry more and more.

3

Mrs Bullitt remained silent, busying herself with the preparation of the cups, saucers, and teapot.

After a while Ivy controlled her sobbing, and watched Mrs Bullitt, who had still not said another word, making final preparations for the tea.

It was while sitting thus, in the fire-lit gloaming of the warm, charming, cottage sitting-room, that Ivy (in so far as anyone so weak and irresolute could do such a thing) made a resolution.

This was to the effect that she would never return to her father. *Anything* rather than that. *Anything*. She would work her fingers to the *bone*!

Ivy kept this resolution.

It is doubtful whether anybody on earth has ever enjoyed a freshly-made, very strong cup of tea (with sugar and milk) more than Ivy did the one which Mrs Bullitt gave her, from a large old-fashioned teapot, and in a large old-fashioned cup. To enjoy a cup of tea, with just that particular sort of intensity, it is necessary, first of all, to be tied up cruelly in a wood during the winter, robbed, and abandoned. And this happens to few women.

The cup was so cheering that it would be fair to say that it inebriated, and soon Ivy was telling Mrs Bullitt, as well as she could, her full story.

She could not have had a more sympathetic listener.

Ivy even explained her violent repugnance against the thought of returning to her father, and Mrs Bullitt said that she need not do so. She could stay with Mrs Bullitt. There was plenty of room.

'Well,' said Mrs Bullitt, when Ivy had more or less finished her story. 'Let's wait till Stan comes back, and see what he says.'

This surprised Ivy.

'Isn't he too young?' she asked. 'Would he understand?'

'You don't know Stan,' said Mrs Bullitt, in a rather grim way.

Chapter Eighteen

I

A word or two should now be said about the general character of Stan Bullitt, who was something of a phenomenon.

He was sixteen years of age, and known in the neighbourhood of Little Bedmonton as a 'holy terror'.

He certainly had abundant vitality.

His parents were dead, and he kept his grandparents, with whom he lived, in a perpetual state of almost abject intimidation.

He knew everything, he did everything, he managed everything. He had, therefore, to be obeyed, in the long run, without question.

He was, undoubtedly, a 'terror'. The trouble was that he was also, in his own extraordinary way, rather holy as well.

He was, as his grandparents were compelled continually to testify, a 'good' boy. He gave them most of his very hard-earned wages: he mended anything in sight (most competently): he was helpful in illness, or in trouble.

He was kind, clever, humorous, and energetic. Above all he was energetic. His voice, which had only recently cracked, and his feet, which were extremely heavily booted, resounded through Three (and Two and Four) Old Mill Cottages quite abominably whenever he was at home.

At such times the only peace for his grandparents was when he was asleep. But he seldom slept more than six and a half hours.

Neighbours would often say that what this boy required was proper parental discipline. But such words had hardly left such people's mouths before he had thundered round and brilliantly mended something (or made something) for them, or assisted them in some other way, in his spare time.

They had therefore to concede that he was, after all, as his grandparents had so often said, a 'good' boy.

He had countless hobbies. At the time at which he met Ivy he was mostly interested in chemistry and photography. With both he made atrocious messes and atrocious smells. But he always opened windows in order to clear away the smells, and he always cleared up his messes. And, when his chemical researches brought about most startling explosions, he never failed to hasten to bang round in his bicycle-clips to apologize for any inconvenience he might have brought to sensitive listeners.

To put the matter briefly, there was no doing anything with him. Anybody who tried to do so soon found that they were getting the worst of it, and abandoned their project.

At six o'clock that evening, as Mrs Bullitt and Ivy were still lingering over their tea and their talk, the front door was heard being opened (and then being slammed), and a peculiarly glazed, pensive expression came over Mrs Bullitt's face.

The master had returned.

2

'Well,' said Stan, as he entered the sitting-room, which was now greenly lit by an incandescent gas-mantle. 'What're *you* two young ladies gossiping about?'

'Nothing, really, Stan,' said Mrs Bullitt. 'We were just gossiping – that's all. Nothing, really.'

' "Nothing will come of nothing, speak again",' said Stan, who was interested in Shakespeare and could quote from him extensively. 'Well. Come on now. What *have* you been talking about? The matter in hand?'

'Yes, we have, really, Stan,' said Mrs Bullitt, as she rose to get him his tea, which he liked to have served to him almost immediately upon his return.

'Good. To any purpose?' said Stan, as he flung himself into the armchair from which his grandmother had just risen.

'Yes, Stan,' said his grandmother, humbly, while again stirring the fire and putting on the kettle. 'She's told me the whole story – from beginning to end.'

'Excellent,' said Stan. 'I've always been told that confession is good for the soul. And may I be permitted to hear the tale as told?'

Here he smiled, with enormously soothing charm, upon Ivy, who smiled back but was quite unable to speak.

'Well – it's a very long story,' said Mrs Bullitt.

'I like long stories,' said Stan, still looking in a friendly way at Ivy. 'So go ahead and tell it to me. Will you, Grandmums?'

His tone, although kind, was also considerably stern. And so Mrs Bullitt, haltingly, and as she gave him his tea, began to tell her grandson Ivy's story.

She was sharply cross-examined on several points, but on the whole came through pretty well. She was assisted every now and again by Ivy, who, encouraged by Stan's grey, shrewd eyes and kindly, knowing smile, put in a word or two of explanation or elaboration.

At the end of the story Stan, who had by now finished his second cup of tea, put the cup down and looked at Ivy searchingly.

'And so The Honourable Gerald Claridge wasn't so honourable after all, it seems,' he said.

'No,' said Ivy. 'He wasn't. He was anything *but* honourable.'

'And he's gone and done a bunk with fifty pounds of yours, and two hundred pounds of your father's. Correct?'

'Yes,' said the half-happy, half-miserable witness.

Stan by this time had all the facts at his command.

'And you don't want to go back to your father. Correct?'

'No. I don't if I don't have to,' said Ivy, visited, for a moment, by the terrible fear that Stan might send her back to London at once.

'And according to Grandmums you don't want to go to the police about it?' said Stan. 'Because that's what you ought to do, you know, and do it quickly.'

'Oh no!' said Ivy, looking at him with wild pleading in her eyes. '*Please*, not the *police*! Please don't make me go to *them*! It'd all come out – about me being tied up and all that. I don't think even my father would want that. In fact I *know* he wouldn't!'

'Very well, then – we'll drop that just for the moment,' said the all-wise, all-powerful, and all-merciful Stan. 'And so let's sum up, as a judge would say.'

He proceeded in a way to sum up, in a way to continue to cross-examine, and in a way to lead the witness.

(It should perhaps be mentioned here that Mr Bullitt, the grandfather, was on a shopping trip to Reading and was not expected back until ten o'clock. But Mr Bullitt was well over seventy, and a mere cypher in this household.)

Ivy, Stan said, could stay at Three Old Mill Cottages as long as she liked, as far as he was concerned. But where was she to go afterwards? Had she any relations or friends?

Ivy said Yes, she did have some relations she believed she might stay with. She had an aunt who lived in Bradford, and who was very kind.

But was she kind enough to allow Ivy to live with her for the time being?

Ivy replied Yes, she thought she was, but she (Ivy) had no money to get there with, as she only had a wrist-watch in all the world.

At this the judge sharply rebuked her, saying the matter of wrist-watches was neither here nor there. Would her aunt take her in or would she not? That was the question which had been put to Ivy.

Ivy replied that she was almost sure that she would. But how was she to communicate with her aunt, and how was she to get to Bradford?

Here the judge pointed out, rather sarcastically, that there happened to be such things as telegrams. He knew for a fact there were. Also it was possible to borrow from the people one was staying with. Wrist-watches or no wrist-watches.

In delivering his final verdict he said that a telegram would be sent that very night and that it would reach Ivy's aunt early in the morning. He would undertake the matter himself, *now*, and if anything went wrong somebody was going to get what for. He was sure that her aunt would take her in all right.

Stan Bullitt could never be contradicted, and Stan Bullitt was never wrong. What he said he would do he did, and what he prophesied would happen inevitably came true.

On the next morning, at about eleven o'clock, Ivy received a reply to her telegram (dictated and sent by Stan) welcoming her to come and stay at Bradford tomorrow.

Just before Stan went off on his bicycle to busy himself with the sending of the telegram, Ivy burst into tears once more.

Stan Bullitt said, as he had said on the lonely road where he had first met her, that it was useless to turn on the waterworks. She was in safe hands. Waterworks were unnecessary.

As usual, he was right. It would have been almost impossible for Ivy to have been in safer hands than those of Stan's grandmother.

The two assisted each other in preparing an evening meal for themselves, for Mr Bullitt and for Stan.

And there were no more waterworks.

Chapter Nineteen

1

Thus this curiously involved, grotesque and unhappy little story – itself very much like something which is read and marvelled at on a Sunday in the *News of the World* – came to a not unhappy ending.

Before going to Bradford, Ivy spent the next day and night with the Bullitts, with whom she was amazingly happy.

There was plenty of room, for the Bullitts in fact inhabited three cottages cleverly knocked into one (on Stan's advice), and let rooms in the summer.

Ivy's bedroom overlooked a stream and was within pleasant earshot of the watermill from which the cottages had obtained their name.

The sense of release, relief and peace which came over Ivy in this room was never again equalled in her life.

For she was going to her aunt, whom she loved, and she was not going to return to her father, whom she hated and dreaded unutterably.

There was not even much urgency in the matter of writing to Wynch Street, for there she was believed to be safely staying with Gorse's aunt.

However, two letters were composed, with Mrs Bullitt's aid, to her mother and to her father.

These were read by Stan, approved of (thank God), and posted by him.

2

Ivy's mother was not very much upset by Ivy's news: she was a woman who was more or less beyond being upset by anything. Moreover, she did not miss Ivy a great deal, for, even when they were living under the same roof, they were both so busy that they saw practically nothing of each other. And it was one mouth less to feed.

Mr Barton's immediate reaction to the news was that a kindly fate had sent him a glorious opportunity for gloating over Ivy – for jeering at her and tormenting her for the rest of his days.

This was because he did not at first realize that he himself was financially involved. He had made out his cheque to Lord Lyddon. Therefore there was no need for him to worry. Lord Lyddon was safe enough – that he knew.

He discovered in his mind that he had always suspected that young Mr Claridge, who had, however, not succeeded in doing any harm to himself.

Mr Barton, therefore, instead of going at once to the police, let twenty-four hours go by without doing anything at all.

Then some instinct made him telephone Lord Lyddon, who was in the telephone book.

He was hoping to be able to deliver some bad news which did not affect himself.

He was unable to get Lord Lyddon, but was answered politely by Lord Lyddon's secretary (a man), who said that he would make inquiries, and who asked Mr Barton to telephone again two or three hours later.

This Mr Barton did, and he was told by the secretary that Lord Lyddon – who was in the country but whom the secretary had succeeded in getting on the telephone – knew nothing whatever about the matter. He had had no cheque from Mr Barton and was completely mystified. He had had a joint account with Mr Gorse, that was all. He was certainly not in any way responsible for anything.

On hearing this Mr Barton lost his head, and was rude, almost to the point of being menacing, to the secretary. The secretary kept his temper very well, and told Mr Barton that he must write to Lord Lyddon. It was Mr Barton, not the secretary, who finally banged the receiver down in a fury.

Then Mr Barton lost his temper in a manner even more damaging to himself. He lost it in a slow, smouldering way, and he carefully invented, and wrote, a long letter to Lord Lyddon. He was unfortunate enough not to have sufficient restraint not to post this.

The letter was illiterate, silly, complicated, and, in a lurking way, abusive and threatening. Lord Lyddon, on reading it, could hardly understand it but was quite certain that he did not like it. He explained the whole matter, as well as he could, to his secretary, who gave the letter to Lord Lyddon's solicitors.

Lord Lyddon's solicitors took an even worse view of the letter than Lord Lyddon had. They wrote, on behalf of their client, an extremely sharp letter to Mr Barton. It was, indeed, as menacing as Mr Barton's letter – but menacing in a sophisticated, knowledgeable, cultured and typewritten way. It scared Mr Barton out of his wits.

The tragedy, from Mr Barton's point of view, was that if only he had approached Lord Lyddon on this matter in a seemly and gentle way, Lord Lyddon would have almost certainly given him, out of pure generosity, the two hundred pounds for the loss of which he was not in the smallest way responsible either legally or morally.

Instead of this Mr Barton had a letter from a firm of solicitors which made him think that he might, if he was not careful, before long be in prison on account of a charge of defamation of character.

Also Mr Barton was unwise in another way. So obsessed and absorbed had he been by his letter-writing to Lord Lyddon that he completely neglected to go to the police about Gorse.

Not that it was likely that this would have done any good, for Gorse had, by now, covered up his tracks and beautifully concealed himself.

As he nearly always did before committing a robbery and hiding, he had made arrangements to exchange his car for another one, and he was now living, on the outskirts of Birmingham, in a small boarding-house, in which he was looked upon as a decided dog and wag.

Mr Barton did not even go to a lawyer. He suffered from the foolish delusion (certainly foolish with him) that 'every man should be his own lawyer', and he believed that he knew a great deal about the law.

Then Mr Barton wrote to Mr Kayne. He addressed this letter to the Mayfair block of flats, and so it took two days to reach Mr Kayne, who was at this time in Walsall.

Having learned his lesson from Lord Lyddon's solicitors, he was not abusive to Mr Kayne. He made, however, the mistake of telling Mr Kayne that he knew that Mr Kayne was 'as straight as a die and as honest as the day is long'.

Mr Kayne was much too shrewd a man not intensely to dislike being told by someone that he was as straight as a die and as honest as the day is long. (That he was both was beside the point.)

Mr Kayne, therefore, was at once put on his defensive. Also he did not like a great deal of Mr Barton's letter, which, if not abusive, was distantly menacing. Also, at the time of receiving the letter, Mr Kayne was just about to sail to America on business. He therefore gave the letter to his principal secretary (a woman) asking her to deal with the matter during his absence. Mr Kayne's woman secretary was much less easy-going than Lord Lyddon's man secretary. She took a very bad view indeed of Mr Barton's letter, and made very clear to Mr Barton, in a letter, what her view was. A few further letters were exchanged between these two, and at last Mr Barton savagely resigned himself to defeat.

Thus, through sillily abusing Lord Lyddon, and falsely flattering Mr Kayne, Mr Barton lost his chance of recovering his money from two men who would otherwise have willingly given it to him.

All that was left to him now was to go, fruitlessly, to the police, and to sit down and write a long, abusive, quite filthy letter to Ivy.

Chapter Twenty

I

At the time at which Ivy received her father's letter she was quite incapable of being hurt by it.

She had just obtained an admirable and extremely well-paid position as a barmaid in a public house in Bradford, and was enjoying life to the full.

She showed the letter to her aunt, who had always detested Mr Barton, and who advised her not to answer.

Ivy accepted her advice and, instead of writing to her father, answered, at great length, a brief letter from Stan Bullitt asking her how she was doing.

In this letter she enclosed the final instalment of her monetary debt to himself and his grandparents, and then went on to gossip at great length.

On the second evening of her stay at the Bullitts' – that is to say the evening before she had departed for Bradford – Ivy had played draughts with Stan.

It would be a waste of time to tell the reader that he was a profound master at this game. And it also goes without saying that he not only let Ivy win the last game but convinced her that she had done so on her own merits. Consequently, her letter mentioned draughts a good deal, and she told him of recent victories (authentically secured) over her aunt at Bradford.

Although Ivy never met Stan again she kept up a correspondence with him until he died, which he did, as a soldier, in the quite early days of the Second World War.

The news of his death made Ivy bitterly unhappy, and yet perhaps, seen objectively, it was not an entirely unhappy thing.

Whom the gods love, it is said, die young. And Stan was peculiarly fitted to do this – to die in all the glory of his boisterousness, cleverness and superb physical health. Stan, if he had lived, would probably never have been able to adjust himself to the harsh exigencies of maturity, and, later, of middle or old age. And, if only doing what he did for Ivy, if only for enabling her, with his overwhelming personality, to escape permanently from her father, he had not lived in vain.

2

What made the not unhappy end of this story even more happy still was the fact that *You and Me*, the musical play in which Mr Barton had failed to invest, turned out to be an enormous success.

This greatly enriched the good, struggling Lord Lyddon, and, better still, hideously wounded the bad, vain Mr Barton.

Having boasted so strongly about his investment in *You and Me*, what was Mr Barton to say at The Unicorn?

Round there he was questioned about the matter in the most friendly way – questioned so amicably and so constantly that he at last came to believe that his questioners were intentionally tormenting him.

He was forced, eventually, to resort to a lie.

Exuding a great air of esoteric knowledge of the theatre, he said that, to tell the truth, he had got *out* of *that* one – and only just in time. It might look as though it was being successful enough – but there was more behind it than most people knew. There was trouble coming up, and he was glad to be out of it. As for Lord Lyddon – well, he didn't want to say anything rash – but Lord Lyddon was going to get it in the neck before long, and well he deserved it. Mr Barton *knew* something about Lord Lyddon. He knew Lord Lyddon only too well. Yes – he could tell some stories about Lord Lyddon – but he wasn't going to – he wasn't going to just at *present*, anyway.

Because, with all his faults, Mr Barton seldom lied, he was a very bad liar, and he did not convince his listeners at all.

On the contrary they realized at once that the man was plainly lying to protect himself from some hurt he had received; and, instead of challenging him on the matter, they showed great forbearance and never alluded to *You and Me* again.

This forbearance Mr Barton mistook for the victory of his falsehood. He had, he thought, fooled them all right. And he would go on fooling them – wouldn't he just . . .

3

Rather strangely, Lord Lyddon, as well as being passionately interested in the theatre, was even more passionately interested in pictures and drawings, and he was, in a small way, an exceptionally good draughtsman.

On the strength of the money he was making out of *You and Me* he allowed himself to be persuaded, by flatterers and by himself, into fulfilling a life-long secret ambition – that of giving a modest exhibition of his drawings at a small gallery.

The exhibition was, unexpectedly, most successful, and was given publicity out of all proportion to its real merits. Because Lord Lyddon was a peer it was even given considerable attention in the popular press. Hence it came to Mr Barton's notice.

By this time Lord Lyddon was on Mr Barton's mind to such an extent that he could hardly think of anything else; and he simply could not resist going to the small gallery, which was near Leicester Square, in order personally to see Lord Lyddon's drawings.

He paid a shilling for this inverted pleasure and came away with a catalogue, on the cover of which one of Lord Lyddon's drawings had been reproduced.

This he took round to The Unicorn.

The reproduction was one of a nude figure.

A majority of Lord Lyddon's drawings were of nude or semi-nude figures, and this gave what Mr Barton thought was a strong weapon with which to vent his spite against him.

As soon as he had ordered his beer, and was sitting down, he showed the catalogue to his acquaintances.

He pointed to the reproduction and said that they were all like that. Every one of them. All in their 'birthday suits' – every one of them.

Mr Barton's acquaintances looked with interest at the catalogue, while Mr Barton raged against Lord Lyddon.

Mr Barton thought it was disgusting. He, speaking for himself, thought it ought not to be allowed.

He did not call it art. He called it indecency.

Rather strangely, Lord Lyddon, as well as being passionately interested in the theatre, was even more passionately interested in pictures and drawings, and he was, in a small way, an exceptionally good draughtsman.

On the strength of the money he was making out of *You and Me* he allowed himself to be persuaded, by flatterers and by himself, into fulfilling a life-long secret ambition – that of giving a modest exhibition of his drawings at a small gallery.

The exhibition was, unexpectedly, most successful, and was given publicity out of all proportion to its real merits, because Lord Lyddon was a peer. It was even given considerable attention in the popular press. Hence it came to Mr Barton's notice.

By this time Lord Lyddon was on Mr Barton's mind to such an extent that he could hardly think of anything else, and he simply could not resist going to the small gallery, which was near Leicester Square, in order personally to see Lord Lyddon's drawings.

He paid a shilling for this morbid pleasure and came away with a catalogue, on the cover of which one of Lord Lyddon's drawings had been reproduced.

This he took round to The Unicorn.

The reproduction was one of a nude figure.

A majority of Lord Lyddon's drawings were of nude or semi-nude figures, and this gave what Mr Barton thought was a strong weapon with which to vent his spite against him.

As soon as he had ordered his beer, and was sitting down, he showed the catalogue to his acquaintances.

He pointed to the reproduction and said that they were all like that. Every one of them. All in their birthday suits – every one of them.

Mr Barton's acquaintances looked with interest at the catalogue, while Mr Barton raged against Lord Lyddon.

Mr Barton thought it was disgusting. He, speaking for himself, thought it ought not to be allowed.

He did not call it art. He called it indecency.